THE

HARVEST HOME.

A Romance.

———————

LONDON:

PUBLISHED BY E. LLOYD, SALISBURY-SQUARE, FLEET-STREET.

THE
HARVEST HOME.

A DOMESTIC TALE.

"Crowned with the sickle and the wheaten sheaf,
While Autumn, nodding o'er the yellow plain,
Comes jovial on."

THOMPSON.

CHAPTER I.

THE FARMER AND THE STEWARD.—THE LORD OF THE MANOR.—A COCKNEY SPORTS-MAN FALLS INTO A DILEMMA.

ROWLAND BROUGH was one of the best practical farmers in the North Riding of Yorkshire, where tillage is perhaps carried to as high a state of perfection as in any English county that can be mentioned. He had been successful too, for, though not what may be called a wealthy man, he had realized a handsome sum, which was one day or other to come to his niece, Mary Everett, who had been brought up by him ever since the death of her parents. Each year had added something to the store he was laying by, and the harvest to which we now more particularly allude was one of the most abundant that had occurred within his memory. The getting of it in, too, was favoured with the finest weather, and a happy grateful man was farmer Brough as he watched the last waggon load of corn drawn towards the homestead, and escorted thither by the men and women who had laboured to bring about this much desired result. He was still occupied in his own pleasing reflections when a friendly voice struck upon his ear, and looking around he saw approaching, Mr. Reves, the venerable steward of Derwent Hall, which might be seen at the distance of a few fields off.

"So, neighbour Brough," exclaimed the old man, "I have again to congratulate you on having gathered in the best crops of any other farmer on the estates of my young master."

"Aye, aye," answered the other, returning the shake of the hand with warmth, "I have indeed much to be thankful for, not only as far as my prosperity in life goes, but for everything else that I most place my dependance on."

"You have an excellent farm, and your rent is certainly very low," observed the steward.

"Why, I can't complain of the rent," answered Brough; "and what is still better, I am not likely to pay a higher one, for the lease is long enough to last my time, and Mary's after me. The wench, I suppose will soon mate with young Frank Marldale, of the Willow Farm, which adjoins mine, and then I shall give up business, so that the two estates may be made into one."

"But are you aware that his landlord, Cecil Derwent, wants the Willow Farm for himself, and will not give another lease when the present one is expired."

"Squire Derwent would not be so unjust as to turn out a tenant who has made the farm one of the best on his estate."

"I don't know that," replied the steward! "for there has long existed a great coolness between my master and Frank Marldale, and it may be that the young man will by and by find out that he has done wrong in treating with contempt a person who may do him a serious injury."

"Well," exclaimed the farmer, "I don't know much of this Cecil Derwent, for he has not been long with us, but as he was not always the rich man that he now is, I should think he will have some little compassion on those who have to labour hard to pay him his rent. At any rate his cousin, the late Mr. Clement Derwent, though he unfortunately spent the greater part of his time in travelling abroad, was a kind hearted and indulgent landlord. But he had his reasons for leaving England, I believe, for they say he wronged some poor, over-confiding girl, who died of a broken heart when she found that he refused to marry her."

"Ah!" sighed Reves, "the girl died, and Clement Derwent went abroad to seek oblivion for a crime that, when too late, he deeply deplored. At length chance threw in his way a young female child, whom he resolved to adopt, and if report speaks truly, he loved her as if she had been his own daughter."

"She disappeared mysteriously, did she not?"

"It is supposed she was stolen," replied the steward, "but upon that point, all darkness and uncertainty. However, be that as it may, Clement Derwent soon afterwards died, and on his will being opened, it was discovered that he had left the whole of his property to the child we are speaking of."

"Then how is it that his cousin, Mr. Cecil Derwent is the possessor of all these estates."

"By the will,'" answered Reves, "it was ordered that the child should have all the property if she was found within a certain number of years. In the event of nothing being heard of her, Mr. Cecil Derwent was to become the owner of the property, but on condition that if the girl should ever be found, he is to give to her one half of that which he now holds."

"Well," observed the farmer, "at any rate it dont seem very likely that she will be found now."

"I think not," replied Reves, for large rewards have been offered for any information that might lead to her discovery, and, strange to say, no one has yet com-forward to claim it.

"Perhaps, whoever stole the child murdered her for some reason or other."

"Well," exclaimed the old man, "it must be confessed, my own thoughts have sometimes turned in that direction, but, on further consideration it seems to me that no one can have had a motive for such an act."

"Not to get possession of her money, think you?" asked Brough.

"Nay, my good friend," exclaimed the steward, "my master, Mr. Cecil Derwent, is the only person interested in the matter, and he, though somewhat wild in his habits, is one of the last persons in the world who would commit such a crime as you allude to."

"Then its my opinion the girl will one of these days be found."

"At any rate," answered Reves, "I can undertake to say that my master will be well pleased if your prediction should happen to be fulfilled. It is true he would lose one half of the estates if such an event should take place; but the property is a very large one, and sufficient still remains to support him in gentlemanly independence. For my own part, however, I have no expectation that the girl will ever be heard of, for if still living, it is most likely she has been taken to some far distant country, where she will be kept in ignorance of the fortune to which she has so just a claim.'"

"Still," replied Farmer Brough, "whoever it was that stole her away, must have done so for the sake of becoming possessed of the property that has been left her."

"It is impossible to say what the motive was," returned the steward, "but I have sometimes thought there may have been a feeling of revenge in it, for the friends of the girl were entire strangers to Mr. Clement Derwent, and some of them may have attributed improper motives to his kindness. If I am right in that motive there is at once an explanation of that which has for so long a time been enveloped in mystery."

"I don't think you have guessed it though, friend Reves."

"Why not?"

"Because if the girl was alive she would have been produced before now for the sake of the reward."

"So she would, under ordinary circumstances, perhaps," answered the steward; "but remember, she was stolen, and those who were guilty of the act know well the punishment that would fall on those who were concerned in the transaction. However, just at present everything is so wrapped up in impenetrable mystery, that we must wait with patience till chance affords us some clue by which we may effect a discovery."

"Surely you don't mean to say that 'Squire Derwent is anxious for her to be found?"

"Indeed, my friend, but I believe he is though," answered Reves, "for anything is preferable to suspense, and as I before observed, the property is so large that he can part with half of it, without any inconvenience. Besides he is now spending only his share of it in the expectation that some day or other the lawful claimant will make her appearance."

"Then the 'squire is an honest man, though people hereabouts do say that he pays rather too much attention to their wives and daughters."

"A little harmless gallantry, my dear fellow, believe me," said the stewrad, smiling. "Remember, he is young, handsome, and has not long emerged from comparative poverty to almost unlimited wealth. Let those, then, who are jealous, be watchful, and by and by their anxiety will cease, when they see him married."

"Is there any chance of there being a mistress at the hall."

"Upon my word I am unable to satisfy you on that point," answered Reves, "for the truth is the squire is not over communicative, and it is not for a dependent like me to pry into affairs that belong not to the situation I hold."

"That's a sly rub at me, Master Reves," exclaimed the farmer, "but for all that I have perhaps as little curiosity as most folks. I merely asked the question without having any particular object in it, and you, like a prudent man, as you always are, don't choose to know anything of your master's affairs."

Mr. Reves smiled in reply to this, shook hands with the farmer, and then continued his way towards the hall. Farmer Brough then took the path which led across the fields, and had not proceeded very far when he was encountered by his young landlord, 'Squire Derwent.

"So I see you have made good use of the fine weather we have been favoured with, and got in your crops whilst most others have scarcely got half through their harvest," said Cecil Derwent as he came up to the sturdy yeoman.

"Aye, squire," he replied, "thank Heaven the corn is safely housed, and as to-morrow will be the first of September, the fields are all ready for you to shoot over, if you have a mind to try the flavour of your own partridges."

"I shall pay an early visit here in the morning, depend on it," replied Mr. Derwent, "for the sport is one that I am passionately fond of, and my steward tells me that game is particularly abundant this year on my estate."

"I neve saw it more so," returned Brough, "for within the last ten minutes I ave seen four coveys of birds that rose almost from under my feet."

"Are you among those who raise an outcry against the game laws?" demanded the young landowner.

"Why, like a good many other laws, there are faults to be found with it," answered Brough, "but I am not one of those that say a gentleman ought not to lay claim to the birds that are found on his estate. Those who have property have a right to keep off intruders who would shoot over their lands without either with your leave or by your leave. But I dont like the system of preserving game, for it's the tenant-farmer that is obliged to keep it, at an enormous sacrifice of his crops, and yet, if he ventures to kill so much as a single bird he is liable to be treated as a common felon."

"Well farmer," exclaimed Derwent, "neither you nor any of my other tenants shall ever have reason to complain of me in that respect. On application to my steward, leave will always be given to sport over my lands; and as for hares, which are the greatest of all destroyers, I give my free permission to shoot them wherever and whenever they may be found."

"That's kind of you, squire, at any rate," said Rowland Brough, "and it's just the sort of conduct that all landlords ought to pursue towards their tenants. You'll have many friends about here for it, depend on it, sir, and especially if you fix your residence at the hall, instead of going abroad to spend your money as our late landlord did."

"I intend to do so," answered Cecil, Derwent; "but my cousin had some excuse for leaving the neighbourhood, since it brought reflections to his mind that were unendurable."

"You have heard then about the poor girl who died of a broken heart when she found that he had deceived her with a false promise of marriage?"

"I have read it all," replied the 'Squire, but though my cousin had some faults, they were counterbalanced by many very excellent qualities as you no doubt know. But to change this melancholy subject, farmer,—it is usual, I believe, when the last load of corn is carried to the barn, to give what is called the Harvest-home supper."

"Oh yes, sir, that's always done in these parts.'

"And you, who appear to be such a genuine sample of the old English farmer, do not of course mean to break through so commendable a custom?"

"While he lives," exclaimed the other, "you will never find Rowland Brough give up any of the good old habits of his ancestors. I could almost as soon foresware my religion, which Heaven forbid! as omit the hospitality that our ancestors took so honourable a pride in. Aye, sir, we shall have real, substantial fare at the farm-house to-night; all my people are invited to partake, and hanged be he man, woman or child that don't kick care to the devil on so happy an occasion."

"And suppose an unbidden visitor should appear there?"

"He'll be welcome to the best I can put before him."

"Say you so! " exclaimed Cecil Derwent," then I will be there to put your hospitality to the test."

"Will you though, squire ?"

"In good truth, I will," he replied, "though I was not honoured with a formal invitation."

"Why, you see, sir," exclaimed Rowland Brough," I had a great mind to take the liberty to ask you, but I thought it might give offence to invite a gentleman so far above me."

"There can be no offence in a well meant compliment," answered Derwent, " and as I wish to live upon the best terms with all my tenants I will become one of those that are to partake of your hospitality this evening."

"I'm glad to hear you say so," exclaimed Brough, " but I hope you'll excuse my throwing out a little hint."

" To be sure I will, what is it ?"

" To remember that my niece, Mary Everett, is engaged to marry Frank Marldale, one of your tenants."

"Aye, aye," laughed Cecil Derwent, " I'll not abuse your confidence, depend on it. But what induced you to imagine that I should pay particular attention to the young lady ?"

"Why the truth of it is," he replied, " rumour says you are rather fond of the female sex."

"Then for once rumour has told the truth," exclaimed Derwent. " I love all the dear creatures who are not very old or ugly, but am, not so dishonourable as to injure the reputation of any woman. Besides, her lover will of course be present, and he would be a sufficient check even were I inclined to play the gallant with your pretty niece."

"That's just what it is that makes me feel rather uneasy," answered the farmer. Frank Marldale hasn't a very high opinion of you, and I was afraid of a quarrel taking place if he suspected you had any designs upon his intended."

" The foolish fellow might say what he liked," answered Cecil Derwent, " but I should have sufficient command over myself not to resent it. In good truth, farmer, I know not of any reason for his dislike of me."

"Well then, I can tell you how it began," replied Brough. "The Willow Farm, which he holds has been tenanted by his family for something more than a hundred years, and he thinks it a hard thing after all this time, that you should talk of turning him out of it on the day that his present lease expires."

"The truth is," answered Cecil Derwent, " I want to add that farm to my park, which is too small in proportion with the hall. That is my only motive, and if Marldale thinks himself aggrieved he ought to have spoken to me upon the subject, instead of showing his resentment by sulkiness."

" It would have been better to have done that certainly," exclaimed Brough ; "but perhaps he didn't think of it, and as we are all of the same opinion, I hope his conduct in this case will not make you think any the worse of him."

"As for thinking ill of the young man for his being loath to leave the farm it is impossible that I can do so," answered the 'squire. " It is only natural that he should wish to continue in the house of his ancestors, and if any other plan can be thought of for the enlargement of my park, I will give Frank Marldale another lease, for any reasonable term that he asks for."

"Oh !" exclaimed farmer Brough, " when I tell him this how differently he will think of you."

"It must not be mentioned to him yet."

"May I ask why not ?"

"Oh there are reasons for it," replied Cecil Derwent ; " in the first place I would not purchase his honourable opinion by doing what, after all, may only be an act of justice, and secondly I may find it necessary to take his farm for the purpose I have mentioned. However, be that as it may, I will take care that he has another in every respect as good."

"That won't do, sir," returned the farmer, shaking his head.

"Why not."

"Firstly, because he'll never feel himself at home in any other house than the one he was born in."

"Well ?"

"And secondly, squire, you must turn out some other tenant to make room for him, and Frank Marldale will never accept your offer, if that's to be the case."

"But I will inquire of Mr. Reves if I have not a farm that is vacant."

"I can save you the trouble, 'squire, by telling you that there is not one," exclaimed Rowland Brough.

"Humph ! you seem to be acquainted with my affairs."

"I know them as well, and perhaps rather better than you do yourself," replied the yeoman; " for after being on this spot for nearly three score years, there are few persons or places that I dont know, for miles round the neighbourhood. In a word 'Squire Derwent, there is only one farm on your estate that will be vacant within the next dozen years, and that happens to be the land held by Frank Marldale."

"At any rate I have no wish to be unjust towards him," said Derwent, "and will think this matter well over before I decide upon what is to be done. To night, farmer, I mean to avail myself of your hospitality, but remember, not a word must be said to your young friend as to the conversation that has passed between us."

They then parted, and Cecil Derwent directed his steps homewards, but scarcely had he proceeded a couple of hundred yards than he was startled by hearing a couple of loud reports, as if from a double barrelled gun. The sound came from the adjoining preserves, and the squire was angrily making his way towards it, when a singularly looking being was seen hastily leaving the place in pursuit of his servant, who appeared to have been wounded ; as they approached, Cecil Derwent drew himself aside in order to escape observation, and from the conversation that followed he discovered that one of the strangers was a cockney sportsman from London, and the other, his groom, or tiger, who had received a few spent shots in his head, which fortunately was too thick to have sustained any very serious injury. Having ascertained these facts, Mr. Derwent stepped forward and demanded the names of the persons who had intruded on the estate.

"What do you want to know our names for !" inquired the one who seemed to be the master.

"To take the necessary means to convince you that private property is not to be intruded on with impunity."

"Intruded on ! Do you call our being here an intrusion ?"

"I do indeed," answered Cecil Derwent, "and I rather think the magistrate will be of the same opinion when he hears the case."

"Magistrate !" exclaimed the cockney ; what has any magistrate to do with a gentleman that has got his shooting certificate in his pocket ?"

"The certificate ;" answered Derwent, "does not authorize you to traspass upon private property, nor to kill game earlier than the time prescribed by law."

"Stuff !" exclaimed the other, " dont the almanac tell us us that partridge shooting begins on the first of September ?"

"True, but this happens to be only the thirty-first of August."

"What of that ?" demanded the cockney quickly. "A day can make no difference, surely ;—and even if it did, I've shot nothing except my own servant, which I suppose I have a right to do as I like."

"I have asked you for your name, sir, and it seems you want to shuffle out of giving me a direct answer."

"Why should I answer a mere gamekeeper ?" demanded the other with ludicrous pomposity. "I am a gentleman, sir, and shall tell my name to no one but your master."

"Indeed ! then it so happens that you are now standing in the presence of

Cecil Derwent, the owner of the property on which you have thought proper to intrude."

"Oh! that's quite another thing?" exclaimed the cockney, drawing himself up. "You should have told me before who you are, and then all this disagreeable misunderstanding would have been avoided. Here is my card, sir :—Brassy Popjoy Esq. That's my name, sir, and the object that brought me here is to kill a few birds by way of bringing my hand in against I come to the place I have taken in the Highlands of Scotland for the shooting season."

"It seems then, Mr. Popjoy," replied the Squire, "that we are not to be honoured with a long visit."

"Oh, dear no," he replied, "I've paid a hundred pounds for the right of shooting upon some moors in the north, and I only just stopped here for a day or two, because I heard there was very good sport to be had on the Derwent estate."

"Your sport," laughed Derwent, "appears to have been rather in earnest, if one may judge by the woeful looks of your groom."

"What, poor Trubbs ?" exclaimed Popjoy, "Oh, it was all his own fault, the foolish fellow, I told him to go and beat some bushes, and at the moment that some birds flew out he must needs pop up his head, which received some few stray shots from my gun; luckily for him, however, there was no making any impression, and all he has to complain of is the loss of a little of his mad blood. But upon my life, Mr. Derwent, this is a very pleasant meeting, and you have no idea of the pleasure it would afford me to have your permission to pay you a visit at the hall."

"You forget, sir, that we are perfect strangers to each other."

"And yet we may have been often in company together."

"How so ?"

"Because my father was a pawnbroker, and we who are in that profession often meet with gentlemen who have favoured them with a call on business matters."

"Believe me, sir, it cannot have been so in the present instance."

"Very possibly, sir, very possibly," answered Popjoy, "so I beg you will not be offended at a little passing joke of mine. Besides sir, you are not talking to one of your every-day common sort of people, for though my father was a pawnbroker, his son scorned the vulgar trade, and when the old man popped himself off to another world, I, his only son and heir, cut the concern, and set up for a gentleman."

"Which," observed Cecil Derwent, "is a part that I dare say you find it more difficult to sustain than the former one."

"No," he replied, "I find it easy enough, for the old man died worth plenty of *tin*, and thats' always a passport you know, with good society."

"If by tin you mean money," said Mr. Derwent, "it will only admit its possessors into a certain species of society, that your well born and highly educated gentlemen avoid, Not that I doubt the respectibility of the class of persons you speak of, Mr. Popjoy."

"I should think not," exclaimed the cockney, "or my old man must have worked to very little purpose, when he was scraping and scraping to leave all he could to his son and heir, which, as I said before, sir, is no other than myself."

"I am glad to hear sir, that your circumstances are so good."

"Well, eight hundred a year ain't to be sneezed at, you know, Mr. Derwent," answered the other pompously, "and as I flatter myself my face and figure are somewhat more than passable, I expect by and by to make it about three times as much."

"By a wealthy marriage, I presume."

"You presume very correctly," answered Popjoy. "There's three or four rich gals ogling at me already ; but poor things I pity them, for they are all doomed to disappointment, and perhaps broken hearts."

"Because you cannot return their affections ?"

"Exactly so," replied the cockney conceitedly. "if there's one thing that I detest more than another it is vulgarity.   You understand what I mean, Mr. Derwent; a man should never marry into a low family."

" The young ladies you speak of then cannot boast of their birth or pedigree?"

" I know nothing about pedigrees," answered the other, " but the son of a rich old pawnoroker ain't going to throw himself away upon common riffraff.   Now there's Susan Dawks, rather a good looking girl, that will have about a thousand a year when the old chap drops off the hooks.   But then Dawks was a tallow chandler, and I could never bear people of that trade after passing the melting house in St. Paul's-churchyard; the very thought of a tallow chandler's daughter makes me sick."

" But she may be a very amiable girl."

" She's a girl of sound judgment or she would never have set her cap at me," continued Popjoy.   " And for that matter, so was Selina Higgins, whose father had grown wealthy on the profits of a green grocery business.   She was fond of me, as I thought, and the match was almost as good as made up, when one day I met her in Newgate street, leaning upon the arm of a dandy looking counter jumper."

" A counter jumper! "exclaimed Mr. Derwent, " and pray what species of animal is that?"

" A very common one, sir, that is seen prowling about the streets of London, chiefly by night," answered the cockney.   " They are most of them linendrapers' shopmen, and it was with one of these sort of chaps that I met Selina Higgins."

"But I suppose she could give a satisfactory reason for having been seen walking with him."

" The pride of the Popjoys could never stoop to ask for an explanation," replied the other.   " From that day I cut the connexion, and bestowed all my attentions upon Miss Sarah Swankey, the daughter of a respectable publican, who used to serve our house with beer.   She was a strapper, sir; weighed fourteen stone, but was unfortunately rather what people call dumpy."

"Your love for her I suppose was sincere?"

" I believe it was, too," answered Popjoy; " for every body said her father was one of the richest men in the parish, and if that warnt enough to make me have her I don't know what would be."

" Have you quarrelled with her too?"

" Why, we didn't exactly quarrel," he replied, " but we broke off the acquaintance rather suddenly, and now, if we happen to meet in the streets we always turn our heads in opposite directions, just to show how little we care for each other."

" Did you suspect her of jilting you, like Miss Selina Higgins?"

" No," exclaimed Mr. Brassy Popjoy, " but I found out that her father had made a regular plant against me."

" What do you mean by a plant."

" Why he wanted to gammon me into marrying his daughter."

" And that it appears you had been very willing to do."

" Right, but I was a deluded young man," replied the cockney; " I believed he had plenty of money, till one morning while looking through the gazette of that day, I saw among the list of bankrupts, the name of Samuel Swankey, licensed victualler, as large as life.   From that moment I cut the connexion, and am now at liberty to offer my hand, heart, and fortune to the first young lady of wealth and respectability who may be desirious of taking to herself a husband."

" Well, Mr. Popjoy "exclaimed Derwent, " you have afforded me so much amusement, that I freely forgive your intrusion upon my property.   Nay, to-morrow shooting will begin in earnest, and if you will favour me with a visit for a few days at the hall, I shall be happy to give you all the sport you desire.   This evening I cannot invite you, for I have to go to farmer Brough's yonder, who holds a merry making in honour of harvest home, and it will probably be late before I take my leave of the company."

"My dear sir," replied Popjoy, " nothing could have happened more apropos, for I have myself received an invitation from farmer Brough to spend the evening with him. So we shall meet again, and to-morrow I pledge myself to make my appearance at Derwent Hall as a visitor there for a few days. So, for the present, farewell, and you may rely upon it, as I pass through your preserves I shall respect your game out of sheer regard for the very gentlemanly owner."

In this manner did they part on the most friendly terms, and no sooner was the 'squire out of hearing than Trubbs, who by this time had recovered from his fright, advancing towards his master said :—

PEEP'S EXHIBITING HIS TEMPLE OF THE ARTS.

"Well, sir, I never saw the likes of you in all my life, for though you at first put yonder gentleman in a towering passion, you have managed to gammon him at last into the best possible humour."

"Trubbs," exclaimed the cockney, with affected dignity, "when will you attend to the advice I have so often given against making use of these coarse expressions? I have used no *gammon* to Mr. Derwent, but brought him into good humour entirely by the force of my own insinuating manners. And you see the advantage I have gained by it; an invitation to his house followed, and I shall have the privilege of shooting over one of the finest manors in the whole county."

No. 2.

"I hope better luck is to come sir," exclaimed the imperturbable groom, "for though you have had at least twenty excellent shots in the course of the last three hours, my game bag is as empty as when first we came out."

"That's through my being rather nervous to day, Trubbs," answered his master. "Besides, I've had no practice since last year, and my aim is a little unsteady.'

"So it seemed when you just now hit me instead of a partridge."

"Hush," exclaimed Popjoy, "you must'nt go telling everybody about that little accident. You are not hurt, sirrah, though you had the impertinence to say you were; but I am you master, sirrah, and ought to know best what damage has been done."

"Hist, sir, here's some one coming."

"Who is he?"

"It's a she, sir, young, pretty and—"

Before he could conclude his description, Mary Everett, who had come out to meet her lover on his return home, passed through the gate near which they were standing. Finding herself in the presence of strangers she would have retreated, but Popjoy was too gallant to let such an opportunity pass, and advancing towards her he gave utterance to such a torrent of unmeaning nonsense, that poor Mary became still more uneasy at finding herself in such disagreeable company. Again she would have retreated, but the cockney was not to be thus foiled, and once more he broke forth in that peculiar jargon which is an offence to females of a sensitive mind. She replied to him with dignity, reminding him that they were strangers, and that, under those circumstances it was rude and uncourteous thus to thrust his conversation upon her. Popjoy, however, could not be made to feel the force of this argument, and as she was turning away to leave him, he seized the maiden's hand and forcibly detained her. But his temerity had nearly cost him dear, for at that moment Frank Marldale arrived at the spot, and would have inflicted a severe chastisement upon the stranger had not Farmer Brough made his appearance just in time to prevent the collision. Upon his interference the affair was patched up, and the young man, supporting Mary on his arm, proceeded on his way to the farm.

This done, Rowland Brough called about him a number of poor persons who were waiting near, and having given them all permission to gather up the ears of corn that lay scattered in his fields, he accompanied Popjoy to his own home.

CHAPTER II.

A TRAVELLING SHOWMAN AND HIS FAMILY.—HOW TO COLLECT AN AUDIENCE.—
THE ARRIVAL OF A SUSPICIOUS STRANGER.

At a later hour of the day other visitors were attracted towards the hospitable roof of Rowland Brough. Many a weary mile had Peeps and his wife travelled that day, but in vain had they endeavoured to persuade the rustics to part with their pence for the wonderful exhibition that he boasted it was in his power to exhibit to them. In a word Peeps was the owner of a portable show, which he carried on his back, whilst his better half carried before him the folding tressel on which his load was made to rest whenever there was a probability of an audience being collected On arriving near the homestead of Farmer Brough, the showman came to a full stop, and his temple of arts, as he called it, was placed ready for exhibition.

"And what good do you expect to get here?" demanded Mrs. Peeps, who by the way, was a bit of a Tartar. "There ain't a soul about the place, and yet you would dawdle away your time here when we ought to be making the best of our way to the next town, where there is a chance of our picking up something in the way of business."

"My dearest Angelina," replied her good tempered husband, "you are a wide awake woman, a very wide awake woman, but you don't know everything."

"I know we are not likely to get any money in this place."

"There you are wrong, my love," answered her husband, "for there is a merry making going on, and as of course there'll be lots of people, we may expect that some of them will have taste enough to patronize our temple of the arts."

"Not they, when they've got something better to do," exclaimed Mrs. Peeps. "There'll be plenty of eating and drinking going on, which will be more than we shall be able to say for ourselves, if you persist in idling away your time here."

"Angelina, my best love,' exclaimed her husband, "you are always twitting me about my idleness, and yet I don't believe that in all our travels you ever met with a more industrious fellow. Look at that magnificent temple of arts, for instance, warn't it formed by my own hands, from my own designs! Didn't I paint all the scenery, and don't I carry it about with me on my back for miles and miles every day of my life? Don't I exhibit it to delighted audiences; and don't you, Mrs. Peeps, ungrateful as you are, act the part of money taker without my ever seeing the colour of the coin?"

"Well, and dont I take care of it, for you."

"You do, my love, for none of it ever finds its way into my pocket. But never mind, Mrs. P. we'll not get into an argument about that now, but commence business at once, so here goes for a tune on the mouth organ, which you, as usual, will delightfully accompany on the triangle."

"And what good will that be," demanded the wife, "when Amy is not here to dance to our music. I wonder where she can be loitering all this time?"

"She's not far off," replied the owner of the temple of arts. "Like me, Amy is a lover of nature, and she has only stopped a little by the roadside to gather a few of the wild flowers that are growing in the hedges. Bless her little heart; I love her as if she was really our own daughter, instead of being the child of somebody else whose name we never heard."

"And most likely never shall."

"Well I am almost in hopes we never shall," answered Peeps; "for somehow I fancy it would break my heart if she was to be claimed and taken away from us."

"Psha! exclaimed Mrs. Peeps, "depend upon it if ever that girl's parentage should be discovered, she will turn out to be a rich heiress, and then, as a matter of course, she would do something handsome for us in gratitude for the care we have always bestowed upon her."

"And why, my Angelina, do you believe she comes of a good family?" he asked.

"Because the man that gave her into your hands made such a mystery about it. Then he kept part of the locket that she wears in order that he might be able to recognize her at any time when it may be convenient, and he would hardly have done that if she had been the daughter of any poor persons."

"Mrs. P.—Mrs. P!" exclaimed her husband, "who is it I should like to know that is wasting time now? Here we have been wasting this quarter of an hour with business at a complete stand still; so accompany me while I play, and the sound of our music will soon bring Amy to us."

And he was right in his anticipations, for no sooner were the shrill notes of the pipes heard than a young and beautiful, though somewhat coarsely clad, girl came bounding with a joyous step towards them.

"Now, my little dear," exclaimed the showman, "you ought to know that business is business, and pleasure is pleasure. You have been stopping on the way to gather wild flowers, and at the same time have been stopping the laudable efforts of Mrs. P. and myself to collect those useful coins without which we find it impossible to carry on the war."

"Alas!" sighed the girl, "then I have made you angry with me?"

"No, no, we are not angry with you, my dear child," exclaimed Mrs. Peeps;

"but we have a chance of making a little money here, and when that is done we have some few miles to go before we reach the next town."

"Ah !" cried the showman, as he saw Amy look round about her, "I know well enough what you are thinking of. You wonder where our audience is to come from. But never mind; dance to our music, my girl, and you'll soon see a most respectable company before you."

This was no sooner said than done; Peeps and his wife contrived to make most discordant music, and Amy danced gracefully, though paying little heed to the sounds which were calculated rather to mislead than assist her. As had been anticipated, a number of the farm servants quickly congregated on the spot, who being overpowered by the eloquence of the showman, paid the sum demanded into the hands of Mrs. Peeps, whose good humour was completely restored on seeing the rapid increase that was made in her almost exhausted treasury. In the midst of all this, Farmer Brough and Mary Everett made their appearance, and in the fear that all further business was put an end to, the proprietor of the exhibition stammered out the best apology he could make.

"Beg your pardon sir," he said;—"I hope there's no offence; but you see this temple of arts of mine aint one of your common every-day, trashy affairs. It possesses genius and a dewelopement of the fine arts combined, and has been exhibited before all the crowned heads in Europe. The charge, sir, is only a penny, but if you'll not be offended, I'll place you on the free list, and you shall see the whole performance free, gratis, for nothing !"

"My good fellow," exclaimed farmer Brough, "I have no wish to interfere with your business, nor the pleasure of those who are in my service. Let them enjoy themselves, but I would rather it was not in this place."

"Any where you please, sir," returned Peeps;—"perhaps you will give me permission to make use of your barn ?"

"The barn, I am happy to say, is better occupied," answered the farmer; "but you shall come into my house, where you and your family shall be heartily welcome to partake of our hospitality. This is the night for our harvest-home, and I would have no one pass my door when all within is joy and merriment."

"You are very good, sir," Mrs. Peeps ventured to say, "but we have a long distance to go before we reach the next town."

"Then, make up your mind to stay here for the night," exclaimed Rowland Brough, "we have plenty of beds for the accommodation of those who choose to remain, and to-morrow when you leave you shall have five shillings to make up for any loss of business that may happen through this whim of mine."

"There, Angelina, my dear," whispered Peeps, "didn't I tell you there was money to be made here?"

Whilst this conversation was going on, the attention of Mary Everett was directed towards Amy, who, seated on the ground, was so absorbed in her own reflections that she heeded nothing of what was doing around her. Mary, however, advanced, and raising her gently up, led her towards the showman.

"Who is this?" she asked; "it seems that she travels with you, and yet from her appearance I should imagine that her condition has not always been so lowly."

"Why, to tell you the truth, she ain't exactly our daughter," replied Peeps, "but she has been with us so long that we look on her almost as such. She was placed under our care about sixteen years since by a chap that I have never seen since, and whether she was his own child or that he had stolen her from somebody, I could never find out."

"Why, Mary, my child," exclaimed Farmer Brough, "you seem to be quite taken with the young stranger."

"I own it, dear uncle," she replied, "for she seems care-worn and full of sorrow."

"And yet, lady," exclaimed Amy, "I have everything to be grateful for to these kind friends, who have ever treated me as their daughter.

"Have you no recollection of events that occurred before you were placed under their care."

"None," she replied;—"at least none that I can rely on ; all seems to me like a dream, and I can remember nothing but the scowling countenance of the man that placed me with those who have since been as parents to me."

"Well, my poor girl," exclaimed the warm-hearted farmer, "if you have any griefs you must forget them to-night, for I would see every face about me smiling and joyful. It shall be the care of my niece to keep you amused, so follow us into the house, for by this time supper must be on the table, and I dare say my friends here are ready to do justice to it."

"Has that strange looking person from London come yet?" asked Mary Everett.

"Oh yes," answered her uncle, "I met Mr. Popjoy on my way, and brought him home with me. Mr. Derwent too will soon be here, so, in doors with you, and hang the man or woman that would look unhappy at our harvest merriment."

All present entered the farm house, and hardly had the place been cleared than a man of peculiarly dark and sinister appearance reached the spot. From the pack which he carried on his shoulders, he seemed to be a hawker, and the name on the licence which was affixed to it was Caleb Kestrel. He looked around him as if almost afraid of being seen, and muttered, as sounds of laughter came from the house :—

"So, at length I find myself once more in my native village. The people though seem to have forgotten me, for I have spoken to many, and not one has yet recognized the voice or features of Caleb Kestrel. Well, so much the better for the purpose I have on hand ; time, and the hardships I have gone through will so far assist me in the business I have to do. But where the devil have the people hid themselves that I trusted the girl with. From one end of the kingdom to the other I have traced them, almost step by step and yet when it seemed certain that I was on the eve of pouncing on them, they have disappeared, as if they knew my purpose, and endeavoured to avoid me. But let them beware how they play any of their tricks on Caleb Kestrel, for he is not used to be trifled with, and if he finds out that they are making a fool of him, he'll—Pshaw ; whats the use of giving way to all this ill humour, like a spoilt child? My first business is to discover them, and my next to act according to circumstances. Let what will happen, the girl must be found, and when that is done it will be easy to extort a large sum of money from this 'Squire Derwent as the price of my silence. Ah! he little thinks of the mischief that is plotting against him, but when my time comes he will make the notable discovery that he must either pay me handsomely or give up half his estates to the adopted child of his late cousin."

As he arrived at this conclusion, the very person of whom he was speaking passed on his way to the house of Farmer Brough. He, however, knew him not, and throwing himself in his path, he said :—

"Pardon me, young gentleman for interrupting you, but I am a stranger in these parts, and want to be directed the nearest way to the mansion of one 'Squire Derwent."

"Indeed!" exclaimed the young man eyeing him with some little distrust; "is your business of so much importance that you must needs see him at this late hour of the day ?"

"Why, you see sir," answered Kestrel, without betraying the least sign of confusion, "I live by my honest toil as a travelling hawker, and must seek my customers wherever I can find them. I have some fine linen in my pack that may suit the 'squire, if he is in want of such an article, and would see him to-night that may start early to-morrow morning on my journey."

"Humph!" returned the other, "from what I know of Mr. Derwent, he is not very likely to purchase goods from a man who hawks things about the country."

"At any rate there can be no harm in trying to do business with him," answered Caleb, "for I have a good tongue of my own, and may persuade him to be a customer, even though he may not be in immediate want of my goods. Besides, I was abroad some years ago, and have often seen his cousin, Edmund Derwent, who, just before his death, charged me with a message to the 'squire here, which I was to deliver as soon as possible after my arrival in England."

" Why, he has been dead sixteen years," exclaimed Cecil Derwent, " so you have taken your time to consider his request."

" Aye, that's true enough," answered the other, " but there are sufficient reasons, when I choose to explain them, for not having performed my promise sooner. In short, my intentions were good enough, but your confounded laws brought me to a full stop almost as soon as I set foot on English ground."

" How long ago was that ?"

" Within a twelvemonth after I had undertaken to convey the message, I returned to this country a poor and friendless man. But I was determined to keep my promise, and immediately commenced my inquiries after Cecil Derwent. But according to the terms of his cousin's will he had not then taken possession of the property which had been bequeathed him, on certain conditions, and as he was then in a state of absolute poverty, he was supposed to be residing in some out of the way place till the time arrived when he was to take possession of his estate."

" And then I suppose, your inquiries ended ?"

" Why to tell you the truth they did," replied Caleb Kestrel, " for I had no money to pay the expence of travelling about from place to place in search of him ; and as it seemed that he was too poor to give me any, even if he should be found, I gave up the pursuit, thinking it the wisest course to wait till he came out of his obscurity."

" But how is it that you have suffered fifteen years to elapse since that time ?" asked the 'squire.

" Oh, it would take a long while to explain that."

" You have been abroad since, I suppose ?"

" Right; I have been abroad," he replied, " and the worst of it was I was obliged to go against my own inclination."

" How, have you been convicted of a crime ?"

" It was all the same thing," answered Kestrel, " for people thought me guilty, and all my own assertions of innocence were listened to as so many idle words. I was sentenced to be transported for fourteen years ; have suffered my punishment, and having only just returned to England, took up the trade of a travelling hawker, and made my way to this place in order to have an interview with 'Squire Derwent."

" You will scarcely be able to see him to-night, my friend," exclaimed Cecil, " for he spends the evening in yonder farm-house, and therefore will not be disengaged till to-morrow."

" You speak, young gentleman, as if you knew Mr. Derwent's thoughts upon the subject."

" I perhaps know them as well as any body can," replied Cecil, " and you will therefore do well to take my advice."

" Which is, not to see him till to-morrow."

" Exactly so," replied the 'squire, " and even then I think your trouble will be taken in vain, for a message can be of very little consequence after sixteen years have been suffered to intervene since you were intrusted with it."

" Perhaps I am the best judge of that."

" It may be so," replied the 'squire, " and you are still at liberty to pursue your own course. Go to the hall if you please, in the morning, but I have very strong doubts whether Mr. Derwent will think it worth his while to give you an interview."

" But he must give me an interview."

" Must !"

" Aye, he shall do so," answered Kestrel.

" He will do as he likes about that, I suppose ?"

" Let him, and it will be the worst day's work he ever did for himself."

" Your words are full of mystery," exclaimed Cecil, " but entrust me with a portion of your message, and as I shall see him presently, I will carry it to him. Perhaps, if there is anything of real importance in your visit, he may be inclined to leave the company and give you the interview you ask for."

" What I have to say," answered Kestrel, " must be whispered into no ears but his own Unconsciously he stands upon the brink of ruin, and it will be his own fault if he does not avoid the destruction that threatens him."

" Nay, ruin he cannot have to fear," exclaimed the 'squire, still resolved not to discover himself; " for the fortune he possessed was bequeathed to him, and no law has the power to deprive him of it."

" You appear to know his affairs, young man ?"

" I am perfectly acquainted with them all," he replied, " for I am particularly intimate with Mr. Derwent, and know all the circumstances of his past life."

"You are aware then that he inherits the property of his cousin on certain conditions."

"Yes, it was to be equally divided between him and a child who in an unaccountable manner disappeared, and has never since been heard of."

" And perhaps never may."

" That remains to be proved," answered Cecil. " Some reports, it is true, say that she was murdered for some motive that has never been explained. Mr. Derwent, however, believes that she still lives, and should she ever appear and her identity be proved, the half of his estate will be given up to her."

" So he may say," exclaimed Kestrel, " when there seems to be but little probability of her being alive, but he would change his opinion upon that matter if ever the girl should be brought forward to make her claim."

" Your words have a meaning in them that I cannot discover."

" Nor do I wish you to do so," answered the stranger. " The squire is the only man that I shall open my mind to, and he is so wrapt up in the company he is keeping yonder that he will not come forth to hear the message I have to deliver. But you, sir, had better say that you have seen me, and that all I ask is a few minutes audience with him."

" I shall not even mention the affair to him," exclaimed Cecil ; " so you ma rest assured that Mr. Derwent will know no more of your presence here than he does at this moment."

" Then I must wait till the morning, when I shall not fail to pay him a visit at the hall.

"Do so, and it will then be at his own option whether he sees you or not."

" I have said before he must and shall see me."

" You had better not send in such a message as that," returned Cecil ; " or the chances are a hundred to one that, as a magistrate, he will make inquiries into your character, that may lead to no very pleasant results."

" But suppose I have no more to fear from 'Squire Derwent than he has from me ?" demanded the other.

" Does he know your name, if you should wish to be announced ?"

" I can't say whether he does or not," replied Kestrel, " but its likely enough he may, for there was one time in my life when it was tolerably notorious. Be that as it may, however, I have important business with him, and if he refuses to see me, it will be all the worse for him before he's many hours older."

" Or, in plain words, you want to extort money from him, for some sort of information that he probably cares as little about, as I do myself."

" H e may be made to feel, whether what I have to say is not worth caring about."

" At first," exclaimed Cecil Derwent, " I thought your motive for coming here was a friendly one; but your words now convince me that you are here for no good purpose. I shall therefore deem it my duty to inform him of all that has taken place between us, and, if he takes my advice, he will give orders for your being turned away from his door."

"Then your advice will be the most unneighbourly you could give," answered the other. "It would be far better if you persuade him to hear what I have to say, that he may judge for himself as to what course he had better pursue. I bear him no ill-will, but on the contrary, the trouble I have taken to see him ought to be a convincing proof, that the message I have to deliver is a most important one."

"Whatever may be its importance," exclaimed Cecil, "there is surely no need for it to be delivered to night."

"And why should I wait the leisure of any man?" demanded Kestrel. "I am poorer than he is, it is true, and my character has perhaps suffered; but, with all his wealth, this Cecil Derwent has not a prouder spirit than that dwells in the heart of the despised fellow before you."

"Surely you have no reason to complain of a little delay when the person you wish to see was engaged with company before your arrival here."

"Psha," what has pleasure to do with business? I have journeyed far enough to see him, and there ought to have been no delay, when I have other matters that call me home immediately."

"It is not for me to make an apology for my friend," exclaimed Cecil, "but I can take upon myself to say, that on no consideration will he be induced to see you this evening. What he may do to-morrow, a few hours will show."

"He will refuse me audience then, perhaps," answered Kestrel, "and if he does I will not leave this neighbourhood till I have made him feel that I possess the power I boast."

"Do you wish me to convey that threat to him?"

"I care not whether you do or do not," returned the other, "for if he was now standing before me I should not express myself in any other words. I have nothing to fear from him, but he must look to himself, lest pride and insolence make him bow his head to the very earth."

"Upon my word!" exclaimed Cecil; "to hear you talk, any one would suppose 'Squire Derwent had been guilty of some great crime."

"I don't accuse him of crime," answered the other, "but his fortune is in my power, and he shall return to his former insignificance if I am to be treated with scorn."

"And the advantage you boast of possessing has been given by the message that was intrusted to you by the late owner of these domains!"

"Come, come," exclaimed Kestrel, "you and I are strangers to each other, and I am not fool enough to explain my business expect to the person I have come so far to see. He will not be rash enough, I should think, to have me turned away before he hears what I want to speak to him about, and if he chooses to grant me an interview, he will learn in a few words the situation in which he stands. To night he may enjoy the festivity in which he is engaged, but in the morning I promise him food enough for his most serious reflection. You smile sir, and seem to doubt my word, yet if you are in the confidence of Mr. Cecil Derwent you will learn from his own lips, that I can put my foot upon his neck as if he was my slave."

"I rather think you will not find it easy to make him yield by threats and intimidation. His character cannot be injured by the malice of a foe, for he has always been esteemed an honourable man, and possesses the happy consciousness of never having been guilty of an unworthy action."

"Humph! Mr. Derwent is fortunate in having so thick and thin a friend."

"I should not have ventured to speak quite so much in his praise," answered the other, checking himself, "but that I saw reason to believe his character is about to be assailed by some unknown foe. What your purpose is in coming here I know not, but in the name of Cecil Derwent, I warn you not to injure one who, when once roused, is fierce and implacable in his wrath."

"We shall see who is to have the best of this," muttered Caleb Kestrel sullenly.

"Aye, we shall see," replied the other; "and for my own part I have not the least fear for the result.   Nay more, I will undertake to promise you shall be permitted to have an interview with him in the morning; but be guarded in your conduct, or you may chance to get the worst of it in the meeting you are so anxious for; and now, sir, I take my leave, for my friends will begin to grow alarmed at my absence, and some of them may presently come out in search of me; away then, and at nine to-morrow you shall find ready admittance into the house of Mr. Cecil Derwent."

AMY THE DANCING GIRL RECOGNIZES KESTREL.

With this he hastened to the scene of festivity, leaving Caleb Kestrel not a little perplexed at what had taken place; little, however, did he suspect that he had been conversing all the time with the person of whom he spoke; and exulting in the prospect of speedily achieving the design that had brought him there, he looked around for some place in which he might obtain shelter for the night; the only place he could see was a barn, which he entered, and, throwing himself down on a heap of straw once more gave a free current to his thoughts,

No. 3.

CHAPTER III.

HARVEST HOME FESTIVITIES.—MARY EVERETT, AND HER NEWLY-FOUND FRIEND—
A DANCE.—A CAPTURE, AND A DISCOVERY.

THE festival given by Farmer Brough to his neighbours and labourers was provided with no niggard views of economy ; of good, solid, English fare, there was
an abundance, even to profusion, and the strong ale that had been brewed expressly
for the purpose, was served round with a liberality that would have shocked our
water-drinking teetotallers.   When the supper was over, Mary Everett was glad
to leave the table, and was soon joined by Amy, who being asked if she had no
clue by which to discover her parents, replied that hitherto all her efforts to do so
had ended in disappointment.

"'Tis strange," exclaimed Mary, "that the people who have brought you up
made no inquiries of the man by whom you were placed under their protection."

"I have heard them say that they did ask him some questions, but he refused to
give them any explanation."

"How is he to prove your identity, should he ever wish to claim you from them?"
asked Mary.

"By means of this broken locket," she replied, showing one which was suspended round her neck. "The half you now look on I have constantly worn ever
since, and the other he kept to compare with mine, should he ever demand me
from those to whom he entrusted me."

"Which, I suppose, you hope he never may do."

"Alas !" sighed Amy, "the saddest moments I have are those in which I look
forward to the chance that I may some day be removed from those who have ever
treated me as their own child. They are poor, young lady, very poor, but whatever they have is shared with me without a murmur."

"That is as it should be," exclaimed Mary Everett, "for it seems to me that
you do your proportion of work towards providing the means of subsistence."

"It is but little I can do," answered Amy, "and I cannot but feel that I am a
heavy burden to my kind-hearted protectors."

"Have you any recollection of the home you dwelt in, before you were placed
under the care of this man, Peeps, and his wife?"

"Very little," she replied, "but I remember our house was a large one—that it
was richly furnished, and that there were many servants in attendance."

"Then of course you belong to a good family."

"I believe so ; but all that concerns that part of my life is veiled in mystery and
doubt."

"How came you to leave your once happy home?"

"I was stolen."

"Stolen !—by whom?"

"Ah !" exclaimed Amy, "that is what I am afraid will never be discovered,
for the villain who took me away has never since been seen or heard of."

"Have you any recollection of his features?"

"Very slight," answered Amy ; "and yet if he were ever to stand before me, I
think I should be able to recognise him."

"Well," exclaimed Mary Everett, "it is to be hoped you never will see him
again, for that he was your enemy has been pretty clearly shown by his acts."

"And yet," sighed Amy, "it is through him alone that I can ever hope to discover the secret of my birth."

"True, that is one reason certainly why you should wish to meet with him again,
although, perhaps, if he were to seek after you, it would only be for the purpose of
taking you away from the people who have treated you with so much kindness."

"That is what I am afraid of," she replied, "for it would break my heart to be taken away from my friends. Ah! young lady, they are odd people in their way, but they have good hearts, and never can I be grateful enough for the kindness they have always shown me."

"Had they any previous acquaintance with the man who placed you under their care?"

"I believe they had known him before."

"Then of course you have heard the name of your foe."

"Only once," replied Amy, "and that was by accident, for it seems they were bound in some way or another never to divulge that secret to me.

"Perhaps they would tell my uncle if he were to put the question to them!" observed Mary Everett.

"Do not ask him to do so," exclaimed Amy, "for if the man we speak of were to hear that they have betrayed his secret it might lead to the most fearful consequences. For their sake then I am content to remain in ignorance of that which might have a most important effect on my future fate."

"Well, my dear girl," answered Amy, "you need be under no apprehension that I shall do anything to cause you a moment's uneasiness. Here, however, I hope you will consent to remain for some time to come, and it shall be our endeavour to make amends for all the misfortunes you have undergone."

"Thanks, generous lady," exclaimed Amy! "I feel for your kindness, but cannot avail myself of it. Those who have so long had the care of me would not part with me without sorrow, and never will I give a pang to those whose every thought has been to render as smooth as possible my path of life."

"But surely if they really love you they would not throw any obstacle in the way of your future prospects."

"They would not," exclaimed Amy; "I know they would not, but they would feel no less acutely my ingratitude in being willing to leave them from motives of self-interest. No, no, dearest young lady, I feel your kindness, but nothing will ever tempt me to leave those I am so deeply indebted to."

"At all events I will speak to them on the subject, and I dare say they will gladly avail themselves of the offer, since it will be so much to your own advantage."

"Indeed, indeed, I should be very sorry if you were to carry your generous intentions so far," cried Amy earnestly. "I love them as a child should love its parents, and to be separated from them now would be the greatest misfortune I have yet known."

"What!" exclaimed Mary Everett; "greater than the one that dragged you from your home?"

"Far greater," she replied, "for at that time I was too young to feel the cruelty that had been inflicted on me. A few days with those worthy people served to allay all my griefs, for they were kind and indulgent, and did all they could to render less painful the change that had taken place in my condition. To them I owe a heavy debt of gratitude, and now, when age is advancing upon them, I will not afflict them by throwing myself upon the protection of others. Think no more of it, then I entreat, for I must bear them company to-morrow when they set forth to resume their humble occupations."

"At present I will not urge my request any further," said Mary, "but you will not feel offended, I hope, if I speak to you once more on this subject before you go?"

The reply of Amy was prevented by a general rising of the guests from the supper table, and the musicians having been desired to take their places, preparations were made for concluding the evening with a dance. This arrangement was relished exceedingly by Mr. Brassey Popjoy, who had a great desire to show off his own graceful movements, though not in a country dance, as was proposed, for that, he thought, would be vulgar. The polka, he declared, was the only dance which he could join in, but as the polka required more than one person, and there was no one in the room who knew anything about it, the young gentleman saw with no little chagrin that there was no chance of his showing off before the present company.   Fortunately for his vanity, however, Mrs. Peeps stepped forth to the rescue.

" Ah !" she exclaimed, " what a lucky thing it is that I can help you at such a time as this.   Two can dance the polka, and I—"

" Mrs. Peeps," exclaimed Popjoy, interrupting her, " I beg you will proceed no further with your proposition, for, anxious as I feel to luxuriate in my favourite dance, I have no wish to take you for a partner."

" Me !" she exclaimed with surprise.

" Ah !" interposed her husband, " what a ninny you must be to suppose that Mrs. P. was able to go through the polka.   No, no, her chief occupation in life is to take money from those who patronize our Temple of Arts, and the dancing part of the business she leaves to our little Amy."

" Amy !" exclaimed the cockney ; " what the girl that has been talking so long to the farmer's niece ?"

" That's the identical girl I mean."

" But surely the daughter of a travelling showman can't know anything about the polka."

" Only try the travelling showman's daughter," exclaimed Peeps, " and when you have seen her paces—steps I mean—I think you will pronounce her to be nothing less than an out and outer."

" Is this true, or is the old 'un only trying to gammon me ?" asked Brassey Popjoy of the young girl.

" He would not have told an untruth," she replied ; " and since you have appealed to me, I confess that I know the dance perfectly well ; though, having a dislike to it, I have not danced it for some time past."

" Well, oblige the gentleman for this once," exclaimed Mrs. Peeps, " show him what you can do, my dear," she added in a whisper, " and perhaps he may reward you with a handsome present."

" I don't know what the old lady means by whispering before company," said Popjoy, " but I hope, since you appear to know the dance, you will not refuse to go through it with me."

Amy without making any reply to this, suffered herself to be led to the upper end of the room, and luckily for Mr. Popjoy, the musicians were able to play his favourite polka.   His ridiculous pretensions, however, soon became manifest, but Amy proved herself to be a graceful dancer, and at the end of the performance she was honoured with most tremendous applause from the company.   To this succeeded a country dance, which was led off by Cecil Derwent and Mary Everett, to the no small mortification of her lover, who intended for himself the honour which had been conferred upon another,   He sullenly refused to join in the dance, and withdrawing himself into a corner of the room, sat watching the movements of the young couple with feelings of the greatest exasperation and jealousy.   At length the dance ceased, and Mr. Derwent smilingly approached him.

" How is it, my good sir," he asked, " that you alone refuse to join in the amusement of the evening ?"

" Am I expected to give reason for pursuing the bent of my own inclination ?" demanded the young man, haughtily.

" Certainly not," answered Derwent, " but I had no notion that you felt offended at my having opened the dance with a young lady to whom you are engaged."

" I am not offended, sir," replied Frank Marldale ; " but a gentleman like you, I should have thought, might have known better than to deprive me of my partner."

" Come, come," exclaimed the squire, " don't let there be any ill feeling between us about such a trifle as this."

" A trifle ?"

" Yes, lovers are not expected to dance together the whole of the evening, and I as the greatest stranger here, made use of my privilege to open the dance with the e of our excellent host.   The young lady made no objection, and I am sure you will not make her uneasy by a display of jealousy that is wholly uncalled for."

" You are the last person in the world whose advice I should ask," muttered Frank Marldale.

" Indeed ! then now I see this is not the first time I have given you offence."

" It is not the first time."

" Then all I can say is that I am not aware of any act of mine that you have cause to complain of."

" Have you then so soon forgotten that at the expiration of the present lease I have been threatened to be turned out of my farm?"

" I am not aware that any threat has been made use of," replied Mr. Derwent ; " but I admit that, for the purpose of enlarging my own park, I have spoken to Mr. Reeves, my steward, about applying your farm to that purpose."

" Then I can only say,' returned Frank, " that it is most unjust to turn me out of my land after the care of myself, and those who held it before me, to bring it into a state of good cultivation, and make it one of the best farms on your estate."

" It may appear hard, I dare say," answered Mr. Derwent, " but you had no right to expect that new leases should be given for ever to the present tenant and his successors ; I may want it for a purpose of my own, but whenever you may be called upon to leave the Willow Farm, I pledge myself to put you in another, that shall be in every respect as good."

" I'll accept of no favour from you, squire," exclaimed Frank Marldale, " for I can feel nothing but hatred and contempt for the man who would heartlessly turn me out of the house in which I and my forefathers for between two and three generations were born. And Mary, too, though she knows how bitterly I feel the conduct you have pursued towards me, could take you by the hand with as much kindness as if you had been our best and most sincere friend."

" Poor girl !" exclaimed Mr. Derwent, " do not blame her for an unintentional affront. I was the first to ask her hand in the dance, and, to say the least of it, it would have been most discourteous had she refused, when I knew she had not been previously engaged."

" I dare say," replied Frank, with a sneer, " you know better than I do the forms and customs of fashionable life. But Mary and I are humble people, who have been brought up in a plain homely way, and she ought to have refused to dance with you when she knew I expected to be her partner all the evening."

" Well really, my good sir," exclaimed the squire, " you are carrying your notions to the height of absurdity.'

" Perhaps you may think so," retorted Frank Marldale, gloomily, " but our country customs may not be worse than your London ones, and we don't want to be guided here by what people do in fashionable life. In a word, I look upon you as a foe, and from this time forward I never want to speak to you except when I come to pay my rent, and from present appearances it seems that I shall not have to do that much longer."

" You are a strange, impetuous fellow, Marldale," exclaimed the squire. " and yet with all your insulting words I am determined not to take an affront from you whilst you are in this humour. Upon reflection you will think better of it, and for my own part I will consult with Mr. Reeves upon the possibility of your remaining at the Willow Farm if some other place bordering on the park can be made to answer my purpose."

" Don't deceive yourself by supposing that I would remain there after knowing that you want to get rid of me," replied Marldale, " I am as proud a man as yourself, in spite of the difference there is between our stations in life, and rather than live under a man who has given me notice to quit, I'll go and work as a common labourer for my daily bread."

" Psha ! you will think better of this when you have given yourself time for cool reflection."

" Cool reflection," answered Frank Marldale, " will never change the contempt I feel for you into respect."

" We shall see about that," exclaimed the squire, " so we'll speak further upon this matter some other time. These angry words of yours will presently reach the ears of the company, and we should be ungrateful towards our host to say or do anything to mar the pleasure he has prepared for us."

" Oh, there's no fear of our being overheard," replied Marldale, " for every one is too much engaged in the dance to pay any attention to us. I have, however, said all that I wished, and now, as you know my mind upon the subject, I hope you'll never so far lower yourself as to try to win back the respect I once bore to your family, by making an offer of another lease of the farm. I'll leave it, though my heart will be there as long as I live, but anything is better than receiving favours from a man that I utterly despise."

" Why Frank, what in the name of fortune is the matter with you now ?" exclaimed Farmer Brough, who, unseen, had been a listener to a considerable portion of the foregoing conversation. "I invited both the squire and you to be my guests to-night, and yet you have been quarrelling with him for the last quarter of an hour, though for the life of me, I can't discover why."

" Humph !" returned Marldale, " Mr. Derwent knows the reason, if you don't."

" Well, I believe it began something about Mary opening the dance with him."

" Ay, I told him my mind upon the matter."

" And very foolishly, in my opinion."

" You may think so," replied Frank, " but I've had it on my mind for some time past to have my say out, and to-night will serve to let him know exactly what I think of him."

" Psha !" exclaimed Farmer Brough, " didn't I hear him say that he would consult with his steward about giving you a new lease for the Willows ?"

" He did say so," answered Frank, " and I, in reply, told him that I wanted no favours from him, and what's more, that I would not accept any, if I had to starve for it."

" Then, in my opinion, Marldale, you are a very foolish and impetuous young man."

" So you may think," he replied, " but I don't want anybody's advice upon this affair. The squire now knows my mind, and as I intended to affront him, my heart feels all the easier for having spoken out boldly. This is the last time, I hope, that words of any kind will pass between us ; but I would have him remember that till the last hour of my existence I shall never regard him with any other feelings than those of hatred and contempt."

With this he strode fiercely away, took an abrupt farewell of Mary Everett, and then let himself out at the door, after directing one more look of withering scorn at the person who had unconsciously given rise to all this anger. In the meantime the dance proceeded as if nothing had occurred to disturb the harmony of the evening, and shortly afterwards Cecil Derwent took his leave to return home. Farmer Brough then busied himself in assisting his domestics to hand refreshment round to the dancers, and was in the midst of this occupation when Joe, one of his farm servants, came rushing in to announce that a suspicious-looking stranger had just been captured as he was leaving the farm, to follow, and perhaps rob Squire Derwent.

" How do you know the man intended any harm ?" demanded the farmer. " He may have merely sought rest and shelter there, and may be as honest a fellow as any in this room."

" You will not say so when you see him," exclaimed Joe, " for he beats all the fierce-looking fellows that I ever clapped eyes on."

" Who has taken him into custody ?"

" Henry was the first who seized him," answered the man, " but bless you! he was so strong that he would soon have broken away, if it had not have been for Mr. Frank Marldale, who was just going home ; however, he is safe enough now and they are going to bring him here, that he may answer any questions that you wish to put to him."

"It will not be many that I put to him," exclaimed farmer Brough, "for I don't know much about the laws, and shall therefore leave the management of the matter to the magistrate. But here he comes, I see, and an ill-looking scoundrel he is, too, as ever I saw in all my life."

During the time that he was speaking, Caleb Kestrel was led in by Frank and one of the farm servants. His look was fierce and malignant, and on being brought forward, he stood firm and resolute, as if prepared to make a desperate effort to escape should an opportunity present itself.

"Now fellow," exclaimed farmer Brough, "you have been arrested, I hear, under very suspicious circumstances, and before you can expect to be set at liberty, we must know your name, what your occupation is, and why you were found lurking about my premises?"

"In the first place then," he replied in a low whisper, "my name is Caleb Kestrel."

"Very well, Mr. Kestrel," said the farmer, "and pray how do you contrive to get a living?"

"By hawking goods about the country."

"I see no pack in your possession," observed farmer Brough.

"No, that's left behind me in the barn, where it may be found if you think proper to send any of your people to look for it."

"That," observed Frank Marldale, "may only be carried about with you to deceive people as to your real character."

"Oh, if you doubt my word," exclaimed Caleb Kestrel in a tone of indifference, "I have my license in my pocket, which any one may read, to convince himself that I have told no lies either about my name or my business."

"It is sufficient," said Brough, after glancing over the contents of the paper, "but I should now like to know why you were found lurking about my premises?"

"Oh, that's easily enough answered," he replied. "The fact is I had no money to pay for a bed, so turned into your barn to get a cheap lodging for the night. In the morning I was going to the hall yonder to see Mr. Cecil Derwent, and its most likely I should have come back with my pockets better filled than they are at present."

"How were you to get money there?"

"How?" exclaimed Caleb Kestrel, rather confused by this unexpected question, and then recovering himself, he added, carelessly, "you forget that I travel with goods, and having some linen of very fine quality in my pack I make no doubt he would be tempted to buy a bargain."

"Squire Derwent left this house not long since," exclaimed the farmer.

"I know he did," answered the ruffian, "for I saw him pass as I stood at the barn door, and was just following him when one of your fellows laid hold of me."

"You knew the squire, then?"

"I know the former one," answered Caleb, "but this one I never saw in my life before."

"Then how were you aware that it was Mr. Derwent who passed the barn?" asked Farmer Brough.

"Because one of your people mentioned his name on parting after he had seen him safe on his way to the road. I didn't see his face though, and it would have been all the same if I had, for I shouldn't know him from Adam."

"Are you aware," asked farmer Brough, "that we suspect you had a design to rob the squire?"

"I can't help the evil thoughts of people," asnwered Kestrel, "but my intentions were not dishonest, whatever your people or you may choose to think of me."

At that moment Peeps, the showman, blew a few shrill notes on his mouth organ, and the sound seemed to have an instantaneous effect upon the prisoner, for he started, and looking round, gazed with amazement upon the person who had excited within him these strong emotions.

"Peeps!" he exclaimed, "is it possible that after a long journey I have had after you, we have at length met together by accident?"

"Oh, I knew you, my boy, the moment you were brought in, though you didn't happen to see me and the old woman," replied the showman. "So I waited till it seemed certain that you had not been taking to any queer business lately, and then resolving to acknowledge our former acquaintance, I gave a few notes on this favourite instrument of mine, and the magical effects were immediately to be perceived."

"Leave this showman's jargon," exclaimed Kestrel, "and tell me of the girl I left in your charge?"

"There she is, right afore your eyes," answered Peeps, as Amy advanced from another part of the room. In an instant the features of the ruffian became known to her, and uttering a cry of terror, she would have sunk to the floor, but for the timely assistance afforded by farmer Brough, who, amazed at what had taken place within the last few moments, demanded an explanation from the prisoner.

"If an explanation is wanted," replied Caleb Kestrel, "you must wait till I have time and opportunity to enter into a very long story. At present it must suffice you to know that the girl you are supporting in your arms is my daughter."

"'Tis false!" exclaimed Mary Everett, vehemently.

"Indeed!" returned the ruffian with a sneer; "and pray what know you of the girl's history?"

"I have heard enough to convince me that there is no foundation for the claim you have made," she replied. "Amy has a distinct recollection of having passed the first three or four years of her life in a large, handsomely furnished mansion in which a large establishment of servants was kept. From that house she was stolen, and if I am not mistaken, you are the person who did the act, and afterwards placed her under the care of Peeps and his wife."

"I acknowledge that it was I, who gave her to their protection," answered Caleb Kestrel. "But I stole her not, and will maintain before all the world that she is my daughter. Nay," he added, taking a small piece of gold from his pocket, "this is a portion of a trinket that I see hanging round her neck; compare them together, and you will see that I am not wrong in the identity."

Farmer Brough and a few of those who felt most interested in what was going on, examined and compared the two pieces of gold, and it was acknowledged by all that they had at some time or another belonged to the same trinket. Caleb watched the countenance of each spectator, with an anxious air, and after hearing all of them express an opinion favourable to his own assertions, he said in a tone of evident satisfaction,—

"Ah! I thought I should find myself among reasonable people, who are to be convinced when fair proof is laid before them. Besides, you all saw just now that she recognised me, in spite of the number of years since we last saw each other."

"Oh, it's plain enough that she remembered your face as soon as she saw you," answered Brough, "but to confess the truth, I thought she seemed to be rather alarmed than pleased at a meeting that was so unexpected."

"What can there be to alarm her?" demanded Caleb Kestrel, quickly.

"How should I know, who am a stranger to you both?" exclaimed Farmer Brough; "the reasons, if there be any, are best known to yourself, but to speak my mind truly, it don't seem that you could have cared much about the girl, since you have left her for fifteen or sixteen years under the care of these people."

"It would be a long story if I were to enter into any explanation now," replied Kestrel, "but the truth is the child had no mother living, and as my daily bread depended upon my travelling through the country, I found it impossible to take her round with me, so I thought of Peeps and his wife, whom I knew to be kind-hearted people, and they readily undertook the care of her on condition of receiving certain fixed sums of money for her support, at periods that were then agreed on between us."

"Which arrangements by the bye, Mr. Kestrel, you own to have entirely forgotten, except as far as the first payment was concerned."

"Wait patiently a few days," answered Caleb, "and when the contents of my pack have been sold, all the arrears you speak of shall be settled to your satisfaction."

BRASSY POPJOY DISPLAYS HIS NOVEL SPORTING COSTUME.

"But," asked Mr. Peeps, "how long do you expect it will be before you have got rid of your goods?"

"Oh, sometime in the course of to-morrow," he replied, "I shall see Squire Derwent in the morning, and shall not come away from his house empty handed."

"You speak as if he was compelled to deal with you," observed farmer Brough.

"I only speak as I suppose will be the case," answered the other, "the articles

No. 4.

I carry are worth his attention, and I know my business well enough to persuade a customer into dealing with me."

" And this girl, your daughter, as you call her, is she to accompany you on your travels ?"

" I have not made up my mind about that."

" Then to-night, at least, you will allow her to remain where she is ?".

" Yes," he replied, " I shall not remove her to-night; and to-morrow I shall make up my mind what to do with her."

" Why you wouldn't be so cruel as to take her away from us ?" cried Mrs. Peeps, with alarm.

" No, no, you must not do that, my boy," chimed in her husband.

" And why mustn't I take her away ?" answered Kestrel. " I only left her with you for a time, and have a right to demand her whenever I think proper."

" But Amy has been so long with us, that we now look upon her as our own daughter."

" Well, well, we wont talk about that now," answered Caleb, " for I have not yet made up my mind what to do with her. In a few hours, however, I shall have arranged my plan for the future, and then, whatever I may resolve on must be considered a law that no one is to gainsay. So now I shall take my leave for the night, and as I don't prove to be the thief I was at first taken for, I suppose there's no longer any objection to my resting in the barn."

" Aye, you can sleep there, if you like," replied Farmer Brough, " but you'll be disturbed at an early hour in the morning, for my workpeople are no sluggards, and some of them will be here as early as five o'clock to begin threshing some corn for the next market day."

" I shall be away before they come," returned Caleb, " for I have much to do to-morrow, and shall need a long day to get through it all. And as for you, Pees, you understand what I have said ? The girl may perhaps remain with you for some time, but if things don't turn out as I expect she must go with me, and travel nobody knows where, or how far."

Without waiting for any reply to this, Caleb Kestrel left the house to proceed to the quarters where he was to take up his night's rest. His absence seemed to afford relief to all, but more particularly to Amy, who had thrown herself into a chair and buried her face in her hands, as if to screen from her eyes the sight of the man whose presence had filled her with so much dismay.

" Come, cheer thee, my girl," exclaimed the farmer in accents of kindness, " and don't let this man, whoever he is, throw a damp upon your kindness."

" Alas !" she cried, " in spite of the relationship he claims, he is as a stranger to me, and yet he may insist upon my following him upon his travels."

" Take my word for it he will do no such thing," answered Brough, " for he wants no incumbrance in his wanderings through the country, and will upon further reflection, be glad to let you remain with the worthy people who have bestowed so much kindness upon you. So, come, let us forget our troubles in another dance, that our festivities may not be broken up by what has just taken place."

The musicians again played a lively air, and the dance was renewed, but it was easy to see that no one entered into it with the former spirit. It was in vain too that Mr. Brassey Popjoy endeavoured to make himself amusing, for all his pleasantries failed to excite even a smile, and he saw with no little vexation that the pleasures of the evening were at an end. In short the company soon afterwards separated, and those who were invited to sleep at the farm house, retired to bed.

CHAPTER IV.

THE MEETING.—THE PROPOSAL.—THE VOW OF VENGEANCE.—MR. BRASSEY POPJOY
APPEARS IN A NEW CHARACTER.

On the morning following the eventful harvest-home, Mr. Derwent left his dressing room for the library in which he usually took breakfast. For some little time he employed himself in reading the newspaper which had just been brought in, but his attention could not be drawn from the singular interview he had on the preceding evening with the pedlar. The man's determination to see him in the morning was most extraordinary, for they were perfect strangers to each other, and he could see that his plea of coming to offer his goods for sale was a mere excuse to enter upon business of a very different nature. But the nature of that business it was impossible to guess, and Mr. Derwent had involved himself in a labyrinth of conjectures, when they were broken in upon by the entrance of one of his domestics with letters that had just been received. These were perused and thrown aside, but the last one, which had not come through the post, was from Mr. Brassy Popjoy, announcing that he intended to avail himself of the polite invitation to spend a few days at the hall, and that he and his servant would arrive there in the course of the morning.

"The gentleman has lost no time in availing himself of my offer," he said, smiling at the recollection of the cockney sportsman's eccentricities, but I am not altogether sorry that he has determined to pay me this visit, for he will help to keep up my spirits, which are sadly deranged, though I scarcely know why. Surely this pedlar can have no very important communication to make, for we are perfect strangers to each other, and even if he had any thing to disclose, it could have been done when we met as well as at any other time. Yet I am forgetting myself," he added, after a pause, "for I revealed not myself to him, and he left in utter ignorance that I was the person whom he was so anxious to see."

A servant at this moment entered the room and announced that a stranger desired to speak to him, and would take no denial, though he had been informed that Mr. Derwent was engaged.

"What sort of person is he?" asked the squire.

"He is a poorish looking man," answered the footman, "and by the pack that he carries, I suppose he is a travelling hawker."

"Is he alone."

"Yes sir."

"Well then, you may show him in," answered Mr. Derwent, "for I suppose he has some request to make since he is so resolute to intrude himself upon me. But you will remain within call, Swift, and immediately upon my summons you must hasten here to learn why your presence is required."

The man retired, and in a short time returned with Caleb Kestrel who started with unfeigned surprise on recognising in the squire the person whom he had met on the preceding evening. Quickly recovering himself, however, he said :—

"Have I the honour of standing in the presence of Mr Derwent, the owner of this mansion?"

"My name is Cecil Derwent," he replied, "but what you have to say to him, I own passes my comprehension."

"Can't you guess?"

"No; your plea for coming here is business, but that would hardly be a sufficient excuse for thus forcing yourself into my presence against my own inclination.

"You have forgotten then, already, that I told you yesterday I had a message to deliver from Mr. Clement Derwent?"

"True, you did say something of the kind," he replied ; "but as the message must have been entrusted to you at least sixteen years ago, it cannot be of much importance now."

"I told a falsehood when I said that I had a communication to make from him," replied Caleb Kestrel, "but I thought it was the best way to get an interview. Though I knew not that you were Mr. Cecil Derwent, I fancied you might be a friend of his; and, that you would most likely inform him of the conversation you and I had together."

"Come to the point at once, man," exclaimed the squire, "and let me know without further trifling, what motive you have for thus forcing your way into my presence."

"Well then, the truth of it is," replied Caleb, "I come to tell you that you are in my power."

"In your power! what mean you, sirrah."

"I mean, that unless certain demands are complied with, you will no tremain much longer the master of this house."

"Ha! you have come then to extort money."

"Money I certainly must have," answered the pedlar, "but it cannot be called extortion when I have it in my power to do you a most important service."

"Psha! what service can you render me?"

"A very great one; you are threatened with the loss of half your property, and can put you in a way to prevent it."

"There was but one person who could lay claim to half the fortune of y cousin, Clement Derwent, and she was stolen from him shortly before his ath."

"I know it," answered Caleb Kestrel, with a grin of triumph, "but the girl lives, and it is in my power to bring her forward at any moment I please."

"How will you prove, to the satisfaction of a jury, that she is the same girl who was stolen?"

"Oh, there will be no difficulty about that," replied the pedlar, "for it was I who stole her, and the persons I placed her with are close at hand to declare th fact that she is the same person who, as a young child, I placed under their protection."

"You acknowledge then that you are the villain who were base enough to steal the girl from my cousin."

"Whether the action was a base one or not is very little to the purpose," returned Caleb. "Revenge was my object, and I had the gratification of seeing that grief for the loss of his young favourite soon brought Clement Derwent to his grave.

"Had my cousin ever injured you?"

"He had," answered Caleb Kestrel, "I was once in his service and was detected robbing him. For that I was prosecuted, and being found guilty, was sentenced to imprisonment. At the expiration of my punishment, I found that Mr. Derwent had gone abroad to reside; I followed him there, watched my opportunity, and, as the severest blow that I could inflict upon him, stole the child he had adopted."

"And did you leave her abroad?"

"No; I brought her over to England, that she might be at hand whenever my plans were ripe for execution. Under the idea that she was dead, you have taken possession of your cousin's property as heir-at-law, but half of it at least must be surrendered to her if I announce that the adopted daughter of Clement Derwent is now living."

"Nay," exclaimed the squire, "there is falsehood upon the very face of it, for had she been still in existence you would long ere this have endeavoured to extract money from me."

"All that can be easily explained," answered the other, "for the truth is, I was soon afterwards tried for a felony, found guilty, and the last fourteen years of my life have been passed abroad as a convict. Upon being released I returned to England, but all trace of the child, and those I had placed her with was lost, and it was not till last night, after you had left the house of farmer Brough, that I discovered those for whom I had been so anxiously searching."

"Was she there at the time I was?"

"Yes," answered the ruffian, she was in company with a travelling showman, and his wife named Peeps, the very persons, in fact, with whom I trusted her between fifteen and sixteen years ago."

'And did you claim her?"

"I did, aye; by means of a broken locket, one half of which was suspended round her neck, and the other in my own possession, I convinced every one present that my claim was a legal one, nay if further evidence had been neccessary, Peeps and his wife were there to prove that she was the same girl that I had committed to their charge."

"Did you also explain the fact of her being the adopted child of my cousin, Clement Derwent!"

"It's hardly likely that I should have been fool enough to do that," answered Kestrel, "for if that secret had been made known there would have been an end to the design I had on your purse, in short Squire Derwent, you have only to give me a sum in satisfaction, and the girl shall never trouble you."

"Villain, would you murder her?"

"No," he replied, "I would not do that, because while she lives I shall always have a claim upon you. All I shall do will be to take her away from this place, and henceforward she will pass as my daughter. So, now, squire, you know my plans, and for the sum of two thousand pounds the estates will remain in your hands."

"I will be no party in such an act of villany," exclaimed Cecil Derwent. "Half this property will still remain mine, as her claim was not made within the period named in the testament of my cousin, and the other I will cheerfully surrender to her as soon as it is satisfactorily shown that she is the person in whose favour the will was made."

"Upon my life, you are a very libera sort o a gentleman," sneered Kestrel, "but as that arrangement would not put a single coin into my pocket, I shall take care to prevent it."

"Nay, I will take immediate steps to ascertain if she is the person you represent."

"Your trouble will be taken in vain then," retorted the other, "for unless we make a satisfactory bargain before I leave this house, I shall, without delay, take her to some distant place—perhaps abroad—where you will never hear of her. So, now, squire, as I see there are writing materials on yonder table, sit down and write me an order on your banker for two thousand pounds, and you and I perhaps may never see eachother again."

Cecil Derwent hesitated for a few moments, and a sudden thought then striking him, he sat down and wrote—not as he had been desired—but a note to the constable of the parish, desiring him to apprehend the person, whom he described with as much accuracy as he could. This done, he objected to give the order which had been demanded of him, under the plea that he required a few hours of deliberation.

"What occasion is there to hesitate?" demanded Caleb Kestrel, sullenly, "when you know as well now as you can a few hours hence that you must come to my terms. Besides, the girl will never feel the wrong since she believes herself to be the daughter of a poor man, and if I have the two thousand pounds I ask for, she will of course share in my good fortune.','

"Nevertheless," exclaimed Derwent, "I must have time to think over your proposition."

"Then I foresee plainly enough that it will end in a refusal," answered Kestre "and the moment I leave this house I shall go far away, and take with me the girl that you are so much concerned about."

"The threats you use will not intimidate me." exclaimed Cecil Derwent who hoped to have him in custody within an hour or two. "In fact I have already thought better of this affair, and will not enter into a conspiracy to defraud this helpless girl of her just rights."

"Very well Mr. Derwent," muttered Kestrel, "then you'll see before long which of us has most cause to regret the turn that matters have taken. I asked but a moderate sum for making you secure in your property, but having met with a refusal, I shall next try whether other steps cannot be taken that you will have reason to be sorry for. I will, however, remain in the neighbourhood a couple of hours, and if at the end of that time I neither see nor hear of you, I shall take the girl with me to some place where you will never be able to find her."

Caleb Kestrel then left the room, and as he did so Mr. Derwent rang the bell for his valet."

"Swift," he exclaimed, giving him the note which he had just written, "I want you to carry this to the constable immediately, and tell him from me that it is a warrant which must be put into force without loss of time. The man herein described must be secured within two hours, as he will have left the place, and I am fearful he meditates some act of violence against a young girl whom he falsely asserts to be his daughter. When secured, he must be conveyed to a place of safety, and to-morrow I will take other means to prevent the mischief I fear he meditates."

The man hurried away to perform his errand, and scarcely had he left the library than another of the domestics entered, conducting Mr. Brassy Popjoy, who, as if to render himself a laughing stock, had attired himself in full Highland costume. He did not, however, appear to be very comfortable under the change, though he rattled on as usual, to the great amusement of Mr. Derwent, who, in spite of his recent anger, could not help bursting into a fit of laughter at the ridiculous figure his new acquaintance cut.

"My dear fellow" exclaimed Popjoy, "what in the name of fortune is there to laugh at. They tell me the dress is common enough in Scotland, and my maxim is that those who go to Rome should do as Rome does."

"True," answered Cecil, "but the garb is not the most convenient one in the world for a sporting gentleman."

"Well, never mind, I shall wear it at any rate, for between ourselves, I think I don't look so much amiss in it."

"But I think you'll find yourself rather cold in it when you get upon the bleak moors in the Highlands."

"That's exactly what I thought about it, myself," replied Popjoy, "so I put it on here just by way of getting accustomed to the change. And after all, my dear fellow, there's nothing like novelty, especially as I want to astonish the people in the north a little."

"I should have thought," answered Derwent, "that as a keen sportsman, you would have preferred a garb better suited to the business you are going on."

"Better suited," exclaimed the cockney, "can any dress in the world give more freedom to the limbs than this dress? It's the very thing, my dear fellow, I tell you, or I should not have been flat enough to give fifty guineas for it only a week ago, in order that I might show my sporting brethren the sort of style that is best adapted to this kind of business."

"You seem to be strongly prepossessed in its favour," returned the squire, laughing, "but I would not mind laying a trifling wager that you will be heartily sick of your new costume before this day comes to an end."

"Nonsense! what's to make me sick of it?"

"The inconvenience it will put you to!" answered Derwent, "remember, we are now in the autumn of the year, and that the mornings and evenings are often exceedingly cold in the northern parts of England."

"But you forget the exercise, my dear sir. We shall walk perhaps thirty miles in the course of the day, and if that won't keep your blood in a glow, I don't know what will."

"You are ready then to start with me exactly as you are?"

"Quite," replied Popjoy, "by the bye, though, I hope you won't think my question too great a liberty, but what could that man, a travelling tinker I think he is, want with you?"

" Oh, nothing but to offer his goods."

" And you did not deal with him, I suppose, for he went way in a towering passion, and was muttering all sorts of horrible things as he passed me."

" Did you hear what he said ?"

" No," answered Popjoy, " nothing but oaths, and all that sort of thing. But I know he's a bad one, and you would have been of the same opinion too, you had seen him last night when he went to the house of farmer Brough."

" It seems then, you were present at the time ?"

" I was."

" How come he to show himself there ?"

" He was forced to do it, whether he liked it or no," answered the cockne; " he was seen coming from the barn under very suspicious circumstances, and young Frank Marldale with the assistance of one of the farming men brought him into the house to give an account of himself."

" The fellow told me something of that," exclaimed Mr. Derwent, " and also that he had met there some persons of whom he has been a long time in search."

" Aye, and nicely he frightened everybody," returned Popjoy, " for would you believe it, he claimed as his daughter the little wench that I danced the polka with.'

" He told me that also, but did he succeed in proving to the satisfaction of every one that his claim was good ?"

" Oh, there could be no doubt that he was right enough there," answered the other, " for both Mr. and Mrs. Peeps acknowledged that he was the person who had left her with them when she was a mere child, fifteen or sixteen years ago. And as a further proof, he produced a piece of broken gold from his pocket which upon examination, exactly corresponded with a locket that the girl wore round her neck. So after that, of course everybody was obliged to admit that he had succeeded in making out his claim."

" He must bring forward more direct evidence than that," replied Mr. Derwent, " before he is permitted to take the girl with him."

" Well, the poor girl will be glad enough of that," exclaimed Popjoy, " for it put her into a terrible fluster, when she found that the evidence was going in favour of the claim that had been made by this Caleb Kestrel, I think he calls himself. By the bye, Mr. Derwent, the looks of that man are not very much in his favour, and I have a pretty good notion that he don't get his living altogether in an honest way. In short, travelling about the country with a pack is only an excuse for picking up waifs and strays whenever he can find them."

" I have no doubt of it," answered Mr. Derwent ; " and in order to prove whether my suspicions are correct, or not, I have just sent one of my servants with a warrant to the constable, authorising him to arrest and keep in safe custody the man of whom we are speaking."

" But you have no charge to make against him, have you ?"

" I have, and a very serious one it is to," replied the 'squire, " he claims that girl as his daughter ; but I believe evidence can be brought forward to prove that he stole her, and afterwards placed her under the care of the showman and his wife as his own offspring."

" Why you don't mean to say that he is a child stealer ?"

" I mean to say that there are sufficient grounds for detaining him upon suspicion, and the scoundrel may soon find that all his evil plottings are at an end."

" Oh," exclaimed Popjoy, " then it appears you and he have been having a word or two of a sort together, well, I thought so when he passed me just now, I was sure there had been a rumpus, and it's perfectly astonishing how very seldom I am mistaken whenever I form an opinion about anything."

" It shows the keenness of your perception," answered Mr. Derwent, unable to suppress a smile at the egregious vanity of his guest, " and I am most happy in making the acquaintance of a gentleman who knows the the world so well. But we are wasting time that should be employed in the field, so excuse me for a few minutes whilst I go to change my dress, and in the mean time amuse yourself with any of the numerous books that you see about you."

"Thank you, my good sir, for the offer," replied Mr. Brassey Popjoy ; "but books are my greatest aversion, and reading was never an amusement that I could take delight in. When I was an apprentice to my father,—worthy man !—I used to pore for days together over his day book and ledger, but then there was some pleasure in that, for I had the satisfaction of seeing that things were going on satisfactorily."

"Do you never read, then ?"

"No," he replied, "I don't mind sometimes looking over the pictures, if they are pretty ones, but even they seem to me like the sugar that they give with physic, to take away its unpleasant taste."

"But you will find here some light reading that may amuse you against my return."

"Thank you, but I would rather not have anything to do with them," replied Popjoy. "I can occupy myself very well with my own thoughts till you have got yourself ready, and if they should fail, why then I can take a turn round the library, and examine the family portraits of which I see you have got a great many."

"And some of them having been painted by the first masters, are said to be very valuable."

"Well, I should think they are," answered Mr. Brassey Popjoy. "At any rate, if I had not retired altogether from the pawnbroker business I should not have minded lending a good round sum of money on the lot."

"From the nature of your business," exclaimed the squire, "I should suppose you are a tolerable judge of pictures."

"Why I won't boast much about that," replied the other ; "for to let you into a bit of a secret, sir, whether an article is good, bad, or indifferent, people in our line have only one system of advancing money on it."

"And that I suppose is to give as little as possible."

"Exactly so," answered Popjoy, "it prevents losses in trade, for if the article is ever so bad we are always sure to sell it for the amount advanced, with interest, and sometimes it happens that the picture, or whatever else it may be, is worth a great deal more than the person that pledged it imagined."

"I am afraid, Mr. Popjoy," exclaimed Squire Derwent, "this pawnbroking business is not a very honest one."

"Well," he replied, "as I have quite given it up, I dont mind confessing to you in confidence that there is a great deal of roguery practised in it. Between ourselves, my dear sir, I'll tell you two or three little manœuvres if you promise not to let it go any further."

"I can safely make that promise," replied Mr. Derwent, "for it's a chance if I remember a word of what you are about to communicate. So proceed, for we are already late to take the field, considering this is the first day of partridge shooting.

"Well," replied Popjoy, "a good many people in our line are not very particular in their dealings with the chance customers that present themselves in their shops. A good many thieves get rid of the proceeds of their robberies in shops of that kind, for when chaps like them present themselves at the counter, no questions are asked them for fear it should hurt their feelings."

"But how do the persons who carry on that sort of traffic manage to avoid discovery."

"Because the business is so contrived that no one can suspect that anything is wrong," answered Mr. Brassey Popjoy. "For instance, a well-dressed man comes into a shop, and from his appearance no one would ever suspect him to be a thief. But he is so for all that, and down he puts a lot of plate upon the counter, which the pawnbroker knows well enough has been stolen only perhaps an hour or two before. I-want ten pounds for these, says the man; and the pawnbroker pretends to look at the goods as if in his own mind calculating their value, though at first sight he sees they are worth double what has been asked for them."

"Then of course he gives, without further hesitation, the sum that has been asked for them."

"Not a bit of it," answered Popjoy; "he offers him just half, and no talking to him afterwards make him budge a bit from what he said at first."

"And does the man who offers the goods for pledge always take the lower sum?"

"Bless your heart, my dear sir, he cant help himself," replied Popjoy. "He knows that he is suspected, and it would be as much as his life is worth to refuse."

"At any rate," observed Mr. Derwent, "he has the privilege of redeeming the things whenever he pleases."

"No, he cannot."

"How is that?"

"Because in transactions of that kind, the pawnbroker considers that he buys the goods out and out. Of course; he says to the chap, 'if I lend you five

No. 5.

pounds for this you wont want a ticket?' 'Oh yes but I do, though,' the man is perhaps simple enough to say, and then the pawnbroker pretending that he is going to weigh the plate, removes it to a counter at the back of the shop."

"And keeps the goods?"

"To be sure he does, for he threatens to send for a constable, declaring loudly that he is sure the things have been stolen, and that as an honest man he is bound to give the thief into custody. You may be certain the chap don't stay long after he hears that,—away he cuts, and is never seen again anywhere in that neighbourhood."

"And the pawnbroker gives the stolen property up to the police as a matter of course?,"

"Not he," replied Popjoy. "He knows well enough that there's no one to say a word against him, for you may be sure the thief himself cant go and make a preaching about it, so the silver is melted down, and all clue to robbery is at an end."

"Surely all pawnbrokers are not such villains?"

"No," replied Popjoy, "there's very few chaps that follow the sort of business I've been speaking about, and even they are obliged to be more careful than they used to be, on account of the police. So now, sir, having let you into this little secret, I am ready to start whenever you are."

Cecil Derwent left the room, and returned in a few minutes afterwards in a dress suitable for the occasion. The two sportsmen then left the house, and calling heir dogs about them, made their way towards the moor, followed by Trubbs.

CHAPTER V.

THE PARTING.—AMY'S SACRIFICE.—THE WARRANT.—A MARTYR.

A little later in the day Caleb Kestrel repaired to the farm house, and in a conversation with Amy informed her that as his business with Squire Derwent was at an end, he was about to leave that neighbourhood immediately. In order however to afford her time to part from her friends, he proposed to set off first and to wait for her near the deserted hut on the moor to which our two sportsmen had not long before directed their way. He then took his departure, and Farmer Brough seeing her affliction, inquired with all the generous warmth of his heart if there was any way in which he could assist her.

"I know," he said, "that you are unwillingly about to accompany this man—your father, I was about to call him,—but I have my suspicions that he is no more related to you than I am. Only say, then, that you would rather not go with him, and hang me if I dont keep you here in spite of the fellow."

"Alas! I dare not refuse," answered Amy; "for he has claimed me as his child, and even those who have hitherto protected me have declared that he is the same person who placed me under their protection."

"But for all that they dont know that you belong to him," exclaimed the yeoman, "and from what you told my niece last night, I have a notion that you were stolen away from home during your infancy."

"So I have thought myself," answered Amy; "but we have no proof of that having been the case, and I must therefore follow, him as he has commanded."

"Nay, only say you wish it, my girl, and neither he nor anybody else shall make you quit my house."

'And why should I wish to remain here," she asked, "when I know the trouble and perhaps danger it would bring upon you? He has said that I shall bear him company in his travels, and, from the little I have seen of him I feel well assured that he would not hesitate even to commit an act of violence rather then be thwarted in his design."

"Why, he is a roughish customer to deal with, I dare say," replied Brough "but I dare say we could manage to be even with him if we went the right way to work. For instance, a hint whispered in the ear of a magistrate would lead to an inquiry that might relieve you from this man for all the rest of your life Mr. Cecil Derwent, for instance, is in the commission of the peace, and if I was to make him acquainted with my suspicions, there's no doubt he would soon learn who this man is, and whether he has any real claim to call himself your parent."

"Oh, pray do not speak to him upon the subject," exclaimed Amy, "for whatever may be the faults of this man, it is not for me to involve him in trouble."

"Then you can leave, without regret, those who have so kindly acted the part of parents to you?"

"Indeed, farmer, I am not so ungrateful as you imagine," exclaimed Amy "for I feel that no trouble could have afflicted me so severely as to be torn from those to whom I owe a heavy debt of gratitude. I would have died for them but cannot endure the thought of their having,—through me,—to suffer the vengeance of him who has claimed me from their hands."

"Do you remember being first placed with them?" demanded the kind-hearted farmer.

"I have a very indistinct recollection," she replied; "but I know that just before that time I was conveyed through many countries, and crossed the ocean to England during a fearful tempest that lasted many days."

"And was this man, Kestrel, with you?"

"He was," answered Amy, "for, young as I was at the time, I never can forget the terror with which his harsh repulsive features inspired me."

"Yet still you are resolved to follow him!"

"I know not how it is," She replied, "but it seems to me that his commands cannot be resisted. And well he knows it too, for he has gone on before, and has left me to follow, as if he knew that I dare not refuse."

"Then let him see that you are not so completely in his power as he imagines,' exclaimed Farmer Brough. "Remain where you are, my poor girl, and if he should venture to return to force you from us, he will find more trouble then he perhaps expects."

"You forget then that, if baffled in one way he would have recourse to secret violence; and, being once removed from the protection of my friends, I should have to endure his cruelty for having dared to disobey him."

"Cruelty!" exclaimed the farmer, "and would you go and place yourself under the power of a person from whom you expect ill usage? No, no, if that's the case, you had better remain where you are, and if he should return to fetch you, why I will give him such an answer as he little expects."

"By which you would bring upon yourself the deadly hatred of a man who I fear would not hesitate at an act of violence to accomplish his revenge."

"You speak as if you knew the character of the fellow."

"I speak only as I have heard both Mr. and Mrs. Peeps report of him,' answered Amy. "They told me some particulars of him last night after he went away, and from their description he has always been a man of violent, wayward habits."

"Then he is the more unfit to have the care of you, my poor child," exclaimed the farmer.

"True," she replied, "but he asserts that I am his child, and if there's truth in it, then am I bound to obey him, however much it may be against my own inclination."

"The feeling is a good one, and does you great credit," answered Rowland Brough; "but I cannot help saying that he has shown very little affection in the matter, since it seems he left you in the care of strangers for I don't know how many years. So now, as you wish to continue with them, do so, and I'll take care that no harm happens in consequence."

"Indeed, sir, I dare not follow your advice."

"Humph ! then you are determined to follow him ?"

"So much so," she replied, " that even if death were to be the certain consequence, I would brave it rather then break the word I gave him before he started." ·

"Well, if you are determined to keep faith with him," answered the farmer, "go and overtake him, and when you have done so, tell him that you have thought better of it, and are going to remain with your friends."

"I am sorry that I cannot do so," answered Amy, "but believe me, sir, go where I may, I never shall forget the kindness I have received from you. May Heaven reward you for it and shield you from all evil."

"Hilloa ! I say, Amy, dont leave me in that way," exclamed the farmer, calling to her as she suddenly hastened from his presence. His words, however, were unheeded, and Amy made the best of her way along the bridle road that led from the farm house to the moors. But she had not proceeded very far when a gate on one side was opened and Mary Everett, who was returning home from the neighbouring village, stood before her.

"Whither are you going so fast, Amy !" she asked.

"To overtake my father, who has gone on before, whilst I remained to bid farewell to Farmer Broug."

"What do I hear ?" said Mary ; " are you then really going to leave us so soon ?"

"Alas ! there is no alternative."

"And that too, I suppose, through that surly looking brute that made his ominous appearance among us last night ?"

"He declares himself to be my father," she replied, "and I must obey him, even at any sacrifice."

"Take care, my dear girl, that it is not the sacrifice of your life."

"I am not afraid of receiving any injury from him," answered Amy ; "for though harsh in his manners there must be some feeling of affection in him, or he would not have travelled so long and so far in search of me."

"That depends upon whether he has any motive for it that we are not aware of," replied Mary Everett. " Besides, his anxiety could not have been so very great, since he has taken fifteen or sixteen years to look after the daughter for whom he now pretends so much affection."

"I believe," exclaimed Amy, " there was some reason for the delay, which will be by and by explained."

"Aye, aye, but of course he will give the explanation in a manner to suit his own views ;" exclaimed Mary Everett. " You are vexed with me, I see, for speaking my mind so boldly, but I have a very indifferent opinion of that strange looking man, and as sure as that I am now telling you so, his presence here bodes you no good."

"And not much harm I hope."

"It has done that already," answered Mary, "for no sooner has the meeting taken place then he orders you to follow him no one knows where, as if you were a dog. But if he had me to deal with instead, he would have found a little more opposition in the way of his plans."

"If I had opposed him," exclaimed Amy, " it would only have provoked him to use force."

"Then you could have sought the protection of the law."

"Against my father !"

"Aye, why not, if he wants to play the part of a tyrant over you. Besides, I don't believe a word of his assertion that you are his daughter, and I wish my uncle Brough had told him as much when he so impudently made his claim."

"That would only have led to a quarrel," exclaimed Amy ; "and why should the festivities of last night have been disturbed on my account ?"

"Because," replied Mary "if this man is, as I suspect, an impostor, it is only proper that he should have been shown forth in his own colours."

"Have you any ground for believing him to be an impostor ?"

"I have," answered Mary Everett, "for all the time he was here I watched him narrowly and could observe the restless motion of his eye, that showed he was not altogether easy in the position in which he found himself. Besides, to tell you the truth, I have a notion that he would not mind committing a robbery."

"A robbery !" cried Amy in trembling accents ;—"why do you think he would be guilty of an evil deed.""

"I am not the only person," she replied," for Frank Marldale, and the man who assisted to capture him, declare that when first seen he was creeping stealthily after Squire Derwent, who had only a few minutes before left our house to return home. So now Amy, you know why I suspect this man of being a thief."

"Have you forgotten," cried Amy, "that the person you speak of is my father ?"

"He calls himself so," exclaimed Mary Everett, "but, as I have already said, I have not the slightest faith in a word that he says. Depend upon it there's a plot at the bottom of all this, and if you will only go back with me and stop at our house a few days, I'll ask my uncle to see Squire Derwent,—who is a magistrate, and between them I think this affair will be sifted to the very bottom."

"I dare not remain after he has bade me follow him," she replied, after a brief pause.

"And yet it is only a few hours since you acknowledged him as your father."

"But I have now acknowledged him," answered the girl, "and having done so it is my duty to obey him. I am, however most grateful for the friendship you have shown me, and, should I ever have occasion for your assistance or advice, will lose no time in either coming here or sending to you."

"Why, that is well said," exclaimed Mary, "though I had rather you had said at once that you accepted the offer to remain at the farm, for my uncle would have taken care that no injury should happen to you, and as for Frank Marldale, he would have died in your defence if I had only given him a hint that danger was to be apprehended."

"I have good reason to believe that both of them would have afforded me protection," answered Amy ; "but it is better that I should go away in obedience to the commands of my father than occasion trouble in a family where I have found such unexpected kindness."

"And have you bid good bye to those good-natured people that you have been with so long ?" asked Mary.

"No," she replied, "I was afraid to trust myself with a parting interview lest I should betray the weakness that I wish to conquer."

"And you are really going away without seeing them ?"

"I am," answered Amy, "but they will know my motive and pardon an act that they will feel assured was not occasioned by any want of gratitude towards them. You can make an excuse for me to them, and say to them as I do to you, it is in all probability,—farewell for ever !"

She darted away with the speed of lightning, and Mary Everett stood gazing after her retiring form, as if uncertain whether to follow or not. At length however, she was roused from her reflections by approaching footsteps, and looking round she perceived Frank Mardale approaching with a gun in his hand.

"Well, Mary," he exclaimed, "I'm glad chance has thrown me in your way, for I have just been down to your uncle's farm, and was much disappointed at not finding you at home, for I called on purpose to inquire whether you have seen or heard anything of that strange man whom we took into custody last night."

"He is gone away for good I believe," she replied.

"And has taken the girl with him ?"

"Yes ; at least she is now on her road to overtake him," answered Mary Everett.

"And does she really believe that extraordinary tale he told, about her being his daughter."

"It seems she does, or she would hardly follow him in his long, weary journeys."

"And yet," observed her lover, "there is so much improbability in it, that, for my own part I cannot believe a word of the fellow's statement. He tells us that he has not seen her for a period of sixteen years, and yet, strange to say, he is able to identify her the moment they met."

"I have just been telling her that I don't believe he has any right to claim her," replied Mary.

"And what said she to that ?"

"Only that his assertion was rather confirmed than disproved ; she considered herself bound to obey his command to follow him. I tried my very best to convince her that she would afterwards have reason to repent the ready belief she had given to his artfully devised scheme ; but all was useless, and she left me only a minute or two before you came up to me."

"Do you know where he is to wait for her ?"

"I believe somewhere on the moors yonder."

"Then I shall make it my business to follow them," replied Frank Marldale, "for I suspect the fellow has some villany in contemplation, and if I find him out he may expect to receive from my hands as sound a drubbing as ever he had in his life."

"For goodness sake, Frank, take care what you do," cried Mary with alarm, "for he is the most desperate looking ruffian I ever saw in my life, and neither in size nor strength are you any match for him."

"But in spirit I may be, though," replied her lover, "and in a just cause I believe I could overcome a bigger and stronger man than he is. So let him beware of what he does, or we may come to closer quarters before long than will be pleasant for him."

"Nay, dear Frank, don't be so rash, or you'll terrify me out of my wits," cried Mary Everett, entreatingly. "The girl we both take so much interest in will, I dare say, be safe enough, for she seems to possess plenty of coolness and courage, and the moment she discovers that he is not what he has pretended, she will leave him and return without delay to my uncle's house."

"Did she promise to do so ?"

"No ; but she was very much pressed to stay with us some time, so that she knows that she will be received with a welcome, come when she may."

"She was a simpleton to go away with the fellow."

"So I as good as told her," replied Mary, "but all the persuasion I could use was of no avail ; for, believing him to be her father, she deems it her duty to obey him, however arbitrary his commands may be."

"Has he said where he is about to take her to ?"

"I believe not," answered Mary. "All she yet knows is, that henceforth she will have to tramp with him from one end of the kingdom to the other, and as it seems he has been abroad on former occasions, I should not be surprised to hear that he has taken her from England."

"Then if I overtake them on the moors," exclaimed Frank Marldale, "I shall take the liberty of telling the girl that she has done wrong to trust herself with a stranger, whose own assertion that he is her father is as yet unproved."

"Pray mind you don't get into a quarrel with him," said Mary, "for he looks like a desperate ruffian, and notwithstanding your declaration to the contrary, I fear he would prove too much for you. So leave your gun at the next cottage, Frank, for you cannot want that now, I am sure, and the 'squire would be angry if you passed over any of his property with a weapon of that kind in your possession."

"To tell you the truth, Mary," replied her lover; "I brought the gun with me on purpose to annoy him if we should happen to meet in the course of our walk."

"Nay, it is he who will have the best means of causing annoyance."

"In what way?"

"By means of the law."

"Aye," replied Frank Marldale; "I thought that was what had got into your head; but I have no intention of putting myself in his power. Surely I may carry a gun about with me without asking his leave."

"It is not loaded, then?" she exclaimed.

"Oh, yes, but it is though," exclaimed the young man; "but for all that I have no intention of declaring war against any of Mr. Derwent's game. All I want is to show him that I will carry my gun whenever and wherever I please, so that I don't break the law by killing any of his partridges or pheasants."

"Then I must say, Frank," she replied, "that it is very foolish of you to get into a quarrel with a person who has never given you any cause of complaint. He seems, on the contrary, inclined to be on peaceable terms with you, and yet there is this determination to make him regard you as a foe."

"He may do as he pleases about that," answered Frank, "for I cannot think that man my friend who takes the first opportunity to turn me out of my farm."

"Indeed you are greatly mistaken in the 'squire," cried Mary. "He is not the harsh landlord you take him for, and my uncle says he is sure you will have the lease renewed even without asking for it."

"I'll not take it from him as a favour," exclaimed Frank, "and that is one reason why I am going to set his orders of defiance by walking over the moors with a gun in my hand. Aye, and he shall hear me fire it off too, though I'll not put myself in his power by shooting at any of the game that he is so chary of."

"And this is only done to vex your neighbour?"

"Nothing more, Mary, depend upon it," replied her lover; "he knows I owe him no good will, and my spirit is too proud a one to yield to him merely because he happens to be the richer man of the two."

"Surely you are not jealous of him, because he is the more wealthy man?" exclaimed Mary Everett.

"Nay," he replied, "you cannot believe me so paltry as that? I grudge not his possessions, though, between ourselves, I have a notion that it will not be long before he has to divide them with some one else."

"Ah, Frank!" she exclaimed. "You are thinking of the long lost girl, I suppose? But people have now given up all idea of her ever being found; and, even if she should happen to be discovered Squire Derwent is too honourable a gentleman to withhold from her the property bequeathed to her by his cousin's will. Be that as it may, however, she is supposed to be dead, so that your anticipations of Mr. Derwent's being obliged to give up half his estates will never be realized"

"Then I shall be very much mistaken, that's all," replied Frank, laughing.

"Is it possible that you would feel a pleasure is seeing him deprived of half his fortune?"

"No, no, my dear Mary," he exclaimed, "my dislike of the squire don't carry me quite so far as that. But right is right, you know, and if the girl we speak of is still alive, it is only fair that she should enjoy the property her adopted father left for her use. But here we are, at your uncle's door, so at this spot we will take leave till to-morrow, for I must return home early this evening, or it's likely enough I shall be caught on the moors by the storm that I see is gathering yonder in the south."

"Had you not better leave your gun at our house, Frank?" she asked, entreatingly.

"No; I shall want it in the morning," he replied; "for, as often as I meet uire Derwent on his estates, he shall see that I persist in carrying my gun in spite of his prohibition to the contrary. So good bye, Mary, and try if you cannot drive from your mind that foolish notion of yours that mischief must follow from my carrying this weapon through the lands of our worthy neighbour."

They had by this time reached the door of the farm-house when the lovers parted, and Frank Marldale throwing the gun across his arm, passed out of the garden gate and made his way by the nearest road towards the moors which he had to pass over on his way home.

We must now return to Mr. and Mrs. Peeps, whose sorrow for the loss of Amy was so great, that the proprietor of the Temple of Arts could find no consolation but by indulging in deep potations through the agency of a few shillings which he had managed at various times to put away without the knowledge of his better half. Long was the search of Mrs. Peeps for her missing husband, but at length she met with him just as he was returning from the village where he had been enjoying himself ; and great was the indignation of the worthy lady when she saw that he was by no means so sober as he ought to have been.

"Oh, Peeps! Peeps!" she exclaimed, "whatever have you been a-doing with yourself all day ? Why I declare if you ain't quite fuddled, though where or how you got the money to make such a beast of yourself is more than I can guess."

" The money my love, was my own," he replied with drunken gravity. "I've saved it up from time to time, and it's hard if a man can't enjoy himself now and then without being blowed up by his wife."

"And how can you enjoy yourself, as you call it," she demanded abruptly, " when we have just lost the poor girl who was like a daughter to us?"

" That's just what has done it all, my love," answered her husband. " Sorrow is dry work, so, as I couldn't help thinking about Amy, I just took a drop to try if that wouln't comfort me in my affliction."

"Mr. Peeps, I am ashamed of your goings on!" exclaimed the indignant lady. " What right, sir, have you to squander away your money in drink, and then call it comforting yourself for the loss of Amy?"

" Haven't I a right to do as I like with my own?" demanded the showman, with more courage than he usually manifested in the presence of his wife. "Am I always to be under petticoat government, Mrs. Peeps, and to be doomed from one week's end to the other to carry the Temple of Arts at my back without ever oeing allowed to spend a shilling with a friend. But I'm determined not to put up with it any longer, ma'am ;—I'll be master of my own actions from this time forth, so you may preach away and be——"

" Peeps,—if you say another word I'll be divorced from you," exclaimed the lady, interrupting him just in time to prevent the conclusion of the sentence. "Your conduct is most scandalous, and I only wish it lay in my power to get you put into the stocks that I see yonder."

" Perhaps you would like to see me put into the cage that stands close by 'em."

" I should indeed," she replied, " but I'm afraid there's no such good luck for me. Indeed, if people always got their deserts you would have a good whipping for this ; and if they would only trust me to do it there should be no strength of arm wanted, I can tell you."

"Upon my life, Mrs. P. this is very unkind of you," exclaimed her husband. "But you can't mean it —I know you can't, or I should think you worse than a Hottentot ! And only to think too that you should give me this blowing up just at a time when I am so deeply afflicted for the loss of our little favourite."

" You afflicted!" cried the lady, indignantly ;—" I believe you are glad she has left us, for now you can come out in your true colours, and ill-treat your unfortunate wife without anybody being the wiser. But never mind, Peeps, I shall leave you if this is the sort of game you are going to carry on, and—"

" Stop a moment, my dear," interrupted her husband, " and don't take any rash oaths till you have well weighed in your mind the consequences of leaving me. Dont it strike you, Mrs. P. that if you go away and leave the Temple of Arts behind there'll be some difficulty in getting such a decent, honest living as you do now?"

"I don't dare about that," she replied, "if it rids me of such a worthless, idle fellow as you are."

"How can you call me idle, my dear Angelina, when I am always doing something for a living?" demanded the showman. "Isn't the Temple of Arts a specimen of my own ingenuity and labour; didn't I construct it after designs of my own, and are not the scenes it contains all painted by my own hand? And yet

after all it comes to this, that I am to be called a worthless, idle fellow, by my own wife."

"And isn't it enough to make me call you so," asked Mrs. Peeps, "when after looking about for you all the morning, I at last find you in this state of—of—"

"Fatigue, my love, it's nothing else I can assure you," interrupted her husband. "I've been wandering round about the neighbourhood to try and forget

Amy. But somehow there's no getting her out of my head, and the thought of the troubles she may have to go through made me giddy, which you are uncharitable enough to tell me is caused by too much drink."

"Didn't you acknowledge, only a little while ago tha tyou had been drinking sir."

"Why yes, I did admit that I had taken just a drop or two."

"Which drop or two made you in a state that you never ought to have been seen in."

"I can't help it, my own Angelina," answered her husband in a tone of drunken gravity. "It was no fault of my own that you did see me in this state, for if you had not come hunting after me in this way, I should have laid down under a hedge to recover myself, and then you would never have known that I had been exceeding in my potations to day. But never mind, my dear, I'm not often guilty of this sort of thing, so say no more about it, and we'll set off on our travels to see what sort of luck we may meet with in the next town."

"Don't be too sure about that," exclaimed a voice close by that made both Peeps and his wife start with alarm.

"Who and what are you," demanded the showman, as soon as he recovered himself, "and why do you come here to frighten honest people out of their lives ?"

"Honest people," exclaimed the man, with a sneer. "You must be very honest when I have the squire's orders not to let you leave this neighbourhood till he has had a word or two of a sort with you."

"With both of us ?" cried Mrs Peeps.

"No," replied the man, "I suppose you are not wanted, for there's only one person mentioned in the warrant."

"What do you mean, fellow, by a warrant ?" demanded Peeps, with all the indignation he could muster.

"Oh, Mr. Innocence, so you would gammon me that you don't know what a warrant is, eh ? You'd have one believe that you never were in a prison in your life."

"Before I answer that question I must know who you are."

"Well then, my name is Smith."

"Indeed ! then perhaps Mr. Smith you'll next tell me what you are ?"

"A constable to be sure."

"A constable !" cried Mrs. Peeps, "and pray sir what have you to do with my husband."

"Only to take him into custody that's all."

"Well, if ever I heard anything so cool as that," exclaimed the showman. "Take me into custody indeed ! why I've never done anything to deserve such treatment."

"And what's more, he shall not go with you, so that's flat !" cried the lady, placing herself between her husband and the constable.

"I'll tell you what it is, ma'am," growled Smith, pushing her on one side, "I have orders to lock this man up in the cage, and I shall do my duty in spite of what you say ; so don't throw any obstruction in my way, or I shall be obliged to take you as well, to keep him company."

"Come, come, old fellow, this is only a little joke of yours I know. There's some mistake in this ; so go back to the squire and make my compliments to him, and say, if he particularly desires to see me, I'll do myself the pleasure of calling on him in the morning."

"You must go with me, I tell you," replied the constable, "for you are the stranger I was desired to lock up for the night, and if I was to let you go, a very pretty row I should get into for it."

"But you must be mistaken," exclaimed Mrs. Peeps, "for my husband has done nothing to deserve this."

"I can't help that, ma'am," answered Smith drily. "He may be innocent for aught I know ; but its not for me to inquire into such matters, so he must explain matters to the squire, who is a magistrate, and if he can persuade him of his innocence he'll be set at liberty, and there won't be much to complain of, seeing that he will be provided with a night's lodging, and nothing to pay for it."

"That may be all very well, my fine fellow," exclaimed the showman, "but consider the injury my character will suffer if I should be locked up in your cage."

"Psha!" retorted the constable, "you have only to leave the neighbourhood, and you'll soon find yourself among people that know nothing about it."

"Can't you take bail for my appearance in the morning?"

"Not by no manner of means," he replied. "My orders are as plain as a pikestaff, and if I don't obey them I know what the consequences will be to myself. So don't delay me with any more of this nonsense, but come along with me and submit to the law quietly."

Both Mr. and Mrs Peeps still remonstrated, but without effect, and the former was at length transferred to the cage instead of Caleb Kestrel, for whom he had been mistaken by the constable. For nearly an hour afterwards did Mrs Peeps remain talking to her husband through the bars that divided her from him, but finding at length that he was to be locked up for the night she went to fetch him the refreshment he would need.

CHAPTER VI.

A STORM ON THE MOORS.—THE COCKNEY SPORTSMAN'S DILEMMA.—THE DESERTED HUT.—AMY'S PERIL.—THE MURDER AND THE ACCUSATION.

THE tempest which had been threatening all the latter part of the day at length broke forth with terrific violence whilst Cecil Derwent and his London friend were returning to the hall across the moors. To add to their perplexity, too, the night was pitch dark, so that even the squire, well acquainted as he was with the place, was compelled to acknowledge that he knew not which way to direct his footsteps towards home. In this extremity he proposed that Brassy Popjoy and his groom should remain near a deserted hut, before which they had just arrived, and requesting that they would not stir away from the spot till he returned, he set out with the faint hope that he might meet with some one who would be able to direct him on his way.

Cold and bleak as it was, Popjoy had long since found out that the Highland costume he wore was most ill suited for the situation in which he was placed, and bitter were the complaints he gave vent to, as he stood shivering and trembling in the blast for which he was so indifferently prepared. Trubbs, the groom, however, had little compassion for his master, for he had taken care to provide himself with sufficient clothing in case of rough weather, and the more the cockney gave utterance to his complaints the more amusement did he find to pass away the time of the squire's absence."

"I told you how it would be, sir," he exclaimed, in reply to some of the doleful observations of poor Popjoy, "but you would'nt take advice, and now I suppose you'll be laid up with a cold, and then a pretty time I shall have of it with your grumbling and lamentations.

"Hold your tongue, scoundrel, and learn the proper respect that is due to your master," returned the other angrily, "I know you told me I should suffer from the bleak winds of this infernal place, but I did'nt expect to find myself suddenly transported to a Siberian climate."

"But you might have taken my advice for all that."

"Advice from our equals is all very well," answered Popjoy, "but when it comes from a servant it is apt to sound too much like impertinence. You forget Trubbs the respect that is due to me, and I often feel a very great inclination to chastise your impertinence by knocking you down."

" Don't say that, sir," exclaimed the groom, "or I shall presently be tempted to do something very desperate."

" What do you mean by that, sir ?"

" Why I shall run away, and leave you to find your way out of this place as well as you can."

" Unfeeling monster ; would you desert me in such a dreadful extremity as this ?"

" I'll not if you don't blow me up," replied the other, "but remember, I'm only flesh and blood, and a man can't stand still to be abused when he knows he has got it in his own power to prevent it by running away. So, if you don't want to be left here all alone you'll not treat me as if I was a poor ignorant nigger."

" You forget, Trubbs, that I have not the patience of Job, and even if I had, this is a place to try it most confoundedly. These bare legs of mine are suffering the agonies of martyrdom from the excruciating winds, and as for my body, I am as wet through as if I had been dragged through a horsepond."

" What of that sir ?" exclaimed the groom. " A genuine sportsman never thinks anything of such trifles, especially if he happens to have had a good day's sport."

" Aye, if he has had a good day's sport there may be some little consolation for him," replied Mr. Brassy Popjoy, "but I don't happen to have killed anything, so there's nothing to console me for the annoyance I suffer."

" You haven't heard the squire grumble, sir."

" The squire has shot something," answered Popjoy, "and therefore he would be a most ungrateful fellow if he was to say a word about getting a wet skin. Besides, he's used to tramping over these horrid moors, and use, they say, Trubbs, is second nature."

" But it don't make a storm like this any the more bearable," replied the other. " Perhaps though he's a philosopher, for they say its wonderful what them chaps can suffer before they begin to grumble."

" I dont know about his being a philosopher, Trubbs," exclaimed his master, " but he's a long time gone, seeing that we are left here to shiver by ourselves in the cold and rain."

" Then why not go into the hut to see if there is a corner of it where we may find shelter?"

" Because with such a wind as there is," replied Popjoy, " I should expect every moment to see it come rattling down about our ears. Ugh! I hear the walls creak, and presently there wont be one stone standing upon another."

" Why not move on then, sir, and keep ourselves warm with exercise?"

" If we did that, Mr. Cecil Derwent would return and leave the place again, under the impression that we had gone away to look after him. In short, Trubbs, we are in a very disagreeable situation here, and, what is still worse, I know not how we are to get out of it."

" Why, if you won't leave this spot, we must stay here I suppose till the squire comes back," replied the other. " Its unpleasant enough, it must be confessed, but its no use grumbling when people find themselves in a scrape, so we had better take things as we find 'em, and when Squire Derwent returns he may perhaps have discovered the road that will take us back to the hall."

" I wish, with all my heart, we were there now," exclaimed Popjoy; " for, besides being wet through to the skin, I feel a most enormous appetite coming on, and from a sly look that I ventured to take into the pantry, I've a notion there's something very good for dinner waiting our arival. Among other things there was a noble pair of capons, and I have been thinking all day of what a glorious dinner I should make off them."

" Don't mention it, sir—pray don't !" exclaimed Trubbs, "for I myself am suffering terribly from a craving appetite, and you have set me longing more than ever for my dinner. This shooting over the moors is a mighty pleasant way of passing one's time for those that like it; but, for my own part I think there's nothing like home, where we can always have our dinner as soon as we are ready for it. In short sir, if ever we are lucky enough to get back to our home, I shall enter into another arrangement, and have it understood that I am not to go out on any more shooting expeditions with you."

" I believe Trubbs, you may spare yourself the trouble of making any bargain of that sort," replied his master, " for I am quite sick of sporting, and shall dispose of the remainder of my shooting term as soon as ever I can meet with a customer."

" And that queer outlandish dress of yours ?"

" Will be disposed of also."

" At a great sacrifice, I suppose ?"

" Yes Trubbs ; the same gentleman that buys my right of shooting can have the kilt and philabeg into the bargain."

" Oh, sir !" exclaimed Trubbs, " I told you you would soon be tired of the dress after one day's experience upon these moors. I knew it well enough, but you would insist that it was the best sporting costume that a fashionable gentleman could possibly wear."

" And so I still say," answered Mr. Brassy Popjoy, who never would admit that he had been in the wrong. " I contend that it is the lightest and most convenient shooting dress that can be worn,—but I confess it would take more patience than I possess to get used to it ; so I desire, sir, that you will throw out no more of your sneers on a subject upon which I pride myself."

" I was not the only person that laughed at it," replied the groom, " for I thought Mr. Derwent was going to laugh himself into convulsions when he first saw you in it,"

" Am I to be laughed out of my own opinion by Mr. Derwent or any body else, sir ?" exclaimed Popjoy, in a tone that he intended for one of very great severity. "Every gentleman has a right to do what he pleases, so long as no one else suffers by it, and if I thought it would vex him I'd wear my Highland costume as long as I honour him with my company."

" But the punishment would fall upon yourself, sir, if this cold weather should last."

" In that case, Trubbs, I might perhaps feel inclined to give way to him. It is wise to yield when our own personal convenience is concerned."

" Oh, sir !" exclaimed the groom, " I only wish he would think of our personal convenience now. It seems, however, that he don't care for our sufferings, or we should not have been left to shiver in all this rain, without a place to shelter ourselves in except yonder deserted hut, and even that seems to have got hardly any roof to it."

" Do you think he's doing this that he may afterwards have a laugh against me ?" exclaimed Brassy Popjoy, whose self-conceit had instantly taken fire.

" I don't know how that may be," replied Trubbs, " but I should hardly think he would venture to laugh at a gentleman who might resent it in a manner that would not be very pleasant to him."

" In other words," exclaimed his master, " you think it very likely I should call him out ?"

" I do."

" And no doubt I should," replied the cockney conceitedly, " but that his hospitality disarms my anger. It was very polite of him to invite me to his house, especially after the few warm words we had when he found me banging away in his preserves."

" Perhaps, sir, he thought you wouldn't do much harm among his birds."

" If he thought anything of the kind, Trubbs," replied his master, " it was only through his ignorance of the man he had to deal with. However, we'll not say anything about that now, for I am much pleased at his having taken me into such comfortable quarters, and to prove to him that I am pleased, I shall not be in any hurry to move from them."

"I'm sorry to hear that, sir," exclaimed the groom, "for though the place seems to be well enough in its way, I'm almost tired of being out of London, where you may travel about for a whole lifetime, and never find yourself in such an out-of-the-way place as this."

"True," answered Popjoy, "but even this moor is well enough in the day time, if there's plenty of sport, and no rain to soak you through. By the bye, talking of that reminds me that he has kept us waiting here a long while, and if he don't make his appearance presently I shall leave the place and find my way back to Derwent Hall the best way I can."

"Hush!" whispered the groom, stepping gently forward; "I hear some one coming this way."

"Then of course the squire has returned according to his promise."

"No, sir, its not him," replied Trubbs, "for I could see by that last flash of lightning that there are two people, a man and a woman."

"What can they be here for, at this late hour?"

"That's more than I can tell you, sir," replied the groom, "but I could almost swear that the man is no other than the travelling hawker that we saw last night at the harvest home."

"And the female is the young girl that he claimed as his daughter. The fellow is a roughish chap, sir, I think, to meet in a lonely place like this; so, begging your pardon for the hint, I think we can't do better than make ourselves scarce while our shoes are good."

This suggestion was no sooner uttered than acted on, and stealthily making their way by the deserted hut, the master and man speedily disappeared. As they did so, Caleb Kestrel, with Amy leaning upon his arm for support, approached the place which had just been left vacant.

"Come my girl, we shall do well enough now," exclaimed Caleb; "here is the place where I said shelter might be found, and whilst you remain there I'll go and find the road we are to take, for in spite of the darkness, I know we can't be very far from it."

"Why need we have travelled on such a night as this!" cried Amy, shivering beneath the blast which seemed to pierce into her very limbs.

"Because I want to get far away from this place," he replied. "The people hereabouts look upon me with suspicion, especially Squire Derwent, who I happen to know has made out a warrant for my apprehension."

"Then you have been guilty of some lawless violence," cried the trembling girl.

"Paha! we had a few words together, that's all," answered Kestrel. "He was not pleased with a proposition that I made, and we parted in anger."

"But surely that would not justify him in depriving you of your liberty."

"You know so little of the world, Amy," he replied, "that it would only be a waste of time to explain the various motives that may urge a man to do that which he has no right. To be brief then, this Squire Derwent knows he is in my power, and to get rid of me he would be guilty of any wrong act."

"And yet the people speak of him as being liked by the whole neighbourhood."

"That's because they don't know him so well as I do," replied the pedlar.

"You are in possession of some secret then?"

"I am."

"Has he been guilty of any evil deed?"

"So the world would say if the fact was generally known," answered Caleb Kestrel. "He has robbed the girl, to whom those estates belong, of her rights; and I believe if that was to be let out, he would not only lose the esteem of those he now calls his friends, but he would be stripped of half of that which he holds by fraud."

"You speak harshly of him, father," exclaimed Amy, "but still I feel assured in my own mind that there must be some mistake in this."

"What mistake can there be when I know all the facts from the beginning to the end?" demanded Caleb.

"Does he know the power you boast of?"

"To be sure he does. I went to his house this morning; saw him, and explained what had caused my visit."

"Was he not alarmed?"

"No, he treated me with contempt, and I came away vowing to be revenged!"

"But you have thought better of it, have you not."

"No;" exclaimed Caleb Kestrel, fiercely; "I am now his sworn foe, and never shall I desist from my designs till I have accomplished them."

"Take care then," cried Amy, "or you may fall into the pit you have been preparing for another."

"There is no fear of that," he replied, "for I can work my plans without thrusting myself very forward. You, Amy, will be able to assist me greatly in this design."

"In what way?" she faintly asked.

"You will represent yourself as the girl to whom the late Clement Derwent bequeathed a large portion of his property. I can swear to the fact, and in a short time you will be mistress of Derwent Hall."

"Then the story you told about my being your daughter was a falsehood?"

Caleb Kestrel knew not what reply to make to the question, for it might ruin his plans if an explanation took place before the time he intended. For some few minutes he stood, considering what excuse he could make, and then, determined to keep up the imposition for the present, he said :—

"Its true enough, Amy, that you are my daughter, but there will be no difficulty in satisfying the world that you are the girl who was adopted by Mr. Clement Derwent whilst he was abroad. The present squire can have no proof to the contrary, and it only requires the slightest degree of produce and ingenuity to make you one of the richest women in this country."

"And would you," she asked in a tone of admonition, "would you persuade me to commit so heinous a fraud against one who has never injured us?"

"Psha! I want no preaching from you, girl," exclaimed Caleb Kestrel. "I have a right to command your submission to my will, and if you hesitate it will be all the worse for yourself, and will not in the slightest degree serve this Squire Derwent."

"But he knows you have already claimed me as your daughter," she replied,

"What if he does?—Can't I at any time say that it was only done to answer my own purpose, and that I am ready at any time to prove that you are the girl who was stolen from Clement Derwent, and to whom he left so much of his property in the event of your ever being discovered. So you see, Amy, I am armed at all points, and there is nothing to prevent my depriving this squire of half the possessions of his late cousin."

"But you have acknowledged to me that you are actuated by a feeling of revenge."

"Why I don't deny that there is a little feeling of that kind," answered the pedlar, "but that is not the only motive that has stirred me up to take this course. I want money to assist me out of my poverty;—I told Squire Derwent so; explained to him the means I possessed to make him surrender up half his wealth, and thought by that means to bring him to his senses. But he has defied me to do my worst, and now he shall see that I am not a man to break my word."

"But surely," cried Amy, "you will not persist in making me the instrument of your revenge?"

"Who else have I a right to command, if not my own daughter?" he exclaimed.

"I have taken you away from those who might have persuaded you to pay no heed to my commands, and now girl I shall expect your ready obedience to whatever I insist on."

"Alas!" sighed Amy, "and all this bitter animosity has been produced by the refusal of the squire to resist an act of extortion."

"What extortion can there be in it," demanded the pedlar, "when I promised on certain conditions that he should not be disturbed in his possessions."

"And so," cried Amy, "if I had really been the adopted child of Mr. Clement Derwent, you would have bartered away my right, for a bribe to keep the secret?"

"There you are mistaken," he replied, "for had you been the girl you speak of, I should still have had it in my power to extort a considerable sum of money for the evidence it would have been in my power to give in your favour. But why am I to listen to your reproaches, when my only anxiety is to do you good? I would raise you from poverty to wealth; aye, and will do so if you are not fool enough to throw away the chance."

"Is not poverty far better than wealth, if the latter is to be acquired by dishonest means?"

"Why, how like a simpleton you talk," exclaimed Caleb Kestrel in a tone half bantering, half angry. "I have not yet proposed anything that would injure Squire Derwent, for he well knows the terms upon which the estates came into his hands, and it can cause him neither vexation nor surprise whenever a claim is made for the portion which belongs to the adopted child of his cousin. He has known all along that he has been holding it only upon sufferance, and, from what he told me this morning there is every reason to believe that he will not hesitate to yield up the half that I am about to demand in your name."

"But not for my advantage, I hope!"

"You can do as you please about accepting it," he replied, "but I shall know how to make use of it if you don't choose to accept the produce of my scheme. However, you'll think better of it when you see how willing he is to give up the property, and, then if you think proper to give me five thousand pounds for the service I have done, why I'll take myself off, and you shall never see anything of me afterwards."

"Would you thus desert your child?"

"Why, the truth is, I don't like anything like restraint," he replied, "and I fancy your temper and mine are so opposite, that we should be all the happier apart. Besides, I'm a rough-spun sort of fellow, and it would be a disgrace to have me in your fine house, where all sorts of great people will be visiting."

"Alas!" exclaimed Amy, "I feel that the change of fortune you speak of will never make me happy."

"How do you know it won't?" he demanded abruptly. "You have always lived in poverty with Peeps and his wife, and would perhaps be content to do so for the remainder of your days. But only once taste the comforts that wealth only can bestow, and you will make the important discovery that I did well in changing your condition in life."

"But whither are you now going to take me?"

"Oh, only a little distance off," he replied, "that you may be in readiness when I see that it is time to bring you forward to make your claim."

"How am I to make the claim when I know not that it is founded in justice?"

"Psha!" he exclaimed, "what an eternal preaching you make about justice; as if it was likely that I would persuade you to do anything wrong! Besides you will have no trouble in the matter, for the proof will lie with me, and with the assistance of Peeps and his wife I think we shall be a pretty good match against any opposition that may be offered."

"May I ask one question without giving offence."

"Certainly;—a hundred if you like."

"Am I then the person to whom Mr. Clement Derwent left so large a share of his property?"

"I have told you that you are my daughter," replied Caleb, "but even if you were not it could make no difference whatever, since I should bring you forward as the girl, and there is not a soul in the world that would be able to contradict my assertion."

"Nor could you perhaps prove it if a strict examination should happen to take place."

"But the squire is not likely to cause any inquiry to be made," replied Kestrel, "for he is willing to give up the half which he has no right to, and the slight evidence I shall bring forward will be quite sufficient to convince him that the just claimant has been discovered. But we are wasting time that is precious, so away with you to the hut, and there wait for me till I return with a clue to the right road to the next town."

"You are not surely going to desert me now that I have been taken away from my friends?" exclaims Amy, into whose mind a horrible suspicion had rushed that some treachery was intended,

No. 7.

"Desert you, eh!" he replied with a derisive laugh. "Is it likely I would play so scurvy a trick on my own child;—especially when I have such brilliant hopes that she will be the means of helping me out of this state of poverty and daily toil?"

"It was wrong of me to suspect you;" returned Amy; "and yet you have said such strange things within this last hour that I scarcely know whether to believe that we are so nearly connected as you assert."

"Come, come," muttered Caleb Kestrel, "I must not hear these doubts my girl. If I have spoken strangely as you say, enough has been said to convince you that I have your interest as heart, and its a hard thing to be suspected when one is about to do another a service. So learn to think better of me, Amy, and, as I live, I'll return to you as soon as I have found out the road,"

"Why may I not go with you?"

"Because this is no weather for a woman to be out when there is a place of shelter at hand."

"Nay," she "replied, the storm has passed away, and the moon, bright and cheerful is breaking through the scattered clouds."

"It matters not for that," he replied. "I am not used to be contradicted when once I've said a thing, so stay where you are, and make yourself quite easy about my return. I believe the road lies somewhere about yonder hollow, and if I find that I am right, I shall be back in a few minutes to take you away from this gloomy looking place. Here is my cloak for you to lie down upon in the snuggest corner you can find in the hut, and as we have travelled some little distance in the course of the day it will be well for you to take the opportunity of resting yourself while I'm absent."

With these words he led her to the ruined hut, spread his cloak upon the floor where no rain had penetrated, and having seen her lie down upon it, he left her with another promise that he would soon return. This done, he examined the staff which he used when walking, unscrewed it, and having deposited a therein, proceeded to pump in a sufficient quantity of air to perform all the usual purposes of a gun.

"There," he muttered to himself, when these arrangements were completed, "I am now ready for anything that may happen to come before me. If a few birds or a hare were to start up I should let fly at them without the fear of the report of my gun being heard, for these things make little noise, and we can carry on a poaching expedition without any one being the wiser of it. Aye, and chance too, may throw me in the way of this Squire Derwent, who was so imperious with me this morning. Well be it so; I should have him within shot, with all the advantages in my favour, and I should not fail to make good use of them, for if he was but dead, Amy would claim all the property instead of half of it, and I should share it with her, without the fear of being suspected of having any hand in the death of this Cecil Derwent. The dog snarled at me this morning, and threatened me with punishment; but only let us meet together this night, and we shall see who has the best of it—he or I! And yet, confound the girl; she must raise all sorts of scruples, and throw a thousand impediments in my way though what I am about to do is as much for her advantage as my own. Well, she must be humoured, I suppose, for the present, but the time may not be very far distant when an opportunity will offer itself for me to get rid of her, and make myself master of all these broad lands. Aye, and I will do so, for she suspects me, and there will be need to look out for myself, lest, by and by, she should discover that it was I who stole her in infancy from the house of her adopted father."

He strode away as he muttered the last few words; but his actions had not been so unnoticed as he imagined, for no sooner had he left the hut, than Amy rose and watched him from a window that overlooked the spot, where he was standing. She saw him load and prepare the air gun, and instantly a thought flashed across her mind that he was out for some evil purpose. She would have uttered an exclamation, but that terror seemed to have sealed her lips, and leaning for support against the wall, she stood trembling, yet unable to move from the spot where she had been watching him. At length, however, as he moved away, some little strength returned, and with faltering limbs she made her way from the hut, and followed him with her eyes, as he pursued his course silently towards the spot where he had said he expected to find the road. She then mounted a small eminence that stood near, and had scarcely taken her place there, when footsteps were heard in another direction, and looking round she perceived by the moonlight that it was Mr. Derwent who was approaching. Alarmed, though scarcely knowing why, lest her supposed father should see him, she was about to call to him, when the thought crossed her mind that by appearing to interfere she might rather injure than serve the person of whose safety she had so many painful doubts.

On arriving near the deserted hut Cecil Derwent paused to look around him for those he had left there no very long time before. As they were no where within sight, however, he made his way towards the path which had been previously taken by Kestrel, and precisely at that moment our heroine perceived the pedlar lurking behind a large tree, and pointing a weapon which was similar in appearance to a gun, at the person against whom he had sworn vengeance. Horror struck, she could utter no sound of warning, but her eyes were fixed glaringly upon the two persons before her, a sharp peculiar sound was then heard, the man who held the weapon bounded away, and at the same moment Cecil fell with an exclamation of agony to the ground. Amy could no longer support herself, for all power seemed to be taken away, and for some few moments she lay apparently lifeless. At length, however, she slowly recovered herself, and her first thought was to descend from the eminence from which she had witnessed the tragical scene, and to ascertain how far her assistance might avail the unfortunate victim of her father's revenge. On reaching the spot she found him, to all appearance on the point of death ; all power of utterance had failed him ; and in the last remaining hope she was about to raise his head, when some one was heard approaching, and the voice of Caleb Kestrel sounded harshly in her ear.

"What foolery is this?" he exclaimed. "A man has been killed it seems, and you must needs raise him in your arms that the blood being found upon your clothes may be produced as an evidence that it was you who took his life."

"And why," she asked, "should I not endeavour to afford assistance to the unhappy man who has perished through your blood thirsty vengeance?"

"Hah!" he exclaimed fiercely, "dare you say that it was I who did this deed?"

"Alas! I witnessed it all," she replied, "and, if called upon, must denounce you as the murderer!"

"Would you destroy your father?"

"Aye," she replied, "you would now appeal to my feelings ; but, by this last act you have estranged them from you for ever. It was you who fired the fatal shot, and alone must suffer for the crime."

"Hear me girl," exclaimed Caleb Kestrel, "for your threats have driven m to madness, and it may be that I shall not stop short at this one deed of blood. There are others who have been marked out for vengeance, and if you promise me not to keep this matter a secret from the world, you will have the shedding of human blood to answer for. Swear then never to reveal what you have seen to-night, or a father's curse shall cling to you evermore. Speak girl ! for I will not ask you a second time to save your father from the gallows."

"I will—I will do all that you ask me," she replied, in a voice scarcely audible from emotion.

"'Tis enough, Amy," he exclaimed :—"I will take your word, but be assured I shall henceforth keep a watchful eye upon you. That which has been done cannot be recalled, but a single word incautiously spoken would send your father to meet an ignominious fate."

"The secret will be hard to keep," exclaimed Amy, "yet I will not break the solemn pledge I have given."

"It may be even harder to keep than you imagine," returned Caleb Kestrel,

" for suspicion will soon fall upon some one, and even though you know him to be innocent, you must not speak the word that would save him."

" Then you would make your daughter a participator in a second murder?"

" Why there's no help for it," exclaimed Kestrel. " Some one must be punished for this act, and surely you would not have that person your own father."

" Pray Heaven I be not tried to the fearful extent you speak of," she replied.

" Humph! I am to understand then that in the event of any one else being accused, you would not hesitate to come forward to assert his innocence?"

" What else could I do in so fearful an extremity?'

" It is not for me to tell you what should be done in such a case," he exclaimed. " You know, without my instruction, the duty that a daughter owes to her parent, and I need only once more remind you that if you assert the innocence of one person, it must lead to questions that in the end must criminate me."

" I have said that you may rely upon me."

" Aye," he replied sternly, " and you also said that you hoped to be spared the trial; by which I can only understand that in the event of suspicion being directed towards another person, you would not hesitate to save his life at the sacrifice of mine. However, I shall not beg and pray of you to remember the duty of a child to her parent; but of this be assured, Amy,—I am a desperate man, who has been obliged to do desperate deeds before now, and I will not fall without taking fearful vengeance."

" Let your vengeance then light only upon me," cried the maiden, " for surely the punishment should fall upon the person who has done you the injury."

" Again," exclaimed Caleb Kestrel, " your words confirm me in the belief that I am to be sacrificed."

" It will not be till driven to the last extremity," answered the trembling girl, " and surely before that necessity occurs you may escape to some far distant place, where the laws of this country cannot reach you."

" No, no," exclaimed the pedlar, " I am not to be hurried from place to place in that way either. If the worst comes to the worst I shall remain here to take my chance of whatever is to follow, so now you understand that if a death of ignominy is to be my lot, you, and you alone, will be the cause of it. Besides, who and what was this 'Squire Derwent that you should feel so much for his death? He was no better than other men, and might have been alive at this very moment but for the insult he this morning chose to pass upon me."

" And think you any imagined insult can justify the act you have been guilty of?"

" Come, come, girl," he replied, " I am not to listen patiently to the reproaches of her whose obedience I have a right to command. There was a quarrel between Mr. Derwent and me, and when once I have received a deliberate insult, it is blood only that can wipe it out."

" Alas!" sighed Amy, " then how bitterley do I regret the hour when you discovered, and claimed me as your daughter."

" Aye," he replied, " I have but little of your love, I believe, and yet you cannot bring the same charge against me, after the years of wandering through many lands that I have passed in searching for you. But why," he added on perceiving that she was gazing intently at the body;—" why is it, Amy, that you keep your eyes so fixed upon the form of him who has fallen by my hand?"

" It was in the hope," she replied, " that he might exhibit signs of returning animation."

" Then cheat yourself no longer with so vain a notion," answered Caleb Kestrel, " for he is dead, and in a few minutes I shall place him in some spot where there will be no chance of the body being discovered. Thus the secret will be kept safely enough, and I shall have no discovery to apprehend."

" Do you then believe that his absence from home will not lead to a suspicion that he has been murdered?"

"I care nothing for what people suspect if there is no evidence to be produced." he replied. "Let them think or say as they will, for it will be all one to me so long as I know there's no danger of being laid hold of."

"But there *is* danger."

"Who from?" he demanded, sternly. "Am I to take that, girl, as a threat that the accusation will come from your lips."

"No," she replied; "as Heaven is my witness I meant no threat by the words I uttered. Unhappily, the secret is in my possession, but never, shall my tongue pronounce the accusation that would send you to meet the punishment of this crime on the public scaffold."

"Why, that is well said, Amy," he exclaimed, in a tone of less severity; "and I was perhaps wrong to believe it possible that you could be guilty of an act that would send your father to the gallows. The fearful secret will remain locked up in your own heart, and in return for it,—if any person should be suspected of the deed, I will do all that may lay in my power to save an innocent man from punishment."

Amy's reply to this was interrupted by the loud report of a gun, and the pedlar, startled by this unexpected warning of approaching danger, exclaimed :—

"I must fly, girl, for if seen near this spot, suspicion will surely light upon me, and I am lost! You must also fly, but in a different direction;—return to the farm-house where you slept last night, and to-morrow, if all things go well, I will meet you there. But remember your promise of secrecy, or I shall soon have more than the blood of that one man to answer for."

These words were uttered menacingly, and the next moment he darted off at his utmost speed towards a coppice at some little distance off, where, for the present, he might conceal himself from observation. Amy also turned away to return to the farm house, and as she glided from the spot perceived approaching Frank Marldale, carrying in his hand the gun which Mary Everett had vainly urged him to leave at the first cottage he happened to pass. Amy then discovered that it was he who had just fired his piece; but, wishing to avoid a meeting with him, she hurred away lest the discovery of the murdered body of the Squire should lead to questions that she would not know how to answer.

Little suspecting the horrible sight that awaited him Frank continued to advance to the very spot on which lay the bleeding form of Squire Derwent. Owing to the darkness of the night he would have passed on without observing it, but at that moment the moon burst forth from the clouds with extraordinary brightness, and revealed to his eyes a spectacle that filled him with horror. Stooping, he at a glance recognized the man against whom he had long felt a mortal hatred, but every unworthy thought was instantly banished from his mind, and stooping down he raised the body in his arms to discover if the vital spark had indeed fled. A little warmth seemed at first to afford some slight hope; but the limbs were without motion; the pulse appeared to be stopped, and all confirmed him in the painful impression that Cecil Derwent had ceased to exist. As he came to this conclusion other persons were heard approaching, and the next moment he found himself in the firm grasp of two of the Squire's gamekeepers.

"Villain!" exclaimed one of them; "this is your doing; you have always hated our master, and now, midnight murderer as you are, have accomplished your revenge by waylaying and murdering him!"

"By Heaven 'tis false!" returned Frank Marldale, struggling to release himself. "I found him lying as you now see him and was endeavouring to render him assistance when you came suddenly upon me."

"Aye, aye, that's a very fine tale to tell," answered the man, "but I and my mate here, heard a gun discharged not many minutes ago, and on hastening in the direction of the sound we find our master murdered, and you standing by him."

"Yet in spite of all these cruel suspicions, I swear to you that I am innocent!"

"Of course you wouldn't mind swearing that to save your life," replied the man ; " but we are not such fools as to let you go when there's such evidence against you. Dont we know that you have always been upon bad terms with our master, and can any body in his right senses believe that he was murdered by any other person than the one we find on the spot ?"

" So far appearance may be against me," exclaimed Frank Marldale ; " but by the heaven above I am guiltless of this dark deed of crime."

" Do you deny that it was your gun that was heard just now ?"

" I certainly discharged it," he replied ; " but it was merely because I would not carry it loaded into my house."

" You must get the magistrates to believe that story," exclaimed the chief gamekeeper, " for I must confess it don't seem very like that you discharged it for nothing. Besides, don't we afterwards discover Squire Derwent murdered, and you standing on the very spot."

" Which is quite enough to warrant us in apprehending him," observed his companion. "So you see, Mr. Marldale, we are bound, whether right or wrong, to carry you before some one who can judge this matter better than ourselves."

It was in vain that the young man protested his innocence of the foul crime that had been committed ; the two men persisted in their belief that he had been instigated to perpetrate the murder through motives of revenge, and in spite of all his remonstrance they expressed their determination to convey him in the morning before a magistrate, and thus place the affair in a train for a searching enquiry. Seeing the uselessness of any further opposition, Frank submitted to this hard destiny, and consented to accompany them to a place where he might be secured or the night.

" I'm really very sorry for you, Mr. Marldale," said the principal of the two men as they went along, " but there's so much suspicion in the case that we should have been blamed if we had pursued any other course in such an affair as this."

" But what ?" asked the young man ; " is to become of the body of your unfortunate master ?"

" Oh, that must remain where it is till we can send some of the people to remove it to the Hall," he replied ; " the poor fellow is dead enough, so he wont suffer much for lying a few hours in the cold."

" And where am I to pass the night ?"

" At my house," he replied, " for you would not find the cage a very comfortable place to lodge in. You can lie down on the bed if you like, and I and my comrade will sit up to watch in case any attempt to escape should be made."

" You have no reason to be afraid of that," answered Frank Marldale, " for why should I desire liberty when all those who I have most respected will believe the charge that is made against me. From this moment there will be neither man nor woman in the world that I can call my friend."

" I should hardly think you are right there sir," replied the gamekeeper, " for you have been keeping company a long while with Mary Everett, and when once a girl is over head and ears in love, it's not easy to make her believe anything against the person she has set her affections on."

" Alas !" sighed Frank, " it is on her account that I feel with double force the degrading position in which I am placed. Her heart will surely break when she hears that I have been accused of this murder. That I am innocent of it she will readily believe, but of what avail will that be if I am deemed guilty by all the world beside."

" Well, it aint for me to ask questions," said the other, " but if this act was not yours, can you say who else is likely to have done it ?"

" At present," he replied, " there is no one upon whom my suspicions rest."

" Nor can I think of any one," exclaimed the man, " for Squire Derwent was so generally respected in those parts that I believe there was not a man besides yourself who had any ill feeling against him."

"And mine," answered Frank Marldale, "would never have urged me to take his life."

"Yet you were near him at the moment when I and my companions arrived at the place."

"I was there, indeed," he replied, "but only reached the spot a few minutes before you."

"And he was then dead ?"

"He was."

"Did you hear the report of any gun besides your own ?"

"No."

"Then that, I'm afraid, will go very hard against you, for it seems quite certain that he met his death by a gun shot wound, and your weapon was the only one that I and my companion heard discharged."

"It is true," replied Frank Marldale, "that circumstantial evidence will at first appear to be very strong against me. But Heaven will not desert the innocent, and there is a hope strong within me that the real perpetrator of this villanous deed will yet be discovered."

"Well," exclaimed the gamekeeper, "all I can say is, that I heartily wish your words may come true, for, barring your dislike of Squire Derwent, I've always heard you spoken of as one of the most peaceable and quiet men in our neighbourhood. But revenge, Mr. Marldale, is a very horrible passion, and when once a man gives way to it, there's no saying how far it will carry him."

"Then you still believe that, carried away by the passion, I took the life of Mr. Derwent ?"

"Why, I don't want to hurt your feelings by saying what I think about it," he replied, "It's not for the like of me to judge between the guilt or innocence of another man, but it must be confessed there's something in this matter that wants clearing up."

"Aye," answered Frank, "and I fear not but all will be satisfactorily explained before long."

"And what will be the use of that if the explanations should happen to come too late ?"

"You mean if I am pronounced guilty and receive the dreadful sentence of death ?"

"Aye, that's what I meant, but I could hardly find it in my heart to give utterance to the words."

"I believe," exclaimed Frank, "that there is one faithful friend who will never give up the pursuit till my innocence has been satisfactorily proved."

"You mean Mary Everett."

"I do," he replied. "Grief for my helpless condition may at first bow down her spirit to the earth, but in a short time she will recover all her energy, and then no difficulties will deter her from the task of discovering the villian by whose hand your master fell."

"The poor girl must mind what she's about there," exclaimed the gamekeeper, "for if there is really such a person as you speak of, she may meet the same fate as the unfortunate Squire Derwent has. However, she is a shrewd, free-hearted girl as ever lived, and I dare say don't require any instruction from me as to what she should do."

"Will you see her and break, as gently as you can, this unfortunate business ?"

"Bless your heart; 1 couldn't do it for the world," replied the other. "You must know, Mr. Marldale, I have an uncommon tender heart of my own; and to see the poor girl take on when she hears of misfortune would be more than I could bear. But we'll talk over this by and by, for here we are at my house where you'll have to pass the time between this and your appearance before the magistrate in the morning."

By this time the door of the cottage was opened, and Frank Marldale was conducted to an upper room to ensure his safe custody. Refreshments were directly offered but declined by the captive, who preferred resting himself upon the bed, though he had little expectation of being able to sleep. The two men then left him and proceeded down stairs to keep watch and ward over their prisoner.

CHAPTER VII.

MORNING AT THE FARM HOUSE.—AMY AND HER FRIEND.—THE ARRIVAL OF HEAVY TIDINGS.—WOMAN'S CONSTANCY.—THE PEDLAR AND HIS VICTIM.

FEVERISH from want of rest, Amy was one of the first up in the farm house on the morning that followed the deed of crime discribed in our last chapter. Hitherto she had not found courage to inform Mary Everett of the murder she had seen committed, for the warning of her supposed father still rang in her ears, and she trembled at the thought of the retribution he might take he discovered that she had confided the secret to another person. Of the accusation and arrest of Frank Marldale she of course knew nothing at present.

In a few minutes after she had left her room she was joined by Mary, who on this occasion happened to be in more than her usual good spirits; and who, perceiving the gloom and despondency that hung upon the mind of her young companion, rallied her upon the subject, and endeavoured by every means she could think of to restore her to better spirits. Perceiving, however, that all was of no avail she asked to be made her confidant, if anything of serious consequence had occurred in the interval since they had last met.

" Believe me there is nothing upon which I need ask counsel or advice," replied Amy. " I greive at the separation that must so soon take place between us; but fate has decreed it, and I must submit."

" Or rather this strange man, who claims you as his daughter, has decreed it," exclaimed Mary, taking her hand, " and for once in my life I would advise flat rebellion against paternal authority."

" But he insists upon my following him in his long and wearisome wanderings."

" Then I would first of all make him prove his right to insist upon it."

" He tells me that has been already done by the evidence of Mr. and Mrs. Peeps."

" And are you sure," asked Mary, " that Mr. and Mrs. Peeps have not been bribed by him to support a false statement."

" How can I doubt those who have ever been to me the kindest of friends?" exclaimed Amy. " It is with real grief that they part from me, but yielding to the superior claims of a father, they consented to yield me to his care."

" I am afraid his care of you will not be very great," answered her friend, " for I have taken a strong prejudice against that man, and, from a few words that have dropped from my uncle, I believe he suspects him to be a worthless fellow, who once lived in this neighbourhood, and was compelled to leave on account of some evil practices that he had been guilty of."

" My father has admitted as much," exclaimed Amy, " but having been punished for his faults, he has now returned as he says, a better man."

" A better man !" cried Mary Everett. " Nay, asking your pardon for my freedom of speech, I can see nothing in his countenance that might lead to the conviction of his having reformed."

" Perhaps you judge him too severely."

or your s ke Amy, hope I do; but it must be confessed I have taken a trong prejudice against this Caleb Kestrel. His appearance here was altogether a mystery, and some of our people still think that when they found him on the night of our harvest-home, he was prowling about the premises for the purpose of committing a robbery.

"Nay, you forget that it is of my father you speak," exclaimed Amy, reproach fully.

"I speak of him," replied her friend, "who I believe has no claim to the relationship you speak of."

"If he has no claim to me, what motive can he have for making it? I have been

brought up in poverty, and therefore he can have no interested designs of his own."

"Ah! my dear girl," answered her friend, "there is no being aware of the motives or designs of bad men. You and I cannot see any reason for the claim he has made, yet I could stake my life for it, there is something concealed which is yet to be brought to light."

"But my friends say that he is certainly the person who many years ago trusted me to their care."

No. 8.

"And so he may be; but it is at least as likely that he had stolen you from your own parents."

"How!" exclaimed Amy, "do you really then believe that I may again be able to throw myself upon the protection of those to whom I am under so many obligations."

"I at least fancy so," answered Mary, "and have also a very strong suspicion that the notion will, upon inquiry, be found correct. In short, the man appears to have always borne a very bad character, and this may only be one of many other schemes to extort money.

"If so, surely Mr. and Mrs. Peeps would have suspected something of the kind."

"So they might," replied Mary, "but they seem to be a couple of those easy sort of people who are content to take any person's assertion without troubling themselves to make further inquiries. They have, in fact, all along believed you to be his daughter, and now give up their charge on the first demand that is made upon them."

"How could they have refused him," asked Amy, "when they acknowledged that he was the person who, during my infancy, placed me under their care?"

"Perhaps they lacked the courage to do so," replied her friend, "but had I been in their place this Mr. Caleb Kestrel, as he calls himself, would not have succeeded quite so easily. However, we will not discuss this part of our subject any further at present; so now listen to a proposition that my uncle sends you through me."

"A proposition from Farmer Brough!"

"Yes;—he offers you a home in his house till I am married, and then you are to go and live with me.

"Impossible."

"And why should there be any impossibility in the matter?"

"Because I have to obey the commands of my father, and am to leave this place with him in a few hours."

"Believe me Amy, if you do anything of the kind you will bitterly repent it," exclaimed Mary Everett. "The man has villain written in his features, and there is some plot going on that you at present little suspect."

"Do not, I implore you, do not fill my mind with more dread than I already feel of that man," exclaimed Amy, unable any longer to restrain her emotion. "I know that in some things you have judged of him but too correctly; he is a man of evil passions; yet destiny has thrown me in his power, and I feel myself utterly helpless."

"Then accept the protection of those who are so anxious to assist you. Here is a home offered where you may dwell in security, for Kistrel will not attempt to remove you by force when he knows the resistance he would meet with."

"Indeed, indeed, I dare not accept your generous offer."

"Then he has used intimidation to compel you to leave those who would protect you?"

"Do not ask what has passed between us in conversation," cried Amy, "for he has said and done much that I dare not repeat."

"You acknowledge then that if you accompany him from this place it would be through fear?"

"I do, my dearest friend; but let him not know that I have said so, or I know not the dreadful consequences that would follow such a disclosure."

"And yet with such a man you would trust yourself?"

"Tell me any way to avoid it," cried Amy, "and most gladly would I avail myself of your counsel. I would do anything to be free from that man, and yet dread to excite his wrath."

"Well," answered her friend, "all that you have been saying only serves to confirm me in my opinion that you should accept the offer of a home in this house. Do that, and when Kestrel finds you have friends, he will quietly disappear, no one knows whither."

"But only to return when he is least expected."

"We will always be on our guard against that," replied Mary Everett; "and should there be grounds for suspecting him at any time of evil practices, he may be handed over to those who have the power to restrain him. So now hesitate no longer, but when my uncle returns, as he presently will, let me have your permission to tell him that his offer of a home has been accepted."

"I will think of it," replied Amy, "but I fear the step is too dangerous to all parties to be ventured on."

"Rely upon it there is not so much to be afraid of as you imagine," exclaimed her friend. "The man is rough and savage enough in his disposition, I dare say; but like others of the same description, he will become reconciled to the disappointment when he finds there is no help for it."

"I have seen little of him," answered Amy, "but quite sufficient to convince me that resistance to his commands would be followed by violence."

"Why then there is the more reason that you should refuse to follow such a man; I, however, have formed my own opinion upon the subject, and it is my belief that nothing is to be apprehended from him if we only proceed with firmness and decision. Depend upon it, Amy, he has no wish to come in collision with the law, for I believe he has already been punished with transportation, and he will not venture a similar doom a second time."

"Have you certain intelligence that he has ever been convicted of crime."

"My uncle says he is sure of it, and he is not a man to make such an assertion lightly. His long absence from England—which he himself admits—confirms the belief, and you have, therefore, to consider whether he is a person who you ought to trust yourself with."

"If he is my father I dare not refuse."

"A little patience," exclaimed Mary, "will soon set us right upon that subject, for if resistance is offered, he will be obliged to bring forward evidence to prove his assertion. Besides, we may be able to ascertain if our suspicion of your having been stolen by him is correct, and should that turn out to be correct, he will be sent abroad again for some years, and the chances are that we shall never hear anything more of him."

"But what has put the notion into your head that I was stolen?" asked Amy.

"Why to confess the truth," answered her friend, "I was unable to repress my curiosity on this subject, so I questioned Mr. and Mrs. Peeps as to whether they could throw any light upon the affair."

"And could they?"

"Not much; but the little they did, was quite sufficient to convince me that our trouble would not be thrown away if we carried our enquiries a little further."

"What did they tell you?"

"That, though very young when first placed with them, you used often to prattle about your former house and the comforts you had had there. Now that, in my opinion, may fairly give rise to surmises; when, according to the account given by Peeps, the man who calls himself your father was never far removed from absolute beggary."

"It may be as you say," sighed Amy; "but even if your suspicion is a correct one, all clue to my family and connexions must by this time be lost."

"Then you have no hope of being restored—supposing I am not wrong in my conjectures?"

"Not the slightest."

"Well, then, I confess to having very exalted notions upon the matter," answered Mary Everett, "and that is one reason why I am so anxious that you should not be lost to us. Caleb Kestrel knows well enough that we suspect him of evil practices, and rely on it, my dear girl, if once he gets you out of our sight, he will take care that we should not discover you again very easily."

"I fear not," sighed Amy, "and yet such is my destiny, that I dare not refuse to obey his commands."

"Nay, that is acknowledging that you believe he has a right to claim your obedience."

"Or rather it is a proof that I fear the man into whose power I have so unfortunately fallen. The claim he has made is hitherto uncontradicted, and I have no alternative but to obey."

"You have friends, though, my dear Amy, who will aid you in resisting him."

"I have indeed found friends where I least expected to meet with them," she replied, "but I will not subject them to the violence of the man whom I myself so much dread."

"Am I then to understand that you leave us, to trust yourself with a man whom we feel certain is an impostor?"

"I must," she replied, "though Heaven knows I do so most unwillingly."

"And well you may, for we know him to be a man who has forfeited his character."

"et he claims me as his daughter, and no proof can be brought forward to justify me in refusing obedience to the commands he has laid upon me."

"Unhappy girl," said Mary Everett, "I fear you will soon have bitter reason to repent this rashness."

"No one but myself knows the terror I feel at the thought of leaving this place with him," exclaimed Amy, "and yet, such is the influence he has obtained over me that I dare not say nay to his commands."

"Can you not find some excuse for remaining here a little while longer?"

'I have tried to prevail on him to let me do so," replied Amy, "but he has met me with a stern refusal, and even threatened me with violence if I show any disposition to dispute his will. In a short time he will be here, and then I leave you for ever."

"Would not a magistrate, if applied to, render you some assistance in the hour of need?"

"I know little of the law," she replied, "but I do not think that assistance could be afforded in a case like this, as the supposed daughter of this man I am bound to obey him, and any resistance that I might offer would only bring upon me the violence I have been threatened with."

"Well," exclaimed Mary, "I don't know what my uncle will say to this when he hears of it, but I have a notion that he will not suffer you to be taken away from his house quite so easily as this Kestrel imagines."

"Then bloodshed may follow, and I shall be the cause of it!" cried Amy, clasping her hands in terror.

"There has been enough of that already," exclaimed Farmer Brough, who entered the room as these last words were pronounced, "murder, my dear children has been committed whilst we slept, and suspicion has fallen upon one on whose innocence I could stake my life."

"Murder so near us!" cried Mary Everett, startled by the utterance of such fearful words.

"Aye," he replied, "squire Derwent was shot last night as he was returning home across the moors."

"By whom was the fearful deed committed?"

"That's just what I should like to know," answered her uncle; for they have arrested one whom we all know well, and whom I am certain had no more to do with it than any of us who are here present."

"His name," gasped Mary, who seemed to have a fearful presentiment of evil.

"Come, come," exclaimed the farmer, "don't be alarmed at what I am going to tell you, for I have already said that I know he is innocent, and this affair of the arrest can only injure him for a few days. In short, Mary, your lover, Frank Marldale has been accused, and is to be taken before the magistrate this morning."

At this terrible news Mary Everett sank back upon her seat, and was for some time unconscious of all that was passing around her. At length, however, by the united efforts of her friends she was partially restored, when a violent flood of tears relieved her throbbing brain.

"Forgive me, my dear girl," exclaimed the good farmer, pressing her to his bosom, "forgive me for the evil news I have brought, but the truth must have come out sometime or another, and I thought it would be better from me than anybody else ; th poor lad will soon make his innocence clear, and there's some consolation in knowing that there's not a friend or neighbour but believes that the deed was committed by some one else."

"Is any person in particular suspected ?" exclaimed Amy, in a tone of intense anxiety.

"At present I have heard no name mentioned," answered Farmer Brough, "but there are plenty of people out in pursuit, and it is expected that the real criminal will soon be in some of their hands."

"And Frank," sobbed Mary Everett, "have you yet been to see and console him in this dreadful affliction."

"I tried to do so," answered her uncle, "but they'll not let any one have an interview with him till an order to that effect has been given by one of the magistrates. By-and-bye, however, I shall see him, and in the mean time shall employ a lawyer to watch the evidence that is to be brought forward against him."

"Evidence !" cried Mary, "can there be any to throw suspicion upon Frank Marldrle ?"

"Why, for that matter," replied the farmer. "any trifling thing will be taken as proof at this stage of the inquiry."

"Was he near the spot where the murder was committed ?"

"He was; and that's the only thing that can at present be brought against him, except indeed, that he had discharged his gun just before the keepers came up and discovered their master weltering in his blood."

"Did he not deny any participation in the foul deed ?"

"Yes," answered the farmer, "he denied it stoutly, but what was the use of that when he was found standing close to the body."

"My life for it," cried Mary, "he was endeavouring to assist the unfortunate sufferer.

"There's very little doubt about that, I believe," answered her uncle, "but be that as it may, he was immediately laid hold of and accused of having murdered the squire. And what made the suspicion all the stronger was, that he did not deny having fired off his gun only a few minutes before. Then it was known too, that he and the squire have not been upon the best terms for some time past, so that one thing added to another seemed to form a plausible ground for taking him into custody."

"But his being near the spot can be but a slight ground of suspicion," cried Mary Everett, "for his way home lay across the moors, so that there is nothing extraordinary in his having been there."

"That's all true enough as far as it goes," answered the farmer, "but it don't save him from the consequence of being taken up as a suspected murderer. Poor fellow ! my heart bleeds for him when I think of the agony of mind he is suffering during this terrible suspense."

"You have not yet told us what they have done with the murdered body," exclaimed Amy, who had listened to this recital with emotions of mingled agony and horror.

"That," he replied, "is because neither I nor anybody else can discover what has become of the corpse. The two gamekeepers swear to its being there when they came away with Frank Marldale, but when some other persons were afterwards sent to take it to the hall, it was not to be found anywhere about the place."

"Doubtless," cried Mary, "the real assassin had in the meantime taken care to remove it."

"That is just what I myself suspect," answered the old man, "for by removing the body the principal part of the evidence will be destroyed, and no conviction will follow. In short, a lawyer would argue before the judges, that the squire may still be alive, though both the gamekeepers swear that they saw him lying dead upon the ground."

" Then the person who committed the deed cannot be punished if the body is not found?" exclaimed Amy, in a tone of deep anxiety.

" Clearly not, for there is no proof of the crime having been committed."

" Your lover then, is in no danger," she cried, joyfully pressing the hand of Mary Everett, " and I shall leave this place without the agony of knowing that my best friends are plunged in grief for the misfortunes of one who is most dear to them."

" But you will also know," answered farmer Brough, " that whilst the mystery remains unexplained there will be some to suspect him of having committed the crime. For that reason I could have wished the body had not been removed, since I know Frank would have been able easily to convince a judge and jury that he was not guilty of taking away the life of a fellow creature."

" And you say," exclaimed Amy, " that no one is at present suspected, except the person who has been unjusty accused?"

" I have not heard of any one," he replied, " and indeed, I hardly know how it should be so, for a terrible tempest raged all the earlier part of the evening, and few persons I should think would venture out on such an open place as the moors at a time like that."

" And yet," observed Mary, " it is but too evident that both Mr. Derwent and Frank were there."

" True, but what do you infer from that, my dear girl?"

" That others were as likely to be there as themselves," she replied, " and consequently that there is the greater probability of the act having been committed by other hands than those of Frank Marldale."

" My dear girl," exclaimed her uncle, " you may take my word for it that no one believes Frank guilty, though unfortunately he happened to be near the spot at the time. A few hours may serve to put the real perpetrator into the hands of justice ; and for my own part I care not how soon, for I am afraid our poor young friend will not be set at liberty till the actual assassin has been taken into custody."

" Then you think it possible he may be sent to prison on this horrible charge?" cried Mary Everett, again becoming alarmed for the safety of her lover.

" Why I don't understand enough law to answer that question," returned the old man; " but I should say that if the body of 'Squire Derwent is not found they will soon give the person accused his liberty."

" How soon?"

" In a few days at farthest."

" And must Frank remain for days in prison?"

" At present he is confined at the house of the principal gamekeeper," answered her uncle, " and I dare say they will not want to remove him from it whilst there is so little evidence against him. So you see there will not be much to complain of, particularly as every one is convinced that he has been accused wrongfully."

" May I not be permitted to go and see him in this hour of trial and adversity?" asked Mary.

" Till the examination takes place, no one will be allowed to visit him," answered the farmer. " The poor fellow is solitary and unhappy enough I dare say, but I'm not sorry that you can't have an interview with him just yet, for your grief is yet young, and in a few days you will be able to present yourself before him with more firmness than you could display now. Besides it will be better for me to visit him first that he may have the consolation of knowing that he is pitied and respected in spite of the cloud that has so suddenly come over him.

" And you may tell him from me, sir," exclaimed Amy, " that let the evidence against him be as strong as it may, I will assist him if there should appear to be need of it."

" You assist him, my poor girl!"

"Aye," she replied, "the promise may appear impossible to be performed, but the kindness I have received here prompts me to do that which would save the life of one who is so dear to you and Mary."

"Why what in the name of fortune is the meaning of all this!" exclaimed the farmer, raising his eyelids with wonder and astonishment. "You speak confidently of preserving our poor Frank Marldale, as if you knew by whom the murder was committed."

"Remember, sir," answered Amy, perceiving that she had said rather too much, "I do not admit that I know any more of this dreadful affair than you do yourself. I believe, however, that Mr. Marldale had no hand in it, and it will therefore be my duty as well as my inclination to do all in my power to discover who it was that sent Mr. Derwent to an untimely grave."

"Thanks, my good and grateful girl," exclaimed the farmer, warmly grasping her hand; "your resolution does you credit, and I shall fully rely on your promise, should there hereafter be any occasion for it. So now make up your mind to accept the offer I sent you through my niece;—make this house your home, and think no more of wandering like a vagrant through the world, with that man who calls himself your father."

"Nay, dear sir," she replied, "I believe there is no alternative but to follow him."

"Reflect a little, my dear child," exclaimed Brough, "and I believe you will by and bye be of the same opinion that I am. For the present I leave you, for I have some few things to speak to Mary about, but remember I shall fully expect a favourable answer when we meet the next time."

He then left the room with Mary Everett, and Amy was about to retire to the chamber in which she had rested the last two nights, when a hand was laid upon her arm, and a gruff voice saluted her with :—

"How now girl! What devil's tricks are you up to now? Have you so soon forgotten your promise of secrecy that I am to be sacrificed for the sake of saving the life of a youngster in whom you can feel no interest?"

"I will not injure you," she replied, returning the gaze with which he regarded her; but if he can be saved without harm to yourself, I will spare no pains to preserve one who is so dear to those who have received me beneath their hospitable roof."

"Psha! let him take his chance, and if matters should be likely to take an unfavourable turn against him it shall be my task to get him out of the scrape."

"Alas! I fear you would not perform your promise."

"Indeed!" he muttered; "so it seems then your father's word is not to be believed!"

"I would fain believe you," she replied; "but how can you aid him when by doing so you would bring upon yourself the suspicion of being Mr. Derwent's murderer."

"Hush!" he whispered, "don't speak such words as those so loud, or we may be overheard. Would you ruin me, girl, by letting these people suppose that I had any hand in the unfortunate gentleman's death?"

"If there is danger," demanded Amy, why do you not fly from this spot while there is yet an opportunity?"

"I mean to do so in a few hours" he replied, "but I must first see your old protector, Peeps, who will be able to assist me in a little affair I have in hand."

"No more crime I hope?"

"Oh no," replied the pedlar, "if there was any crime in contemplation, Peeps is the last person in the world that I should think of making my confidant. He's too addle-pated to be trusted where life is endangered, but I believe in the matter I am going to consult him about he may be able to do good service."

"Why not see him then at some other place far away from here?" demanded Amy. "Both of you get your living by travelling through the country, and surely it would be easy to appoint some spot, miles away, where there would be little or no danger?"

"Why, the truth is," answered the pedlar, "what I have to do is just in this immediate neighbourhood. A few hours may serve to settle the business, and then you, my girl, will have reason to confess that I am not indifferent to your interest."

"I neither ask nor desire any favour from you," she exclaimed.

"And why not?"

"Can you ask that question after the fearful scene I witnessed last night?" she demanded, in a low, hollow tone, that seemed to thrill through every vein.

"Let me har no more taunts like that," growled Caleb Kestrel, "or I may be tempted to do that which I am most anxious to avoid."

"Do your worst," answered Amy, regarding him with a firm and stedfast eye; —"slay me if you will, but ask me no more to leave this place with you."

"That will depend upon the result of my interview with Peeps," exclaimed Kestrel. "If he falls in with my views you may remain in this neighbourhood, and become the golden calf for all men to fall down and worship."

"You have before hinted that I was born to great wealth," returned the maiden; " and if there is any truth in your words villany must have been practised towards me when I was too young to know the wrong that was inflicted."

"And who do you suspect of having done the wrong."

"You."

"Ha, ha, ha!" laughed Caleb Kestrel; "a likely story, indeed, that a father should injure his own child."

"I do not believe that you have any right to call me your daughter," she exclaimed.

"Indeed! And who pray has put this foolish notion into your head—Peeps or his wife, perhaps?—If I thought so they should bitterly suffer for it."

"They have never breathed such a hint to me," answered Amy; "but, on the contrary, since your appearance here they have assured me it was you who placed me under their care, and that they have always believed me to be your daughter."

"Then why did you just now throw a doubt upon the claim I have made?"

"Because I have an indistinct recollection that when very young I lived in splendour and affluence."

"Your memory serves you well, my girl," he replied, "for I was not always the poor miserable outcast that you now see me. I was once rich, and you, I suppose, have a faint recollection of the time; however things took an unfavourable turn—I sank from affluence to poverty, and no longer having a home of my own, I placed you with Peeps and his wife, who I know to be very honest, worthy people in their way. So now, Amy, you see how easily I have cleared up the mystery that has so sorely puzzled you."

"My doubts are not yet removed," she exclaimed, "for I have reason to believe that there is not one word of truth in all that you have been uttering."

"Why do you doubt me?"

"Because from all I have heard, you were never in better circumstances than you are now," she replied. "Farmer Brough and many others remember your living in this neighbourhood years before I was born, and all of them say that you were poor in the extreme,

"And did'nt they tell you that I went abroad?"

"Yes."

"Very well then," he exclaimed, "what was to hinder me from growing rich?" Suppose now that I was a gambler, and lived well upon the money obtained from the fools who ventured their stakes against mine?—But why should I enter into explanations with one who has no right to demand them from me? I have claimed you as the child I left with Peeps and his wife; they acknowledge that my claim is a fair one; and I defy all the world to prove that my assertion is false.

"And you are determined that I shall accompany you when you leave this place."

"To be sure I am," he replied, "for I should always be in fear of your betraying me were I to lose sight of you for a moment. That affair, of last night has thrown me in your power, and now you doubt my being your father, there is but too much reason to believe that you would not hesitate to denounce me as the man who took the life of 'Squire Derwent,"

"Have I not promised though sorely against my will, to keep the dreadful secret?"

"Aye, aye," he replied, "you certainly gave me your promise, not to blab what you saw ; but since then young Marldale has been taken into custody on suspicion of being the murderer, and I have reason to suspect that you would save him from the gallows by sending me there."

"If you suspect that," said Amy, "why do you not seek safety by immediate flight."

No. 70.

"Because there is something for me to do that requires my preesnce here," he replied, "I will make you wealthy Amy, and you shall assist me with the means of living abroad by bestowing upon me a handsome share out of your fortune in return for my sevices."

"I will not accept of your services for any such purpose," answered Amy, "wealth I have never expected to be mine, nor have I ever desired it, and were it to come through your means I should have but too much reason to believe that the fortune would not be acquired honourably."

"But I tell you it is your own," exclaimed Kestrel, "and might have been yours years ago if I had known where to find you. I sought Peeps and his wife throughout the whole length and breadth of England, but no tidings could I hear of them till chance threw me in their way in this outlandish place. And now, Amy, that we have met, I will claim for you a fortune, such as, for amount, you can form no conception."

"Once or all," she replied, "I decline your offer; for, even if I could, I have no desirt o take the property you speak of from its present possessor."

"Oh!" exclaimed Caleb Kestrel, "there's no occasion to be squeamish about that; for it so happens that, at the present moment, the property is not in anybody's possession. So no harm will be done, and, with very little trouble, you will be converted from a poor girl to a wealthy one."

"I have never coveted wealth."

"Perhaps not," he replied; "but you shall have it though, in spite of yourself. However, this is no place to enter into an explanation, so meet me an hour hence at the entrance of the village, and I will then give you certain information that, I think, will serve to change your present determination."

He then abruptly left the house, and Amy fell into a train of thought that his mysterious words had given rise to. At first she resolved not to keep the appointment he had made, but, on further consideration, determined 'to hear his explanation."

CHAPTER VIII.

HE FAITHFUL STEWARD. — A MYSTERIOUS VISITER. — A STRUGGLE, AND THE RESCUE.—CALEB KESTREL IS ONCE MORE AT LARGE.

For some reason or other, which he refused to explain to all inquisitive inquirers, Mr. Reves had locked up one of the apartments in the Manor House, the key of which he kept in his pocket, desiring that no one would approach the prohibited spot till permission was given him to do so. But, as it always happens where there is mystery, the servants kept a continual watch upon the place, and, though they could not dive into the secret cause of all this extraordinary caution, they saw quite enough to convince them that there was something which they must and would—by hook or by crook—find out. In fact, the interdicted chamber was the one in which the body of their master had been deposited, and they could see no reason why Mr. Reves should be the only person allowed to pay their respects to one who was equally respected by every member of his household. Even the sagacious Mr. Brassey Popjoy was sorely puzzled when the singular fact was related to him, and as he could not untie the Gordion knot himself, he resolved to cut it at once by demanding an explanation from the steward. Full of this thought he went in search of Mr. Reves, and at length ound him in the library busily engaged in looking over a number of papers that were spread out on a table before him.

"Pray, my friend," he said, "are you very much occupied at present, or ma

I ask for an explanation of a mystery that, for the life of me, I am not able to find out."

"If your question is of importance," replied the old man, "I can spare a few minutes, but will not promise to make any revelations unless your questions are totally unconnected with the affairs of this family."

"Humph!" returned the cockney, "you are a plain spoken old gentleman I find; but as a particular friend of your late master, I think myself justified in asking why you will not suffer any one but yourself to enter the room where the body is lying?"

"That is a question that I must be excused answering."

"Indeed! Then suppose I insist upon seeing the remains of the man whose hospitality I have been receiving?"

"Believe me, I should be sorry if you were to do so."

"And why?"

"Because," replied the steward drily, "I should be under the disagreeable necessity of giving you a point blank refusal."

"Come, come," said Popjoy, assuming an air of authority, "it may be all very well for you to speak in this way to your underlings, but as an intimate acquaintance of the late Mr. Derwent, I have a right to expect a satisfactory answer to my question. Had your master been alive you would not have dared to treat me with this insolence."

"Insolence!"

"Yes, sir, what can be more impertinent than to refuse a reply to a reasonable question?"

' Had your question really been a reasonable one, you should have had no cause to complain of my silence," replied the old gentleman. "There is, however, sufficient ground for the secrecy you speak of, and until that is removed I refuse either to give an explanation or to suffer any other person than myself to enter the room that is the subject of so much curiosity."

"Then suppose I go before a magistrate, and inform him that I have reason to believe that something wrong is going on here?"

"Do so if you please, by all means," answered Mr. Reves; "and when the magistrate arrives I will, in a private audience, satisfy him that I have only acted as a faithful servant. However, it is useless to carry this subject any further, because neither threats nor promises shall induce me to reveal a secret that it is absolutely necessary to keep for some little time longer."

"Oh, I sharn't be kept long in suspense then?"

",Probably only a few hours; but at present it is impossible to say when I shall be at liberty to answer your question."

"Very well," replied Popjoy; "then I suppose I must yield to this extraordinary whim of yours, though it must be confessed I do so with a great deal of uneasiness. However, there's one other question that I suppose you'll not object to reply to?"

"What is it?"

"Is there any truth that the young man charged with the murder of my friend Derwent is to be discharged out of custody?"

"I believe Frank Marldale is already at liberty."

"How is that?"

"Because we could not too soon render justice to a man, whose innocence was manifest."

He innocent!" exclaimed Popjoy; "wasn't he found stooping over the body when nobody else was near the place?"

"Aye," answered the other, "that looked very black against him at first, must confess, but circumstances have since occurred that prove he was no more guilty of the act he was accused of than you or I are."

"Pray may I ask what the proofs are?"

"Just at present I cannot answer that question."

"Humph! so there's another secret, is there?"

"Aye, but it is one that must soon be revealed," answered the steward, "and therefore your curiosity in this instance will not be very severely taxed."

"I suppose the truth is, you have got your eye upon the person that committed the murder."

"We have merely a suspicion against a person," answered the old man, "but at all events we are perfectly well convinced that Frank Marldale was merely the first person who happened to arrive on the spot after the crime had been perpetrated."

"Are you sure of that?"

"Quite."

"Well, at all events there seems to be plenty of mystery," exclaimed Brassey Popjoy, "for hang me if I can tell how any witness can be found to prove that young Marldale is innocent, unless, indeed, some one happened to be by that witnessed the murder without attempting to prevent it."

"If there is some little mystery in the affair," returned Mr. Reves, "it may be some consolation for you to know that a very brief period will serve to clear it up to your entire satisfaction, as well as to that of every body else."

"For my part," exclaimed the cockney, "I don't see what occasion there can be for any mystery in this case. My friend Derwent has unfortunately been murdered by some cold blooded villain, and there can be no sufficient reason for keeping the facts of the case so secret."

"You forget, my good sir, that if too much is said, the ends of justice may be defeated."

"Then why not before now have caused the arrest of the other fellow that you suspect?"

"Because our evidence against him is not yet quite complete, and if he was once discharged out of custody for want of proof, he would take care to keep beyond reach of danger should we afterwards want to lay hands on him."

"Who is the man you suspect?"

"One who is almost a stranger."

"His name?"

"I cannot just yet explain.

"Hang me if I know what you will explain," returned Popjoy, impatiently. "I have asked three or four questions of you, and not to one of them can I get a reply—except that I must be content to remain in ignorance, whilst you are privaleged to know everything. Ah! it's all very well, old gentleman, for you to trifle with me in this way, but had my friend Derwent been alive you would not have dared treat me in this manner."

"Mr. Derwent was master of his own actions, which is more than can be said for myself," replied the steward.]

"But he is dead, and you can therefore have no orders of his to obey now."

"True, I am at liberty to do as I please," answered Reves, "but duty tells me that I ought to act precisely the same as if he was here to lay his commands upon me. I know the mischief that might be caused by suffering an incautious word to escape, and a little patience, Mr. Popjoy, will serve to convince you that I am acting perfectly right in not letting this secret go beyond myself."

"You talk about a *little* patience," retorted the other, "but egad I think you have tried mine to the very utmost."

"And yet, after all, sir," observed the steward, "you cannot be at all interested in what you are so anxious to learn."

"Not interested!" exclaimed Popjoy; "do you suppose I am a stock or a stone that I can feel no interest in discovering the murderer of my dear friend?"

"I don't in the least doubt your kindness, sir," answered the old man, "but an explanation of what you are so desirous of learning, would rather injure than assist the inquiry that is now going on. So I entreat of you to ask no further questions, and you have my word that in a day or two at the furthest, the whole mystery shall be satisfactorily explained."

"I don't know what you may mean by a satisfactory explanation," retorted the baffled cockney, "but, hang me, if I can see any satisfaction in the fact that my hospitable entertainer has been murdered by some ruffian. However, I see nothing more is to be got out of you, so I shall wish you a good day, Mr. Reves, and I hope, [the next time we meet, you will be a little less reserved than you are at present."

Mr. Brassey Popjoy then flounced himself out of the room, in no very good humour; and the steward, nothing disconcerted by this slight explosion of anger, resumed the task in which he had been interrupted. He had not, however, been long thus engaged, when the door of the room was once more opened, and on raising his eyes to see who the intruder was, he perceived Caleb Kestral advancing with a look expressive of firmness and determination.

"You see I have not used much ceremony in introducing myself," said the pedlar, in his usual off-handed manner, "for, the truth is, my business is of importance; and I thought, if I sent a formal message, you would only put me off to some other time."

"Which I must do now," answered the steward, "for I am just now particularly engaged in affairs connected with the property of my late master."

"Humph! that's the very business that has brought me here."

"And pray what have you to do with the affairs of the late Mr. Derwent?" enquired the steward.

"Not much, myself, certainly," answered Caleb Kestrel, "but I know a young girl that will soon claim all this property; and I want to hear whether peaceable possession will be given her."

"That will depend on what sort of proofs she may bring forward, as evidence that her claim is a just one."

"Oh, never fear but I shall be able to make that clear enough," exclaimed the ruffian, "I've known the girl from her infancy, and there's two people that can prove she is the same person that I trusted to their care when she was a mere infant. Besides, your late master had many letters from his cousin, in which the child was spoken of as joint heir to all his property, both in England and abroad."

"But such evidence will not prove the identity of the girl you are speaking of."

"How do you know that?"

"Because I have just been reading them, and the last letter sent speaks of the child as having been stolen, and expresses a fear that she has been made away with."

"Where are the letters?"

"Safely locked up, and in my custody."

"Give them to me."

"Indeed I shall do no such thing," answered Mr. Reves, rather startled by the tone in which this demand was made.

"But you *must*," retorted the other, "for I am here on behalf of the girl, to demand all papers and documents that may be required to put her in possession of her rights. They belong to her, and I will not leave this house without them."

"You will not have them from me," exclaimed the steward, becoming more and more alarmed at the awkward situation in which he found himself.

"Come, come," retorted Caleb Kestrel, "you'll do no good by opposing a man that is never to be thwarted when once he has made up his mind to anything. So quick, man, and despatch me about my business at once."

"Once for all, I will not give up a single paper, till well satisfied that the claimant is justified in making the demand."

"Well, and haven't I told you that the girl was stolen from Mr. Derwent's cousin, when he was in Italy?"

"And how am I to know that you are not endeavouring to impose upon me for purposes of your own?"

"Because, not being the claimant for myself, I can have no purpose of my own to serve," answered Caleb Kestrel. "I am here only to perform an act of justice, towards a girl that is almost friendless; and I shall not leave this house till you have given me the letters you have in your keeping."

"I will never give them into your hands," replied Mr. Reves; "and even if I did comply with your demand, I can see no use that you could make of them."

"But they will be of use though," exclaimed Kestrel, for I mean to put them at once into the hands of a lawyer, who will lose no time in restoring the girl to her rights."

"That is the way in which I myself intend to dispose of all the papers in which the child is mentioned," answered the steward. That an infant was adopted by Mr. Derwent, during his absence abroad, we have his own frequent testimony, but this young girl's identity must be satisfactorily proved before she is permitted to enjoy the property you have claimed."

"Have'nt I told you that there are two other witnesses besides myself that can prove it?"

"You have, but where are they?"

"Oh, near enough to be brought forward at half an hour's notice. They were going to leave for a distant part of the country, but I prevailed upon 'em to remain where they are, under a promise that they shall be well paid for any inconvenience they may be put to."

"In all probability then you have bribed them to support the falsehoods you are prepared to utter."

"Well," exclaimed Kestrel, "you will soon have an oprortunity of judging for yourself whether I have made any false statements about this girl. But I see plainly enough how it is ; you are now master of all Mr. Derwent's papers, and would keep his estates to yourself if I would stand idly by and suffer it."

"Say and think what you will of me," exclaimed the steward, "for my character is too well known in this neighbourhood to be easily injured by the false accusations of a man like you."

"A man like me, what do you take me for then?"

"It matters not," returned Mr Reves, "for if an explanation of my meaning was given it would not be received as a compliment, I can assure you. Be that as it may, however,, I have given an answer that neither persuasion nor intimidation will never change, and you will now, therefore, be pleased to leave a house where your presence is not required,"

"Humph," ejaculated the ruffian, you might be a little more civil I think. But never mind, the hall will soon be in other hands, and I shall then take care that you no longer hold your present office in it. It will then be my turn to tell you to leave a house where your presence is not required."

"If you have anthority given you to do so," answered the steward, "I shall not require a second bidding. But mark me, fellow, there is a secret yet to come out that will entirely overthrow all your plans for putting your claimant into possession of the estates of Mr. Derwent."

"Fool! can you set yourself up against the will of your late master's cousin?" exclaimed Caleb Kestrel. Didn't he leave half his property to the young girl he had adopted, if ever she should be discovered, and don't I tell you that I am ready to bring her forward at a moment's notice?"

"So you say," replied the old man, "but I may be permitted to suspect that, to serve your own purposes, you are about to bring forward an impostor."

"But I have two witnesses."

"Both of whom, for the hope of gain, may have entered into a vile conspiracy. In short," continued the steward, "I am determined to sift most deeply into this claim of yours, and shall put the affairs into the hands of a person who will only yeild up possession when he sees that the girl is justly entitled to the estates."

"We shall see about that before long," exclaimed Caleb Kestrel. "But what's the use of talking when I want to be *doing*? You have got these letters, it seems, so give 'em to me for I wont leave the house without 'em, any further obstinacy may cost you your life."

"Ha!—would you murder me, villain?"

"Perhaps so ; for when a desperate man, like me, is roused into a passion, he's not very particular about what he does. So, now I have spoken out pretty plainly and it will be best for you to give me the papers 1 have demanded."

"Never!"

"Then you have pronounced you own doom!" exclaimed the ruffian, and bounding forward, he seized Mr. Reves in his powerful grasp, and in an instant hurled him on the ground, ere he could defend himself.

"Now 1 will give you one more chance of saving your life" he muttered, "tell me where 1 may find the papers, and no further violence shall be offered."

"I will perish first!" returned the old man, vainly struggling to release himself from his perilous situation.

"Die then," exclaimed Kestrel, grasping his shrieking victim by the throat; and so tightly were his fingers compressed, that a few minutes must have accomplished the murder, but for the fortunate interposition of Martha, who, alarmed by the cries, rushed in, just in time to save the old man's life. Alarmed by her exclamations for assistance, Caleb Kestrel immediately relaxed his hold, and starting upon his feet sprang towards an open window, from which he leaped into the garden beneath, and from thence commenced a rapid flight from the scene of danger.

In the mean time, every asssistance was rendered to Mr. Reves, who, fortunately, had not received so much injury as had at first been apprehended. He was soon able to explain all that had taken place, and having described the person who had attempted his life, all the male portion of the household were despatched in search of the villain who had made so daring an attempt to commit murder. Then turning towards Martha, he poured forth his most heartfelt thanks for the preservation which he owed to her.

"Oh, sir," she replied, "a little longer and it would have been all over with you; for the wretch seemed determined to take your life, and all I wonder at is, that he should have been such a coward as to run away at the sight of a woman."

"It must have been your cries that alarmed him," replied the old man, "for he knew that further assistance would immediately arrive, and to that circumstance I owe not only my life, but the preservation of certain documents that he came here to demand from me. But how happened it," he added, "that you were in the hall at the time?"

"I came here," she answered, "from Mary Everett, to learn if it is indeed true that young Mr. Marldale has been discharged, and that the magistrate said he left the court without a stain upon his character?"

"Yes," replied Mr. Reves, "it is all perfectly true, and I am most happy to confirm the fact, because, in my own mind I felt convinced that Frank Marldale was as free from guilt as I was myself."

"But, as some one must have committed the murder, have you any notion who that some one was?"

"At present all is mystery."

"Can't you think of any body, Mr. Reves?"

"Indeed, my dear, I cannot."

"Then what do you think of my being shrewd enough to have formed a notion upon the subject?"

"Do you mean that you suspect some person of having fired at Mr. Derwent?"

"I do."

"Who is it?"

"The man that would just now have taken your life."

Mr. Reves paused for a few minutes, to reflect upon these words, and at length upon a repetition of them he said :—

"To tell you the truth, Martha, a suspicion of the sort has more than once crossed my mind, but the notion has been no sooner formed than abandoned."

"You don't think him capable of such an action then, I suppose?" said the girl.

"His recent voilence is enough to convince me that he would not hesitate to commit any crime," answered the old man, " I know him to be a ruffian, but still nothing has occurred at present to fix upon him the crime to which you have alluded. '

"But perhaps if he was to be taken up something might be found to prove his guilt."

" Our mere suspicions, reasonable as they may be, are not sufficient to deprive the man of his liberty," replied Mr. Reves. " Our inquiries, however, may go on, and if a chance should offer itself, the fellow shall be immediately taken into custody."

" Ah sir, but take my word for it, he'll not remain long in a place that's too hot to hold him."

" He will not leave the place for some little time I know," replied the steward.

" Did he tell you so."

" Not exactly in words ; but he is about to claim this estate for the young girl that slept a night or two ar Farmer Brough's and till he has made the attempt he will not leave this neighbourhood."

" Is it Amy you are speaking of ?"

" Yes ;—the man asserts that she is the girl who was adopted by the late Mr. Clement Derwent."

" And do you think there is any truth in it ?"

" The story seems improbable," answered the steward, " but tho fellow offers to prove the assertion, and it now remains for us to hear the evidence of the two persons that he says can substantiate his words.

" He means Mr. and Mrs. Peeps I dare say.

" No doubt of it, for it seems she has been with them the greater part of her life ' '

" And a very nice, quiet, modest little body she is too," exclaimed Martha. " She's quiet a favourite at the farm, I can tell you, and it will be a sorrowful day there if the pedlar—who calls himself her father—should persist in taking her away to travel over the country with him."

" Ah !" cried the steward, " that suggests something to me that I thought not of before. The man certainly did claim her as his daughter on the night of Farmer Brough's harvest supper, and if there is any truth in what he said there is an end at once for the claim that he is going to set up for her !

" But I don't believe a word about her being the daughter of that man," exclaimed Martha.

" What reason have you to doubt it ?"

" A very sufficient one, I think," she replied. " The girl, though roughly brought up, seems to have high blood in her ; and I heard her say yesterday that she has a faint recollection of being, when a child, in a large and richly furnished house."

" It would be strange," muttered the steward, " if she should prove to be thu long lost child."

" Very strange indeed," interposed Martha ; " and very lucky too for her, for now that Squire Derwent is dead, instead of having only half this estate, the whole of it will belong to her."

" You think nothing less than all ought to satisfy her ?"

" If it's her right she ought to have it," replied the girl. " Not but what I'm very sorry poor Mr. Derwent has been murdered, for he was very much liked by all but Frank Marldale, and his dislike only arose from a little bit of jealousy."

" And a serious dilemma that jealousy got him into," exclaimed Mr. Reves, " for it seemed to strengthen the case against him when he was suspected of having caused the death of the man whom he had been frequently heard to denounce."

" So it did with a great many people," answered the girl, " but for all that, he was not without friends, who put no faith in the reports that were spread abroad against him. Nothing would ever have convinced Farmer Brough that his favourite would be guilty of such a crime as murder, and as for myself and poor Mary Everett, everybody might have been against him, but still he would have had true staunch friends to stand up in his behalf.

"And yet," exclaimed the steward thoughtfully, "how many innocent men have been sacrificed upon no better evidence than there was in the case of Frank Marldale."

"So I'm afraid sir," returned Martha, "but for all that they were not called

murdered men because it was the law that had put them to death. Now poor Frank might have met with the same fate, but for some strange chance that no one seems able to explain. By the bye, Mr. Reves, perhaps you can tell me what proof there was that the young man had nothing to do with shooting the Squire?"

"I certainly know all the circumstances of the case," replied the old gentleman, "but there is a secret connected with it which I am not just now at liberty to reveal."

No. 10.

" A secret !—Dear Mr. Reves, how very much you would oblige me by letting me know what it is.

" Were I to do so," he replied, " I fear it would not be a secret much longer. In a little while, however, you and all the rest of our neighbours will see to the very bottom of the mystery, and a very agreeable surprise it will prove to be, I can promise you."

" Now my dear friend, do just oblige me."

" I am forbidden by a solemn promise," he replied, " and you must there rest satisfied till the time arrives when the prohibition will be removed, perhaps your curiosity will be kept on the rack no longer than to-morrow."

With this he turned away and went towards the chamber which none were allowed to enter but himself.

CHAPTER IX.

PEEPS IN THE CAGE.—LIBERTY OF THE SUBJECT,—CALEB KESTREL'S INTERVIEW WITH AMY,—AN EXPLNAATION.

CRIBBED, cabined, and confined within the narrow limits of the village cage, the situation of Peeps was an exceedingly uncomfortable one. He, however, had philosophy enough to endure the misfortune with tolerable patience, for he doubted not that his liberatlou would soon take place, and there was besides some little in the idea that he would have good grounds for damages against the over officious constable. At length that important personage was seen approaching ; the door was presently afterwards opened, and Peeps was informed that as no charge would be made against him he was at liberty to leave the place as soon as he pleased.

" And pray," asked the proprietor of the temple of arts, " what reason had you for locking up a gentleman a whole night in this infernal cage of yours."

" Oh, it all happened through a mistake," replied the man.

" You'll be made to pay for your mistake, my fine fellow."

" It was no fault of mine," replied the constable. " Squire Derwent made out a warrant to arrest a stranger, and as you happened not to be known in the neighbourhood, I naturally supposed you must be the person he meant."

" Oh, oh ! the squire, ah ?" chuckled Peeps ;—" he is a rich man, that can afford to pay damages, so I shall soon set a lawyer to work at him."

" You'll be puzzled to do that, I'm thinking," replied the constable, " for Mr. Derwent is dead."

" Dead !" why he was well enough at the harvest supper.

" So he was after seven or eight o'clock last night," returned the official, " but some villain murdered him as he was going home across the moor."

" You don't say so !" exclaimed Peeps, with mingled horror and astonishment. " And pray, Mr. Constable, who do they suspect is the assassin ?"

" A person that is about the last that I should have thought would have been guilty of such an act," answered the other. " You recollect, I dare say, a young man named Marldale that was at farmer Brough's the other night ?"

" Yes."

" Well he's in custody for the murder."

" Then my life on it they've got hold of the wrong man."

" That's what everybody else says," exclaimed the constable. " Nobody will believe that Frank Marldale committed the murder though there are a few strong points against him."

" What are the strong points ?" demanded Peeps.

" Why, in the first place, it's well known that Frank had a very great dislike to the squire,'

" Humph ! that may be, but it don't follow that he would be villain enough to murder him."

" But he was found near the body by a couple of gamekeepers who had hastened to the spot immediately after they had heard the report of a gun. The men it seems, thought there were poachers about the place, but upon coming up they found Squire Derwent shot, and Frank Marldale standing close to the body."

" Well, that looks rather suspicious certainly," exclaimed Peeps ; " but its just possible that the young man might have been passing the place a little after the crime was committed."

" That's exactly the excuse he makes," answered the constable, " but the game-keepers, who are the principal accusers, say, that though they had been going their rounds some hours before, they had not seen any other person than Frank any where in the neighbourhood of the place."

" And what have they done with the young fellow ?"

" Oh, they have put him in confinement, and to day he will be taken before one of the county magistrates, who is to go to Derwent Hall for the purpose of having the depositions of the two witnesses."

" And when they have heard the evidence, what is there in it ?" demanded Peeps. " The young man was likely enough to have been passing the spot, and if he saw a fellow creature lying upon the ground murdered, it would have been strange indeed if he had not stopped to see if it was not possible to afford assistance. However, if he can prove his innocence, he has likewise, a capital case for damages for false imprisonment."

" You dont mean to take advantage of a poor fellow like me for a mistake ?" exclaimed the constable.

" Well upon second thoughts I don't know that I shall," replied Peeps ; " for though the imprisonment was anything but pleasant, you may have been the means of keeping me out of mischief, who knows but I might have been upon the moors, and that they would have accused me of the horrid crime."

" Ah ! that's the way to look at it," exclaimed the constable, well pleased at t' turn affairs had taken.

" And if anything of the kind had happened," continued the other, " there's no saying what effect it would have had upon the delicate nerves of the affectionate Angelina Peeps. It would have killed her out right, and then what should I have done for a treasurer to the temple of arts ?"

" You make light of this affair, considering what a very serious one it has turned out."

" On the contrary," answered Peeps, " I feel my heart like a lump of lead in my bosom. The poor young fellow that has been accused seems to be a nice chap enough, and as for the squire I was quite delighted with him for his affability in dancing with my Angelina on the night of the Harvest Home."

" Aye," returned the constable, " everybody liked him, except Frank Marldale, and he, I believe, only felt a little vexed because the squire wanted his land, and, it was thought, wouldn't let him have a new lease for the farm, when the old one expired."

" Well," exclaimed Peeps ; " but his being vexed about a matter of that kind would not have driven him to murder Squire Derwent. He might not have liked leaving the farm, perhaps, but I dare say if he wanted one, there were plenty of others to be had in the neighbourhood. But be that as it may, I wouldnt mind betting my temple of arts against a farthing cake that this Frank Marldale is as innocent of the crime of murder as I am."

" Every body believes him to be innocent," replied the constable, " but that's poor consolation, seeing that he is deprived of his liberty, and that, too, upon a charge that, go which way it may, will go against him all the rest of his life."

" Then he had better leave the neighbourhood," observed Peeps, " and go to some place where he's not know."

" But that's not all," returned the constable, " for we don't know what effect this affair may have upon Mary Everett, the young girl that he was courting. She may not choose to marry a man that has been charged with murder, and—"

"If that's her temper, I've done with her!" exclaimed Peeps, interrupting him. "And yet I mustn't be too fast about saying that," he added, checking himself, "for she has been kind to my little Amy, and if she had a thousand faults I could overlook 'em all for that."

Just then Mrs. Peeps was seen bustling towards them, and the constable, probably dreading a volley from the lady, bolted off as if he was in danger of being shot.

"Peeps at liberty," she exclaimed, throwing her arms about his neck in true melo-dramatic style, "why how in the name of fortune has all this come about?"

"Why the truth is," my dear Angelina," answered her affectionate husband, "the constable discovered that he had made a little mistake—that he had laid hold of the wrong man, so he has just been and let me out of the cage."

"And warn't you very uncomfortable all night in that nasty, cold, damp place?"

"Particularly so my love," he replied, "for I thought what your sufferings must be on my account, and wondered what the deuce you would do with the Temple of Arts if I happened to be locked up till the next assizes."

"But I hope you mean to make some of 'em smart for this false imprisonment."

"False imprisonment!" exclaimed the showman; "between ourselves, Mrs. P. there was a good deal of *reality* about it. Besides, its no use going to law with, people that have no money, and, unfortunately, the only one who had the means of paying damages has been murdered."

"Ah! then you've heard what has happened to the poor Squire!"

"Yes," he replied, "I have heard all about it."

"And you've heard who they've taken up on suspicion of being the assassin?"

"To be sure I have, but I dont think he would be guilty of such a wicked act."

"That's what almost every body else says about it," exclaimed Mrs. Peeps. "There's Farmer Brough in a fine way about it, and as for his niece, I think it would break her heart if she was to hear of his being committed."

"She's a good creature, that Mary Everett," returned the showman, "so I'll tell you what I've been thinking of doing. We'll give up the profits of the Temple of Arts for a few days, and I'll fill up the time in trying to find out who murdered the Squire."

"Peeps! Peeps," cried his wife reproachfully, "do you want to get yourself into trouble again? Is'nt it enough that you have just got out of one scrape, but you must foolishly run headlong into another?"

"Angelina Peeps I'm ashamed of you!" exclaimed her husband, "Where's all your fine womanly feeling gone to, that you would have me forsake a poor fellow in his misfortune? Hav'nt you said yourself that you don't believe young Marldale had anything to do with the murder? and yet you would have me leave him to his fate.",

"As for that matter," she replied, "he has got plenty of friends to lend him a helping hand without your troubling yourself with what don't concern you. Besides, we depend upon the profits of our business, and as no more customers are likely to be found in this place, we must get on to the next town as soon as possible."

"You forget, ma'am," exclaimed her husband, "that the sooner we go away, the sooner we shall be obliged to part from our little favourite, Amy."

"Do you mean then to give her up so easily to that surly looking fellow, Caleb Kestrel?"

"Why, the truth of it is, there's no help for it when a certain old gentleman dies," answered Peeps. "He left her with us, you know, and, as her father, has a right to claim her whenever he thinks proper. For my own part I've always expected it would come to this some day or another, and now that the evil moment has arrived we must submit to give her up to her father."

"But she don't want to go away with him."

"So she says," answered her husband, ' but what help is there for it if Kestrel chooses to resist? The law won't assist us in such a case as this, and if we were to take her away with us on the sly he would be sure to trace us out, and then the poor girl would be worse off than ever."

" What a wretch the fellow is," exclaimed Mrs. Peeps, grinding her teeth with fury.

" My dear Angelina, there's no denying that fact," he replied, " for we know he used to be years ago, and I don't suppose he has improved since last we saw him. But, for all that, he claims her as his child, and it would be the worse for us all if we refused."

" You are afraid of him then ?"

" Not a bit, my dear, but its no use putting ones hand into a lion's mouth. Caleb Kestrel is not a man to be baulked when once he has set his mind upon anything, so the best thing we can do will be to let her go away with him and if he don't beheave to her with kindness we'll persuade her before we part, to leave him at the very first opportunity that offers itself."

" Ah, Peeps !" she exclaimed; " you never cared about the poor girl.—You only pretended it like a hypocrite as you"are !"

"Angelina," retorted her husband indignantly, "If you say that again I'll punish you by throwing myself into the first pond I meet with ! Not care about the girl ! why hasn't she always been to me like a daughter of my own, and am I now to be told that all this time I've been acting the part of a hypocrite ! But I'll talk to you further upon this subject as we go along, for yonder is Caleb Kestrel coming this way, and I don't want to meet him just now for fear I should tell him too much of my mind."

Upon this he hurried off with his better half, but his good prevailed over his momentary anger, and upon Mrs. Peeps's promise never to repeat the offence, he became quite appeased, and instead of giving a lecture, proposed various schemes by which to prevail on the pedlar to let the girl remain for some little time longer.

Scarcely had Caleb Kestrel reached the place of appointment than Amy also made her appearance there. Her manner towards him was timid and distant, but feigning to take no notice of this he said :—

" So, I see you know how to keep an appointment punctually, and it is well that you have done so in this instance, for I have that to say which concerns you nearly. In short, Amy, to keep you no longer in suspense, I am about to reveal a secret that will cause you no little surprise."

" I can guess it already," she replied, " for you have said that it is in your power to make me rich."

" Exactly so.—Now look around you."

" I do," she replied.

" Well then, all that you can see, as far as the eye reaches is your own domain."

" Nay, that is impossible," exclaimed Amy, " for all I am gazing on belonged to the man you last night mur——"

" Hush !" muttered Kestrel, grasping her arm tightly, " mind you have pronounced a word that might send me to the gallows. You say this estate belonged to Cecil Derwent, but 'tis false, for whilst you lived he only held it on sufferance."

" How can that be if you are my father ?" she asked.

" It is now time that the delusion I have practised on you should be at an end," he replied. " I can claim no kindred to you, Amy, for you were the adopted child of the late Clement Derwent, who died abroad more years ago than your memory can go back to."

" This is some one's trick to impose upon me in furtherance of your own selfish schemes."

" For once girl, you may believe me," answered Kestrel, " and a few hours will serve to prove that I am in earnest ; I repeat, you were adopted by Clement Derwent from whom I stole you when an infant in revenge for an injury that he had done me. And my revenge was complete, for the loss he had sustained broke his heart, and the triumph I felt was such as those only can feel who labour successfully towards a certain end."

"Wretch!" cried Amy, "can you exult in the villany of which you have been guilty?"

"Come, come, my girl," he exclaimed, "I must not hear reproaches uttered, when I had no other object in meeting you here than to do you an important service. Remember, I am about to make you mistress of these broad lands, and surely that deserves some better reward than to be called hard names, and to hear myself eviled."

"I will not accept the service you have proffered me," replied Amy, "for I know well that there is some trick in this, to enrich yourself rather than me.'"

"Why, I certainly expect to share in your good fortune," exclaimed the pedlar, "for every labourer is worthy of his hire, and I have been for years past endeavouring to discover you in order that I might gather in the harvest I have been working for. And now, girl, you see the time has at length arrived when you may shake off for ever the bonds of poverty."

"Away!—leave me!" cried Amy, turning away with disgust. "You would impose upon me by an artfully devised polt, but I will make no party in it when I have reason to believe that you would put me forward to make a claim for which there is no just ground."

"Do you think then I have told a falsehood in asserting that you are the person to whom Clement Derwent left his large property?"

"I do."

"Then a little reflection will serve to convince you that I am no impostor," answered the pedlar. "Peeps and his wife can both swear that you were the child I placed under their care some years ago, and if further corroboration should be required, it is to be found in the broken locket, half of which is in my possession, and the other half is still suspended round your neck. These things will have their weight in a court of justice—if it should be necessary to have recourse to one, and a few weeks at the very farthest, will see you established in Derwent Hall as its mistress. So come, Amy, acknowledge that I am your friend, and that it will be better for us to be upon good terms, than that we should part in anger."

"How is it possible," she asked, "that I can be upon good terms with a man whose hands are red with the blood of a fellow creature?"

"Psha!" exclaimed Kestrel impatiently, "why remind me of what I would fain forget? Cecil Derwent provoked me to the violence by his own insolent conduct, when I called upon him yesterday morning. Nay, he even went so far as to issue a warrant for my apprehension; and where is the man that would not seek revenge when an injury is attempted against him?"

"Would you attempt to palliate the shedding of another man's blood?"

"Why, for the matter of that," he replied, you, at any rate, have no right to reproach me for what has been done. Whilst Cecil Derwent lived, half the property of his deceased relative was his own, because you had not been discovered within a certain time specified in the will, which had been made in your favour. Now, however, that he is dead, you will enjoy the whole of it, and that, too, without any reproach to yourself, since it was my hand that sent Cecil to his long account."

"But am I not equally guilty," she asked, "to know who the murderer is, yet withhold the secret, when an innocent man is now in custody on suspicion of being the assassin of Mr. Derwent?"

"What matter is it to you who is in custody for it?" demanded the other. "Wont his being so prevent suspicion falling upon me, who can assist you so materially in establishing your rights?"

"You think, then," she replied, "that I would be guilty of concealing your rime for the sake of any benefit you may have it in your power to confer upon me."

"I don't know how far your inclination may carry you," answered Caleb Kestrel, "but your sacred promise has been given to keep the secret, and you will break it at your own peril."

"In other words," exclaimed Amy, "you would sacrifice me as you did Mr. Derwent, if you thought there was danger of my revealing what I saw last night."

"It's likely enough I should," he replied carelessly, "but that is not the subject I wish to speak upon just at present. The question is this; will you accept my services in obtaining the large property left you by the late Mr. Clement Derwent?"

"Why are you so anxious for me to do so?'

"Oh, you know well enough why I am so anxious," he replied. "Have'nt I said that I shall expect to be handsomely rewarded for performing a service that no other person in the world besides myself can do?"

"Then," exclaimed Amy, "your assertion being unsupported by other evidence, will find few believers."

"And why shouldn't people believe me?" demanded the ruffian sullenly. "I suppose I'm as likely to speak the truth as any body else, and especially in a case where I am trying to to serve another person."

"Aye," returned Amy "but self-interest is at the bottom of all, and I can see, if nobody else does, that you are only anxious to urge this affair on for the sake of what you might afterwadrs be able to extort from me. In short, having confessed one part of the deception you have practised, I now place no reliance on the assertion you have made, that I am the person to whom the Derwent estates were bequeathed."

"Fool!" muttered Caleb, "would you throw away the golden prize that is to be had for stretching forth the hand?"

"If it is not mine by right and justice," she replied, "I will not consent to be put forward as a claimant of that which belongs to another."

"Psha, would you stand in your own light, then, now that there's a chance of making your fortune."

"It is in vain that you urge me," exclaimed Amy, "for having been brought up in poverty, and humility all my life, I have no desire now to change it for the most brilliant prospects you have brought before me."

"But I must see the prospect change though," returned Caleb Kestrel, "for matters are begining to grow desperate, and I must have money enough to live abroad. There will be awkward inquiries I expect, about the death of Squire Derwent, and if once suspicion should happen to fall upon me, the game would soon be up."

"So, you would go abroad, then?"

"To be sure I would," he replied, "for where else can I be so safe?"

"You may be safe there from the vengeance of the law," answered Amy, "but if you have such a thing as conscience, you will never again experience either peace of mind or happiness."

"What! you think, then, I must always have my thoughts turned to the affair that took place last night?"

"It is impossible that you can forget it, even for a moment." she replied, "Sleeping or waking that one thought must always be uppermost in your mind. embittering the remainder of your days, and rendering every hour of your life an, intolerable curse."

"Come, come," exclaimed the ruffian, "let's have no more of this, for its time enough for a man to look his troubles in the face when there's no help for it. As for my conscience, I don't know that I shall feel very sore upon that point, for it's a commodity that I'm not much annoyed with, and if once I can find myself safe on the other side of the Channel, I shall soon forget Squire Derwent, and the means that brought our short acquaintance to an end. So now accept my offer without any further murmur, and before a week is over your head, you shall be one of the richest women in the whole county of York."

"Is it not enough that I have said I covet no higher station than that which I at present occupy?"

"I know you have said so," replied Caleb Kestrel, "but it don't follow that a foolish notion is to be persisted in for ever. Besides, you possess a great deal of regard for the people that brought you up, and how can you so well reward your friends as by raising them from poverty to comfort? So you see, my girl, there are more persons than yourself to consider in this matter."

"For their sake I might be induced to listen to this project of yours," answered Amy. "At present, however, they know nothing of the news you have brought me, and I can scarcely expect them to believe my assertion when I tell them that I am the heiress of the late Squire Derwent."

"But they'll believe it fast enough when they hear all the particulars from me," exclaimed Kestrel. "Besides, the locket I have spoken of is known to have been worn by the child on the day she was stolen, and part of it having been in your possession ever since will be pretty good evidence in coroboration of the assertion I am about to make. Besides, there are at the hall still some of the domestics who lived with Mr. Clement Derwent up to the time of his death, and they will be able to confirm the statement that is to make you their mistress."

"Then you are determined, in spite of all remonstrances, to pursue this matter to an end?"

"To be sure I am," he replied. "You heard me speak the plain truth when I said I needed the money you are to give me for the part I am about to take in the transactions, I must have it too before many hours have passed away, for it may be too late to escape if the innocence of young Frank Marldale should be made manifest. When he is set at liberty I must look out for myself, for suspicion will be sure to fall upon me next, and if they make me change places with him there's little mercy to expect from those that would have the trying of me."

"Thus knowing your danger, why do you remain so near the scene of your crime?"

"Why there are two reasons for it," he replied. "One of them is that I can't move away from the place without money; and the other, that if I was to leave so very suddenly, it would at once direct suspicion against me, that I was the cause of Mr. Derwent's death. So in spite of the danger, I shall remain here a few days longer, and if the worst should happen, it will be something in my favour that I didn't run away."

"But are you sure," asked Amy, "that no one besides myself saw you commit the deed?"

"Oh, yes, I'm quite certain about that," he replied, "for I was watching my victim a long time before he fell, and I took good care that no one should have it in his power to come forward afterwards and denounce me."

"Yet there was one that saw you."

"Aye, but that one I am in no fear of," he exclaimed. "You, Amy, are the only person who can denounce me, and I know well enough that so far as you are concerned I have nothing to be afraid of."

"Yet we are almost strangers, and, even according to your own acknowledgement, I have received a most severe injury from your hands."

"Aye," he replied, "you have led a hard and wandering life through me, I am ready to admit; but the time has now come for reparation, and I am ready to make it in a way that ought to bury all recollections of the past in oblivion. You will be the mistress of all these broad lands, and that too through information that no one but myself has the power to give."

"But the information you speak of would never have been given, had you not expected to receive a large proportion of the property for a reward."

"Never mind the motive," he replied, "since the benefit will last as long as you live, and may very likely be the means of your marrying some high-born man, who has a title to share with you."

"And what right have I to aspire to a title?"

"Why as much as half of those that flaunt through the world like so many painted butterflies," he replied. "Besides money is an excellent passport, and no sooner will it be known that you have wealth, than a score or two of noblemen will be eagerly endeavouring to worm their way into your good graces."

"For which reason," exclaimed Amy, "I would much rather remain in my present obscurity."

"Psha!" returned the other, "such a notion may have been very well whilst

AMY FINDS THE BODY OF DERWENT, AND IS SURPRISED BY CALEB KESTREL.

you were the supposed daughter of Peeps and his wife; but now things have altered, and knowing yourself to be the lawful heiress of the late Mr. Clement Derwent, it would be madness to throw away the chance that is before you. So remember, to-morrow morning you will meet me at the Hall, and I'll then introduce you to Mr. Reves, the steward, as the person he is henceforward to look upon as his mistress."

Amy knew that it would be in vain to urge any further objections, and she therefore suffered him to take his departure under the impression that she would

No. 11.

obey his last injunction. In her own mind, however, she determined to reflect well before she made herself a party in the ambitious design of the pedlar ; and it was not till she had revealed the whole affair to Mary Everett, and heard her opinion upon the matter, that she resolved to keep the appointment that had been made.

CHAPTER X.

POPJOY GROWS SICK OF A COUNTRY LIFE.—A SECRET DISCLOSED.

ON the following morning, when Mr. Reves, the steward, went to the room occupied by Brassy Popjoy, he found him labouring under the effects of a violent cold that he had caught during his rambles over the moors on the night of the tempest. The cockney, like most invalids, was not in the best possible humour ; and in reply to a question from his visitor, he exclaimed :—

Is it necessary, sir, to ask a man in my situation after his health ? Don't I look horribly bad—and is that to be wondered at after taking physic enough to kill an elephant ? This cursed visit will be the death of me ; and all through my own folly in leaving London, which is the only place where a man can be said to exist."

"And yet, sir," answered the steward, " this neighbourhood is reckoned to be remarkably healthy."

"They may say what they like about it," exclaimed Popjoy, " but let any sensible man look at me, and then hear what he would say about the place."

"Pardon me for the suggestion, Mr. Popjoy," returned the steward, " but I have rather a notion that you owe your illness to the light clothing you wore on the day you went out shooting."

"Well," he replied, "it must be confessed the Highland costume was not exactly the thing for my delicate constitution, and yet I dont know that my cold was caught through that means either, for isn't the dress worn farther north, and yet I never heard of the people suffering any inconvenience through it."

"That is, no doubt, from habit."

"Perhaps so," replied Popjoy, " but, be the cause what it may, I shall not stop here after to-day, when there's a decent place like London to live in, and plenty of people there that will be glad enough to see me go back."

"Then you have quite given up all notion of shooting over the moors, that you took for the season ? "

"Yes, Mr. Reves, I have indeed," answered the cockney, " I've had a regular sickener in the short time I have been here ; and this very night will see me and my servant on our way back to the metropolis. My right of shooting over the bleak moors, I shall dispose of to some greater fool than myself, and, in future, no one shall have it in his power to laugh at Brassy Popjoy for leaving the only place in this world where real pleasure and comfort are to be found."

"I am sorry, sir," exclaimed Mr. Reves, " that your visit here has been so unpleasant."

"Unpleasant !" returned the other, quickly ; " can anything be more unpleasant than the miserable plight I am now in ? Then there's your master—who was kind enough to invite me to his house—loses his life through his civility in accompanying me on a day's shooting excursion ! And of all men in the world, who should have committed the murder, but the young fellow I met at the harvest supper, and who was to have married that pretty little girl, Mary Everett."

"So it was suspected at first," replied the steward; " but I am happy to say Frank Marldale has been discharged from custody on the clearest evidence of his innocence."

"Nonsense!" exclaimed Popjoy, "how can he be innocent, when he, and no other person was found close by the murdered body of poor Mr. Derwent?"

"If you promise not to let it go any further, I'll convince you that young Marldale is guiltless of the crime that he was charged with."

"Oh, as for keeping your secret you may safely enough trust me with it, " replied Popjoy; "but before you begin, I tell you, old gentleman, you'll have a hard job to convince me of Marldale's innocence."

"Nevertheless, I shall do so to a certainty," answered the steward, and then putting his mouth to Popjoy's ear, he added in a whisper,—"What should you say, sir, if I tell you that Mr. Derwent is at this moment alive?"

"Why I shouldn't believe you," replied the other, "for I myself saw him brought dead into his own house."

"So we all thought," replied Mr. Reves, "but upon going into the room where we had left him, I afterwards found that life had not fled, for there was a slight motion in the heart that assured me there was still some hope of his recovery. Luckily, I had known some little of surgery in my younger days, and setting myself the task, I at length had the satisfaction of seeing my master revive from the death-like torpor in which he had been lying."

"Surely you must be joking with me," exclaimed Popjoy, almost breathless with astonishment.

"The subject is not one for joking on," answered the steward, "nor is it likely I should tell you a falsehood that must so soon be discovered."

"Is the squire able to leave his room then?"

"Not at present," replied the steward, ".but he will do so presently; for I expect the person who really attempted the murder will be here this morning, and he will not be suffered to leave the place till he can satisfactorily prove that he is innocent of the crime."

"Upon my life this is a strange improbable story of yours, Mr. Reves," exclaimed the cockney. "If the man you expect here was really guilty of the deed, he would be a precious fool to come to a place where there's so much danger."

"But he is not yet aware of the recovery of his intended victim," replied the steward; "and he is going to bring with him a young girl, who he says he can prove is the heiress to all these estates.''

"How do you know he is going to do that."

"Because he came here last night to tell me so, and he expects that I and the domestics will receive her as our future mistress."

"Then I suppose he'll find himself most confoundedly mistaken?" exclaimed Popjoy. "Egad! how the fellow will stare when he finds that the owner of the property is still in the land of the living."

"True," answered the other, "but his surprise will be still further increased when he is accused of being the person who attempted the murder."

"And who is to accuse him?"

"Mr Derwent himself. In the midst of our conversation he is to come into the room and accuse the villain of having attempted to take away his life.''

"By-the-bye," exclaimed Popjoy, " you have not yet told me who the fellow is."

"The pedlar that calls himself Caleb Kestrel."

"What! the fellow that claimed a young girl for his daughter at the harvest supper?"

"The same; and it is the girl you speak of that he says is the heiress to these estates."

"Then the fellow must be mad to make such an assertion."

"At all events," answered the steward, "he tells a very plausible story, and Mr. Derwent is inclined to think there is truth in it. One thing is quite certain—a female infant that was adopted by the late Mr. Clement Derwent was stolen from him, and at his death which happened shortly afterwards, it was found that he had left the chief part of his property to the child in the event of her ever being discovered."

"Oh, I see through it all, plainly enough," exclaimed Popjoy "This Kestrel has heard of the story, and so trumps up a lie for the sake of putting her into possession of the estates.' But he'll find himself preciously mistaken though, when instead of being allowed to remain in this house with his pretended daughter, they give him a different sort of lodging in the county jail."

" As far as the man is concerned, I believe you are right," answered the steward ; " but with respect to the girl there seems to be a probability that she is the person who was taken away during her infancy, and, if that can be proved, it is the intention of Mr. Derwent to surrender up the property to her without going through the trouble and expense of a long lawsuit."

" Why then he'll make a beggar of himself."

" I don't exactly see that," answered Mr. Reves, "for he was much struck with the beauty of the girl when they first met, and if they should happen to make a match of it, why the property will still remain in the same hands."

"Egad! old boy," exclaimed Popjoy, taking his hand, and shaking it violently, " you have told me such strange things, and it seems so much more remains behind, that hang me if I have not a mind to change my resolution, and stay here a few days longer, just to see how all will turn out."

"You can banish yourself from your favourite London for a little while?"

"Yes, just for a day or so," he replied. "There's plenty of excitement going on here I see, and as the Squire has not been murdered, the house wont be so dull as I expected. So my man may unpack my trunks again, for I shall remain here the full time I expected ; and now, if you will just conduct me to his room, I'll congratulate him on his fortunate escape from the assassin's hand."

"At present, you cannot see him." answered the steward, "for he is particularly engaged with Frank Marldale, and has desired that no one shall see him till the moment when he suddenly presents himself before the man that he suspects attempted his life. Besides, you promised to keep the secret I have trusted you with, and Mr. Derwent would be displeased if he found that I had mentioned it to any one."

"Oh, very well, then I'll wait till he has shewn himself," replied Popjoy, "but for the life of me, I cannot see his reason for keeping up so much mystery."

" Why, the truth of it is," answered the other, " he wants to keep the secret of his recovery from this Caleb Kestrel, till he has ascertained on what grounds he lays his claim on behalf of the girl. He will be in an adjoining room while the man is stating his case, and after hearing all that is necessary, he will suddenly come forward, and denounce the villain who attempted to murder him."

. " Did he see the man who aimed the bullet at him ? "

" No," replied the steward, " but this Kestrel had vowed to be revenged on him not many hours before, and he is the only person who owes a grudge to Mr. Derwent. Besides, the walking staff which the pedlar carries is supposed to be an air-gun, and the attempt must have been made with an instrument of that kind, because my master is quite certain there was no report when he received the wound."

At this moment, Mr. Reves received a message that the two persons he expected had arrived, and he immediately hurried away, to learn the important facts that were to be disclosed. Almost at the same moment Trubbs entered the room, to announce that the trunks were all packed, and every thing was ready for their departure for London.

"Very well, Trubbs," replied his master, "you have done well to obey my orders, but you may now amuse yourself with unpacking them, for I have changed my mind, and intend to remain here a few days longer."

"What!" exclaimed the groom, "didn't you tell me just now, sir, that you couldn't stay in a house where the body of a murdered man was lying ? "

"Perhaps I did," answered his master, "but circumstances alter cases, and I have just now heard something that has changed my determination. Oh! Trubbs! Trubbs! I've been told a secret, and am bursting to tell it, but dare not for my life."

"Well, I don't know how it is," exclaimed the other, "but everything about the place seems to be full of mystery for the last few hours."

"Why what has happened, Trubbs?"

"Ever so many things, sir," he replied. "Maybe you haven't heard the report that young Marldale has been suddenly discharged from custody, though it seems almost certain that he committed the murder."

"But it seems quite certain that he did not do it," replied his master, "and he was discharged because there was clear proof of his innocence. However, there's a secret at the bottom of it, Trubbs, that I dare not tell, but in a little time, something will come out that will fill your weak mind with astonishment."

"Well, for my part, I'm astonished enough already," replied the groom ; "and so are a good many others besides me, for, among other things, the steward has locked up the room in which they have placed the body of Squire Derwent, and not a soul is allowed to go into it except himself and young Mr. Marldale, who, I believe, is there at this very minute."

"He is," answered Popjoy, "and I could tell you the reason of it, if it had not been for my promise of secrecy. However, there's one consolation, my lips will not be sealed much longer, and then there's a secret to come out that will astonish a good many people. But I mustn't speak out now, Trubbs, so answer me this one question. Did you see two persons that arrived here just now, to see the steward?"

"I did."

"Do you know them?"

"Yes ; one of them is that black-muzzled fellow, the pedlar, and the other the girl he claimed as his daughter."

"Well then," exclaimed Popjoy, "it will be some relief to me to tell you what they are here for, since I was not asked to make any secret of that part of the business. The girl is going to lay claim to all the Derwent property, and the pedlar is to prove her right to it."

"Oh, as for that matter," answered the other, "I dare say he would not mind swearing to anything, if money is to be made by it. In my opinion, he is a precious scoundrel, sir ; but I rather think he'll find more trouble than he expects to make people believe that the girl has a right to the estates."

"Nevertheless," exclaimed Popjoy, "the steward tells me there is a chance of her being the heiress, who was lost some years ago, and has never been heard of since. Mr. Reves tells me she was stolen, and, if so, take my word for it the pedlar will turn out to be the man that took her away."

"And what will they do with him if it should turn out so?" inquired the groom.

"Why, if they do as they ought, they'll put a halter round his neck, and hang him," replied his master.

"But I never happen to have heard of an instance of a man being hung for child stealing."

"Perhaps not," answered Popjoy, "but it don't follow that it ought not to have been done, though. Besides, there's another reason for believing that the pedlar will stand a chance of going to the gallows before many weeks are over."

"Has he done anything else besides stealing a child, sir?" asked the groom.

"Why, he's very strongly suspected of being concerned in a murder, and if that notion should turn ont to be correct, he'll be sure to—but what am I about! I had almost babbled the secret, and broken the pledge that I just now gave to the steward."

"Pledge, sir!" exclaimed Trubbs. "You'll excuse me, sir, for the liberty, but I was desired always to correct you whenever you make use of words that are in any way connected with the pawnbroking business."

"You are right, Trubbs," answered his master, "and you may consider that I owe you half a sovereign for having attended to my orders. Always perform your duty with the same zeal, and by and by I shall be deeply indebted to you."

"Very good, sir," replied the groom, "but I hope you'll not be offended with me if I should now and then take the liberty to rub up your memory about payments. And now, sir, I would ask if you are serious in your intention of remaining here a few days longer?"

"Of course I am, for there'll be nothing but rejoicing going on for the next week or two to come."

"Rejoicing in a house of mourning?"

"Aye, Trubbs, there's mystery in it I know, but presently you'll be as wise as myself, and then you'll make one of the most extraordinary discoveries ever heard of. I tell you that not only the people in the house, but the whole neighbourhood will be almost frantic with joy, and that's all I dare say; so if your curiosity has been excited, you must wait till the whole affair comes out in due course of time. And now, Trubbs, you may go and unpack my boxes."

The groom, thus dismissed, retired, but not just then to perform the task set him. He was, in fact, inquisitive to learn something of the mystery, and, in order to possess himself of the facts, went to listen at the door of the room, where the meeting had taken place between the steward and the pedlar.

CHAPTER XI.

THE PEDLAR AND HIS VICTIM.—THE THREAT.—A SURPRISE.—THE ACCUSATION. —JUSTICE TO THE INNOCENT AS WELL AS THE GUILTY.

HAVING been ushered into a room where they had to wait some few minutes for the arrival of Mr. Reves, the pedlar took the opportunity of urging upon Amy the absolute necessity that there was for her to persist in the claim he was about to make in her behalf.

"Remember," he exclaimed, sternly, "there must be no child's play—no woman's fears—no scruples now! A great stake is to be gained, and if we lose it through any folly of your's, I'll not answer for the consequences."

"Your threats will not intimidate me," she replied, "but if I find there is sufficient foundation for the assertion you are about to make, I will not throw any obstacles in the way."

"Why," asked the pedlar, "should you doubt my word, when I have so often, and so solemnly declared that you are the adopted child who was stolen from the house of the late Mr. Clement Derwent?"

"Because," said Amy, "it is your interest to assert it; and, but for that fact you would have left me in the same poverty in which you lately found me."

"So you have been pleased to tell me before," exclaimed the other, "and my reply still is that my motives can make very little difference, so that I succeed in getting you acknowledged as the mistress of this noble house and its broad domains. There are no difficulties in the way if you will only act with firmness, and surely the prize is worth trying for."

"Not if I am to be continually haunted with your presence," she replied.

"You will not be troubled with me any long time," answered Caleb Kestrel, "for this country is no place for me, and as soon as the money I demand is paid, I shall leave England for ever. So having removed that impression, I suppose I may expect that you will not throw any doubt upon the assertions I am about to make?"

"In that I shall be entirely guided by circumstances," she calmly replied; "for if the claim you are about to make, is not satisfactorily made out, I shall not hesitate to abandon it."

"Oh, you needn't have any doubt about that," exclaimed the pedlar, "for every thing is clear enough to secure you all that I am seeking for. Besides Mr. Derwent is dead, so that you will not have anything to reproach yourself for in depriving him of an inheritance that was never justly his.

"Aye, he is indeed dead," replied Amy; "but how can you speak so calmly of a fact that your own hand—"

"Hush!" he exclaimed interrupting her, "not another word for your life! We may be overheard here, and if listeners should be about, you know what the consequence would be to me."

"You know it also," she exclaimed, "and therefore do not provoke me to do that which you would afterwards have bitter reason to repent."

"Are you mad, that you utter these threats to me?" muttered Caleb Kestrel between his clenched teeth.

"They are no threats, as you may hereafter find out."

"I see how it is," he replied, drawing a knife from his pocket, and presenting it threateningly at her, "I am unfortunately in your power, and you hope to alarm me with menaces. But think not to intimidate one who would bury this weapon in your heart, the instant a word was pronounced that would hand him over to the tender mercies of the law. I am provided with such a weapon, as you see," he added, "and, if need be, both you and I will perish by it, rather than I would yield myself to the gibbet."

"If you would escape that fate, why do you still urge me to do that which is repugnant to me?" she asked. "I never dreamt of, or desired riches, and if my own wishes were consulted, I should continue under the care of those kind people, who have acted the part of parents to me."

"Aye, aye," exclaimed Kestrel, "its all very well to say you prefer poverty to a life of ease and affluence, but, for my own part, I see no reason why you should not have that which is justly your own. Clement Derwent made his will in your favour—your identity can be clearly proved, and it is only justice that you should enjoy you own."

"It is well for *you* to say so, who have been the cause of all my misfortunes."

"I have been the cause of them," he replied, "but is it nothing in my favour that I am now willing to make you all the reparation in my power?"

"Aye, but is it not done to serve yourself rather than me?" demanded Amy. "You require money, and to serve your own convenience, I am to be thrust forward into a situation that I would gladly avoid."

"Hush! say no more" whispered Caleb, "for I hear footsteps coming this way, and we must not be found wrangling. Recover your composure, Amy, and speak not unless I ask any question."

The door now opened, and Mr. Reves made his appearance.

"So," he exclaimed, "this, I suppose, is the young female of whom you spoke to me yesterday?"

"It is," he replied, "and I am now here to assert her claim to the Derwent estates. When we last spoke together upon the subject, you seemed to doubt the truth of the claim I made in her behalf, but of course you have read the will of Mr. Clement Derwent, by which he bequeathed his property to a female child whom he had adopted."

"He certainly left his property as you say," replied the steward, "but if after the lapse of a certain number of years, the child was not discovered, then the estates in question were to be divided; one half going to his cousin, Mr. Cecil Derwent, and the other to be retained for the use of his adopted daughter, in the event of our search for her proving successful."

"Exactly so, but your master, instead of complying with the terms of the will, has taken the whole of the estates into his own hands."

"That he did so, there is no denying," answered Reves, "but in justice to him I must add that he did not take that step till all hopes of finding the girl were at an end. Had he lived he would cheerfully have resigned her share, upon the claim being substantiated."

"And I am the only person that can do so," exclaimed Caleb Kestrel, "for now that no danger is to be apprehended from the confession, I acknowledge myself to be the person that took her away."

"What motive had you for such an act of cruelty?"

"Revenge!—Clement Derwent prosecuted me for a trifling theft that was committed during the time I was in his service, and no sooner was the term of my punishment at an end, than I took away the child, because I knew she was the dearest object of his regard. I afterwards brought her over to England and placed her under the care of a couple that I had formerly known, and passed her off to them as my own daughter. They are both at hand to prove my assertion that she is the same child that I left with them."

"All this may be perfectly true," answered the steward, "but we must have good proof that she is the child who was adopted by the late Mr. Clement Derwent."

"Which is not so difficult as you imagine," replied the pedlar, "for with a view to what might afterwards be required, I broke a locket which she wore, half of which, as you see I have kept till now, and the other is still suspended round her neck. Thus there can be little doubt of her identity, and I therefore formally demand in her name, the property to which she is justly entitled."

"And pray have you no selfish motives of your own, for making this claim?"

"It matters little, whether I have or not," answered the pedlar. "Let it suffice you that the girl needs some friend to assert her rights, and who is so proper a person to take that duty upon himself as the man who for many years past has been the cause of her living in poverty?"

"You speak with seeming fairness," said the steward, "and I dare say if upon inquiry your story turns out to be correct, Mr. Cecil Derwent will not hesitate to yield to the demands that are made upon him."

"Mr. Cecil Derwent is dead."

"No, villain, he is not," exclaimed the Squire, who at that moment entered the room, leaning on the arm of Frank Marldale. "He yet lives to denounce you as the would-be assassin who sought his life!"

For a moment Caleb Kestrel seemed to be completely paralysed by the suddenness with which his villany had been confounded. He stood aghast as if the grasp of justice was already upon him, but quickly recovering his usual audacity, he said :—

"Who is there here, besides yourself, who dares accuse me of the crime of meditated murder?"

"I do," exclaimed Amy, "for I was present, and saw you aim your weapon against the life of Mr. Derwent!"

Pale with rage, Kestrel directed towards her a look of withering hatred, and darting towards her he would have plunged his knife into her heart, but for the timely intervention of Mr. Derwent, who, foreseeing the design, stepped forward and prevented the fatal blow. In another moment Caleb was secured by a couple of constables who were in attendance for that purpose.

"Your villany has been again defeated," exclaimed Cecil Derwent, "and it now only remains for the law to deal out the punishment you deserve."

"Still I can be revenged on yonder girl," cried the defeated criminal, "for I now withdraw all that I have been saying in her favour, and declare that she is not the child adopted by Clement Derwent."

"Your malice will be defeated there also," returned the Squire, "for I am satisfied that she is the person we have so long sought after in vain, and I am ready to give up to her that portion of the property to which she has an undoubted right. The man and woman who brought her up have satisfied me that she is the same person whom you left in their care, and with that assurance I will not deprive her even for a moment of her rightful inheritance. You are therefore baffled on every

every side, and she whom you have so deeply injured, will at length obtain the justice which has hitherto been denied her."

"And now that all has been discovered," demanded Caleb, "how is it that you have survived the blow I aimed at your heart?"

"To explain that," answered Cecil, "would occupy more time than I am at present inclined to bestow upon the subject. Suffice it, therefore, to say that I revived under the skilful hands of my steward, and happily live to witness the pun-

(Caleb Kestrel taken from Derwent Hall for the attempted murder of the squire.)

ishment of the assassin who would have destroyed me. You will now be conveyed to prison, and my last advice is that you repent the evil life you have so long led."

On a sign being given, Caleb Kestrel was now dragged from the room in spite of the violent struggles with which he endeavoured to break away from them. Amy would then have taken her departure, but Cecil Derwent perceived her intention, and taking her hand, he said :

"Nay, my dear girl, you must not be permitted to leave a house which from this moment is your own. That you are the adopted daughter of my cousin Clement I do not hesitate to believe, and you will, therefore, take that share of his property which it was his intention should be yours."

" Indeed, indeed sir," she cried, "I covet neither riches nor grandeur, far far happier shall I be to pass the remainder of my days with those to whom I am under such heavy obligations."

" And what is to hinder your being with them ?" demanded Cecil. "I am convinced they deserve the gratitude you feel towards them, and what better fortune can befal them, than to reside under your roof, and exchange a wandering life for the comforts it will then be in your power to bestow upon them? I see that argument, at least, has some weight with you, and that you will not refuse to accept that to which you are so justly entitled, and which I am most anxious to surrender to the adopted daughter of my relative."

" And between ourselves, squire," whispered Frank Marldale, " more unlikely things have come about, than that all the property will still remain in your own hands. The girl is pretty, and her wealth will make her a fitting match for the owner of the other half of these estates of Derwent."

Cecil smiled at this remark, and then taking Amy's hand, he said to her,—

" I hope, fair cousin, if you will allow me to call you so, you will not refuse the proposition I have just made. Remember, in acceding to it, you will only take that which is your own by right, and by doing so, you will be able to show your gratitude to those who deserve to be rewarded."

" For their sake I yield," murmured Amy, " but be assured I do so with reluctance, for how shall I, who have been used to poverty and hardship, be able to support a station so new to me."

" Oh, never fear," he replied, "but the customs of a higher grade in society will come sooner and more naturally than you think for. In a little time you will be able to acquire the accomplishments necessary for your new station, and people will forget the poverty that has marked the first few years of your life."

" But I shall not easily forget it myself," she replied, and therefore in my new station, I shall avoid that society for which I feel myself totally unfitted."

" Ah!" exclaimed Cecil, " but at present you little dream of the inducement that high life offers to enter into the gaieties that fortune only can compass. In short, wealth can bestow no happiness unless it procures for its possessors those things which are beyond the reach of their poorer fellow-creatures."

" My chief pleasure," answered Amy, "will be in making those happy to whom I am so much indebted for the kindness they bestowed upon me."

" And they are both in another room anxiously awaiting to congratulate you on the improved state of your fortune. I sent for the worthy couple, and my steward has already informed them of what has taken place."

" Then I will see them without delay," she exclaimed, " for I long to tell them that their wanderings and privations are now at an end for ever."

And with those words she left the room and hastened to meet her two anxious friends."

" I see how all this will end," said Frank Marldale, as soon as she was gone. "You are already head over ears in love with the pretty Amy, and by-and-by you will marry her, and thus possess yourself of an excellent wife, as well as that share of the property which you have just given up."

" More unlikely things have come to pass, certainly," he replied, " for, to confess the truth, I was much taken with the girl the first moment I saw her at Brough's. And if my suit should prove successful we will marry on the same day that makes Mary Everett your wife. So now the foolish jealousy that existed between us is at an end, and you shall remain tenant of the Willow Farm at a reduced rent. That I know is the best news I can possibly give you; so soon as the first burst of their transport is over, we will go and see how the ex-showman and his wife receive the intelligence that they are not to be separated from the girl whom they have so long regarded as their own daughter."

On entering one of the smaller rooms of the mansion, they found Peeps and his wife congratulating Amy upon the extraordinary turn of fortune of which she had just been telling them. The ex-showman was most vociferous in his expression of pleasure at the change which had befallen his young favourite, but his better half was more mild in the method of showing the joy that the recent news had inspired her with, and taking the hand of Cecil Derwent as he entered the room, she said :—

"Ah, squire, how kindly you have acted to our poor girl when we thought she had not another friend in the world besides our two selves. But she will be grateful, I know, for all favours, and it will be a consolation for you through the rest of your life, to know that you have done justice to an orphan girl."

"For which I deserve no praise," he replied, "since I have performed nothing more than my duty."

"Perhaps it may be, so far as that goes," exclaimed Mrs. Peeps, "but you were not bound to show all this kindness to myself and my husband, as well as to Amy. And, to speak the truth, I don't know how we can ever make amends for it, unless Peeps throws open his Temple of Arts for your inspection as often as you may feel inclined to see the exhibition."

"My dear friends," returned the squire, "believe me, the offer I made you and your husband of a home in this house was instigated by the fact' that I knew it would afford the highest degree of satisfaction to Amy. Indeed, there is not the slightest merit to me, since this house and all that it contains belongs—not to myself, but our young friend."

"Mr. Derwent," exclaimed Amy, advancing timidly towards him, "I have already received too many favours from you, and will not hear of any further sacrifice. This house has been your home almost from infancy, and were it really mine by right, I would at once quit the roof rather than you should leave it."

"You think I should regret taking my departure?"

"I am sure you would."

"Well," he replied, "under other circumstances I might, perhaps, feel sorry at leaving a place that is endeared to me by many recollections of the past. I have, however, an idea of travelling abroad three or four years, and on my return to England it will matter very little where I fix my home."

"Are you going to leave the country, sir?" inquired Amy, in a tone of earnestness that she found it impossible to repress.

"Why," he replied, regarding her with no little surprise, "I have almost made up my mind to take that step, but if there was only one friend to whom my absence would occasion grief the plan should be instantly abandoned. How say you, Amy, have you any wish that I should remain in England?"

"Excuse me, sir," exclaimed Peeps, coming to the rescue at this rather awkward point, "but of course Amy, as well as the rest of us will feel sorry if you go away from us."

"And why should you feel sorry, my friend?"

"Well," he replied laughing, "hang me if I can give any reason at this moment, though a thousand might be found if I had only time to think of 'em. However, I'm sure you won't go away when you come to consider that people may say you left England out of sheer vexation at having lost half your fortune."

"I care not what the world would say of me," he replied, "for I have at least the satisfaction of knowing that I resign without a single regret that which has been too long withheld from its real owner. In short, have I not been living for years in luxury, whilst poor Amy has been dragging on a wretched existence of toil, penury and want."

"I may have endured hardships, sir," exclaimed our heroine, "but has it not been my good fortune to find friends who have toiled hard and suffered privations themselves in order that my affections might be as few as possible? Nay, Mr. Derwent, if fortune had never smiled upon me I could never have had anything regret while such kind protectors were left me."

"And can you forgive us," asked Peeps, "for having made you tambourine player and dancer to our establishment?"

"Why should I have been excused performing my share towards obtaining the money necessary for our support?" she inquired, "Caleb Kestrel gave you no money to defray the extra cost of my maintenance, and I always felt that the trifling task entrusted to me went but a little way towards making amends for the privations I often caused you."

"But didn't your music and dancing, and, above all, that pretty face of yours bring lots of customers to our Temple of Arts?" inquired Peeps. "Why to be sure it did, and many and many a time we should not have been able to get an audience together at all but for your attractions, added to the other wonders of our exhibition. So don't talk any more about favours, my dear girl, for if we make any inquires into the subject we shall find that they mostly lie on the other side. But come, we must return, or Farmer Brough will begin to think we have taken French leave without so much as thanking him for the hospitality he has been kind enough to bestow upon us."

"Farmer Brough," observed the squire, "has heard by this time that you will not return to his house except as occasional visitors."

"Who has told him so?" asked Amy.

"A servant of mine, who was despatched for that purpose," answered the squire. "In short, this house is now your home, and if I remain in it a few days longer, it will be only as the guest of its honoured mistress.

"Nay, I beg—I entreat of you——"

"In this instance," he replied, "I must be allowed to act without contradiction, though I will not say the time may yet arrive when I should be delighted to return and remain a permanent inhabitant."

"I say, Peeps," whispered Mrs. P., nudging her husband, "I declare if that aint as much as to say he'd be glad to marry the girl."

"Well, I dare say that will be the end of it," he replied; "and she seems to understand the hint, too, for see how she blushes and holds down her head, as he draws her to a part of the room where we can't overhear what passes between them. And young Marldale, too, is pretty well up to the game that's going on, for he is coming towards us because he don't want to be a Marplot."

"My good friends," said Frank, shaking them both by the hand, "I think I can now congratulate you both upon the certain happiness of your adopted daughter. In short, they have loved each other from the moment of their first meeting, and I believe Squire Derwent will not find it a difficult task to prevail upon the young lady to accept the offer of his hand."

"And then," sighed Mrs. Peeps, "I suppose we may reckon that our stay in this house won't last much longer?"

"Nay," answered Marldale, "if the squire really loves Amy, he will not deprive her of the society of those who are so dear to her. On the contrary, he will endeavour to render your residence as happy as possible."

"You think he won't turn us out, then?"

"Be not alarmed about that," returned the young farmer, "for he has too generous a heart to be ungrateful to those who have been such steadfast friends to the woman of his love. So make up your mind to remain in these comfortable quarters as long as you live. But see, he comes this way, and Amy leaves the room by herself."

"Which looks very much as if he was going to tell us what has been passing between them," observed Peeps, with a sly wink at his wife. Then, turning towards Cecil Derwent, he added—"Well, squire, so you had a secret to tell Amy, eh?—Something that a couple of old 'uns, like Mrs. P. and I, had no business to hear?"

"The secret is one that may be told in a few words," he replied. "Your adopted daughter and I love each other—both have just now confessed as much, and she has left the room that I may ask if you have any objection to the proposed union ?"

"Objection !" exclaimed Mr. Peeps and his wife, in a breath.

"Aye ; you have been her faithful guardians so long that you may well claim a right to have a voice on the subject."

"Perhaps so," replied Peeps, "but do you suppose we could have a word to say in a case of this kind? No, no, both Mrs. P. and myself are too well satisfied to make any objection, when we see plainly enough that her happiness depends upon her marrying you. Besides——"

He was here interrupted by one of the men who came running in almost breathless with haste to announce that Caleb Kestrel had been rescued by a couple of men who rushed out upon them as they were conveying him along a lonely part of the road.

"Then let the information be immediately conveyed to the nearest magistrate," exclaimed Cecil Derwent, "for whilst that man remains at large, Amy will not be safe. Nay, more, let a reward of fifty pounds be offered in my name, and to be paid immediately on his being placed in safe custody."

The man disappeared on receiving these instructions, and Mr. Derwent continued to those about him, —

"The escape of this reckless villain fills me with apprehension and alarm, for we know him to be a vindictive, and I fear lest the first object of his revenge should be the girl we have just rescued from his power."

"He shall not be much longer at liberty if I have the power to prevent it," exclaimed Marldale, snatching up his hat and making towards the door.

"Where are you going to?" demanded the squire.

"In pursuit of Caleb Kestrel," he replied, "I know every lurking place for miles around, and will hunt him out if he remains anywhere in the neighbourhood. You remain where you are, for Amy may require the aid of a protector, and it will not do for all of us to be absent from the house in case of need.

"Before any remonstrance could be offered, the young man had left the room, and was making his way towards the moors in some part of which he expected to find the object of his pursuit. The squire immediately afterwards left Mr. and Mrs. Peeps, to console themselves as they best could, and went to inform Amy of what had occurred.

CHAPTER XII.

THE FUGITIVES.—THE DESERTED HUT.—PAST, PRESENT, AND FUTURE.—A PURSUER.
—FRANK MARLDALE FALLS INTO BAD HANDS.—THE NIGHT EXCURSION.

AFTER the rescue of Caleb Kestrel, which we have briefly alluded to, he and his friends fled with all their speed towards that wild part of the country where the attempted murder of Squire Derwent had taken place. It is true there was no occasion for any extraordinary haste, for the men who had charge of the prisoner ran off like so many startled hares as soon as the report of a pistol was heard, and the others were allowed to pursue their own way without much fear of interruption. At length they reached the moors, and from thence directed their way towards the deserted hut in which it will be remembered Amy took shelter on the night of the murder by her supposed father. Arrived there, the three men entered, and for the first time broke the silence which had been observed from the moment when the rescue had been suggested.

"Well," exclaimed Kestrel, "here we are at last, but the next thing to ask ourselves is how long they will let us remain here in quiet. I suppose they wont suffer an escape without an attempt to recapture their prisoner, and this I should suppose is about the first place they'll think of searching for him."

"And if they do," retorted one of his companions, " I suppose we must have a good fight for it. We wont yield very easily, and with plenty of arms at our command, I think we can put half-a-dozen of them to flight, as we did those fellows just now."

" Don't make too sure of that, Dick Ratcliffe," exclaimed Kestrel, " for they may send men that are armed as well as ourselves, and then what sort of a chance should we have with 'em ?"

" How is this Caleb ?" demanded George Layburne, the other stranger, " you used to be as stout hearted a fellow as any among us, but now you seem to be afraid of your shadow. Have you turned coward all of a sudden ?"

" No more than you have yourself," he replied sullenly ; " but when a man finds that all his favorite plans fail one after another, he begins to feel nervous and uneasy. I've at length discovered that girl you have so often heard me speak about, and now she has just slipped through my fingers when I thought everything safe."

" Well," demanded Dick, " and what good was to come of it after you found the wench ?"

" A great deal of good," he replied, " the girl is rich, and I meant to have half her money."

" Why not all, while you were about it ?" asked George Layburne.

" Oh," he replied, " I dare say that would have been the case in time. But it don't ao to appear to be too greedy, so I thought it would be better to demand half now, and the remainder when that was spent. But all that was upset by a strange circumstance that I should never have dreamt of."

" What was that ?" asked George.

" Why, it would be a long story if I was to enter into all the particulars," he replied, " but the truth is, I shot Squire Derwent, who owns the other half of her estates, and just when I thought she had a good claim to the whole of the property, hang me if I didn't discover that he was still alive."

" Psha !" exclaimed Dick, " there may be some mistake about it."

" How can there be any mistake," he asked, " when I saw him face to face, and he denounced me as being the man that had attempted to murder him."

" And that I suppose is how we came to find you in custody ?"

" Yes," he replied, " they were going to take me before a magistrate, and it's likely I should have found myself in jail by this time, if you had not suddenly pounced on my convoy and put 'em to flight."

" What do you think of doing next," asked Dick Ratcliffe.

" Why, that is a matter that requires some little consideration," he replied, " but I suppose we must not leave this place without trying to carry the girl off with us."

" Humph !" retorted the other, " what good would you get by that ?"

" A great deal," replied Kestrel ; " we could demand money by way of her ransom, and I'll answer for it they would not mind coming down pretty handsomely rather than leave her at our mercy."

" But is it easy to get hold of her ?" asked George Layburne.

" Yes, it will be easy enough, if we go boldly to work."

" Does she ever go out to take a walk ?"

" She did," replied Kestrel, " but I dare say they'll persuade her to keep in doors now that I am at large again."

" Then how do you mean to manage ?"

" Take her from Derwent Hall, to be sure," he replied, " I've had the forethought to make a pretty accurate examination of the buildings, and there is one window in particular that we might get in at without fear of being disturbed. A vine grows up and forms as excellent a ladder as we could wish for."

" And does that window belong to the room the girl is to be found in ?" demanded Dick Ratcliffe.

" That I don't know till we try."

" When is the attempt to be made ?"

"To-night. Delays are dangerous, and we ought to be far enough from here before twelve hours pass over our heads."

"And what if we should happen to be surprised!'

"Why then we must fight for it," answered Caleb Kestrel. "The prize is worth some risk, and I think is to be mine if we only set resolutely to work."

"And what are Dick and I to get for our trouble?"

"Oh, I shall not fail to reward with a liberal hand those who make themselves useful to me," answered the pedlar.

"But it may be many months before you can bring the girl's friends to your own terms."

"If once we get her out of their hands it will not be long before they pay down the money for her release. They look upon me as a sort of fiend in human form, and rather than suffer her to remain in my company longer than need be, they'll come to terms, though perhaps they may appear to be a little bit extortionate."

"All this may seem easy enough to talk about," observed Layburne, "but how are you to make a bargain with the squire when it's most likely he'd give you into custody the moment you venture to go before him?"

"Psha! he'll not dare to do so."

"Not dare?"

"I tell you," continued Caleb Kestrel, "he would rather cut off his right hand than detain me a moment longer than may be necessary to give an answer to my demand."

"You have him somehow under your thumb then?"

"Not at present, but I soon shall."

"Why not speak out plainly to the point at once?" exclaimed Dick Ratcliffe impatiently. "You expect us to join you in this affair, and yet we are to be kept in the dark as if we were a couple of pals that are not to be depended on."

"As for that," he replied, "I know both of you to be true men enough, and my only reason for not enlightening you sooner was that I thought it was of no use to enter into particulars till we had made sure of laying hold of the girl. However, to let you into the secret, I mean that Amy herself shall demand from the squire the money that is to purchase her deliverance."

"You'll find it rather a hard matter to do that, I'm thinking," exclaimed Ratcliffe incredulously.

"So you may fancy now, old fellow," laughed the pedlar, "but do you think she'll refuse to write a letter to the squire, making the demand, when she finds herself in our power, and that there is no other way left to get out of it."

"Aye, aye," answered Layburne, "she may write such a letter as you speak of, but the person that's fool enough to deliver it into the hands of Squire Derwent would be detained as a hostage, till she is restored to her friends."

"That shows you don't look at the question on its right side," exclaimed Kestrel, "It's true, as you say, that the squire would make use of any advantage we might throw in his way; but I don't mean to give him the chance, and, whoever goes to him on the message, will return, either with the money, or a promise that it shall be paid immediately."

"And how is all that to be managed?"

"Oh, easily enough," replied the pedlar; "when we get Amy here, she shall be compelled to write a letter, from my dictation, to Squire Derwent, informing him of her condition, but of course giving no clue to the place where she is to be found."

"But that information he will easily be able to extort from the person who goes on the errand."

"That's true enough Dick," replied the the other, "but she will add something more to the letter, that will make the bearer of it safe enough you may rely on it. She will write a postscript, my boy, conveying the rather startling information that her life will be certainly sacrificed if at the end of three hours the messenger does not return to his companions in safety."

"You don't mean to kill her though, I hope ?" exclaimed Layburne.

"Not I," he replied, "but the threat will answer the purpose just as well as if I did. Squire Derwent will, I dare say, be frightened into our terms, and if not, why I know of a cave a few miles off on the sea-coast, where we can keep her safe enough till the money we demand is paid down."

"Its all very fine talking about carrying the girl away with us," exclaimed Dick Ratcliffe, "but when our funds are out how are we to support this girl as well as ourselves till the gentleman you speak of comes to your terms ?"

"There'll be no difficulty about that," he replied, "for near the cave lives a number of smugglers that know me well enough, and they'll not let me want for anything if I promise to make it all right with 'em when matters are squared between Mr. Derwent and myself. Besides, these friends of mine may be useful to us in another way, for if there should be any danger of our being traced to the cave, they could launch their boat, and take us all over to Holland in a few hours."

"You seem to have arranged everything pretty well at any rate," observed George Layburne, laughing.

"That's because I never like to do things by halves," he replied. "If you take an affair in hand, make all sure before you begin, and it will be brought to a close more to your satisfaction. In the present instance, you see how complete all my arrangements are, and I could almost lay my life that before this time to-morrow, the money I am going to demand from Squire Derwent will be ours."

"Very likely," replied Ratcliffe, "but the moment the girl is safe out of our hands he'll be sending the police after us."

"Let him ; I care not what he does, nor who he sends for when once I have the money, I shall not stay much longer in a country where I am not safe. There is plenty of places abroad to live in if we have but the means, and when mine are gone, I shall get some of my old friends in England to try how much more they can frighten Amy out of. Ha, ha, ha ! she has managed to keep out of my way a long time, but now that I have found her she is as good as a fortune to me."

"Don't you think it would be rather too bad to come upon her again, if you get money from her once ?"

"Not at all, for she will be able to afford it ?"

"That depends on how far your demands extend."

"True, but I am not so hard to satisfy as you seem to think," said Kestrel. "My expectations are not excessive, and if I make a second demand on her, or get others to do so, it will only be on some particular emergency."

"But won't it be cruel," said Ratcliffe, "to keep the girl in constant terror ?"

"What's the use of preaching to me about such nonsense as that ?" demanded Caleb Kestrel. "I neither like the girl, nor the man that was going to bring her up as his adopted daughter, for it was all through that same Clement Derwent that I suffered a long and wearysome imprisonment. However, he gained nothing by it, for it was while I was in confinement that I formed the plan that afterwards brought him to his grave."

"Did you murder him ?" asked Richard Ratcliffe.

"No," replied the pedlar, in a tone of fiendlike exultation, "but I stole from him the child he was so fond of, and when every chance of finding her had failed he died of grief and a broken heart. However, it seems he clung to the hope that she was still alive, for he bequeathed to her all his property, if she was found within a certain time, and half of it only if the period he named had elapsed, As soon as I learnt that, I went in search of the people I had left her with, intending to make money through her, but somehow I never could find any trace of her, or them till a short time ago, when I happened to meet them at a Harvest Home in this neighbourhood. So now you know the whole history of the affair, and must see by this time, that my chance of getting money from the squire is pretty certain."

"Hush!" interrupted George Laybourne, "some one is coming this way as if in search of you."

"Aye, aye," returned Caleb, after looking out to see who it was, "it's young farmer Marldale coming to see if we have taken shelter in this deserted hut. Well, he'll pay dearly for his rashness, for we must make him our prisoner here, while we go to-night for Amy."

"How are we to keep him here unless one of us stays behind to watch over him?" demanded Ratcliffe.

[The ruffians obtain access to the apartment of Amy.]

"Have a moment's patience, and you shall see how it is to be done," answered the pedlar, as he took from his pocket a coil of stout cord, which he threw towards his companions in crime. "Just you get that undone against I want it, and this meddling fellow will soon find himself powerless in our hands."

"Did you expect him to follow us here, that you came provided with the means of stopping his mischief?"

"Why, I can't say I gave it much thought," answered Caleb Kestrel, "but

No. 13.

the truth is, I always carry an article of that kind with me, because there's no knowing when it may be useful."

" And you mean to bind him hand and foot ?"

" Have patience, and you'll know all about it in a brace of shakes," whispered his friend. " So now not another word, for he's close by, and if he should hear us, a whistle or any other signal might bring more people to his assistance than we should know how to deal with. Mum's the word, you know, and both of you be ready to give me your assistance the moment I lay hands on him."

A dead silence ensued, which was broken only by the footsteps of Frank Marldale, as he cautiously approached the place where he thought it likely the pedlar had sought concealment. At length when he had come sufficiently near, Kestrel rushed forth with the speed of an arrow, and ere his victim could make an effort to protect himself, he was securely grasped in the arms of the man whom he had come forth to capture. At the same instant, Laybourne stepping forth, presented a pistol at the head of the prisoner, and the other ruffian stood ready with the rope, which he had disentangled ready for the purpose it was intended for. Seeing himself thus unexpectedly overpowered, the young man shouted out lustily for assistance, upon which Kestrel placed his hand over his mouth, exclaiming in a hoarse, threatening tone,—

" Madman !—another sound like that, and it will be the last you ever make in this world. Remain silent and your life is in no danger, but attempt to raise an alarm, and you die like a dog."

" Why have you thus seized me, villain ?"

" In self-defence to be sure," answered the pedlar. " You came here in search of me, but I have managed to turn the tables on you, and as the chance is now in my favour you must make up your mind to remain here till some of your friends happen to discover the place where we have left you in captivity."

Whilst Kestrel was thus speaking, he dragged the young farmer into the hut, and with the assistance of his comrades bound him to a post, which, standing in the middle of the room, had once formed the principal support of the roof. It was in vain that Marldale struggled and remonstrated, for he was overpowered by numbers, and they were deaf alike both to his threats of punishment, and his promises of a liberal reward as the price of his immediate liberation.

" What's the use of any sum of money that you can offer me, when I am going to do that to night that will soon put me in possession of more than all your farm and stock to boot are worth. The game I'm playing is for thousands, and you, I suppose, would be generous enough to offer me somewhere about a hundred."

" I understand you," exclaimed the young man, " there is still a design against Amy, who you think is to be frightened into giving up half her property on condition that you will annoy her no more with your hated presence ?"

" Tush ! why should my presence be hateful to her, when but for me, she never would have been known as the heiress to those estates ?"

" But for you," answered Frank Marldale, " she would not have been a wanderer all these years on the face of the earth. It was you who stole her from a peaceful home, and never would she have been restored to her rights through your means, but for the large sum of money you expected to make by it."

" Oh ! 'tis all very well to throw that in my teeth young fellow," exclaimed the pedlar carelessly, " but isn't it the way of the world to fancy that one good turn deserves another, and why have not I as much right as anybody else to expect a reward for my services ?"

" Because there would have been no occasion for your services, but for the villany that prompted you in the first instance to take away Amy from the protection of her adopted father."

" But there was my own revenge to serve, young man," answered the pedlar, exultingly, " and when once I had made up my mind how that was to be carried out, I never rested till the girl was taken away from the house of Clement Derwent. Not that I owed any grudge to the child herself, but as she was more dearly valued by her protector than anything else he possessed in the world, I knew the loss would be the source of such constant grief, that he would never hold up his head again. And it turned out that I was right too, for when there seemed to be no chance of ever seeing her again, he sank under his misfortune, and shortly afterwards I saw him carried to his grave in a foreign land. I followed at a distance, and my heart exulted at the sight, for I knew that it was I who had sent him broken-hearted out of the world."

"Wretch!" exclaimed Frank Marldale; "your triumph was short lived, for in the meantime the child had been taken away by those you had trusted her with, and you were thus deprived of the rich harvest you hoped to make on announcing her to be the heiress who had been stolen from the house of Clement Derwent."

"It can't be denied that it gave me a great deal of trouble," answered the pedlar; "but never mind,—it's not worth looking back now, for the girl has not only been found, but has been acknowledged, and I don't mean to take my leave of this neighbourhood till she has recompensed me for all the toil and anxiety I've had."

"If you remain here many hours longer," replied Marldale, "it will be at the hazard of falling into the hands of some of the numerous persons that are looking after you."

"There's not much fear that any of the cowards will venture near me," he exclaimed; "for it's pretty well known that I carry arms to be in readiness at any moment of need. And what's more, I believe it is also understood that I shall not hesitate to use 'em if I should find myself too closely pressed. So you see, young gentleman, you may reckon yourself a very fortunate fellow in finding me in a humour merely to keep you in confinement when it would have been easy to have put you out of the way at once."

"Had you done so," exclaimed Frank Marldale, with more boldness than discretion, "the murderer would soon have been made to answer for his crime."

"Psha!" retorted the other, "what would be more easy than to conceal the deed if one felt inclined to do so? Here are plenty of deep ravines that the footsteps of man never penetrated, and in one of them your bones would have whitened with little chance of ever being discoverd. And even supposing that the body was found, where is the evidence to connect me with being the cause of your death?"

"You would be suspected by those who knew that I came out upon the moors for the purpose of looking for you."

"Upon my word young gentleman, I think you might easily have found more profitable employment," exclaimed Caleb Kestrel. "You and I are strangers to each other, and yet you seem to have taken a great deal of pains to get me into a scrape that might perhaps have cost me my life. But never mind, we have you here safe enough, and there's the consolation for you to know that there's a chance of staring to death, for we are not going to return, and perhaps none of your friends may think of coming here till it will be too late to save your life. So now, young fellow, you see what you've got into through troubling yourself with things that don't concern you?"

"I feel no regret for what I have done," answered Marldale, "for the purpose that brought me here was a just one, and if I have failed in accomplishing it the fault was none of my own."

"Yes it is," exclaimed the pedlar, "for who but yourself would have thought of coming single-handed against Caleb Kestrel? You ought to have known better, young man, and I suppose by this time you would give all you possess in the world to be back safe and sound in your own farm-house."

"I would not return there," he replied, "till I had succeeded in placing you in the hands of the law."

"The law!" exclaimed Kestrel derisively, "why I have managed to keep pretty clear of it for a good many years past, and with the experience I have gathered I should say there's not much chance of my getting into a dilemma now. And what's more, I am determined never to be taken within the walls of a prison, for the moment I see myself without a chance of escape, a pistol placed at my head will soon cheat the hangman of his victim. So you see my plans are all formed for every kind of difficulty I may happen to find myself in, and, even supposing you had come suddenly upon me to day, with people behind ready to give you their assistance, I should, with these two bull dogs, have first shot you and then myself."

"Aye," interposed Dick Ratcliffe, "you ought to consider yourself a d—d lucky fellow to have got off so well. Sometimes you might not have found us in good humour, and in that case our friend Kestrel would have made short work of it with you. No one need ever have been the wiser, and even if the murder had been discovered, and ourselves suspected of having done it, we should have taken ourselves far enough off from the scene of danger."

"Well gentlemen," exclaimed George Layburne, "I don't know what you may both think of it, but in my opinion we are acting like three infernal fools in talking here when there's so much business to be done. For my own part I don't like the notion of leaving this youngster behind us, for he may contrive to break the cords, and then we know what would be the end of it : we should lose our chance of carrying off Amy, and then of course away goes the money that has been proffered for the help we are to give."

"Let him understand then," returned Caleb Kestrel, "that if we are interrupted either by him or anybody else, we mean to protect ourselves to the very last. We have six pistols amongst us, loaded with balls, and when they are no longer of any use, why then we'll begin with our knives, and I'll be bound we shall be able to keep off the enemy if they are ever so strong. They must remember they have desperate men to deal with, and if once we are put on our defiance it will be all the worse for those that drive us to extremities."

"There is little chance of my being able to take any part against you," exclaimed Frank Marldale, looking down at the cords that bound him to the post.

"So much the better for yourself," replied the pedlar, "for while you are there you will be out of harm's way, and it's more than likely that if you had been free you would have been meddling in affairs that you have nothing to do with."

"What !" he exclaimed, "have I no right to interfere when I see a weak, defenceless woman about to become the prey of ruffians ?"

"Take my advice," answered the pedlar, "and have nothing to do with matters that don't concern you. If you had been the girl's sweetheart there'd have been some sort of excuse for taking part with her, but she is almost a stranger to you, and of course has no kind of claim upon you."

"Her chief claim upon me is that she is nearly friendless."

"The few she has are quite enough for me to cope against," replied the pedlar, "and for that reason I think myself fortunate in having put it out of your power to rank yourself among their number. The squire and his servants are able to take care of her, I should think, and now that she has taken up her abode at the hall I should suppose there's not much fear of her being run away with."

"And yet," exclaimed Marldale, "judging from what I have heard, there seems to be but too much reason to believe that you have some such object to carry out this very night."

' Nonsense ! I only want to see her in order that I may know whether she means to reward me for having helped to make her one of the richest heiresses in this country."

"Leave that to her own generosity," answered Frank Marldale, " and I'll pledge my very existence itself that you will have no reason to repent having given her your confidence. Nay, set me at liberty and I will undertake to convince her that her future peace of mind is to be purchased by giving you the sum of money that has been demanded."

"What a precious fool you must take me for," exclaimed Kestrel after having indulged himself with a hearty laugh at the expense of young Marldale. "Set you at liberty, eh! Come that's rather too good a joke, considering the advantage I should give away after having got you under my thumb. However, we have no time now to argue this matter any further, so we'll leave you to enjoy yourself whilst we go to finish our business, which I should think may be all brought to a comfortable conclusion, if we have any luck, in about a couple of hours or so."

He now examined the cords that bound his prisoner, and having found that they were quite secure, he and his two companions left the deserted hut in order to complete the task they had undertaken to accomplish. For some time they moved on in perfect silence, but at length Caleb Kestrel, addressing himself to his two companions, inquired if he might depend upon their sticking to him in case any of the people at the hall should be disturbed.

" Did you ever know us to be cowards when our courage was needed?" demanded Dick Ratcliffe, rather piqued by the want of confidence implied by these words. " We always stick to our work whatever it may be, and we are not likely to flinch from our duty now that we have been promised something worth while as soon as you get the young woman's money."

" Humph! so you are offended are you?"

" Not exactly offended," answered Ratcliffe, " but people don't like to be suspected when there's no reason for it, and both George Layburne and myself knows that we have as good a share of courage as you yourself can boast of. However, we don't want any quarrelling when there's business to be done, so lets say no more about it, but come to some understanding among ourselves as to how we are to act when we get to Derwent Hall?"

" Why, in the first place we must all three climb up to Amy's chamber window, which can easily be done, as I told you before, by means of a tree that climbs up the house."

" And when we get into the room?"

" We must first wake the girl if she happens to be asleep, and then threatening her with death if any alarm is made, I shall desire her to follow us without offering any resistance."

" Which, as a matter of course," observed Layburne, " we may suppose she'll refuse to do."

" I shall be much mistaken if she does," continued Caleb Kestrel " for the girl holds me in the greatest dread, and I expect, if a promise is made that no violence will be offered, she will not venture to refuse that which we can have the power to compel."

" May I ask where you mean to take her to?"

" I have already told you our course will be toward the sea coast."

" Aye but to what part?"

" Why to a large excavation in the rock that overlooks the sea," replied Kestrel, " I suppose neither of you are so ignorant of this part of the country as not to have heard of Robin Hood's cave."

" I've been there," answered Dick Ratcliffe, " and a capital place it is too, for half-a-dozen well-armed men would easily defend it against the attack of fifty, and if you once get the girl there she may be kept your prisoner as long as you like."

" What do you want her to do when we have taken her there?" asked Layburne of the pedlar.

" She must write to Squire Derwent," he replied "desiring him to pay the bearer of the note, a certain sum of money, and informing him at the same time that if a refusal is sent back, she will be carried over to some part of the continent where she will never be found."

" That's all very fine, returned Layburne, " but who the devil is going to be fool enough to take the note."

" Why what is there to be afraid of?"

" A great deal, in my opinion, he replied. " What's to hinder the squire giving the messenger into custody, and thus keeping him shut up in jail, till he confesses where the girl has been taken to."

" That might be very possible, if care was not taken to prevent such an advantage being taken," answered Kestrel. "But you seem to have rather a short memory, for I told you before that the note shall contain a caution, warning Squire Derwent, that if such a step is taken it may cost Amy her life. He'll hardly feel inclined to run such a risk when he knows the consequence, and I rather think we may comfort ourselves with the hope that the money will be sent back, or at least that we shall have a promise that it shall be paid within a few hours afterwards. But hist! I hear people coming this way, so let's hide beyond yonder clumps of furze, till they have got out of our sight.'

The three concealed themselves, and within a few minutes about half a dozen men were seen to go by. These by their conversation were discovered to be some of the people that had been sent out to search for Caleb Kestrel and his companions, and it was not until all appeared to be quite safe that they ventured to leave the spot which afforded them the concealment they required.

CHAPTER XIII.

AMY TAKES POSSESSION OF HER NEW HOME; AN ALARM; SLUMBER DISTURBED; THE ABDUCTION; CECIL DERWENT AND HIS FRIENDS COMMENCE AN ACTIVE PURSUIT

BEAUTIFUL as was the hall and the pleasure grounds which surrounded it, Amy would have preferred some less ostentatious abode in which to pass the remainder of her days. The representations of Cecil Derwent, however, prevailed over her own inclinations, and in deference to his wish she consented to accept of that portion of the house which she was to occupy till the arrival of the not far-distant day which had been named for their nuptials. But she felt dull and oppressed, for her lover accompanied by Brassy Popjoy, and Peeps, had gone out in quest of the fugitive pedlar, and being left alone she retired to her chamber with Mrs. Peeps at an early hour in the evening. Here seating themselves at a window that overlooked the shrubbery, they conversed of all that had taken place, contrasting the past with the present, and even endeavouring to dive into the future, which in the imagination of the elder lady, was to bring with it all the happiness and pleasure which ample means can alone bestow.

"Ah! my dear Amy," exclaimed Mrs. Peeps, after a pause, " who, a week ago, could have believed what was about to come to pass. Then you were the poor and adopted daughter of a couple of strolling vagabonds, and now you are the mistress of a large fortune, and one of the finest houses in all Yorkshire."

"True," said our heroine, "but I much doubt whether I shall ever be half so happy as I was when we used to wander through the country without either care or anxiety."

" Bless the girl! what can she be thinking of?" exclaimed the worthy lady, with unfeigned surprise. " Ain't this a perfect paradise of a place to live in, and can any body in their senses prefer going about from place to place, to being in a mansion with plenty of servants at command, and all the luxuries that can be enjoyed only by the wealthy. Besides, I thought you really loved this Squire Derwent, who every body says is such an excellent young man."

" I do love him," answered Amy, "but it is for his goodness of heart, and not for the wealth he is said to possess. Had fate ordained it otherwise, I would rather have been united to one whose living depended upon the labour of his own hands."

" My dear, that is a ridiculously romantic notion.'

"I know I am romantic, but that is scarcely to be wondered at, when you remember that I was born in sunny Italy, where all things in nature and art assume a different complexion to what they do in less favoured countries."

"But you left so young that it is hardly likely you can remember anything of the land you speak of."

"Ah!" replied the maiden, "but the feelings that were born within me cannot be obliterated by my removal to another country. Nay if ever I had one wish stronger than another, it was that you and Mrs. Peeps might go to my loved Italy, and that I might be allowed to accompany you."

"And do you really think Peeps's Temple of the Arts would have met with encouragement there?"

"Why I can't say there would have been much chance of that."

"You think his paintings are not quite finished enough?"

"Pardon me for changing the subject," exclaimed Amy, "for indeed my dear madam, I am not a sufficiently good judge to give an opinion upon a subject of so much difficulty. But if I cannot express myself upon that point, I can at least say that the poor neglected orphan girl found the most affectionate of parents in you and your warm hearted husband."

"Is there anything deserving great praise in acting kindly to an unfortunate child who was thrown upon our care?" demanded the good lady. "Peeps and I took a liking for you at once, and to tell you the truth we purposely kept out of the way as much as possible because we were afraid some day or other that fellow, Caleb Kestrel would come forward to claim you from us."

"And at last your fears were realized;"

"So they were," replied Mrs. Peeps, "but things turned out very differently to what we had imagined, for, instead of taking you away with him he was the means of putting you in the way of receiving a large fortune."

"Which was done only for the most selfish motives," exclaimed Amy. "Too indolent to work himself, he thought to possess himself of half any fortune that might be coming to me, and hence his anxiety to prove the claim that he made in my behalf."

"Ah! he has alway been a worthless fellow, my dear," returned Mrs. Peeps, "and that was another reason why I and my husband tried to keep out of his way. But never mind, I think there's not much more to be feared from him, for if he should be taken it's not likely he'll ever have his liberty again, and if he escapes from the hand of justice he'll never dare show himself any more, so that you may make your mind quite easy and comfortable as far as that part of the question is concerned."

"Has it not struck you that he may employ agents?"

"Agents are not easily to be found for a man that is locked up on a charge of felony," observed Mrs. Peeps.

"Perhaps so, but this man is not yet in custody, and we know well enough that he will never be taken unless some stratagem is employed for the purpose."

"At any rate he must leave the neighbourhood," observed the old lady, "and then I don't see what reason you can have for being afraid of him. Besides, you will by and bye be the wife of Squire Derwent, and then I should like to see if this insolent pedlar will dare to annoy you. Then its well known too, that he is the man that attempted to murder the squire, and, though I am not quite certain what the law would do with him if he happens to be caught, I should say good care will be taken not to let him have another opportunity of taking his revenge into his own hands."

"Look!" exclaimed Amy, in a tone of alarm, and pointing towards a thick clump of evergreens in a distant part of the garden;—"did you see nothing move yonder across the path, where the moonbeams fall so brightly!"

"What do you mean, my love?" demanded Mrs. Peeps, participating in the alarm of her foster child, "I have neither seen nor heard anything, and yet I was looking nearly in that direction almost at the moment you spoke."

"Still I am certain I saw something move."

" What was it like ?"

" It seemed like the shadow of a man creeping in a stooping posture behind yonder thicket of shrubs."

" Oh," exclaimed Mrs. Peeps, " then I'll be bound I can unriddle the mystery without much trouble. It's only the house-dog prowling about the premises, for I fancied I saw him myself not long ago just about the place you speak of. So get rid of this foolish alarm, my dear Amy, for there's no reason to suppose that robbers are on the premises at this hour in the evening."

" Have you so soon forgotten Caleb Kestrel ?"

" Simpleton !" exclaimed the good lady, " what can have put such a foolish notion as that into your head. Caleb Kestrel knows that all the country is up in arms against him, and is it likely he would come into the midst of the greatest danger. However, I shall keep my eyes in that direction, so let us change this disagreeable subject, for I declare you have made me feel quite nervous with this strange notion of yours. By the bye, my love, how much longer is that strange gentleman from London going to remain here."

" I have not heard Mr. Derwent say," she replied, " but as he has ordered his luggage to be unpacked again, I suppose he means to avail himself of the invitation to enjoy the sport that is to be found on the moors at this season of the year."

" Is he an old acquaintance of the squire's ?"

" No," replied Amy, " Farmer Brough told me that they were quite strangers till a few days ago, when an odd circumstance led to his being invited to partake of Mr. Derwent's hospitality. In short this London sportsman was found trespassing in the preserves, but his manner and conversation proved to be so eccentric that Mr. Derwent invited him to spend a few days at the Hall."

" And this Mr. Brassy Popjoy was with him on the day of the attempted assassination ?"

" They had left this house together," answered Amy, " but separated in the storm that overtook them, and Mr. Popjoy and his groom returned home alone after having wandered about on the moors nearly all the night. Next day when news of the supposed murder reached here, the visitor ordered his servant to make immediate preparations to return to London, but on the discovery that Mr. Derwent was not killed, he gave a sudden order to unpack all his boxes and trunks. So here he seems likely to remain as a fixture for some time to come, and I have a notion that, eccentric as he is, he will not prove a very disagreeable addition to our domestic circle. At all events, Farmer Brough seems to have received a visit from him regularly during the three or four last seasons, and from what he says, the Londoner has no worse faults than vanity and eccentricity."

" Well, he must be a strange gentleman, that's certain," exclaimed Mrs. Peeps, " for, would you believe it, he seriously proposed to my husband this morning that they should both travel together round the country for the next three months, and live upon nothing but what they could make by exhibiting the Temple of Arts."

" And what said Mr. Peeps to that ?" asked Amy.

" Why, he told him he would consider the proposition and let him know the result of his deliberation in the course of a few days. But, Lor' bless you, my dear, what business would P. be able to do with a chap like that dangling at his heels."

" Perhaps," laughed Amy, " he might find him useful if he could only persuade him to do the hardest part of the work.—That is to say, Mr. Popjoy might have no objection to carry the Temple of Arts on his back from town to town."

" That hint was thrown out," observed Mrs. Peeps, " but the gentleman's pride rebelled, and he refused to perform any other part than the one you used to do."

" What ! play the triangle and dance ?"

" Yes !" exclaimed the lady indignantly ; " only think of the man's presumption in supposing that he was able to follow in your footsteps ! However Peeps would'nt give a reply at the moment, but promised him one when the matter has been properly considered."

" Poor Mr. Popjoy !" laughed Amy ; " I am afraid like too many wealthy idle people he studies only how he may make himself most ridiculous. He is not the only one who has sought notoriety by committing acts that there is reason to be ashamed of in an after period of life. However, I suppose Mr. Peeps has no intention of indulging his foolish whim."

"You may make yourself quite easy there, my dear girl," replied the other, "for now that through your kindness our circumstances are so greatly altered, we must do nothing that will bring disgrace upon our benefactress."

"Benefactress," exclaimed Amy; "and who, think you, has most reason to be

grateful. Do I not owe all the blessings I have enjoyed to the kindness of yourself and Mr. Peeps, and shall I now receive your thanks, when I have not yet half repaid the heavy debt I owe you? deserted by the man who represented himself as my father, you still struggled on to support me, though at that time I must have been a heavy tax upon your exertions,"

"Well my dear," replied the kind hearted woman, "and do you suppose either Peeps or myself grudged the little you shared with us? No, no, we have at any rate the satisfaction of knowing that whatever we gave was bestowed with a free heart."

No. 14.

"For which you have won my never ending gratitude."

"If you were to talk of gratitude," exclaimed Mrs. Peeps, " I wonder how I and my poor old man can ever express half the thanks we owe you. Look at the home you have given us ;—the ease and comforts that we shall enjoy all the rest of our days, compare them with the trifles it has been in our power to do for you, and then tell me on which side the balance turns. Why in one day, Amy, we shall be more than repaid for all the eighteen years of care that we bestowed upon you."

"Aye," replied Amy, " but your favours were granted at a time when you could barely support yourselves, and yet never did I go without my full share of whatever it was in your power to give. It is now my turn to repay those favours, and there is the less reason for your gratitude, because I cannot experience the same inconvenience that you were compelled to endure. So never, my dear mother, let us speak upon this subject again, for my chief pleasure will consist in seeing you enjoy with me the fortune that has so unexpectedly befallen me."

"Well, my love," replied Mrs. Peeps, "I'll say no more about it since you wish it, but poor dear Peeps and I shall think of it the more, and it will be strange indeed, if ever we forget the kindness that induced you to offer us a home in your house."

Amy was going to make a reply to this, but a sudden exclamation escaped her lips, and starting from her seat, she whispered :—

" There it is again, dear mother !—Do you not see it yonder ?"

" See what, my child ?"

"The shadow of a man stretching across the moonlight on yonder gravelled walk !"

"Oh, I see what you mean," exclaimed Mrs. Peeps, also rising and looking in the direction pointed out. "There certainly is something like a shadow in the place you speak of, and if it isn't the house dog, as I before observed it must be some of the shrubs throwing a black looking shade across the pathway."

" That is impossible," returned Amy with increasing terror, "for see, it has disappeared, which could not have been the case if it had been a tree, as you would have me believe."

"Well, my dear," exclaimed her companion, "I'm sure I can't make out what it can be. All I know is that its very foolish for people to frighten themselves with mere shadows."

"But you forget that where there is a shadow there must be a substance to cause it. In truth, I have at least one enemy to be afraid of, and if he should have formed any plot against me, I fear he will not desist till he has accomplished it."

"Ah!" said Mrs. Peeps, " now you are thinking again of that Caleb Kestrel, I'll be bound."

" I am, indeed," sighed our heroine.

"And do you think there's any occasion to be alarmed about him ?"

" Have I not but too much reason ?"

"You had, it must be confessed," answered the lady, " but now he's got quite enough to do to take care of himself. It's a likely thing that he should stay prowling about this place, when a reward has been offered for his apprehension !"

"Ah!" sighed Amy, " you little know how far the vindictive passions of that man are capable of carrying him. He can set little value on his life when I have heard him say, that, when hard pressed he will shoot himself rather than fall into the hands of any persons that may be sent in pursuit of him."

"Then all I can say is, I hope he may soon have an opportunity of putting his boast into effect."

" I know not how it is," sighed Amy, " but, kind as you have always been to me before, you now treat my fears with a levity that I never till now experienced."

" And if I do so now, my dear child," exclaimed Mrs. Peeps, kissing her, "it is done only that I may drive from your mind all notions that serve to make you uneasy. You thought just now there was a shadow on the path yonder, and, if I laughed at your notion, it was partly that I saw nothing to be afraid of myself, and partly that I wanted you to be of my opinion."

"But surely I could not distrust my own eye sight?"

"You would be very foolish if you did, my dear," answered the good lady, "but we are not to be frightened at every trifle that we see and can't account for at the moment. For my own part I confess myself to have been as foolish as any one ; I've been startled if a mouse did but run across the room, and fancied that nothing but robbers must have been coming to murder me. However, Peep's, who's frightened at nothing, laughed me out of it, and now nothing alarms me ;—no, not even if that horrid, good-for-nothing pedlar was to appear before us."

"Oh, don't speak of him !" cried Amy in terror.

"My dear child, you alarm yourself about that man when I'm convinced there's not the least occasion for it. There was once a reason to be afraid of him, it must be confessed; but now he has quite enough to do to look after himself, and I'll be bound, if the truth were known he's far enough away before this time."

"Then you think it quite unlikely that he is at this moment lurking about these premises."

"I should think him a very great fool if he was," replied Mrs. Peeps, "for who can ever believe that he would be such a madman as to come into the very midst of danger."

"But he may have disguised himself so that no one would know him."

"He must be a cunning chap indeed, if he can deceive my husband," exclaimed the other. "Peeps would know him under any disguise that he might put on; and for that matter so should I, so he had better not show himself where people are on the look out for him. Ah, Amy," she continued after taking breath for a moment, "you shake your head as if in doubt, and yet in all the years that we have known each other you have never found me deceive you."

"True," sighed the maiden, "you have acted towards me as a kind and affectionate mother, but for all that I cannot help thinking you have too much confidence in your own opinion on this particular occasion."

"You still think, then, Caleb Kestrel is lurking in this neighbourhood for some bad purpose ?"

"I feel convinced of it."

"Well then, all I hope is, that he may be," answered the old lady.

"Why do you wish that ?"

"Because there would then be some certainty of his falling into the hands of those that are looking after him," she replied. "The whole country is up in arms, and if he is any where within half a dozen miles from this spot, we may hope to hear of his being in custody before another day has passed over our heads. However, my dear, child, we'll not say anything more upon this subject at present, so as it's growing late, take my advice, and go to bed, for Squire Derwent, and those that went with him, may not return till they have either taken the pedlar, or satisfied themselves that he has left this part of the country."

"But suppose that Kestrel should be near ?"

"I tell you again, my love, that's not at all likely," answered Mrs. Peeps. "Besides, I am going to sleep in the next room, and if anything should happen to alarm you in the night, the slightest noise will immediately bring me to your side. To be sure, there are only the female servants left in the house, but women can shout out lustily when there's danger, and that would be sufficient to put Caleb Kestrel to flight, supposing he should be hardy enough to come when he is sure to meet none but foes."

Kissing her young favourite with all the fondness of a parent, Mrs. Peeps retired to her own dormitory, leaving Amy still watching from the window, and keeping a constant gaze towards the spot where she had twice seen the shadow. The moon was still shining brightly, so that if anything had been stirring about the grounds she could not have failed to see it; but though an hour passed away, all without remained still and silent as the grave itself. Becoming somewhat less uneasy, Amy now began to undress herself, and went to bed, having first put out the lamp, as she feard it might act as a guide to Caleb Kestrel, in the event of her former suspicion being correct. Overpowered by her long watching, Amy soon sunk under the influence of sleep; but she had not been in this state more than half an hour, when she was awoke, and, to her horror, beheld three men, who had just entered by the window, standing round her bed. Her first impulse was to raise a cry of alarm, and as she did so, Kestrel sprang forward, and placing his hand upon her mouth, exclaimed in a low, menacing tone,—

"Another cry like that, girl, and you perish. Be silent, I command, for you have no violence to fear, unless we are forced to resort to it through any disobedience to the warning I have given."

"Why are you here?" she demanded, in a voice that excessive terror had rendered nearly inaudible.

"Question me not now," he replied, "for there is no time to enter into an explanation of the motives that have brought me here."

"Have you come to rob the house?"

"No," he replied, "not a thing will be removed by any of us."

"Then what is your object?"

"To remove you to some far distant place, till Squire Derwent thinks proper to yield to my demand. So we will retire to the next room while you dress yourself, and see that you are not long about it, for we have no time to waste, and must be miles away from here before the return of those that are gone out in search for me."

At this moment, a sudden apparition appeared before them, in the form of Mrs. Peeps, who, having awoke by the outcry of her young friend, had hastily put on a few of her clothes, and proceeded to ascertain the cause of her alarm. No sooner, however, had she entered the room than the two companions of Caleb Kestrel seized her in their arms, muttering at the same time the most fearful threats of vengeance if she ventured to utter a word above a whisper.

"Oh, you three villanous robbers!" exclaimed the lady, scarcely regarding the threats; "so it was you that have been lurking in the garden, and then stole upon us, when you thought all in the house were asleep?"

"Silence, woman!" muttered the pedlar, levelling a pistol at her head; "silence, I say, for if your voice disturbs any of the servants, I will myself quiet you for ever."

"Oh, shoot me, if you please, Caleb Kestrel," she replied, in a more subdued tone; "shoot me, but do not injure the poor girl that has been to me as a beloved daughter."

"Observe my injunctions," exclaimed the ruffian, "and no harm will befall either you or her. All I want is, to remove Amy to a place where she will remain concealed till Mr. Derwent thinks fit to come to the terms I have already proposed. She will be treated with kindness and consideration, and if, for a time, she is deprived of her liberty, the 'squire may blame himself for it, since I warned him, the last time we met, that I should proceed to the utmost extremity, unless he gave me the sum of money I demanded."

"And so," cried Mrs. Peeps, wrathfully, "villain that you are, this poor girl is to suffer because you cannot come to terms with Mr Derwent? But you shall not carry your wicked plans into execution, for even though I die for it the next moment, I'll raise an alarm that shall soon bring people to her assistance."

"Gag the noisy Jezabel," exclaimed the pedlar, "and then drag her into the next room, where we will watch over her whilst this girl prepares herself for the long journey she has to go." Then addressing himself to Amy, he added, in a stern, threatening tone, "You will not fail to use all diligence in getting yourself ready, for we have not an instant to lose, lest the return of your friends should spoil a plan that has so far been carried on with success. And above all, make no attempt to escape, for we are prepared to prevent it, though we may be forced to sacrifice your life."

Having gvien utterance to this menace, he followed his two companions, who by this time had dragged the resisting Mrs. Peeps into the room which she had not long before left. Terrified at leaving the house in company of the three ruffians, yet not daring to disobey the commands of a man in whom she stood in so much dread, Amy began to dress with all the speed she could. This, however, was not enough for Kestrel, who two or three times whispered to her through the door to make more haste, and at length entered the room just as she was ready to accompany him she knew not whither.

"Now," he exclaimed, "put on your bonnet, and whatever outward clothing may be required, for you have a long way to travel, and by the clouds that are gathering, we are likely to have a rough night of it. And above all, keep silence, lest this adventure should turn out worse than there is any occasion for."

Pale and trembling with apprehension, Amy followed all his injunctions, and being at length ready, she was assisted by Caleb Kestrel to descend from the window, into the garden, when being quickly joined by the other two men, they paused for a moment to look round to see that nobody was near to to watch them. Having, satisfied themselves upon that point they made the best of their way to a bye lane within a short distance from the house, where horses were found in readiness to convey them on their journey. Amy was placed upon one which was provided with a side saddle, and the men having mounted, they all set off, at a slow pace at first, but more rapidly when they reached the moors, over which from their being intersected with a great number of paths, there was little probability of their route being traced by any of those who might be induced to follow in pursuit. For nearly an hour they proceeded in silence that was broken only by the quick trampling of their horse's hoofs as they galloped onwards towards the place of their destination. At length the pedlar, who had throughout kept close by the side of Amy, said in a low suppressed tone :—

"You now see, my girl, what an act of folly it is ever to set at defiance one who never yet was defeated in any plan that he had undertaken. Years ago I succeeded in carrying you away from the house of your adopted father, and now, even though a reward has been offered for my apprehension, I have ventured into the midst of the enemy's camp, and taken you away from those you thought yourself so safe amongst."

"Alas!" she sighed ; "why taunt me now that I am unhappy ?"

"I don't want to taunt you, my girl," he replied, "but a man can't help giving utterance to his triumph when he sees that everything has succeeded to the utmost of his hopes. Squire Derwent thought to have taken me, or, at the very least, to have driven me out of the country, and I can't help enjoying the idea of the consternation he will be in when he returns home and finds you have been carried off by the man whose demands he treated with scorn."

"Do you think, then," asked Amy, "that he will make no efforts to snatch me from your hands ?"

"Oh, as for that," answered the ruffian with indifference, "he may do as he pleases, because I know he'll never dream of the place we are going to, and, even if he did, such a strict watch will be kept up, that we should know when to expect him, and before his arrival you would be transported to some other place."

"Whither are you going to lead me ?"

"Why," he replied, "that's a question I don't mind answering now, because you'll have no means of communicating the secret we wish to keep from your friends. Know, then, Amy, that your abode for some little time to come will be at a place called Robin Hood's cave ; a large hollow space in the cliffs that face the sea, and from whence we can remove you in a boat to the opposite coast at any time when there may be reason to suppose that the place of your retreat has been discovered. I dare say, my girl, you think it very hard to be kept there as my prisoner, but, remember, all the annoyance might have been avoided if Squire Derwent had thought proper to have yielded to my demands."

" You wanted to extort money from him ?"

" I did, and he chose to ride rusty about it, and thence arises the difficulty you are now in."

" Name the sum you want," exclaimed Amy, " and I pledge myself it shall be yours, on condition that I am immediate y set at liberty."

" Set you at liberty !" retorted the other with a sneer ; and why should I take your word when I know well enough that the squire would never let the money be paid.   No, no, I have got you now safe enough, and you'll never be set free till the sum demanded is placed in my own hands."

" And what reason will Mr. Derwent have to believe that you will keep your word after he has yielded to your demand ?"

" Ah, there's no occasion to be afraid of that," exclaimed the ruffian, " for all I want is the money, and when that's paid I shall go abroad, and you will return to Derwent Hall."

" Your scheme then will fail," answered Amy, " for he will not submit to extortion whilst there is the law to aid him in discovering the place I have been taken to."

" Humph !" exclaimed the pedlar, " he must be a strange sort of lover then if he suffers you to remain in my power when it only requires a sum of money to buy you off.   Besides, I shall dictate a letter that you must write, describing the misery of your situation, and earnestly entreating him to lose no time in acceding to the only terms that can restore you to freedom."

" I would rather perish," cried Amy, " than make myself a party in so villanous a transaction.   Unhappily you have succeeded in carrying me away from the protection of my friends, but no selfish consideration shall ever induce me to demand such a sacrifice from Mr. Derwent as you have proposed."

" Aye, so you think now," exclaimed the pedlar, " but your notions will be much altered before you have been in the cave a week.   There the wealth you have just succeeded to will be utterly useless, and after a little reflection you will acknowledge that it will be better to sacrifice half your property than remain cooped up in a cave that is visited by none but smugglers."

" Smugglers !" cried Amy with alarm ; " am I then doomed to the society of such lawless villains."

" You are indeed, my dear," he replied with a chuckle of delight at the terror she had manifested.   " They are not exactly the sort of people that you would choose for your companions, I dare say ; but needs must when the devil drives, and it will be in your own power to shorten your visit at Robin Hood's cave, whenever you think proper to send the note I have spoken of."

" Villain !" exclaimed Amy, " you can see only the triumph that is so far yours ; but be assured the hour of retribution is nearer than you imagine.   Every exertion will be used to discover the place you are conveying me to, and when once a clue has been obtained, no time will be lost in bringing to justice all those who have been concerned in this cruel outrage.   Agree you then to my proposition ; suffer me to return to the home you have taken me from, and I promise any sum of money you may think proper to name, even though it should amount to half my fortune."

" All that sounds very well, Amy," he replied, " and I dare say there may be some fools in the world that would be taken in by your fine promises. I, however, must have the money paid down beforehand, and when that has been done you may go your ways, whilst I betake myself abroad, where I may enjoy my fortune without fear of being laid hold of by the law."

" How do I know that my liberty would follow when once you have received the money you want to extort from me."

" Humph ! you doubt my honour then ?"

" Honour ? what honour can I expect in the man that has by force carried me from my friends and home ?"

" Aye, aye, my girl," exclaimed Celeb Kestrel, " it may be all very well to blame me for what has been done ; but a desperate man like me can't stand upon trifles, and as there was no other way to bring Squire Derwent to his senses, I determined on a bold plan at once, and have taken away the woman that he was about to marry. He little thought to lose you in this way, and when he finds there is no other way to get you back, he'll give all I ask, as well as a promise not to take further proceedings against me. So take my advice, Amy,—write the letter I spoke of as soon as you get to the cave, and if it's delivered to the squire in the course of to-morrow, you may return to Derwent Hall with no further cause of complaint than a few hours confinement. What say you, girl, will you follow the counsel that is to set you free?"

"If I reply now," said Amy, "it would be to reject your proposition with all the scorn it merits. Unfortunately, however, I shall have time to consider what you have said, and when the proposal has been considered, I will let you know the result."

"Ah," he exclaimed, "then I may consider the thing as settled."

"Do no such thing," she replied, "for if I do yield it will only be at the last extremity, when no other chance of my rescue remains. But I feel assured it will not come to that, for Mr. Derwent will never relax in his endeavours to find me, and you will then be compelled to restore me to that freedom of which I have been unwarrantably deprived."

"Don't make too sure of being rescued by your lover," exclaimed Caleb Kestrel, "for there is little chance of his ever finding the cave, and even if he did succeed in such an attempt, I should have plenty of time to remove you from it before he could reach the place. And mark me, this is no vain boast of mine, as my two companions here can bear witness if you ask 'em."

"Be that as it may," answered Amy, "I can at least bear my misfortunes with resignation."

"Yes, yes," he replied, "its easy to say so now, but confinement will soon grow wearisome, and particularly to you, who have always been used to a constant change of scene with the people I placed you with. They took you about from place to place, and now, when you find yourself shut up in a cave, the contrast will be so great that you would rather give up your whole fortune, and return to your former wandering life, than be for ever deprived of the liberty that forms a part of your being."

"You have judged me wrong, if you believe that I am to be influenced by a little inconvenience and restraint," answered the girl. "Hardships I have been used to all my life, and it will now be easy for me to suffer all your malice can inflict, rather than yield to the cruel extortion you have proposed."

Just then, Dick Ratcliffe, who had been a little in advance, rode back and with some consternation, announced that he had just seen a couple of horsemen riding at great speed across the moors, and suggesting that they should slightly change their own direction, and pursue the remainder of the journey in silence. Kestrel quite coincided with him, and after giving the necessary orders with respect to their route, they set forward at increased speed to reach the cave, which was now not more than five miles off.

We must now return to Cecil Derwent, who with his friend arrived at home at an early hour in the morning, after an unsuccessful search for Caleb Kestrel. It was sometime before he could rouse the still sleeping inmates, but at length on gaining admittance to the hall, he was startled by hearing a moaning noise as of some person endeavouring to call for assistance. Peeps was also struck by the same sounds, and after listening for a moment or two, he exclaimed in a tone of alarm,—

"If that ain't the voice of Mrs. P, I'm a Dutchman! The poor dear woman has been taken ill in our absence, and them sleepy servants havn't heard her."

With this he bolted up-stairs, closely followed by Mr. Derwent, and made his way to the room from whence the notes of tribulation seemed to proceed. On entering the apartment his consternation and alarm may be imagined when he beheld the helpless situation in which his better half had been left by the thre ruffians who had visited the house during the night. The handkerchief that secured her arms behind her, and the one which had been placed over her mouth to prevent an alarm being raised, were quickly removed, and a glass of wine having been administered as a restorative, the poor woman was soon able to give in a hurried manner the details with which the reader is already acquainted. At the first word that intimated the violence which had been used to carry off Amy, the squire rushed into the chamber she had occupied, and there saw quite enough to convince him of the truth of all he had heard. Maddened by the dreadful misfortune that had occurred he flew back to the room he had just quitted, and in hurried accents demanded if Mrs. Peeps knew who had been guilty of the outrage that had been committed during his absence from home.

"Oh yes, sir," she replied, "that villain Caleb Kestrel, as you may suppose was at the head of the mischief. He and two others got in at the window of Amy's room, and nothing would suit but she must dress herself, and go away with them."

"Did you hear anything by which we may form a notion of where they have taken her to?" demanded Cecil Derwent, with breathless haste.

"Lor' bless you, no, sir," she replied, "they only said something about having a long journey before them, and they were in a terrible hurry to be sure to get away before you returned."

"And you made no attempt to alarm the servants?" he exclaimed in a tone of reproach.

"Don't fancy anything of the kind," replied Mrs. Peeps, "for I began to scream out as loud as I could, and I had no sooner done so than two of the fellows presented their pistols at my head, and threatened to blow out my brains if I attempted to make the least noise again. Then they gagged me to prevent any alarm being given, and my arms were tied behind me, to make sure that I should not be able to remove the handkerchief from my mouth till they had got far enough away to make their escape certain."

"And what of Amy?"

"Ah, she was terribly frightened, as you may suppose, sir," answered the lady. "The poor girl looked as pale as death with fear, and yet she managed to command herself so as to appear as if she was not a bit alarmed."

"What reason did Kestrel give for the violence he offered?"

"A very bad one."

"Was it revenge?"

"Partly so," replied Mrs. Peeps, "but I think his principal motive was to extort money from you as the price of her deliverance.

"My whole fortune then shall be devoted to that purpose, if I can only find the means to negociate with him," exclaimed Cecil Derwent. "Aye, I will give all I possess in the world to purchase Amy's liberty, even though I become a beggar ever afterwards."

"Between you and I, sir," interposed Peeps, "there ought to be no occasion to do anything of the kind. The magistrates will give orders for all the assistance you want, and I think with a little management we may soon hear something of this Caleb Kestrel, and of course wherever he is, poor Amy is sure not to be far off."

"You forget, my dear friend, what an artful scoundrel we have to deal with."

"Ah, that he's a cunning chap there's no denying," answered Peeps, "but still there may be others in the world quite as deep as him. Now, for my own part, I've had a pretty fair share of experience in the world, and as I mean to take an active part in the pursuit of this precious villain, I think it likely enough it will not be long before we hear something of him."

"In all your travels through this country have you ever met with a place where he would be likely to seek concealment?"

"Oh, yes, sir, plenty," replied Peeps;—"there's lots of old stone quarries and mines that have been long since disused. Then there's the Deserted Hut on the moors, which is a likely place for a man to hide himself in if he wanted to keep out of sight for a little while."

"We have already searched the Deserted Hut when we first went in pursuit of the pedlar."

"Very true, sir, but it don't follow that he's not there now. It's nearly twelve hours ago since we were there, and he may have taken the poor girl there, to remain till there's light enough this morning to make his way across the moors."

"At all events, we'll take the place in our way," answered Mr. Derwent, "but from the little I know of the man, I think he is more likely to have taken her some distance at once. Besides, your wife says Caleb Kestrel made a remark that no time was to be lost as they had a long journey before them."

"And yet the fellow may only have said it to deceive us," observed Mrs. Peeps. "He's as cunning as a fox, and must have been lying wait some hours in the garden before he and his comrades ventured to break into the house."

No. 15.

"Why do you think they were lurking about the premises?" asked the squire

"Because Amy herself almost as good as told me so."

"Ha! how could she have been aware of it?"

"Why, I'll tell you all about it, sir," replied Mrs. Peeps. "I was sitting with Amy in her own room just before she went to bed, and all of a sudden, in the midst of our conversation, she started up, 'and pointing towards the shrubbery, asked me if I didn't see something like the shadow of a man stretching across the gravel path."

"And did you see anything like what she said?"

"I saw a shadow, certainly," she replied, "but I couldn't make out whether it was a human being's or not; so I tried to laugh her out of the notion, and by way of making her mind more easy, told her that it was nothing but the house-dog prowling about the premises."

"Was anything more seen of it?" asked Mr. Derwent.

"Yes," she replied, "and the next time I thought it looked like the shadow of a tree, or something of that kind. However, I now feel pretty certain it was Caleo strolling about the place till the servants were gone to bed."

"Had that thought struck you before," exclaimed the squire, "our poor Amy would have been spared all her present anxiety and alarm."

"Very true," observed the ex-showman, "and poor Mrs. P. would have escaped being gagged and having her arms tied behind, for all the world as if she was going to be hanged. But never mind, it's too late to think of those things now, so let's see if something can't be done to discover Amy and get her away from that black muzzled fellow of a pedlar."

"Aye," sighed Mr. Derwent, "that is my most anxious desire, but how can we hope to prosecute a successful search when we know not even which way they went after leaving this house."

"I think I may be able to assist you, then," exclaimed Mr. Brassy Popjoy, who till now had not ventured to interpose a word. "The fact is, when I lost you last night, I could see no fun in wandering by myself over the moor, so I made my way towards the place you call the Deserted Hut, because from that spot I happen to know my way pretty well to Derwent Hall."

"Well," exclaimed the squire, impatiently, "what did you see there?"

"Why, at the distance of a few hundred yards from the place where I was standing, three or four persons on horseback gallopped by me, and made their way across the heath."

"Could you see whether there was a female among them?"

"I'm almost sure there was," replied Popjoy, "for one of 'em wore a veil, or something of that kind that streamed out like a flag at the masthead."

"Did she call out, or make any other signal of alarm?"

"Not that I heard," he replied, "but as she was surrounded by men, it's likely enough she may have been frightened into silence."

"Were they going in a direction towards the sea coast?"

"I should say they were," answered Popjoy, "but perhaps you had better not take my word for that, for I dare say as you go along you'll meet with more people that will be able to assist you in the right way to take. And now, with your permission, Mr. Derwent, I'll go and lie down for an hour or so, for hang me if this hasn't been a night of fatigue such as I never experienced in London."

As he was considered rather in the way than otherwise, when anything of importance was to be done, no objection was made to this, and the cockney having taken his leave, Mr. Derwent inquired if all who had accompanied him in his former search were willing to go again to recover Amy from the hands of the villain who had treacherously stolen her away. To this a cheerful response was given in the affirmative, and the squire, having first provided each man with a brace of pistols and sufficient ammunition, proposed that no time should be lost in commencing a task that had so important an aim in view.

"That's exactly what I've been thinking of myself, sir," exclaimed Peeps, "for if the girl is to be rescued from Caleb Kestrel, there ought not to be a moment lost in setting about it. Mrs. P. will remain behind to look after the household matters, and if she feels rather uneasy at my running into danger, she has only to recollect that it's done for the sake of our poor Amy, and then I'm sure she'll rest quite satisfied."

"To be sure I shall," replied the lady, "but for all that, Mr. Peeps, you needn't run yourself into unnecessary danger. I know what a foolish, hot-headed fellow you are, and when it's to serve the poor girl that has been with us so long, I shouldn't wonder if you was to place yourself at the head of the party instead of remaining beyond the reach of danger till you see whether your services will be required or not."

"Don't make yourself at all uneasy about that, my loved Angelina!" returned her affectionate husband, "for when there are so many other people willing to take a good share of the risk, you may be sure I shall not put myself too forward in this affair."

"In that case," observed Mr. Derwent, "we had better dispense with your services, for we shall require a great deal of courage as well as prudence, and unless all are ready to come to blows at the requisite moment, we may as well remain where we are, and leave everything to chance."

"Oh, never mind what I say before Mrs. P.," whispered the proprietor of the Temple of Arts. "I'm obliged to gammon her a little you see, sir, or there might be fits of hysterics, and swooning away, and all that sort of thing, which are very unpleasant to the nerves when a man is going out on a dangerous duty." Then addressing himself to his better half, he added. "My love, you had better not give way to lowness of spirits during my absence, for there'll be enough of us to gain an easy victory over the enemy if there's only three of them, as Mr. Brassy Popjoy reports. So make yourself quite easy, and expect us to return with Amy — that is to say, if we happen to meet with Caleb Kestrel and his comrades, and can persuade 'em to give up the girl."

Mrs. Peeps was, or at least pretended to be, quite satisfied with this promise on the part of her liege lord and husband; and soon afterwards the squire, followed by all who were to accompany him, proceeded to the stables, where the requisite number of horses were saddled and brought out for the conveyance of the party to their place of destination, wherever it might happen to be. Mr. Derwent was the first to mount, and his example was followed by all the rest except Peeps, who, never having been on horseback, was sorely puzzled how to find his way into the saddle. This affair was, however, soon managed through the assistance of one of his companions, and all being now ready for the march, Mr. Derwent and his followers commenced their journey in search of the lost Amy.

CHAPTER XIV.

THE LOVERS.—FUTURE PROSPECTS.—NEWS OF THE LOST ONE.—FRANK MARLDALE TAKES HIS DEPARTURE IN SEARCH OF AMY.—HIS ARRIVAL AT THE END OF HIS JOURNEY, AND THE REASONS HE HAS FOR BELIEVING THAT HIS TROUBLES WILL NOT BE WITHOUT ITS REWARD.

IT may appear extraordinary that Frank Marldale should have remained at home when everybody else had manifested such laudable zeal to assist in the recovery of Amy, but the truth is, he had important duties to perform on his farm, and his services, though freely offered, were refused by Mr. Derwent, on the ground that there were already sufficient persons engaged in pursuit of the pedlar and his confederates. Mary Everett, however, thought it a reproach that he should be almost the only person in the neighbourhood, and when he visited her as usual in the evening, she laughingly asked him if he had lost all sense of gratitude, that he alone remained at home when his services were so much required to assist in the recovery of the unfortunate Amy. Frank felt rather abashed at the question, and, with some confusion, explained to her that his assistance had been offered to the squire, and refused, on the ground that his presence was required at home.

"But," added he, on seeing that his excuse was hardly satisfactory, "my heart is as much in this cause as if I was more actively engaged in it; and if it will afford you any gratification, Mary, I will set out this very moment, and continue my search till I have either learnt tidings of Amy, or have heard that she has been found, and once more restored to the protection of her friends."

"And you would do that to please me?"

"Entirely so."

"Then, my dear Frank, I'll impose no such task upon you," she replied. "In truth, I see no necessity for you to go, when so many have kindly volunteered their services; and the reproaches you just now listened to, were intended more in jest than in earnest. In a few days, however, we may expect the return of our friends, and, then, if they should bring no good tidings, you may go in search of Amy; and, from the interest you feel in the cause, I am assured you will discover the place where she is concealed, be it ever so difficult to trace out."

"And as my reward, you will no longer postpone the day that is to make me the happiest of men?"

"That will depend upon circumstances," laughed the maiden; "for you know the understanding between us is, that our marriage shall take place at the same time that Amy gives her hand to the squire."

"Which, no doubt will be as soon as she is rescued from that ruffian, Caleb Kestrel," returned her lover. "As her husband, Mr. Derwent, will be able to protect her from all further violence, and the pedlar will cease his persecutions as soon as he finds they can no longer be carried on with impunity. So as their union is not likely to be long delayed, I'll wait with all the patience I can for the period that is to make you mine. And I think, Mary, I can promise you a happy home, for the farm is a profitable one; and now that the squire has promised me a new lease, upon the most favourable terms, I shall make great improvements upon the land, in the hope, that by and by it may rival your uncle's farm."

"Ah, dear Frank," she exclaimed, "who, only a few days ago, would have anticipated such a delightful change as this? You were then suspected of being the murderer of Squire Derwent, and now you have found him your kindest friend and benefactor."

"And did you, Mary, believe the charge made against me?"

"Never for an instant."

"But there were many that did; and yet they ought to have known that I was incapable of so dreadful an act."

"Nay, Frank," answered Mary, "people may have been afraid you were carried away by a feeling of revenge against the squire, but I can boldly assert, that every one sincerely felt for you, and that all hoped you would be able to prove your innocence. And it was proved, too, and that by the very man you were supposed to have slain."

"And during that period of terrible suspense, you never once thought I committed the act?"

"I was sure you did not," she exclaimed, taking his hand, "for have I not ever found you kind and gentle? Harbouring no bad thought against your fellow men, and always endeavouring to do a service to those who needed assistance. These things came into my mind, Frank, and I could not believe the charge, though, it must be owned, my heart was almost breaking when I reflected that many a one has been sacrificed by circumstantial evidence, that there is no means of contradicting. You, however, were more fortunate, and having already established your innocence, the esteem of all your former friends has been fully restored. Still, the perpetrator of the act is at large, and appears to be as determined on mischief as ever, though one would have thought his chief care would have been to remove himself as far as possible from the neighbourhood where his crime was committed."

"Aye," replied her lover, "but the thirst for gold is strong upon him, and he will run any risk to to extort from Mr. Derwent the price of Amy's future safety. He has even gone so far as to demand half the squire's fortune, and I believe it would have been given to him but for the last act of violence he has committed. As it is, however, it is to be hoped he will not remain much longer at liberty, and then effectual means will be taken to prevent a repetition of his infamous designs."

" By transporting him for life I suppose ?"

" That is the mildest punishment he can expect," replied Frank Marldale " and far beneath his deserts, for though he did not absolutely kill his victim, there can be no doubt as to what his real intention was."

"But suppose after all, he should succeed in baffling the search of his pursuers ?"

" Then the squire and Amy will be in as much danger as ever, for revenge will urge him on to accomplish his blood-thirsty design. So you see, Mary, no trouble must be spared to lay hold of him, in order to prevent a crime that I tremble to think of."

" If you are speaking of Caleb Kestrel, I fancy there's not much doubt that we shall hear of his capture before long," exclaimed farmer Brough who had entered the room unperceived by them.

" You have heard tidings of him then ?" asked the young man.

" I have ; and my only wish is that Squire Derwent knew as much as I do, for then he would know what direction to follow, and Kestril would soon find himself in the strong grasp of the law."

" Is your information to be relied on, uncle ?" asked Mary.

" Oh yes, there can be no doubt of that," he replied, " for two farmers of my acquaintance happened to be riding across the moors last night, or rather at an early hour this morning, and they saw three horsemen with a mounted female among them, and from their description there can be no doubt as to who the person's were ?"

" Did they make no effort to rescue the poor girl ?" asked Frank.

" They would have been troubled to do that," replied the farmer, " for just as they were going to ride after them, the others changed their direction and galloped across the moors at their utmost speed, seemingly with the intention of making for the sea coast. Now that is a piece of information that would be useful to the squire, who might make inquiries in the quarter, and perhaps rescue the girl from the villian's that have taken her away by force."

" Good heaven's !" cried Mary, " suppose their next step would be to take her across the sea ?"

" That's exactly what I'm afraid of," answered her uncle. " They may take her over to a foreign land, and then make what bargan they please with Mr. Derwent for her restitution. At any rate poor Amy's situation is a very terrible one, and the sooner a search is made along the sea coast, the greater chance there will be of releasing her from the danger."

" Then the task of proceeding there shall be mine," exclaimed Frank Marldale. " I will return home, mount one of my strongest horses, and if I obtain no information it shall be through no want of exertion on my part."

" That's spoken like a noble, generous hearted fellow as you are," cried farmer Brough, shaking him violently by the hand. " I expected nothing less from you Frank, and egad I wish you may have the honour of finding the girl, for I know nothing will give you greater satisfaction than to be the means of restoring happiness to those that are now suffering as much anguish and distress. By the bye, though," he added, so suddenly recollecting himself, " the sea coast extends many miles, and I'm afraid you'll find it no easy matter to pitch upon the exact spot where they are to be found."

"If you are only certain they have gone in that direction it shall not be long before I hear something of the fugitives."

"Do you know any likely place where they may shelter themselves."

"I do," answered Frank Marldale, "for two years since, when I was ordered to the sea side on account of my health, I went to a retired place, the neighbourhood of which was infested with a daring band of smugglers, and it strikes me as being more than probable that Caleb Kestrel may have taken his victim among that lawless horde. At any rate I will make strict inquiries there, and perhaps the promise of a handsome reward may procure for me all the information I require."

"But will you not run great risk in going there ?" asked Mary in no little alarm.

"Why, I don't think there's much danger," answered her lover, and even if there was, something must be hazarded where there is such an important object in view. Beside, the men we are speaking of are only to be feared by those who go to interfere with their unlawful calling, and as I have no such purpose, I may expect to be treated with courtesy, if not with respect."

"Yet, if they are friends of Caleb Kestrel they will not give you the information you require, and may perhaps make you their prisoner in order to prevent your designs against the man you are seeking for."

"Nay, there your fears are groundless," answered her lover, "for were they to be guilty of an act like that, it would be sure to bring people in search of me, and in the end involve themselves in trouble. So now having, as I hope, relieved your alarm on my account, I suppose I may go on my errand without leaving you in much doubt as to the success of my mission."

"So that I can be assured of your safety, Frank," she replied, "I will offer no opposition to a plan that I am most anxious should come to a successful termination. I, however think it would be prudent for you to seek for Mr. Derwent in the first place, and then with his assistance, and that of the persons that are with him, you might venture among the smugglers without danger, and make more sure of relieving Amy from the evil men into whose hands she has so unfortunately fallen."

"Well, exclaimed Father Brough, "I must say there's some reason in what the girl says, and I join with her in recommending that you first seek the squire, and then proceed to the other business just as he may think proper to advise. It would look like meaning something if several persons accompany you, and there'll be less risk of being roughly handled by these smugglers than if you should rashly venture among them alone."

"Your advice is too good to be lightly thought of," answered Frank, " but the difficulty is—where am I to look for Mr. Derwent, who is himself following an uncertain pursuit?"

"Oh, I dare say he's not far off from the same place," exclaimed the farmer. "No doubt he has met with persons who have seen the fugitives, and in that case, he'll not fail to make his way to the sea coast. So follow your first plan my boy, and in case there should be occasion for their use, don't fail to take with you a couple of pistols for your protection."

"Alas!" cried Mary, "of what use would they be in the event of falling in with a number of lawless men, who hesitate at no crime in the pursuit of their business."

"Are you still in fear for me then ?" asked Frank.

"I cannot but confess my weakness," answered the maiden, " and it is scarcely to be wondered at when I know that in a cause like the one you have undertaken, no sense of danger will deter you from bringing the inquiry to a successful end."

"Had I no one but myself to care for," he replied, "there might be some ground for your alarm. As it is, however, my thoughts will be directed towards another object, and for your sake, Mary, I will run no further danger than may be absolutely necesary for the restoration of your friend, so let that be your consolation during my short absence, for I feel certain that if vigorous measures are taken, the task I have now in hand will be brought to a successful termination before many hours have passed away."

"The lad's right enough there," exclaimed Farmer Brough, "for if any time is wasted, he had better by half not undertake the affair at all. Caleb Kestrel must not know that the enemy is near till the moment he is ready to pounce upon him, or there'll be a sudden shifting of quarter, and then it may not be so easy to discover where Amy has been removed to."

"True, farmer," returned Frank, "and for that reason, my first care shall be to find Mr. Derwent, whose caution and judgment in an affair of this kind, will be better than my own. I will act throughout entirely under his control, and no doubt we shall return before long with a good account of the errand we have been upon."

"And accompanied by Amy," I hope," observed Mary Everett.

"Aye," joined the farmer, and what would be almost as good, with Caleb Kestrel as a prisoner. Hang the fellow! he has caused nothing but confusion and alarm in the neighbourhood ever since he first made his appearance here, and I suppose we shall never be restored to our former quiet till he is transported. In short, we must lay hold of him by hook, or by crook, or we shall always be having the same trouble to go through over and over again."

"There now," exclaimed Frank Marldale, "as my plans are all arranged I'll lose no time in putting them into operation. I have but to return home, give a few necessary orders to my people as to what is necessary to be done during my absence, and then set off for my place of destination as fast as a swift horse can carry me. In the mean time, Mary will remain under your charge, Farmer Brough, and I shall rely upon you not to suffer her to give way to feelings of alarm or despondency on my account."

The farmer promised to pay strict attention to to the charge that was given him, and Frank took his leave to return to his own home, where the few arrangements he had to make were soon settled, and he set forth on his journey through the darkness of night had set in some hours previously. However, the country he had to travel over was well known to him, and he proceeded at a rapid pace across the moors, taking a path that would save him some few miles in reaching his place of destination. During three or four hours he proceeded on his way without meeting any person, and just as daylight was appearing, found himself near the place where his inquiries were to be carried on. Another quarter of an hour brought him to a small lonely public house near the sea-side, the landlord of which was up, and attending to a customer who had gained admittance even at that early hour of the morning. His horse having been taken to a shed that served the purpose of a stable, Frank Marldale entered the house, ordered breakfast to be provided for him, and then seating himself beside the man, bethought himself how he should contrive to introdue the questions he wished to put to him. It was easy to see, in fact, that the fellow belonged to the band of smugglers, and he was, therefore, just the very person of all others that Marldale wished to speak to. It was true Farmer Brough had recommended that no step should be taken till Mr. Derwent had been consulted, but here was an opportunity that had not been anticipated, and Frank determined to open the business as soon as he could find a favourable opportunity. At length, finding no other way to open the subject, he commenced the conversation b y inquiring of the man if he lived in that neighbourhood.

The man grumbled out an affirmation.

"Then of course you know most of the people hereabouts."

"Yes, I know a good many on' em."

"Have any strangers arrived here within the last few hours?"

"What do you want to know for?" asked the man, turning round and staring him hard in the face.

"I had a motive for asking the question," replied Frank, and I thought you could have no objection to answer it."

"Humph! but I never make myself too free with strangers."

"Nor do I ask questions without expecting to pay for any information I may receive," replied Marldale ; and then finding that no attention was paid to his hint, he added :—"I see friend, your mug is empty ; will you suffer it to be filled at my expense?"

"No," was the gruff reply.

"You are high-minded methinks."

"At any rate I can pay for what I drink," replied the fellow ; and its not my way to take a favour from anybody."

"If that's the case, Master Jabez Thompson," exclaimed the landlord, rather piqued at losing an order for more ale, and you are so very full of cash, I'd be glad if you'd just settle that trifle of three and tenpence that has been so long scored up against you,"

"I didn't say I was full of cash," replied the countryman, somewhat surprised by the demand. "But never mind, if I haven't any money, I've money's worth about me, so give me five bob for this little bit of gold that I picked up yesterday afternoon, and you may make me quits by taking the three and ten pence out of it."

To the surprise of Frank Marldale, he recognized in the bit of gold, as the man called it, the identical portion of a locket that he had seen Amy wear round her neck. Here then was a proof that she had been in the neighbourhood, and it now remained to discover where she had been taken to. Requesting to look at the trinket, he inquired of the landlord if he intended to purchase it.

"Not I," he replied. What's the use of a thing like that to me, when I'm hard up for money. So you may keep your rubbish for me Jabez, and you can pay your score the first time you're in cash."

"Will you sell it to me?" asked Frank of the man. "I'll give double the price you have asked for it."

I believe the price you first fixed upon is nearer the real value, he replied but the truth is it closely resembles one that belonged to a female friend of mine, and if it should turn out to be hers she will be glad to have it restored."

"Does the lady live far from here.?"

"She did."

Then how can it be hers when I tell you I found it in this neighbourhood no longer ago than yesterday?"

Frank Marldale counted out the silver he had offered for the trinket, and having paid the man, inquired of him if he had seen a female thereabouts to whom a jewel of that description was likely to have belonged."

"No," he replied, we've very few women in these parts that can afford to dress themselves out in finery."

"Have you heard that any such person as I speak of has been seen near the spot where you found the piece of gold?"

"Well, if you must know," replied Jabez Thompson, I have been told that a female came here yesterday."

"How did she come?"

"On horseback."

"Was she alone, or accompanied by any person?"

"I tell you I didn't see her," answered the man, but I have been told there were three or four persons with her."

"All like herself, on horseback, I suppose."

"Well I rather think they were. But I say, Mister Stranger, what are you asking all these questions for?"

"Because there is no doubt the lady is a person of whom I am in pursuit."

"The devil," exclaimed Jabez Thompson, then may be she's a runaway wife of yours."

"She is no relation to me whatever," answered Frank, but having fallen into bad hands, I have followed to rescue her."

"Then I doubt, sir, you'll have some trouble."

" Why do you think so, my friend ?"

" Because if anybody has run away with her as you say, he'll take precious good care not to let any one find her."

" Harkee, my good fellow," exclaimed Frank Marldale ; " the person I am seeking has been stolen from her home by a villain, for the purpose of extorting money. I am determined to release her from his hands, and any assistance or information you may afford shall be paid for at any price you choose to name.'"

" What if I was to ask a hundred pounds ?"

(Marldale recognises the locket in the possession of Jabez.)

" It should be in your hands within twelve hours."

The man paused, scratched his head, and then said with a cunning expression of countenance,—

" Well, this is a darnation good offer of yours, young gentleman, and I only wish I could tell you where to find the lady. To be sure I might get shot by some of our chaps here for telling tales, but then with a hundred pounds in my pocket I might go somewhere else and live."

No. 16½

"Are you willing to assist me in discovering the place she has been taken to ?"

"Yes, sir, I'm willing enough to assist," he replied, "but the truth of it is I don't know where she's gone."

"But you could hear, I suppose ?"

"Perhaps I might," answered the countryman ; "but our people hereabouts are precious close chaps, and if I was to put questions to any of 'em, they'd think there was some reason for it."

"But if proper caution were to be observed, I don't see how any suspicion could be awakened. Besides, the promised reward is worth some little trouble, and if the matter is brought to a satisfactory termination you shall have fifty pounds more than I have already offered."

"Hang me if I know how to find the lady," exclaimed Jabez, evidently willing to give his assistance, but alarmed at the consequences it might bring upon him if it should be known to his companions that he had given any information. Then, seeing that the landlord was no longer in the room ,and that they were quite alone, he said, putting his mouth to Frank's ear, "There's a great many pits and caves, sir, in these parts, where a person might be hid for years, and no one would ever be able to find him."

"And you think the lady has been taken to one of them ?"

"I'm almost certain she has."

"Can you direct me to the right one ?"

"No ; and even if I knew I wouldn't tell you."

"Why not ?"

"Because if you were seen going there, some of the people would be sure to shoot you ?"

"Then I must wait till the arrival of further assistance," exclaimed Frank Marldale. "Some friends will soon join me, and when we can go in a body there will be little to fear from any violence such as you speak of. By the bye, I suppose you will undertake the task of guiding us to all the places where the lady is likely to be concealed."

"Oh, yes, I'll do that if you like," he replied, "but I must have half the reward paid down before I stir an inch with you."

"I dare say that can be managed easily enough," exclaimed Frank Marldale; "for one of the gentlemen I am expecting to meet has provided himself with a large sum of money for the purpose of defraying any expense that may occur."

"Then I'd advise him to take care of it," answered Jabez Thompson, "for people aint particularly honest down in these parts, and if it was known he had money with him, he'd be sure to lose it, and very likely his life as well."

"You don't give the neighbourhood a very good character."

"Bless your soul, sir, it don't matter," replied the man, "for every body knows what sort of a place it is, and what I say wont damage its character much. But you don't know yet, sir, where to find me when I'm wanted."

"I suppose we can have no better meeting place than this ?"

"Yes, this will do very well," answered Jabez ; "only, mind you, the landlord mustn't know that I'm going to be your guide, for he's as big a rogue as ere a one of us, and would just as soon send a bullet through my head as look at me."

"You needn't be afraid of my saying anything about it," replied Marldale, "for I have an interest in keeping the affair as close as possible, for should my designs be made known care would be taken to foil me."

"And when do you think I shall be wanted ?"

"That is quite uncertain at present ; you will, however, remain about here till the time comes, so as to be ready to accompany us at a moment's notice."

The landlord entering at this moment with his guest's breakfast, Jabez Thompson left the room, and was presently afterwards seen loitering towards the sea shore. Frank then commenced his morning's meal, which, after his long ride, he was able to do ample justice to, but had scarcely got half through it when the ned to say that two gentlemen had just arrived, who had also ordered breakfast, which, with the first guest's permission, they would take in the same room with him. Frank Marldale could not of course object to so reasonable a request, and presently afterwards who should present themselves before him but Mr. Derwent and the former proprietor of the Temple of Arts. The surprise occasioned by this unexpected meeting did not exceed the pleasure it afforded, and in explanation Mr. Derwent informed his young friend that the search had hitherto proved unavailing, but that they had been assured on pretty good authority, there was every reason to believe the young lady had been carried to that part of the sea coast, and was concealed in one of the numerous caverns that there abounded.

"Your information is certainly correct, sir," replied Frank Marldale, "for I have just been informed that a female, mounted on horseback, was brought here yesterday by three men, and I have the most positive proof that the female was Amy."

"What is your proof, my dear sir?" asked the squire.

"This broken locket which she constantly wore round her neck," answered Frank, exhibiting the trinket which he had just before purchased of Jabez Thompson. He then related the circumstance under which it was found as a confirmation of the fact that the person they were in search of had been there.

"That's certainly the identical locket of our poor little Amy," exclaimed Peeps, after examining it with great attention. "I could swear to it from among a thousand, and so could Mrs. P., too, if any further proof was wanting."

"The finding of this jewel is a most extraordinary piece of good fortune," observed Mr. Derwent, "for it serves to convince us that we have pursued the right course in coming here, and that fact alone will inspire us with fresh determination to bring our search to a successful termination. But the next question is, how are we to discover the right cave, when it seems there are so many of them in the neighbourhood?"

"All that may be more easily managed than you think for," replied Frank Marldale, "for I have seen a man who has undertaken to make the necessary inquiries as to where the young lady has been conveyed, and when he has ascertained that fact, he will guide us to the place."

"Is the fellow to be relied on?" asked Mr. Derwent.

"I rather think he is," answered Frank, "for the truth is I have taken it upon myself to offer him a very large reward in consideration that he performs his duty faithfully. In short, a hundred and fifty pounds is the sum, half of which he insists upon receiving before he goes a step to serve us."

"Is the man one of the smugglers I have heard so much talk about?"

"Yes, and glories in the name of Jabez Thompson."

"Excuse me for interfering, gentlemen," exclaimed Peeps, "but I really think it's hardly respectable to have to do with a smuggler."

"Perhaps so, under most circumstances," replied the squire, "but in the present instance there's no one that can serve us so well as a man that knows all the hiding places in the vicinity. My friend has therefore done well to engage him, and I am now all anxiety to commence a search, that is to restore the lost Amy to us."

"We must not be in too great a hurry about that," exclaimed Frank, "for the man tells me the smugglers will stoutly resist us, and that they will not stop short even at bloodshed rather than suffer us to enter any of their retreats."

"Then what is the course you advise?"

"Why, in the first place, one of us must ride over to the next town, which is not more than five miles from hence, and there represent the whole affair to a magistrate, who will of course send a number of constables to aid us in the rescue. Not that I should hesitate to accompany you alone in such a course as this, but prudence ought not to be neglected when the consequence of a defeat would prove most disastrous to the young lady."

"This affair begins to look rather alarming!" exclaimed Mr. Peeps, whose fears had been roused by the mere hint that a stout resistance was probable

"Perhaps, then, you had better remain behind, whilst we take the brunt of the business upon ourselves," said the squire gravely.

"Pardon me sir," exclaimed the ex-showman, "but I'm no coward, as a certain person at home would tell you. But I've a blessed wife to consider, and poor Mrs. P. has always expressed a most decided objection to being obliged to disfigure herself by wearing a widow's cap."

"And you, I suppose, have an equal objection to render it necessary to comply with the fashion?"

"It must be confessed, sir," answered Peeps, "that I have no wish to afflict my Angelina in a matter which so nearly concerns myself. Besides, you have been so kind and considerate as to promise that my future life shall be passed in comfort, and I've no wish to die just when I'm likely to enjoy myself."

"My good fellow," answered squire Derwent, "I see nothing at all to fear from this adventure, because in the first place we shall have every assistance afforded us by the constabulary of this district, and secondly the smugglers will hardly risk a conflict with us, merely for the sake of preventing the capture of a female for whom they can feel no interest. So now, as you know exactly how the affair stands, you can give it all the consideration you please, and then decide upon whether you will aid us, or remain safely in this house till the danger, (if there is any) is over."

"Oh, as for that," exclaimed Peeps, somewhat ashamed of having shown the white feather, "I'll prove myself as courageous as the best of you; and will make one of the rescuing party in spite of all the widow's caps in the world. Haven't I always loved Amy as if she had been my own daughter, and is it likely I'd hang back when she's in the hands of that infernal villain, Caleb Kestrel?"

"Well said, old gentleman!" exclaimed Frank Marldale, gently tapping him on the back; "I thought you had too much pluck to desert us when there's most need of your services. You love the poor girl;—have brought her up from childhood though ill able to bear the expense, and I was sure it was not in your nature to desert her at a moment when she needs the assistance of all her friends."

"Psha! is it likely I would desert her when I know what a rumpus Mrs. P. would kick up if I was to forsake her?"

"Then you have no longer any fear?" asked Mr. Derwent.

"I never had any," he replied; "but you must own it makes a man feel rather queer when he knows there's a chance of being killed."

"Nay, never give way to a notion of that kind, my good fellow," exclaimed the squire. "Mr. Marldale is going to give information to a magistrate, and it's pretty certain he'll come back with a posse of constables at his heels. We shall then have plenty of strength on our side, and with a good cause to fight for, it will be strange indeed if we can't rescue Amy in spite of any resistance that may be offered by the smugglers and their friend Kestrel."

"And when may we expect your return, young gentleman?" asked Peeps of Frank Marldale.

"Soon after dark sets in to night," he replied. "In the meanwhile Mr. Derwent will see Jabez Thompson, inform him of what we are about to do, and make arrangements with him as to where we shall all meet together, and at what hour the attack shall be made. On my return I will have my men in a wood that I passed through in my way here, and will then proceed to this house to ascertain what plans have been formed in my absence."

Frank Marldale rose, left the place, and having saddled his horse, set off with all speed towards the town from whence he was to bring his expected assist-ance,

CHAPTER XV.

THE MAGISTRATE AND HIS CLERK.—RUMOURS THAT THE SMUGGLERS HAVE AGAIN DEFEATED THE LAW.—A VISITOR BRINGS FURTHER ALARMING INTELLIGENCE.—ASSISTANCE ASKED FOR AND GRANTED.—MARLDALE SETS OUT ON HIS RETURN, AND LEAVES HIS MEN IN AMBUSH.

JUSTICE CAPSICUM, to whom we are about to introduce the reader, had been long resident in India, where he made a large fortune, and then, growing tired of a country that is so injurious to most constitutions, returned to his native land, there to enjoy himself for the remainder of his days. Being wealthy he was of course looked up to in the neighbourhood in which he had settled, and his importance was afterwards still further increased by being appointed a magistrate for the county in which he resided. By the poor, he was regarded with a feeling that almost amounted to awe; but to those who were above him in rank and station, he could be absolutely servile. Yet taken altogether, the good points in his character may be said to have preponderated.

On the same day to which the incidents of our last chapter belonged, the magistrate sat reading the paper after breakfast, which on this occasion had occupied a longer time than usual. This was caused by the absence of his clerk, who had not arrived at the usual time, and great was the anger of Mr. Capsicum thereat, for he had a matter of some importance to speak about, and the nabob had no idea of being kept waiting by a man that he regarded as his inferior, and who consequently could have no excuse for not keeping his time with more correctness. At length the clerk arrived, and the anger of the great man exploded.

"Really, Mr. Jones, this is too bad," he exclaimed, looking at his watch. "Here's eleven o'clock, and it was your place, sir, to have been here an hour ago. Ain't you aware, Mr. Jones, that you ought to have been at your post at ten?"

The clerk was used to these humours, but he was a nervous man, and in the trembling accents of a criminal, he replied:—

"I'm very sorry, sir, but—but—"

"Do pray leave off your butting, and come to the point at once," interrupted the irritable old gentleman. "Pray, Mr. Jones, why have I been kept waiting all this time?"

"The truth is, sir, my wife has just been confined, and—"

"What have I to do with that?" again interrupted the magistrate; "is the law of the county to be kept waiting because your wife chooses to be confined at an inconvenient time like this. No, Mr. Jones, you must find some better excuse than that, or you and I shall have a little serious talk together."

"Indeed, sir, there was no help for it," replied the clerk, "It is very seldom that I am a minute over my time, but my wife was in great danger, and I thought you would not be displeased at my remaining with her as long as I could."

"And have you been cruel enough to leave her in danger?" exclaimed Mr. Capsicum, in the very spirit of contradiction.

"No, sir, she was better when I left home."

"Glad to hear it, very glad to hear it," returned the old gentleman, whose better points were coming out now that his ill-humour had had its full vent. "I'm sorry to hear she has been so ill, Mr. Jones, but take home this guinea to her when you go, and don't be afraid to ask for another if you should find money run short, as it will do on occasions of this kind. By-the-bye, didn't you think I spoke a little bit sharp to you just now?"

"Rather so, sir."

"Well, never mind, forget it, for after all it was only my hasty temper, and that I could not help. And now to business, Mr. Jones; you have heard, of course, that the smugglers have been at their old work again, and that a large cargo was landed the night before last, and disposed of before the revenue officers had the least notice of what was going forward ?"

" I have heard something of it," replied the clerk, " but no blame can be attached to you, as your duty only commences after these lawless men are taken and brought before you."

" Humph ! do you think it is not the duty of a magistrate to take means to prevent a robbery on the revenue?"

" I know your worship's anxiety to perform your duty," answered Mr. Jones, submissively ; " but the government has provided a body of men for the especial purpose of guarding the coast against smugglers, and it is they who have neglected their duty, and not you. Besides, sir, the fellows that were engaged in the affair the other night are pretty well known, and there is every reason to believe that a great many of them will soon be brought before you."

" So much the better, for if the evidence will bear me out, I'll commit every one of 'em for trial. I am sorry the neighbourhood is so full of these worthless rascals, Mr. Jones, but they'll find no quarter from me, for I'll do my part towards clearing the place of the rascals, if I have only the opportunity."

" I am afraid, sir, we shall never be able to get rid of them entirely," observed the clerk.

" You think then, the law is not strong enough for them ?"

" When they are caught, the law is quite sufficient," replied the other, " but these men are difficult to find, for they have a great many hiding places about this part of the coast, and whenever a search is made for them they seem to burrow into the earth like so many wild rabbits."

" Aye, so they may, so they may," exclaimed Mr. Capsicum, " but they can't cheat and laugh at us for ever, and by-and-bye, we shall find where it is they contrive to hide themselves. I've been used to hunting out criminals in India, and it will be hard if I suffer myself to be defied by such fellows as these."

" I have no doubt of your zeal, sir," replied the clerk, " but unfortunately these fellows have formed themselves into a very large body, and even the coast guardsmen confess that the smugglers on this part of the coast are more difficult to entrap than any others they have ever heard of. Now and then, to be sure, a solitary one is caught, and perhaps, transported, but its no warning, for others are always found to fill up the vacant places."

" Are none of the men known ?" asked Mr. Capsicum.

" Oh, yes, sir," replied the clerk, " there are a good many fellows that never think of getting into any sort of employment, but are always in readiness to assist whenever the signal is given that a cargo is about to be landed. These men are known smugglers, but there's no doing anything with them unless they are caught in the fact. Sometimes, to be sure, when hard driven, they will commit a robbery, and when found guilty they are always transported, in order to keep them out of harm's way as long as possible."

" And I believe more than one murder has been committed in former times ?"

" There have been several," answered the clerk, " and in every instance the perpetrators, and all that could be proved to have been out with them, have suffered the extreme penalty of the law."

" I wonder at that, too," exclaimed Mr. Capsicum, " for one would have thought they would have sought concealment in some of the secret hiding places you have been speaking of."

" And its most likely they did," answered the other, " for in every case it was a long time before they were captured, and then, not till they thought the affair had blown over, and that they might venture to come from their hiding places. But even the example of hanging has had no good effect, for smuggling goes on as briskly as ever it did, and this affair of the night before last, is said to have been one of the boldest and best contrived that has taken place for many years."

" Well, we shall see which is to get the best of this, they or I," exclaimed Mr. Capsicum. " I have been used to deal with fellows quite as cunning as they are, and have always succeeded, so that it will be hard if I can't prove my zeal by capturing a few of the rascals that have so lately defied the law. Egad! if nothing else will do, I will myself head a party of the revenue officers, and go in search of the fellows."

"I hope you will not do that sir."

"Why do you hope that, Mr. Jones?"

"Because you will always be a marked man afterwards," he replied; "these men are said to have sworn to be revenged against all who take an active part against them, and one magistrate has already been sacrificed by them for no other reason than that he was known to have said, that he would never relax his efforts till he had succeeded in entirely breaking up the bands.".

"And were the murderers suffered to escape with impunity?"

"Only one of them was caught," answered the clerk, "but the evidence against him being very conclusive, he was convicted and executed. The affair, however, caused a great deal of uneasiness, for all that had taken any part in the prosecution, received letters threatening them with dreadful retribution, and many persons were obliged to leave the neighbourhood because they could not venture to leave their houses without danger of assassination."

"But surely this lawless system may be put an end to?" exclaimed the magistrate; "there must have been great weakness manifested somewhere, and it shall now be my business to try whether the place cannot be cleared of such a nest of scoundrels."

"I'm afraid, sir, you will not succeed," answered the clerk, "for the truth is there is not force enough hereabouts to do any good. The smugglers are well aware of that, as they continue the old game, land their cargoes every now and then, and laugh at the authorities for the weakness they cannot help."

"At any rate," exclaimed Mr. Capsicum, "I have learnt something from this conversation, and shall lose no time in endeavouring to bring this state of things to an end. In short, I shall write to the secretary of state, explaining the impossibility of upholding the authority of the law, and requesting the aid of a small military force to rid the coast of these dangerous men."

"That has been done before, sir," returned the other, "but those in power seem to expect that the smugglers can be dispersed without any additional aid, and we have been left to carry on this unequal contest for years."

"Yet the coast guard is said to be a very efficient body of men."

"And it is said with truth," answered Mr. Jones, "but they are not a sufficient force here, and it is seldom they are able to do any good on land. At sea, to be sure, they often give chase to the luggers that are laden with contraband goods, and the cargo is always thrown overboard, but the vessels are notoriously fast sailors, and in nearly every instance they and their crews get clear off to try their luck another time."

"Then hang me if I don't make a stir that shall put a stop to their infamous doings," exclaimed the old gentleman. "They'll find me a determined enemy when once I begin, and if it costs me a thousand pounds out of my own pocket, I'll rid the country of the intolerable pest. A body of daring fellows shall be collected together at my own expence, I'll offer rewards for the apprehension of all that are known to be engaged in smuggling, and particular care shall be taken to secure those that assist by concealing the contraband goods that are landed. These measures will soon have a beneficial effect, and I flatter myself that within twelvemonths, I shall be the means of making this neighbourhood what it ought to be."

Mr. Capsicum was here interrupted by the entrance of a servant to announce the arrival of a stranger, and orders having been given for his admittance, Frank Marldale was immediately afterwards ushered into the room. The old gentleman eyed the new-comer with a scrutinising glance, and desiring him to be seated, inquired if he came to ask his magisterial assistance.

"I should not otherwise have taken the liberty of intruding upon your privacy, sir," answered the visitor. "In short I have an exceedingly difficult task to perform, and as it will require a few constables to bring my designs to a successful termination, I came to request as many men as you can spare."

"Ah, I perfectly understand," exclaimed the magistrate, "you are here upon the very business I and my clerk were just speaking of."

"Can it be possible that you have heard of the young lady's abduction?" asked Frank with surprise.

"My good sir, I know nothing of any young lady," replied Mr Capsicum, gravely putting on his spectacles. "It was of the smugglers that we were speaking, and I thought that you, as well as myself, were anxious to assist in taking them."

"You have not heard then anything of a young female who has been brought into this neighbourhood!"

"No;—where is she?"

"That is exactly what I want to discover."

"And you thought I must certainly know all about it?"

"I was in hopes you might have received information upon the subject," answered Frank Marldale; "for I have myself, though not long since arrived, ascertained that the female I am in quest of, has been seen at a place about five miles off, where all clue to her is at an end, except that it is supposed she has been taken to one of the caves that are used as places of concealment by the smugglers."

"My dear sir," exclaimed the magistrate, "your search is a hopeless one I fear, if she has fallen into the hands of those men. They have baffled every attempt that has been made to disperse them for years past, though, I have great reason to believe the day that is to rid us of their presence is not far distant. That, however, is but poor consolation to you, who of course must be most anxious to rescue the young lady without delay. By the bye you have not yet told me whether she was taken from her home by force."

"She would not have accompanied the ruffians but for the violence that was used to drag her away."

"Were the men that committed this act, smugglers?"

"No."

"I perceive;—some rejected lover has carried her off."

"There, sir, you are again wrong," said the young man. "She has been taken away by a villain whose only design is to extort money as the price of her liberty."

"Phew!" whistled Mr. Capsicum; "this is an awkward affair, I'm afraid. Pray, sir, how far off did the young lady reside?"

"About five and twenty miles from hence."

"And what reason have you for supposing that she has been brought into this neighbourhood?"

"This locket, which she wore constantly round her neck, was picked up by a man near the sea shore."

"That looks like a confirmation of the surmise, certainly," replied the old gentleman. "It is sufficient to prove that she was brought this way, but then, for aught we know, she may have been taken miles off by this time."

"I have reason to believe otherwise," answered Frank Marldale, "for the man who found the locket seems pretty confident that she was taken to one of the hiding places."

"Do you know the man's name?"

"Yes; it is Jabez Thompson."

"Jabez Thompson," exclaimed the magistrate; and then turning to his clerk, he added, "Have you ever heard of such a person?"

"I have, sir," he replied; "and he bears the character of being one of the most desperate smugglers in the place."

"Whether or not," exclaimed Frank Marldale, "I saw him with this jewel in his possession, and that is quite sufficient to prove that the young lady was not long since at the spot where he found it."

"Did you seize the fellow?"

"There was no occasion to do so," replied Frank, "for I have offered him a liberal reward on condition that he will guide myself and a party to the cave where she is concealed."

"Well, hang me if this is not just the very opportunity I have been wishing for," exclaimed Mr. Capsicum. "You of course require the assistance of some constables to go with you to the rescue of the young lady you are in search of?"

"That was indeed the object that brought me here," answered Marldale, "and I have now to request that no time shall be lost, as every moment is of the utmost consequence."

(Kestrel in the cave alarmed by the sudden appearance of the Smuggler.)

"If I may be allowed to offer an opinion," observed the clerk, diffidently, "I would suggest that some of the coast-guard would be of most service in a case like this."

"You are perfectly in the right, Mr. Jones," exclaimed his superior, readily catching at the idea. "A stout resistance may be expected if the smugglers are concerned in this affair, and as the coast-guard will be well armed for the expedition, we shall not only make sure of rescuing the unfortunate female, but may also

No. 17.

capture some of the fellows we have been so anxious to lay hold of. By the by, though, what reliance can be placed on the promise of this Jabez Thompson?"

"I think there can be little fear of him, when so large a sum as a hundred and fifty pounds is to reward him for his trouble."

"Aye, that indeed may make him honest," exclaimed the magistrate. "However, at all events, the thing is worth a trial, so do you, Mr. Jones, run instantly to the station of the coast guard, and ask for such a number of men as the officers may think necessary for the undertaking. Say also, that I shall accompany them, to lend my assistance towards capturing as many of the smugglers as we possibly can."

The clerk was not long in obeying these orders, and, snatching up his hat, he left the room.

"Now, sir," said the magistrate, addressing his visitor, "may I inquire how it was that the young lady's friends allowed her to be carried off so easily?"

"The truth is, they were absent at the time, in pursuit of the very man that took her away," he replied.

"And the scoundrel's motive is supposed to be the good bargain he would make as to the price of her release?"

"Exactly so."

"Has the man any claim to her?"

"Not the slightest. He has, in fact, been her most bitter enemy through life, having stolen her, when a child, from the house of a wealthy gentleman who had adopted her. That crime occurred when she was living abroad, and, bringing her over to England, he placed her under the care of an itinerant showman and his wife, who brought her up with as much tenderness as they could, though her situation must have been hard enough to bear, as she was obliged to travel with them from place to place, for the means of obtaining their miserable pittance. During several years this man, Caleb Kestrel, was unable to find them, and it was not till a very short time ago that he accidentally encountered them at a harvest home supper that was given by a neighbour of mine."

"Did he claim the girl from the people he had left her with?"

"He did," replied Frank Marldale, "but it was only for the purpose of extorting all the money he could from her."

"What money could he expect to get from a poor girl like her?" asked Mr. Capsicum.

"It would be a long story to enter into now," replied the young man, "but, for the present, it may suffice to tell you, that she proved to be the long lost heiress of Derwent-hall, in this county, with the extensive domains belonging to it. This was well known to Kestrel, who immediately formed his own plans for enriching himself at her expense."

"By Jove then we must lay hold of the villain, that he may receive the punishment he deserves."

"If he gets all the punishment he deserves, Mr. Capsicum," returned the other, "he will make his exit from this world by means of the gallows. In short, he has been guilty of an attempt to murder, and, for some time, I was suspected of having committed the crime."

"Bless my heart!" exclaimed the old gentleman, "whose life did he attempt to take?"

"The assassin's aim was directed against a Mr. Cecil Derwent, who stood in the way as having a claim to half the property, which was bequeathed to him in the event of the girl not being discovered within a certain number of years. Kestrel determined that she should have all, in order that he might lay claim to a larger sum, for which purpose he waylaid him on the moors, discharged an air gun at him, and effected his escape, leaving his victim, as he supposed, dead."

"Oh, the poor gentleman recovered then?"

"He was revived by the skill of a faithful steward, who, in his youth, had made considerable progress in surgery. The secret, however, was not made known, and, to the astonishment of everybody, Mr. Derwent one day suddenly made his appearance among his friends, and denounced Caleb Kestrel as the man that had treacherously sought his life."

"Was that done when the villain was present?"

"It was."

"And yet he was suffered to escape?"

"Unfortunately he contrived to get away, or this fresh trouble would not have befallen us," answered Frank Marldale. "There is, however, the satisfaction of knowing, that we are not very far from him, and if success attends us this night, we will hold him with so strong a grip that it shall never again be in his power to do mischief."

"Well, my good sir," exclaimed the magistrate, "your story has interested me very much, and you may rely upon it, that I will do all in my power to assist you. But you must need refreshment after your ride, so be my guest till the arrival of our expected reinforcement, and, in the meantime, we will so arrange our plans of attack that there shall be little fear of a failure."

He rung the bell, ordered a substantial luncheon to be brought in, and whilst he and Frank Marldale were doing justice to the good things before them, proceeded to discuss the business that now occupied all their attention.

"I have been thinking," he said, "that we must not place too much reliance in the man that has undertaken to guide you to the place where the young lady is supposed to be concealed. Rogues are seldom unfaithful to each other, and I am afraid he will want the reward first, in which case he will not be likely to fulfil his contract."

"He has only stipulated for half of it to be paid in advance," replied the young man, "and the remainder he is not to receive till his promise has been performed."

"And half will be a handsome sum for doing nothing," exclaimed Mr. Capsicum. "The fellow will be well satisfied with his day's profit and will then lead us a pretty dance from place to place, that will end all in smoke."

"You think then our trouble will be in vain, and that it will be useless to prosecute the search."

"Nay, I don't go quite so far as to say that, my young friend," answered the magistrate ; "but something strikes me that we shall do more by our own exertions than by any assistance we are likely to receive from this Jabez Thompson, who is one of the most notorious among the gang he belongs to. Be that as it may however, we'll have a good search while we are about it, and perhaps chance, or fortune may lend us to the very place we are anxious to find. The men I have sent for will soon be here, and we will then march to the place you came from, which we shall reach, I should suppose, just about nightfall, which will suit our purpose to a nicety."

"By the by," observed Frank, "I forgot to tell you that we shall there meet a couple of friends."

"Are they likely to be of good service in case of need?"

"Both of them are friends of the young lady," answered Frank, "and therefore every reliance may be placed in them. One of them is her lover, Mr. Cecil Derwent, and the other the travelling showman, who so long and faithfully discharged towards her all the duties of a parent."

"Aye, aye," exclaimed Mr. Capsicum, "there can be no doubt about either of them, and I dare say they will render very efficient aid in the cause of one who is so dear to them. But in case of an encounter, we must prepare for a very desperate resistance, because the men who will be opposed to us have every thing at stake, and if victory should declare in our favour, they know well enough what will be their subsequent fate."

"For my own part," replied Frank Marldale, "I anticipate less difficulty in this affair than you seem to do, for the smugglers are likely enough to hear of our intended movements against them, and they will hardly risk a conflict which may turn so fatally against themselves. But at any rate, we will be prepared for the worst, and if every heart is animated by feelings like my own, we will all perish rather than fail in our enterprise."

"Excellent, i'faith !" exclaimed the magistrate. "Your spirit pleases me, young gentleman, and I feel confident in a cause like this we shall come off with flying colours. Egad ! a man must have a heart of stone in his bosom if he wouldn't risk everything for the sake of rescuing a helpless woman, when she has fallen into trouble. So, here's success to our undertaking, and may villany be forced to yield to the cause of justice and humanity."

"I drink your toast with all my heart, sir," replied Frank Marldale, raising the glass to his lips, and draining its contents to the very bottom. "The girl we are in search of is, it is true, nothing to me, for our acquaintance has been a very short one, but I feel deeply interested in her fate, or I should not have left my home, where my presence is just now] so much required."

"Perhaps you are partly actuated by feelings of friendship towards Mr. Derwent ?"

"I certainly would go through fire and water to serve him," answered the young man ; "yet strange to say, it is not long since I looked upon him as my bitterest enemy."

"Which probably arose from rivalry in love ?"

"No," he replied; "but he is my landlord, and as my lease was about to expire he sent me a notice that he should not renew it, as he intended to add my farm to his park. This may seem to be a very slight ground for so rooted a dis-like, but the truth is, sir, the house and estate had been held by my family for three or four generations, and it wounded me to the quick when I found that I was to be turned out [of it like a dog. I, and those who went before me, had by our labour and skill, made it one of the best farms in the neighbourhood, and it was hard to be forced to leave it when I knew that my landlord had not a single com-plaint to make against me. However, that's all over now, and Mr. Derwent and I are upon the best of terms."

"I suppose your lease will be re-granted ?"

"Yes," replied Frank, his eyes sparkling with pleasure, "I am to remain in the old house that I have loved so well from my boyhood upwards. Everything has been given in my favour with the utmost liberality, and that too, in consideration of my having been unjustly accused of having been the assassin that attempted the murder of Mr. Derwent."

"Ah !" exclaimed Mr. Capsicum, "how strangely things turn out sometimes. One hour you were the bitterest of enemies, and the next the warmest of friends, through an event that it was impossible to have foreseen. But everything happens for the best, as it is no doubt in the present case, for through the carrying off this young lady, it's more than likely we shall get rid of the scoundrels that have so long been the pest of our neighbourhood. But I see my clerk coming across the court-yard, so now to hear what success he has met with in his mission."

He had scarcely done speaking when that person came red-hot with haste into the room.

"Well Mr. Jones," exclaimed the magistrate, "what news do you bring us from the station ?"

"Very good sir," he replied ;—"the lieutenant has spared you twelve of his best men, and they have his orders to put themselves entirely under your command."

"How soon will they be here ?"

"They are here already, sir," answered the clerk. "I ventured to hint that there was not a moment to lose, and they were sent off without any de-lay."

"Are they well armed ?"

"Yes sir, each man has an extra brace of pistols."

"Then I think we may fairly begin to flatter ourselves that success is certain," exclaimed the magistrate, turning to Frank Marldale. "We needn't mind meet-ing double our numbers now, for the smugglers will take alarm when they see us so well prepared to meet them, and when once they are beaten, there will not be much difficulty in rescuing the young lady you are in search of. As for Kestrel, or whatever the fellow's name is, we must on no account suffer his escape, even if we have to shoot him through the head to prevent it."

"We must not, indeed," replied Frank Marldale, "for if once he gets at large, it will be to resume his persecution against his unfortunate victim. Besides, he merits death, and shall have his deserts, even though my own hand robs him of life. But excuse me, sir, if I venture to hint that it would be as well for the men to march at once towards the place of destination, for my friends are anxiously expecting my return, and it would be advisable for us to make our search at as early an hour in the evening as possible."

"Where had they better wait for us?" asked Mr. Capsicum.

"At a wood that lies about a quarter of a mile from the public house where I met with Jabez Thompson. I know not the sign of the place, but they cannot mistake it, as it is the only house of the kind in the neighbourhood."

"I know the exact spot you mean, very well," answered the magistrate, and then, turning to his clerk, he added :—"go, Mr. Jones, and direct the men to commence their march forthwith. This gentleman and I shall immediately follow on horseback. For this day, sir, your services will be no longer required; so return home to your wife, and if she is better in the morning be here at the usual hour, for if we make any of the smugglers prisoners, you and I shall have a busy day of it."

The clerk bowed and retired, and then Mr. Capsicum, whilst putting on his wrapper and great coat, said :—

"I think, sir, we may reckon upon giving these fellows a smart peppering if we happen to be fortunate enough to light upon'em ; I say if we happen to light upon 'em, because, I have no great faith in the promises of the man that has undertaken to be your guide. He belongs to a very bad lot, and in my opinion, he means to deceive instead of to guide us."

"At all events we must appear to place some reliance in him, or he will be sure to lead us into some ambush," exclaimed the young man. "Like yourself I place but little reliance on him, but we must depend somewhat on our own judgment, and if there be any reason to suppose he means to play us false, it will then be imperative on us as a matter of self preservation, to punish him on the spot with instant death."

"Which act," exclaimed Mr. Capsicum, "will most likely be retaliated by his companions in iniquity. However, be that as it may, I am quite ready to take my share in the danger, and if we get the best of the affair, nothing will afford me greater satisfaction than to have been the means of ridding the country of a set of scoundrels that have too long been suffered to have their own way."

"And I think, sir," exclaimed Frank Marldale, "you will not have much reason to complain of those who are willing to assist you in the undertaking. Our sole object is to release an unfortunate girl who has fallen into the hands of evil men, but as there appears to be another duty to perform, you shall find that we are as ready to join in your cause as you have been to assist in ours. But these protestations of mine are vain ; a few hours will prove our sincerity, and I trust that this night will show that our zeal is as great one way as the other."

By this time both the gentlemen were ready for a start, and their horses having been brought to the door, they mounted and set forth on a journey that if succesful was to lead to the most important results.

CHAPTER XVI.

JABEZ THOMPSON PROVES TO BE DOUBLE-FACED;—THE PEDLAR BECOMES ALARMED, AND RESOLVES TO CHANGE HIS QUARTERS;—THE FLIGHT.

IN spite of his seeming candour, Jabez Thompson, as the reader may already have foreseen, was a hypocrite at heart, and had no more idea of assisting in the recovery of Amy than he had of flying. The reward that had been offered him, however, was too tempting to be rejected, and as there was little chance of the full sum being paid him in anticipation of the service he had promised to perform, he proposed that half should be paid him in advance, considering within himself that even that sum would amply repay him for doing absolutely nothing. With his mind thus made up he strolled towards the sea-side, where he wandered about for some time to ascertain if any watch was set upon him, and being at length perfectly well satisfied that he had nothing to fear on that score, he began to climb a very precipitous and narrow path, that led by a circuitous route to the place which we have before designated as Robin Hood's cave. Why it was called so nobody knows, except that a legend existed of its once having been a retreat of the far-famed outlaw whose name it bore, and as many murders were reported to have been committed therein, no one in the neighbourhood except the smugglers, would ever venture within its narrow entrance. So far the place might be considered an excellent hiding-place for those who had reason to conceal themselves from the officers of justice, and as the spot had years before been known to Caleb Kestrel, it was the first he thought of as a tolerably secure retreat when first he made up his mind to carry Amy away from the house. He accordingly sent word to the smugglers that he intended to seek an asylum among them for a time, and no sooner had the girl been secured in the manner already detailed, than he commenced his rapid career across the moors, in the direction of the spot where he felt satisfied he might keep his prisoner till arrangements were made for extorting the large sum of money he expected to make by her capture.

It is unnecessary to detail the journey beyond the point where we left him, and we will therefore content ourselves with observing that he was met near the cave by a man generally known as Tom Teazle, who conducted them by the pathway before mentioned to the cave where our heroine was to be detained a close prisoner. Owing to the rapidity of their flight and the terror she felt, Amy was insensible long before she arrived at the place of destination, and her horror may be well imagined when recovering from her swoon she found that she was far beyond the reach of those who would have rescued her, had there been any clue by which they might ascertain the place where she had been taken to. In a short time, however, she discovered the loss of her locket, and then a faint hope inspired her, that, in case of a pursuit in that direction, the trinket might fall into friendly hands, and thus might ultimately lead to her discovery. During the period of her insensibility, Caleb Kestrel watched over the rude couch that had been made up for her, and it was whilst he was thus occupied that Jabez Thompson crept stealthily into the cave. Uncertain whether it was a friend or foe that had thus intruded, the pedlar snatched up a pistol, and was about to fire, when Jabez in the utmost consternation implored him to desist.

"Who is it, and what brings you here?" demanded Kestrel.

"Who should it be but a friend?" returned the other; "and as for my business, it is to tell you, Caleb Kestrel, that the enemy is close at hand, and that you must lose no time in leaving this place, unless your life is no longer of any value."

"Fool!" exclaimed Kestrel, "what enemy can so soon have traced me to this outlandish spot?"

"I can't pretend to tell you his name," replied Jabez;—"but a chap—looking very much like a farmer—met me in the public house this morning, and asked me a great many questions, to discover whether any strangers had lately arrived, bringing with them a female that seemed to be a prisoner."

"Ha! and what reply did you make to that?"

"Why, it was no use denying the truth," answered the other, "for he happened to see that I had part of a gold locket in my possession, which he knew belonged to the female he was looking after, and I was obliged to confess when and where I had found it."

"Did it belong to the girl I brought here?"

"I suppose so, for he knew it in a moment."

"Then of course you told him that the young lady and her companions had gone further along the beach?"

"I should have done so," replied Jabez Thompson, "but that he seemed to be of a different opinion, so I put the best complexion I could upon the affair, and told him I had no doubt I could guide him to the very spot where you were to be found."

"Villain! then you have betrayed me?"

"Softer words, if you please, Mr. Kestrel," exclaimed the other. "I may be a villain, perhaps, but not quite so great a one as to get one of my own sort into trouble."

"What motive had you, then, for leading him to suppose that I was to be discovered?"

"The truth is, he promised me a large reward to assist him in his search after the young lady you brought here."

"And you would earn it by giving me up?"

"Not quite so fast, if you please, till you have heard what sort of an explanation I have to give," replied Jabez Thompson. I saw plainly enough what sort of customer I had got to deal with, and as it was no use denying that I could give him all the information he wanted, I thought the best thing I could do was to appear willing to earn the hundred and fifty pounds that he offered. But you know me too well to believe I would betray a friend, and I hardly need say that I promised to guide him to the retreat only for the sake of pocketing the reward, and not with any intention of giving you up to your enemies."

"But how are you to help yourself?" demanded Caleb Kestrel. "My pursuer, whoever he is, is no doubt armed, and if he sees you are false to your promise, he'll shoot you like a dog."

"I know all about that," answered the other, "and I must therefore bring him to this place."

"And so give me up to him?"

"What nonsense you are talking," exclaimed Jabez; "aint there plenty of other hiding places in this neighbourhood, and can't you be in one of 'em while I bring him here?"

"And why should I be hunted about in that way?"

"Because you'll be all the better off for it," replied Jabez. "The chap will think I've kept my faith with him if I show him the way to this place, and that will so far satisfy him that he'll go away without wishing to look for you any where else in this neighbourhood. Now, in my opinion, Caleb, my plan will turn out to be the best one after all, for when once this part of the country has been searched, they'll never think of coming again, so that you may remain in safety here as long as you choose to stay."

"How far from here is the nearest place that I can retreat to?"

"Oh, there's plenty close at hand," answered Jabez Thompson, "but to prevent any awkward mistake, I think you had better go to another cave about half a mile off. It's quite as good as the one where you now are, and I can take you to it by a path where no one will be likely to see you."

"Can I depend upon you?" exclaimed Caleb Kestrel, eyeing him with a scrutinizing glance.

"Depend upon me? I should think so."

"But suppose the bribe should be increased to a larger sum, on condition that I am taken?"

"Why I would pretend to accept it," answered Jabez, "and, after all, they would be no nearer their mark. No, no, my boy, you and I have no great reason to respect the law, and I'd sooner lose my right hand than betray an old friend."

"Well, I begin to think better of you than I did at first," exclaimed Kestrel, " and yet I fancy this affair might have been differently managed. What occasion was there to rout me from this place where I felt myself tolerably secure."

"There was the best of all reasons," he replied. "Others, as well as myself knew of your being here, and who can answer for it that some one of 'em wouldn't have betrayed you in real earnest instead of pretending to do so, as I did. But enough of that, Master Kestrel, for there's other things to think of now, and I want to know, in the first place, what you are going to do with that girl, now that you have been at so much trouble to take her away?"

"I shall keep possession of her to be sure, till her friends choose to come to my terms."

"And that, perhaps, may never be."

"Then I'll take her abroad, and they shall never hear of her more."

" Which will be only adding an incumbrance when you may want to move about from place to place."

"Don't it strike you then," asked Kestrel in a subdued tone, "that there is a way to get rid of her when all hopes of getting the money I expect is at an end?"

" Why, you wouldn't murder her surely?"

" Fool !" exclaimed the ruffian, "what is it to you if I dispose of her in my own way? I have formed my own plans with respect to this girl, and will carry them out too, or she shall be made to bear the torrent of my vengeance."

"Oh, with all my heart," exclaimed Jabez. "Do as you please, and then I suppose you'll be satisfied. But, remember, you must not stay here too long, for I have got to see the strange gentleman again presently, and I don't know but he'll have a few more to assist him in the search."

" Hah ! what makes you think that ?"

" Because I saw two other chaps go into the public-house soon after I left it, and as one of 'em rode off to the next town about half an hour afterwards, I took it into my head that he was going to fetch further assistance,"

"And if your surmise is correct, will your people join together to give them a warm reception?"

" I can't promise that," replied Jabez, " for the long and the short of it is, they have got themselves to look to, and if any rumpus should take place the end of it would be that the whole band would be at once broken up."

" Then I am not to expect any assistance ?"

" I don't see why you should when their own interest is so much concerned," answered the other. "Indeed they are not best pleased at your coming here at all, for they see nothing but danger and trouble coming of it, and, but for you, they might have remained undisturbed for years to come."

" What do the fellows want more?" demanded Caleb Kestrel. " I have promised to pay them all well when I have brought my bargain to conclusion, and yet they begin to grow dissatisfied, though I have been here but a few hours."

" That's because they'd rather have the money now than wait for it nobody knows how long. However, that's not my business with you now, Master Kestrel. I come to do you a service, and it will be your own fault if any mischief should happen through your staying here too long."

" How am I to depend on you ?" asked the pedlar. " You have already promised to bring my enemies to this cave, and for aught I know you may next lead them to the one you have proposed as my next place of concealment."

" Do have a little reason, and ask yourself a question or two," exclaimed Jabez Thompson. " If I had intended to have given you up to your pursuers, it is little likely I should have come to tell you that it's high time to be off."

" That certainly is a point in your favour," returned Caleb, "but still as these men have been tampering with you I have not much confidence in anything you say."

Well, then, if that's the case you had better follow your own notions and remain here till it's too late. It won't be long before they come, and when they do make their appearance you must remember there's no back door for you to make your escape from."

"But I am armed though, and they shall find that I'll not yield myself up till overpowered by numbers."

"And what's the use of fighting w   get off to a place as snug as this, if you'll only think proper to follow   ."

PERILOUS DESCENT OF AMY FROM ROBIN HOOD'S CAVE.

"Wait till th s girl recovers from her swoon," answered Caleb Kestrel. "We shall hear what she says upon the subject, and can afterwards act accordingly."

"Are you going to ask her if she will accompany you."

"I'm not quite such a fool as to do that," replied the other; "but if Amy can be persuaded to accompany me without offering any resistance, I think half my difficulties will be got over. She is over head and ears in love with Squire Derwent, and if I threaten to make him the first victim of my vengeance, I think it will not be difficult to keep her quiet."

No. 18.

"And would you kill the gentleman ?"

"Would I, aye. Who and what is he that I should spare his life, any more than he would mine if he had but the opportunity of taking it ? Besides I have once attempted the thing, and as I know he wants to be revenged upon me for it, I know of nothing better to prevent it than to send a bullet through his body."

"D—m me, Caleb, if ever I saw such a cold blooded fellow as you are," exclaimed Jabez Thompson. "If a man offends you, you no more mind shooting him down than if was a dog."

"Aye," he replied, "but that's only when I know him to be an enemy.   Now this Mr. Derwent is trying to hunt me into the hands of the law, and as I happen to know that they'd send me to the gallows if they could only lay hold of me, I think no way is left but to put an end to the man that is leading on the pursuit."

"It's no business of mine to be sure," exclaimed Jabez Thompson, "and there ain't many people that will accuse me of being particularly soft hearted, but between ourselves Kestrel I cannot help thinking that this chap would never have thought of hunting about for you if the girl hadn't been carried away from him."

"Yes, but he would, though," returned the other. "He took a mortal dislike to me from the moment when he discovered it was I that stole the child in her infancy, and that dislike grew into hatred when I fired at and wounded him. Curses on my arm, say I, for not having made a better aim at his heart, for if I had but succeeded in that, the girl would have come in for all his property, and I might have made a good bargain with her without much trouble."

"What a hungry fellow you are after money, Caleb," exclaimed his companion.

"Why the truth is I am in a fix, and can't get out of it without money," answered Caleb. "I want to go abroad to be out of harm's way, but how am I to do that when my pockets are as empty as your head ?"

"I don't know anything about my head," replied the other, "but rough as I am, my heart ain't quite so black as your own.   However, I've not come here to quarrel or be insulted, but to warn you that this place wont do for you to remain in."

"Through your own foolery in promising to bring my pursuers here," exclaimed Kestrel.

"Foolery !—show me the man, will you, that could refuse the offer of a hundred and fifty pounds."

"Psha !" retorted the pedlar, "I would have given double that sum if you had kept your tongue quiet about these caves."

"How was I to know that you have so much ?"

"I have not got it in my possession at present," answered Caleb Kestrel; "but if matters don't turn out worse than I expect, it will not be many days before I can boast of being the master of a few thousands."

"Nonsense ! how are you to extort such a large sum from Mr. Derwent, I should like to know ?"

"Such a simpleton as you are, might be puzzled how to go to work," answered the pedlar; "but I know the world a little better, and if I can only escape the fellows that are coming after me, you shall see that half the gentleman's fortune at least shall be given me as the price of Amy's safety."

"But he may not heed your threats."

"Ah, but he will though, when he finds that the girl's life will be sacrificed if he chooses to be obstinate."

"You wouldn't surely be coward enough to murder a poor helpless girl," exclaimed Jabez.

"Why shouldn't I, if they try to thwart me?" demanded the ruffian. "An attempt may be made to hunt me into some corner, and if so the girl will be an incumbrance, and then there'll be no other way left but to kill her."

"For which they'll send you to the gallows."

"As for the gallows, its the last thing I ever think of," replied Caleb, in a tone of indifference. "The tree is not yet grown from which I am to swing, for, when the worst comes to the worst, and I can see no way of escape, I'll put a pistol to my head and blow out my brains. So you see if my enemies happen to get the best of it, they won't have the gratification of seeing my carcase dangling in the air."

" How can you talk so lightly of death ?"

" Because I never had any fear of it," he replied. " I never knew indeed what it was to be afraid of anything, so you may suppose from that there'll be a pretty stout resistance if my pursuers should happen to hunt me to my den. And should that ever occur, Jabez Thompson, don't let yourself be seen among 'em or you would be the first man to fall by my hand."

" Humph ! you still think then that I'm going to tell the people the exact spot where you are to be found."

" Why else have you agreed to accept the bribe ?"

" For a very good reason, as I think," he replied ; " if I hadn't jumped at the offer some one else among our people would, and then you might have been worse off, for you would most likely have been taken prisoner, whereas now you have had sufficient notice of the intended visit, if you'll only think proper to make the best use of it."

" That excuse may be all very well," exclaimed Caleb Kestrel, " but I've not yet heard any reason given why my pursuers could not have been taken to some of the other caves, just as well as here ? They would have gone away satisfied, and I should have remained undisturbed in my snug retreat."

" Not quite so snug as you think," answered the other ; " for the gentleman I met with this morning, had heard of Robin Hood's cave, and before he reached this place he seems to have made up his mind that it should be the very first place he searched. So you see, Caleb, you might have been suddenly pounced upon, but for my luckily getting at the secret."

" Is there no way of deceiving the stranger into a belief that one of the other caves is the one he wants to search ?"

" I don't think there is," he replied, " for he seems to be a wide-awake sort of chap enough, and if he happens to find out that I have been gammoning him, he'd order me into custody, and I should be chiselled out of my money."

" Not if you have it beforehand."

" But they'd take it away from me again if they discovered that I had not performed my part of the contract," replied Jabez Thompson. " So I thought the best way was to make myself safe, and that can only be done, by bringing the gentleman and his friends to this place."

" By which I shall be routed from my place of concealment, almost as soon as I have taken possession of it."

" Well Caleb," exclaimed the other, " and ain't it better to put up with that than to run the risk of being shot, or at the very least taken prisoner? However, all I know about it is, that I have done everything for the best, and as for bringing your pursuers here, there's no help for it, unless I choose to be worse than my word, and that's not a very likely thing, when there's a hundred and fifty pounds hanging to it."

" D—n it, man, I would have given anything almost rather than this should have happened."

" How was I to know that ?" demanded Jabez. " The bargain seemed to me too good a one to be rejected, and I agreed to it at once, though reserving to myself in my own mind the right of giving you notice of all that is going on. I have done so, Caleb, and now if anything disagreeable should happen, the fault will be yours and not mine."

" You have already heard me say what will follow if I should find myself too closely pressed by my enemies."

" Yes, you talked something about shooting me."

" It would be something more than talk if it was ever to come to that," answered Caleb Kestrel, " for with one of my pistols I would take your life, and with the other place myself beyond the vengeance of those that would take me."

"All this is very well, but its mere braggadocio," exclaimed Jabez Thompson. "You know well enough that I would't take any body to a place where you might me concealed, so make your mind easy upon that subject, and prepare to follow be with the young lady, for the sooner we leave this place the better. And see, she is now recovering from her swoon, and will be able to walk with us from this cave to the one we are going to."

Amy had indeed shown signs of returning animation for some time, and hearing these latter words, she demanded of Caleb Kestrel where he was next going to take her.

"Don't trouble your head about where we are going to," he replied sullenly, "for whether you like it or not, it will be all the same in the long run."

"Alas!" she sighed; "when will these persecutions cease."

"When you and your friends come to reason," answered Caleb Kestrel. "You all know well enough what will satisfy me, and yet the devil a bit can I bring anybody to terms."

"And to gratify your avarice," exclaimed Amy, "I am to be dragged away from home; carried across the country no one knows where; and upon rousing from my fainting fit, I find myself in a cave, where I suppose you mean me to pass away the remainder of my miserable existence!"

"You are mistaken there, my girl," answered the pedlar, "for it's neither my wish nor my interest to remain in a place where there is so much danger. In short the pursuers are already on our heels, and I expect them here this very night."

"Heaven grant it may be so," she exclaimed, and then recollecting herself, she added with a sigh;—"but it is impossible;—my friends know not where to find me, and, little suspecting that I am so near, they will pass on to prosecute their inquiries elsewhere."

"I wish I could be as sure of that myself," returned Kestrel; "but the truth of it is they have proof of your having been in this neighbourhood."

"What proof?"

"Look if you have not lost something since you left home."

"Ah! my locket is gone!" she exclaimed after a hurried examination, "Some one has taken it from me, knowing that I cherished it as the only keepsake I had of him who first pitied and protected me."

"Its a pity some one had not taken it from you," answered Kestrel, "for then the fellows that are after us would have gone on their way without dreaming that you were in this neighbourhood. But the trinket was picked up in the place where you lost it, and from information this man brings me, it's pretty certain the cave is to be searched before long."

"Would that my deliverers were here now!"

"Oh, I dare say you would like to get away from me," exclaimed Caleb Kestrel; "but there's no chance of it, so don't deceive yourself with a parcel of vain hopes that will only end in smoke. This man is to guide us to another cave some little distance from this one, and then as he is afterwards to bring the enemy to this place, they will go away satisfied, and I shall be left to perform the rest of my plan in leisure and safety. But there is one caution to give you, Amy;—no cries for assistance must be uttered as we go along, or your life will pay the forfeit of your temerity."

"My life!" she replied;—"and of what value is that to me, now that I am torn away from all that I hold most dear?"

"You will not surely be fool enough to tempt my vengeance?"

"I fear it not."

"Come—come," exclaimed Kestrel, in a more soothing tone; "it's all nonsense, Amy, for you to make so much fuss about an affair that after all is but a trifle. No further violence is intended, if you will only submit to remain quiet for a little while; and as for the few hundreds that I want from Squire Derwent, I don't see why he should grudge me, since I have been the means of making a discovery that afforded him a great deal of satisfaction."

"Have you so soon forgotten the attempt that was made to take away his life ?"

"No, no, my girl, I've not forgot it," he replied, "but who is there to prove whose hand aimed the bullet ?"

"I can."

"You !—would you send me to the gallows?"

"What reason have I to spare you ?" demanded Amy. "Are you not a villain, that would spare no one, even if it was his own brother that stood in his way? Are you not still my unrelenting persecutor, and is it not your present design to rob Mr. Derwent by extorting money from him as the only terms upon which I can ever hope to be set at liberty? Do I not know all this, Caleb Kestrel, and is it to be wondered at, therefore, if I take the first opportunity that offers to hurl destruction upon you ?"

"All this may be easy to say," he replied, sneeringly, "but I shall take care to prevent the mischief you would like to do me."

"But there are others that will never rest satisfied till they have brought my enemy to justice."

"Let them beware," exclaimed Caleb, "or they may fall into the tiger's den when least they are expecting danger. And yet how easily and satisfactorily all may be arranged, if they will but fall into my views, and accept a proposition that will only take a few hundred pounds from the squire's pocket."

"Mr. Derwent will not submit to extortion," replied Amy ; "and, therefore all the trouble you have taken to carry out your plot will be in vain. Besides, he has but to apply to a magistrate for assistance, and all he requires will be granted."

"Will he run the risk of having you taken away to some place where the laws of this country cannot reach me ?"

"I understand the hint," replied Amy, "and now I tell you, once for all, that no threats shall ever intimidate me into giving you my aid to prevail on Mr. Derwent to submit to your extortionate demands. You would have me believe that it is your intention to take me abroad if your demands are not complied with, but sooner will I perish by my own hand, than become the slave of such a villain as you have proved yourself."

"I'll tell you what it is," exclaimed Jabez Thompson, interposing, "we are wasting time here that ought to be better employed. So, one word for all, Kestrel, you must either leave this place directly, or take the chance of finding another retreat without my assistance."

"Why are you in such a hurry when the people we expect can't set out on their search till you go to guide them?"

"Don't make too sure of that," answered Jabez, "for if I don't go back there's plenty of our fellows to be found that would be glad to stand in my shoes if they had the chance. So follow me, both of you, and I'll soon take you to another place, where you may remain secure enough till after the search is over, and then you may both go to Jericho for aught I care."

Finding that it would be in vain to resist, Amy rose from the piece of rock on which she had been seated, and Kestrel, after having placed himself by her side, drew a pistol from his belt, and then led her towards the mouth of the cave.

"Mark me, girl," he said, in a low, threatening tone, "there should be no misunderstanding between us now, for life and death will for a time depend upon yourself. Our way must be pursued in silence, for if but one exclamation is suffered to escape your lips, that moment will be your last in this world."

Amy made no reply to this, and she remained firm and unshaken, though the words were intended to strike terror into her heart. Leaving the subterranean retreat, they proceeded along a narrow winding path that had been cut out of the solid rock about midway between the summit and the base. Once or twice she cast her eyes anxiously towards the beach below to see if any one was there who might afford assistance in this hour of need. The place, however, seemed to be deserted ; not a human being met her gaze, and now for the first time she began to despair of that rescue which till then she had relied on. At length, on turning a projecting mass of rock, they descended by a rather steeply-inclining path, which in a few minutes brought them to the cavern they were in search of. This they entered, and soon found themselves in profound darkness.

"Is this the den we are to conceal ourselves in?" demanded Caleb Kestrel, sullenly.

"Aye," returned the smuggler, "and I don't know that a place better suited for the purpose could have been found if you had searched the world through. To be sure it's rather gloomy, but what of that? Its only to stay in till your pursuers have left the neighbourhood, and as that's not likely to be long first, you ought to be content, and bless your lucky stars that you have found such a capital retreat. So, for the present, I shall bid you both good by, and as soon as the coast is clear again, I'll come back and let you know what, in the meantime, has been done."

Jabez then made his way towards the entrance, which was just discernible, and the pedlar leading Amy slowly onward, struck his foot against a large stone which would serve for a seat. Throwing his cloak over it to protect her from the damp, he desired her to sit down and wait patiently till the time came when they could seek a more comfortable and equally secure asylum. Nearly worn out with the exertions she had gone through for some time past, she obeyed him, and the ruffian in a tone of triumph then proceeded,

"You now must admit, Amy, that all hopes of rescue are at an end; your friends, it is true, are near, and in sufficient numbers to have borne you off, had they but the means of tracing you to this place. That, however, can never be, for they will presently search the cavern we have just left, and failing in their object will be easily persuaded by the fellow who brought us here, that your captor has conveyed you to a distant part of the kingdom. They will then go away, never to return, and I can enter into a treaty with Mr. Derwent that will at once put money into my pocket, and give you the liberty you must so anxiously desire."

"Rest satisfied with that notion," she replied, "for I feel assured Mr. Derwent will not submit to your extortion."

"He must be a pretty sort of lover if he leaves you in captivity when a few hundred pounds would restore you to him."

"You think he will make no exertion to discover the place where you have concealed me?"

"Oh, he may do that if he pleases," exclaimed Kestrel, "for I shall always have people to watch his movements, and should he ever approach us too near, it will at any time be easy for me to remove you somewhere else. So, my girl, make up your mind never to get out of my hands till the ransom I demand has been paid up."

With these words he left her to her own reflections, and groped his way towards the entrance of the cave, in order to listen for and prepare against the approach of an enemy.

CHAPTER XVII.

A CONSULTATION;—ARRIVAL OF JABEZ THOMPSON;—KEEPING TO A BARGAIN;— SIGNS OF WAVERING;—THE SEARCH AT ROBIN HOOD'S CAVE.

HAVING disposed of the small force they had brought with them, Frank Marldale and the magistrate made their way towards the public house that has already been mentioned, where they found Squire Derwent and the ex-proprietor of the Temple of Arts, anxiously awaiting their return. Mr. Capsicum was formally introduced, and a few other preliminary matters having been gone through, the four gentlemen began to consult upon the means that would be most likely to bring their labours to a successful termination. There was one thing, however, that they could scarcely account for—Jabez Thompson had not yet made his appearance, and Mr. Derwent gave it as his opinion that the man had made a promise he never intended to fulfil. Frank Marldale on the other hand placed the utmost reliance in his promise.

"Had there been nothing to gain, gentlemen," he exclaimed, "I should have begun to think as you do about the fellow, but he has made a good bargain for himself, and as half the reward is to be paid to night, before he takes upon himself the office of our guide, I think we may pretty safely reckon upon seeing him before long."

"But he ought to have been here before now," observed the squire.

"Perhaps he may have delayed it from prudential motives," interrupted Mr. Capsicum. "It is not quite dark yet, and he may be afraid of being seen by any of his companions to enter this house. Not, by the bye, that much reliance is to be placed on a man of that kind, for even if he should come here according to promise, I should still suspect some foul play is intended."

"Mercy on us, you dont say so!" exclaimed Mr. Peeps in alarm, "may I ask, sir, what you think he means to do?"

"Why there, my good sir, I own you rather puzzle me," returned the magistrate, "for not knowing exactly what the man's thoughts may be, I know not what design he may have in his head. One thing, however is certain;—the smugglers gather here in great force, and if they choose to unite in a body, they may oppose our passage to the cave, and give us a great deal of trouble."

"And perhaps murder all our party!" exclaimed Peeps.

"Really, my good sir," laughed the magistrate, "I don't think there's much fear of that, for the men we have in ambush are well armed, and know well how to use their weapons, in case of need. All I meant to say, was, no great deal of reliance can be placed on the fellow who has undertaken to be our guide, and it will be necessary to keep a vigilant eye upon him in order to foil him, supposing my suspicions are at all correct."

"We must keep him constantly near us," observed Mr. Derwent, "and on the first appearance of treachery I will myself shoot him through the heart. A hint of that kind may as well be given him, as no doubt it will have a marvellous effect towards keeping him true to the promise he has made."

"Especially as the money he is to receive, will be of no use to him," suggested Mr. Peeps. "'Fore George! what trouble that peddling fellow has given us to be sure, ever since that unfortunate night when first he showed his ill-looking face at Farmer Brough's harvest-home supper. But he has always been the same ever since I have known him, and that's a good many years since, now."

"By the way, sir," exclaimed Frank Marldale to the magistrate, "this is the person I told you of, who brought up the girl that was stolen from her adopted father by Caleb Kestrel. He is an honest worthy fellow, as ever lived, and brought Amy up to the best of his means, though unfortunately they were limited."

"And the child he reared, is as you say, the present possessor of the Derwent property."

"Half of it is her's," replied Frank, "but I rather think if the ' course of true love should run smooth,' after all their troubles, she will soon call herself mistress of the whole estate. But a truce to this, gentlemen, we have now serious business to occupy our attention, and I think if our plans are well laid at the commencement, it will not be long before Amy is released from the hands of the villain that has carried her off."

"That is to say," exclaimed Mr. Capsicum, " if they have not taken her far beyond this place."

"Do you think that probable?" asked the squire with alarm.

"It will depend entirely upon whether this Kestrel has received intelligence of your being in pursuit of him," replied the magistrate. "If he has received news to that effect, it is only reasonable to suppose that he will fly with her to some distant place."

"In that case," sighed Mr. Derwent, "she will be lost to us for ever."

" Not so, my dear sir," exclaimed the old gentleman, " for though the recovery of the young lady may be postponed, it cannot be long before we hear tidings of her, Nay, she may even find means to escape from her persecutor, and should that happen, I don't think it very likely Kestrel would venture again to take her from her own home."

" I'm not quite so sure about that," observed Peeps, " for Caleb is a regular devil-may-care sort of fellow, whenever he has made up his mind to anything, and as there is a large sum of money depending upon his keeping the poor girl in his hands, he'll not stick at trifles for the sake of making a profit by her."

" Then all I can say is, we must take care not to let him escape if we should be fortunate enough to come within reach of him," exclaimed the magistrate. " I should like to take him alive if we can, in order that he may be made an example of, but, rather than suffer him to slip through our fingers, we must shoot him."

" That is to say," suggested Mr. Peeps, " if some of his vagabond companions don't prevent it by shooting us instead."

" There's very little fear of resistance from men that know what would be the consequence of being taken," answered Mr. Capsicum. " Conscience makes cowards of such people, and the moment they see we are prepared to give them a warm reception, they'll seek for safety in flight. At least I have always seen it to be the case, and I know of no reason why it should not be so in the present instance."

" It may be so with the others," exclaimed the Squire, " but Caleb Kestrel, if driven to extremities, would fight to the last, and when every hope failed him, I fear he would sacrifice the unfortunate Amy to his infernal thirst for vengeance."

" I dare say, from all I have heard of him, he is a very desperate character," returned the magistrate; " but he must be a black hearted villain indeed, if he would murder a female that has never been guilty of an offence against him."

" Alas! you know him not," exclaimed the squire.

" Quite enough, for all that," replied Mr. Capsicum. " He is a thorough paced bad fellow there's no doubt; but as bad as he is have been brought to their senses before now, and if we only act with a little courage and discretion he will not much longer have it in his power to trouble or annoy you. By the bye, I wish this guide of yours would make his appearance, for I long to begin the search, and if we should be fortunate enough to meet with him in the cave, there'll be no chance of his escape if we take sufficient care to keep the entrance well guarded. But this man, Jabez Thompson, don't seem to come, and if he plays us false, I'm afraid, all our notable plans will be of no use."

" He will be here presently, I have no doubt," said Frank Marldale.

" But his long absence is enough to make one suspect that he has some plot brewing," exclaimed the magistrate.

" What sort of plot ?" demanded Peeps with alarm.

" That remains to be proved !"

" But what do you think he may do ?"

" There are a thousand different ways to do mischief when a man is resolved upon it," replied Mr. Capsicum. " I have a notion, however, that he may have a design to lead us into ambush, and in order to avoid that it will be necessary for us to keep in as compact a body as possible when we are following him to the place where he says this Kestrel has secreted himself. Each man of us must also carry a pistol in his hand, to fire at the assailants if they should appear, and if that should fail to disperse them we must immediately rush upon them sword in hand, and that, I'll answer for it will soon send them scampering away."

" Mecry on us," groaned poor Mr. Peeps, " what a very desperate affair this seems likely to turn out !"

" Not at all, if we only show a little courage," answered the old gentleman. " They know what would be the consequence if they are taken prisoners, and believe me there's not a man among them that will stand his ground if we do but exhibit a determination not to suffer a defeat. So take heart, my good friend, and to-morrow we shall have a good laugh at the discomfiture of the enemy."

"Laugh!" responded Peeps, "I never expect to laugh again."

"Nay, if you feel at all afraid, I should recommend you to remain here till our return."

"Remain here alone!" exclaimed the ex-showman, more terrified than ever at the bare suggestion. "I think I see myself stopping by myself, when for aught I

know the place may soon be filled by a score or two of smugglers! No, no, if I must perish in this disagreeable affair, it shall be in plenty of company, so with your leave, gentlemen, I'll make one of your party."

Before any reply could be made to this, Jabez Thompson entered the room, and with all the familiarity of an old acquaintance took a seat by the side of Frank Marldale.

"Well gentlemen," he exclaimed, helping himself to two or three glasses of No. 19.

wine in succession, "I suppose you all know what I have undertaken to do, and the terms that have been agreed on?"

All turned their eyes towards him in mute surprise, and the young farmer perceiving that they knew not what to make of the new guest, informed them that he was the person they had expected, and who had ome in fulfilment of his promise.

"Oh," said squire Derwent, "this then is the Jabez Thompson that you told us of ?"

"That's my name sir," replied the smuggler. "I've no reason to be ashamed of it, and especially among gentlemen that I am going to oblige with my services."

"Are you not rather going to oblige yourself by accepting a reward?" asked the magistrate.

"Put it any way you like sir," replied Jabez, now helping himself to nearly a rummer full of brandy. "I ain't any ways particular about trifles ; only let it be understood that I don't stir a peg till I have half the money down."

"If that was the bargain, I don't know that there will be any objection made to it," replied Squire Derwent. "We'll keep faith with you at any rate, but how are we to be satisfied that you will fulfil your part of it."

"I'll tell you," answered the fellow with easy indifference ;—"you want to go to Robin Hood's cave, don't you ?"

"Aye, if the person we are in pursuit of is there."

"Well, I suppose he is," replied Jabez, "for I know he and the young lady were there an hour or two ago."

"But," replied Mr. Capsicum, looking shrewdly at him, "Caleb Kestrel would not be there now if you, or any body else, have given him a hint of our intended visit to his retreat."

"Do you think I'd be guilty of such a thing ?" exclaimed the fellow, shrinking under the keen glance of the magistrate, but at the same time endeavouring to screen himself by an appearance of innocence. "No, sir," he added, "this Kestrel, or whatever his name may be, is nothing to me, and if I get paid for my services, you may depend upon my performing them faithfully."

"Answer me just one question," cried the magistrate, still eyeing him with a steady glance, "have you and I ever met each other on any previous occasion."

"You mean have I ever been brought before you on any charge ?"

"Exactly so."

"Then I'm happy to say we have never met under such circumstances, and I think I may say we never shall."

"Hump ! you mean to leave this part of the country, then, I suppose, when you have pocketed the reward?"

"I dare say I shall," replied Jabez Thompson, "for as I mean to give up my old ways now, there's no harm in confessing that I have been one of the smugglers that you and a good many other magistrates have been so long looking after. But that's all past now, and as I think of turning over a new leaf, it would never do to stay with a parcel of chaps that would be jealous of the little sum I'm to make by this bargain."

"Then you really mean to perform your promise honourably ?"

"I do."

"You know what would be the consequence if we had reason to suspect that you were going to play us false ?"

"Perhaps you would shoot me, and so save the reward that I was to have?"

"That might occur as a last resource," answered Mr. Capsicum, "but you have nothing to fear so long as everything appears to be fair and straightforward in your conduct. A reward has been promised you on certain conditions ; half is to be paid you before you leave this house, and the remainder as soon as the young lady has been delivered safely into the hands of her friends. When you have received the full amount, my advice is, that you go to some far distant place, where you will be removed from your old companions, and may perhaps support yourself in respectability in some honest employment."

"That's just what I thought of doing, sir," exclaimed Jabez, in a tone of apparent sincerity. "You see, sir, I've grown tired of my old way of life, and I should now like to be doing something o make amends for the past."

"We shall see by and by whether you are sincere," returned the magistrate ; "so now to come more immediately to the business we have in hand. Have you seen anything of this Caleb Kestrel since your conversation this morning with this gentleman ?"

"Yes," he replied, after some little hesitation ; "it must be confessed I have just given a look in at the cave."

"Indeed ! and what did you go there for, my man ?"

"Oh, nothing particular, sir," he replied ; "only to see if Kestrel was there, that was all ?"

"Did you see him ?"

"Yes, he was there safe enough."

"And the young lady ?"

"Was there also—I saw them both."

"You mean to tell us, then, that you said nothing to the man we are seeking, of our being here ?"

"How could I ?" exclaimed the other, "when I was not aware of anybody being in the neighbourhood except the person that spoke to me early this morning ?"

"Well," exclaimed Squire Derwent, "I for one place no great reliance in your promises after once the money has been given."

"What ! not when I should forfeit the other half if I don't take you to Robin Hood's cave ?"

"You are equivocating with us already," exclaimed the magistrate. "It is likely enough you may take us to the place you have named, but I can almost venture to say we shall find neither Caleb Kestrel nor his victim there."

"If they are not, how can I help it ?"

"Aye, that remains for us to find out," returned the old gentleman. "You may not be quite the rogue I expect, but somehow there's a very strong suspicion in my mind that you have been to the cave to put the pedlar on his guard."

"Why should I do that ?" demanded Jabez Thompson, "when I never saw anything of the man till he came here yesterday evening ? Besides, is it likely I should take part with him when so much money depends upon my delivering him up ?"

"And would he give you nothing," answered Mr. Derwent, "for giving him notice to make his escape ?"

"He might if he had the means," replied the fellow, "but I don't see how he's to bribe me when he has no money."

"You are not aware, then, that he expects to extort a large sum of money from me as the only condition on which he will part with the young lady he has stolen away."

"Kestrel has not let me into any of his secrets."

"I see plainly enough that nothing is to be got out of this man," exclaimed the magistrate. "He is too cunning to admit anything that will militate against him, and it therefore only remains to trust him just as far as we can see, and no farther. Thus we have no choice but to place ourselves under his guidance, and if any trickery should be intended we shall know how to punish him."

"Upon my life, gentlemen," muttered Jabez, "this is not exactly the way to treat a chap that is ready and willing to do you a service. However, if you repent your bargain, have nothing to do with me, and then Caleb Kestrel will be able to carry the girl somewhere else, where you'll never be able to find her."

"The fellow speaks but too truly there," exclaimed Squire Derwent, "and we must, at all hazards, trust to the honourable performance of the duty he has undertaken. At any rate we shall be too many for him if he proves false."

"I know what you mean," replied Jabez, "you've brought some of the coast guard with you, and think to frighten me into doing my duty, though there's no reason why I should be doubted."

"How do you know we have assistance at hand ?"

"Why, the truth is, I'm not quite such a sleepy-headed chap as you take me for," answered the fellow, "I saw the gentleman that I first spoke to this morning ride off towards the town, and the thought then struck me that he was going to ask for help in case the smugglers should prove too many for him. So to make myself quite certain about it, I watched for their return, and about an hour ago I saw a lot of chaps hide themselves in the wood till they are wanted."

"And have you informed your companions of it ?" asked the old gentleman.

"Not I," he replied, "for it was nothing to me, and if I made any stir about it there's no telling what mischief it might do. I should, however, advise you not to let any of our chaps know what sort of people are in the neighbourhood, for there's a strong body of 'em when they are all collected together, and if it comes to hard fighting I know which side would get the worst of it."

"The smugglers of course."

"Not a bit of it," exclaimed Jabez Thompson, "everything would depend upon gaining the victory, and they'd fight like desperate men as they've always proved themselves to be."

"So I expect," replied Mr. Capsicum; "and we have come here prepared accordingly. Our men are well armed in case of an emergency, and should we come to blows they are ordered to spare none that are found with arms in their hands. In short the presence of these daring smugglers is found to be a most intolerable nuisance in the neighbourhood, and if they think proper to give us the opportunity we want, by appearing in a hostile attitude, we shall unshrinkingly prepare our duty by exterminating the whole band at a single blow."

"Well, I've nothing at all to do with it," returned Jabez Thompson, "but it seems to me that talking is the easiest part of this business, for our people are as well armed and as courageous as your's when once driven to fighting. However, that's not the question just now; here am I ready to perform my part of the contract, and when half the reward has been paid into my hands, I'll go and lead you to Robin Hood's Cave."

Without making any reply to this, Mr. Derwent took out his pocket-book, and counting the amount in bank notes, handed them over to the fellow who was to act as their guide. These Jabez crammed into his fob, and then drinking off another rummer full of brandy, hastily rose from his seat, exclaiming,—

"Now then, gentlemen, I'm your humble servant whenever you are ready to go with me. I've been suspected, it seems, of intending to play a double game in this business, but you'll soon have reason to acknowledge that I'm a man of my word. At all events, I'll take you to the place, and if the persons you are seeking don't happen to be there, it will be no fault of mine."

While he was speaking the party rose from their seats, and looking to their arms to see that they were in proper condition in the event of their being required, they followed Jabez from the house, and made their way towards the place where they were in hopes of discovering Amy and rescuing her from the hands of her captor. In a few minutes afterwards the landlord and Dick Ratcliffe came forward from an adjoining room, where they had been listening to a great part of the preceding conversation.

"Who'd have thought of Jabez Thompson turning out to be such a confounded villain as to betray his comrades ?" exclaimed the former, as he fastened the door to prevent the sudden return of any of the party. "He has actually sold 'em all for a bribe, and, I suppose, the next thing we hear will be that the whole of the poor fellows will be either killed or captured."

"Oh, you needn't be afraid of any harm befalling them," returned the other, "for they know the enemy is too strong for 'em, and not a man among the gang will venture out to oppose them, when there's not a chance of doing any good."

"How do you know that ?"

"Because we've held a consultation together, to be sure," answered Dick Ratcliffe. "I happened to watch Jabez to the cave, and suspecting something was wrong, I softly crept in after him, and overheard all that passed between him and Caleb Kestrel."

"Well, and what took place?"

"Why, I learnt pretty well the same things that we heard to-night," answered the other. "Thompson has undertaken to lead the party to the hiding place, in consideration of a large sum of money that has been promised for his services. However, the fellow is not quite as bad as you suspect, for he has given Kestrel notice of what is about to happen, and he and the girl are now in another hiding place, where they will not be very easily found."

"But he'll let the preventive service's chaps into the secret of one of our best haunts."

"It can't be helped if he does," replied Ratcliffe, "and I don't know that it will matter much, seeing that we have plenty of others that we can always defend against greater numbers than they are likely to bring against us."

"And is Jabez to be the only one that is to make a profit of this?"

"The truth is he thinks himself devilish cunning," exclaimed the other, "but it will be a strange thing to me if he don't find out before long that he has got quite as knowing ones to deal with. In short he shall divide the money among us, or his life won't be worth a week's purchase."

"How much has he promised him?"

"A hundred and fifty pounds."

"And part of that he has received to-night."

"Yes, he has got half of it, and I fancy that's all he is ever likely to have."

"Will they break their word with him then?" asked the host.

"I have a notion they will," answered the other, "for when they find the man they are after has fled, they'll begin to suspect that their guide has been playing a false game, and then Jabez may hook for the rest of the promised reward. However, the sum he has already received is a pretty large one, and we must go snacks with him, or he'll lose it all, as well as his life."

"What will be the use of either one or the other to us if we are to have our business here knocked on the head?" asked the landlord. "The coast-guard people have been long wanting to find out some of our secret hiding places, and when once they've made a beginning it won't be long before they entirely rout us."

"Hang it," exclaimed Dick Ratcliffe, "what a fellow you are for always looking at the worst side of a question. We have carried on our business here for more than a dozen years without anybody being able to rout us, and it will be hard if we can't stand our ground now as well as we ever did."

"You may accuse me of looking at things on the worst side," retorted the other, "but we have found out that Jabez Thompson can act the rogue towards us when it suits his own pocket, and who can say that he won't betray the whole band if these people offer money enough to make it worth his while."

"We must keep a sharp watch on him to prevent anything of that kind," returned the other, "and the moment there's any reason to believe that he intends treachery to his old comrades he shall have a bullet through his head, if there's no other hand besides mine to do it."

"And poor satisfaction that will be when the mischief's done."

"It will be our own fault if we let the matter go too far," answered Dick Ratcliffe, "and the best thing we can do will be to give him a broad hint that we suspect him, and are not to be trifled with if we should find our notions are correct."

"But what if he chooses to cut our connection and give the information when he is out of our reach?"

"All these ifs and buts show you to be a coward in your heart," exclaimed the smuggler. "For my own part I think there's nothing to fear from Jabez when he finds that we suspect him, and are keeping a close look out upon all his actions. Besides, he knows there's a good cargo to be landed on this coast as soon as we can find an opportunity, and he'll hardly be fool enough to lose his chance of the profits when it's likely to be so well worth the having. But enough of this, my boy, let us once see the enemy sheer off, and then we'll soon come to a close understanding with Jabez Thompson. By the bye, who is this chap that has brought a woman amongst us?"

"I know nothing about him, but what I've heard from Jabez himself," replied the host. "He speaks of him as one Caleb Kestrel, and a rough sort of chap he is too, by all accounts."

"And the female?"

"Oh, he makes a mighty secret about her, but I believe he has carried her off from her home in order to get hold of a large sum of money by way of ransom."

"She's rich, then?"

"I believe she is," replied the host, "but whether or not, there's plenty of money to be found somewhere, and Caleb Kestrel don't mean to let her off till her friends come down handsomely. Indeed, from all accounts, I believe he reckons upon receiving some thousands."

"Humph! he reckons his chickens before they're hatched."

"I don't know how that may be, but he has the girl under his thumb, and if the money ain't forthcoming very soon, he means to take her abroad to some place where she'll never be found till all his demands have been agreed to."

"And in the meantime," observed the smuggler, "Jabez Thompson, without consulting us upon the subject, has presumed to give him an asylum in one of our hiding places."

"Yes; he was promised something, and thought to pocket all that money himself, as well as the reward that was offered by the people that were here just now, for taking them to the cave where they were concealed."

"The fellow has been trying to outwit us then?" exclaimed Dick Ratcliffe. "He thought to keep all the profits of this affair to himself, but he'll find himself most confoundedly deceived, for he shall either act fairly towards his comrades or meet the reward of his intended treachery. But I say, old boy, you must not say a word about this to him, or he'll vanish with what he has got, before we can make him disgorge any of it. Keep him in the dark as long as you can, and when the proper time comes we'll manage to bring him to a correct reckoning."

"We shall have some trouble to do that, I'm thinking," returned the landlord.

"Then he shall die like a dog that he is!" exclaimed Ratcliffe. "The fellow that would deceive his friends deserves no pity, and as Jabez Thompson knows that I am not a chap to be trifled with, he'll not be mad enough to refuse us our fair share of the money that he ought to divide among us."

"Aye, aye, its all very well to say so," exclaimed the other, "but how shall we be able to help ourselves if he should bolt away to night, as soon as he has led his party to the cave?"

"That shall be managed easily enough," answered Ratcliffe, "for I'll presently follow 'em to the place they are going to, and if Thompson attempts to run away, I'll bring him down with a bullet, like a scoundrel as he is."

"And get taken up as a murderer?"

"Nonsense!" exclaimed the other, "who can tell in the dark whose hand it was that did it? Besides, I'll take good care not to show myself till the coast is clear of our enemies."

"Which I fancy will not be for some time if you are rash enough to commit a murder.'

"Murder! I call it nothing but justice, though it may be a little sharpish. However, be that as it may, I shall go and keep a look out after him, for the fellow is not to be trusted now that we have found him out at double dealing, and we must be prepared for the worst in case he should be persuaded to betray us to the party."

"Shall I go with you to watch him?"

"You may if you like," exclaimed Dick Ratcliffe; "but mind we must manage this affair very cautiously, for if they should see us prowling about there's no knowing what would come of it, for it seems there's a strong body of the coast-guard to assist in case of need, and our party would have but a poor chance against fellows that are armed to the teeth."

Whilst uttering these words Ratcliffe and his companion left the house and cautiously took their way towards the rocks from whence they could see all that was going on. In a short time afterwards Jabez and the party he had been guiding emerged from the cave, and as they passed near the place where the two men were concealed, the latter could hear enough to convince them that the search had ended in disappointment. On arriving at the beach, the magistrate separated from the party to return home, whilst Derwent and his friends, vexed and chagrined at the result of their expedition, returned to the public-house where it was agreed they were to pass the night.

CHAPTER XVIII,

JABEZ EXCUSES HIMSELF AND MAKES FRESH PROMISES ;—THE PURSUERS RETURN HOME AFTER A PROFITLESS JOURNEY ;—AN ATTEMPTED EXTORTION.

On entering the room appropriated to the use of travellers, Squire Derwent and friends seated themselves round the fire to talk over and deplore the total failure of the errand on which they had started. Indeed, so totally were they engrossed with this all absorbing subject that they were unconsious of having been followed into the house by Jabez, until that worthy individual abruptly demanded the fulfilment of the contract that had been entered into between them.

"When your part of it is completed," replied the squire, in no very good humour at the interruption, you will find that mine will be strictly complied with. In one word, assist in the recovery of the young lady we are in search of, and I will even go so far as to double the sum that has been promised."

"Then you don't mean to pay me the remainder of the money?"

"Not till you have led me to the place where Caleb Kestrel has sought concealment."

"I have done that already," answered the fellow, "and its no fault of mine that the bird had flown."

"But I begin to suspect that he left the place in consequence of information received from you.

"That's not very likely," exclaimed Thompson, "when I must have known that you would suspect me, and then that all chance of getting the remainder of the money would be at an end. I've acted fairly and honourably to you sir, and I hope you won't wrong a poor fellow like me out of my rights."

"You must not call them rights before you have fully completed your bargain," answered Mr. Derwent, "nor shall I be moved from my present intention till you have afforded me all the assistance you promised. Besides, the man we are in search of is no doubt lurking somewhere near the place, and I dare say if the task is set about with determination you will be able to ascertain where he is to be found between this time and the morning."

"How am I to know where to find him ?"

"It's not for me to tell you how it's to be done," answered the squire, "but I should imagine that the secret is easily to be come at if you inquire among your companions."

"What companions do you mean ?"

"The smugglers, to be sure!"

"Smugglers !" exclaimed Jabez with well feigned indignation. "Do you take me for one of those sort of chaps, then ?"

"It matters very little what I take you for," laughed Mr. Derwent, "for I am not likely to act upon my suspicions so long as you shew a readiness to assist me in the purpose I have in view. In a word, will you earn the remainder of the reward by continuing the search ?"

" Of course I will," he replied, " though, for that matter, I consider the bargain, as far as I'm concerned, has been completed. I've taken you to the cave where I know he took the young lady, and if he has taken her away again, it's a hard thing to punish me for it."

" The punishment, as you call it," returned Mr. Derwent, " will be of very short duration, if you think proper to perform all you promised. Learn where this Caleb Kestrel is, and you shall not have long to complain of being treated with injustice."

" And supposing the smugglers have taken him and the young lady over the water in one of their vessels ?"

" Hah ! you are aware then that they have done so ?"

" Indeed, I am not aware of anything of the kind," replied Jabez ; " but I have heard that such a scheme has been talked about, so you had better make up your mind never to seen the young lady again, unless you are prepared to come down handsomely."

" I should not heed what this man says," interposed Frank Marldale, " for he seems to be concerned in the affair, and only throws out this hint for the purpose of exciting your fears, and thus extorting a large sum of money."

" But we know the desperate character of Caleb Kestrel, and if ever he takes Amy away from this country, all hope of her recovery will be for ever at an end. Nay, I have even fears that he may have recourse to assassination, in order to complete his revenge."

" Believe me, there is no ground for so horrible a suspicion," exclaimed Marldale, " for money seems to be his object, and he only wishes to keep her in his custody till he has wrung from you a large sum as her ransom. That he is a villain of the deepest dye, we have unfortunately too much proof, but he will never take her life, so long as there is a prospect of enriching himself through her means."

" Then why not come to his terms ?" suggested Brassy Popjoy.

" I would do so this instant," answered Derwent, " but that no faith can be placed in the scoundrel's word, even if I should agree to pay him the sum he wishes to extort."

" That may be," observed Frank Marldale, " but he would take yours, I should suppose, if you promise to accede to his demands immediately upon the young lady's restoration to freedom."

" If you think that, gentlemen, you are uncommonly mistaken," exclaimed Thompson, " for he's an artful card, and aint to be deceived by promises. No, no; you must down with the money, and trust to his honour afterwards, or the girl will be taken to some outlandish place, where all your cunning will never find her."

" How is it that you apear to know the inmost thoughts of this ruffian ?" demanded the squire.

" Lor' bless you ?" he replied, " I know no more about 'em than any gentleman here present. But I know how I should act in the same case, and can suppose that Kestrel will not be quite so soft as to give up the girl till he has got all the ready he asks for."

" Will you endeavour to see him and make the best terms you can ?"

" Will you pay me if I do ?"

" Aye, liberally."

" And the other money that I was to have had to night ?"—

" Shall be paid to you at the same time."

" Then it's a bargain," exclaimed Jabez ; " but it must be on condition that you do one thing I ask."

" What is it ?"

" That you and the other two gentlemen leave this place to-morrow morning."

Why do you desire our absence?" asked Mr. Derwent.

" Because while strangers are about, the smugglers will refuse to give me any information as to where Kestrel is to be found. They look upon your presence here with suspicion, and I've had a hint from 'em that they've a notion I'm going to betray 'em."

" But how am I to know the result of your inquiries?"

" Oh, don't trouble yourself about that," replied the fellow, "for I promise you shall have all the particulars as soon as I have any to inform you of."

MR. TRUBBS ALARMS THE DOMESTICS OF DERWENT HALL.

" Do you know me then?"

" I know well enough where to find Derwent Hall," he replied. " Your friend let me into a few secrets this morning; so, as there will be no difficulty in finding you out, you may return home quite satisfied about hearing from me as soon as I have made Caleb Kestrel acquainted with your proposition."

" Cannot one of us remain here whilst the others return home?" demanded Frank Marldale.

No. 20.

" You can do as you please about it, gentlemen," answered the other, " but I shan't attempt to do anything, so long as any of you remain in this neighbourhood."

" Perhaps you think we should watch you ?" exclaimed Mr. Derwent.

" I shouldn't at all wonder but you might," he replied. " However, you wouldn't get much good by that, for I should take care to prevent any discovery by not doing anything so long as there was a chance of being followed. So now you know my mind, and can do as you think proper in the matter."

" How are we to know that you will perform what you have undertaken ?" demanded the squire.

" Oh you needn't have much doubt about that," he replied, " for when a liberal reward is promised for my services, I'm not very likely to break my word. Do as I have said ;—go from this place to-morrow morning, and I dare say within three days you'll hear something from me."

" Well," exclaimed Mr. Derwent after a pause, " though greatly against my own inclination, I agree to your terms. But mind, there must be no trifling or unnecessary delay, for we pretty well know the lawless life you have been leading, and it will be in our power at any time to bring you to punishment."

" I don't like to be threatened," muttered Jabez sullenly ; " but never mind, I suppose it must be put up with, so, to avoid coming to a quarrel I shall take my leave. Only remember, you must be away from here in the morning, for I shall not move a step till I find the coast is quite clear."

Having given this intimation, Jabez Thompson took his departure, leaving the three gentlemen to discuss the proposition he had made. Brassy Popjoy was delighted at the prospect of so soon getting out of a neighbourhood where he apprehended no little danger to himself, but his companions entertained opinions quite the reverse, expressing the greatest reluctance to leave the place till they had accomplished the purpose for which they had set out. However, the more they argued the question the more they became convinced that if anything was to be expected from the assistance of Jabez Thompson, it would be through compliance with the terms he had laid down. It was therefore resolved, much to the gratification of Popjoy, that they should return home in the morning, and wait, with what patience they could, for the information promised by the man who had undertaken to act as their agent for the recovery of Amy. By the time this resolution was adopted the landlord returned, and refreshments having been placed before them, they shortly afterwards retired to their several apartments, each to ponder over the events of the day, and to form his own conclusion as to what would be the result of the affair they were engaged in.

The next morning they all three met again at the breakfast table, where the matter was again discussed, but without arriving at any conclusion that appeared to be satisfactory. At the conclusion of the meal they settled the somewhat extravagant demands of the landlord, ordered their horses, and immediately set out on their return home, which they did not reach till a late hour in the evening. There numerous inquiries awaited them, to which they had no satisfactory reply to give, and the fate of the unfortunate Amy appeared to be more than ever involved in darkness and obscurity. The general impression however was that Kestrel would remove her to some place which would not be easily discovered, and that consequently it might be weeks or months before anything was heard of her. To Cecil Derwent this suspense was torture of the most cruel description, yet he determined to wait the three days mentioned by Jabez Thompson, and then, if nothing was heard from him, to visit Mr. Capsicum, the magistrate, once more, and to request his further assistance to discover whether Kestrel was still concealed 'in the neighbourhood.

Heavily and wearily passed away the hours, and the anxiously expected third day had nearly come to a conclusion, when, as Cecil Derwent was sitting alone, a servant entered to announce that a stranger requested an immediate interview with him. Not doubting but it was the person he was so much wishing to see, he ordered him to be shown in, and scarcely had this direction been given than—not Jabez Thompson, but a stranger,—entered the room. On the attendant disappearing, the stranger threw himself into a seat opposite to Mr. Derwent, and introduced himself as one Richard Ratcliffe, who had come on a special mission to treat for the release of Amy. The squire looked at his strange visitor with suspicion, and then demanded when, and upon what terms she was to be restored to the protection of her friends.

"The when will depend upon yourself," answered Ratcliffe, with cool insolence; "the terms are arranged by Caleb Kestrel, and may appear rather exorbitant;—but, when favours are asked—and especially such a one as this—people must not hesitate about trifles."

"Is the young lady still in this country?" demanded the squire.

"She is."

"And upon my complying with certain arrangements, Kestrel will surrender her up?"

"Yes."

"What sum of money would he extort?"

"Rather a large one, as I before hinted," replied Ratcliffe. "He has opened his mouth rather wide, it must be confessed,—and yet, under all circumstances, I don't know that ten thousand pounds ought to be considered too much."

"Ten thousand pounds!"

"That's what he told me to demand," replied the fellow; "and I may add, that he is determined not to accept of a shilling less, because he knows well enough that you'll pay it rather than let the girl remain in his hands. By the bye, if you have not so large a sum of money in cash, you may give him one thousand pounds only, and the remainder he will be satisfied with in such a portion of your estate as will amount to the value. So you see, after all, he is not inclined to deal very hard with you."

"And what," asked Cecil Derwent fiercely, "if I call for assistance and order you into custody, as an accomplice of the scoundrel who broke into this house and stole from it a helpless female?"

"This is my reply," exclaimed the ruffian, starting up from his seat and presenting a pistol at the squire's head:—"Stir from that sofa at your peril; utter a sound of alarm, and that moment you are a dead man?"

"Villain!" cried Cecil Derwent, "did you come here to murder me?"

"No," he replied; "I don't want to harm you, so long as there's no danger to myself. I came here to be the means of restoring a young lady, who, I understand, was destined to be your bride. Whether she is worth the sum that has been demanded is a question for you to answer, but all I can say is, that Caleb Kestrel will never part with her under the terms he has proposed."

"Then I must procure assistance that will force him to deliver her up to me."

"What will assistance do for you when she is hundreds, or it may be thousands of miles away?" exclaimed the other, "You have no child to deal with in Caleb Kestrel, but a man that knows how to meet greater difficulties than you are likely to throw in his way."

"But there are those watching in the neighbourhood where he is supposed to be concealed, who will never give up their object till he has been secured and the young lady rescued."

"Kestrel is aware that he has enemies abroad," answered the other, "and it's not likely that he'll show himself when he knows the danger of it. Besides, he has the ready means of getting abroad with his prize, and if once the girl leaves England, it's certain she'll never see it again."

"What motive can he have for taking her abroad?"

"He has two," replied the ruffian; "one is that she shall be beyond your reach, and the other that, in order that he may possess this property, he may by and by force her to become his wife."

"Hah!" exclaimed Derwent, startled by these words. "Does the villain dare to presume so far?"

"Presume! is there any great presumption in his seeking the hand that has wandered through the world with travelling show-people ? Isn't the pedlar as good as her any day ?"

"It was his villany that forced her to adopt a wandering life," answered Cecil Derwent. "To him she owes all the sufferings and privations she has endured, and yet he now has the unparalleled baseness to contemplate forcing her into a marriage with him. But his intention will be frustrated, for Amy would rather perish than wed herself to the man whom she can only look upon with loathing and disgust."

"Oh, it may be all very well for you to say so, Mr. Derwent," exclaimed the other, "but girls are not so fond of dying as all that comes to. Besides, if she don't like her husband she needn't live with him, if she chooses to give up all her property for his use. You look daggers at me, Mr. Derwent, but I am a plain-spoken fellow, and would rather tell you how matters are likely to turn out, than go away, leaving you under a mistaken notion that Caleb Kestrel is to be foiled."

"This is only done to intimidate me."

"I have told you nothing but the truth," replied Ratcliffe; "if you are obstinate, the girl may soon be the wife of Caleb Kestrel, and yet you hesitate to give him the ten thousand pounds he has demanded for her release!"

"What time does he give me to consider his proposal?" demanded Cecil Derwent.

"Not an hour," he replied. "The matter requires no consideration, for you must either agree to his demand, or the girl goes abroad in less than a week from this time. So you see parleying in this case is out of the question, and you must make up your mind without any nonsense or dilly-dallying."

"Let him come here, then, and we may come to terms."

"Come here, eh?" exclaimed the ruffian. "Is it likely he would trust himself among you and your friends?"

"Then, be the danger what it may," returned Mr. Derwent, "I will meet him in any place we may appoint."

"Do you think that would be prudent?"

"Perhaps not; but at any rate I am willing to run the risk."

"Aye, aye, you may be mad enough for anything," retorted Ratcliffe, "but I don't think it's very likely Kestrel will let an enemy know where he is to be found. And even if he does, you may be sure he would not let you go loose again till he and the girl were beyond your reach."

"But I believe an arrangement might be made between us that would ensure her immediate release."

"It dont matter to me what you believe, Squire Derwent," exclaimed the other, "for I'm sent here to make the bargain for him, and if I don't take back a satisfactory answer, you'll have reason enough afterwards to be sorry for it."

"And how," asked Mr. Derwent, "am I to be satisfied that he would give up Amy, even supposing I agree to his terms?"

"Why, I suppose you must rely upon his honour for that?"

"Honour? Can I expect it from a man who has proved himself to be a villain in so many instances?"

"I'm not here to argufy that matter," exclaimed Ratcliffe; "but it's my opinion that if he gets the money, he'll not want to encumber himself with the girl. All he thinks about, is getting safe across the herring-pond, where he may live like a gentleman upon the portion he expects to get out of you."

"Then tell him from me," answered the Squire, "that I'll make no terms except with himself. I am willing to meet him when and where he pleases; and nothing shall induce me to part with a single coin till the female he has carried off has been safely surrendered into the hands of her friends."

"Then you mean to say I am to tell him that there is no chance of a ransom being given for the girl?"

"When she is free I will make him a liberal offer," replied Derwent; "but it is impossible to trust to the word of a man who would have no scruple in breaking it."

"And yet," returned the other, coolly, "it strikes me you will find yourself obliged to take it, if he continues obstinate."

"We shall see that before long," exclaimed Squire Derwent; "for he may be the first to yield, when he makes the discovery that I am not to be forced into his terms."

"I believe you profess to love the girl?"

"So much so that I would willingly sacrifice my life to extricate her from the peril into which she has fallen."

"But you may release her upon much easier terms than that."

"So you would make me believe," replied Mr. Derwent; "but I have good reason to suspect that if the money is paid the young lady will be no nearer to her release than she is now. In one word, you may tell Caleb Kestrel that I am willing to come to terms with him, but they must not be altogether of his own dictation."

"And if I do tell him so," answered Dick Ratcliffe, "I know well enough what the consequence will be. But that's no business of mine, and I only give you the hint in order that you may consider the matter before you send back such a message by me. The young lady is completely in his power, and this is not a time for you to irritate him by a refusal."

"Am I, then, to be forced into a concession?"

"You know better than I do what ought to be done," exclaimed the other. "I'm only giving a hint of what will follow in case of a refusal, and if you don't choose to take it, there'll only be yourself to blame for whatever may be the consequences. In five minutes you must come to some decision or another, for at the end of that time I shall be off to inform Kestrel of what has taken place."

"You have already received my answer," replied the squire.

"Then you have determined to abandon the young lady to her fate?"

"On the contrary, I have resolved to take speedy and effectual measures for her relief."

"By going in search of her, I suppose?"

"Aye, and that, too, without delay."

"Then take my word for it, you will not succeed," replied the fellow "Caleb Kestrel is not a customer to be dealt with quite so easily as you fancy; and as I shall reach him before you can possibly do so, he will have plenty of time to carry off the wench and convey her to some place where neither you nor your friends will ever be able to find her."

"Wretch!" exclaimed Mr. Derwent, "you shall not be permitted to leave this place till my object has been accomplished."

"Who is there to hinder me?"

"I will," replied the squire; "I have assistance enough in this house to secure you, and—"

"Don't be too fast in your notions about that," interrupted Dick Ratcliffe. "I have not come here unprovided with the means of defence, and if any tricks are played, yours will be the first life sacrificed in the struggle for liberty. Besides, Kestrel is expecting my return every moment, and if he don't see me by a certain time he'll guess there's mischief brewing, and will put himself far enough beyond your reach. So keep your temper, Squire Derwent, and try if you can't be a little more reasonable."

"On one condition no violence will be offered," he replied. "Go back to him who sent you, and endeavour to persuade him into giving me a meeting, and, in return, I promise to take no advantage of his being in my power."

"Do you think he'd believe your promise, even if I was to take him such message?"

"Then there's an end of our conference," exclaimed Mr. Derwent. "Go back to him who sent you here, and say that, skilfully as he has woven this infamous plot of his, I will yet find means to foil him. Aye, even though I have to follow him to the further end of the globe, I'll have that vengeance that his crime merits.'

" You'll not be very likely to find him," returned the other ; " and now, as I see there's no chance of doing anything with you, I'll tell you a secret that I think will cause no little surprise. What should you say, Mr. Derwent, if within a few minutes I bring the girl into your presence ?"

" Deceive me not with such a hope," he replied ; " for all you have been saying proves that she is still with Kestrel."

" So I wanted you to suppose ; but the truth is I brought her with me, and she is now within call."

" Hah !" exclaimed the squire, " convince me of that, and fifty pounds shall be your reward."

" When ?"

" The moment she is restored."

" Then the money will soon be mine," exclaimed Ratcliffe. " You look as if you doubted me, squire, but for all that, I've told you nothing but the honest truth, as you'll presently see."

" Impossible. Caleb Kestrel would not have restored her without first receiving the ransom he had demanded."

" But she comes with a message from him, and it is expected that the confidence he thus places in you will not be without its reward. He has, therefore, sent her back by me on these conditions :—That you take no further steps against him, and that the sum of money demanded shall be immediately paid to him."

" How long a time does he give me for consideration ?"

" Three days ; and if at the end of that time the terms are not fulfilled, means will be taken to carry off the girl again, and you will never have another chance of seeing her."

" Am I to understand then," demanded the squire, " that all you have been telling me is false ?"

" Certainly."

" What was your motive ?"

" To work upon your fears, and extort the money that Kestrel has named as her ransom. You, however, choose to be obstinate, and as every thing had failed I was at last obliged to confess that the girl has been sent back on the condition I have mentioned. But I warn you, Squire Derwent, not to hesitate longer than the three days that are given, for, if the terms are not agreed to by that time, Amy will once more be in the hands of Caleb Kestrel, or perish before your eyes. So now you understand the matter in its true light, and if you promise to consider it fairly, I am ready to produce the girl, who no doubt will prevail upon you to take the step that alone can save her from further persecution."

" Where is she ?" demanded Mr. Derwent eagerly.

" So near that if I but open that window and give a signal, she will in a few moments be in your presence."

" Why did she not come with you ?" asked the squire, still doubting the truth of what he heard.

" Because I thought it best to try what could be done, whilst you believed her to be in the hands of Caleb Kestrel," he replied. " So I left her in the shrubbery under the care of a comrade, who has my strict orders not to let her move from the spot, till he hears my signal."

" Then in Heaven's name delay no longer."

" You forget our bargain, squire," he replied ; " give me the fifty pounds you promised, and Amy shall be here directly."

" May I rely upon your word ?"

" To be sure you may ; I'm telling no lie now, Mr. Derwent, though you may perhaps think I'm only telling you this story, for the purpose of getting the money."

Doubtful of the truth of what he heard, yet unwilling to throw away even the slightest chance, Mr. Derwent opened his desk, took out the required sum, and placing it in the hands of the ruffian, demanded the fulfilment of the promise that had been given. Having deliberately counted the gold, Ratcliffe carefully deposited it in his pocket, and then opening the window gave the signal whistle that had been previously agreed on. For a moment or two afterwards he watched to ascertain if it had been heard, and having satisfied himself on that point, he left the room, without giving utterance to another word. Within a few seconds Amy rushed in, pale and exhausted, and sank faintingly into the extended arms of Cecil Derwent.

CHAPTER XIX.

A CONSULTATION IN THE KITCHEN.—AMY'S RETURN DISCUSSED.—AN APPARITION, OR SOMETHING VERY LIKE ONE.—BRASSY POPJOY TALKS OF RETURNING HOME, BUT CERTAIN WEIGHTY REASONS INDUCE HIM TO PROLONG HIS VISIT.

NEWS, whether good, bad, or indifferent, generally travels quickly, and in the present instance it was not long before the unexpected return of Amy was known to all the servants in the establishment, through John the footman, who had been a listener in an adjoining room during the whole period of the interview, between Mr. Derwent and Dick Ratcliffe. No sooner had he witnessed the departure of the visitor, and the re-appearance of our heroine, than down he went into the kitchen, and there related before a full conclave, the extraordinary news of which he was the bearer. Some expressed their surprise, and others their disbelief of the story, but, whichever way their opinion went, all were ready enough to question and cross-question him, as to what he had seen and overheard. Mrs. Nicely, the housekeeper, in particular, was very sceptical, as to the probability of John's extraordinary narrative, and absolutely refused to believe a word of it, till the fact was demonstrated before her eyes.

"Very well, ma'am, of course you can do as you please about that," exclaimed the indignant footman, "but seeing 's believing, and if what I've been telling you aint true, may I be eternally ——"

"For shame, John!" cried Martha, putting her hand over his mouth, just in time to prevent the escape of the last word; "I declare it's quite horrid to hear you swear so before females, that you ought to treat with decorum and respect.

"It's enough to make a parson swear, when one's doubted after speaking nothing but the truth. However time will show, which of us is right, and which wrong, and then you'll all be ashamed of yourselves, for doubting my word."

"Are you sure the person you saw was not some other person?" asked Mrs. Nicely.

"To be sure I am," he replied; "I saw her as plainly as I do you this moment, and if that's not enough, I heard master call her by name, when she fell fainting into his arms."

"This is the most marvellous thing if true, that I ever heard of," exclaimed the housekeeper. "First of all a villain takes the young lady away for the sake of the money he may be able to make by it, and then he sends her back again without receiving even so much as a silver sixpence! But I'm sure there must be some mistake about it; you must have been dreaming, John."

"So you may think," he replied, "but I was wide awake enough to hear every word that was said, and at one time I was just going to rush into the room, for the strange chap pulled out a pistol, and threatened to shoot master, if he uttered a word, or tried in any other way to raise an alarm."

"Then why did'nt you come and tell us of what was going on?" asked Tom Thornley, the groom. "There's enough of us men folks in the house to protect the governor, and hang me if we wouldn't soon have given the fellow a lesson, that he'd not have forgot in a hurry."

"I'd a very good reason for what I did," answered John, "for I heard the chap threaten master that he'd shoot him dead on the spot, if any body came to take him, and that he'd afterwards serve all the rest the same, if they tried to prevent him leaving the place."

"What a horrible ruffian!" exclaimed the housekeeper.

"Oh! so you begin to believe me at last, do you?" cried John. "Your opinion is changing, is it, about the young lady's return."

"Why yes, I'm rather in hopes you are right," she replied; "but really the story is such a strange one, that you can hardly wonder at people fancying you must have made a mistake. So the young lady fainted in master's arms, did she?"

"Yes, as true as you are sitting there."

"That was improper," exclaimed Mrs. Nicely, prudishly.

"But suppose she couldn't help herself."

"Don't talk to me about being unable to help it," retorted the housekeeper. "Young ladies can't be too particular about whose arms they faint in, and as for Mr. Derwent, I'm surprised and shocked, that he has not rung the bell for me or some other female, to take charge of Amy and bring her to."

"There's no occasion for all this virtuous indignation, old lady," replied the footman, "for I saw Mrs. Peeps run into the room directly afterwards, and if she cant take care of the girl that she has brought up as her own daughter, I don't know who can."

"Oh, if Mrs. Peeps is with them, there's an end of the matter," exclaimed the old lady in a calmer tone. "She seems to be a good motherly sort of body enough, but for all that I wonder master can demean himself by making companions of such low people as this showman and his wife."

"Don't you know why he likes 'em?" asked Martha.

"No."

"Then I can tell you," she continued; "he feels grateful to the people that have acted with so much kindness towards the girl he is going to make his wife, and for my own part I admire him for not being too proud, to offer a home to those who have proved themselves so well worthy of his kindness."

"And I'm sure both of 'em conduct themselves," added John, "which is more than can be said for Mr. Brassy Popjoy and his groom, who both of them, and the last in particular, keep the house in a constant broil with their queer doings."

"But they are going away soon," exclaimed Mrs. Nicely, "and a good riddance too, for Mr. Trubbs is too fond of his monkey tricks to please me, and seems to be never so much delighted as when he's doing something to frighten people out of their shoes."

"Aye," returned Tom Thornley, with a sagacious shake of the head, "but let him look out for squalls, for I've a rod in pickle for him if he and his master dont take themselves off to London pretty soon. Its only a few days ago that he rode master's favourite mare, without either with your leave, or by your leave, and brought her home with both her knees broken."

"And what did the squire say to that?" asked John.

"Nothing at all," replied the groom, "for it seems that he and his master can do just as they please, and a tolerable use they make of their privilege, hang 'em."

"And yet Popjoy has done one good act, too, since he has been here," observed John.

"What's that?"

"Why, he was one of the first that offered to go with master, when he was about to set out in search of the young lady."

"That may be all very well so far," returned Tom Thornley, "but I'll answer it he hung back whenever he saw there was any danger in the way. He's a regular coward, I can see, and if he made the offer, it was only because he was ashamed to stay behind when everybody else was willing to lend his assistance. However, it appears Miss Amy has come back to the old hall safe and sound, and now, I suppose, to prevent her being carried off again by that pedlar fellow, master will make her his wife without delay."

"And what good will that do?" asked Mrs. Nicely, "when the man knows that any sum of money he likes to ask would be given him, on condition of her being restored? No, no, take my word for it, her troubles are not over yet, nor will they be, in my opinion, till the rascal swings on the gallows."

"Which don't seem likely to be the case just at present," observed Martha,

AMY'S INTERVIEW WITH THE OLD GIPSEY WOMAN.

"for he takes care to keep out of the reach of his enemies, and from what I heard Mr. Peeps say this morning, he has all sorts of hiding-places in different parts of the country, so that people may search about for years without finding him."

"Don't they know which is his favourite one?" asked the housekeeper.

"No, they all seem to be alike to him," replied the girl, "and to deceive his pursuers, he sometimes goes to one, and sometimes to another."

"What was that I heard about Robin Hood's cave?" asked John.

No. 21.

"Why," she replied, "some man—a smuggler, I believe, told Mr. Marldale, that if he was well paid for it, he would guide him to the place where Caleb Kestrel was concealing himself. So when he was afterwards joined by our master, Mr. Peeps, and the cockney gentleman, they got the assistance of a magistrate and some of the preventive service men, and went in a body to Robin Hood's cave, guided by the smuggler I just spoke of."

"Ah!" ejaculated the housekeeper, "he deceived them, I believe, after receiving a great part of the money."

"At any rate," answered Martha, "when they got to the place the bird had flown, and it is thought the guide gave information of what was about to happen, so as to give him plenty of time to escape before the expected visit. Be that as it may, however, no Cabel Kestrel was to be found, and everybody gave up all hope of seeing Miss Amy again, unless by some miracle."

"And by a miracle it seems she has found her way home this very night," observed Mrs. Nicely. "But how is it, Martha," she added, "that you have got hold of all this information?"

"Mr. Peeps told me, and he ought to know something about it, seeing that he went with the pursuers."

"Humph!" exclaimed the old lady, "you seem to be mighty thick with Mr. Peeps! I wonder what Mrs. P. would say if she knew it."

"She *does* know it," answered the girl, "and both she and her husband are very kind to me, because I treat 'em with more respect than the other servants. Aye, and among other things, they've put me on their free list, as they call it."

"Free list!" exclaimed John, "what the deuce does that mean?"

"Why, that I am to see their performance in the Temple of Arts for nothing, and as often as I like."

"Pshaw: rubbish!" ejaculated the housekeeper.

"Oh, shouldn't I like Mr. and Mrs. Peeps to hear you call their Temple of Arts rubbish!" cried Martha. "However, be whatever it may, they were able to make an honest living by it for a good many years, and as they don't like to be ungrateful to an old friend, they keep it in their bed room as an ornament, and to remind them of the hardships they were obliged to go through before they were lucky enough to fall in with our master."

"In my opinion it was our master that was lucky in falling in with them," replied John, "for if it hadn't happened that they were invited to Farmer Brough's harvest-home, the girl would have gone away with 'em the next morning, and the discovery of who she was would never have taken place."

"Which would have saved her all the suffering she has since gone through," observed Mrs. Nicely.

"So it might," observed Martha, "but it don't follow that her troubles are to last for ever, and now that she has been restored to home, I should hope there's a chance of her being suffered to remain here in peace and quiet."

"That will depend upon circumstances," exclaimed John, "so don't make yourself too certain about her troubles being at an end."

"Why they wont carry her off again, will they?"

"They'll try it at any rate," he replied, "for I heard the chap say just now, that if an arrangement is not made with Caleb Kestrel within three days, she'll either be dragged away by force, or murdered in the midst of those that attempt to resist them."

"Mercy on us," exclaimed Mrs. Nicely, "then the house is going to be attacked by robbers."

"That will depend upon whether Mr. Derwent will agree with the terms that have been proposed by Kestrel," answered John. "What do you think of the fellow's modesty in demanding ten thousand pounds to give up the persecution?"

"Ten thousand pounds!" exclaimed every voice.

"Yes nothing less will satisfy him, I can assure you," he replied. "I heard the man just now utter those very words, and as a sort of favour, he added that, Kestrel will be satisfied with one thousand in cash, and the remainder in land of equal value. A very pretty thing indeed, to divide the estate into two that a rascally pedlar may be able to live like a gentleman."

"But it must be done, I suppose," exclaimed Tom Thornley, "or the young lady will be the sufferer."

"How is it our master don't apply to a magistrate for assistance?" demanded the housekeeper.

"That's just what he said he would do," answered John; "but the man only laughed at him for his pains, and told him that Caleb Kestrel was not to be caught quite so easily as all that comes to, so you see there's only one way left to deal with the matter. The money, large as the sum is, must be paid, or there'll never be an end of this trouble and annoyance."

"Well," exclaimed Tom Thornley, "I suppose the governor is the best judge of what ought to be done, but, if I had been in his place the chap that came with the message should not have gone away quite so easily."

"How was it to be helped," demanded the footman, "when he was armed with pistols, and Mr. Derwent had nothing to protect himself with. It's all very easy to say what ought to have been done, but for my own part I don't see any fun in risking one's life, when there's no chance of getting the best of it."

"Ah!" exclaimed the groom, "you are a coward."

"No more a coward than you are," was the angry reply, "I can boast as much courage as any one, and as for—"

Here the bravery of the speaker and his listeners was put to the test, for while he was speaking, a figure clothed in white and bearing a lighted candle, glided with slow and solemn steps into the kitchen; at this sight the whole of the assembled persons rose from their seats with exclamations of terror, and rushed tumultuously towards the door where a scramble took place for precedence in escaping from the presence of the object of their alarm. In the midst of this confusion, however, a loud laugh caused them to look round, and as the supposed ghost threw aside the sheet that had enveloped him they discovered that all their alarm had been occasioned by the mischief-loving Mr. Trubbs. Of course all were now anxious to make it appear that they suspected from the first who it was, and that they only pretended to be frightened in order to humour the joke. Mrs. Nicely was one of the loudest to assert that she had not been in the least alarmed, but at the same time she thought it highly necessary to read the delinquent a very sharp reproof for what she called the folly and wickedness of his conduct. This was only laughed at by Trubbs, who thought it a hard case if a man could not have a little bit of fun without being taken to task for it."

"Fun!" exclaimed the indignant housekeeper, "do you call it fun when some of us might have been frightened into fits, and perhaps out of our lives? But them sort of goings on won't do here, and I shall tell Mr Derwent that either you or I must leave the house immediately."

"What?" demanded Trubbs, "for a little prank like this?"

"These are not times to play pranks, I can tell you, sir," retorted the old lady, warmly. "Aint we all in trouble about the young lady that has been carried off, and are we to be annoyed with the monkey tricks of a jackanapes like you."

"Oh, don't be cross with him, now we've found out he's no ghost," exclaimed Tom Thornley. "It was only done in a bit of a lark, and I for one will forgive him if he promises not to play off any more of his tricks to frighten us."

"You needn't be alarmed about that," replied Trubbs, "for my master talks of getting back to London, and if his present mind holds good, he and I shall leave this place to-morrow. So I determined to have one good bit of fun before I go away, and have had it. But I must be off now, for Mr. Popjoy wants to see me about getting his trunks packed up, and when that's done, I'll return and spend a jolly evening with you all."

Saying this, he ran off in search of his master, who he found walking up and down the shrubbery.

"Trubbs," he said, as his groom approached, "I've changed my mind about going away tomorrow, for Miss Amy has returned home, and I've a notion that things here wont be quite so dull as they have been. In short, I fancy there'll be a wedding, and if so, I should like to be one of the guests."

"What, the squire and Miss Amy are going to marry, I suppose."

"I don't know it for a certainty," answered his master, "because Mr. Derwent and I have not met since the young lady came back. It however, seems very likely, and as my company here don't appear very disagreeable, I shall intrude a little longer upon the hospitality of my friend Derwent."

"Do you happen to know how Miss Amy got back, sir?"

"No, I have only heard the news from Mr. Reves, the steward, who is as much in the dark as any of us. He, however, saw her come into the house and go towards the room where his master is."

"Then somehow or other Caleb Kestrel must have let her slip through his fingers."

"If so, he was less watchful than usual," returned his master. "But be that as it may, something strikes me the squire will marry the girl immediately, to prevent her being taken away again, and for that reason I have determined not to return to London for a few days."

"But do you think the marriage of Miss Amy will put a stop to the goings on of Caleb Kestrel?"

"If that don't, I know not what will," answered Brassy Popjoy. "The pedlar, perhaps, may not have a fancy for carrying off another man's wife, and even if he should be inclined that way Mr. Derwent can easily put him into a different humour by giving him a good spanking sum of money to keep him quiet."

"Then why hasn't he done that before?" asked Trubbs.

"Aye, that's just what I've been puzzled at myself," answered his master. "He's rich enough to pay for peace and quietness, and if he don't do it, whatever may happen afterwards will be his own fault."

"That's very true, sir, but in my opinion the best way to make all things safe, would be to pop Caleb Kestrel in prison."

"He has got to catch him first, though," returned his master, "and that don't seem to be quite so easy a task as you fancy. The fellow he has to deal with is a shy bird, and will keep out of harm's way in spite of all that may be done to snare him. So, after all, I don't see any better plan than that a marriage should take place at once between Mr. Derwent and the young lady, and afterwards it may be as well to try the effects of money upon the pedlar."

"If I gave him any," observed Trubbs, "it should only be just enough to buy himself a rope with."

"Leave him alone," answered Brassy Popjoy, "and one will be provided for him at the expense of the country. The rascal, by all accounts has deserved it this long time past, and, cunning as he is, he may get his deserts at last. Drat the fellow, he has completely put an end to all the pleasure that I expected to have had here, and if it were only for that reason he ought to be made to feel the full vengeance of the law."

Having given vent to this opinion, the cockney turned away, and entering the house, was met by Mr. Reves, who was searching for him to deliver a message from the squire, requesting to see him immediately. In the belief that his advice was about to be consulted, the self-important Mr. Popjoy followed the steward to a room where he found Squire Derwent and Amy seated together.

CHAPTER XVII.

AMY'S UNEASINESS AS THE TIME FOR THE FINAL ANSWER APPROACHES.—A MORNING WALK.—ENCOUNTER WITH A GIPSEY.—A HINT AS TO THE FUTURE, AND THE THREATENED CONSEQUENCES OF NEGLECTING THE WARNING.

Two days out of the three that had been given to consider the proposition of Caleb Kestrel, passed away, without the occurrence of any event that requires mention. Amy herself,—though really very much alarmed as the time approached—

refrained from speaking upon the subject to Squire Derwent, because she had the most implicit reliance upon whatever measures he might contemplate ; she avoided even the slightest hint upon the subject, and even affected an air of cheerfulness, that she was far from feeling. Mr. Derwent, however, knew the feelings of anxiety that must of necessity fill her heart, and taking the opportunity of their being alone on the morning of the third day, he inquired if she had any suggestions to make as to the course she wished him to adopt. She answered that she had none, being perfectly well satisfied to leave the entire management of the affair in his hands.

"You think then," he said, "that I am acting right in resisting the extortionate demands of your persecutor ?"

"I am certain," she replied, "that you would not adopt the course unless certain of being able to carry out your views effectually."

"This generous confidence, my dear Amy, is most gratifying to me," exclaimed Mr. Derwent, "and be assured I will do nothing to forfeit the good opinion of one whom I so much love. Had Kestrel been more moderate in his demands, I would before now have acceded to them, but when he insists upon such an extravagant sum of money, I feel it my duty to defy him to the worst—being pretty well certain that he will not dare to carry his threats to take you away again, into effect."

"Yet he has succeeded in one attempt."

"True," answered her lover, "and for that very reason he is the less likely to succeed in a second, I am now prepared for him—my servants are all armed in case of a night attack upon the house, and should he venture to show himself here, there is every reason to believe that it will be no easy task for him to escape falling into our hands. At all events, we are determined to give him a warm reception such as he little dreams of."

"Do you not think then," she asked, "of the danger you are running ?"

"I can have no such selfish feelings," he replied, "when the danger—if there is any—is incurred to protect you from the violence of this bad man. Nay, to tell you my mind, I feel almost certain that he will not again attempt violence, though I should not be altogether sorry if he did so, because I feel quite certain it would be the last effort he would ever be able to make."

"Are your people then to be depended on ?" she asked.

"I can place the most implicit reliance in their firmness and determination, in the event of an attack," answered Mr. Derwent. "Indeed, my steward, Mr. Reves, has sounded them on the subject, and so inveterate are they against the pedlar, that they have expressed a determination either to take or kill him if he is hardy enough to come here in quest of you."

"It may appear bold for me to offer a suggestion," exclaimed Amy, "but I should have thought it better to have asked the assistance of a magistrate in such a case as this."

"The notion struck me also," he replied, "but, upon further consideration I saw that such a step would do more harm than good. The circumstance of my applying for aid would most likely come to the ears of Caleb Kestrel, who would then change his tactics, and perhaps come upon us when least expected. So, under all the circumstances, I think it better to let things take their course, and, with heaven's powerful aid, the cause of rectitude cannot fail."

"Would it not have been better for me to have sought a temporary shelter some - where else ?" she asked.

"If you had done so, Kestrel might have heard of it, and in that case his success would have been almost certain, because you would have been away from your protectors."

"Alas ! sighed Amy, "how bitterly do I regret the trouble and annoyance that my presence has brought with it. Far better would it have been to have remained in poverty, to which I was brought up, than to feel that I am the cause of anxiety, if not danger, to one who has proved himself my faithful friend."

"Nay, dearest Amy," exclaimed the squire, pressing her hand, "my love would be ill-deserving of the name, if I was not willing to endure all for your sake. The task of offering myself as your protector is one most gratifying to me, and the reward for my poor services will be great indeed, when the happy moment arrives that will allow me to call you mine.'

" Do you not think Kestrel will take every means in his power to prevent our union?"

" He would if the opportunity were given him," replied Mr. Derwent, "but he has got nearly to the end of his tether, and perhaps before many hours have passed away he may be deprived of all power to do further mischief. At all events he has got those to deal with who are determined to pursue him to the very utmost, and even if he should not come here in pursuit of you, I will not cease to follow him till he is in the strong hands of the law."

"But he has accomplices who are perhaps to be as much dreaded as he is himself."

" There is little to be apprehended from them," answered Cecil Derwent, " for when once the head is taken away the others will have no motive for keeping up this cruel persecution. For that reason I have marked out this Kestrel, and if once he come within reach of my arm, he shall either yield himself my prisoner, or die for his obstinacy."

" Oh, let there be no bloodshed !" cried the trembling girl, " at least let it not be by your hand that even such a villain as Caleb Kestrel meets his death."

" Believe me, Amy," he replied, "nothing but an extreme emergency shall drive me to do that which would cause you pain. Besides, I believe there is no reason to anticipate a tragical termination of this affair, for my plans have been carefully considered, and my people all appear to be so zealous in the cause that no doubt Kestrel will be easily made a prisoner if he ventures to repeat his violence against you. So console yourself, my dear girl, and endeavour to look with confidence to the protection promised by your friends.

" How can I do otherwise than confide in them when I have had such ample proofs of their kindness?"

" Ah, Amy !" he exclaimed, " how could we do otherwise than advocate your cause, when we saw you the victim of Kestrel's avarice and villany ? Common humanity dictated the course we ought to pursue, and had we acted otherwise we should have been no less guilty than the wretch of whom you have such bitter cause to complain."

" But you are in danger through me."

" Not so much as your fears lead you to imagine," answered the squire, " and even if I was, my heart must be base indeed to shrink from its duty. Besides, I am not the only one willing to serve you, for our friends Marldale and Peeps are equally sanguine in a cause that we have entered into heart and soul."

" Mr. Peeps," she replied, " has ever proved a faithful friend ; I owe him a heavy debt of gratitude, so heavy, indeed, that no act of mine can ever repay it."

" But the good man is already more than repaid in seeing you restored to your rights ; knowing, as he does, that he performed an act of noble generosity in acting the part of a protector when he could not by any possibility have suspected that you would ever have it in your power to repay him. And he seems still determined to carry out his good intentions, for, zealous as all are in your cause, there is not one more so than he is in our endeavours to rid you of the persecutions of Caleb Kestrel. Then there is his excellent wife too, who, if she cannot fight in your cause, will at least prove a kind friend to console you in the midst of your afflictions."

" Is she not alarmed at the expected attack ?"

" Only for you," replied Mr. Derwent, " for herself she has no fears, and I almost fancy if the worst should happen she would prove as courageous in your defence as many of us. Nay, it is not an hour since I heard her declare that if Kestrel comes within her reach she would fix him with so firm a grasp that he should never escape from it whilst life remained within her."

" Surely," cried Amy in alarm, " she will not risk her life by coming in conflict with that desperate man !"

"There is no occasion to make yourself uneasy on that point," answered Mr. Derwent, "for, as I said before, I do not think the pedlar will venture on an attack if he should hear, as no doubt he will, that we are prepared to resist him. He will deem discretion to be the better part of valour, and, I even venture to hope, may perhaps satisfy himself by accepting a moderate sum of money to quit this country for ever."

"But even at a distance he may employ agents to carry on his foul designs against me."

"Even if he did so, we could defy them," answered Cecil Derwent. "Fellows of that description, too, expect to be liberally paid for their services, and they are not then to be depended on, unless the employer is near to look after them. However, to make all sure, it is my most anxious wish to make Kestrel our prisoner, for we have charges heavy and serious enough against him to send him away from this country for the remainder of his life. Could we only see that take place, Amy, you would not have a single care left to embitter a heart that ought to be all joyousness and peace."

"I should indeed be most happy," she sighed, "but for the dread that fearful man has inspired me with."

"Do you still apprehend danger from him whilst surrounded by so many of your friends?"

"How can I help it," she asked, "when I know the lengths to which desperation will carry him?"

"But all his desperation cannot succeed in a bad cause," replied her lover. "The fellow's avarice has defeated all he intended to do, and we have only to remain firm, to show him that vice can seldom triumph over virtue and innocence."

"Do you think," asked Amy, after a pause, "that there will be any danger if I walk through the grounds?"

"There will be none till the period for deliberation has expired," replied the squire; "but after then I should not advise you to leave the place unless accompanied by some of your friends. I would have you keep within sight of the house, too, so that you may hasten back in case any suspicious persons should appear in sight. To-morrow, however, will serve to show the intention of your enemies, for if we neither see nor hear anything of them when the night has passed away, we may conclude that Kestrel has perceived the folly of attempting violence, and is waiting to hear what proposition I have to make with respect to making him an advance in money."

"Will he venture here to speak to you upon the subject?"

"I should imagine not," answered Mr. Derwent, "for an evil conscience has made him suspicious, and I fancy he would prefer sending the man that brought you back the other evening, to make a bargain for him."

"And in that case you would bribe Caleb Kestrel to abandon his persecution?"

"If there was any other way to make you secure, I would see him hanged before I would encourage his villany. As it is, however, I suppose the wisest plan would be to make a bargain with him, though it must needs be confessed I should part with money to him with a very bad grace."

"And yet my security may depend upon it," she cried. "Nay, so little do I heed wealth, that I would freely give him all that has so lately fallen to me, in exchange for that peace which I enjoyed as the supposed daughter of Mr. and Mrs. Peeps."

"Aye, my dear Amy," answered Mr. Derwent, "but you forget that in doing so you would be rewarding a scoundrel that deserves the heaviest punishment that can be inflicted on him. That is my reason for having resisted the demand he made upon me, and I can scarcely regret my refusal, even though it may have been the cause of adding to your uneasiness and alarm. Besides, if he had found me yield too easily, it would not have been long before he came upon us with another demand. Such is the cause of my apparently strange conduct in refusing to come to his terms when your safety seemed to depend upon my acquiescence."

" You thought it would be better to watch for an opportunity to make him a prisoner ?"

" Yes, Amy," he replied, " and if Caleb Kestrel don't mind what he is about he will not be suffered much longer to enjoy the same liberty he does at present. Through his messenger he has threatened to come and drag you away if his proposal is not complied with at the end of three days, and all I can say is, that I hope he will keep his promise, for, if he does, it will be a strange thing to me if ever he gets away again."

" But he will not suffer himself to be taken without offering the most desperate resistance."

" Which I am prepared for, and therefore feel no apprehension whatever for the result."

" Alas !" sighed Amy, " armed as he will be, may you not lose your life in my cause ?"

" And if I do," replied her lover, " will it not be sacrificed in the cause of jus‧ tice ?"

" But could I ever be happy afterwards ?"

" Well, well, my dear Amy," exclaimed Cecil Derwent, " we must not look on the worst side of things when the chances are all on our side. Villany has rarely courage to support it, and you will find it so in the present instance, if Kestrel has the temerity to attempt carrying his threat into effect. But it is idle to talk of that now, for my opinion is that the ruffian will not dare show his face here, knowing, as he well does, that we will never surrender you again into his power."

" Yet I have heard Mr. Peeps say he always fulfils his threats in spite of any danger that may oppose him."

" Perhaps," observed Mr. Derwent, " that may only be when he has timid people to deal with. In the present case, he would discover his mistake, and therefore, I more than half suspect he will take care to keep himself out of the reach of danger. At any rate, my dear Amy, I would have you await the issue of this affair with firmness, for, come what may, you shall not be dragged from this spot while I have life to support me."

Having afforded her this slight consolation, he took leave of her for a short time, and Amy once more fell into a train of painful thoughts that had been conjured up by the perilous situation in which she found herself. In the presence of her lover, she had sufficient command over herself to maintain an appearance of tolerable composure, but no sooner had he taken his departure than all her worst anticipations returned with double force. At length, however, anxious to recover herself, she attired herself for walking, and strolled for a short excercise in the park, choosing a route she had once taken before, and which offered so many beautiful points of scenery, that she hoped to forget for a while the deep affliction into which she had sunk. In half an hour she had traversed the plantation that crossed the domain, and then found herself at a gate that led into a lane, from whence a most delightful prospect was to be obtained over the adjoining country. Regardless of any risk she might run, Amy passed through, but had not proceeded many paces, when she suddenly found herself near a gipsy tent, before which a woman was seated, engaged apparently in superintending the preparation of the mid-day meal. Startled, and somewhat alarmed, Amy hurried to retrace her steps, but the attempt was a vain one, for the hag had instantly followed her, and in a whining way asked her if she would not like to have her fortune told.

" No, my good woman, no," she replied, endeavouring to pass on, " there is nothing but sorrow in the future for me, and that has been already revealed to me more clearly than any words of yours can do."

" Won't you cross my hand with a piece of silver this morning ?" asked the woman, in a half supplicating, half threatening tone.

" Yes, there is half-a-crown," replied Amy, taking the money from her reticule, and placing it on the palm that was extended before her. " Take it, my good woman, and let me pass on my way."

" Aye, aye," answered the old woman, " I never refuse good money when it's offered ; but I should like to earn it too, so let me see the lines on your hand, and I'll tell you how you'll fare in this business with Caleb Kestrel."

"Ah! you know him then, and have heard of the persecution I have suffered from him ?"

"To be sure I have," she replied, "or I should have followed him all the way to this place to very little purpose. We travelled together for many a long year but at last he grew tired of me, I suppose, for all of a sudden he was missed, and it was not till lately that I heard he was to be met with in the wilds of Yorkshire.

"Have you seen him yet ?"

"Yes, on the very day that he carried you off."

"Know you where he is now ?"

"Not exactly," replied the gipsey, "but he'll not be very far off if he mean to put into practice his threat of taking you away again if certain demands of his be not agreed to."

"You have not seen him then since the time you just now spoke of ?" asked Amy.

No. 22.

"No," she replied, "he chose to be angry because I had followed him, and his ast words were never to thrust myself into his presence again. Ha! ha! those were brave words to come from the man I had once given my heart to, so I determined to stay here till he comes back, and then to have my revenge."

"Surely you would not take away the life of even such a villain as he is?"

"No, no, not I, young lady," she replied. "There's no occasion for me to stain my hands with his blood when the art I possess tells me that he is doomed to meet his death on the gallows. I have warned him of his fate, but the fool turns a deaf ear to me, and follows his own mad course in spite of the danger. But how was it, young lady, that he let you escape when you were so completely in his power?"

"He sent me back, accompanied by two of his companions to act as my guides."

"What reason had he for doing that?"

"Self interest," replied Amp; "he found there was no chance of extorting money whilst I remained a prisoner in his hands, and I was sent back in the expectation that his extravagant demands will be acceded to."

"And suppose they are not?"

"In that case he threatens to take me away again."

"Aye, aye, I know that," replied the old woman; "but are there any in Derwent Hall that are ready to risk their lives in case he should attempt to carry out his threats?"

"I believe all would die in my defence."

"Then there is a chance of his not coming," exclaimed the gipsey, "for, though always scheming mischief, Caleb Kestrel would rather shun than seek danger. For the present, keep within the house—it may be only for a short time, for I have myself a reckoning to settle with your enemy, and will not leave this place till I have seen him locked up in your county jail."

"But knowing that you are near at hand, he will take care to keep beyond your reach."

"True," she replied, "but when cunning is matched against cunning, mine may in the end prove too much for him. Besides, Caleb knows what I am when revenge once gets into my heart, and he'll quail before me like a cowardly hound as he is, when he finds I'm bent upon his destruction."

"Are these words spoken in truth," asked Amy, "or are they only uttered to deceive me into a belief that you would be my friend."

"How can I be your enemy when we never met till now?"

"Forgive the suspicion," exclaimed Amy, "but surrounded as I am with dangers, I thought you might still be the friend of Caleb Kestrel, though professing the greatest hatred against him."

"Deceive yourself no longer then," exclaimed the woman, "for I am his mortal foe, and he guesses as much, though so far he knows not the hatred my heart has conceived against him. But the time may not be far distant when he will feel the vengeance of the woman that he has abandoned through mere caprice."

"Take care that he suspects you not," returned Amy, "for if he do the revenge will be all on his own side."

"I know him too well, to give him such an opportunity."

"And you think he will not attempt to make his threatened attack on Derwent hall."

"I think," replied the woman, "if it had been intended, he would have keep the secret carefully locked up in his own heart. The threat may have been only made to frighten the squire into paying the sum of money that has been demanded. However, don't remain too secure upon what is only an opinion, for this is a desperate game that Kestrel is playing, and he may risk an attack upon the house, when he finds there is no other chance of getting the gold that he wants to support him in some foreign land."

"You know not then, whether he has left the cave he took me too?"

"I can well believe he has," replied the gipsey, "for its not very likely, he would remain in a place that you could point out to those that wish to go in pursuit of him."

"I could not point it out."

"How so ?"

"Because my eyes were bandaged, and I was not permitted to look about me till my guides had, led me at least a mile from the place where I had been imprisoned."

"But you know the neighbourhood, and I should suppose it would be easy to find the cave you were taken to. However, let that be as it may, Caleb Kestrel will not remain there at the risk of being taken, and its not at all unlikely, that he may direct his steps hither to learn how matters are going on."

"If he come here, I am lost!" exclaimed Amy.

"That," replied the gipsey, "will depend upon yourself. From this time you had better not leave the house, till you hear that Kestrel is in custody, which, if my hopes deceive me not, will be in the course of a very few days. At all events, maiden, your best security lies in my feelings of hatred against that man."

"But since he knows you are in this neighbourhood he will be upon his guard.

"That will depend upon whether Squire Derwent will assist."

"How can he assist?"

"By pretending to consider the proposal that has been made about the money that is demanded. If he do that, Caleb may be thrown off his guard, and he will venture here in the hope that all his expectations are about to be realized."

"Mr. Derwent," she replied, "will not practice deceit, even to rid himself of an enemy."

"But he may when it is to rid you of one."

"I would not ask him to do an act that he would regard as dishonourable," answered Amy.

"Then he does not love you?"

"It is because I know he does, that I would not put his feelings to too severe a test," exclaimed Amy. "Short as our acquaintance has been he has honoured me with his regard, and it would be a poor return were I to urge him, from selfish motives, to do that which he might afterwards bitterly regret."

"You care not for yourself, then?"

"Not when his honour is concerned."

"And what sort of honour can his be," demanded the gipsey, "if he would suffer you to remain in constant danger, when he has it in his own power to prevent it."

"Mr. Derwent has done all in his power to prevent it," replied Amy. "He, at great personal risk, pursued the ruffian who had carried me away, and his now prepared to offer the most determined resistance if the attempt should be repeated. Nay, he has declared himself ready to sacrifice his life rather than suffer me to fall again into the hands of my cruel oppressor."

"He must be watchful," exclaimed the woman, "or the wolf may be in his fold before he is aware of the danger. Let my warning then be taken in time, for so sure as it is neglected, so surely will both he and you have heavy cause to repent it."

"Perhaps you know of some other plot that you have not yet thought proper to reveal?"

"I know nothing more than you have heard," she replied, "for angry words passed between Caleb Kestrel and myself the last time we met, and it is therefore not very likely that he would let me into any secret that might turn out against himself. No, no, the villain now looks upon me as his enemy, thought the time has been when we were the best of friends."

"Was there no quarrel before you parted?"

"Not the slightest."

"And has he never given any reason?"

"Yes, his excuse is, that he was anxious to go in search of some people tha he had trusted you with a few years ago, and that I was an incumbrance upon him at a time when he wanted to get quickly from place to place. But I have followed him, though, and, having once more met, will soon see which is to get the upper hand in the matter."

"Beware how you excite his fury," cried Amy, "for, short as his stay in this place has been, he has already nearly succeeded in committing a foul and deliberate murder."

"I have heard of it ; Squire Derwent was shot whilst pursuing game upon the moors, and an innocent man had nearly suffered for the crime. But how was it ever known that the crime was committed by Caleb Kestrel ?"

"He admitted almost as much, and there was strong circumstantial evidence to prove him guilty of the deed. He has, however, been suffered to escape, not, I am afraid, to repent the evil of his former ways, but to form new projects against those who have never harmed him by word or deed."

"Aye," exclaimed the gipsey, "but he must mind what he is about though, or the plotter may fall into his own snare."

"So you would have me believe," answered Amy, "but I fear he will have an opportunity of doing a great deal of mischief before he falls into the hands of the law."

"Wait patiently three days, and it is likely you may then hear something that will alter your opinion."

"What mean you ?"

"Don't ask me, now, what I mean, but wait the time I have mentioned," answered the woman. "I have counselled the Book of Destiny, and in its dark pages I find that just at this time Caleb Kestrel is likely to be in great danger."

"That which you call the Book of Destiny, I place little reliance on," answered Amy.

"Aye, and many others besides yourself pretend to treat lightly the art that I have studied so long," exclaimed the gipsey. "However, I ask you not to believe it now, but wait till the three days have come to an end, and then, if Kestrel should happen to be in the hands of his enemies, you will admit that the words I have uttered must have had something for a foundation."

"I should rather be inclined to suspect that certain facts have come to your knowledge that you have not thought proper to acquaint me with. However, I must now return home, lest my longer absence should give alarm to those who are at all times most anxious in my behalf. Come to the hall, if you think proper, and any service you do shall be richly rewarded."

Amy then passed on, and had hardly got through the gate that led into the park, than she was met by Mr. Peeps, who had been for the last half hour hunting about for her in every direction.

"My dear girl," he exclaimed, "where have you been hiding yourself all this time ? They are all in consternation and alarm about you at the hall, as I came out to see what the deuce had become of you."

"Have I been absent so very long, then ?" asked Amy.

"Not such a long time, certainly," answered Peeps; "but when we know there's danger, it's apt to put a thousand strange notions into our heads that we should never have thought of at any other time. There's the squire, too, in a rare fidget about you, and he was coming out full tilt to look round about the place, only that I laughed him out of his fears, and offered to take upon myself the task of taking a turn round the park to see where you had got to. Bytheby, my dear child, what has kept you so long ?"

"I have been talking to a gipsey woman that I met."

"Ah ! been having your fortune told, I'll be bound."

"Indeed, my dear sir, I have something of more consequence to think of, just at present."

"Then what could you possibly want with a gipsey woman ?"

"She accosted me," replied Amy, "and from her first few words I discovered that she was acquainted with Caleb Kestrel."

"Then all I can say about it is, that the acquaintance don't add much to her respectability," exclaimed Mr. Peeps. "A man like that can have no decent friends, I'm sure; and as for this woman, whoever she is, I suppose she's only here to assist in all the dirty work he undertakes."

"On the contrary, she speaks of him with the utmost bitterness."

"Humph! She don't like him, eh?"

"She holds him in perfect abhorrence."

"Does she give any reason for it?"

"Yes; he deserted her after they had been living some years together."

"Ho, ho!" exclaimed Peeps, "if that's the case, I fancy she may be of more use than I at first thought for. If there's revenge to be sought she'll be an able assistant, so let's go back and try whether our offer of money will buy her over to our side."

"There's no occasion to go back, my dear sir, because I have already gleaned quite sufficient to convince me that the woman has no other desire but that of revenge. She has told me more about Kestrel than I knew before, and I now feel but little fear of the attack he has threatened to make on the hall."

"You think it was all bombast, then?"

"I think he will scarcely venture to show himself where he may be sure a resolute resistance waits him," answered our heroine.

"Does he know anything about our preparations?"

"If he know not of them now, he soon will," answered Amy; "and even if we should escape from our danger, it will only be to fall into another. This gipsey woman is determined he shall not escape, for she has followed him to this place for no other purpose than to give him up to justice."

"But how do we know she is telling the truth?"

"It is not very easy to decide, I must admit," replied Amy, "but there was a bitterness in the woman's words and tone that made me believe she must have some private revenge of her own to carry out. Be that as it may, however, she has cautioned me to remain in the house for some few days so as to thwart the schemes of Caleb Kestrel if he has plotted to carry me off a second time."

"And what does she say about his coming here to assist in that piece of villany?"

"Her opinion is that he will not venture to show himself where there is so much danger to be apprehended."

"Why the affair then is likely to end in smoke?"

"I cannot venture so far as to say that," she replied, "because he has accomplices, and they may not have the same means to be afraid of coming here that he has."

"Does he know the woman is waiting here?"

"Yes."

"And I suppose guesses her errand?"

"I believe he does."

"In that case, depend upon it he'll be rather inclined to walk in any other direction than to show himself here. And that proves the remarkable acutenes of poor Mrs. P. for she said, only just before I came, she was quite sure Caleb Kestrel would never dare come near the old hall."

"Why does she think so?"

"Because there's such a number of women in the place that it wouldn't be wel for him to go there."

"Has he any reason to be afraid of women?"

"Why, not of their fighting perhaps," answered Peeps, "but where there's a good many women there may be a great deal of noise, and that mould bring assistance from all round the neighbourhood sooner than would be pleasant."

"And you really think that would deter him?"

"It's Mrs, Peeps opinion, my dear, and you know she's never wrong, at least she says she never is—and I don't contradict her, for if she; don't know I should like to know who does."

"Still we must be prepared, for Kestre. is playing for a heavy stake, and I think it hardly likely that he will be induced to give it up merely because it cannot be gained without some risk ?"

"Risk ! why he's sure to be either killed or taken prisoner."

"The latter will be quite sufficient for the ends of justice," answered Amy, "and I trust, whatever violence these men show, Mr. Derwent and his friends will have compassion on the unfortunate men who have undertaken this enterprize in the expectation of gain."

" Ah, its little compassion they'll meet with, if they come to disturb our peace and quietness," returned Mr. Peeps. " Besides, what right have scoundrels like them to expect quarter, when they'd cut all our throats, if we only gave 'em the opportunity."

" Let them all be taken," answered Amy, " and the law is sufficiently strong to punish them. But I know Mr. Derwent will not be revengeful, for he can pity the weakness that has led these wretched men into a career of crime and violence."

" Will he think nothing then of their breaking into the hall, and carrying you off ?"

" He will pardon all in the remembrance that I was allowed to return to my home ?"

" Yes," replied the old gentleman, " but not till you had been kept away from it three or four days, and it was found there was no other chance of bringing the squire to his terms. Besides, he knew pretty well that a sharp look out is kept up round the neighbourhood of Robin Hood's cave, and though he may manage to escape when he has nobody else to care for but himself, he would have found it a hard matter to get clear off, if he had had a woman to take away with him. So you see, after all, there is not much to thank him for, since whatever has een done was through selfish motives."

" Well," said Amy, " all I hope is that the affair will pass over better than we thought for."

" At any rate, my dear, there is nothing to be afraid of, since you will be protected by people that are determined not to let you fall into the hands of the enemy. Even Mr. Brassey Popjoy, and he don't seem very remarkable for courage either, has declared he'll fight for you to the very last."

" He has my thanks for his good will," she replied, " b it I trust there will be no occasion to put his courage to the test."

" Well, I hope not, I'm sure," exclaimed Mr. Peeps, " for to tell you a bit of my mind, I never had a very great stomach for fighting, and the thought of having a parcel of desperate ruffians to deal with, has made me feel uncommonly queer. However, never mind, I shall get over that in time, and if matters should happen to come to the worst, perhaps, I may be able to do my duty, as well as any of them."

" Heaven forbid that you should be put to the test."

" So say I with all my heart," he exclaimed, " for putting myself out of the question, I don't know what would become of Mrs. P. if a scrimmage was to take place in the house. It would be the death of the poor dear soul, for we have travelled through life, as well as through the country together a good many years, and in all the time I dont think either of us have so much as dreamt that we were tired of each other."

" May you live many years longer to enjoy the easier circumstances in which you now find yourself," exclaimed Amy.

" Well, I hope so too," answered Peeps, " for in spite of matters looking rather cross at present, I have a notion that they'll soon mend, and then only think what a pleasure it will be for me and Mrs. P. to witness your happiness as the wife of Squire Derwent ! Ah ! my dear Amy, who would have thought a few week ago that you would be, before long, one of the richest girls in all Yorkshire ?"

" Who indeed," she replied ; " but if proof was wanting, have we not one in the present instance, that wealth seldom if ever brings peace of mind with it ?"

" But the peace of mind will come 'by and by for all that," exclaimed the ex-showman. " I like people to look forward with hope and I'm sure you have every season to do so Amy, for though the sky may appear to be a little overcast at present, the sun will soon break out, and then you may look back upon the past with a smile at troubles that you now take so much to heart. But here we are at the old hall again, my dear, and see yonder comes Squire Derwent to hear from your own lips where you have been and why you were so long absent."

Cecil now approached but he felt too happy a t seeing that she was safe to ask either of the questions that had been suggested by Mr. Peeps. He merely expressed his satisfaction at her return, and them gave utterance to a hope that she had not been detained by any unpleasant adventure.

" No," she replied, " nothing that was by any means unpleasant. I met, indeed, with a gypsey woman, who began by asking me to let her tell me my fortune, and ended by giving me some information about Caleb Kestrel."

" Some old crony of his I'll be bound."

" I believe she had been acquainted with him many years,"· answered our heroine, " judging from what she said, her feelings towards him are now anything but friendly."

" Is she likely to give evidence against him ?"

" I think so, and if she do, it will be of the greatest importance."

" Then I'll immediately seek her and ascertain how far she will be able to criminate him."

" Take my advice and do no such thing," exclaimed Peeps, " for if any of the pedlar's folks should see you speaking to the woman, he'll be sure to hear of it and prevent any scheme that you many place for getting him into your power. So leave it till to-morrow squire, and then I'll see this old woman and get out of her how far she is willingly to assist us against her old crony."

" Will there not b e the same danger of your being seen to talk to her as if I was ?"

" Certainly not," he replied, " for nobody could suspect anything from chatting with an old fortune teller. It would be supposed that I was consulting her pro-fessionally, and nothing more would be thought of it."

" Do you not think it would be better for no one to see her for the present ?" asked Amy. " I have myself heard quite sufficient to convince me that the woman will be ready to give all necessary evidence whenever you find yourself in a position to proceed against Caleb Kestrel."

" But I must first ascertain how far she is able to aid us," exclaimed the squire. " For aught we know, she may be scheming against us, in order that we may be put off our guard, and that the man she professes to hate may have an opportunity to carry out his evil designs."

" Then have her taken up and brought before you," suggested Peeps.

" What plea have I for depriving her of liberty ?"

" A thousand may be found if you have a mind," answered the other. " She has no right, for instance, to be travelling about the country as a vagabond, and it's for you to question her as to her motive for lurking about your pre-mises."

" But if she have any guilty design in view, is it likely she will confess what it is ?" asked Squire Derwent. " Besides, it would not be advisable to irritate a person from whom we suspect some important information is to be obtained."

" You don't think then there is any chance of her being frightened into telling all she knows ?"

" These people are seldom to be frightened so easily as all that comes to," answered Mr. Derwent, " and in the present instance, the gipsey is well aware that we have not the slightest ground for making an accusation against her."

"And even if we have," interposed Amy, "it would be foolish on our part to proceed harshly against one who may have it in her power to assist us in a most important degree."

"You think then she really has important revelations to make ?"

"I can see no reason to doubt it," she replied, "for the woman spoke of Caleb Kestrel with unfeigned bitterness, and I believe if left to herself, she will before long disclose facts that will enable you to commit him to prison on a serious charge."

"Then, in your opinion, it will be better to let matters remain as they are at present ?" asked the squire.

"I do, indeed," she replied, "and in the meantime, I will take another opportunity to see her without letting it appear that my visit has any particular object in it."

"Nay, that must not be," exclaimed Derwent, "for there is danger of your falling into the hands of Kestrel, or some of his equally wicked companions. For a few days, at any rate, you had better remain in the house, and in that interval I will exert all my best energies to place your enemies within the strong grasp of the law."

By this time they had entered the hall, when Amy went to her own room, and her two companions proceeded to another apartment, where they found Frank Marldale waiting their return to relate some important information of which he had become possessed.

CHAPTER XXI.

DANGER INCREASES.—A COUNCIL OF WAR TO PREPARE AGAINST AN EXPECTED HOSTILE VISIT.—THE NIGHT ATTACK AND ITS RESULTS.—VICTORY DECLARES ON THE SIDE OF JUSTICE, AND THE PEDLAR FINDS HIMSELF IN AN AWKWARD POSITION.

THE news brought by the young farmer was most alarming, for he had not long before been told that Caleb Kestrel had been seen crossing the moors, and as some of his companions had been met not far from the same spot, there was but too much reason to fear that some desperate scheme was on the eve of exploding. Mr. Derwent paced up and down the room, scarcely knowing what plan to adopt, but resolutely determined to oppose the utmost resistence in the event of any attempt being made to force Amy from her home. As for Brassey Popjoy, he did nothing but curse his own folly for having remained in the house where there had been nothing but alarm and danger from the first day of his arrival.

"We shall all of us be murdered, for certain," he added, during a pause, "and the young lady will be taken away and forced to marry this fellow whether she likes it or not."

"Never, whilst I have life to prevent it ?" exclaimed the squire.

"Aye, continued Popjoy, "it's all very well to put a bold face upon it, but how are we to protect Amy if these villains are determined to take her away ? For my own part I was never used to fighting, and should expire with terror if they were to get into the house."

"Then, between you and I," said Peeps, "we should do much better without, than with you. Perhaps, if the truth was told, I've not much more courage than yourself, but if matters come to a push, hang me if I don't do my best towards rescuing my poor little Amy from the scoundrels we are expecting."

"At all events," observed Frank Marldale, "it will be better not to let her know of this expected danger as long as it is possible to keep it from her. We may be altogether wrong in our anticipations, for a thought has just struck me that Caleb Kestrel may have returned to this neighbourhood only to try whether he cannot conclude the negotiations for putting an end to his persecutions."

"Would that he came alone," exclaimed Squire Derwent, "and I would submit to any sacrifice rather than suffer Amy to be kept in this continual state of alarm. Nay, I will freely give up the whole of my fortune, if, by doing so, I can but purchase for her that peace of mind that has been so terribly disturbed of late."

(Caleb Kestrel defeated in his villanous designs.)

"Perhaps," said Frank Marldale, "it would be as well for one of us to see if we can obtain an interview with Kestrel."

"Which is the one that's likely to run such a risk as that?" demanded Brassey Popjoy.

"If no one else is willing to make an effort for the poor girl, I'll go myself," exclaimed Peeps. "I happen to know something of the chap, and he may perhaps argue the matter over with me, when he wouldn't with anybody else."

No, 23.

Should it be thought advisable to take such a step, it shall be done by no one but myself," exclaimed Cecil Derwent.

"But he has attempted your life once, and may do so again."

"The thought of that will not intimidate me from the performance of my duty," answered the squire. "Single-handed, I hope to be at least a match for him, and if he has the assistance of any of his people, I'll prove that in a good cause I can fight even to death."

"Don't talk of death in that light manner, my dear sir," exclaimed the alarmed Brassey Popjoy; "just be good enough to consider my nerves, and speak of something else not quite so disagreeable."

"It is not my wish to increase your terror," he replied, "but we are now driven almost to the last extremity, and it is necessary to arrange such plans as may appear best to meet the emergency."

"But it may be all a mistake about Kestrel's return."

"There can be no mistake," answered Frank Marldale, "because the man that gave me the information is most positive as to having seen him. For my own part I have not the least doubt upon the subject, and it is therefore imperative that the friends of Miss Amy take immediate steps to preserve her from the expected violence."

"And at all risks she shall be preserved from it," exclaimed Cecil Derwent. "I believe even those who are in the house are sufficient for its defence, in the event of an attack; but if the night passes over quietly, I will to-morrow apply for further assistance, and take such steps as will add to the capture of Kestrel and his associates."

"But how are you to find them?" asked Popjoy.

"Through an old gipsey woman, who seems to have followed him to this neighbourhood for no other purpose than to be revenged for some injury that he has done her. She will be a useful agent in this business, and, from what I can understand, will very readily give us all the assistance that is in her power."

"Upon being well paid for it, I suppose?"

"No sum will be considered too large if she affords the aid I expect," replied Squire Derwent. "All my thoughts—all my care are directed towards this one object, and neither expense nor trouble shall be spared, if I can only accomplish it."

"Then you really expect to lay hold of this pedlar?"

"I think there can be very little doubt of it, if we go the right way to work," replied Mr. Derwent, "but it is unnecessary for me to say that success will entirely depend upon the assistance I receive from my friends, when the moment for action arrives. If they are but true to me—and I have every reason to believe they will be—we shall soon see this troublesome affair brought to a close."

"And then," exclaimed Popjoy, "I hope the wedding will immediately follow, for, after so much bother and annoyance, it's high time that we should see smiling faces about the place. Ah, Mr. Derwent, you'll be a happy fellow yet, depend on it."

"I hope so; but we must not reckon too much upon that till our enemy is deprived of all further power of doing mischief."

"In other words," observed Peeps, "till he's either hanged or transported, one of which I hope will be his fate before long."

"Well," exclaimed Brassey Popjoy, "all I can say about it is, that the sooner he meets one of those fates the better it will be for all of us, for nothing else will put an end to his confounded plotting and mischief."

"Do you apprehend any mischief from him, my dear sir?" inquired Squire Derwent.

"Why, there's no saying where the villany of a fellow like that will stop," he replied, "and as I was one of the party that went out in pursuit of him, he may take it into his head to do me some mortal injury. However, I can get out of his reach by returning to London, which I have serious thoughts of doing immediately, unless this Caleb Kestrel is taken."

Mr. Derwent could not restrain a hearty laugh at this candid admission, and soon afterwards they separated, with an understanding that they were all to meet again at ten o'clock in the evening, to keep watch, in case any attempt should be made to enter the house by violence. During the remainder of the day, Amy remained in her own chamber, anxiously waiting a result upon which her future destiny depended. That she had true and resolute defenders she well knew, but then Caleb Kestrel was no common enemy to deal with, and his associates were of that ruffianly class, that the attack, if one was to be made, would be of a most violent description. It was in vain that she endeavoured to console herself with the hope that they would not venture upon so bold a step, because the pedlar had already given proof that he was willing to run any hazard rather than be defeated in the diabolical plot in which he was engaged. From him, therefore, it was quite clear she had no quarter to expect, whilst he remained at large, and it was with no little apprehension that she looked forward to the coming night, when a desperate effort would no doubt be made to drag her by violence from those to whom she could alone look up for protection. As she gazed around upon the splendidly furnished room in which she was sitting, she could not forbear a sigh as the recollection crossed her mind of the happy, careless days she had spent, previous to her unfortunate meeting with Caleb Kestrel. The contrast was indeed a sad one, for with wealth at her disposal, and all the luxuries of life about her, she was surrounded with difficulties, and could look for nothing but misery and despair. She felt deeply grieved, too, at the trouble and inconvenience she had been the means of bringing upon those who had so generously advocated her cause, and at one time had nearly made up her mind to surrender herself into the hands of the pedlar, as the probable means of turning away his fury from those who had offended him, merely by interposing to rescue her from his villanous schemes. On the other hand, however, she knew that his principal design was to extort money from Mr. Derwent, and that if she again fell into his power, he would never restore her to liberty till the large sum he had demanded should be paid to him. She trembled at the bare thought of being compelled to pass the rest of her days in the society of so remorseless a ruffian, and at length resolved to remain where she was, till it should be known whether Kestrel would dare commit the violence that was expected. At the time appointed, Mr. Derwent met his friends, all of whom were furnished with a good supply of arms, to resist any attack that might be made upon the house. All of them, except Mr. Brassey Popjoy, were tolerably assured that they were in sufficient force to deprive the enemy of any chance of succeeding in their designs, and it was resolved, at any rate, to give them a warm reception if they ventured to intrude themselves into the house. By turns some of them went to look round the premises, to see if Caleb and his accomplices had not made their appearance, but two hours passed away without the occurrence of anything particular, and at that time they were joined by all the domestics belonging to the establishment, all of whom were supplied with arms to assist, in the event of their services being required. At length a loud and sudden crash was heard, the hall door flew open with violence, and the sound of heavy footsteps announced that the expected attack had commenced. In an instant all started to their feet, and rushed towards the head of the stairs, from whence they perceived Kestrel and a number of other men preparing to ascend. Mr. Derwent called upon them peremptorily to retire from the house under pain of instant death, but his command was unheeded, and, as no other alternative remained, a volley was discharged at them, the effect of which was instantaneous, for the villains staggered back as if all had been wounded, and commenced an immediate retreat, struggling, amidst oaths and imprecations, for precedence in getting out of the house. Taking advantage of this confusion, Mr. Derwent and his party rushed down the stairs and succeeded in securing Caleb Kestrel, after a desperate resistance of some few minutes. The rest were pursued by the servants, but all managed to get clear off, in consequence of the darkness of the night. As for Caleb, his arms were secured behind him in order to prevent any further violence, and in that state he was led to the room where they had been watching, and where they found Amy in a state of indescribable alarm at the volley she had just heard. In a few words the whole affair was explained to her, and she was then prevailed upon to retire to her own apartment, upon an assurance being given that all present danger was now at an end. Then, turning towards the prisoner, he said sternly—" You now see, Caleb Kestrel, the termination of a career that has been as reckless as it has been wicked. You are in the hands of those from whom you have no mercy to expect, unless under certain circumstances, and it therefore only remains for you to obtain your liberty by a solemn promise to leave England for ever, and to cease your persecutions against Amy both by yourself, and your accomplices."

" I shall make no promise of the kind," answered the ruffian, " for I fear nothing that either you or the minions of the law can do against me."

" Then transportation for the remainder of your life has no terrors for you?"

" If I thought there was any chance of such a punishment I might perhaps listen to your proposal," he replied, " but as I can yet defeat those that want to crush me, I shall make no such promise as the one you would extort from me."

" Do you think we cannot produce sufficient evidence?"

" Oh, I dare say you may be able to do that," answered the prisoner, " but if matters should come to the worst, I can at least die by my own hand, and there's no one that can prevent me."

" You will be strictly watched."

" Perhaps so, but they can't make me eat against my will; and though death by starvation may be a lingering and painful one, I can meet it willingly rather than be sent abroad as a convict."

" And yet," observed Frank Marldale, " you have been offered liberty on the easiest terms ?"

' They may seem easy to you," answered the pedlar, " but they are not such as I feel inclined to accept. Besides, though I may be for the present in the hands of those that owe me a mortal grudge, it is not certain that I shall remain long under bondage ; and, if I should be fortunate enough to escape my enemies, shall be made to feel what sort of revenge still remains in my power."

" Why, you don't expect to escape ?" exclaimed Brassey Popjoy in accents of the greatest dismay.

" I throw not my words away upon such an idiot as you are," returned the other, scornfully.

" Idiot ! do you dare to call me an idiot ?"

" I dare speak the truth at all times when it pleases me to do so," replied Caleb Kestrel, and then, turning towards Mr. Derwent, he added—" You must not imagine, squire, that because fortune has so far declared in your favour, I am rendered quite powerless. The snake that has been lying in your path is only scotched, not killed, and before long you will have reason enough to be sorry for not having closed with my proposition instead of treating it with neglect."

" Think you I would stoop to parley with a villain like you ?" demanded the squire.

" Prudence, at least, ought to have inclined you that way," exclaimed the prisoner, " and since you have thought proper to take up the defensive, the consequences must fall upon your own head. By a sacrifice that ought not to have stood in the way, you could have purchased peace and security for Amy, but the gold was not forthcoming, and the chances were that this night you had lost her for ever."

" Now it strikes me, old fellow, that the chances were altogether the other way," interrupted Mr. Peeps, " for we suspected what sort of schemes you would be up to, and having prepared ourselves for the worst you now find yourself on the wrong side of the hedge, in spite of all your cunning."

" Pshaw ! I'm only defeated for a little while."

" You seem to imagine that there are neither bolts nor bars strong enough to deprive you of your liberty," observed the squire.

" That's just what I do believe," replied Kestrel, with a grim smile of defiance ;

"I have my own hands, and good fortune to depend upon, and neither of them are likely to deceive me when there is so much reason to make a bold effort to escape from captivity."

" Yet the time has been when you were obliged to go through the full term of punishment awarded you," observed the squire.

"Ay," he replied, "you are speaking of the time when your cousin, that is now dead, caused me to be transported for a trifling robbery that I had committed on him. And you say truly that on that occasion I was obliged to endure the sentence which had been passed upon me, but have you forgotten the revenge I took against him as soon as the law had been satisfied to the fullest extent ?'

" Like a base-hearted coward as you were, you hurled your vengeance upon an innocent child.'

" That child was Amy, the adopted daughter of your cousin Clement," answered the pedlar, exultingly. " I know she was the treasure he most dearly prized, and when I had removed the girl, and all hope of discovering what had become of her was at an end, I had the satisfaction of seeing my former persecutor sink rapidly under an affliction that he was unable to bear. Then it was my turn to triumph, and my exultation knew no bounds when I at last heard that Clement Derwent had died of a broken heart, brought on by excessive grief."

" Why did not your malice end there ?" asked the squire.

"Because I saw clearly that I had opened the way for my own fortune," answered Kestrel. " I knew the terms of your cousin's will, and determined to keep Amy under a cloud till the time came when I might hope to make what terms I pleased with you. You are aware that I lost sight of the girl for some years, and that when, at length, I discovered her still under the protection of the people I had placed her with, I lost no time in taking those steps that were to convert me from a poor wandering pedlar into a wealthy gentleman."

" By demanding half the fortune that had been left by my cousin ?"

" Exactly so."

" But you have been foiled ?"

" Not quite so completely as you imagine," answered Kestrel, " for though Fortune has frowned upon me this night, my imprisonment will not last any very long time—I shall yet be free ;' and, when the hour comes, you will have reason to repent the obstinacy that induced you to reject the fair proposition I have made."

" Was it fair to demand half the gentleman's property?" inquired Peeps.

"I am not inclined to answer that question to any one but the person I have been speaking to," replied the prisoner. "Squire Derwent knows best what value ought to be put upon the future happiness of the young lady he professes to love ; and, since he has not thought proper to accept my terms, he cannot feel suprised at my having taken the only means in my power to bring him to his senses."

" But she whom you tore from her home has never injured you."

" What has that, to do with it?" demanded the ruffian. " Do you suppose I reflected whether she had ever harmed me, when I knew there was no other way to bring you to my terms except by working on your fears for her safety ? Ay, and I should have succeeded, too, but for the cursed piece of ill luck that turned to-night's attempt against us."

" And now," exclaimed Mr. Derwent, " finding yourself defeated and wholly in my power, would it not be the wiser course to accept my offer of immediate lberty, in a solemn promise being given never again to molest Amy ?"

" What would be the use of liberty to a man that has not a halfpenny in the world to help himself with ?"

" You mistake me, for I am willing to purchase your forbearance, though not at the extravagant price you ask for it."

" Then," replied Caleb Kestrel, " differing as we do on so important a point, our treaty may be said to be at an end ? You have heard my terms, Squire Derwent, and, even if there was not a single hope left me, I would not purchase my freedom by giving way in the most trifling degree."

"Remember, fellow," exclaimed the other, "this is your last chance of escaping a fate which, if it overtakes you, will render you a miserable slave for the remainder of your days."

"Haven't I told you that my fate is not in your hands, but in my own?" demanded Kestrel. "What matters it that I now happen to be your prisoner, when I feel certain that in a very few hours I shall be in the enjoyment of as much freedom as you have?"

"Impossible!"

"So you may suppose; but I happen to be of quite a different opinion, and that being the case, Squire Derwent, I don't see the use of our carrying this argument any further. A little time will show which of us is in the right, and if it should happen that I have been too sanguine in my expectations, there is still one way of escaping being sent abroad as a convict, and that is by refusing to take food till death comes to put an end to my sufferings."

"It's all very fine to talk about starving yourself to death," exclaimed Mr. Brassey Popjoy, "but I rather think that you will grow heartily tired of it before you have proceeded very far with the experiment. Hunger, my boy, will soon bring you to your senses, and a good thing, too, for I don't think you have any great share of 'em, or you wouldn't have been playing off your tricks with people that have proved themselves to be more than a match for you."

"In one word," interposed Mr. Derwent, "you must either give the solemn promise I have demanded, or my servants will be desired to convey you immediately to the cage, there to await the hour for your examination before a magistrate in the morning."

"To prevent all chance of that," answered Squire Derwent, "a sufficient guard will be placed round the cage; and even if an attack should be made upon them by any of your associates, it will be with little probability of success, since a signal will quickly bring sufficient assistance to back our people. You see, therefore, the utter hopelessness of your situation, and it only remains for you to say whether the terms I have offered are to be accepted."

"You have already had my answer," replied Caleb Kestrel; "and if this conversation was to be carried on for a month longer you would get nothing more out of me."

"Then you will repent your obstinacy."

"Why should I repent it, squire?"

"Because you will find, in the end, that it would have been far better to have closed with a good offer."

"A good offer!" exclaimed the pedlar. "Do you call it a good offer to promise a man a small sum of money when he has demanded a large one? But it serves me right, too, for I ought to have kept the girl when I had her in my power, and not have sent her back to your house under the expectation that you would act towards me with the greater liberality."

"You should have known better than to place your reliance upon a man from whom you had neither favour nor gratitude to expect," answered the squire. "The truth is, you knew I was determined to rescue the girl, and having no means of preventing her discovery beyond a few hours, you made a virtue of necessity, and sent her back, under the erroneous impression that you might afterwards enforce the sum of money that had been demanded as the price of her liberation."

"Ay," he replied; "and there was every chance of my succeeding, too, if it had not been for your suspecting that a visit would be paid you to-night."

"How could I do otherwise than suspect it, when you sent word that such would be the case if the ransom money was not sent to you before the expiration of three days? However, I have to thank you for it, since, had it been otherwise, it might have been some few days before we should have been able to discover the retreat to which Amy was conveyed."

"Then you never could have found her," exclaimed the ruffian; "for I should have taken her over to the opposite coast, and then you might have hunted long enough before you found any trace of her. So you see I have not gone so far as I might have done; and the only reward I have got for my forbearance is, to be sent to prison as a felon."

"What right have you to complain," demanded Squire Derwent, "when all your acts have been of a violent and vindictive description, not only against the young lady herself, but against me also, as the protector of helpless innocence?"

"Was I to expect no reward, then, for my services?"

" I am not aware of any services you have performed."

"Indeed! then it was nothing to have been the means of discovering who and what she was?"

"That was merely the effect of chance," replied Mr. Derwent, "and, therefore, little merit is due to you for it. However, even admitting that we owe you some thanks for what has been done, enough has been already offered to recompense you for the benefit conferred."

"Humph! my only recompense is the being made a prisoner."

"What other alternative had we, after the desperate attack that has been made upon this house?"

"I'm not going to argue upon that point, Mr. Derwent," exclaimed the ruffian; "but it must be confessed, that no attack would have been made if anything like a fair offer had been made, as an acknowledgment of the services I had performed in sending the girl back, when there was nothing to hinder me from carrying her to some place abroad, where she never could have been found. And that's just what ought to have taken place, for then, instead of being your prisoner, I should have been enjoying my liberty, and you must have come to my terms, extraordinary as they may appear to be."

"And no doubt you would have done so," answered Mr. Derwent, "but that there were difficulties in the way which you were not inclined to encounter."

"What difficulties could there have been?"

"More than you think for," replied the squire. "For instance, you knew that Amy's friends would never have relaxed their exertions till they had brought her enemies to condign punishment."

"They must have been first of all caught."

"Would there have been any difficulty in that?"

"The greatest."

"How could you, for any length of time, have avoided the pursuit of those who were determined to rescue the young lady from your hands?"

"Oh, that would have been far more easy than you seem to imagine," answered the pedlar. "But why should I talk of these things, when there are others of more importance that ought to occupy your attention? Why not come to terms with me now, Squire Derwent, and secure your own comfort, as well as that of the young lady, by paying down the money I have asked for, as the price of my future forbearance?"

"Is it for you, a prisoner, to name your own terms?"

"To be sure it is," replied Kestrel, with the insolence of demeanour that he had displayed throughout. "I am a prisoner, it is true; but what difference does that make, when I have comrades still at large who have received my instructions, and are ready to act upon them as soon as they see that I am no longer able to assist myself. In a word, squire, there's half a dozen as reckless fellows as ever you saw in your life, who will dare any peril to carry Amy off at the first opportunity, even though they have to wait months for it."

"Your idle boastings will not intimidate me," exclaimed Mr. Derwent, "for now that we know the sort of ruffians we have to deal with, every precaution will be taken to prevent a repetition of the violence that has already been committed. So now, Kestrel, for the last time, I ask you if you will agree to accept of liberty on conditions such as those I have just mentioned?"

" No," he replied, doggedly; "I shall not yield an inch."

" Then here our conference ends," exclaimed Mr. Derwent ; " and you must submit to the consequences, though they will harass you for the remainder of your days." Then addressing himself to his domestics, he added, " let the prisoner be immediately conveyed to the village cage, where he will remain under your custody till the time arrives for his examination before the magistrate. Guard him well, and let no communication take place between him and his friends, or he may yet find means to escape, and then all our present advantages will terminate in utter discomfiture."

The men promptly obeyed the commands of their master ; but, in spite of their superiority in point of numbers, it was with no little difficulty that they succeeded in preventing his breaking away from their grasp. His struggles to shake them off were indeed so great that Frank Marldale saw the necessity of tendering his services, and even then it was not without the most violent efforts that he was at length dragged from the house, and from thence to the place where he was to pass the time that intervened till the hour arrived for his examination.

" Depend on it we shall have more trouble than enough with that fellow," exclaimed Peeps, as soon as he saw that the pedlar had been taken from the house. " He's the most resolute chap I ever saw in my life, and if your people ain't very careful we shall hear in the morning that the bird has contrived to escape."

" Not after the strict charge I have given them to keep a strict watch over them," replied the squire. " Besides, they know what danger would follow to themselves if he should get loose again, and the risk of their own personal safety will alone be amply sufficient to keep them watchful over the charge they have been entrusted with."

" It may be all very well to say so, my dear sir," exclaimed Mr. Brassey Popjoy, " but suppose he should happen to escape in spite of all their watchfulness,—what would become of us then, I should like to know? Why, we should be worse off than ever, and every one that has taken part against him might look upon himself as a dead man."

" Really, sir," replied the squire, " I see no grounds [whatever for even the slightest apprehension."

" Hasn't he got plenty of friends that are both ready and willing to assist him ?"

" Their assistance would be of very little service against those that have been set to guard him," replied Mr. Derwent. " Besides, there are plenty of men in the village where the cage is, and on the first signal, by firing a pistol, they would immediately assemble, to prevent the escape of so desperate a ruffian."

" Then I may set it down as being all right ?"

" Most certainly you may," replied the squire, " or I should not treat the affair with so much indifference."

" Well," exclaimed the cockney, " there's some consolation in hearing you say that, at any rate ; for, to tell you the truth, I began to feel heartily sorry that I had come so far in the pursuit of game only to find everything at sixes and sevens. But never mind ; I'll wait and see what to-morrow brings with it, and then, if matters don't take a more favourable turn, I shall direct my men to pack up my boxes and portmanteaus and hurry back to dear, delightful London as fast as four post horses can carry me."

" You seem uncommonly careful of yourself, sir," observed Mr. Peeps, with a sly leer.

" And so I need be," replied the cockney, " for in all my experience I never saw such goings on as since I've been in this confounded neighbourhood. Talk of the quiet of a country life !—why, there's been nothing but confusion and violence ever since I first set my foot in Derwent Hall. By the by, I mustn't say that, either, or the squire will begin to think presently that I am not grateful for his hospitality."

"On the contrary, my dear sir," exclaimed Mr. Derwent, "I cannot but admit the force of your observation, for there has indeed been little else than trouble and vexation, though my friends will do me the justice to say that it has not been through any fault of mine. In general all goes on smoothly enough, and so it would have done still but for the unfortunate appearance of Caleb Kestrel at Farmer Brough's harvest home supper."

"Unfortunate in some respects, but fortunate in others," interposed Mr. Peeps

[Kestrel's examination before the Magistrate.—See page 197.]

"for, had it not been for his arrival in this neighbourhood, we might never have known that Amy was the long-lost adopted daughter of your cousin Clement Derwent."

"True," answered the squire; "but it may still be doubted whether she would not have been far happier in her former sphere than she has been in her new one. With you and your worthy wife she probably knew scarcely an hour's unhappiness, but the moment her real station in life became known she has been the object] of Kestrel's cruel and unceasing persecution."

No. 24.

"There's no denying that," replied the ex-showman ; "but then, on the other hand, we have the consolation of knowing that the rascal is now in limbo, and long may he continue so, say I ; for if he should happen to break loose again there'll be the deuce to pay among us all."

"For goodness sake, my dear Mr. Peeps, don't remind us of it," exclaimed Brassey Popjoy. "I've been trying to forget our trouble, but, somehow or another, you seem to take a malicious pleasure in making people remember that they are in hourly danger of having their throats cut."

"I don't think there's much danger of your being served so," observed the showman.

"And why am I any more safe than anybody else?"

"Because you'll take care to keep on the right side of the hedge if Kestrel should by any chance escape from those that have the charge of him," replied Peeps. "Not that I blame any man for looking after himself, so long as he don't run away like a coward, when his assistance might be of use to his friends."

Brassey Popjoy was about to reply to this with some warmth, but Mr. Derwent prevented what might have proved a disagreeable termination of the day's triumph, by observing that the hour was very late, and suggesting that it would be advisable to retire to bed, in order that they might be prepared to perform the new duties which awaited them in the morning. This hint was promptly acted on, and the friends having separated, Mr. Derwent proceeded to the apartment occupied by Amy, whom he found in earnest conversation with Mrs. Peeps on the events of the day and the probable effect that it would have on her future destiny. On observing the approach of her lover, she rose to meet him, and, in a tone of diffidence, inquired if he thought she had at length seen the climax of her misfortunes.

"I believe you may now rest assured that there is no longer any danger to be apprehended," he replied ; "for even should your persecutor find means to escape, he will never dare return to a place that his crimes have rendered too hot to hold him."

"So it was thought after his unsuccessful attempt against your life," she replied, "and yet how few hours afterwards was it that he, and his equally desperate comrades, broke into the house and carried me away, in open defiance of all danger !"

"You speak truly, my dear Amy," answered Cecil Derwent ; "but then the villain took the opportunity of coming when he knew that there was not a male person in the place to defend you from his attack. Now, however, it is far different, for, under no circumstances, shall you be left without a sufficient number of persons to guard you, in case any farther attempt should be made to tear you from your home."

"Believe me, it is not for myself that I feel this alarm," exclaimed Amy, "but for the sake of you, who I know to be the object of his most inveterate hatred."

"Ay, ay, my dear child," interposed Mrs. Peeps, "the devil has shown his cloven foot, sure enough ; but for all that, I don't think he is so much to be feared as you may fancy."

"What grounds have you for fancying so?"

"Because, generally speaking, fellows like him, are great cowards when they know danger is in the way ; and it's my opinion that, even if he managed to get loose, which, by the way, is not very likely, he would make all haste to leave a country where he must look upon every person he meets as an enemy. That's my opinion mind, but whether I'm right or wrong, I should advise you to keep within the house for some time to come, or at least till it is satisfactorily proved that Caleb Kestrel and the whole of his villanous comrades have left the country for ever."

"Which, I rather think, will be the case before long," observed Mr. Derwent, "for all of them are well known to have been guilty of crime, and it shall now be my chief object to pursue them with untiring energy, till they have been deprived of the power of doing further mischief. That task, I believe, will not occupy any very long time, and probably less than a month may see all danger from them at an end; at all events, it shall be no fault of mine, if they are at large a longer period than I have named."

"Do you really think my troubles are so nearly at an end?" asked Amy, with a sigh.

"I, at least, venture to hope so."

"Alas!" she replied, "hope has so much deceived me of late, that I have now cease to place the slightest reliance on it. Once, indeed, my heart was full of it, but it was before wealth brought upon me all its curses, and embittered days, which, but for my change of circumstances, might still have been happy."

"Do you then despair of those brighter hours that may succeed the clouds with which the horizon of your life is just now overrun?"

"How can I do otherwise than despair?"

"Bless the girl," exclaimed Mrs. Peeps, "how she gives up all at once."

"Have I not experienced enough to make me do so?"

"Why," replied the old lady, "it must be confessed, matters have not been running very smoothly of late—but what of that?—If you have got into trouble one day, you have managed, by some means or another, to scramble out of it the next, and you will do so again, I dare say, so never look at the dark side of a question, while there's a chance left that matters may make a favourable change."

"What probability is there," asked Amy, "that any favourable change will take place in my lot?"

"There's every reason to hope it," replied Mrs. Peeps, "for they say, when things get to the worst they must mend. Now, in my opinion, nothing can possibly be worse than you have lately gone through, and if I am right in that, you ought to look forward to better days, instead of giving way to despair."

"Argued like an able logician, Mrs. Peeps," exclaimed the squire, in a tone of cheerfulness, that was intended to inspire the heart of Amy with lighter feelings; "by Jove! our young friend is in most excellent hands, so long as she has you for a guide and counsellor; and I most earnestly hope she will be induced, through your example, to believe that the termination of her trouble is near at hand, if not, indeed, already past. At any rate, she may rest assured that she is now surrounded by zealous friends, who are, one and all, willing to shed the last drop of their blood in her service, rather than allow her to undergo any further persecution."

"I know and feel the kindness of my friends," answered our heroine, "and I may be believed when I say that my heart feels deeply grateful for the generous support they have afforded me. The remembrance of their favours is never absent from my mind; yet I cannot but regret that I have caused them so much trouble, and even danger, to protect me from the insidious attacks of my enemies."

"Surely," exclaimed Mr. Derwent, "you would not have expected them to stand quietly by, when, by an exertion of their own, they had it in their power to rescue you from peril?"

"If they had," observed Mrs. Peeps, sharply, "they would not have deserved to be called men, and I should not have scrupled to tell them so, too, if any of them had shrunk from their duty, when a poor, defenceless girl needed their services. However, there's no occasion to say anything about that now, for everybody came forward boldly, and you, Amy, have good reason to thank them for their courage, since to it you entirely owe your deliverance from the hands of Caleb Kestrel."

"I do, indeed, thank them for what they have done," answered Amy; "but I cannot yet believe that I am no longer in danger from him."

"Why, you surely don't believe it possible that the pedlar can ever escape from the custody of the people that have him in charge?"

"Has he not already escaped most marvellously, when it was thought no human power could aid him?"

" Exactly so, my dear," answered Mr. Peeps; "and who knows but that it was some superhuman power, since it's exactly such people as Caleb Kestrel that the devil most delights to assist? For my own part, I shouldn't wonder at it a bit, so you may consider yourself very fortunate in having escaped from such a half-demon as he is."

" I am, indeed, most fortunate," sighed Amy, " but the future is still dark and uncertain; and I feel convinced, that, severe as my sufferings have already been, they are nothing to what I have to endure, if Kestrel should ever again be at liberty to indulge his revenge."

" Nay," exclaimed the squire, "how is it possible that he can escape from those who have him in charge?"

" I know not that it may be so in this instance," replied Amy; "but I have heard of people, before now, who have been acquitted of heinous offences, because sufficient evidence could not be brought forward to convict them of their crimes."

" But in the present case, there is no chance of anything of the kind," exclaimed Cecil Derwent, " for out of the three or four charges we have to bring against him, there is not one that we cannot prove by the clearest evidence."

" His attempt upon your life is one instance," observed Mrs. Peeps.

" Yes," he replied, " that can be proved by Amy herself, who, unseen herself, was a witness of the discharge of the air-gun by the hands of Caleb Kestrel, who, at that time, was supposed to be her father."

" Then," continued Mrs. Peeps, " there was his breaking into this house, and carrying her off by force of arms."

" Which can also be easily proved."

" And, thirdly," added the old lady, " there's his attack upon the Hall to-night, which I should think will send him abroad for life."

" There can be no doubt of it," returned Mr. Derwent; " so that, upon three such charges as we have to bring against the scoundrel, I think it would be strange indeed if he should escape with impunity. At any rate, I, for one, have no doubt upon the matter, and it is my most earnest wish that Amy should look forward to the future with less alarm than she has hitherto done."

" Believe me I will do so," she replied, " for I should be ungrateful indeed; were I to doubt the zeal of those in whom I have so much reason to rely. I leave myself in the hands of my friends, with a firm reliance that they will leave no effort untried in order to rid me of the foe that has robbed me of my happiness.'

" That's right, my dear girl," exclaimed Mrs. Peeps, " rely upon those that are willing to assist in this cause of yours, and you will never have reason to repent your confidence. In the future, I feel certain, there's plenty of good in store; and in order to convince myself that it is as I have said, I intend going to-morrow to see the gipsey-woman you have been telling me about, in order to learn from her what sort of a destiny yours is to be."

" And why," asked Mr. Derwent, " should you consult one, who knows no more about the matter than you do yourself?"

" What!" exclaimed the old lady with astonishment, " do you place no belief in the words spoken by fortune tellers?"

" Not the slightest," he replied, " for I know them all to be nothing but cheats and impostors."

" Then what a number of people must be taken in by them every year!"

" Many thousands, I am sorry to say," replied Mr. Derwent; " and what makes the matter still worse, is the fact that a great number of the deluded fools are to be found amongst a class of persons who, from their station and education, ought to know better."

" Then how," asked Mrs. Peeps, " did the gipsey woman happen to tell Amy so many things that were true?"

" Because she was acquainted with Caleb Kestrel many years ago, and is acquainted with almost every event of his life," replied the squire. " The art she professes did not assist her in the least, as Amy herself can testify."

"I can," replied our heroine, rousing herself from a sort of reverie, into which she had fallen ! "the woman spoke only from facts, and her words were intended but to warn me against the attack which was afterwards made upon this house."

"And the warning seems to have done good too," exclaimed Mrs. Peeps, "for it put us all upon our guard, and was the means of getting Caleb Kestrel into trouble."

"More easily," observed the squire, "than he will be able to get out of it. At any rate, if he escape, it must be by means of his former good luck, for the strictest watch will be kept over him and his comrades till he is removed on board the convict ship where he will have very little chance of eluding the vigilance of those whose duty it is to convey their prisoners to the place of destination."

"But do you think he will be sent away for life?" asked Mrs. Peeps.

"What less punishment can be expected in so bad a case as his?" demanded Cecil Derwent. "Has he not been guilty of almost every crime, and will justice be satisfied unless means are taken to prevent the repetition of his heinous offences?"

"That may be all very true, sir," exclaimed the old lady, "but do we not frequently hear of prisoners being acquitted altogether through some little loose hole that the lawyers find for them? Ay, and that, too, though their guilt is as clear as the noon-day."

"That such is too frequently the case, cannot be denied," answered the squire. "but in the present instance I think there is very little fear of such an event taking place. Caleb Kestrel is now within the strong grip of the law, which will never be relaxed till the moment when he yields up his miserable existence. And be assured, my dear Amy," he added, turning towards her, "that I am not uttering these words merely to relieve your fears, but because I feel satisfied that the end of your persecution has arrived. Caleb Kestrel no longer possesses the means to injure you, and I now look forward with a confident hope to the perfect restoration of peace and happiness, that the presence of that vindictive man has for, a brief period, suspended."

"Having thus endeavoured to restore her confidence, Cecil Derwent took his leave for the night, and the two females remained for some time longer in earnest conversation upon the subject which just then occupied all their thoughts. At length, wearied both in body and mind, they retired to bed, and soon forgot in sleep the cares that harassed them.

CHAPTER XXII.

CALEB KESTREL BEGINS TO SEE THAT MATTERS WEAR AN AWKWARD ASPECT ; HE TRIES THE EFFECT OF BRIBERY, BUT FAILS IN HIS OBJECT.—THE EXAMINATION, AND COMMITTAL.

BOLD and resolute as had been the conduct of the pedlar during the time that he was in the presence of Mr. Derwent and his friends, he no sooner found himself alone in the cage than uneasy reflections upon his present situation began to occupy his mind. That an incessant and strict watch would be kept over him was a fact upon which there could be no doubt, for his designs against Amy were too well known to admit of any carelessness that would allow him a chance of repeating the violence of which everybody knew him to be capable. Rendered desperate by the thoughts that rushed tumultuously through his mind he tried the windows and the door in the faint hope that they might yield beneath his strength ; but they were too well secured to afford him the least chance of escape by either of those means, and, even if he could have made his way from the cage, there would still have been the difficulty of fighting a passage through the numerous persons by whom the place was surrounded.

Opposed, then, by difficulties, whichever way he turned, he even began to think of submitting to the terms that had been proposed by Mr. Derwent. Pride, however, would not permit him to yield after the resolution he had expressed; and still being of opinion that his own proposition would be ultimately acceded to, he finally resolved to await the result of his examination before the magistrate, in the hope that his comrades would form some scheme to affect his rescue on his way to the prison. In that case, he would still be at liberty to urge the payment of the sum of money he had demanded and, in the event of a refusal to carry Amy to some distant place where he would be able to defy any search that might be made for her. These thoughts occupied his mind till sleep came upon him, and upon waking in the morning she was still more confirmed than ever in the views he had taken upon the subject. Whilst he was thus brooding over the future, and plotting all sorts of wild schemes for the perpetration of further iniquities, he was interrupted by the entrance of the constable with the breakfast. This being placed upon the small table that formed part of the scanty furniture of the place, the man was about to take his departure, when the prisoner stopped him by inquiring what time the examination was to take place.

" At eleven," was the brief reply.

" Who is the magistrate?"

" Mr. Borrowdale."

" Humph! I've heard of him, and report says he's very severe to the poor unfortunate devils that are taken before him."

" I don't know much about that," replied the constable, " but folks tell me he is very just in all his decisions, and it's only the guilty that have any reason to charge him with being severe."

" In that case I have nothing to be afraid of."

" What! can you deny breaking into Derwent Hall?"

" It would be of no use if I did," replied Kestrel, " but I can say that I didn't break into the place to commit a robbery, and the mere getting into the house can't be punished as a crime."

" Well, I don't know how that may be," exclaimed the constable, " but I've been told you meant to carry off a young lady, and that her friends are determined to get rid of you, if they can."

" That's true enough," answered the pedlar; " they only want to send me away in order to avoid paying a sum of money that I have demanded of Mr. Derwent, as my own right. It is I, in truth, that have most cause to complain, since I have been locked up here like a criminal, for no other reason than that I have made a demand which the squire chooses to resist."

" Prove that to the magistrate, and he'll soon set you at liberty."

" What's the use of attempting proofs when no one will listen to 'em?" asked Kestrel. " I should only get laughed at for my pains, since, as a matter of course, my accuser's word will be taken before mine."

" The truth of it is," replied the constable, " there's no denying that you broke into the house, and as that is an offence against the law, Mr. Derwent had no choice but to send you before a magistrate."

" But the offence is not a very serious one."

" Perhaps not, if you have never done anything worse."

" The truth is," replied Caleb Cestrel, " I have always got an honest living by travelling through the country with my goods. Chance, at length, brought me to this village, where I discovered a girl that I had long been in search of, and through my means she has come into possession of a large fortune that was left her by a cousin of the man that is now persecuting me."

" Did you ever see Mr. Derwent till lately?"

" Never!"

" Then he can have no spite against you."

" His bad feeling has arisen from no other grounds than that I have demanded a sum of money that I believe myself entitled to, and which he refuses to give, though I promised to leave the place immediately, and never to molest him any more."

"I suppose that's because you've asked him too much?"

"If I have asked him too much, he has offered me too little," replied Caleb Kestrel; "and now, in order to get rid of me entirely, he's trying all he can to get me out of the country."

"Well, that's a question that must be settled between yourselves," exclaimed the constable; "but you know as well as I do, that he can't have you punished, unless he's first of all able to prove that you have done something to deserve it. An innocent man never need be afraid in this country, for the laws are made to protect everybody, till it has been proved that they are not worthy of it."

"Humph!" ejaculated the pedlar; "to hear you talk, one would suppose that no man was ever punished wrongfully."

"Such things may sometimes happen," answered the other, "but that's no reason why such a fate should be yours."

"You could prevent it if you like," exclaimed Kestrel, plunging boldly into the subject he was anxious to speak about.

"I?—What do you mean?"

"Why, that you might as well do me a good turn, and earn something that will be worth your while."

"Oh, oh! You want me to let you out of this place, eh?"

"Exactly so—the service is one that will not cost you much trouble, and I will pay liberally for it."

"It's all very well to talk about pay," exclaimed the constable, "but it would be at once supposed that I had suffered you to escape; and what would be my fate then, I should like to know?"

"Pshaw! it could be managed easily enough, if you thought proper to assist a poor fellow out of his trouble. Forget to lock the door when you go away; and then meet me afterwards at the deserted hut on the moors, and I'll raise twenty pounds for you."

"Fifty pounds wouldn't prevail upon me to do anything of the kind."

"Then what's to hinder me from taking the keys from you, and leaving you here in my place? I'm the strongest if we come to a struggle, and, once at liberty, my enemies should never have a chance of laying their hands upon me again."

"You may be the strongest," answered the constable, eyeing him keenly, "but I can shout loud enough to be heard, and there's plenty of people that would come to my assistance if you were to play off any of your tricks."

"Well, then," exclaimed the prisoner, suddenly altering his tone, "since threats are of no use, why shouldn't you and I talk over this affair a little rationally? I've offered to pay for any service you are inclined to do me, and surely it will be better to find yourself richer by some few pounds, than to see me sent to prison with a chance of being obliged to pass the remainder of my days as a miserable convict."

"It's all very well to talk about paying for my service," exclaimed the man, "but where's your money to come from, I should like to know?"

"Oh," he replied, "that may be easily managed by the time I have been at liberty an hour. My friends can soon get the money together, and every coin of it shall be yours, on condition that I can be allowed to get myself out of this confounded place."

"Well, then," exclaimed the constable, "the best way is for you and I to come to an understanding at once, by my telling you that I am not inclined to get myself into a scrape, by suffering the escape of a prisoner that has been committed to my custody."

"Who is to know that you had anything to do with it?"

"People must be confounded fools if they didn't suspect it," replied the man, "and I'm not going to run any risk for the sake of a few pounds."

"Then you have the satisfaction of knowing that my friends will not fail to revenge themselves upon all that have taken part against me."

"That is to say if they be allowed to have their own way."

"And what's to hinder them having their own way, when they'll work in darkness and secrecy?" asked Caleb Kestrel. "The chaps you'll have to deal with are not to be easily threatened when they have an object in view, so you had better give the matter a little more consideration, before you make up your mind to refuse my offer."

"What good would it be if I were to let you out, when I know there's plenty of people outside ready to pounce upon you in a moment?"

"That's my affair," replied the pedlar. "All I want is, that the chance shall be given to me, and then I'll trust to the swiftness of my own legs to get out of the reach of my pursuers. By Jove, old fellow, I can run like a deer when there's danger behind, and my enemies would have but a poor chance of overtaking me, if once I have the good fortune to get a few yards in advance of 'em. So now, make up your mind at once to stand my friend, and I'll answer for it the thing may be so managed that no one will ever think of suspecting that you had any hand in assisting me to escape."

"Do you suppose Squire Derwent wouldn't guess that some one had given a helping hand? And who is so likely to be suspected of the act but myself?"

"But suspicion is no proof."

"May be not," answered the constable; "but I might find myself in a very awkward situation for all that."

"Pshaw! you have not the courage of a mouse."

"I can't help that," answered the constable; "but whether I've courage or not, I'm not going to bring ruin on myself and family, by helping a man that has got himself into trouble by his own bad actions."

"My bad actions have never harmed you."

"Very true, and I mean to take care they never shall, and the only way to make myself sure is to keep you here, under lock and key, till the magistrate sends you to some other place, where there'll not be much chance of your making your escape."

"Then you had better look to yourself," exclaimed Caleb Kestrel, "for from the moment that I am committed to prison, my friends will let no opportunity pass to avenge themselves upon all that have taken any part in bringing me into trouble."

"In that case, there is no reason for me to feel any alarm," answered the constable, "for I have done nothing more than my duty in refusing to let you out of my custody."

"Are you always as strict in performing your duty?"

"I am."

"You never took a bribe then?"

"I was never offered one before," he replied.

"But, suppose I was to increase my proposition?"

"Increase it?—Where's the money to come from, I should like to know?"

"From Squire Derwent, to be sure."

"Squire Derwent!—Why, he's the very man that sent you here."

"I know it," replied the prisoner, "but for all that he would be glad to give me any sum of money I might choose to demand, if once I manage to get out of his confounded grasp."

"Has he any reason to be afraid of you, then?"

"So much, that he would refuse nothing if he find himself again at my mercy. He knows pretty well that I am not to be trifled with; and as the breach between us has been widened, he would see that my terms must be yielded to."

"There must be some good reason for it then," replied the constable, "for I've always heard that Mr. Derwent is a man not easily to be moved by threats, and he bears so good a character in this neighbourhood, that I'm sure he has never been guilty of any act that he need be afraid of."

"What he has been guilty of is no business of ours just at this moment," exclaimed Caleb Kestrel. "Let it satisfy you, that I have it in my power to do him a most grievous injury, and that he would rather thrust his hand into the fire than provoke me to do him all the mischief that is in my power."

"Has he wronged you?"

[Amy's visit to Caleb Kestrel, in Prison.]

"To be sure he has."

"In what way?"

"Oh," exclaimed Kestrel, "it would take a long time to relate all the causes of complain I have to bring against him. We hate each other thoroughly, and at present I happen to have got the worst of it; but only give me a chance of getting out of this infernal den, and if I don't make him yield to all my demands, you may set me down as a liar, and a vain boaster."

"And what, if he don't give way?"

No. 25.

"Why, then there is a certain young lady, that he is very fond of, who would be carried away, and taken to some place where he would never be able to find her, search for her as long as he may."

"Don't you think yourself a pretty sort of fellow to make an innocent female suffer?"

"What have I to do with innocence when my own interest is concerned?" demanded Caleb Kestrel. "He knows what sort of man he has to deal with, and may yet be sorry for having obstinately refused to do the only thing that can secure a quiet life for himself and the girl that I have been the means of restoring to her rights."

"You are speaking of the young female that they call Amy?"

"I am."

"They say she was stolen away from her friends when quite a child?"

"So she was," answered Caleb, "and it was through me that a short time ago she was discovered to be the heiress of half the Derwent property."

"Then you knew the girl before?"

"To be sure I did; and for many years past I have travelled from place to place through England, in search of her. At last, chance took me to the house of Farmer Brough on the night of his harvest supper, and there, to my surprise, I discovered the girl with the very people she had been living with ever since the time of her mysterious disappearance from the house of her adopted father. So I made known who she was, and the only reward I have got for my services, is to be locked up like a felon in this vile dungeon of yours."

"That," observed the constable, dryly, "is because you, and some of your people, broke into Derwent Hall."

"But not to rob the place."

"Then what took you there, I should like to know?"

"To take away the girl, when I found that my restoring her to her rights was to be treated with ingratitude. In truth, I thought it was the only way to bring the squire to his senses; but somehow, fortune deserted me, and instead of taking Amy away, I was captured by the enemy, who sent me here with the uncomfortable prospect of being banished from England for the remainder of my days."

"Which, I suppose, will be nothing more than your deserts."

"So you may think," exclaimed Kestrel, "but for my own part, I look upon it as a very base return for the services I have performed. In short, I might have claimed Amy as my daughter, and no one could have contradicted my assertion, seeing that the people she had been brought up by always looked upon her as my child. However, I see my folly now that it's too late, and it only remains for me to get out of this precious scrape as well as I can."

"Which you want to do by bribing a man to forget his duty."

"What has duty to do with it, when your own interest stands in the way?" demanded Caleb Kestrel.

"Why, the truth is, I have no wish to lose either my character or my situation," replied the other, "the one has been a tolerably good one all my life, and the other goes a good way towards the support of myself, my wife, and my children."

"You have forgotten then that I have promised to pay for your services."

"Promises, Master Kestrel, go for nothing between strangers," answered the other, "and, even if the money were laid down before me this very minute, I should prefer doing my duty faithfully, to neglecting it for the sake of a bribe. So now, I suppose, as we understand each other, you'll not try any more to lead me away from my duty."

"Can you blame a man for trying hard to get his liberty?"

"Not I," replied the official, "but I should blame myself, though, if I were weak enough to yield, when I know you are plotting mischief against people that have never done you any injury. Why, let me ask you, should I set a man at liberty, when I know the only use he wants to make of it, is to do mischief to others?"

"I don't want to do any mischief," muttered Kestrel, "if people will only do me the justice I ask for."

"But what you call justice others may reckon to be nothing but downright imposition and extortion."

"If you know all," exclaimed Caleb Kestrel, "you would acknowledge that I have a right to expect some return from the squire for the services I have done him. But for me, he never would have known that Amy was the heiress of immense wealth, and in that case he never would have thought of making her his wife."

"But he would have had all the property instead of only half of it, and then the advantage would have been entirely on his side."

"And won't he have all of it as it is, if he marry the girl that has been so long kept out of her rights?"

"Very true," answered the constable ; "but suppose the young lady should be already engaged, or, which is just as likely, suppose she should not feel inclined to become his wife."

"Not so fast, my good fellow," exclaimed Kestrel, "for I happen to know that she is very fond of him, and has promised to go with him to the altar as soon as they are safe from the plotting I have been engaged in against them. Now I have no objection to their matrimonial project on condition that I receive some fair remuneration for all the good I have done them."

"You reckon nothing, then, for all the alarm and uneasiness you have caused to two persons that have never injured you?"

"As to that," answered Kestrel, "I don't see that they have much to complain, when I could have gone much further if I had liked. The girl was entirely in my power a few days ago, and I might have taken her where she would never have been heard of again, but that I expected to have received a fair reward for all I have done."

"Well," exclaimed the constable, "and you may depend now upon receiving your full deserts, for the charge against you is a very heavy one, and the squire will hardly be satisfied unless you are sent out of the country for the remainder of your days."

"What have I done to deserve such a punishment?"

"It's not for me to tell you what you have done," answered the other, "and even if it were there's no time to do so now, for here comes my mate, to take you before the magistrate, and if he should happen to hear what you've been talking about, he'd be sure to relate it at head quarters, and then good care would be taken to prevent your offering a bribe to the person who has the care of you next."

The entrance of the headborough prevented any reply to this, and as Caleb had by this time finished his breakfast, he was secured to prevent any attempt to escape, and conveyed through the village to the house of Mr. Borrowdale, who happened to be the nearest magistrate in the neighbourhood. On entering the room in which the examination was to take place, the culprit saw that it was already occupied by Mr. Derwent, Amy, Frank Marldale, and the other persons who were able to give any evidence against him. Still the pedlar maintained all his usual firmness of demeanour, and upon being asked his name and occupation, he replied to the questions without betraying the slightest signs of fear or emotion. This done, Mr. Derwent was called upon to make his charge, which he did in as few words, and with as much conciseness, as the extensive nature of the charge would admit of. After this, Amy was desired to step forward and corroborate the accusation, and the statement she made was so clear and decisive, as to leave no doubt that the present case was a proper one to be sent before a higher tribunal. Other witnesses were, however, heard, and when all the witnesses had been heard, the magistrate inquired of the prisoner, if he had anything to say before he was fully committed to take his trial on the charges he had just heard.

"What can I say?" he asked, "when such a dead set is made against me by people that care not what lies they tell so long as they can get me out of their way

All I know about it is, that I never intended to rob Mr. Derwent, unless the taking away a young woman may be called so."

"Had you any right to claim the guardianship of the young lady, that you attempted to remove by violence?"

"That is a question I am not bound to answer, since it may be made use of against me when the day of trial comes."

"The truth is, sir," exclaimed Squire Derwent, addressing himself to the magistrate, "this man has admitted the fact that it was himself who stole Amy from my cousin when she was a child."

"And afterwards," said Mr. Borrowdale, "he trusted her to the care of the persons with whom she was lately found?"

"He did."

"And were the persons kind to her?"

"So much so," replied Mr. Derwent, "that she regards them with as much affection as if she were their own child."

"Which is a proof that I have not done her any injury," exclaimed the prisoner. "In short, I had no evil feelings against the girl, and she would never have been stolen from Mr. Clement Derwent but to revenge myself for a wrong that I had suffered from him."

"A very lame excuse that, for inflicting a heavy injury upon an innocent girl who never wrongd you," observed the magistrate.

"I am not trying to excuse what I have done, nor is there any reason why I should do so," answered Caleb Kestrel, haughtily. "My motives none have a right to inquire into, though the squire could, if he think proper, tell you why I have tried to take her away from him."

"Which I will do in a few words," said Mr. Derwent, accepting the challenge that had been thrown out. "The truth is, your worship, this man has been endeavouring to extort money from me, and when all other means failed, he carried Amy away, with the view of forcing me to consent to a large ransom, that he expected for her deliverance."

"Has he obtained money from you by threats?" asked the magistrate.

"He has not," answered the squire, "though it must be confessed I have been several times almost inclined to yield, rather than subject a timid female to his continual persecutions. The thought, however, that I should be encouraging villany restrained me, and I resolved to resist his demands, in the hope that, by watchfulness and care, I should be able to counteract his evil practices."

"But you would not have succeeded but for the friends you had to assist you," exclaimed Kestrel with a sneer.

"I don't know, prisoner, whether you exult in the base course you have pursued," said the magistrate, "but if so your triumph will be of short duration, since there is sufficient evidence to ensure your conviction and consequent punishment. Mr. Derwent has just cause to feel aggrieved at the violence he has described, and the steps he has since taken will, it is to be hoped, prevent all further attempts that you or your associates may have intended."

"As for me," he replied, "there's little chance of my being able to do anything now that the law has laid hold of me; but let Mr. Derwent and the young girl look to themselves, for I have friends ready and willing to follow out my plans, and it will not be long before they find means to carry the girl away from those she calls her protectors."

"'Tis a vain boast," exclaimed Cecil Derwent, "for the ruffians he speaks of are well known, and if any of them should be seen lurking about the neighbourhood, they will be immediately apprehended, and lodged in jail. In short, they last night received so warm a reception when they attacked my house, that it is hardly likely they will again venture to carry out their infamous projects."

"Do you think them cowards, then?" demanded Kestrel.

"None but cowards would have dared to direct their attacks against a helpless female."

"If that sneer is attempted for me it fails in its object," retorted the prisoner.

"I have, it is true, endeavoured to carry Amy away, but the fault was your own, since no violence would ever have been offered her, but for your obstinacy in refusing to pay me down the sum of money I wanted. It is you, therefore, that she has to thank for all the annoyance she has suffered."

"And why should Mr. Derwent have submitted to so infamous a proposition?" asked the magistrate.

"Because, by listening to my terms, he would have insured my immediate departure] from England, and of course there would have been an end of all further trouble."

"In my opinion he acted perfectly right," observed Mr. Borrowdale, "for, had he acceded to your demands, he would have been holding out an encouragement to other extortioners. However, that is not the affair we have to do with at present, so, if you have no other explanation to give, it will be my duty to com mit you to prison, where you will await your trial before a higher authority."

"If you expect an excuse from me I have none to give, except that Mr. Der went has only himself to blame for all that has taken place. A fair offer was made to him, and as he didn't think proper to come to any terms, it was not to be wondered at that I took the only means in my power to make him suffer for it."

"But the girl, who never did you any harm, has been the greatest sufferer by your infamous proceedings."

"And is this the first time you ever heard of the innocent being made to suffer for the guilty?" demanded Kestrel, insolently. "I knew the girl was an especial favourite of his, and it was only by persecuting her that I could hope to bring him to his senses. To be sure I have not yet succeeded, but there's others left besides me, and if they don't carry out my views, it will be something very wonderful."

By the desire of the magistrate the depositions of the various witnesses were read over to them, and having been signed in taken of their perfect correctness, the prisoner was led from the room, and from thence conducted to the prison, where he was to remain till the ensuing assizes. As soon as he was removed, Mr. Derwent and his friends also left the house, on their return home, which they reached without the occurrence of any adventure worthy of being recounted. On retiring to his own room, however, the squire was quickly followed thither by Mr. Reeves, his faithful steward, who, with evident traces of alarm, inquired if he had been accosted on his way by any of Kestrel's accomplices.

"No, Mr. Reeves," he replied, "I have not met any of them, nor is it very likely that we shall ever see them again, for the scoundrels know the penalty that awaits them, if they should fall into the hands of those from whom they have no quarter to expect."

"The fellows are lurking about though, sir, for all that," exclaimed the steward; "in short, one of them met me in the park about an hour ago, and from what he said, I'm afraid there's mischief in the wind."

"What passed between you?"

"Some hard words I can assure you, sir," answered Mr. Reeves, "and the rascal had the insolence to tell me, that if Caleb Kestrel was committed to prison, you, and all other persons concerned in sending him there, would, to a certainty, very soon repent it."

"Did you make no attempt to secure the fellow?" asked his master.

"I would, if there had been the slightest chance of succeeding," he replied, "but what would have been the use of an old man like me contending with [a fellow that had youth and strength on his side? Besides, he was armed with a brace of loaded pistols, which he took good care to inform me, would be brough t into use, if I attempted either to lay hands upon him or to call for assistance."

"Where were all my men servants?"

"You forget, sir, that they went to give their evidence against Caleb Kestrel before his worship, the magistrate. The man I am speaking of knew that perfectly well, and took the opportunity of accosting me, when there was but little danger to himself."

"Did he speak of the young lady who has so cruelly suffered from the persecution of his companion in crime?"

"He did."

"And threatened to wreak his vengeance upon her, I suppose?"

"Yes, sir; he said if Kestrel was sent to prison we might expect to receive another visit, that would not be quite so unfortunate to himself and his comrades as the last was."

"There is sufficient in all this to create uneasiness," exclaimed the squire; "but I am still of opinion that the threats are not intended to be carried into effect. Indeed, we may be pretty well certain of that; for when people really intend to do mischief, they never go beforehand to give information of it to those who are most concerned. However, it is well to be prepared for the worst, so I shall take care that no precautions are taken to prevent any act of treachery that may, by chance, be in progress against us."

"And what do you think, sir, will be Kestrel's fate?"

"Conviction will, of course, take place, because the evidence we have to produce against him is so clear, that no doubt of his guilt can possibly exist in the mind of a jury."

"But we have heard of flaws in indictments before now," exclaimed the steward, "and, if that should happen to be the case in the present instance, Kestrel would be set at liberty, and you would not be allowed to enjoy another moment's tranquillity."

"That, my good sir," replied Mr. Derwent, "is placing matters in the very worst light, and I see no reason, just at present, for believing that the enemy of our peace will have the opportunity you speak of. Nay, there are more charges than one against him, so that, if he should happen to get over the first indictment, there are others to follow, which it will be more difficult to evade."

"I'm glad to hear you speak so confidently," exclaimed Mr. Reeve, "for, to tell you the truth, I was very much afraid your troubles were not over, though your principal enemy in under lock and key. By-the-bye, sir, I hope they'll keep a good-look out upon him, for Master Job Smith, the constable, has spread a report abroad that Kestrel tried to bribe him this morning, to let him out of the cage."

"Perhaps Smith only says so, in order to give people a higher notion of his rigid honesty."

"I don't know how that may be, sir," answered the steward, "but I can't help thinking that the pedlar will try his hardest to get out of the clutches of his gaolers, and, if he should succeed, we know pretty well what sort of trouble and mischief he would cause us."

"My good sir," exclaimed Mr. Derwent, "don't let that give you any uneasiness, for I can assure you there is not the least fear that the prisoner will be suffered to escape. Those who have the care of him know perfectly well the sort of person they have to deal with, and so strict a watch will be kept upon him that if even the thought of getting out of prison should enter into his mind, it can only end in disappointment and mortification. No, no, Kestrel is safe enough now, and I am much mistaken if his companions are not under the same roof with him, before they are many hours older."

"But where are we to look for them?"

"That is a question that I am unable to answer just at this moment," replied the squire; "but when once we commence our search, the fellows must soon be taken, unless, indeed, they make their escape from the neighbourhood, which would be just as well for us, since they would not be able to injure us."

"Well, you know best how that may be, sir," answered Mr. Reeves, "but, if I might take the liberty of giving an opinion, I should say that danger can never be over, so long as those fellows are at large."

"Then I suppose we must take steps for their immediate capture, and then, at east, we may sit ourselves down, tolerably well assured that we have nothing more to apprehend."

"And, till then, I suppose the young lady will not venture abroad, unless well attended?"

"I have requested her to remain within doors, for the present," answered Mr. Derwent, "and, though confinement is extremely irksome, she readily assented to my suggestion, and will not leave the house, till every one of her enemies is in custody."

"Which, I hope, will be very soon," exclaimed the steward, "though it must be confessed I have very little expectation of seeing so desirable an object speedily accomplished. They are artful scoundrels that we have to deal with, and unless the greatest secresy is observed in all our actions, the proceedings we are about to adopt will be known, and our labours rendered useless."

"Then will you undertake to make the necessary inquiries, as to where they are likely to be found?"

"I would do so cheerfully," answered the steward, "but it unfortunately happens that I know not where to commence my inquiries."

"In that respect I can assist you," replied Mr. Derwent. "Go to the Eagle gate, on the south side of the park, and you will there meet with a gipsey-woman, who, it seems, has known enough of Caleb Kestrel to hate him most inveterately. Say you come from me, and, upon learning your errand, she will—if it be possible—inform you where these men are most likely to be found."

"Are you sure she is to be depended on?"

"I have a notion that she may," answered the squire, "for it seems she owes the pedlar a long grudge, and is determined to gratify her revenge, at the first opportunity that offers. Nay, so deep is her feeling of hatred, that she has resolved not only on the destruction of Kestrel, but of all those who are connected with him."

"And you wish me to see this woman immediately?"

"There ought to be no delay about it," answered Mr. Derwent, "for the enemy is no doubt upon the alert, and any time that we may lose will be so much to the advantage of the ruffians we are anxious to ensnare in our meshes."

The steward readily undertook the task that had been entrusted to him, and, within a very few minutes afterwards, he was making the best of his way towards the gipsey's tent.

CHAPTER XXIII.

CALEB KESTREL RECEIVES A STRANGE VISITOR IN HIS CELL.—AN OFFER OF ASSISTANCE.—THE MEANS OF ESCAPE ARE PLACED AT HIS DISPOSAL.—HE HEARS NEWS THAT REVIVES HIS ALMOST SINKING HOPES.

NOTWITHSTANDING the bravado with which the pedlar had met the accusation made against him, he no sooner found himself confined within the narrow limits of his prison cell, than his spirits seemed to forsake him at once, and he could no longer look forward to his deliverance, with even the slightest degree of hope. The strong walls and massive iron bars that guarded the window, were indeed enough to appal the stoutest heart, and as often as he gazed around him, he felt the more assured that the period of his iniquities had arrived. On the following morning his despondency had increased, and when the turnkey entered his cell, he found him gloomily brooding over the altered aspect of his future prospects.

"So your courage is beginning to ooze out, is it?" exclaimed the man, in a half bantering tone. "Yesterday, whilst before the magistrate, you pretended to treat the affair very lightly; but if anything will take the pluck out of a man, it's when he finds himself in a place like this, where he can't go in and out just when he pleases."

"Is it any part of your duty to insult those who have the bad luck to get into your clutches?" demanded the prisoner, sullenly.

"No," he replied, "but it's a hard thing if one may not have a joke now and then with the gentlemen we have to attend on," answered the turnkey, rubbing his hands as if he had said something very smart. "However, as you don't seem inclined to join me in a laugh, we'll drop the subject, as Jack Ketch said when he turned off the unfortunate malefactor."

"Has anybody been here to inquire after me?" asked Kestrel.

"Yes, there's a person at this very time wants to see you."

"Do you know who it is?"

"No, I didn't ask her any questions."

"_Her_!—It's a woman, then?"

"To be sure it is, and a tolerably pretty one, too."

"Did she send any message to me?"

"Nothing more than that she wanted to see you about something very particular."

"Then why didn't you bring her?"

"Because I thought she might be some old flame of yours, that you would rather not see."

"Fool! are you still jesting with me?"

"Come, come, master, we must have more civil language here, if you please," exclaimed the turnkey, "or you and I shall not agree, and then, I know which will get the better of the quarrel."

"I am treated here like a wild beast," muttered Kestrel, "and yet you wonder that I grow impatient."

"What do you mean by being treated like a wild beast?"

"Am I not secured to the wall by a chain, as if there were any chance of my breaking out of this place?"

"You must blame the governor for that," replied the man, "for he ordered that everything should be done to prevent your escape."

"But I suppose, upon my promise not to attempt anything of the kind, he'll not mind giving me a little more liberty?"

"I don't know how that may be," replied the man, "but I'll put the question to him on condition that you give me your word not to abuse the favour. The fact is, however, you are looked upon as a very dangerous character to deal with, and that chain was put upon you in order to prevent any mischief."

"I suppose in consequence of something that my enemy, Mr. Derwent, has been saying?"

"Squire Derwent is a gentleman, every inch of him," answered the turnkey, "and I don't believe he has had anything to do with it. You, however, seem to have taken a dislike to him, though for what reason I neither know nor care."

"But I know very well, though," replied Caleb Kestrel. "It was he that brought me to this plight, for had he given me the sum of money I asked for, I should have been far enough away before this, and he would have been left to enjoy the society of Amy in peace."

"All this is like Latin and Greek to me," exclaimed the man, "for I know nothing of your quarrels, except that people say you wanted to frighten him into giving you half his fortune."

"Had he done so it would have been well bestowed," answered the pedlar, "for he would have got rid of a plague, and I should not have seen the inside of this cursed dungeon."

"Ay, but you wanted too much, and he was not inclined to give way to extortion."

"Extortion! Why, I had a right to expect half his fortune, at the very least."

"But he didn't think so, it appears, upon which a quarrel takes place, in which you have come off second best. And it's right that it should be too, for the squire has a high character as a man of honour, whilst you are said to be one of the greatest rogues under the sun."

"Ay," exclaimed Kestrel, "you can insult me now as much as you please; but if my limbs were free, I'd soon show you that words like these are not to be spoken with impunity."

"What!—you are growing rusty again?"

"How can I help it, when you say everything to rouse my passion?" demanded the prisoner. "However, I shall see the governor one of these days, I suppose, and then I shall ask him whether I am to be treated worse than a dog."

"You can do as you please about that," he replied, but it's little good you'll get by it, I can tell you. Besides, the governor don't often come round among the prisoners; so if you have any message for him you had better send it by me and then it's sure to be delivered all right and properly. And now, my fi fellow, just tell me, if you please, whether you have thought of making any preparations for your defence against the day of trial comes."

"What is it to you, whether I have or not?"

No. 26.

"Ah, of course I have nothing to do with it," replied the turnkey, "but I thought it just as well to thow out the hint, because a good many chaps like you have been sent over the herring pond, when they might have been acquitted, but for neglecting to engage the assistance of some blustering counsellor."

"Humph!" ejaculated Caleb Kestrel; "you are engaged, I suppose, to recommend some such person as you are speaking of?"

"Not I," answered the other, somewhat taken aback by this latter remark. "It's nothing at all to me whether prisoners engage counsel or not; but I don't like to see people sacrificed while there's a chance of their being acquitted by the skill of a lawyer."

"Well, then, make yourself easy," replied Kestrel, "for it appears to me that I shall not stand in any need of advice."

"You mean to defend yourself then, of course?"

"Perhaps I may; and what is it to any one if I do?"

"Oh, nobody has anything to do with it; but I don't see what reasons you have for being so short with me."

"Nor am I going to take the trouble to explain myself upon that subject," exclaimed the prisoner. "You told me just now that some female is waiting to see me; go and ask her name, and, when I have heard it, I'll tell you whether the interview will be agreeable or not."

"I asked her name before," replied the turnkey, "but she refused to tell me—so it is no use putting the same question again."

"Then, at all hazards bring her here; and if it should be any person that I don't like, you may take her back, for not a word will she be able to get out of me."

The man disappeared on receiving this instruction, and Caleb Kestrel occupied the intervening time in wondering within himself who his visitor could be. Presently afterwards footsteps were heard approaching, and, on the door being opened, the prisoner saw, to his utter amazement, Amy follow the turnkey into the cell. Struck dumb by a circumstance so little expected, Caleb gazed upon her with a look full of mingled emotions of wonder and doubt—he saw that her eyes were suffused with tears, and thought he could detect in her countenance some trace of pity for the position in which he was placed. At length, approaching him more nearly, she inquired tremulously if she could not be permitted to speak with him alone for a few minutes.

"I know nothing about that," he replied, "for I'm no longer allowed to do as I please; so, if you wish for any favour, you must ask my gaoler, who will either comply with your wish or refuse it, according to the humour he happens to be in."

"Do you wish particularly to be alone with the prisoner?" asked the man, doubtfully.

"I do."

"Well, then, I suppose it must be so," he replied, "for he's secured safely enough to the wall; so all you've got to do is to keep beyond the length of his chain, and then no harm can possibly happen. But what you've got to say mustn't last too long, for we turnkeys have strict orders not to leave their prisoners with visitors more than a few minutes at a time."

Amy promised compliance with this, and when the man had withdrawn from the cell, she inquired of Kestrel in a whisper if he would accept of liberty on certain conditions that she had to make.

"Name your conditions," he replied, "and then I'll tell you whether I can agree with them or not."

"In the first place," exclaimed Amy, "you must promise to leave England immediately, and for ever; and secondly, never again to subject me to your cruel persecutions."

"How am I to leave this country," he replied, "when I have not a shilling to keep me anywhere else?"

"That shall be provided for," she replied ; "so now tell me whether you will cease to pursue me with your wrath ?"

"If the first proposition be carried out, you may depend upon my letting you remain at peace for the rest of your days."

"Then your liberation is near at hand."

"Who sent you here to tell me so ?"

"A certain gipsy woman, who is known by the name of Deborah."

"Ah !" exclaimed the pedlar, "is she so near me, then ?"

"Yes ; she has followed you to this neighbourhood, and it is by her counsel that I am here."

"But she and I have long been sworn enemies."

"And, judging from her language, she still remains hostile to you," answered Amy.

"Then why does she wish me to regain my liberty ?"

"I cannot pretend to understand her motives, unless they are grounded upon former friendship, and a hope that; from gratitude, you will cease to persecute and annoy me."

"You are some especial favourite of hers then, I suppose ?" exclaimed Caleb Kestrel.

"I know not whether I have even her regard," replied our heroine, "but the woman seems to feel a warm interest in my behalf, and has gone thus far out of her way, in order to serve me."

"And it was she that sent you here ?"

"It was."

"Were there no other conditions than those you have named ?"

"None."

"Humph!" exclaimed Kestrel, "she is liberal enough to propose my release from this place, yet has it not in her power to afford me even the slightest assistance."

"But she has sent the means by which you may help yourself."

"Is it money, by which to bribe my gaoler?"

"No, for that would have been useless," replied Aamy. "She has, however, sent, through my hands, this small file, which may be easily concealed till the time for using it arrives, when some of your companions will be close at hand to render any help that may be required."

"What are the conditions she expects for this service ?"

"I have already informed you."

"Well," exclaimed Caleb Kestrel, as he examined the file, which had been placed in his hands, "this is certainly one step towards the object I had in view, but I'm almost afraid Deborah must have some scheme in her head that I'm unable to fathom."

"I have said she has not lost all her former affection for you ; added to which, she is not without hope that, in gratitude for her services, you will suffer me to pass the remainder of my days in peace."

"And the money that I shall require to carry with me abroad?"

"Will be supplied, to any reasonable amount, by Mr. Cecil Derwent."

"Then he also is in this secret?"

"At present he knows nothing about it," answered Amy, "but there is every reliance to be placed on his assistance when he finds that it will rid me for ever of an enemy."

"Has the old woman named any time when I am to attempt my escape from this place?"

"She leaves that to your own judgment," replied Amy, "but told me to suggest to-night, because the less delay there is in these things the greater chance is there of their being brought to a successful termination."

"Is she to meet me, supposing I should be fortunate enough to get clear away from my prison ?"

"No, she has no wish ever to see you agai.

"Ha, ha, ha," laughed Kestrel, "there she and I exactly agree on this subject, though we have not done so for many a long day before. We grew heartily tired of each other, and that which once was love grew into the fiercest hate."

"On your side, perhaps," replied Amy; "but how can this woman hate you, when she is so anxious for your deliverance?"

"Ay," answered the prisoner, "the question seems natural enough, but the sex she belongs to is so fickle that there's no accounting for the extraordinary things that sometimes happen. The time has been when we used to fight with such fierceness that any looker-on would have supposed that one of us must have died, and yet now she feels pity for me when she sees I am in trouble."

"And you laugh at her for her pains!"

"Because I can't help suspecting that there's something more at the bottom of all this than I can well see through, at present."

"Then you give no credit for good intentions?"

"If you had seen as much of this world as I have, you would learn to think as I do," answered Caleb Kestrel. "There's deception to be found every where, and more particularly when it is least suspected."

"You are speaking of the female sex as if women were more deceitful than men, and yet I believe, upon examination, it will be found that exactly the contrary is the fact."

"Well, we won't dispute upon that subject," he replied, "because it's not very likely we should agree if we were to carry it on for a week. If I should contrive to get out of this infernal den, may I depend upon receiving money from Mr. Derwent?"

"You may," she replied; "but let me tell you before hand that the amount will be trifling in comparison with what you demanded from him when you were at liberty."

"Well, that must be an after consideration; but you may tell him from me that I must have enough to keep me without work, or by-and-bye I may find it necessary to appear on the scene again."

"Mr. Derwent will act in this affair as he thinks proper," answered Amy; "but whatever the amount of money may be it shall come out of the fortune that has so unexpectedly come to me. This I shall insist upon, or I should not have come here to make an arrangement of which he is, up to this moment, entirely ignorant."

"If you are to give the money," exclaimed Kestrel, "why may not the sum be agreed upon at once?"

"Because you may not be able to effect your deliverance, and, in that case, any bargain we might make would be of no use. Besides, I made up my mind, before coming here, not to come to any conclusive terms till I am sure that you will honourably keep your promise."

"Ah," replied the pedlar, "as for that, you needn't be afraid about my leaving England, for the cursed country has grown too hot to hold me, and I shall be glad enough to get to any other place where the infernal officers of the laws are not constantly looking after me. But hush! my gaoler is coming back, and we must change our conversation to some other subject."

The man he spoke of now entered the cell, and, addressing himself to Amy, informed her that the time allowed for visitors had expired; then, turning towards the prisoner, he added,

"I've just seen the governor about what you were speaking of just now, and he says, that as you have behaved yourself pretty well since you have been here, I may give you a little more liberty, by releasing you from your chains."

Whilst saying this, he selected a peculiarly constructed key from the bunch he held in his hand, and in another instant Caleb Kestrel was so far free as to be able to take what little exercise the narrow limits of his cell would allow. This done, the gaoler beckoned Amy to follow him, and having seen her to the outer door of the prison, he returned, bringing with him the coarse fare allowed for dinner.

"There," he said, placing the contents of his basket on the table, "you see,

Master Kestrel, I've not forget you; and the governor desires me to say, that if you conduct yourself well, he will, in a day or two, permit you to take, every day, an hour's airing in the yard."

"He's very good," replied Caleb with a sneer; "but, perhaps, I may not care of availing myself of his indulgence."

"What! are you going to turn refractory, just when you ought to be most submissive?"

"Submissive!" exclaimed the prisoner, contemptuously; "I never yet submitted to any one, and it's not likely I'm going to begin now, when I find myself caged like a wild beast. Don't you know that confinement makes all things more savage? and is it to be wondered at if it has the same effect upon me?"

"As I never had anything to do with wild beasts, I can't say much as to their habits," replied the turnkey; "but this I do know, when people are brought here for their misdeeds, they must submit quietly to the rules and regulations of the prison or take the consequences, which are not very pleasant, I can tell you."

"I have always heard," muttered Kestrel, "that prisoners are held to be innocent till a jury has pronounced them otherwise."

"So they are," answered the gaoler; "but we must have laws to govern them, or a pretty state of confusion we should soon be in. Why, the governor is a sort of king within these walls, and to disobey even his slightest orders is to bring down punishment that may last as long as he thinks the case deserves. So now you understand how the case stands, my boy; and if my advice is worth following, you'll submit quietly to all orders, and then you may expect to be made tolerably comfortable as long as you remain here."

"When are the assizes to come on?" asked Kestrel.

"Oh, not for a month," replied the turnkey; "and that, I'm thinking, will be quite soon enough for some that have got to be tried.'

"Perhaps so," exclaimed Caleb, indifferently; "but for my own part I care not how soon the time comes, for I'm heartily tired of being shut up in this gloomy place."

"Then you expect to be acquitted?"

"Of course I do; don't all men look forward to the best, however black things may be against 'em? Besides, what great offence have I committed? I tried to carry off a female, was prevented doing so by superior numbers, and, for my pains, have been sent here to be tried as a felon. Now, perhaps you can tell me what great harm there is in what I did?"

"It's not for me to argue with you upon that point," exclaimed the official; "but as you have asked me the question, I must needs say, that Mr. Derwent did perfectly right in sending you here, when he found there was no other way of getting rid of a troublesome fellow."

"But he might have given me what I asked for, and then he would never have had again to complain of any annoyance."

"Perhaps you wanted too much?"

"I only wanted what I considered a fair reward for the services I had done," replied Caleb Kestrel. "But for me the girl would never have come to her birthright; and surely it was not too much to expect that I should be treated with something like liberality. Instead of that, however, I'm looked upon as a ruffian, and, in order to get rid of me, have been sent here, in the hope that I may afterwards be sentenced to transportation for life."

"I can't say how that may be," answered the other; "but one thing is very certain, the judge that tries you will not pass a more severe sentence than he thinks the offence deserves."

"There you and I must differ," exclaimed the prisoner; "for this will not be the first time I have stood at a bar, and I can speak from former experience as to whether the sentence is always in proportion to the offence."

"What did they do to you?"

"Transported me for seven years, on a slight charge, though there was no other evidence against me than the cousin of Squire Derwent."

"Oh! then now I can see the cause of your dislike towards the squire. There' a good deal of revenge in this, I find, and you must needs carry your ill feelings against the young lady he's about to marry."

"Perhaps you are not altogether wrong there," he replied ; "for the truth is I have been treated with scorn and contempt by the very girl I have so greatly served. She would still have been a beggar but for me, and yet no reward has been given for my services."

"And I dare say, if the truth was known, you have been in too much of a hurry in making your demand."

"I have not shown any more impatience than my necessities urged on me," answered Kestrel. "I wanted to get out of this country as quickly as possible ; and as that could not be done without money, I demanded my reward, as the only means of carrying my views into effect."

"But you asked too much, and met with a blank refusal."

"I only asked what I considered to be fair, under all the circumstances ; and Mr. Derwent, in order to save the money, has basely made this charge against me."

"Ay, ay, Master Kestrel," exclaimed the turnkey, "it's all very well for you to say that the squire has bad motives for what he has done, but the fact is you have driven him to it by your violence, and then complain when you find yourself defeated. However, here you are, and whatever the consequences may be you must put up with them."

"But suppose I happen to be acquitted?"

"Well, suppose you are?" returned the other ; "you'll begin your old games over again, and be brought back before you have been out of it a week."

"Do you take me for a fool, then, that I must needs fall into the same trap that I've once escaped from? No, no, only let me get clear out of this place, and I'll warrant you will never see me in it any more."

"Then you don't intend to annoy the squire any more?"

"Not in a way that he shall get any advantage over me," answered the pedlar, "for experience has taught me a lesson that I'm not likely to forget in a hurry ; and if another opportunity should be offered me I shall so contrive matters that Mr. Derwent shall be forced to come to terms without having it in his power to send me to gaol, or take any other advantage over his enemy."

"You mean others to do the dirty part of the work?"

"I don't know that there's any dirty work in a man trying to get his rights," answered Kestrel. "I only ask for what may be considered my just reward, and if it's not to be got by fair means I'm not to be blamed for having recourse to foul."

"What is there to hinder your going to law if your claim against the squire is a just one?"

"Law, eh!" he exclaimed ; "and pray what's the use of a poor man going to law against a rich one? I've no money to throw away, and without it I have but a poor chance of obtaining justice. But never mind, I don't despair yet of being able, by my own means, to make Squire Derwent come to reasonable terms with me."

"If your terms are as reasonable as you say they are, I'll be bound you would not have much trouble to bring about an arrangement with him even now, if you promise not to bother him any more."

"How can that be," demanded Kestrel, "when I have been committed for trial through his means ; and he must either follow the matter up, or run the risk of being suspected of having brought a false accusation? Besides; it isn't my present situation that will make me humble myself to him, even though I was sure of getting off scot free."

"That is because you unfortunately make so certain of being acquitted by the jury."

"You are wrong there," he replied, "for juries are sometimes composed of such thick-headed fellows that I should be very sorry to place any reliance in their seeing things in the right light."

"Then how the deuce do you expect to get off?"

"Wait patiently till the time comes, and you will acknowledge that I have not reckoned upon my release without having good grounds for having done so. In short, I have lived long enough in the world to place more reliance in myself than I do in others, and if I can't assist myself I may then make up my mind that all chance is over with me."

"I don't know how that may be," replied the turnkey, "but in my opinion you are a very foolish fellow not to employ counsel to defend you when the case comes on for trial. They are men, recollect, that are regularly brought up to the profession as others are to trades, and seeing as they do every point that may be made use of in their client's behalf, they often succeed in finding out a flaw in the indictment that gets the prisoner out of his difficulty."

"All that may be true enough," answered Caleb Kestrel, "but I'd rather be without that sort of gentry than have anything to do with 'em. Besides, haven't I told you before that it's pretty certain I shall not want anybody to assist me out of this difficulty, as Mr. Derwent, for certain reasons that I could give, will not be anxious to press a charge that he knows to be a most unjust one."

"Unjust!" exclaimed the gaoler; "is there anything unjust in a man trying to punish another one that has injured him?"

"But it so happens that, instead of injuring, I have been the means of assisting him most materially, and the extraordinary part of the affair is that, instead of returning my services with gratitude, he has taken this course to get rid of me."

"What is there extraordinary in his trying to punish a man that broke into his house for an unlawful purpose?"

"I broke in only to carry off the girl I had restored to her rights, and not to commit a robbery."

"Squire Derwent is not supposed to know that, and in order to prevent a repetition of the offence, he has taken the precaution to have you placed under restraint. And for my own part, I think he has acted perfectly right, for who would remain under the dread of a second attack when it is in his own power to prevent it?"

"As far as I am concerned, he may be able to prevent it," replied the prisoner; "but I have friends still at large, and he had better beware of them, for they are desperate fellows, and he may depend on it they'll never rest till they have revenged my cause."

"I know the men you speak of," answered the other, "but a sharp pursuit has been made after them, and they have either fled altogether, or are skulking somewhere about the neighbourhood, afraid to show themselves, for fear of being taken."

"If they are skulking, as you call it, about the neighbourhood, you may rely on it they'll not be long before they pay another visit to Derwent Hall, that will be more successful than the last."

"In which case," replied the turnkey, "you will be the less likely to receive a mild sentence, than if matters are suffered to go on quietly. However, I have no right to interfere with things that don't concern me, so let matters take their own course, and then perhaps those that deserve punishment will meet with it all the sooner. By-the-bye," he added, as he turned to go away, "I believe the governor will visit your cell to-morrow, and if you are wise you'll not open your mind to him quite so much as you have to me, for he'll take notice of every word you say, and, may be, will use the information he receives, if it should appear to be of any importance."

Having offered this hint for the benefit of Cabel Kestrel, the turnkey quitted the cell, and the pedlar found himself left once more to those cogitations which, in spite of his affected innocence, filled him with feelings of alarm, that it was his chief object to conceal.

CHAPTER XXIV.

WAITING FOR TIME AND OPPORTUNITY.—AN ATTEMPT AT PRISON-BREAKING.—
THE FUGITIVES.—A CONSULTATION.—AN APPOINTMENT.—A SEPARATION.

THE intervening hours passed heavily to Caleb Kestrel, for all his hopes were centred in the success of his project, and the scheme was too hazardous a one for him to regard the future with any certainty of success. Ever suspicious, too, that others were as treacherous as himself, he could not but believe that Amy had been sent to him in furtherance of some plan that was in operation, and it therefore occupied no inconsiderable portion of his time to imagine the reason of her not only having counselled his escape, but having also supplied him with the instrument that would, more than any other, assist to afford him the means of leaving the prison. Mr. Derwent, of course, came in for his share of suspicion, for it was not likely that he should remain in ignorance of what was going on, and, supposing him to have a full knowledge of all the facts, what else would be thought of it but that he was first tempting the prisoner to escape, in order that he might afterwards hold him still stronger in the iron grasp of the law? Be that as it might, however, Caleb resolved to run the risk, having first of all determined to defend himself to the very last extremity, in the event of his worst suspicions being realised.

During the remainder of the day he was not disturbed by any other visit from the gaoler, and a portion of the time was occupied by a careful examination of the spot where the cell was situated, so that if he managed to open for himself a way through the bars of the window, he might be at no loss to determine which way to take, supposing an immediate pursuit should be made after him. In this respect his mind was soon made up, and having arranged everything to his satisfaction, he descended from the place where he had been making his observation, and threw himself upon his straw mattress to seek that rest and repose which he knew would be essential before he made his grand attempt. He continued to rest till the chimes, at a quarter of an hour before midnight, roused him, and then, starting up, he began to prepare in earnest for the task he had undertaken. His first care was to ascend to the window from which he was to escape, but which was elevated at least ten or twelve feet above the floor of his cell, and guarded by strong bars thick enough to have intimidated any person less resolute than himself. These difficulties, however, only served to nerve him for the requisite exertion, and having torn up the coverlet of his bed into strips, he rolled them up, threw them to the place to which he was about to ascend, and then, with inconceivable difficulty, succeeded in reaching the ledge, which was on a level with the bottom of the window, and from whence he saw, with no little delight, Dick Radcliffe and George Layburne crawling on the ledge outside, towards the spot where he himself was standing. At the same moment they perceived him, and then, raising themselves on their feet, they, in a whisper, admonished him not to commence filing the bars just then, as the prison watchman would pass under the window in a quarter of an hour.

"Have you ascertained whether all else about the place is safe?" he asked of his companions.

"We have neither seen nor heard anything to give us reason to suspect the contrary," replied Dick Radcliffe; "but you must be very careful, though, when filing through the bars, for if found out on this occasion you'll never have another opportunity afforded you."

"Have you brought any arms with you?"

"We have, and can provide you, as well as ourselves, with a brace of loaded pistols, in case they should be wanted."

"Who told you to come here?"

"Old Deborah, the gipsy-woman."

"When did you see her last?"

"At her own tent, to be sure, where she has concealed us the last three or four days, because it was the last place where our enemies would be likely to look for us."

"Why should they not have searched there as well as anywhere else ?"

"I don't know," answered Radcliffe, "unless it is because the old woman is supposed to be no friend to either you or your comrades."

"At any rate, she can be no enemy of mine, when she takes so much pains to get me out of this infernal dungeon."

"Who knows what mischief she has got in her head?" demanded George

Layburne. "The hag has been seen talking a good deal with some of the people at Derwent Hall, and her being so civil to us all on a sudden would almost make one believe that she has some villanous scheme in her head."

"Only let me find out that she is treacherous," muttered Kestrel, "and a leaden bullet in her head shall make all safe. I have, myself, no great deal of faith in the old woman, but she knows I am not to be trifled with, and that, perhaps, may make her careful of what she does. In short, I am not so suspicious of her as I am of Squire Derwent, who pretends a willingness to assist in my

No. 27.

escape, only, as I fancy, that he may afterwards get me to leave the country in order that he may be fairly rid of me for ever."

" Then the best way will be to remain concealed for a time, and then we two can manage to compel him to give the full amount that you have so many times demanded from him."

" He may depend upon it," replied Kestrel, " that I'll never leave the country till he has given all I ask for."

" That may be," exclaimed Radcliffe, " but the advantages are all on our side, for you will not dare leave whatever place you may hide yourself in, because the only conditions he requires as the price of your liberty, are, that you leave the country for ever, and promise never again to molest either him or the young woman."

" And what right," asked Kestrel, " has he to make conditions when I am not present to hear them ?"

" I suppose he thinks that when a man has fallen into difficulties, he's glad to do anything to get himself out of 'em."

" Then he won't find that it's the case with me," exclaimed the pedlar, " for, let the consequences be what they may, I'll either have the money I demanded of him, or the girl that has caused all this trouble shall not be in England another week."

" Humph !" ejaculated Radcliffe, " you speak with as much confidence as if you were not afraid of being suspected as one in the plot."

" What care I for their suspicions, so long as I can keep out of the reach of danger ?" asked Kestrel. " There's no occasion for me to appear openly in the transaction till everything is ready, " for you and Layburne can do all that's necessary as far as preliminary matters go, and when the affair has gone sufficiently I can come forward and conclude the business in my own way."

" I see how it is," grumbled Radcliffe, " you are willing enough to give us all the rough part of the work, but when money is to be touched, you will allow no one to have a hand in it but yourself."

" Fool !" exclaimed Caleb Kestrel, " the squire, if he comes to terms, would have nothing to do with a third party. The affair has all along been between him and me, and I'm not going to let any one else have the handling of the money, when, by right, it will be my own."

" You don't think of paying those that are ready and willing to run the risk of assisting you ?"

" Haven't I promised that all who have assisted me shall be liberally rewarded ?"

" Yes, you have promised ; but, to tell the truth, I have no great faith in your word, if you can find a loop-hole to creep out of."

" Have I ever deceived you ?"

" I can't say you have," replied Dick Radcliffe, " and there's a very good reason for it, seeing that none of your comrades have ever given you the least chance of cheating them. For my own part, I never trust to any one, even in less important matters than this ; but when I know that you mean to get out of England as soon as the bargain is finished, I should like to know where we are to meet before you take your final leave of this country ?"

" Can't you wait till we see what turn things take ?" exclaimed Caleb Kestrel. " We have not the money yet ; and when we have, it will be high time for us to quarrel about its division."

" Nobody want's to quarrel, so long as you are honest with us," replied Radcliffe, " but when men engage themselves in a dangerous pursuit, it's high time they should know whether there's anything worth while to be expected from those that engage their services. However, we'll not press the subject on you any further just now, so tell us where we shall meet presently, for I don't see that we can do any good at present, since you are more likely not to be observed if we are not with you."

"Meet me two hours hence near the Seven Elms, on the borders of Brooksden Moor; if I escape, I will be there; and if you see me not, rely upon it I shall have been detected in the attempt."

"We will not fail to keep the appointment, so, for the present, farewell, for the watchman will soon go his rounds, and if he should see us, we may be sure the plot is at an end."

"Stay," exclaimed Kestrel, as he saw them about to descend, "how shall I have to proceed, supposing I am so far fortunate as to descend to the ground in safety?"

"There'll be no further trouble or difficulty," replied Radcliffe, "for, if you turn to the right, you'll find a small door that is never used, the lock of which we picked to effect our entrance here. You will find it closed, but not locked, and when you find yourself on the other side, you must make all the haste you can towards the place where we have appointed to meet, lest your escape should be discovered before you have time to leave your pursuers a sufficient distance behind."

"I will not forget your advice," answered Kestrel, "and in the mean time, do you and Layburne repair to the tent of Deborah the gipsy, who may assist us, if she be in a good humour!"

"How can she assist us?"

"That she will be able to explain better than I can, for she is a woman of shrewd wit in cases of emergency, and it will be well for us to humour her vanity by seeming to consult her."

"Can you rely on her?" asked Radcliffe.

"I'm afraid there's very little dependence to be placed upon her," answered the pedlar, "but I am unfortunately too much in her power to offend her just at this moment."

"And suppose she should threaten to disclose the place of your retreat?"

"Then we shall be driven to extremities, and nothing will remain but to take her life."

"Ha, ha!" exclaimed George Layburne, "you begin to talk of murder, do you?"

"Only if driven to it by absolute necessity," answered Kestrel; "I don't like the woman, it's true, but I would not take her life if there's any way to avoid it!"

"And if you do go so far," replied his companion, "neither George nor I will lend you a hand in it."

"Pshaw! you take everything in earnest, though I only spoke of what it might be necessary to do, in case of danger to ourselves."

"Danger to ourselves!" repeated Layburne; "you don't mean to say there's any fear of her peaching?"

"To tell you the truth, I don't think there is," answered Kestrel, "but when people find themselves in a perilous situation, the best way is to be prepared for anything that may happen."

"Why, then, after all, there's very little chance of our having to shorten the days of the gipsy woman?"

"Very little indeed," replied the pedlar, "for I have known her a long while, and from my own experience can declare that she can keep a secret, even though her own life was hazarded by it."

"Then why did you suspect her just now?"

"Only because she and I are not on quite such good terms as we used to be," answered Caleb Kestrel. "We once lived together as man and wife, but when at last our quarrels began to grow too frequent and serious, I suddenly left her, and we have not met since, though I have heard from others that she owes me a heavy grudge."

"Then why, in the name of all that's wonderful, would you trust her with the secret, if you should have the good fortune to escape?"

" Because she may feel flattered if I make her my confidant, and will certainly do her worst against me, if I should seem to treat her with suspicion. In short, Deborah is so dangerous an enemy that I must try to soothe her, even though I must play the part of a hypoerite in order to impose upon her."

" By-the-bye, Caleb," exclaimed Layburne, " it would have been well if you had never played a worse part than that of a hypocrite."

" What !" retorted the other, " must the devil reprove sin ?"

" Come, come," interposed Radcliffe, " this is neither the time nor place for a quarrel, so drop the subject, and let's think of matters of more consequence. We are to meet Caleb at the Seven Elms, and then further arrangements can be made as to what's to be done next."

" That is to say," observed George Layburne, " if the people here will let him off as quietly as he expects."

" If you would have me get clear off, don't throw cold water upon what I'm going to do," exclaimed the pedlar. " At present I feel pretty confident that we shall meet at the time and place appointed, but the moment I hear a doubt thrown upon it, I seem to lose all my courage."

" Then take some of this to revive your courage," said Radcliffe, handing a small bottle of brandy through the bars. " That's the stuff to drink, my boy, when you feel nervous, so don't be afraid to take a good swig at it, for I brought it with me entirely for your use, knowing that you would need something to give you pluck, when the time came for getting out of this infernal place."

" Are you sure nobody saw you come in ?" asked Kestrel, after having taken a pretty good pull at the bottle.

" There can be no doubt about it," replied his comrade, " for if any one had twigged us, the whole prison would have been in a state of commotion long before this time. So make your mind easy about that, and if you'll only go on with your work silently there's no doubt we shall see you at the appointed place."

" How am I to work silently when I have to file through these bars ?" demanded the captive.

" Don't ask me how you are to do it," exclaimed Dick Radcliffe, " but recollect that it must be done, or you won't have such another chance as this given you. A little patience you must have, but the sound may be easily deadened, as you'll find out when you begin to work."

Caleb Kestrel drew the file from his pocket, and drew it three or four times with a heavy pressure across the bars. By placing one hand over the instrument the sound was scarcely perceptible, and upon examining the mark he had left behind, he was surprised at the deep cut he had already made.

" There, now," exclaimed Radcliffe, " you see there's no such great difficulty in it after all, so keep up a good heart, and an hour's labour will remove enough of these bars to admit your body through them. When that's done you'll find the rope that assisted us up here, and will afford you a descent, if you will only act with a little caution. When you reach the bottom, turn off in the direction I told you, and a few yards further on will bring you to the door we will leave open. When you get on the outside, turn the key, and even if an alarm should be raised you'll have an excellent chance to escape, since your pursuers will have to leave by another gate on the opposite side of the prison."

" But if I should happen to be beyond the time appointed, you will not leave the place ?"

" No, you may depend upon our remaining there till you come, or, at any rate, whilst there's a chance of seeing you. In the meantime, we shall not forget our promise to see the gipsy woman, and will try all the means in our power, to persuade her to lend a helping hand towards getting you clear out of the country."

" Then now away with you, my boys," exclaimed Kestrel, " for I'm anxious to get to my work, and it's better not to begin till you are both out of harm's way."

Acting upon this hint, the two men silently descended by means of the rope, and having gained the ground in safety, made their way towards the door by [which they [had entered, and effected their retreat without the slightest interruption [from any one. Caleb Kestrel listened for a few moments afterwards, and finding that all was quiet wthin the prison, he was about to commence his task, when the slow, heavy footstep of the watchman was heard as he went his customary round. Had the man been less drowsy than he was he must have seen the rope that had been left dangling from the upper cornice, but having been just roused from a heavy slumber, he passed quietly on his way, and having, as he supposed, performed his duty in a highly commendable manner, returned to his box and again fell into a deep sleep, leaving the prisoners to take their own chance. No sooner was all quiet again than Kestrel commenced his work in earnest, and so well did he labour that before the expiration of an hour he had removed sufficient of the bars to afford him ample space to pass through. On reaching the outer ledge, or projection, he soon found the rope, by which he descended, and had no sooner reached *terra firma*, than he made all speed to the door, through which he quickly passed, and having turned the key as directed, made his way towards the place of appointment.

We must now, however, follow his two friends, who had proceeded to the gipsy's tent, where they found her in the act of arranging her moveable dwelling, for she was an early riser, and was going to visit a distant village in pursuit of her usual avocation. She was not aware of the approach of visitors till they suddenly presented themselves before her, but, subduing all appearance of surprise, she said—

"You are early comers, this morning; but I suppose there has been mischief in the wind, for men like you are seldom out at night, except for evil."

"Then for once you are mistaken," exclaimed Radcliffe, "for it so happens we have been to help a friend that's in trouble."

"Who is he?"

"Caleb Kestrel."

"Humph! I thought I had sent him all that was required when he received from me an instrument that would soon restore him to liberty, supposing no one interrupted him."

"Ah, we know all about that, of course," exclaimed Dick Radcliffe, "but, then, his window was high up from the ground, and we thought it would be an act of friendship to give him the means of descending in safety after he had removed the bars."

"And has he done so?"

"That's more than we can say," replied George Layburne, "for we both came away just as he was going to begin work, so of course we know nothing about what took place afterwards; but he seemed to be pretty confident of succeeding though, and that's generally half the battle, when people have got any difficult task to do."

"Where is he going to, if he gets out of prison?"

"He's to meet us at the Seven Elms, where our future plans are to be arranged."

"Am I to have no voice in it?"

"To be sure you are," answered Radcliffe, "for that's just the very object that brought us here. He wants to know if you'll be his friend, now that he's in difficulties."

"Indeed!" exclaimed the gipsy, "his spirit, then, can stoop to ask a favour of me that he has wronged and forsaken, though I never gave him cause for unkindness."

"Excuse me, old lady," interrupted Layburne, "but reproaches are out of place just now, when the man you speak of is in need of assistance."

"What assistance can he want from me?" asked Deborah.

"Merely your advice as to what he had better do, and may be a word to Squire Derwent by way of persuading him to secure his own future quiet, by giving him something handsome to live abroad."

"What interest can he suppose I can have with the squire?"

" I don't know anything about that," he replied, " but it has been reported to him that you have been speaking to some of the people down at the Hall, and he fancies from that you are rather thick in that quarter."

" If the report has been carried to him, it must have been by one of you two," she replied. " Be that as it may, however, I have no influence either with the squire, or anybody else at the big house—unless, indeed, it is with Miss Amy, and she neither acts nor speaks for herself, but leaves the management of everything to Mr. Derwent, so that whatever is done must be directly through him."

" And a precious obstinate fellow he seems to be," observed Layburne ; " for though he could have put an end to all the bother, by giving way, he prefers saving his money to parting with it, though by doing so he would prevent all further trouble and annoyance."

" Who can blame him for refusing to give way, when Caleb Kestrel has demanded no less than half his fortune as the price of his future forbearance ?"

" I don't know what sort of a bargain our friend wants to drive," answered Dick Radcliffe, " but if his demand is considered too great a one, why don't the squire make his own offer, to see whether terms can't be come to ? He ought by this time to understand the value of peace and quietness, and if he chooses to be obstinate in his refusal to pay for them, he'll have to blame himself for whatever may be the consequence."

" But who," asked the gipsy, " can blame him for resisting extortion ?"

" And who can say that Kestrel has done, in trying to make the best bargain for himself ?" asked Layburne. " He considers that he had done a great service to the girl, by restoring her to her rights, and that it's d———d hard to be refused his just reward."

" He should have been more moderate in his expectations then, and the affair would have been brought to a close before now."

" Well, you may say what you please about it," exclaimed Radcliffe, " but, in my opinion, there's no excuse for the way in which the squire has treated the whole affair. It seems he's over head and ears in love with the girl, and yet, because a matter of pounds, shillings, and pence stands in the way, he would suffer her to undergo the same sort of troubles that she has already had to suffer."

" Don't deceive yourself about that," returned the gipsy, " for he shall never annoy her again."

" Who's to hinder it ?'

" I will."

" You ! Do you suppose Caleb Kestrel is to be scared from his object by a woman ?"

" I not only suppose so, but am certain of it," answered Deborah ; " ay, and for that matter, Caleb himself knows that he had better thrust his right hand into the fire than drive me to do all the mischief that is in my power. You laugh at my words as if there was no truth in them, but ask Caleb himself if there is not truth in them, and you'll soon find out that I'm not a mere idle boaster."

" All I can say about it is, that, if you speak the truth in this matter, you are about the only person in the world that he cares a rush about," exclaimed Radcliffe.

" Ask him, then, if you like, whether a word spoken by me would not be enough to send him to the gallows."

" Thank you for the permission," laughed Dick Radcliffe, " but, to tell you the truth, I'd rather not put such a question to him. He and I have had words together before now, and sometimes we have even come to blows, but he has always got the best of me, and that's more than anybody else has ever been able to do. Be that as it may, however, if you have got as much influence over him as you speak about, you can't do better than persuade him to be more moderate in his demands upon Squire Derwent, and then perhaps there may be some chance of coming to an understanding."

"Why should I interfere," she asked, "when I know that it is in my power to prevent the violence he threatens ?"

" Because, if you can bring him to reason, it's more than any one else can do, and it would save a great deal of trouble, and perhaps some danger."

" The danger can only be to himself," answered Deborah, " and if he has not wit enough to keep out of it, he must take what follows."

" But I and Layburne must share it with him."

" Then give up all further connexion with him, and you will save yourselves harmless."

" Very good advice that, I dare say," exclaimed Dick Radcliffe, " but it so happens that we have given our word to assist him through this affair, and it would not be right to desert him at the last moment. Besides, he has promised to pay us well for our services, and that's a good reason why we should stick to him till the last."

" Be warned in time," exclaimed the gipsy, " for I can see further into futurity than you do, and I can tell you that the evil practices of Caleb Kestrel are drawing towards a close. Too long already has he been permitted to pursue his career of crime, but all things must have an end, and, before long, he must yield to the destiny that awaits him."

" You don't mean to say that he is going to die ?"

" I am in no humour to answer all your questions now," returned the woman, " but the words I have uttered are founded upon the art I practise, and in a brief time you will acknowledge their truth. Keep you appointment, then, with Caleb Kestrel, and tell him, from me, that if he values his life, he will desist from persecuting Amy, and seek in a foreign country that safety which he can never find in this."

" It might be all very well to tell him what you say," answered Layburne, " but the question is whether he'll listen to it. Besides, what would be the use of his going abroad, when he has not the means of living there ?"

" Only let him promise to go, and I'll undertake to persuade the squire into giving him a sufficient sum of money to keep him from want for the remainder of his days."

" Pshaw ! he'd only laugh at me for my pains."

" Let him do so," she replied, " and he'll soon have bitter reasons to be sorry for his own short-sightedness."

" Then perhaps you'll have the goodness to tell him as much yourself ?"

" Not I," she replied, " for I have no wish to see him again, unless chance should happen to throw him in my way. We parted in anger, and never yet have I been able to forgive him."

" But you would not do him a mischief, I hope ?"

" Not unless he drives me to it," answered Deborah; " and as a proof that I would avoid doing so as long as possible, I have had many opportunities of gratifying my revenge, yet have forborne, in consideration of the love I once had for him. He must not, however, urge me too far, lest I should, in the suddenness of my wrath, give him up to a death of shame."

" Methinks it would be as well if you were to tell him so," exclaimed Dick Radcliffe.

" Have I not just said that I will never see him, except when chance throws us together ?" asked the gipsy. " Yet, seeing the danger he is bringing upon himself, I would have him warned in time, that he may avoid the shoals and quicksands with which he is surrounded. Tell him to leave England without delay, and he may yet save himself."

" Leave England !" exclaimed Layburne; " and how the deuce is he to do that without money ?"

" I will see either Amy or Squire Derwent, and get for him a sufficient sum to supply his present wants. Afterwards, an arrangement can be made to provide for his future maintenance as long as he chooses to remain abroad."

"Then you would have him transport himself?"

" Ay, to prevent that which would be far worse."

" Humph!" ejaculated Radcliffe, "you are again hinting at the gallows!"

" It may come to more than a mere hint," she replied, "if he is rash enough to scorn my advice.   You may tell him so, if you please, that there may be no mis-understanding between us."

" And if did tell him so, 1 should only get laughed at for my pains," replied Dick Radcliffe.

" Is he so reckless as to laugh at danger?"

" Why, the truth is," he replied, "he has been so often in danger, and has gene-rally contrived to escape from it so cleverly, that he new begins to think he'll always have the same good luck.   Still, if you wish the message to be given him, I'll do it, though I don't think it will be of any use."

" But he'll not despise a warning that comes from me," exclaimed Deborah, " for he knows that the mysteries of fate are opened to me, and will he the caution I send him."

" You still have some kindly feeling towards him, then ?"

" Do not deceive your friend by telling him anything of the kind," answered the gipsy, " for I would merely save him from a doom that his long course of crime has richly deserved.   Besides, in wishing him to leave this country, I am chiefly urged by an anxious desire to preserve Amy from those cruel persecutions he has yet in store for her."

" Humph! you take a great deal of interest in the girl."

" I should be a foul discredit to my sex if I felt not for the sufferings of a help-less girl," she replied.   " Years of injustice has she already endured, and it is now high time that she should enjoy the more prosperous condition to which she has just been raised, or it would have been far better that she should have remained as she was."

" But you must own that she would still have been wandering about with those show people, if it had not been for Caleb Kestrel."

" Ay that's true enough," replied the woman ; " but what motive induced him to make the discovery he did? Was it not that he saw in it the means of extorting from her a great part of the money that was to come into her hands?"

"There's no denying that," answered Radcliffe, " but you must also confess that —as every labourer is worthy of his hire—he had a right to expect payment for putting her in possession of a fortune.   And it's my opinion the girl herself would have been inclined to give all he asked for, if it had not been for the obstinacy of Squire Derwent."

" Mr. Derwent would not have interfered in the affair, if the demand had been more moderate."

" I don't know how that might have been," answered the other, " but, for my own part, I think he ought to have felt more interest for the girl than to let her be troubled when it was in his power to prevent it.   And, even now, it's not too late, if he chooses to listen to reason, and reward Kestrel according to his deserts."

" If he had been rewarded according to his deserts, he would not be alive now," exclaimed Deborah.

" What has he done, that you should always be hinting about it?"

" Ask him, if you want an explanation of things that have long passed by."

" I should like to catch myself at it," returned Radcliffe, " for I know pretty well what he is when he's in a passion; and, though older than myself by some years, he has twice the strength when once his monkey's up."

" Then be content to wait a little longer, and your curiosity may, perhaps, be gratified," answered the gipsy.   "So, now, away with you both to keep your ap-pointment with him, and fail not to tell him from me, that there must be no more violence either against Amy or the Squire, or he will afterwards have bitter reason to repent it."

' Well, I don't mind telling him that, if you particularly wish it," replied Dick Radcliffe; " but mind, I shall not take any of the blame upon myself if he should happen to get into a passion about it. So now, before we go, tell me if you will see him, supposing he should have any particular question to ask ?"

"If it can be avoided, I would rather not see him again ; but if he should, for once, be reasonable, and resolve to take his departure from this country, he may come here to receive my directions as to the course he must pursue in future, But he must make up his mind to keep his promise strictly, for, should he break his word with me, it will be the worst day's work he ever did for himself in his life. Fail not to tell him that, for much depends on it."

Saying this, she closed the canvass of her tent, as a hint that she deemed the conference to be brought to an end, and Radcliffe and his companion, seeing that it would be in vain to ask any more questions, took their departure towards that part of the moor where they had appointed to meet Caleb Kestrel. To avoid meeting with any one, they took a bye-path that they knew to be little frequented, and in silence pursued their way till they arrived at the place where the pedlar was already impatiently awaiting them.

"So you've managed to give 'm the slip, in spite of all their watchfulness," ex-

No. 28.

claimed Radcliffe, as soon as they came near enough to be certain that the person they saw was he of whom they were in search. "Egad, old fellow, I was almost afraid you'd have been caught, though I wouldn't say so, lest it might discourage you."

"Nothing was ever done more easily," he replied, "for there was not the slightest interruption from the beginning to the end, and I have been waiting here, anxious to know whether you have seen Deborah?"

"Oh, yes," replied Layburne, "we found her in her den, and, for a wonder, she was in tolerable good temper."

"What does she say about me?"

"That you must not carry on your designs against the girl any further," answered Radcliffe, "for she takes up her cause strongly, and threatens to disclose something that will send you to the gallows if any more tricks are played off either against her or the squire."

"Indeed!" exclaimed the pedlar, rather startled by this announcement. "Did she say what she meant to do?"

"No, she left us quite in ignorance about that."

"And well she might," answered Caleb Kestrel, "for the truth is, it was only a threat to intimidate me, and at the same time to give you both a notion that I have been guilty of some great crime."

"What object could she have for doing that?" asked Layburne.

"How can I tell the motives of a mischievous hag like that?" he exclaimed sullenly.

"It must be revenge, if anything, for she told us you had deserted her after living many years together."

"What business had she to enter upon such a subject as that?" demanded the pedlar. "But I see how it is well enough;—she has been brooding over her revenge, and I suppose the blow will fall upon me when it is least expected."

"There's no fear of that," answered Radcliffe, "though I can't say quite so much if you are mad enough to do anything against her wishes, for she has taken a great fancy for the girl, and will not mind what mischief she does, if any harm befalls her through your means."

"Did you say I want to leave the country?"

"Yes."

"And what does she think of that?"

"She seemed rather pleased at it, and will see Mr. Derwent or Amy on the subject of getting an allowance for you to live abroad."

"A beggar's allowance, I suppose."

"I know nothing at all about that," answered Radcliffe, "for I had no authority to make any bargain with her, or to ask questions that would be much better put by yourself, supposing she would consent to see you, which, by the bye, don't seem very likely."

"Humph! did she tell you she wouldn't see me?"

"Why, she did as good as tell us so," he replied, "but after all, she said that if you are prepared to act by her advice, she will meet you once more, in order to bring matters to a conclusion. But recollect, my boy, Amy must be suffered to remain quiet, or there'll soon be a regular blow-up of everything."

"Does she want me to submit to her like a child?"

"I can't say anything about that," replied Dick Radcliffe, "but she may know more than you would like to have published abroad, and if that's the case, you'll be wise to knock under to her."

"Never," exclaimed Caleb Kestrel, "for rather than submit to that woman, I'll find means to get rid of her!"

"What, would you have the heart to murder the woman that you once professed to love?"

"Let her not enrage me, then, and I shall not trouble myself to interfere with her," answered the pedlar. "I had hoped to have seen the last of her when we parted, and yet now it is my evil destiny to meet her again, just when her presence is most likely to mar my projects."

" Don't you think the offer of a handsome sum of money might induce her to hold her tongue?"

" That question would not have been asked if you had known her as well as I do," replied Kestrel. " She takes strange whims into her head sometimes, and when once she has made up her mind to anything, neither bribe nor entreaties will persuade her to change her plans. It was that that led to our last quarrel, and I left her with an oath never to make peace with her again, even though she begged forgiveness on her knees!"

" Which don't seem very likely," replied Dick Radcliffe; " for if one may judge from her words and conduct to-night, it's pretty certain that she never means to forgive your bolting away from her. However, that has nothing at all to do with the business we have on hand, so make up your mind at once whether you'll leave the country on the conditions she has proposed, or remain here, at the hazard of being taken back to the uncomfortable quarters you have just escaped from?"

" That is a question that must not be decided too suddenly," answered Caleb Kestrel; " for I am unwilling to give up the golden prize that is in view whilst there's a chance of gaining it."

" But Deborah has promised to get something out of the Squire for you on condition of your leaving the country."

" Aye," he replied; " but I should like to know the motive of her great anxiety to get rid of me. There must be something more at the bottom of all this than I am aware of, and I'll know the whole truth before I think of leaving England at her bidding."

" Very well," exclaimed Radcliffe, " If you are determined to see the Gipsey, she has no objection to give you an interview, on condition that it is to be the last you'll ever ask for."

" Does she dare make conditions with me?"

" It seems very like it," answered the other, " for there was no mistaking her words, and she seems to be just the sort of woman that means exactly what she says. For my own part, I like your straight-forward people, that there can be no mistake about."

" Well," replied the pedlar, " I suppose there's no way left but to submit to her humour, so perhaps I may go to see her, if I can only make up my mind to keep my temper in case she should want to act the blusterer over me."

" Are you going to see her to-night?"

" No; I'm in no humour now, for if anything went wrong I should spoil all by flying in a passion. Perhaps to-morrow I may have more command over myself, and then will be the best time to hear what sort of a proposition she has to make."

" And are you going to run the risk of remaining in this neighbourhood?"

" One place is as safe for me as another," he replied, " so, with what money you have got, buy me a suit of clothes such as are worn by the farmers of this county, and I shall be able to disguise myself so that no one will be likely to recognise me. When that's done, meet me in the deserted hut, where we have often concealed ourselves before, and we'll then arrange our plans for the future."

" Why that'll be almost the first place where they search for me."

" Very likely," replied Kestrel; " but even supposing they should go to look for me, there's plenty of ways that we know of getting out of the place before the enemy can come upon us.—But hush!—not another word for your lives, for I hear the distant tramp of horses that seem to be coming this way, and perhaps bearing upon their backs some of my pursuers!"

A dead silence immediately ensued, and the three men crept stealthily forward to reach a thicket that seemed to promise them a temporary hiding-place. This they eagerly plunged into, and had not long thrown themselves down under some thickly-growing shrubs, when the pursuers passed the skirt of the wood at a rapid trot.

CHAPTER XXV.

THE FUGITIVES AND THEIR PURSUERS.—A PERILOUS SITUATION.—AN UNEXPECTED
RELIEF.—SPECULATIONS AS TO WHAT SHOULD BE DONE NEXT.—RETREAT TO
THE DESERTED HUT, AND A FRESH CAUSE FOR ALARM.

For a full hour the three companions lay in their place of concealment, without daring to speak or move, lest anybody should be near to pounce suddenly upon them. It is true that, armed as they were, they had little to fear from a single individual; but in the event of a pistol being discharged, further assistance would speedily arrive, and then the probability was that they would be either taken or killed, in spite of any resistance that might be offered. At length the solemn silence of the night was broken by the voices of many men, evidently advancing towards the wood, and undoubtedly their condition now became one of considerable danger. To escape was impossible, for people were heard calling to each other on every side, and it therefore only remained for them to be where they were, and, in the event of a discovery, to defend themselves resolutely, as the only remaining chance of escaping from those who were in pursuit of them. Presently afterwards they were still further alarmed by the discovery that some of the party had ventured to enter the wood, and they could hear them beating the bushes round about them, whilst the following conversation was carried on among them.

"I say, Job Smith," exclaimed one, "if we should be lucky enough to fall in with the pedlar to-night, it will be a pretty windfall to divide among us, for they say the Squire has offered three hundred pounds for his apprehension, and I don't see why it should not fall to our lot as well as to any one else."

"Aye, aye," replied the person addressed, "it may be all very well to think of the reward, but, for my own part, I cannot help thinking that we are running a very great risk in trying to earn it."

"Why, of course, there's a risk," observed another, but what of that, if we can manage to touch the Squire's rhino. Besides, we must not think of danger when we have a duty to perform, and especially as it can't be very great, since I don't see how Kestrel can have got any arms in the short time he's been out of prison."

"But you forget, Harris," exclaimed the first speaker, "that he has friends lurking about in the neighbourhood, and I dare say they have supplied him with weapons for his defence. But never mind, I mean to take my chance about that, and all I wish is that the fellows and I stood within arm's length of each other.

And little did he imagine that at the moment he spoke, another step would have brought him to the very spot where the object of his pursuit was crouching on the ground. By a singular fatality, however, he turned away in another direction, and once more Caleb Kestrel was relieved from the excessive terror occasioned by his perilous situation. Still the men continued their search round about the spot, as if they felt certain that the fugitive was not far off.

"Has any one been to the old tumble-down hut on the Moors?" asked Job Smith, the parish constable.

"Oh, yes! five or six have gone there," replied Harris, and they wanted me to join their party; but I knew a trick worth two of that, for is it likely Caleb Kestrel would think of hiding himself in a place that it is certain would be the first his enemies would search."

"True," exclaimed Rumbold, the first speaker; "he'd be crazy, indeed, to go there, and I wouldn't mind betting a crown that if he ain't in this wood at the present time, he has been here since he broke out of prison."

"Then go along, my boys, and don't give up till we've searched every corner and crevice of the place," cried Job Smith. "By Jove, it's not long since I ha him safe enough in our village cage, and I only wish I had him there now, for I'd take a little more care to keep him under lock and key than the governor of the jail seems to have exercised."

" Ah !" ejaculated Harris, " you fancy yourself a very clever fellow, I dare say ; but who can blame the governor for what has happened, when he had such a fellow as this Caleb Kestrel to deal with. Why, you might as well throw the fault on me, because I'm turnkey of the prison, though I can swear to having locked him up for the night as safe as possible."

" That may be, old fellow ; but your making the door fast didn't prevent him making his escape from the window. And who could have supplied him with the instrument that he used to file through those strong iron bars with, is a puzzle that I can't get over any how. If I was only certain who it was, I'd——

" Well," exclaimed Job Smith, " what would you do ?"

" Why, send him to keep company with Kestrel, on the other side of the herring-pond."

" Has any one been to see him in prison ?"

" Only Miss Amy, from Derwent Hall, and it's not very likely she would do anything to set her greatest enemy at liberty."

" It would be strange if she did," observed Rumbold, " for I'm sure she has reason enough to wish the fellow to be kept under restraint till he gets sent out of the country for good an' all. But never mind, we've only got to set to work in earnest, and I've no doubt we shall be able to claim the reward before many hours are over."

" I say," exclaimed Harris, " suppose he should be lurking near enough to hear what we are saying about him. It would be rather a pleasant situation for the poor devil, I'm thinking."

" As for that," returned the constable, " he knows well enough what his fate will be if he's caught, so I should say he'll take precious good care to get as far out of the reach of danger as possible."

" But how can he hope to escape, when, far and near, people are looking after him in every direction."

" Why, perhaps he thinks his old good luck will never forsake him," replied Job Smith. " Somehow or another, he has always managed to escape, when everybody else thought it impossible, and if we don't take care, he'll do so this time, for he's up to every dodge, and I dare say will keep himself snug in some out-of-the-way place till we've given up the pursuit, and then it will be easy for him to get abroad, with the assistance of some of those smuggling friends of his."

" Squire Derwent don't think so, though," exclaimed Harris, " for he has a notion that the pedlar will be concealed in the neighbourhood till he has an opportunity to carry the girl off again, and if he should succeed in doing that again, it will all be over, for he'll take her away with him to some place where no one will ever be able to find her."

" Can anybody tell me why he runs so much risk, when it seems he don't care a straw for the young lady ?" asked Rumbold.

" Ah !" exclaimed Harris, " that's just the mystery that no one can see through very clearly. There's a good many stories afloat upon the subject, but the most likely one seems to be that he knows the Squire is in love with the young lady, and no doubt he hopes to get a good thumping sum of money for restoring her to her friends."

" The rascal ought rather to have a halter."

" There we all agree with you, my boy," exclaimed Harris, " but unfortunately the law don't make an offence of this kind a hanging matter, and the worst that can be done is to send him abroad for life."

" Well, and if they can only do that, it will keep him out of further mischief."

" Aye, it would keep *him* quiet enough," observed Smith, " but the fellow happens to have comrades that are as great villains as himself, and Squire Derwent is afraid lest they should keep the game alive, even if Kestrel should be sent out of the country. For my own part, I see no reason why there should be any fear of it, because when they see their principal has been punished, they'll be glad enough to escape to some place where they may not be known as the associates of Caleb Kestrel."

"Have they been long in this neighbourhood?" asked Rumbold.

"Oh, no," replied Smith; "as constable of this parish, I can name pretty well every one in it that bears an indifferent character, and I'm certain these fellows were never seen here till the pedlar first made his appearance."

"Where the deuce could he have picked 'em up?"

"That, I believe, is a question that can be easily answered," returned the other, "for they are thought to be some of the smugglers from Robin Hood's Bay, and if so, they belong to as rascally a lot as is to be found from one end of England to the other."

"Then, as constable, why havn't you taken 'em up before now?"

"Because we've no facts to prove against 'em," answered Smith, "and I should find myself in the wrong box if I was to take up men that the magistrates couldn't commit. Besides, I'm only an underling, and it would be against all rules to act without orders from my superiors."

"Then by and by," observed Rumbold, "the parish may be over-run with smugglers from Robin Hood's Bay."

"There's not much fear of that whilst they've something more profitable to keep 'em in their old quarters," replied Job Smith. "People say they drive a profitable trade in the contraband line, and you may depend on it they won't give that up merely to assist Caleb Kestrel in his mad project of carrying a young girl away from her friends."

"Especially if we should be lucky enough to nab the pedlar," observed Harris.

"Which we must do, for the sake of the peace and quietness of the neighbourhood," exclaimed the constable. "The place has been in a state of constant trouble ever since the fellow first showed his ill-looking face in it, and I, for one, am determined either to take this Kestrel, or make the place too hot to hold him."

"Ah!" returned Rumbold, "the reward offered by the Squire has made you an uncommonly active officer all at once."

"Why," he replied, "the hope of gain generally stirs people up, though, for that matter, I believe no one can accuse me of neglecting my duty, even when reward is out of the question. Indeed, it's not so very long since Caleb Kestrel offered me almost any sum of money I liked to name, if I would let him out of the cage, and I stoutly refused, though no one ever need have known that I had anything to do with it."

"But every one would have suspected as much," observed Harris.

"Very likely they might," he replied, "but why need I have cared about that, when I should have got money enough to go and live somewhere else. However, I've told you nothing but the truth, and Kestrel could tell you the same, if you was to ask him."

"I only wish we had it in our power to ask him," exclaimed Rumbold. But I suppose its no use wishing, for he'll take care to keep himself out of our reach, and by and by we shall find, to our cost, that all this trouble has been taken to no purpose."

"Then you don't think he's skulking about in this wood?"

"I thought he might be here at first," he replied, "but after the search we have made I don't see how it's possible we could have overlooked him, if he had been in the place. In short, he's a great deal too cunning for us, and whilst we have been wasting our time here, he has found some other place to conceal himself in."

"What say you to going once more to see if he is at the Deserted Hut?"

"Those may go that like," answered Rumbold, "but the place has been searched already to-night, and I don't see the use of going there any more, unless we want to make a parcel of fools of ourselves."

"In that case we had better return home," observed Job Smith, "for I don't see the use of wasting our time here any longer."

"Nor I," exclaimed Harris, "for though I am perhaps more interested in capturing the prisoner that has escaped from my custody, than anybody else can be, I'd rather return to the governor to know whether he has any fresh order to give me."

"What orders can he have to give," asked Rumbold, "when he is as much in the dark as any of us?"

"You are going to remain here, then?"

"Not a bit of it," he replied, "for I'm convinced the chap we are seeking for is not here, and instead of giving up the chase, I mean to go elsewhere, and inquire of every one I meet if such a person as Caleb Kestrel has been seen in the neighbourhood. That's the way to hear something of him, so if either of you have a mind to bear me company I shall be glad of your assistance."

"For that matter I don't think it's likely either of us will refuse," answered the constable, "for, in the first place, we are all alike anxious to share the reward, and, secondly, it would be cowardly to leave you to the chance of a struggle with such a desperate fellow as Caleb Kestrel."

"As for that," exclaimed Rumbold, "he would find in me as tough a customer as ever he had to deal with in his life."

"Aye, but suppose he should be armed?"

"Well, suppose he is? Haven't I brace of bull-dogs well loaded, and if he should resist I'd shoot him through the head without taking the trouble of thinking whether I was right or wrong."

"It's all very well to say so," observed Harris, "but Kestrel might not give you the chance of finishing him quite so easily. People say there's more of the devil than the man in him, and as for courage—bad as the scoundrel is—no one can say that he has ever shewn the white feather when once put upon his mettle."

"Very likely," answered Rumbold, "but when a man has a bad cause to defend he can't fight as well as when he has a good one. Besides, he has future liberty to look to, and where's the man that would quietly give that up while he is able to defend himself?"

"But he can't do much if he's attacked by numbers."

"Exactly so," answered Rumbold, "and for that reason I would rather have both of you with me, in case he should feel inclined to make any show of resistance. So, if you like, we'll just make a search round the neighbourhood, and if he's not to be seen or heard of, we'll come and have another look in this wood to-morrow night."

This was readily agreed to by his companions, and immediately afterwards they all left the place to look for the fugitive in another direction. It was some time, however, before Kestrel and his two friends ventured to rise from amidst the bushes which had concealed them, and it was still longer before they spoke, lest any of the enemy should still be near them. At length, when they felt quite assured that all was safe, the pedlar inquired of his two companions what they intended to do next.

"Why, we shall follow your example, whatever it may be," replied Racdliffe. I

"Then I shall remain here till night, and then go to the Deserted Hut, where I think we may remain in safety till we can arrange our plans."

"Don't you think it would have been better to have brought matters to a close just now when we could have done it so easily?" asked the other.

"What do you mean by bringing matters to a close."

"Why, there were only three men against us, and if we had made a sudden attack upon 'em, they would have been so taken by surprise that we might easily have done for 'em all."

"True; but we should have had murder to answer for.

"Not if we had gone the right way to work, answered Radcliffe. "It would have been the easiest thing to have made 'em our prisoners, and then we might have bound the three fellows together to prevent all chance of their pursuing us."

"But they soon would have raised an alarm, and so brought other people to release them."

"Aye, but we might have gagged 'em, and then what assistance could they have brought, I should like to know? I was thinking all the while how nicely they were in our power, if we only went the right way to work, but I was afraid of speaking to either of you, even in a whisper, for fear the fellows should hear me."

"And what good should we have done for ourselves even if we had acted as you say?" demanded Caleb Kestrel. "The men might have been secured, no doubt, but they would have been released before long, and then the pursuit after us would have been hotter than ever. So, after all, it was best to let them go away quietly as they did, because they don't even suspect that we were near the place, and there is consequently the less chance of their coming back to make a fresh search for us."

"You forget, then, that they talked of returning?" exclaimed Layburne.

"No, I don't," answered the pedlar; "my eyes were open to every word they said; but what need I care about what they meant to do, so long as I know they will not find one of us here."

"Very likely," exclaimed Radcliffe, "but for the sake of the reward they don't mind what trouble they take, and you'll find out to your cost they'll never give up the search till they have earned the money Squire Derwent has offered for your apprehension."

"Let them search as they will," answered Kestrel, "for I must be a fool indeed ifl'm not able to avoid three such simpletons as they are. Why, I would hardly mind standing face to face with the three of them, for I could frighten away what little sense they may have by merely presenting a pistol at them."

"I see how it is," exclaimed George Layburne; "you have always had the good luck to escape from danger, and must needs fancy that you will do so on every other occasion. But, remember, fortune sometimes frowns upon a man, and I have a great notion that you will soon find yourself within the walls of a prison again."

"Suppose I do," he replied, "will it be harder for me to get out again than it was to-night?"

"Not if you have the tools to do it with," answered the other, "but you may not always meet with a young lady, kind enough to supply you with a file to cut through your bars."

"Well," exclaimed Caleb Kestrel, "I don't see the use of talking about that, now, so, as you two are not known to be associated with me since my escape, you had better go at once to the next market town, and get a supply of provisions, for we must not starve, as well as hide ourselves from the public. Bring enough to last us a week, that, if need be, we may keep snug till the danger is all over."

"Shall we bring the things here?" asked Radcliffe.

"No," he replied, "watch your opportunity, and when nobody's near, take them to the Deserted Hut, where I'll meet you as soon as possible after the dusk sets in. No one will disturb us there, I dare say, and if matters go on pretty quietly, we shall be able to form your plans for forcing the Squire Derwent to give me all I have asked for."

"And are we to bring you the clothes you want for a disguise?"

"By all means."

"Very well," answered Radcliffe, "we may find money enough to do that, but I can tell you something must be done to get more directly afterwards, or we shall find ourselves completely aground."

"Never fear about that, my boys," exclaimed the pedlar, "for I know the value of the time present, and will not cause any delay where so much danger may follow from it. Go then on your errand, and I will remain here till it is dark enough for me to venture to the place where we are to meet."

The two men now counted over their money in order to make a correct calculation of their expense, and finding that they had enough to answer their purpose, they made their way through the wood towards a road which they knew would lead them to the town where their purchases were to be made. On being left alone Caleb Kestrel began to reflect more seriously on his position than he had hitherto done, and it must be confessed that his cogitation did not in the slightest degree increase the confidence that he generally placed in himself. The fact was not to be denied that he was in a more perilous situation than he had ever been in before, and he saw that it would require the exercise of all his care and circumspection to avoid the rocks towards which he was hastening. The large reward, too which had been offered for his apprehension was the occasion of still further inquietude, for it was possible the sum might prove too strong a temptation for his companions, and if they chose to turn against him what chance would there be for him to escape from the punishment of which he stood so much in need? Still he could not but admit that the men had hitherto been faithful to him, and it was also certain that they might,—had they been inclined,—have betrayed him to the enemy

but a brief time previously. Under all the circumstances, then, he resolved to betray no want of confidence in the men he had hitherto trusted, but rather to exhibit more than usual courtesy, so as to keep them in good humour till their services should be no more required. Another thing, too, in his favour was the fact that they knew not how large a sum he was to receive from Mr. Derwent, except that they believed it would be very considerable, and that consequently their share would be much more than they would get by betraying him. These,

No. 29.

and similar thoughts occupied him through the whole day, and at length when the darkness of the ensuing night had set in, he gladly left his place of refuge, and stealthily made his way to the Deserted Hut. On reaching the door he listened to hear if any person, were approaching, and having satisfied himself that all was right, he entered the hovel, where, by the faint moonlight, he discovered that his companions had arrived before him and were lying asleep on the ground. Almost exhausted by the day's abstinence, he grasped a bottle that stood between the two men and refreshed himself with a portion of the brandy it contained ; he then partook heartily of some food which he found in a basket, and having recruited his nearly wasted strength, proceeded to the door, in order that if any danger should threaten he might be early apprised of it. But all was calm and quiet ; not a sound was heard except the gentle rustling of the leaves, and for the first time since his escape from prison, Kestrel began to feel that he was beyond the reach of danger. After an hour had been passed in this way he returned to the dilapidated chamber, where, seating himself upon a stone between his two sleeping comrades, he took out his pistols and reloaded them, in order to be quite certain that they were ready for use in the event of a sudden attack. Whilst thus engaged he was alarmed by hearing the report of fire-arms at a distance, and starting from his seat, he roused his two companions from the sound slumber in which they had fallen.

"What the devil's the matter now ?" exclaimed Radcliffe, rubbing his eyes and stretching his limbs as he looked and saw that there was nothing to call for immediate fear.

"Matter !" returned Kestrel ; "how should I know what's going to happen next when people are discharging fire-arms, and I can only fancy they are some of the people sent out in search of me ?"

"Have you seen any body ?" yawned Layburne.

"If I had," answered the pedlar, "he would have received the contents of one of my pistols through his body. No, the danger's not quite so near as that just yet, but we must be prepared for the worst, or they may be upon us before we can defend ourselves."

"Don't you think it would be the wiser plan to conceal ourselves till they have done looking for us ?" suggested Layburne.

"It might, if we knew of a safe place."

"Then there's one through yonder breach in the wall," replied Dick Radcliffe, "my comrade and I have been amusing ourselves by breaking a way through ; and it's well we did, for there's a large vault underneath the cottage that's dark as pitch, and at the other end is an aperture large enough for a man to crawl through, and, from what we could see, it seems to lead to a copse where we might be concealed whilst our pursuers are occupied in searching this place."

"This is a lucky discovery," exclaimed Kestrel, after a brief examination of the aperture that was spoken of, "for we may be concealed in the vault below till the enemy are about to seek us there, and then we may effect another retreat through the hole you speak of, which I should suppose can be easily and speedily closed up to prevent our pursuers making their way out by the same way. But what's the matter, Layburne ?" he exclaimed as the other came hastily from the door ;— "have you seen anything, that you seem to be so much alarmed ?"

"Yes," he replied, "people are coming this way with torches, and of course they are in search of you."

"Let them come," answered Kestrel, "for they'll only be disappointed, as has been the case on more occasions than one before. Perhaps another search here may convince them that this is not the place I should choose for a refuge, and if that should be the case, I might hope to remain here undisturbed for some time longer."

"It seems to be a strong party that's coming, at any rate," exclaimed Radcliffe, who had been to the door to calculate whether the danger was very great or not, "for there's no less than a score of them, and if my eyes are not greatly deceived, Squire Derwent and some of his friends are among them."

"Then the best way will be to send a bullet through the squire's head," cried George Layburne.

"Fool!" muttered Kestrel, "would you kill the goose that lays the golden eggs? Slay the squire, indeed!—and supposing that was done, what becomes of the money I'm expecting from him?"

"Why you must get it from the girl, I suppose," he replied, 'for she's rich enough according to all reports, and I should think it was easier to make her pay the money than you've found it with the squire, who has already given us more trouble than enough."

"Be that as it may ' exclaimed Caleb, "there must be no blood spilt to-night, unless there should be no other way to save our own lives. All we have to do is to take care not to fall into the hands of the enemy, and if we manage to do that, I'll take the first opportunity to make him pay down the sum I have demanded from him."

"Take the first opportunity, eh?" muttered Radcliffe. "If we wait for that, we shall tire our patience I'm thinking."

"And if we don't wait for it," retorted the pedlar, "we shall be likely to have thrown away all our time and trouble, for Squire Derwent is the most obstinate chap I ever had to deal with in my life, and nothing can be done with him except by humouring."

"And you are a likely fellow to humour him!" exclaimed Dick, sneeringly.

"Well," answered the other, "it must be confessed its going rather out of my way, but I see plainly enough where my only chance lies, and it would be madness to go headlong to work when all depends upon coolness and a steady judgment."

"Ah!" exclaimed Radcliffe, "I see plainly enough how all this will end. You have taken it into your head that you know but how to manage the business, and, by and by, we shall find that all our splendid castles have been built in the air. In short, we have been fools to take any part in the affair, and if our prospects don't take a more favourable turn before long, I, for one, shall leave you to finish it by yourself."

"And it won't be long before I follow your example," exclaimed Layburne, "for what little money we had is now gone, and I can't see any prospect of getting any more for some time to come."

"Will you both have patience for a few days?"

"For a week, if any good is to come of it."

"Patience, my dear fellows, and everything will turn out as you wish it," exclaimed the pedlar. "Do you suppose I don't feel as much interest in bringing matters to a conclusion as either of you do? and is it likely that I should wish to remain skulking about this place, when I don't know one moment after another whether the enemy may not be just ready to pounce down upon me? Besides, how can I do anything till I have money to go to work with?"

"You are not likely to get any whilst you are hiding yourself instead of trying to get it from the squire."

"Which I hope to do in a very short time," answered Kestrel. "By the bye, have you brought me the disguise I spoke about."

"Yes."

"Where is it?"

"Down in the vault I've been telling you about," answered Radcliffe.

"Why did you put them there?"

"Because we thought it very likely we might be interrupted by unwelcome visitors, and if, in the hurry we had left the things behind us, they would have told a tale that might have ended rather awkwardly. So there they are, ready to put on whenever you please, and if there should be need for it, we have the means at hand to procure a light. That, however, had better be avoided, for we must be careful not to give the enemy an idea that we are concealed here."

"See! they are coming towards us," exclaimed Layburne, who had again been watching from the door, "and if we don't mind what we are about they'll be here before we can get out of the way. D—n 'em! they had best not drive us up into a corner though, for if they do I mean to take care of myself even at the expene of blood."

" You know what I said before?" whispered Caleb Kestrel ;—" there must be no bloodshed unless we are driven to the last extremity, for remember, if so much as our lives should be sacrificed, there will be an end of all hope of getting money from the squire. So control yourselves, and only act in the defensive when every chance of escape is at an end,"

" Very well, answered Dick Radcliffe, " we've put ourselves under your guidance for the present, and neither Layburne nor I wish to disobey orders so long as they are reasonable. It may be as well, however, to come to an under-standing, that if things don't look more promising before long, we shall turn our steps back towards Robin Hood's Bay, where we are always sure of profitable employment, unless, as is now and then the case, the revenue officers get scent that a cargo is to be landed."

" You wish to leave me then ?"

" Not a bit of it, if we can only see [our way clearly," answered Radcliffe. Show us that we shall not have all our labour for nothiug, and I don't mind wait-ing a week or so till you bring Squire Derwent to agree to your terms."

" It will be done in less time than that if it's done at all," replied the pedlar, "for now that I am supplied with a disguise there is less difficulty in the way than there was previously. I may now ride about without fear of being known; and perhaps I may chance to meet the squire when he is alone, which is just the opportunity I want."

The light from the torches borne by the persons who were approaching now flashed through the room in which they were standing, and warned them that it was time to retreat. Radcliffe snatched up the bottle and the basket of provisions, and the three men retreated through the aperture, which, after descending a few steps, led them into a spacious vault, which, however, they had no opportunity of examining just then, as it was enveloped in the most profound darkness. They were, however, soon aware that their escape had not been effected a moment too soon, for hardly had they reached their new retreat than a number of persons were heard rushing into the room above them, and by the quick trampling that followed it was evident that a vigilant search was making throughout every part of the ruined building. Caleb Kestrel and his two companions stood anxiously listening to every sound, and ready to retreat to the second aperture as soon as there should appear to be any necessity for it. They, however, remained per-fectly cool, knowing, as they did perfectly well, that they would have a sufficient good start of their pursuers if they made their way out of the vault when the enemy was preparing to enter it.

CHAPTER XXVI.

MR. DERWENT AND HIS FRIENDS ARE ON THE RIGHT TRACK, AND CALEB KESTREL
HEARS A SECRET OR TWO THAT RATHER ALARM HIM—A RESOLUTION TO
SEARCH THE VAULT, AND THE FUGITIVES HAVE ONCE MORE TO TAKE CARE OF
THEMSELVES ;—THE PEDLAR DISGUISES HIMSELF, AND, ON HIS WAY ACROSS
THE MOOR ENCOUNTERS ONE WHOM HE WOULD RATHER NOT HAVE SEEN.

AMONG the many voices that were heard overhead, Caleb easily recognized that of Squire Derwent, and as every word that was uttered met his ear, he soon learnt quite sufficient to convince him not only that the party was in warm pur-suit of him, but that it was determined not to relax in the search till the object of it was safely in custody. For the first time the pedlar began to wish that he had escaped to a greater distance from the scene of danger, but regret was now all in vain, and making up his mind to defend himself to the utmost in the event of a discovery, he listened to the conversation that ensued, with feelings that it may be easily imagined were far from comfortable.

"So," exclaimed Mr. Derwent, "the scoundrel is not here as I imagined, but that he is not far off I am certain, and if you, my friends, will assist me as you have hitherto done, I hope many hours will not elapse before we have him once more in prison."

"And what will be the use of that?" demanded Brassey Popjoy. "You've had him there already, and yet the infernal careless rascals that had to look after him must needs let him escape."

"I rather think it was not altogether carelessness," returned the squire, "for I find upon enquiry that the prisoner was locked up for the night, and so silently did he file through the bars of his window, that nobody knew of his escape till the morning. By the bye, Mr. Popjoy, I forgot to enquire why you discharged your pistol just as we were turning the corner of the wood?"

"Why," he replied, "the truth is, I fancied I saw a man hiding himself behind a tree, and thinking it could be no one else but Caleb Kestrel I fired in the hope of bringing him down."

"And did it prove that it was a man you fired at?"

"No, my dear sir, it was only the shadow of the tree," answered the cockney, "but I'm not to blame for the mistake, because a great deal of excuse ought to be made for men that act under nervous excitement."

"Were you much alarmed?"

"N—n—no!" answered Popjoy, "only a little nervous; in fact, this is the first time I was ever out on such a desperate expedition, and Heaven knows I hope it may be the last. In London we manage these things very differently, for there we've plenty of police officers, and as they are paid for their services its quite right and proper that they should stand the chance of being killed when a man is to be made prisoner. So, between ourselves, Mr. Derwent, as London is the safest place for a man to live in, I think I shall tell Trubbs to get my travelling baggage ready for a start to-morrow morning."

"Oh, I hope we aint a going to lose the pleasure of your company quite so soon as that, old fellow," exclaimed Peeps, giving him a slap on the shoulder that made the cockney wince with pain.

"Perhaps, my dear sir, you'll make your arguments a little forcible the next time you address yourself to me," cried Brassey Popjoy with ludicrous solemnity, "I am not used to so much roughness I can assure you, but my servant, Trubbs, can bear anything and you can try how he would like it, if you don't mind running the risk of being knocked down for your pains."

"What!" exclaimed the ex-showman, "are you growing rusty about nothing? I only meant to show my friendship by trying to persuade you to remain at the Hall a few days longer."

"I meant to have stopped another month at least," replied Brassey, "but how can I do so when such a wretch as that Caleb what dye call him, is prowling about, seeking whom he may run away with. It was only the other night that he carried off Miss Amy, and I suppose I shall be the next to share the same fate if he only happens to take it into his head that he can make money by me."

"Make money of you!" exclaimed Peeps. "Talking of that, why I could have made a fortune if you and I had only known one another a little sooner."

"How could you have done that?"

"By showing you about the country as a natural curiosity," replied Peeps. Why I should have crowds of country people to visit my caravan, if they could only have seen a real cockney alive."

Mr. Brassey Popjoy looked unutterable things at this affront, and an angry reply would have followed, had not the squire turned off the subject by enquiring if anybody had searched the place underneath where they where standing, and to which the opening in the wall seemed to lead. An answer having been given in the negative, he inquired whether there was anybody that would follow him if he led the way.

"I will go with you, squire," exclaimed Frank Marldale, "or rather I will go alone, for if there is any danger it would be better that only one life should be sacrificed than a number."

"There is no occasion for anybody to run an unnecessary risk, when there are so many here who have so kindly volunteered to assist me in the pursuit of my enemy," replied Mr. Derwent. "We are all anxious to capture the ruffian, and I will not shrink from my duty now that I believe he is almost within my grasp."

"You think then he is concealed somewhere about this place?" exclaimed Frank Marldale.

"I do," replied the squire. "At any rate he has been here within a very short time, for the smell of liquor is still strong in the room, and who else is so likely to have sought shelter here as Caleb Kestrel and his equally scoundrel companions."

"If they are anywhere about the place," cried Brassey Popjoy, looking round him with alarm, "they may presently take it into their heads to pick us out two or three at a time, just by way of punishing us for being such a pack of fools as to follow them here."

"Oh, you need not be afraid of that, my good sir," exclaimed Mr. Derwent, "for even supposing such a thing was possible, we are strong enough to overpower them before they could do much mischief."

"I say old chap," said Peeps laughing, "will you have the kindness to make yourself a target for me, in case these chaps should commence the assault by firing a volley at us."

"Don't be a fool and frighten me so," exclaimed Popjoy; "this is no joking matter I can tell you, and if I had known as much as I do now, before we came from the Hall, I'd have seen all the Kestrels at Jerico before ever I'd have risked my precious life in such a mad affair. Mercy on us, what would my poor father have said, if ever he could have thought I would make such a fool of myself!"

"Come, come, my friend," said Mr. Derwent, "never repent doing a good action. You were kind enough to offer your services in this expedition of ours, and if we succeed—as I believe we shall—in capturing the persecutors of Amy, it will be a pleasant reflection for you as long as you live, to think that you assisted in rescuing an unhappy girl from the oppressions of a villian."

"Well, there's a good deal in that, to be sure," replied the cockney, "and perhaps I might be rather glad that I came out with you, if it wasn't for the uncomfortable reflection that there's a good deal of danger in taking up the cudgels against such a chap as Caleb Kestrel."

"Psha! he is no more than a man, after all," exclaimed Peeps.

"But a very dangerous sort of customer to deal with for all that," retorted the cockney. "In fact, I never have been used to come in contact with such people, and if I have the good luck to get safe back to London, I'll take care never to leave it again for anything."

"Oh, you'll change your mind about that, I dare say, after a time," said Mr. Derwent; "so think no more of danger, my dear sir, but remain here to keep watch, while I and the rest of our party go down below to see if the people we are seeking are there."

Mr. Brassey Popjoy, however, felt no inclination to follow this suggestion about being left above, and no sooner did the others begin to move in the direction of the broken part of the wall, than he placed himself in the midst of the moving party, judging that to be the safest place in the event of a sudden attack being made upon them. Assisted by the torches they carried with them, they descended into the vault in the full expectation of discovering the object of their search concealed there; but, as may have been anticipated, their hopes were again frustrated, for their intended visit was known before hand to Caleb and his two companions, and,

as a matter of prudence, they made a hasty retreat through the furthermost aperture, carrying with them everything that might afford even the slightest evidence
of their having been secreted there.   Notwithstanding this, however, they made
a minute search over the whole vault in the expectation that their task would not
be all in vain, but nothing occurred to confirm their suspicions, and, disappointed
at the result of their labours, they at length left the vault without discovering the
opening by which the three fugitives had affected their escape. All now felt
dispirited at the failure of their task, and urged by the remonstrances 'of several
of his friends as to the uselessness of pursuing the matter any further that night,
Mr. Derwent at length consented to return home on the understanding that the
object they had undertaken should be resumed with increased energy in the
morning.

We must now follow Caleb Kestrel and his friends, who, as may have been
foreseen, had effected a safe retreat to a neighbouring thicket, from whence they
could observe all that was going on at the Deserted Hut, without being seen
themselves. Silently they kept their watch over the actions of their enemy, and
it was not till Mr. Derwent and his party were far out of hearing that Kestrel—
who had been occupied in the meantime in changing his own apparel for the disguise that had been brought him—inquired if there was any probability of the foe
returning to resume their search.

"Not a bit of it, my boy," answered Dick Radcliffe, "they have now reached
the other side of the moor, and its as much as I can do to see the faint light of the
torches they carry with 'em."

"But to-morrow they'll begin again," exclaimed the pedlar, "and as I may
chance to fall in with 'em, the only question is, whether they'll be able to recognize
me under this disguise."

"The devil a bit can they," answered George Layburne, "for I myself shouldn't
know you, if it wasn't that I happen to be aware of the transmogrification you
have undergone. But for all that, old fellow, I'd have you take care not to show
yourself too much, for some people are uncommonly cunning, and if you should
happen to be discovered by any chap, there's no saying what he might do for the
sake of earning the reward that has been offered for your apprehension."

"And what if such a thing should happen ?" asked Kestrel, "haven't I arms
about me, and is it likely I should suffer myself to be taken easily, or without
resistance ?"

"I dare say not," replied the other," but for my own part, I always think
it best to keep out of danger as long as one can.   In short, there's no saying
what may happen when two people come to a wrangle, and the wisest plan
therefore is to avoid meeting with people that may feel inclined to do us a
mischief."

"And yet that seems a cowardly way of getting out of a scrape."

"I don't care what it may seem to be," answered Dick Radcliffe ; "for every
man ought to look after his own safety, since he'll not find anybody else to do it
for him."

"But I can't keep out of danger," exclaimed Caleb, " for come what will of it,
I must see Mr. Derwent face to face, and if that aint going into the very midst of
danger, I don't know what is."

" When do you mean to see him ?"

"It must be early in the morning, because we know very well that he will be
out again to recommence his search, and it would only be an act of civility on my
part to save him the trouble."

"That's all very fine, Caleb," exclaimed the other, " but we happen to know
that your civility goes so far, that you would like to send a knife through his heart
if you could only do it without being found out."

"Well," replied the pedlar, " there may be a good deal of truth in that, my boy ;
but, at all events, I have never been hypocrite enough to pretend any kindness
towards him. He has insulted and reviled me more than once, and now that he
has refused to give me what I ask in consideration of my leaving him and the girl

alone in future, it must needs be confessed that I hate him from the very bottom of my soul."

"Do you hate him so much that you could kill him, if he still remains obstinate the next time you meet together ?" asked Layburne.

"Why do you ask that question ?"

"Because I half fancy it will come to that."

"Have I ever given a hint that anything of the kind may occur ?"

"No," answered the other, "but I know you don't stand upon trifles when once your blood grows warm, and as a quarrel is sure to take place between you on one of these occasions, I thought it very likely that—"

"I shall finish my days as a convicted murderer ?" interrupted Caleb, as he directed a fierce glance towards the last speaker.

"And what, after all, is more likely ?" demanded Radcliffe, as if fully resolved to pick a quarrel with him. "You have been guilty of almost every other crime, and when a man comes to that he don't stand very particular about shedding a little human blood, if it will serve to wipe away an old quarrel. Nay," he added in a bantering tone, "don't look so savagely at me, old boy, we are good friends enough, and it's a hard thing if you and I can't open our minds freely to each other upon all sorts of subjects."

"Aye," muttered the pedlar, "you take advantage of me now because I want your assistance, and have thrown myself more than I ought to have done into your power. Under these circumstances I shall take no heed of your insults just now; but beware how you do it another time, for it will only serve to open an old sore, and I may not then be able to control my passion as well as I do at this moment."

"Pshaw !" exclaimed Radcliffe, "what's the use of two old friends like us quarrelling about nothing. Take my hand, my boy, and if ever I should venture to crack a joke with you again, take it kindly, and don't break out into these thundering rages."

"I don't want to fall out with you," answered Kestrel, taking the offered hand of his comrade; "but hang me if I can put up with what you call a joke, so, if we are to continue friends, never let us say or do anything that is likely to bring on discord. So now, as the day is beginning to break, I'll take my leave of you for a few hours, while I go to Derwent Hall, and if I can only manage to borrow a horse out of some paddock as I go along, I think it would greatly assist in preventing my being discovered, as no one would ever think of looking for Caleb Kestrel mounted on a horse."

"Take care, Caleb," said Layburne, laughing, "or what you call *borrowing* a horse may be called *stealing* one by the wiseacres, if you should happen to be found out at it. But, for all that, I like your notion, for, as you say, no one will ever suspect you for anything else than a jolly farmer, riding about the country on his business."

It was then arranged that their next meeting-place should be at the Deserted Hut, if it should be found safe to do so, and if not they were to repair to the Seven Elms, to discuss the occurrences of the day, and to make their arrangements for the future. This done, Caleb Kestrel bade them good-bye, and left the place to form, as he went along, those plans which were to decide whether he was to succeed in his views upon the purse of Squire Derwent, or to renew his violence against Amy. He had not proceeded very far before he came to a stable by the road-side, the door of which being open, he ventured to enter, having a ready excuse for his intrusion, in case any one should happen to be there. But all was as he could have wished, for the man had gone away to breakfast, and without thinking or caring for the consequences, the pedlar quickly saddled one of the two horses that he found standing there, and then, mounting, he rode off with all speed towards the moors, where, being able to see round him a great distance, there was no chance of being surprised by an enemy in ambush. Having ridden a mile or two onwards, he reined in his horse, and looked about for any well-known object that might serve to guide him in the direction of Derwent Hall, which he thought

he might now venture to visit, without much fear of detection. Whilst thus slowl
riding on, and his mind completely absorbed in the reflection natural to the state
of uncertainty and doubt in which he found himself, he was startled at hearing his
name pronounced in what seemed to him an unearthly tone, and looking up, perceived that he had been accosted by Deborah, the Gipsy woman, who, with arm
upraised, seemed to forbid his further advance till he had first listened to her. A
second glance showed him that he was beneath a gibbet, upon which still swung

CALEB KESTREL AND RADCLIFFE HAVE GAINED ACCESS TO THE BED CHAMBER.

the ghastly skeleton of a murderer, who, five or six years before, had been executed
on that spot, where the sanguinary crime had been perpetrated. Awe-struck at
these combined circumstances, Caleb Kestrel sat mute and motionless, and the
paleness that overspread his countenance betrayed the inward emotion that he
would have fain concealed from her whom, of all others, he would most gladly
have avoided.

"Why do you not speak to me, Caleb?" asked the Gipsy, in a hollow, sepul-
chral voice. "Has the presence of her you have so deeply injured, struck you

No. 30.

dumb, or am I to understand that you have resolved to hold no further communication with me?"

"Avaunt!" he exclaimed, "this meeting was not sought for by me, and at this moment I would rather avoid your presence."

"I know it," she replied, with a laugh that rang painfully through his ears. "You are afraid of hearing my reproaches, knowing as you do how richly they are deserved. But never fear, man, I am not going to speak of the past, for I would rather warn you of the future, which is full of danger to yourself, if you do not abandon the evil designs that you entertain against those who have never injured you."

"What have you to warn me of?" he asked hoarsely.

"Look above you," she replied, pointing upwards, "and gaze upon the marrowless bones of one, who, like yourself, was driven on by the wildest impulses from one crime to another, till he committed that which brought him to a shameful end. Yet even he might have died honoured and respected, but that he scorned the advice of a tender wife, who has since died of grief for the ignominious death of one whom she loved in spite of his cruelty and neglect."

"And what," he asked, "has all this to do with me?"

"Not much," she replied, "if you will not take the warning I would hold out. You are on your way to Derwent Hall, and your errand is one of mischief, for never yet have you been there except for the purpose of spreading consternation and alarm."

"That's no fault of mine," he replied, "for had the squire thought proper to agree to my terms, he would long before now have got rid of what he has since found to be a very troublesome fellow."

"What right have you to extort money from him?"

"About the same right," he replied, "that you have to question me upon the subject. However, since you wish it, I'll give you an answer. I have done more for the squire and Amy than any body else would; for the one I have helped to a wife, and the other I have assisted to a fortune, that never would have been her's but for me. These, in my opinion, are very important services, and ought to have been well rewarded, though hitherto I have not received a farthing."

"That's your own fault," exclaimed Deborah, "for you required too much, and when it was refused, menaces and even violence were resorted to."

"Well, and how could I act otherwise when I saw that all the good I had done was returned with ingratitude?"

"Squire Derwent would have refused nothing in moderation."

"Don't talk to me about moderation," he exclaimed, "because I ought to be the best judge of what my services are worth."

"But why should the heaviest part of your vengeance have fallen upon a weak, powerless woman?"

"Because I knew the squire would be more likely to come to my terms if she was the principal sufferer," answered Caleb Kestrel. "Aye, and he does feel it too, though so far he wont acknowledge it, under the false notion that I shall come down in my terms."

"You are resolved, then, to rush blindly on your destruction?"

"Destruction!"

"Aye," she exclaimed, "what else can you expect after setting the law at open defiance? Recollect, you have wealth and power to contend against, and, if you will madly persist in this course of violence and outrage, the end will be more terrible than you expect."

"Psha!" muttered Caleb, impatiently, "don't begin any of your old fortune-telling tricks, because you know I was never to be deceived by 'em. I can see as far as most people, and being able to avoid danger when any threatens, I'm quite willing to take my chance in what may follow from this affair between me and Squire Derwent. In a word, I am now on my way to see him, and that, too, with every chance of bringing matters to a satisfactory conclusion."

"Believe it not, Caleb," she exclaimed, "for I know the squire has made u his mind to hold no further communication with you, and he has even gone so far as to swear that if ever you should cross his path again he will either surrender you into the hands of justice or loose his life in the attempt. So now you know the worst, and it will be no fault of mine if evil befalls you."

" How came you by this information?"

" It matters not how I came by it," she replied, "for it may be relied on, and bitterly will you repent the rashness should you treat my warning with indifference or neglect."

" Squire Derwent is a vain, empty boaster," exclaimed the pedlar, "for what chance could he have if he and I were to come to a struggle for superiority? True, he is younger by many years, but my strength, even now, is more than equal to his, and in five minutes the fingers clutched upon his throat would leave him a blackened corse."

" And you," returned Deborah, " as his murderer, would be condemned to hang, like the wretched object that swings above your head, as a dreadful warning to others."

" There you are wrong," answered the pedlar," for I know my own destiny too well to believe that the gibbet will be my end."

" How know you that ?"

" Because, even though the judge might condemn me to such a fate, I would take care to spoil the hangman of his job. My hands would yet remain free enough to enable me to destroy life, and even if they were bound, I would rush headlong against the walls of my cell with such force as to spare myself the horror of standing beneath the gallows with thousands of human faces turned towards me."

" 'Tis an easy thing to say all this," she replied, "but should it ever come to such a time as I have spoken of, all this bravado would give way, as it has done with better men before you. Pause, then, before you go too far, and no doubt Squire Derwent will act with all reasonable liberality, when he finds that you cease to extort money from him by a vindictive persecution of Amy."

' Humph ! so you would have me rely upon his generosity ?"

" Why not, Caleb, when it will bring matters to a more speedy conclusion?"

" Oh, as for that," he replied, " I can bring them to a speedy conclusion by following out my own plans, so that Mr. Derwent must not suppose that I am to be kept quiet like a child that is to be threatened into submission. If he has any proposition to make, why has he not done it before now, instead of driving me to extremities by coldly refusing to come to any terms with me ?"

" That is a question that he only can reply to," answered Deborah. "No doubt, he has his own motives, and it may reasonably be supposed that he will consider no terms while they are insisted upon as if you had a right to direct what course he is to take. Tell me, Caleb Kestrel, would not you have shown equal obstinacy had anybody attempted to bully you in the same way ?"

" I can't say how that might have been," he replied, "but it's no satisfaction for me to know that I have been driven to all this violence through the unwillingness of Squire Derwent to make me a sufficient recompense after all I have done."

" You have not given him time enough to consider what a sufficient recompense is," observed Deborah.

" An hour would have been enough for that," exclaimed the pedlar, "and as he has been so long making up his mind, I'm now going to ride over to the Hall to insist upon the affair being brought to a conclusion."

" You will be known, Caleb," she replied, "and the people there have orders to take you the first time you cross their path."

" They'll have sharp work to do it, then," exclaimed the pedlar, "for the next time I'm in danger of being taken they shall find that they have a tough customer to deal with. It may be my fate to be hanged like the poor wretch whose bones are now swinging over my head, but if I am to suffer the extreme penalty of the law I'll at least have the satisfaction of knowing tht I've done all the mischief I could."

"Wretch!' cried the Gipsy, "will you never feel remorse for the crimes you have committed?"

"Call me whatever names you please, Deborah," he replied, suppressing the passion that he would otherwise have given way to;—"call me robber—murderer, if you like, for just now I happen to be in a humour that can put up with anything. In short, I have important business of my own in hand, and will not mar it by quarrelling with an old woman that I can put out of the way any time I please."

"You have tried to do that before now," answered Deborah, "but I know your deadly purpose, and by watchfulness have always contrived to thwart your evil designs."

"Don't be quite so fast," exclaimed Kestrel, "for it may be that you are doomed at last to die by my hands."

"No," she replied, "I can read your destiny in the book of fate which to you is a sealed volume, and there I have long since discovered that your death will be by the hands of the hangman."

' "Never!" he exclaimed vehemently; for whenever I find that all other hope has forsaken me, I will find some means or other to rid myself of existence. I'll not perish like a dog, for the gratification of a blood-thirsty law ; and those that come to witness my execution shall return home without the gratification they expected."

Perceiving that she was about to reply to this, Caleb Kestrel put spurs to his horse and rode off, to avoid further unpleasant truths that he had no wish to hear. Having proceeded some distance towards Derwent Hall, he was suddenly startled from the reverie into which he had fallen by the sound of horses' feet, and being thus made aware that danger was to be apprehended from the direction in which he was proceeding, he abruptly turned across the moors, and galloped with all the speed he could towards a thick plantation of trees, which he remembered to have seen in the immediate neighbourhood of the place he was about to visit. On arriving there he dismounted, and leaving the horse free to return to the stable from whence he had been taken, wandered through the thicket to ponder over his plans till it was time to put them into execution. Whilst thus engaged, a crash was heard amongst the underwood, and before he had time to conceal himself, Dick Radcliffe with one bound threw himself before him.

CHAPTER XXVII.

THE PEDLAR AND HIS ALLY.—A MIDNIGHT VISIT TO DERWENT HALL IS PROPOSED.
—THE SLEEPING CHAMBER, AND A BRIEF CONSULTATION THEREIN.—AMY ROUSES
FROM HER SLUMBER.—THE ALARM, AND HASTY RETREAT OF THE TWO RUFFIANS.

THE unnecessary alarm into which he had been thrown, had the effect of putting Caleb Kestrel into a very bad humour, but presently recovering from this, he inquired of his companion what mischief was in the wind, that he was skulking about so near to the hall. At this question Radcliffe burst into a laugh, and would have replied by putting a similar question, had he not been afraid of bringing on a quarrel just at the very time when everything seemed ripe for bringing their plot to a successful termination. Therefore, seeing the advantages to be derived from a good understanding between them, he briefly informed the pedlar, that he had managed to scrape an acquaintance with one of the female domestics, who, in consideration of a reward that had been promised, had consented to assist them in gaining admittance to the hall, and to give Amy a sleeping potion, that would prevent all chance of her waking if they determined to carry her off with them that night."

" Are you sure the girl is to be depended on ?" asked Kestrel.

" I don't see any reason to doubt her," replied the other, " for she has taken a dislike to Amy for some reason or another, and the twenty pounds I promised her in your name settled the bargain at once."

" How are we to get into this house ?"

" By means of this key," replied Radcliffe, taking one from his pocket. "It belongs to a back door, which she pointed out to me, and if we enter when all the people are in bed we may make our way to Amy's sleeping chamber without fear of our being disturbed."

" But Amy will be sure to raise an alarm."

" Haven't I told you that our female confederate has promised to provide against that, by putting a sleeping powder into a medicine that she takes on retiring to bed."

" That will do," exclaimed Caleb Kestrel, " if we can only make sure that the girl will perform her promise."

" Oh, you needn't be afraid about that," answered the other, " for she seemed pleased enough at having it in her power to do Amy a mischief, and especially as she would put money into her pocket at the same time."

" And does she know that we are to be there to-night ?"

" She expects us at any rate, and everything is to be so arranged, that we may get into the house without noise."

" Aye ; but the question is how are we to get out of it without being discovered ?"

" Why, I don't see much difficulty," replied Radcliffe, " for the girl will be as fast as a church, under the effect of the sleeping draught, and even if she should happen to wake, it will be easy to frighten her into silence by threatening her with our daggers."

" But she knows I would not kill her, because, when she is dead I should have no more influence over Squire Derwent, and the chance of getting the money I want would be at an end. However, I suppose we must try this new plot of yours, though, to speak my mind, I have no idea of its ending to my satisfaction."

" You've made up your mind then to try ?"

" I have."

" That's all right, so now let's away to hide ourselves in the Deserted Hut, for I've a notion that before long people will be coming here to look for us, and if they should this is about the worst place we could have chosen to hide ourselves from the enemy."

" Is Layburne in the hut ?"

" Yes," answered Dick ; " I left him there two or three hours ago, and he's looking anxiously enough for me by this time. But we don't want to have him with us at the Hall though, for you and I will be quite enough to do all the business that's to be done there, and another one added to our party would most likely upset everything."

" Whilst thus speaking they left the thicket, and as the night was very dark they boldly struck out across the moor, proceeding in silence, and listening for any sound that might indicate the approach of danger. At length, without meeting the slightest interruption they reached the desolate cottage in which they had so often found a shelter against pursuit, and where Layburne was impatiently waiting their return. From thence they crept into the vault beneath, where a dim light was burning, and the three friends sat themselves upon the ground to partake of the rough fare which had been left from their last meal. This was washed down with a copious supply of brandy, that had been provided by Dick Radcliffe, who knowing what sort of work they had to go through that night, had procured a fresh store from the next tavern. Over this, and in a tone that could not be heard beyond the dingy vault in which they were assembled, they discussed their plans till it was time for them to take their departure for Derwent

Hall. That night Amy retired to her sleeping apartment rather later than usual, and was accompanied thither by Annette, the treacherous servant of whom Dick Radcliffe had spoken. To appearance the girl was all kindness and attention, but this was only done the more easily to deceive her mistress, who certainly would have suspected any one rather than the person she had most frequently in attendance upon her. It appears, however, that Amy had in some way or another brought upon herself the anger of her servant, who ever since, under the mask of the most devoted attention, was plotting how she might best carry out her project of revenge. The means she at last took are already known to the reader, and having on the night in question mixed some powerful opiate in some gruel which her young mistress was to take, she left the room and proceeded to complete the arrangements in that part of the house by which it was to be entered. Little suspecting the treachery that was in progress against her, Amy stood for some time gazing from the window upon the beautiful scenery, which was now rendered distinct to view by the bright moonlight. At length feeling weary, she partook of the posset which had been prepared for her, and being almost immediately afterwards under the powerful influence of the opiate, she threw herself into bed, dressed as she was, and presently fell into a stupor so intense that it might have been taken for death itself, except for the slight and nearly imperceptible heaving of her bosom. She had been in this state about an hour and a half when the door of her chamber was stealthily opened, and Caleb Kestrel, followed by Radcliffe, cautiously entered on tiptoe. A single glance at the sleeping girl showed them that Annette had been faithful to her promise, and the two ruffians placing themselves at the foot of the bed, conversed together in a tone so low that it was scarcely possible they could be heard in any other part of the house.

"The girl sleeps soundly enough," whispered Caleb, pointing to her, "and by all appearance is not likely to wake for some time to come; but the next question is—how are we to get her out of this house without disturbing the people?"

"Ah, that can be managed easily enough if you only follow the advise I gave some time ago. Let's stay where we are till she wakes of her own accord, and then if she should attempt to raise an alarm, we must first gag, and then compel her to go with us under a threat of instant death if she refuses."

"But suppose she's not to be frightened by threats?"

"Ah!" exclaimed Radcliffe, "you must always look at the black side of everything, as if matters could never by any probability go right. Besides, did you ever know a woman that couldn't be frightened into silence by the sight of a blade of shining steel?"

"Most females are as easily intimidated as you say," returned the pedlar; "but this girl has courage greater than ever I saw in the sex, and you'll find by and by, that when she wakes we shall have more trouble than you expect."

"Humph! we have not much to fear from the people of the house, for they are all sound enough asleep, or they would have heard us as we came up stairs."

"But some of 'em may wake, for all that," exclaimed Kestrel; "and if they should pounce suddenly upon us, what way is there for us to make our escape?"

"What way?—why out of this window, to be sure," answered Dick Radcliffe; "it's rather high," he added after looking out to take a survey; "but when people have their liberty to look after, they must run greater risks than this if they'd get out of the reach of danger."

"It's all very well to talk about jumping out of the window," exclaimed the pedlar, "but if we do so, what's to hinder our pursuers from following our example?"

"Ah, of course, there's nothing to hinder 'em from taking a desperate leap," returned Radcliffe; "but if they were foolhardy enough to do that, and we should find ourselves too hardly pressed, we have each a brace of well-loaded pistols, and four of 'em at least would soon be wallowing on the earth in their own blood."

"And the end of it would be, that we should have to answer for the crime of murder."

"They'd have to catch us first, and, judging from the game at hide and seek that we've been playing for some time, I should say that our chance of getting clear off would be a very good one. But I don't suppose matters will be quite so serious as that, for they know what sort of customers they've got to deal with, so that it's not at all likely they would pursue us, when it would be certain to end in the death of some of 'em."

" Hush!" whispered Caleb Kestrel, " the girl moves, and if she wakes we must be upon the alert, or both of us are lost."

" Then you stand on one side of the bed, whilst I take my place on the other, and if she attempts to raise an alarm you know what we have to do to save ourselves."

The two ruffians stationed themselves by the bedside, and remained there in silence for some time, during which period Amy was gradually recovering from the stupor in which she had so long been lying. The moon was then pouring a flood of rich light into the chamber, so that every object in it was as distinctly visible as in the daytime, and as our heroine turned her eyes towards the casement they encountered the fierce and malignant glance of Caleb Kestrel, who had been watching her with a look something like that with which a hungry tiger gazes upon its destined prey. Yet, horror-struck as she was, no sound escaped her lips save a low wail, like that of a person in the extremity of mortal agony. Her next effort was to spring up, but the firm grasp of her persecutor held her down as if she had been an infant. She made a feeble effort to release herself, but the attempt was in vain, and in her despair she entreated mercy from him who knew not the meaning of the word."

" Listen to me, Amy," he whispered in her ear; " you are to consider yourself my prisoner, and all resistance will now be vain, for I have sworn to take you from this house, and my oath shall be kept, even though I may be forced to shed the blood of your lover. Your cries, it is true, would bring the Squire to your assistance, but the moment he enters this apartment will be his last!"

" You see now exactly how the matter stands," added Dick Radcliffe, " so jump up, my girl, and go quietly with us, or you may soon have to mourn for the loss of some of your friends."

" Villain!" exclaimed Amy, " I will perish rather than go with you."

" Then look at this dagger," exclaimed Radcliffe, holding one before her eyes, " and learn from it that we have come here fully determined to carry out the design we have in view. Caleb Kestrel is determined not to be foiled this time, and as I am to share largely in whatever sum of money he makes, I shall not stop at trifles if you make any uproar to bring the assistance of your friends.'"

These threats, however, instead of intimidating Amy, served only to render her the more desperate, and making another effort to spring from the bed, she raised a cry so loud and piercing that it penetrated even to the most distant recesses of the mansion. Radcliffe lifted his dagger for the purpose of plunging it into her heart, but the weapon was snatched from his grasp by Caleb, who, alarmed by hearing a number of persons hurrying along the corridor, violently dashed open the casement, and, reckless of the consequences, leaped from thence to the ground. Dick Radcliffe, who saw the danger of remaining, instantly followed his example, and the two comrades, after waiting just long enough to ascertain that the room they had just left was filled with people, made the best of their way through the shrubbery, and from thence to the Deserted Hut, where George Layburne was waiting for them.

" How is this?" exclaimed the latter worthy, as they approached him. " Have you suffered the girl to escape you again?"

" There was no help for it," muttered the pedlar, " for we were obliged to save ourselves by making a hasty retreat."

" And a couple of precious fine fellows you must be, to let a female thwart you at every attempt you've made!"

" Aye, jeer at us as much as you like, for I believe we deserve to be scorned and laughed at for our pains," exclaimed Caleb. " For my own p ar, I could go and drown myself from sheer vexation."

"And I suppose your only reason for not doing so, is, that you hope to be more successful another time?"

"You may be sure I shall not be satisfied to let matters remain as they are. I have been fooled enough already by a woman, and it's now time that the triumph should be on my side."

"Oh, it's all very well to flatter yourself with that notion," exclaimed George Layburne, "but you have had opportunities enoguh already, and yet the wench has always managed to slip through your fingers as if she was an eel. But to-night was to do such wonders, that I little thought you were coming back with the same tale, and faces as long as my arm."

"This may be a very capital joke for you," retorted Radcliffe, "but the affair was not quite such an easy one as it may have seemed, and I believe if you had been with us when the whole hall was set in commotion, you'd have been as glad to get beyond the reach of danger as Caleb and I were."

"But you were armed, and hang me if I wouldn't have had a try for it, before I suffered the girl to escape."

"What was the use of our arms against so many?" demanded Caleb Kestrel. "It may be all very well to stand fire when the chances are anything like equal, but there happens to be a determination to take me at all hazards, and if we hadn't made our escape as we did, I should have been in safe custody before now."

"And, as it is, they'll have you before long."

"What makes you think so?"

"Because, as a matter of course, they'll know who it was that has made this fresh attempt to carry off the girl, and if they kept a sharp look-out for you before, they'll be doubly vigilant now that they find that you are as resolute about the affair as ever."

"I don't mean to deny that," returned Caleb Kestrel, "but if you both remain faithful to me, they'll have more trouble to trace out my retreat than they probably expect. In short, I know the sort of enemy I have to deal with, and it will be my own fault if I don't lead 'em a dance from one part of the country to another, that will make 'em heartily tired of the business they've undertaken."

"That may be all true enough as far as Squire Derwent and a few of the others go," answered Layburne, "but it happens that you have got worse fellows than them to deal with ;—fellows that are looking out for the reward that's been offered, and who'll never be tired of looking after you so long as there's money to be made by it. Then there's the governor of the jail, too, likely to lose his situation, all through your having made your escape, and he has offered another reward for your apprehension, so that I don't see how you can expect to be at liberty much longer."

"I see well enough that my course don't run very smooth," answered Caleb Kestrel, "and that this old Deserted Hut, often as it has served me in the hour of need, is no longer a place where I can hope to conceal myself from the people that are pursuing me. Besides, as it would be useless for me to make any further attempts against Amy just at present, I think I shall pay a visit to my old friends, the smugglers, in Robin Hood's Cave. There, at any rate, I may lie safe and snug for the present, and by and by, when the pursuit is not quite so hot as it is now, I may come forth from my den and carry off the girl without trouble."

"You must be a little more venturesome than you seem to have been to-night, then," observed Layburne.

"Come, come, old fellow," exclaimed Dick Radcliffe, "you must not be quite so sharp upon us about what has happened to-night. We made our way into the house as we undertook to do, but it would have been madness to have remained there after Miss Amy had roused all the people with her screams."

"Did the servant-girl assist you as she promised?"

"Yes," replied Caleb, "she left the door so that we could easily get in, and I suppose gave the sleeping draught to her young mistress, for Amy seemed to be lying in a state of stupor for a long time after we had entered the room, and that too, while Dick and I were talking by her bedside."

"Why didn't you gag her, when she awoke ?" asked Layburne.

"It's all very well to ask us why we didn"t," answered the pedlar, "but the truth is, she didn't care for our threats or our daggers; so when she screamed lustily for assistance we were glad to jump from the window and make our escape the best way we could."

THE QUARREL BETWEEN CALEB KESTREL AND JABEZ T OMP SON.

"That will be of very little use, if you [stay here much longer," exclaimed Layburne, "for I see torch-lights yonder across the moor, and, my life for it, your pursuers are already after you."

Caleb Kestrel went to the door for a few minutes, and having watched the lights, he returned to his two companions.

"It's true enough that they are after me," he said, "but even at this distance off I can see that they are following every direction but the right one. However, it's more than likely that some of the fellows may take it into their

heads to come and search this place, so the sooner we make good our retreat -
the better."

"Which way are you going?" asked Radcliffe.

"Where you may both follow me if you think proper," he replied. "I shall
make the best of my way towards the sea-coast, and find my old friends
the smugglers, who will no doubt give me shelter in Robin Hood's Cave
till I can venture once more to show myself abroad. I suppose neither of
you will have any objection to keep me company there, for if any of us should
fall into the hands of the enemy we shall have very little mercy to expect from
them.

The truth of this latter assertion was so evident, that both Layburne and Dick
Radcliffe at once closed with his proposition, and it was further agreed that they
should set forth on their journey whilst the way before them appeared to be
tolerably clear. Their first care, however, was to place their arms so that they
might be ready for immediate use in the event of a sudden attack, and having
thus prepared themselves, they set forth from the Deserted Hut, and crossing the
dismal heath that lay before them, succeeded in escaping from a place that they
had good reason to know was too hot to hold them.

CHAPTER XXVIII.

THE CONFEDERATES SEPARATE.—THE PEDLAR AND DICK RADCLIFFE PROCEED TO
YORK.—THE THREAT.—THE QUARREL.—KESTREL BECOMES VIOLENT.

ALL that night, and the greater portion of the next day, the three comrades proceeded on their way, stopping only occasionally for such refreshments as were
absolutely necessary to sustain them through the fatigue they had to undergo. For
a long time they heard nothing to cause them much alarm, but at length, on stopping
at a road-side public house, they heard conversation going on on the subject which
related to themselves; from what passed they ascertained that bills offering a
reward for their apprehension had been circulated through the neighbourhood, and
that consequently there was every chance of their being apprehended, unless they
separated and took different directions till the keenness of the pursuit began to sub-
side. Alarmed at the imminence of the danger which they had been endeavouring
to escape from, they left the house, when it seemed they might do so without
bringing any particular attention towards themselves, and crossing some fields
made their way towards another road, which their pursuers would be less likely to
take than the one they had just left. Very little conversation passed between
them as they hurried on, but at length, having proceeded about four miles, they
came to a place where another road diverged off at right angles from the one they
had been following. Here Caleb Kestrel suddenly paused—

"I'll tell you what," he said, after looking round to satisfy himself that no one
was watching them, "if we all keep together in this way we shall be sure to draw
the attention of passers by towards us, and if once people begin to suspect who
we are, it will not be long before the game will be over with us."

"That's just what I've been thinking myself," exclaimed George Layburne,
"so I, for one, am quite willing that we should part at this spot, and we can make
a bargain, if you think proper, to meet at the cave in somewhere about a week's
time. We shall then hear how the search goes on, and if nothing particular
happens to alarm us, we may perhaps try some other plan either to carry the girl
off with us, or get the money from the squire, which, by the bye, will suit the
present state of our affairs better than anything else."

"And why should we part," demanded Dick Radcliffe, "when our best security is to remain altogether?"

"You think it best, then, that we should be taken altogether?" exclaimed Caleb Kestrel, with a dark frown.

"If, with arms in our hands, we suffer ourselves to be taken by the cowardly curs that are upon the look-out, we shall deserve any fate that may befall us. I, however, am resolved not to be taken alive, and if ever the enemy and I should happen to come to close quarters, I'll either fall in my own defence or send some of them to the other world as a broad hint to others of what they have to expect if they interfere with me."

"Then, what do you intend to do?" asked the pedlar.

"Go wherever you do, to be sure."

"But I have made up my mind not to go to Robin Hood's Cave till I know how matters are likely to turn out."

"May I ask what direction you are going to take?"

"I shall go direct from here to the city of York," answered Kestrel.

"Where, as a matter of course, you will be recognised and arrested for the sake of the reward that has been offered for your apprehension."

"Perhaps so," answered the pedlar; "but I have not made up my mind upon this subject without first of all considering all the chances both for and against me. Like yourself, however, I am determined not to be taken whilst I have strength enough to fight in my own defence, and when I find that it's of no use any longer to contend against numbers, I'll put the last pistol to my head and blow out my brains!"

"Just by way of letting the world know that you had such a commodity," observed Radcliffe, with a sneer.

"Or rather," exclaimed George Layburne, "to deprive our enemies of the reward they are so anxious to earn. However, we are losing time when we have not a moment to spare in idle talk, so, in a word, I'll let you know what I've made up my mind to. I shall make the best of my way from this place to Robin Hood's Cave, where I shall wait till one or both of you come to let me know how matters have been going on, and what's to be done next."

"And not a bad plan either," returned Dick Radcliffe; "for you will be in a place of safety, whilst we are exposed to danger, through not being quite such cowards as to hide ourselves in holes and corners the moment that we see there is danger."

"I'm no more of a coward than yourself," retorted Layburne, "and perhaps not so much, because I don't boast so much of my courage as you are apt to do. However, 'fine words butter no parsnips,' so, as we are not likely to make matters any better by getting into a quarrel, the wisest thing we can do will be to say no more upon the subject. You, it seems, are going to York with Kestrel; but before we part I should like to know when and where we are to meet again?"

"There's no place better that I know of than the Cave," replied Caleb.

"Good! Now tell me *when* I am to expect you there?"

"There's the difficulty," answered the pedlar; "for everything will depend upon how matters seem to be going on when we reach the city. If the search after us is not very brisk, I shall be with you in two or three days at the furthest; but if there should be danger, we shall of course keep ourselves snug and quiet till we can find an opportunity to get away without being seen."

"But what makes you go to a place where you are so likely to be known?' asked Dick Radcliffe.

"Because it's very likely I may meet an old friend there."

"What old friend do you mean?"

"Jabez Thompson."

"Humph! Are you sure he's a friend?"

"I've never seen any reason to believe otherwise of him," replied Caleb Kestrel; "and if he had been false, I must have found him out before now, when he might have given me up to my foes at the time I was at hide and seek on the sea coast."

" You can think as you like about that," exclaimed Radcliffe; "but I never had a very good opinion of him after he took a parcel of people to look for you in Robin Hood's Cave."

"Perhaps that might have looked rather suspicious," returned the pedlar, "but there couldn't have been any treachery intended, when he came to the place before hand, and gave me notice of what he was going to do. By that means I was able to get away with the girl to another of the caves; and as a proof that Jabez never intended to betray me for the sake of the reward, I was not followed to the spot, though he could have put my pursuers upon the right clue."

" But why was it ?" demanded Radcliffe. " You promised to pay him a large sum out of the money you expected to receive from Squire Derwent, and he thought that would pay him better than taking the reward that had been offered for your apprehension; especially as he would never have dared show himself among his old comrades again."

"You seem to owe him a grudge," muttered Caleb.

"Not I," returned the other; " I never had any quarrel with the man, because we happen to have met together very seldom. However, for all that, I've a notion that he's not to be depended upon, and yet you are now going to York for no other purpose than that you think it's very likely you may meet with him there."

" Do you think I should do so unless I had a notion that he might afterwards be of some service to me ?"

" Service !" retorted Dick Radcliffe. " Yes—yes you'll find him of great service if he takes it into his head to set the infernal police upon you when a visit from them is not expected."

" Pshaw ! why do you think he would be such a scoundrel ?"

" I have told you that already—the reward that has been offered is too tempting for a poor man to resist; and when he has no more honour about him than you, or I, or any of the rest of us can boast of, I have very good ground for saying that he is not to be trusted."

" But I must trust to somebody," answered Caleb Kestrel, " and why not him as well as anybody else ?"

" I don't see the occasion you have for trusting anybody."

" How, then, am I to be aware of what is going on when I am obliged to hide myself night and day ?" asked the pedlar.

" Can't I go out and make the inquiries ?"

" You forget, Dick, that you are as deep in the mire as I am, and if they should happen to set eyes on you, I needn't say what the consequence would be. So now you see the danger, and I hope if we both have the good furtune to reach York in safety, you'll take my advice and keep within doors so long as there is a chance of falling into the hands of the enemy."

" What !" exclaimed Radcliffe, " you are beginning to be afraid, are you ?"

" If I am, it is the first time in my life," answered the pedlar, " and I'll take care that no one shall ever have any real cause to accuse me of cowardice. My whole life has proved the contrary of that, or I should not have been in my present dilemma."

" I don't know what you may hav e been in former times," exclaimed the other, " but of late I have seen quite enough to show that when money is in the way you can be bold enough, though I'm not quite sure whether you mightn't hang fire if there was not a pretty good certainty of securing something worth while."

" And Caleb is in the right there," interposed Layburne, " for a man has no business to run any risk unless there's a fair chance that he'll make something handsome for himself by it. For my own part, I don't mind confessing that I would have had nothing at all to do with this business unless there had been money in the way."

" Who didn't know that without your putting yourself to the trouble of saying so ?" demanded Dick Radcliffe with a sneer. " You are always looking out for yourself, and by and by I should not wonder at your turning round upon your old comrades, if you thought there was anything to be got out of it."

Caleb Kestrel saw plainly that a quarrel was brewing between his two companions, and foreseeing the danger which must arise from such a collision at such a moment, he dexterously changed the conversation by asking Layburne if he knew any of the smugglers amongst whom he was going to seek a temporary retreat.

"Why, I can't say that I have ever seen much of them," he replied; "but I know Tom Hazle and two or three others, who are good fellows enough in their way, and many a time have they wanted me to join their band, because they thought I was just the sort of chap to lend a ready hand when a cargo is to be landed."

"Were you afraid of the consequences?" asked the pedlar.

"Not I," he replied, "but the truth is, I have always been able to make a pretty good living by following my own way of life, and I thought it would be foolish to give up one thing till I could find another. First of all, I started as a poacher, and got imprisoned for it three or four times, which was as nice a school of villany as they could possibly have sent me to. I learnt all sorts of scheming and devilry there, and at last I got to thieving, and have stuck to it ever since."

"Till now," interposed Dick Radcliffe, "when it seems you have given up petty pilfering for the sake of assisting in carrying off a young girl, instead of the booty you have been more used to."

"Well," he exclaimed, "and who can blame me for that, when our friend here offered me such liberal pay for my services?" Besides, I don't see any great deal of harm in it, for the girl has never, till now, known what it was to have a regular fixed home, so that she can't miss the comforts of it as a great many other persons would."

"Aye, aye, that's the right way to look at it, my boys," returned Caleb Kestrel. "As you say, there's no harm in what we've been doing, and especially so when we come to recollect that she would have been nothing better than a wanderer if it had not been for my having discovered her by mere chance on the night of Farmer Brough's Harvest Home. So she has nothing much to complain of, seeing that all the trouble and annoyance might have been avoided, if she or Squire Derwent would have paid me for my trouble. However, we are forgetting ourselves strangely, for I see daybreak beginning to show itself, and we have all some distance to go before we reach the places we have got to go to."

"I, for one, shall be off," exclaimed George Layburne, "and remember, I shall wait at the cave till I see you there, and then, whatever business there may be in hand, I shall cheerfully make one to lend a hand in it."

Without waiting for any reply to this, he turned down the road that diverged off to the right, and at the same time Kestrel and his companion continued that which they had been following for some time previously. For three or four hours they walked on, and at length arriving before a quiet-looking road-side public-house, they entered to procure the refreshment of which they began no stand in need. There were but two or three persons there, but the fugitives thought they occasionally cast suspicious glances towards them, and they in a very short time made a hasty retreat, changing the course they had hitherto kept, and passing through a number of fields, in order that, if a pursuit should be commenced, they might elude those whose suspicions seemed to have been roused. Fortunately for them, however, they met with no interruption whatever, but from that time they took care to avoid all public roads, and to keep only to those bye-ways which seemed to offer the least interruption. They took care also not to stop at any place where they were likely to be recognised, and at length, just after the dusk of evening had set in, entered the venerable city of York, which, for the present, was to be the end of their journey. The next question that perplexed them was to find a place where they might find shelter for the night, and this was a matter of so much doubt and difficulty, that they both paused near the old Mark te Cross and looked around them, wondering which way they should direct their course The more they gazed around, however, the more perplexed they became; and at length Radcliffe, seeing no chance of coming to a speedy decision, proposed that he should go in search of some place, whilst his comrade remained where he was till his return.

"And why should I remain here alone?" asked Caleb Kestrel, as a suspicion of some intended mischief passed through his mind."

"Ah!" returned the other, "you needn't stay unless you like; but I thought if we both went wandering through the streets together, it might attract more attention than if we go singly."

"And what will be thought if people should see me loitering about here alone?" demanded Caleb Kestrel.

"What should they think if you mind what you are about?" demanded the other. "However, if you don't like my proposal, you had better go with me, and we'll try together whether we can't find this Jabez Thompson, though to me it seems like seeking for a needle in a bottle of hay."

"Upon second thoughts I shall remain where I am," exclaimed the pedlar, "for I may see some one pass that I know, and who might be able to direct me to a lodging where we may remain concealed till this pursuit is at an end."

"Or, perhaps, you may see some one that can tell you if Jabez is still in the city."

Having said this with a sort of half sneer, at what he considered the improbability of such a thing, Dick Radcliffe made his way towards an opposite street, which, from the appearance of poverty which it bore, seemed more likely than any other to afford the sort of asylum that he was in search of. The pedlar watched him as he remained in sight, and then slowly pacing up and down, he gave free vent to his thoughts of the past, the present, and the future. In neither of them, however, could he insure anything that afforded him a ray of hope, for by that time his means of subsistence began to grow very limited, and just then he could see no prospect of immediately mending his fortunes, unless, indeed, by any piece of unexpected good luck, he could either cajole or persuade Squire Derwent into giving him the sum of money he had so often and so vainly tried for. But under all the circumstances, this was, perhaps, scarcely to be expected, for many of his recent acts had thrown him more and more into the power of the man from whom he expected this relief; and as for Amy, there was now less chance than ever that he would be able to tear her from the protection of those who were by this time so well aware of the plot he was continually forming against her. Under all the circumstances, therefore, he could not help feeling that his prospects were now more gloomy than ever, and that he must either make one more bold effort at once, or else seek the only means that presented itself for securing his own safety, by immediate flight from the scene of danger. He was thus uneasily occupied in reviewing his own position, when a voice was heard calling him by name, and looking round he, to his great surprise, discovered that the intruder was no other than Jabez Thompson. His first impulse was to advance toward his acquaintance, but to his increased astonishment, the other retreated a pace or two, as if unwilling to be upon too familiar terms with him.

"How is this, Jabez?" he exclaimed, with smothered indignation. "Why do you avoid me, when, for aught I knew, we were as good friends as ever?"

"It may suit your purpose very well to keep me dangling at your heels like a well-bred dog," answered the other, sullenly; "but my patience is at length fairly worn out, and you and I are not likely to be friends again till you have paid me for all the trouble I had when you took up your quarters in Robin Hood's Cave."

"Humph! is that your only grievance?"

"Perhaps I might find more if I was to take the trouble to think for a moment," answered Jabez. "However, the one I've mentioned is quite enough for the present, and, what's more, you'll not be a free man another half hour unless I have the money you promised, or at least a very considerable part of it."

"Am I to understand, then, that you would be villain enough to give up an old friend for the sake of the reward that has been offered?"

"That's just exactly my meaning; so now, as there can no longer be any mistake between us, you'll perhaps cut this matter short by telling me what you intend to do?"

"Before I ask that question," exclaimed Caleb Kestrel fiercely. "I must know whether you are serious in what you have said."

"Serious! do you think this a joking matter, then?"

"Perhaps not, but I can hardly think it possible that you can mean to play the part of such an infernal scoundrel."

"Oh, as for that," exclaimed Jabez Thompson, "business is business all the world over, and if people are wanted to assist in your dirty work, you must make up your mind to pay 'em for it."

"And depend upon it you shall be paid for it," muttered the pedlar in a tone that could hardly be misunderstood. "I have a good memory for all things, whether they may be favours or injuries, and, take my word, you shall acknowledge that I am not unmindful of any vow that I may once have uttered."

"Come, come," exclaimed Jabez, "I've no time to waste over a trifling matter of this kind, so, in one word, let me know whether you are prepared to let me have the money you promised?"

"In one word then—No!"

"Very well," answered Jabez Thompson coolly, "then you know what to expect before you are many minutes older."

He turned round on saying this, and was about to take his departure, when Caleb Kestrel maddened by the thought of his danger, sprung forward, and seizing Jabez by the throat with one hand, applied the other with so much force that his antagonist was immediately laid sprawling upon the ground. Taken thus by surprise, the defeated man remained a few moments as if stupified, but at length recovering himself he was about to call loudly for assistance, when Caleb again clutching him by the throat, commanded him in a tremulous tone to remain quiet or take the consequences.

"Dog," he exclaimed, "if your life is of any value, utter not a sound or a cry, for you have a desperate man to deal with, and by the heaven above, you shall die if any body should come this way to your assistance."

"Are you going to murder me?" demanded Jabez Thompson, almost suffocating from the pressure on his throat.

"I want no man's blood to answer for," returned the other, "but I now know my own danger, and, before I release you, you must swear not to betray the place where I am to be found."

"I—I—do swear it!" gasped the almost choking wretch.

"That promise has saved your worthless life," exclaimed Caleb Kestrel, relaxing the deadly grasp with which he had held his antagonist to the ground. "For the present, Jabez Thompson, you have escaped death, but remember, your oath must not be trifled with, or the next time you and I meet together we shall not part upon quite such easy terms as at present."

"Oh, I shan't forget this interview of ours, depend upon it," returned the other, gloomily, "for it has made one impression upon me that will last out the remainder of my life if it was to go on for another fifty years to come. You and I shall be fast friends in future, I dare say, but mind—no more of these ugly squeezes, Master Kestrel, or our friendship may perhaps come to rather a sudden end."

"Take care, then, never to give me the same cause," exclaimed Kestrel, "for depend upon it, whenever I fancy myself in danger from the treachery of a pretended friend, I shall always take the readiest means that offer to relieve myself from it.   It was you that offered the provocation just now, or I should not have handled you quite so roughly as I did."

" Well, never mind saying anything more about that just now," returned Jabez, " for the thought of it may bring up unpleasant feelings, and in such cases as this, the least said is the soonest mended. So now tell me, what mischief are you next bent upon, that I find you prowling about the streets of York ?"

" Before I answer that question, I must know whether I may depend upon your future services and assistance."

" Aye, on condition that I am to be well paid for what I do."

" You shall."

" Then consider me from this moment at your service," exclaimed Thompson. " Egad! our meeting here was rather a rough affair, old chap, but we begin to understand one another rather better now, and so long as there is a chance of anything being made by it, you may depend upon finding me a faithful ally."

" But suppose you should take it into your head to grow impatient, before I can bring matters to a conclusion ?"

" Oh, you needn't be afraid about that," answered Jabez Thompson, " for I shall watch you as closely as a cat does a mouse, and shall very soon see whether matters are going on right or wrong. However, we'll not say anything more about that now, for we 've had one quarrel already to-night, and, as far as I am concerned, I don't want to get into another for one while to come ; so perhaps you'll now tell me what business has brought you to this city ?"

" I came here because the whole country has been roused by offers of reward for my apprehension."

" Humph !—rather a curious notion, I think, to seek for concealment in a busy populous place like this !"

" The truth is, I thought this the most likely place where I might remain in safety," answered Caleb Kestrel, " for who would even think of looking for me in a place that's thronged with people ?   Besides, to tell you the truth, Jabez, I made my way here because I fancied it was very likely I might meet with you, and that we would arrange some little plan to raise money, for I happen just now to be confoundedly short of the article that alone keeps one going."

" Did you come here alone ?"

" No."

" Who is with you ?"

" An old acquaintance,—one Dick Radcliffe."

" He's one of the right sort, I suppose ?"

" If he wasn't he would not have been received into my councils," answered the pedlar.   " I know him to be as staunch a fellow as ever lived, and if we have only a chance of doing any business, you'll find that he's just the sort of a chap for our line of life."

" And is he the only one that has followed you from the neighbourhood of Derwent Hall ?" asked Jabez.

" Not the only one that came away with me," answered Kestrel, " but the other left me on the road some miles off, and is to wait at the cave till I either go to meet him there or he receives a message to join me in some other part of the country."

" By the bye," exclaimed Jabez Thompson, " it would have been much more prudent if you had gone to the cave as well, for there you might have remained safe and snug till the pursuit was over, and when everything grew quiet it would have been easy to form some fresh plans for carrying off the girl that there's been so much talk about."

" Depend upon it the subject didn't escape my attention," answered the pedlar, " but I knew it would be some time before the search after me was over, and I felt no inclination to be shut up in a miserable cave, for nobody knows how long. So I came here, as I said before, to conceal myself in one of the out-of-the-way streets of York, where I might remain snug till an opportunity offers to ease some one of any superincumbent cash that he or she may have."

"Do you feel inclined to crack a crib?"

"Aye, that or anything else that will put a little money in my pocket, for to confess the truth, it is almost cleaned out. So, if you know of anything that will be worth while, I shall be ready to commence the business without delay."

"Well, then," replied Jabez in a whisper, "to tell you the truth, there's an old gentleman, not far from this city, that I have had a design against myself, and should have managed the affair before now, but that I found one was not enough to be in it."

THE MISER'S DEATH.

"Is the person you speak of rich?" asked the pedlar.

"People hereabouts say he is."

"But does he keep much money in his house?"

"Oh, yes—he's a bit of a miser, I believe, and hoards up lots of gold that he keeps in a strong box in his bedroom."

"Then it shall not be long before we ease him of it," exclaimed Caleb Kestrel "you, of course, will make one in the affair, and if I could only send word to George Layburne in time, I know he'd be glad enough to be another."

No. 32.

"What do we want with him?" demanded Jabez. "Three of us, I'm sure, will be quite enough for a job of that kind, and then there'll be the larger share of booty coming to you and me and Jack Radcliffe.

"That may be all very true," exclaimed the other, "but George may happen to hear of what we've been about, and if he should, I know enough of him to be quite certain that, in revenge, he would give information against us to the police."

"But we shall have no time to let him know, for if anything is to come of this, it must be done at once."

"When do you think of going to work, then?"

"Why, as no time is to be lost, I should say that we ought not to delay the matter beyond to-morrow night. Besides the old man's very ill—some say he is lying on his death-bed, and if he should happen to kick the bucket before we go, we may as well stay where we are, for those that come in for his property will be sure to remove it to a place of greater safety. So we have no time to lose, you see, and therefore the sooner we set to work the better."

"Does he keep many servants in the house?"

"Not he," exclaimed Jabez, "he's too fond of his money to do that, so there's no one about him but a housekeeper, and it may be a niece and nephew, that have lately come from some distance off to be present at the death-bed of their old miserly relative."

"Then we have not much resistance to expect?"

"So little, that we hardly need trouble ourselves to think of it," replied Jabez Thompson. "Indeed, I hardly know whether we need carry any arms with us, unless, indeed, it be as a matter of caution in case there should be more persons in the house than we expect. But that's the last thing we ought to look forward to, for the old man has always had a mortal dislike to having anybody in the place that might be supposed to be spunging on him, and as for the nephew and niece, they will not want a parcel of people hanging about 'em just when they expect to gammon the old gentleman into leaving them the whole of the money that he has been laying by for years past."

"Have you mentioned this affair to anybody else?"

"Not a soul."

"Then we have every reason to suppose that there's not the slightest chance of our intentions being discovered?"

"Who dare suspect anything that I have hardly thought of myself," asked Jabez, "but that perhaps I might never have attempted, if it had not been for our unexpected meeting to-night? All we have to do, then, is to make an appointment as to the time and place of meeting, and all the rest will be easily enough managed if we only keep our own counsel and act with caution."

"In the first place," said Caleb Kestrel, "I would ask if you know of a place where I and my comrade can have a snug lodging while we remain in this town?"

"That can be easily enough managed," exclaimed the other, "for I have a room large enough to accommodate us all, and you and Radcliffe can stop there as long as you like."

"Is it safe, think you?"

"If it wasn't safe it wouldn't do for me," answered Jabez Thompson, "for the police are no friends of mine, and, of course, I've gone to a place that they are not very likely to pay a visit to."

"But what are the people that keep the house?"

"They are pretty much the same as you and I," answered Jabez; "that is to say, they get their living on the cross, and are cunning enough to keep their affairs snug and quiet to themselves. So, in spite of the roughness of our first meeting to-night, it may after all turn out to be fortunate for all of us, since I was as much in want of money as yourself, and was only prevented mending my circumstances by the fact that I could not attempt to enter the old gentleman's house without having at least one or two other bold fellows to assist me."

"You say the house is not far off?" observed Caleb Kestrel.

"Not more than a mile from the city."

" Is the situation a lonely one?"

" Very; there's not another house within five or six hundred yards of it, and even if an alarm should be raised, we can easily enough get away with whatever booty we happen to find."

" What is the old man's name?"

" Stephen Archdale."

" And you are sure he keeps money in his house?"

" So people about this place report," answered Jabez; " and I believe a good many blame him for it, and even venture to prophesy that some time or another his house will be broken into by thieves, for the sake of the property that is said to be there. But hush!" he added, slouching his hat over his eyes to prevent a recognition; " some one is coming towards us, and we must be mum, or we may find all our fine plans brought to a finish sooner than we expected."

" Oh, never fear," answered the pedlar, looking round, " for it's only Dick Radcliffe, my old comrade, come back to me after looking through the town to see if he could find a lodging."

" Which I've not been able to do," exclaimed the other, as he heard the last words; " for somehow people here look suspiciously at me, as if they thought I was here only to do mischief."

" It don't matter, as it happens," answered Kestrel; " for while you have been gone I've met with an old acquaintance in the person of Jabez Thompson, who has just been putting me up to a move that will supply us with an article that we stand greatly in need of."

" You mean money, I suppose?"

" Exactly so."

" Where are we to get it from?"

" You shall know all about that when you get to my lodging," answered Jabez Thompson; " but for the present the less we say about our private affairs the better it will be for all of us. So now, gentlemen, follow me, and if the accommodation I can afford you is not of the best description, it will at any rate stand you in very good stead till you are able to provide yourselves with something better."

Taking a hint from the sign that was made to them by their newly-found friend, they followed him in silence through a number of streets, which were enveloped in a darkness that answered their purpose exceedingly well. Fortunately for themselves, they met no one from whom they had reason to apprehend danger, and at length reached an old dilapidated-looking building, in which they were informed was the lodging they were at present to occupy. From the street they ascended a flight of broken stairs, which led them to a dingy apartment, which was the home of their comrade, Jabez Thompson.

CHAPTER XXIX.

THE THREE CONFEDERATES ENJOY THEMSELVES OVER A MIDNIGHT CAROUSE.—THE PREPARATIONS OF THE SUCCEEDING DAY.—ARRIVAL AT THE APPOINTED PLACE. —THE CHAMBER OF DEATH.—A BOOTY SECURED, AND ESCAPE OF THE ROBBERS FROM THEIR PURSUERS.

THE first thing that Jabez Thompson did after conducting his guests into his barn-like looking room, was to trim the lamp and diffuse a more cheerful light throughout the apartment. This done, he seated his two friends at a table, and then, placing before them such refreshments as his cupboard afforded, bade them enjoy themselves after the long walk they had had. This hospitable invitation, as may be supposed, was cheerfully responded to by the pedlar and Dick Radcliffe, and as soon as the cravings of hunger were satisfied, a bottle of brandy and another of rum were set before them, as their host said, in order that they might drink success to the expedition in which they were to be engaged in on the following night. In short, both the guests seemed to feel themselves as much at home as ever they had been in their lives, and with every succeeding draught that they drank off they became more and more indifferent to any danger that they might incur whilst committing the meditated robbery. Dick Radcliffe in particular, was in high spirits when he had heard the whole plan explained, and declared that for such a scheme as that he would willingly run ten times more risk than they were likely to encounter.

" This is the very thing of all others that we most wanted!" he exclaimed, after drinking off another glass of spirits, " for our means were beginning to run most confoundedly low, and but for a little help of this kind, I don't know what the devil we should have done."

" Don't make too sure of anything till the whole affair has been brought to a conclusion," interposed Caleb Kestrel ; " for there's many a slip you know, old fellow, between the cup and the lip, and who can tell but what we may be routed in the midst of our business."

" Routed !" vociferated the other, who began to grow exceedingly valiant in proportion as he imbibed the potent liquor before him ; " and do you think if ever we get into the house we are going to be driven away like so many rank cowards ?"

" But suppose," asked Kestrel, " we should happen to be attacked by a superior number of the enemy?"

" In that case we must show 'em fight."

" What ! and get killed or made prisoners for our fool-hardiness !" retorted his comrade. " Now, I am as much against giving up a good chance as yourself or anybody else can be ; but when all hope is at an end, I'm one of those sort of people that like to take care of number one, even at the risk of being laughed at for a coward."

" D—me, Caleb," muttered Radcliffe," " I never heard you say anything like that before. But I suppose you only mean to act on the safe side now, and that, whenever there is danger, you'll creep out of it, and leave others to go through the difficult work. Well, of course, you'll do as you like about it; only remember this, if you desert us in this affair that's coming on, I shall do the same by you when next you want to carry Amy away from her friends."

Jabez Thompson saw that a quarrel must ensue unless he took precautions to prevent it, and having filled both their cups once more with liquor, he proposed as a toast—" Success to the project that is now under our consideration."

" Aye, aye, I'll drink that with all my heart," exclaimed Caleb Kestrel, draining off his liquor to the very last drop, " for I'm at least as much interested in the success as either that's here present, and perhaps rather more so, for if we should fail in it, I shall not be able to find either a home or a shelter to shield me from those infernal people that are hunting after me for the sake of the reward."

" In that case," observed Dick Radcliffe, " you must make up your mind to make a bold defence in the event of our being disturbed in the midst of the business we have to go through. Recollect, this old miser has most likely got by him plenty of the stuff that we want to relieve him of, and if, as is very likely to happen, he should take it into his head to offer resistance, we must not hesitate to put an end to it by sending a bullet through his head."

" There you are going too far a great deal, my good fellow," exclaimed Jabez Thompson, " for though I'm about as rough a chap as you'll find here and there, I never could endure the thought of taking a man's life merely because he might choose to defend his property against those that wanted to deprive him of it. Besides, murder is always punished by hanging, and I've a strange sort of dislike to mounting a scaffold for the mere form of what they call being made an example of for the good of society. So now you know my motive upon the subject, and I hope you'll make up your minds not to kill the old man unless there's no othe chance of saving our own lives."

"Oh, never fear about that, man," answered the pedlar, "for Dick, in spite of what he says, has as much objection to taking away life as either of us. To-night he has taken a drop too much, and says things that he would not have thought of at any other time, but to-morrow, when he gets sober, he'll be pretty much of the same opinion with you and me."

"Well, perhaps I may," he replied, "so let's say no more about it till we know better what we're talking of. And now, touching this old gentleman;—is it quite certain that he always keeps a large sum of gold in his house?"

"I can only tell you what I've heard a good many people say," answered Jabez Thompson, "and I think it's likely enough too, when we come to consider that misers generally like to keep their money by them for the sake of having the pleasure of looking at it, and counting it all over every time the fit seizes them."

"That may be all very true," observed Kestrel, "but the gentry you are speaking of are also apt to keep their hoards in strong iron boxes, and if that should be the case with this Mr. Stephen Archdale, there'll be more trouble to get at his treasure than we reckon on."

"Then we must bring box and all away."

"It's a good deal easier to talk than to act in this instance," replied Caleb, "for iron chests are weighty affairs, and I think all three of us would hardly be able to remove this one, especially if it should so happen that an alarm has been raised."

"Very well," exclaimed Dick Radcliffe, "then I supose it will not be very difficult to find the key of his strong box."

"Where are we to look for it?"

"Oh," cried Dick," if you are going to meet me with difficulties at every turn, I've done with the busines at once. Where are we to find the key, forsooth! Why where every careful chap like this Mr. Archdale always puts such things at night, to be sure—under his pillow, because it seems to be the safest place."

"Humph!" laughed Jabez Thompson, "you seem to be wide awake to these sort of things."

"That," replied Radcliffe, "is because this is not the first time I've been concerned in easing a miser of his money. I was once before in a job of the same kind, and in that case we found the key in the place I have named."

"And what became of the person you robbed?"

"Ah, we didn't do him much harm," answered Dick Radcliffe, "because we took care to prevent his raising an alarm by tying a sheet tightly over his mouth. So all we did was to carry off everything of value that we could lay our hands on, and he was left behind to weep and groan for the loss of what was more precious to him than life itself. However, that affair did me very little good, for one of our chaps turned out to be a precious rogue, and instead of dividing the money fairly and honourably amongst his comrades, he bolted off with the whole of the booty, and we never heard of him again till we read that he had safely landed in America."

"And afterwards," observed Jabez Thompson, "I suppose you were more shy about whom you trusted?"

"The truth is," he replied, "I grew so disgusted with the sort of life I had been leading that I gave it up and had serious thoughts of trying what honesty would do for me. But it was a bad speculation, that of mine, for every one seemed to know what sort of character I had been, and go where I would for work. not a soul would listen to me, and I was obliged to wander about almost starving."

"Is it possible," asked Dick Radcliffe with a sneer, "that you ever thought of working for a livelihood?"

"Perhaps the notion mightn't have entered my head," returned the other, "but when our companion ran away with all our money, I was left completely destitute, and there was no choice left between starvation and turning honest. It was a hard struggle, I confess, but at length I was driven to desperation, and in a moment of despair I thought of buying a broom and sweeping a crossing. But pride wouldn't allow me to do that either, and after trying everything else that I could thin of, I took a tour through the country, sometimes picking up such stray trifles as I might happen to meet with on the road-side, and at others, when driven by hunger, begging a few pence from the passengers I happened to meet."

"How long did that last?" inquired the pedlar.

"About a month."

"And what did you do afterwards?"

"Why I reached a place in the neighbourhood of Robin Hood's Cave, where I fell in with three or four chaps that I soon found out were smugglers. So, finding that they led a jolly sort of life, and thinking there was no great harm in helping to cheat the revenue, I agreed to join the band, and from that time to the present I have been a smuggler. And now, gentlemen, 1 believe I have given you a full, a true, and particular account of the principal events of my life."

"But how is it," asked Caleb Kestrel, "that, after having forsworn plunder, you are now so willing to lend a helping hand towards easing old Stephen Archdale of his money?"

"Why," he replid, "the truth of it is, that, after you had been hiding yourself in the cave, Mr. Capsicum, the magistrate, took it into his head that I had been the chief means of screening you from justice, and the constables in that part of the country were particularly desired to seek after and apprehend me with as little delay as possible. Fortunately I got wind of this, and not wishing for a lodging in the jail, I thought it best to show a clean pair of heels, and I wandered about from place to place till chance brought me to this city."

"Where you are as likely to be discovered as in any part of the country that you could have gone to."

"I know that Master Kestrel," he replied, "but what's the use of travelling about in a place where there's no chance of picking up a penny if it were to keep you from starving? In short, I found it a hard matter to keep life and soul together; so, having discovered that country places would not afford me even a dry crust of bread, I made my way to York, thinking it likely enough that I might meet with somebody or other that I knew, and that together we might arrange some plan for bettering my miserable condition."

"And strangely enough," exclaimed Dick Radcliffe, "you have met with two that are willing to join you in the very first plan that you have proposed to them. But remember, my boy, if any mischief should come of this, we are not to be blamed, because the first proposal about the robbery was made by you."

"I know all about that," he replied' "yet how was I to help myself, when I saw hunger and starvation staring me in the face?"

"Hunger and starvation!" exclaimed Caleb Kestrel; "how can that be, when we have just seen such a store of good cheer upon your table?"

"Why," he replied, "the plain truth of it is this—though I'm almost ashamed to acknowledge myself guilty of such paltry actions, I have given myself up to small pilferings lately; fogle-hunting, in particular, I have found rather profitable, having been able through it to provide myself with pleny of everything to eat and drink, besides paying for the lodging you find me in. However, I am anxious to get out of this low way, and for that reason have proposed that we do something that will be better worth our while. Now this affair to-morrow night may bring us in three or four hundred pounds, and if so I shall go somewhere abroad, till the inquiries concerning me are not quite so pressing."

"Don't you think of going back to the coast?" asked the pedlar.

"That's a matter that I have hardly yet decided on," answered Jabez Thompson. "but if you are going there for any particular purpose of your own, it's likely enough I may accompany you. In plain words, Master Caleb Kestrel, for you don't seem to understand me—if you want my assistance there, and have a mind to pay me for it, you'll always find me ready at your beck and call."

"Perhaps I may want you there," answered the pedlar, "but a good deal will depend upon how this affair of ours goes on to-morrow night. If by chance it puts a good round sum of money into my pocket, I shall not care about troubling Squire Derwent for any just at present, but shall go away to some place where I am not likely to be heard of, and when it seems that I am pretty well forgotten by those that I now stand in some fear of, I can return, play off the old game, and if money be not forthcoming from the squire, I'll carry Amy away from him to some place where neither his cunning nor all the rewards that he can offer, shall ever be able to discover her. But enough of this for the present, so, if you have a place that we can lie down upon, we'll rest ourselves for the remainder of the night, and to-morrow we'll see what's to be done about the miser and the chest of treasured gold that you speak of."

Jabez Thompson now bestired himself to make up what accommodation he could for his two guests, and after a great deal of contrivance he managed to make up a kind of an apology for a bed, consisting of a heterogeneous collection of wearing apparel and other matter that happened to come to hand. Luckly, his friends were not at all disposed to grumble at the efforts he had made in their behalf, and after the bottles had been completely emptied of their contents, they threw themselves down, and shortly afterwards a very loud snoring announced that they were all revelling in the mystic regions of slumber.

Being very late when they retired to bed, the sleepers were not at all inclined to rise even at mid-day, and in truth it was not till nearly seven o'clock in the evening that they were once more assembled round the table to partake of such fare as the hospitality, or rather the means, of Jabez Thompson afforded. The meat, in fact, though tolerably abundant, was not of a very choice description, a circumstance that the host deeply regretted, and apologized for, though there was little occasion for it.

"You see, my boys, how it is," he exclaimed, "my cupboard is beginning to wear rather a shabby appearance, and I'm reminded that it's high time for me to be doing something to replenish it. Let us hope for good luck to-night, and to-morrow, wherever we may chance to be, we'll enjoy ourselves handsomely upon a part of the money that old Stephen Archdale has been at so much trouble to scrape together."

"What's the use of making a parcel of rubbishing excuses about what you've put before us?" demanded Dick Radcliffe. "There's nothing here that I can see to find fault with, for there's enough, and more than enough, to fill our bellies, and if the grub ain't of the very choicest description, we can be satisfied with it for the present, and when fortune favours us, why we'll sit down and enjoy ourselves over something better."

"Aye, aye, we shall do well enough as it is." exclaimed Caleb Kestrel, "so now tell us, old fellow, what time do you think of starting upon this expedition of ours?"

"Whenever you like. Directly, if you please."

"How far off do you say the place is?"

"About a mile when we get beyond the city walls."

"Then we shall be too soon if we start now."

"Not if we loiter a little as we pass through the street's, answered Jabez; "and perhaps it may be as well if we do so, for some of the chaps hereabouts are rather apt to watch me about whenever I make my appearance out of doors, and it will be necessary to lead 'em a bit of a dance from place to place, lest anybody should happen to follow us to a certain spot where it wouldn't be very pleasant for us to be discovered."

"You know better than I do whether they are likely to act the spy upon us," exclaimed Dick Radcliffe, "but if I catch any of 'em at it, it shall be the last time they ever do anything of this kind."

"Come, come, old fellow," cried Jabez, "you are getting a little too warm again, I find. You must go steadily to work in this affair of ours, or the game will be lost through your folly. So keep yourself steady, will you? and I dare say the prize we are looking after will be ours."

Both Dick Radcliffe and the pedlar promised to be guided strictly by the advice of their friend, and shortly afterwards all three of them left the house, and proceeded slowly, and with apparent indifference, through the streets of York. People seemed to regard them with looks of suspicion, but that might all be fancy, at least so thought the three comrades, and onward they proceeded, taking, to all appearance, very little heed of those who thought it worth their while to watch them about from place to place. At length, however, everything seemed to be clear for them, as no one was seen that could be suspected of looking after them, and taking that opportunity, they hurried out of the city, and soon found themselves in a dark lonely road, that Jabez Thompson signified led towards the large, though mean looking mansion of Stephen Archdale, the miser. A walk of about twenty minutes served to bring them to the place they were in quest of, and having passed through a pair of lofty iron gates that were dropping from their rusty hinges, the three comrades stood watching and listening to discover whether anybody was still up in the house. All, however, was perfectly silent, and the only sign of the place being inhabited was a solitary light that shone through a window immediately above the spot where they were standing.

"That," whispered Jabez, pointing up to the light, " is where the old gentleman sleeps. No doubt he's in bed and snoring by this time ; if you are both ready, I don't see why we should wait many more minutes in loitering about and doing nothing ?"

"But do you think the other people in the house are up ?"

"Do you mean the nephew and the niece ?"

"Yes."

" Well then," replied Jabez, "I neither know nor care anything about them, for when once we get into the house we have very little reason to be afraid of any rumpus they may kick up to bring assistance to the house. If nothing else will do we must gag them, as I suppose we shall be obliged to do with the old gentleman, for if he should wake, and find us helping ourselves to his precious gold, there'll be such a clatter in the place that we should have but a poor chance of getting clear off."

" He had better mind what he's about, though," muttered Dick Radcliffe, " for if I see any danger of being taken, I shall not stand for repairs, but send a leaden bullet through his brain just by way of putting a stopper on his voice."

" Which will also put a stopper upon us, if you don't mind what you're about." returned Jabez, " for if once we get into the hands of the officers of justice, the only chance we shall have will be——"

" What's the use of looking at the worst that may happen to us," exclaimed Caleb Kestrel, interrupting him, " all we've to do is to mind that everything is done properly, and then we shall leave the house a great deal richer than we entered it. So now, Jabez, show us how we are to get in, for there's not a moment to lose, or some of the people within may chance to find out that they have got some queer customers lurking about the premises.'

Jabez, acting upon this suggestion, led them round to another part of the mansion, where some lattice work over one of the side doors offered a ready means of climbing up to a window above, that, by some accident or carelessness, happened to be left open. Having cautioned his comrades in a whisper to be as silent as possible, he was the first to ascend, and no sooner had he effected a safe entrance, than the others, in turn, followed the example he had set them. Being all now within the house, they stood for awhile to listen in breathless silence, and finding that there was no sound to indicate that anybody was awake, they took off their shoes and glided with noiseless steps along a passage towards a room from whence a dim light was shining. The door stood open, and as the ruffians entered they beheld a sight that, hardened as they were in crime, appalled them, from the unexpected nature of the scene that was presented to their view. Upon the bed lay stretched in death the venerable form of the old man they had come to plunder, whilst over him, with clasped hands and a countenance expressive of the most intense grief, stood a young man, in whom they recognized the nephew of the deceased miser. So wrapt was he in the melancholy thoughts that occupied his mind at the moment, that he heard no sound to warn him of approaching danger. For some minutes, during which the robbers concealed themselves behind a quantity of timber that stood in one corner of the room, the young man remained in the same stupified attitude of grief, and it was not till a flood of tears at length came to his relief that he recovered sufficiently to be aware of the weakness that had overtaken him. Then, taking the shrivelled hand of the old man in his own, he pressed it to his lips, and with a convulsive sob hurried from the room towards his own chamber. During all this time the robbers had been watching him from their place of concealment, and it was not for some few minutes after they had heard

THE RECOGNITION OF KALEB KESTREL.

the door of his apartment close behind him, that they ventured to creep from their lurking place towards the bed on which lay all that remained of the once wealthy miser. They were not, however, to be intimidated from their object by the sight of death, nor by the coffin at the bed side over which they had nearly stumbled, for all of them were silent upon discovering the strong box of which they were in search, and which they soon afterwards found beneath the bedstead which contained the lifeless clay, the sight of which had first filled them with so much dismay. This coffin, though of great weight, was by their united efforts dragged forth slowly and without noise; but the next difficulty that presented itself was

No. 33.

how to open it, for the lock was an extremely massive one, and by its appearance set at defiance all the attempts that might be made to force it open. In this emergency, Caleb Kestrel proceeded to the bed, raised the pillow upon which rested the head of the dead man, and drew forth in triumph the key, which had been deposited there for safety. The task they now had to perform was a comparatively easy one ; the lock immediately yielded, and the lid of the coffin being raised, the robbers gazed with infinite delight and satisfaction upon the glittering treasure that was presented to their view. To help themselves to as much gold as each of them could conveniently carry was the work of a very few minutes, and having thus burdened themselves, they closed the lid, returned the chest to its former place beneath the bed, and then, once more gliding from the room, they were making their way along the passage, when Edward Archdale, the young man whom they had just before seen, rushed out of his chamber and pursued them, at the same time uttering loud cries for assistance. In a moment he was felled to the ground by a heavy blow, and the robbers were again making their way towards the window by which they had entered, when other cries met their ears, and they perceived Marian Archdale, the miser's niece, running from them with frantic exclamations, that threatened them with the most imminent danger, unless the greatest haste was made to escape whilst there was yet an opportunity. In this emergency, therefore, not a moment was lost ; the three men made all possible haste to leave the house, and it was not till they had reached the lodging of Jabez Thompson, that any of them either relaxed their speed, or attempted to give utterance to a word. To all appearance they had not been watched, as they made their hasty progress through the city, but they were far from feeling quite easy upon that point, and they sat for some time looking from the windows, to see if any persons were about, who appeared to be looking for them.

" I rather think it's all right enough," at length whispered Jabez Thompson, " for not a soul, except the watchman have I seen in the street, and if one may judge from his manner, he has nothing more than his usual duty to look after to-night."

" Perhaps so," returned Kestrel, " but we have others as well as him to expect danger from, and I shan't consider myself quite safe till I'm far away from this infernal neighbourhood."

" Who is there that can swear we had any hand in the robbery ?" demanded Dick Radcliffe, gloomily.

" There's no saying how things come out," exclaimed Jabez ; " and as for witnesses against us, there's both the nephew and the niece of old Archdale, that saw us in the house, and it may happen that they'll be awkward customers, if we have to deal with 'em before a judge and jury."

" Psha !" retorted Radcliffe, " they scarcely saw us for an instant, and there was not light enough for 'em to swear to any of us."

" It's all very well to make yourself comfortable upon a notion of that kind," exclaimed the pedlar, " but this is not the first time that I have found myself in a dilemma, and it has always appeared to me to be much easier to get into, than to get out of one."

" Then I suppose, if the truth was known, you want to get away from this place as soon as possible."

" I do ; but it would be madness to make the attempt till we know what sort of a stir will be made about this robbery, and that, I suppose, we shall hear of to-morrow, if any of us like to venture out and make the inquiry."

" In the first place, let's put our money into this hole, that I discovered a day or two ago under the hearthstone," said Jabez. " It will be out of sight there, in case any one should come to make inquiries, and, of course, if any questions are put, none of us will know anything about a burglary being committed at the miser's house."

After a little more conversation, as to their present and future prospects, the three men threw themselves upon the rough beds that had been prepared for them, and in a short time were dreaming of the adventure in which they had been engaged.

CHAPTER XXX.

AN INTERVAL OF DOUBTS AND FEARS.—NEW PROJECTS AGAINST AMY.—PLANS ARRANGED.—CALEB KESTREL VENTURES OUT IN DISGUISE.—AN UNEXPECTED MEETING, AND THE RECOGNITION.—A HASTY RETREAT.

NEARLY a week passed away, and the three robbers kept close within their place of concealment, Jabez alone venturing out, and that, not till after dark, to fetch such provisions as were necessary for their most pressing wants. This, however, began to become exceedingly irksome at length, and Caleb, who was more uneasy under restraint than any of them, proposed that they should now think of removing to some other place, where they might have greater freedom than they had at present. They were, besides, in momentary apprehension of being discovered and dragged away to a prison, which they would have no chance of leaving except to be sent abroad for the remainder of their lives as convicts.

"I'll tell you what, my lads," exclaimed the pedlar, suddenly rousing himself from the unpleasant rumination into which he had fallen, "this sneaking way of hiding ourselves don't suit me at all, so, be the consequence what it may, I shall leave this place and boldly face the danger, if, indeed, there is any."

"Ah!" returned Jabez, "I can guess very well how it is—you are not satisfied with the money we have already got, but must needs worry that poor girl again for the sake of what you may be able to extort from her or her friends."

"And what is it to you if I have such a notion?" demanded Caleb sullenly, "I know my own affairs best ; and if anything is to be got by making another attempt, I surely have a right to do so if I don't ask for your assistance."

"But you are not going to get rid of me quite so easily as that," returned Jabez Thompson, "for I've engaged to lend you a helping hand, and shall not give up my opportunity whilst there's a fair prospect of gaining money by it."

"Nor I," added Dick Radcliffe, "for as I've so often been in the case before, I don't see why I should be left out just when there's a chance of something handsome being made by it. So now, Caleb, let's hear what new notion you've got in your head."

"There's nothing particularly new about it," he replied, "for it's the old story over again; I want to get money from 'Squire Derwent, and if he still remains obstinate, why I'll deprive him of the girl, even though in the end I take her life."

"What!" exclaimed Radcliffe, "have you at last made up your mind to kill Amy ?"

"That will depend upon circumstances," answered the pedlar, "but you may be sure I shall not have recourse to that till every other attempt has proved a failure. I have, however, another project in view that I think may be successful, since we have now a confederate in the service of 'Squire Derwent, and I think we may depend upon her being faithful to her promise."

"You mean the servant girl, Annette, I suppose ?"

"Yes! we have once found her true to her word, and I don't mind trusting her again if she gives a promise to lend us her assistance."

"What do you want her to do ?"

"Pretty much as she did on the former occasion."

"Aye," returned Dick Radcliffe, "she then gave her a sleeping draught ; but I suppose the medicine was not quite strong enough, for Amy woke before we had time to carry her off."

"True," answered Caleb, "but this time I'll take care that the draught shall have its intended effect, for I shall go to a chemist's in this town and purchase it myself."

"Do you know what to ask for ?"

"I do ;—but why do you ask that question ?"

"Because a mistake would be very awkward if it should happen to be powerful enough to kill the girl, instead of only sending her to sleep for a few hours. Unpleasant inquiries would be sure to follow; and if it should be suspected that we had any hand in the affair, we should be sent to the gallows, instead of living to enjoy the money we divided after the affair at the miser's."

"You needn't be under any fear of that kind," answered the pedlar, "for I well know the nature of the medicine I am going to use, and can undertake to say that no worse effects will follow from its use than that of making Amy sleep a few hours longer than she would otherwise have done."

"Well," exclaimed Jabez Thompson, "and when all that has been accomplished, what is to be done with the girl?"

"She must be taken away, if possible, and if we succeed in doing that, the squire shall never see her again till he has given me, in full, the money I have demanded of him."

"And when are you going to get the sleeping-draught?"

"This very morning, if I can."

"What is there to hinder you, then?"

"Nothing more than that it would be madness for me to show myself in the streets till I have disguised myself to prevent every chance of being recognised as one of the men that carried off the gold from the house of old Stephen Archdale. There's a chance that we may have been seen on our return home, and if so, I might be taken into custody when least I suspected such a thing."

"What sort of a disguise do you want?" asked Jabez.

"Nothing more than a cloak, a different sort of hat to the one I've been used to wear, and a pair of riding-boots instead of those I have now got on. These, in addition to a trifling alteration in the method of disposing my hair, will make so great a difference that I might meet even my most intimate friend without much fear of being recognised."

"And how are you to be supplied with these various articles that you have mentioned?" asked Jabez.

"Through your means, if you will undertake the task," replied the pedlar, as he took a bag from his pocket and selected a piece of gold from amongst that which had once formed part of the hoard belonging to Stephen Archdale. "This will provide all I require at present; and if you will favour me by purchasing the articles, I may perhaps return the compliment some other time."

Jabez Thompson, who was a tolerably good tempered fellow at bottom, readily undertook the commission that had been imposed upon him; and having once more gone over the different articles he had to purchase, he left the place under a promise that he would not be gone any very great time. For the next ensuing quarter of an hour neither the pedlar nor Dick Radcliffe uttered a word to each other; but at length the latter, growing tired of so long a silence, ventured to inquire when it was likely they would leave their present gloomy quarters.

"That will depend upon circumstances," was the brief reply.

"And which way are we to direct our footsteps when we do make a move of it?" asked the persevering Dick Radcliffe.

"I'm not quite certain about that."

"Oh,—you haven't made up your mind, then?"

"Why there's not much to take into consideration," answered Caleb Kestrel, "but I suppose we can't do better than make our way back towards Derwent Hall;—taking care as we go along to ask, wherever we are not known, whether the search after us is at an end yet."

"D——n it!" exclaimed Dick, with surprise, "you surely wont be so foolhardy as to do that?"

"How else," he asked, "are we to know whether there's much danger in venturing to return to the hall?"

"By waiting till the news reaches us, as it will, if we have only patience to wait for it a little," answered Radcliffe.

"I don't know how you may feel inclined that way," exclaimed Caleb

Kestrel, " but hang me if I could make up my mind to stay another week in this place, if I was to be ever so well paid for it. So I shall make a move of it without delay, and as for you and Jabez Thompson, you can either follow me or remain behind, which ever you may feel most inclined for."

" You'll not catch me staying here, I can tell you," returned Dick ; " so, if you make up your mind to return to Derwent Hall, I shall go back to Robin Hood's Cave, and tell your friend Layburne, that it's of no use for him to waste his time by waiting for you there any longer."

" Layburne!" exclaimed the pedlar, as if suddenly recollecting himself ; " hang me if I hadn't forgot all about his being there with an understanding that I was to follow as soon as we had ascertained in York whether the pursuit after us was going on as briskly as ever."

" And now that your memory has been refreshed, I suppose you'll go to the cave and keep your word with him ?"

" I think I shall, Dick."

" And being there, don't you think it would be better to remain till everything appears to be safe ?"

" That will depend upon what we hear from George Layburne," answered the pedlar.

" What the devil can he know about it ?"

" Why I should suppose he is in the way of getting the earliest information of what's going on," answered Caleb Kestrel ; " for the smugglers have always got people on the look-out for 'em in the case of any unlooked-for danger, and they would be sure to hear it, if there was any chance of our being traced out by those infernal bloodhounds of the law. However, be that as it may, I'm glad you put me in mind of Layburne, for I don't know that we can do better than go and hide with him in the cave."

" I suppose there's no doubt that the smugglers will do the thing towards us that's fair and honourable ?"

" We have never found them act otherwise when I was at the cave before," answered Caleb Kestrel, " and yet there was then a reward offered for my apprehension just the same as now."

" Perhaps you promised to pay 'em something handsome when you got the money you expected from 'Squire Derwent ?"

" No," he replied, " the only man I bribed was Jabez Thompson, and, to do him justice, it must be confessed that he kept faith with me uncommonly well."

" And yet the poor devil has not yet received so much as a sixpence from you, up to this time !"

" There was no help for that," answered Kestrel, " for I have not yet been able to bring 'Squire Derwent to a reckoning, and of course what Jabez was to receive was to come out of the money that I was in hopes of getting as a bribe not to molest Amy any more. However, be that as it may, Jabez has not much to grumble about, for he was cunning enough to make a bargain with the 'squire, and received half the money down upon the nail, though he knew he never intended to be base enough to betray me—his best friend—into the hands of my enemies."

The other was about to enquire with a sneer how far Jabez was indebted to him for his friendship, when the person of whom they were speaking entered the room with the various articles which he had been commisioned to purchase. These were duly displayed before the pedlar, with many expressions of admiration at the excellence of the things he had brought, and a great many observations upon the extreme difficulties he had to encounter before he could succeed in meeting with the goods which he had been sent out to procure. To all this, however, Caleb Kestrel uttered not a word of reply, but contented himself with trying them on to see how far they would answer the purpose they were intended for. As good luck would have it, everything gave the greatest satisfaction, and even Caleb himself acknowledged that his disguise was as perfect as he could have expected. Dick Radcliffe, however, who seldom thought proper to agree in opinion with any one, chose to say that the disguise was so shallow that any person, who had ever seen him before, and who had a grain of penetration, must easily recog-nize him as the person for whose apprehension a large reward had been offered. Kestrel, however, paid no heed to this, and having in'ormed his companion that he should be back again in a short time, he set out to procure the opiate that he believed was to crown his efforts with success. Having reached the streets, he wandered about the town for some time, scarcely conscious of the purpose which had brought him out. His mind, indeed, was occupied with the various speculations that were continually floating through his mind, and it was not till the glaring colours of various hue that issued from a window hard by, startled him from his reverie, that he remembered the errand upon which he had come out. He paused for a moment to see if anybody was in the shop, and having ascertained that the place was not occupied by any one, he entered, to make the small purchase that he believed was to be of so much importance to him. No shopman being present, he knocked upon the counter, to give notice of the pre-sence of a customer ; still, however, no one came, and he was about to leave the shop, when a door that communicated with the surgery was thrown open. and a young lady and gentleman, who appeared to be some friends taking their departure, came forth, and were about to make their way through the shop, when both of them starting back, with an exclamation of horror, denounced him as being one of the robbers who had stolen the gold from the room of their dead uncle, Stephen Archdale ! Strange as it may appear, though the recognition was mutual, Caleb Kestrel maintained the utmost coolness and composure, in the midst of the peril with which he had been so unexpectedly menaced. It is true he had first of all ascertained that not a soul besides themselves were present, and being thus assured that a chance of escape yet remained, he threw aside his cloak to show them that he was armed, and then as quickly wrapping it round him again, exclaimed in a calm, deliberate tone—

"It seems you both fancy you know me, but as I am not equally anxious to claim an acquaintance, you will perhaps take the hint, when I declare that the first person who approaches to lay a hand upon me, will perish for his fool hardi-ness. Who you take me for, I am not aware, nor do I desire to know, since this is the first, and will probably be the last time of our meeting."

"Have you the affrontery to deny," said Edward Archdale, "that you are one of the villains I and my sister saw, some nights ago, escaping from my uncle's house with the booty you had just taken from the box in which it had been deposited?"

"It is well for you, young man," answered Caleb Kestrel, "that a female is present to protect you from my wrath, for, had it not been for that circumstance, I should not have failed to punish as it deserves the insolence you have been guilty of towards me."

"'Tis well to carry it off with this unblushing assurance," exclaimed Maria Archdale, "but I myself had a clear and distinct view of you on the night of the robbery, and I can swear with a safe conscience that you are one of the three men who broke into our uncle's house, and robbed him of his money."

"So you may persist in saying," replied Caleb, "but my word will be taken as soon as either of yours, and if need be, I can prove by two respectable witnesses that I did not arrive in this town till after the robbery you are speaking of."

"Oh," exclaimed Edward, "it seems, then, that you have heard that a burglary has taken place?"

"I must have been deaf, otherwise," he replied, "for the people hereabouts seem to have nothing else to talk about."

"That," answered the young man, "is in consequence of the peculiar atrocity that marks the case. My uncle was lying dead upon his bed when the robbers entered the room, and yet, undeterred by the appalling spectacle before them, they committed their pillage even in the presence of the dead."

"And what have I to do with all that?" demanded Kestrel.

"I still believe you to have been one of the men that I saw on the night of the robbery," answered the young man. "Your features are exactly similar, and in the assured conviction that I am right, you shall not be suffered to go at large again till my accusation has been laid before a magistrate."

"Have a care of what you are doing, young fellow," exclaimed Caleb Kestrel, his voice trembling with passion that he could no longer subdue, "for though innocent of such crimes as you would lay to my charge, I have passions that are not easily controlled. Nay, if you advance towards me to fulfil your threat, or raise an alarm to bring assistance, the young lady there will be the first object upon whom my vengeance falls."

"Villain!" ejaculated Edward, "would you be base enough to take the life of a helpless female?"

"When a man sees himself menaced with danger," answered the pedlar, "he is not very particular as to the method he takes to extricate himself from it. You have threated me, and I in return have threatened the young lady, which you will find something more than an empty vaunt if you proceed to the foolish extremities you speak of."

"Had you been as innocent of the robbery as you would make me believe," exclaimed Edward Archdale, "you would not have refused to accompany me before a magistrate, who would have inquired into all the facts of the case, and discharged you, had my proofs been deemed insufficient."

"And why should I submit to a disgrace, when it is in my own power to prevent it?" demanded Caleb Kestrel. "I have a character as well as yourself to lose, and, were it once doubted, I might never again be able to hold up my head in society."

"This pretended sensitiveness will not deceive me," returned Edward, "for in spite of your stubborn denial of the fact, I am still convinced that you were among the villains on the night when our house was entered and robbed. You curl your lips in disdain when I repeat the accusation, but I still maintain it, and yet you dare not face it out before a magistrate, though I have challenged you to the trial."

"Take care I don't challenge you in another way," muttered Caleb Kestrel. "You have done all you could to urge me to commit an act of violence, and if I have forborne so long, you have only to thank this young lady, who I would not terrify by any outrageous conduct of my own, so long as there is a possibility of avoiding it."

"And yet," exclaimed Edward Archdale, "in spite of your boasted gallantry, you just now threatened to shoot her if I made any attempt either to capture you or to cause others to do so. But I see well enough that I am not mistaken in the first impression I arrived at respecting you, and though, for my fair young friend's sake, I may now suffer you to depart, I shall keep a look out for you, and it may be that before many hours are over, I shall have succeeded in placing you in such a situation that you cannot so easily elude me as on the present occasion."

Caleb Kestrel smiled scornfully as young Archdale uttered these words, and then turning away without designing to speak another syllable, he left the young people full of amazement. From an interview so full of danger to himself, the pedlar returned to the lodging of Jabez Thompson, where he found his two friends anxiously waiting for his return, and giving way to the most gloomy anticipations in consequence of his having been longer absent than had been expected.

"Well," exclaimed Dick Radcliffe, "you've come back at last it seems, Caleb, and I'm glad to see that no evil has happened to you, for both Jabez and I began to fancy that some mischief had befallen you, on account of your being away so much longer than you expected."

"And you were pretty near right in your notion," answered Kestrel, seating himself upon a log of wood, which was made to perform the uses of a chair. "Egad! I have met with an awkward adventure, and should never have been suffered to return to my friends if it had not been that I had assurance enough to brazen out the affair by threatening those that had me completely in their power."

"Have you been recognized?" asked Jabez.

"Aye, that I have; and by people, too, that owe me neither favour nor affection," returned the pedlar.

"Who were they?"

"The nephew and niece of old Stephen Archdale, the miser."

"That's awkward, indeed," exclaimed Radcliffe; but where was it that you happened to meet with them?"

"In the chemist's shop."

"And are you quite certain they knew you?

"So much so," he replied, "that they boldly charged me with being one of the men that broke into their uncle's house."

"How was it, then," demanded Jabez Thompson, "that they didn't ca l for assistance, and have you secured?"

"Because I took care to frighten them both by showing the weapon I was armed with," replied the pedlar, "and even the young gentleman seemed inclined to do me all the mischief that he could, till I plainly told him that if he attempted to betray me, either by word or sign, I would take the life of the young female that was with him."

"Which, I suppose, had the effect of keeping him quiet?"

"Yes," answered Caleb Kestrel, "it saved me, I believe; but if the threat had been merely against his own life, I rather think the young fellow would have been fool-hardy enough to risk putting me to the proof."

"This is bad news, indeed," exclaimd Dick Radcliffe, who seemed to be greatly disconcerted by what he had heard; "these people will be sure to make a great talking about the wonderful discovery they have made, and perhaps already the police officers are searching for us through all parts of the city."

"It won't be long before they are hunting for us, I dare say," exclaimed Caleb; and I have therefore made up my mind, as I came along, to leave York and find some better place of concealment. You, I suppose, will both go with me, but remember, there's no time to be lost if we mean to distance our pursuers."

"I, for one, am ready to start whenever you like," said Jabez.

"And so am I for another," exclaimed Radcliffe," so now, first of all to take care of our gold, and then to leave this gloomy looking den that no longer offers us a safe asylum."

The hearthstone was then raised, and the three men having each secured his hidden treasure, expressed themselves quite ready to go forth in quest of some other place of shelter. Before starting, however, Jabez inquired of the pedlar, who generally took upon himself the office of leadership, where he thought of directing his flight.

"To Robin Hood's Cave, of course," answered Caleb, "there we shall find Layburne waiting for us, and if he reports favourably of the place, we may remain there till some new scheme can be thought of for taking Amy away from her newly found home."

"Ah!" exclaimed Dick Radcliffe, "you are still harping on that girl, though she has already cost you so much trouble, and is likely to get you into a great deal more if you don't give up this foolish notion of yours."

"So you have told me before," answered the pedlar, "but this is my own affair, and I'm not to be turned from it by the croaking of a coward that fancies there's danger in every step he takes. Are you so blind as not to see that money is to be made by the little risk we run, and are we to throw away a chance like this, when there's almost every certainty of succeeding if we go, cautiously to work?"

"Ain't you satisfied with the money we got from old Archdale?"

"No," he replied, "that won't last us very long, and when it's gone we shall neither find friends nor shelter."

"But we can find others to supply our wants as well as the miser."

"And ain't there as much danger in that as there would be in trying to make Squire Derwent give me the money I have demanded from him?" asked the pedlar. "In the one case we should only get a paltry sum, that would'nt last us a month, and in the other we may get enough to keep us all like gentlemen for the rest of our lives. So don't talk to me any more about giving up my schemes against Amy, for if you don't choose to lend me a helping hand, say so at once, and I'll soon find othersthat will not be quite such chicken-hearted fellows."

" Ah, as for that," exclaimed Dick Radcliffe, " we have both of us, perhaps, got as much courage as you have, but don't boast so much about it. We are no more afraid of facing danger than you are, Kestrel, and not feeling inclined to lose our

share of the money, after running so many risks with you, we shall both of us follow your example, and take our chance, whatever it may be."

"Then go with me now," returned Caleb, "for the darkness of the night favours us, and if Fortune don't desert us just when her favours are most needed, we shall get out of the town without meeting with any interruption."

Silently the three desperadoes descended the stairs, and having reached the, street, which they found nearly deserted, they hurried along with all speed to the further limit of the city. Here they found the road which it was their present

No. 34.

objeet to take, and having listened for a few moments to ascertain whether all was safe, they set forward on their journey in the expectation of reaching Robin Hood's Cave on the followiog evening.''

CHAPTER XXXI.

MR. CAPSICUM IS ONCE MORE ON THE ALERT.—THE ARRIVAL OF AN UNEXPECTED VISITOR.—AN EXPLORING EXCURSION PROPOSED.—THE SMUGGLERS' HOUSE OF CALL.—TOM HAZLE AND THE HOST PROVE TOO CUNNING TO DIVULGE ANY SECRETS, AND THE MAGISTRATE AND HIS FRIEND RETIRE FROM THE FIELD SOMEWHAT DISCONTENTED.

As the subject which once occupied no inconsiderable share of his attention was no longer spoken of in his neighbourhood, Mr. Capsicum had almost forgot that there was such a person in the world as Caleb Kestrel, and he was consequently not a little surprised one morning, on opening a letter which had just reached him by post, to learn that the pedlar was still prosecuting his evil designs against Amy, but that having been thwarted in a recent attempt, he had again been compelled to make his escape, and was supposed to be on his way to his former retreat, Robin Hood's Cave. The magistrate read the letter over a second time, to be certain that he understood every part of it, and then interrupting his clerk, who was busily occupied in writing, he exclaimed rather testily—

" Mr. Jones, how is it, sir, that you have not acquainted me before now that that scoundrel Kestrel is lurking hereabouts again ?"

" Indeed, your worship, this is the first intimation I have received of it," replied Mr. Jones, laying down his pen, and looking as much surprised as his employer. " No one, I can assure you, has whispered such a thing, or I should have thought it my duty to mention it immediately."

" Well, it's pretty certain he's here then," exclaimed the old gentleman, "for I have just received intelligence of the fact from Mr. Derwent, who has succeeded in tracing him as far as York, from whence he is supposed to have hastily retreated after having been concerned in a desperate burglary and robbery."

" Let us hope, then, the villain will soon be taken, sir, replied his clerk, " though, if I may say so without offence, Mr. Derwent seems to have no authority for supposing he has come to this part of the country."

" Where is he so likely to have gone ?" demanded Mr. Capsicum. " Isn't this place unfortunately swarming with a parcel of villanous smugglers, who would readily enough give him shelter in some of their secret caves, if they could only prevent his falling into the hands of the law ? In a word, he has already successfully eluded search in this neighbourhood, and it is therefore the place of all others that he would most likely come to if he should ever find himself hard pressed against by those that are in pursuit of him."

" Perhaps, sir," observed Mr. Jones, venturing a little flattery, "he may not come here after all, for he knows there is an acute active magistrate in this district, and I should imagine that he would rather seek any other place than this."

" Aye, aye, sir," replied Mr. Capsicum, "there's a good deal of sound sense in that observation of yours, but for all that, it behoves us to be on the alert when there is only a bare suspicion that such a scoundrel may be lurking near us, and I shall therefore give orders for a very strict watch to be kept, so that if he should venture to show himself abroad he may be immediately taken and brought before me, to the end that I may deal with him according to the law.''

" If he is here, sir," returned the clerk, " I should think there can be very little doubt of his being taken, for a large reward has been offered for his apprehension, and that will make people vigilant in the discharge of their duty, if anything will."

"And if they should be lucky enough to take him," exclaimed Mr. Capsicum, chuckling at the idea, "he'll have a magistrate to deal with, that will take care he receives his due deserts. Confound the fellow! it puzzles me to think how he has escaped so long, when there has been such a warm pursuit of him!"

"Ay, sir, and it's still more astonishing that they should have suffered him to escape, even after he has been put under lock and key. However, he has now let people know pretty well what he is, and I'll be bound the next time he gets into trouble he'll not find it quite so easy to get out of it as he has done on all former occasions."

"That's very true, Mr. Jones," exclaimed the old gentleman; "you have taken a very correct notion of the matter I see, and it's to be hoped you'll exercise all your vigilance now it's supposed he's lurking about this place. In the first place, I think you had better call on Timothy Snipe, the headborough, to tell him the sort of customer we are likely to have to deal with, but at the same time you must caution him not to go chattering about it to every one he meets, for if the smugglers should happen to hear what's going on, this Caleb Kestrel will be put upon his guard, and he'll be off again before we have a chance of taking him."

"But the reward that has been offered, sir, will make him cautious."

"Ay, that indeed may be as you say," answered Mr. Capsicum, "but still sometimes your over cunning people do as much mischief as those that go to work in a more headstrong way. You will, therefore, do well to remind Snipe that everything will depend upon his own prudence, and that if he minds what he's about, he may put a sum of money into his pocket that is worth looking after."

"Don't you think, sir," asked the clerk, "that it would be better for me to tell him to call here and receive your instructions?"

Before Mr. Capsicum could make any reply to this, the hall-bell was rung, announcing a visitor, and as the magistrate rose to leave the room, 'Squire Derwent, attired in travelling costume, hurriedly made his appearance. The meeting between the two gentlemen was cordial in the extreme, and Mr. Jones having been desired to leave, they at once entered upon the subject that had occasioned so unexpected a visit.

"I think, my dear sir," exclaimed Mr. Capsicum, "I can understand the nature of the business that has brought you here, though your letter contained not the slightest hint that you would follow so soon after the receipt of it. You have ascertained that Kestrel has really made up his mind to occupy his old hiding place, and have come here to obtain my assistance towards causing his immediate arrest."

"Very true, my dear sir," answered Mr. Derwent, "I have, as you say, no doubt that he has made for this neighbourhood, and if my suspicions are correct, we shall soon have the satisfaction of putting an end to the villanous plots he has been engaged in."

"But how do you know he has come this way?"

"Because I followed him to York, as I informed you in my letter," replied the squire, "and from all I could gather in that city, I have every reason to believe that he was one of the men concerned in a robbery that was committed in that neighbourhood an evening or two since. Indeed, the description of his person is so accurate, that I have not the slightest doubt of its being the man I am in pursuit of."

"That may be," exclaimed Mr. Capsicum; "but, knowing, as he does, the danger of a discovery, I should hardly think it likely he would venture to seek shelter where he is almost sure to be followed."

"So I should have fancied myself," replied Squire Derwent, "but upon making enquiries, I found that a person answering his description in every particular, and accompanied by two other men, left York at night, and took the road leading to this place. Acting upon that hint, I of course followed in the same direction, and from what I have learnt on the road, I have not been very far behind them all the way I came. So you see, my dear sir, I have had some ground for this somewhat abrupt visit, and if you can only have with me a little patience, I believe we shall very shortly have to congratulate ourselves upon the capture of one of the greatest scoundrels in the country.'

" But he is a desperate fellow, and we shall not be able to take him without some trouble as well as risk."

" Everything will depend upon the manner in which we go to work," answered Mr. Derwent.   " The object we have in view is, of course, not known hereabouts at present ; and I have a notion that if we can see some of these smugglers, there will not be much difficulty in gaining them over to our side if a liberal sum of money is offered as a reward for their services in causing his capture."

" I see your drift, but the question is, how we are to get an interview with the desperate fellows you are speaking of."

" Do you think there would be any great danger if you and I were to go to the public-house by the sea-shore, where they meet ?"

" As for danger, my dear sir," answered the magistrate, " I have no right to think of that when a public duty is to be performed, and, therefore, if you fancy any good is to be done by it, my services are at your command whenever you equire them.   In short, I am ready to accompany you, either alone, or with such assistance as may be deemed necessary to keep those half savage smugglers, under proper subjection."

" If the choice is left to myself," exclaimed Squire Derwent, " I should prefer you and I going alone, because it would not appear so much like an attempt to intimidate them.   Moderation may do more for us than intimidation, and especially if we give them a sum of money at the commencement of our negociation as an earnest of what they are afterwards to expect if they perform their duty faithfully. In short, I am of opinion that twenty pounds paid down will prove our confidence in them, and that, with men like them, does much more than threats and intimidation."

" Well," exclaimed the magistrate, who now began to approve of the notion, " we'll try this plan of yours at any rate, for, even if the offer is not accepted, we have no violence to fear from men who can be driven away at any time should they defy the law more than they have already done.   Besides, notwithstanding my being in the commission of the peace, I am not altogether unpopular amongst them, because they know I have it in my power to punish them with extreme severity if any of them should come into my clutches."

" Perhaps you would have no objection to go with me at once ?"

" So little objection have I to it," answered Mr. Capsicum, " that I was going to propose the very same thing if you had not have been beforehand with me.   In short, there's nothing like acting with promptitude and decision, in cases where you want to take an enemy by surprise."

" Whilst he was saying this, he put on his hat, and expressing his readiness to go at once, he and Squire Derwent, without telling any one where they were going, left the house, and made their way towards the small public house to which the reader has already been introduced.   On arriving there, they were immediately recognised by the host, who, without betraying the slightest alarm at so ominous a visit, begged them to be seated, and asked what commands they had to give him. On approaching the house, however, they had observed two or three men seated in an adjoining room, and judging that they were some of the people they wanted to see, they opened the door and entered with as much apparent unconcern as if they had merely called at the house for refreshments.   As they seated themselves, the men, who were engaged over some game at cards, eyed them with a glance of suspicion, but not a word did they utter that might be construed into a consciousness of danger from so unexpected a visit.   After a little while, however, all but one of them left the room, and even he was preparing to follow their example, when Mr. Capsicum desired him to remain where he was, and answer two or three questions that he had to put.   The man eyed him with a peculiar glance of penetration, and in a half surly tone, inquired if he knew him.

" Ay," he replied, " as well as you do me—your name is Thomas Hazle, or I am mistaken in the man that has been brought before me on more than one occasion, since I have been in the commission of the peace."

"That can't be denied," answered the fellow, "but there has never been evidence enough against me to commit me to prison."

"So much the better for you, Hazle," exclaimed the old gentleman, "and as far as I am concerned, I hope you may always have the same good luck on your side. You have only to live honestly, my good fellow, and then you'll never have anything to fear from the law."

"Honestly," muttered Hazle, "I never stole anything in my life."

"Perhaps so, but then you violate the laws in other ways, and that's a thing you might avoid, for smuggling is regarded as a very serious offence, and if persisted in too long may——"

"When I am brought before you on a charge of that kind, it w ll be quite time enough for you to lecture me," exclaimed Tom Hazle, impatiently : "I thought you might have something particular to say, or I should not have stopped here so long after my companions had left."

"Come, come," said the magistrate, "there's no occasion for a misunderstanding between us, because I have business to speak about, that you may, if you like, turn to your advantage."

"Is it to split against a comrade ?"

"No."

"Then what else can you want with me ?"

"To tell me where I can find a man named Caleb Kestrel, who there is good reason for believing is secreted somewhere in this neighbourhood. He, I believe, is no companion of yours, and therefore you can assist me without being guilty of treachery."

"To be short with you then," exclaimed Hazle, "I know nothing at all about him, nor where he's to be found."

"Do you mean to assert that he has not arrived in this neighbourhood within the last few hours ?"

"I suppose you wouldn't believe me if I was to say that I haven't seen him," replied the smuggler; "so the sooner this matter is brought to a close the better, for if we talk for an hour we shall only leave off as we began."

"That you do, or will know something of him, I am certain," interposed 'Squire Derwent, "and as it is of the utmost importance that I should trace him out, I am ready to pay you liberally for any service you may feel inclined to do me. Nay, as a proof that I mean what I say, here is a bank note for twenty pounds, which you may receive at once as an earnest of what is to follow, and I will rely upon your own sense of honour to complete the bargain."

"But suppose, with all my trying, I'm not able to discover where he is ?"

"If I see that you really exert yourself to the utmost, I shall not grudge the money even though you may not succeed," answered Mr. Derwent. "However, our host here, I dare say, will lend you all the assistance he can ; and as there's no doubt the pedlar will find his way into this neighbourhood before long, there's an excellent prospect of your both making a profitable affair of this. What say you," he added, turning towards the landlord,—"are you willing to lend your aid towards securing a man who has proved himself to be a most incorrigible villain ?"

"What do I say to it ?" exclaimed the host, "why the man never did me any harm in his life, and hang me if I'm going to betray him, when, for aught I know, he has never done anything to deserve punishment."

"Are we to understand this as your determination ?" asked Mr. Capsicum.

"Certainly you are."

"Then perhaps you would rather afford your assistance to the villains we are in pursuit of ?"

"Indeed I don't know but what I might."

"Then," exclaimed the magistrate, "in order that there may be no mistake between us, I now tell you plainly that a severe punishment awaits any person that either harbours or otherwise assists in his escape from the officers of law who are now engaged in searching for him."

" I don't want to set myself up against the laws, or you either," answered the landlord, " but I am not bound to be an informer unless I like ; and I'd rather suffer my hand to be chopped off, than I'd be scoundrel enough to give a poor devil up when he was not able to help himself."

" Then you must take care, or this obstinacy may prove your ruin."

" Ah, I know all about that, sir," replied the other, " but I must be a short-sighted fellow indeed if I 'm not able to manage matters better than to get myself into trouble when it's so easily to be avoided."

" In plain terms, then, you are determined to run the risk of a long imprisonment, for the sake of assisting a scoundrel whose crimes deserve neither commiseration nor pity ?"

" What have I to do with his crimes," demanded the host, " when he has never done anything to harm either me or mine? For aught I know, he has been wronged by the people that are loudest in their complaints against him, and if that's the case, who can wonder at his having rode rusty about it?"

" You know nothing about the matter, I see," exclaimed 'Squire Derwent, " for he has been the aggressor throughout, and the object of his persecution happens to be a weak, defenceless woman, whom he has once wronged, and would now crush to satisfy his feelings of revenge."

" How do I know but there may be a reason for it ?"

" There can be no sufficient reason for the cruel course he has thought proper to pursue in this instance ;" answered Mr. Derwent, " that, however, has nothing to do with the business that has brought me and my friend here ; we have reason to believe that he either is, or soon will be, in this neighbourhood, and as a reward has been offered for his apprehension, you, or anybody else, that may assist him in eluding justice, will have no mercy to expect if the fact should be clearly brought home."

" It's all very well to threaten us," exclaimed the landlord, " but you have first of all got to prove an offence, before you can punish us for it. Besides, it is not at all likely he would come again to these parts when he has once been routed."

" At any rate," answered Mr. Capsicum, " we have sufficient proof that he left York by the road that leads hither."

" And what can you argue from that ?" asked the other ; " he may have come that way for the sake of deceiving his enemies, and then have turned off into some other road that no one will ever think of."

" Nay," exclaimed Mr. Derwent, " we are not to be misled by a suggestion of that kind, for I happen to have traced him to within three or four miles of this house, and as he has had sufficient time to reach this place, I have a notion that, even while we are talking, he is concealed somewhere about your premises."

" Has any body hinted at such a thing ?" demanded the host, with alarm.

" I have not yet had time to prosecute my enquiries," replied the squire, " but as my suspicions do not appear to be unfounded, we will go back, and, if my friend Mr. Capsicum approves of it, return with a sufficient force to satisfy myself as to the truth of an opinion that may lead to the most important results."

" Indeed !" exclaimed the other sullenly, " I thought every Englishman's house was his castle."

" So it is, as long as he conforms himself to the laws," replied the magistrate " " but where a man not only openly violates these, but sets those in authority at defiance, it is time to treat him as one that is no longer worthy of protection or respect."

" Who, or what have I set at defiance ?" demanded the landlord, " I have only told you that the man you are in search of is not here, and if my word is to be taken, I don't see why I'm to be threatened with having my house searched."

" But if we always took the word of those that we suspect," answered Mr. Capsicum, " we should seldom or never discover the retreat of evil-doers. Be that as it may, however, this Caleb Kestrel is known to have been harboured here once, and we have good ground for supposing that he may come 'here again."

"He was not concealed here."

"I know not how that may be. but at any rate it is well known that you were aware of his being concealed in the neighbourhood, and yet, with the knowledge that he was a fugitive felon, you took no steps to give him up to justice."

"Very well, sir," returned the host; "it may be exactly as you say, but if the same thing was to happen over again, I should act just in the same way that I did before."

"Take care, then, that you don't get yourself into trouble," exclaimed Mr. Capsicum, "for I have entered heart and soul into this affair, and shall not fail to punish with the utmost severity all who may be concerned in screening an offender from justice. There are many charges against this Caleb Kestrel, and a reward having been advertised against him, all those who take part with him will have to answer for the offence in a way they little expect."

"Well, sir," interposed Tom Hazle, "I've told you that I'll give him up to you and this gentleman, if he should happen to come in my way; but if we shouldn't hear or see anything of him, it will be no fault of mine."

"Aye, aye, you have told us so, I know," answered the magistrate, "but, having got the money, the next question is, whether you will be as good as your word. But you are now aware of what will be the consequence of any deception, and if any is practised upon us, I, for one, shall not feel inclined to show you the least favour."

"Nor do I ask for any, because I know you have no reason to feel at all dissatisfied, when you see how hard I mean to work for the sake of proving that I deserve the money you have just given me."

"At the same time," continued Mr. Capsicum, "you have to remember that the reward will be all yours, if you think proper to perform the duty according to your promise. And mind, you are not so much required to take this man yourself as to give early information of his place of concealment to those who will relieve you from all further trouble."

"Then you only want to know as soon as he comes here?"

"That's all, replied the magistrate;" let us know that, and the exact spot where he is to be found, and we'll take upon ourselves all the responsibility of the rest So now you know what is expected from you, and if any underhanded work should be proved against you, you will know what sort of punishment to expect."

"Psha!" exclaimed the landlord, "how is he to know where the chap is to be found unless Kestrel himself is fool enough to go and split against himself? There's a hundred places in this neighbourhood where he might hide himself for months to come, and no one would ever be able to find him, unless they happen to know every hole and corner where a chap might choose to stow himself."

"But Hazle knows all the places, and he has undertaken, in consideration of the reward he has received, to use all his best endeavours towards surrendering this fugitive into our hands."

"And if he does anything of the kind, he'll be a most infernal villain, and no ne ought ever to keep his company again, said the host."

"How is this?" demanded Mr. Capsicum; "are you going to advise him to set the law at defiance?"

"I shall not tell you what my advice to him will be," answered the landlord; "but Tom Hazle knows as well as I do what course he ought to steer in a case of this kind and if he forgets his duty towards a poor devil that's in need of a friend to help him, it will be high time for some one to give him a good broad hint upon the subject."

"It occurs to me," observed 'Squire Derwent, "that, however much he may be nclined to perform his duty in this business, you are determined to prevent it as ar as lies in your power. We shall, however, keep a careful watch over you both, and if anything should occur to prove that either of you are acting with favour towards this Caleb Kestrel, you will have no quarter to expect from those you have deceived."

" But I'm not going to deceive you, master," exclaimed Hazle.

" May I then rely upon receiving from you the earliest information of the fugitive's arrival here ?"

" Of course you may."

" And I have your promise that you will not let him know of his presence here being expected ?"

" Yes, I'll promise that as well."

" Then you are a d—d scamp for your pains !" muttered the landlord, in a surly tone.

" I wish you would mind your own business, and leave me to manage my own," exclaimed Hazle, with a sly wink at his comrade, that was not observed by the two gentlemen. " I know very well that I've been paid handsomely for what I've promised to do, and you wouldn't have me behave shabbily after putting their money into my pocket, would you ?"

" Certainly not," returned the other, taking the hint; " a chap ought to keep strictly to his bargain when he's got the money in hand; but I can't help thinking it's rather hard that this poor devil, Caleb Kestrel, should be betrayed by those that he thinks ought to shelter him."

" If you knew the villain as well as I do," exclaimed 'Squire Derwent, " you would neither shelter nor pity him. His whole life seems to have been spent in doing all the mischief in his power, and now, as a climax to his other crimes, he is persecuting a helpless female for the purpose of extorting money as the price of his future forbearance."

" Oh yes," returned the host, sneeringly, " it's very well to throw all the blame upon him, but I dare say, if both sides of the question could be heard, we should soon discover that there are as many faults on the one side as the other. Kestrel, I suppose, has been kept out of money that he knows ought to have been his long ago, and when he ventures to make a bit of a stir about it, and perhaps demands it rather roughly, he's called a villain, and a hue and cry is raised against him from one end of the country to the other."

" You know nothing of the case, or the person you speak of," answered Mr. Derwent, " or you would not sepak thus of a person who has drawn upon himself the execrations of all who are not equally worthless as he is. We are, in short, pursuing him for his crimes, and I, for one, will never give up my object till I have brought upon him the severe punishment he deserves."

" That may be all very well," exclaimed the host, " but I don't see why you should come here to bribe others to do what you are not able to do yourself. If the man has committed any offence, there are officers enough to perform any dirty work there may be to execute, without troubling people that feel no interest in the matter."

" But if I ask for the service of this man, I have also given him money enough to pay for it."

" Then the long and the short of it comes to this," exclaimed the host, " you have given Tom Hazle the twenty pounds on condition that he does all he can to get Kestrel into trouble ?"

" I have already said so," answered 'Squire Derwent.

" And you must understand," added the magistrate, " that there must be no attempt to deceive us, for a watch will be kept upon both of you, and if it should be discovered that if either have done anything to conceal him from justice the heaviest punishment will be inflicted that the law will allow of. So now, as you know the consequences of acting against this warning, you will do well to keep it constantly in your recollection. As for you, Hazle, you have accepted the reward promised by this gentleman, and if you fail in the performance of the duty you have taken upon yourself, the punishment shall be as heavy as the law can inflict."

Having uttered this threat in a firm, resolute tone, Mr. Capsicum and the squire took their departure, though not without an uneasy feeling of suspicion that they should be followed, and perhaps captured, by those whom they had so daringly set at defiance. Finding, however, that their fears on this subject were groundless, they retraced their steps, and placing themselves in a situation where there was little probability of being seen, they kept a watch upon the house with a feeling of certainty that something would occur to forward the object they had in view. There they remained for nearly an hour, and then, having seen several suspicious-

KALEB RESTREL IN TROUBLE.

looking persons enter the house, they returned home to procure further assistance, in order that they might come back and search the house when such a visit was least expected. We must now, however, return to the two comrades, who having remained silent some little time, in order to satisfy themselves that all was right, began a low whispered conversation about the visit they had just received, and the consequences that might arise from it. Tom Hazle seemed to be quite at his ease about the matter, but it was far different with the landlord, who could not make up his mind as to the part his comrade intended to play in the affair.

No. 35

" What do you mean to do, Tom?" he asked. " Are you going to betray a friend for the sake of the money the squire gave you ?"

"Don't be such a fool as to think so," answered the other gloomily, " for if I had meant to be such a villain, what would have been easier for me to do than to have told them that the man they are in search of arrived here before them, and that he is concealed in the vault underneath the very room in which we are sitting ?"

" And to tell you the truth," answered the host, " that's exactly what I thought you were going to do. However, I'm glad to find that you are not such a confounded traitor as I thought for; and now, I suppose, the money you took from the young 'squire is to be equally divided between us as a reward for our fidelity to an unfortunate fellow creature ? But whilst we are comfortably talking over this matter our friend Caleb must be on thorns, so here goes to let him out of his dreary prison."

With this he removed the chair upon which he had been sitting, and, exactly under the place, succeeded, after some little trouble, in raising a trap-door, so carefully concealed as to defy the closest search of those who were not previously aware of its existence. He then held a light over the darksome aperture, and immediately Kaleb Kestrel emerged from it to receive the congratulations of his friends.

CHAPTER XXXII.

CALEB KESTREL AND HIS FRIENDS DELIBERATE UPON THEIR PROSPECTS, PRESENT AND FUTURE.—A MOST UNPLEASANT INTERRUPTION.—CAPTURE OF THE PEDLAR, AND HIS REMOVAL TO MR. CAPSICUM'S MANSION.—HIS AFFECTED DESPONDENCY, AND THE DETERMINATION HE FORMS UPON BEING LEFT ALONE.

THERE was a dark scowl visible upon the countenance of Caleb Kestrel, as he presented himself before his two companions, and throwing himself upon a seat, in a fit of il.-humour, he seized hold of a tankard of ale that had been left untouched by the recently departed visitors, and he took it not from his lips till every drop had found its way down his parched throat. Then, returning the vessel to the table, he directed an angry glance towards Hazle, as he exclaimed—

" So, it seems, then, I am to be betrayed, and that, too, by the man I placed all my confidence in ?"

" What the devil do you mean by that?" demanded the person he had addressed with so much abruptness.

" Oh, you thought I couldn't hear all that passed amongst you, and that I know nothing about twenty pounds 'Squire Derwent gave you, as an earnest for doing his dirty work ?"

" Psha ! is that all you've got to grumble about? Did I do wrong, then, in taking the money when it was offered me."

" You know best about that," answered the pedlar, " but I came here in full confidence that I should find myself among staunch friends, and it seems,—when too late,—I have found out my mistake."

" Then all I can say is, you have judged wrong of both of us," exclaimed the landlord ; " for never had man better friends than you have, and yet we are to be looked upon with suspicion, though all the while we have been doing our best to keep you safe and snug from those that are hunting for you all over the country."

" Why did Tom take the money, then ?"

" Because it happened to come in very acceptable, and he would have been a great fool to have refused it."

" But the 'Squire expects him to do a service for it."

" So much the better," replied Hazle, " for he'll find out that he's mistaken; and whilst he's depending upon assistance from us, we may find means to place you where you'll be out of his reach."

" It may be all very well to tell me that," exclaimed Caleb Kestrel, " but if my ears didn't deceive me, the two gentlemen that were here just now suspect that I am either in this neighbourhood or shall be here before long. Whilst that's their notion, I can't think myself safe for a moment, and especially if the fine promises they made should stir up your hearts to betray me to the enemy."

" D—n it, Kestrel, what do you take us for?" exclaimed the host.

" It's no use asking me what I take you both for," answered the fugitive, " because where a man finds himself in a situation of danger such as mine is, he don't know how to distinguish between his friends and his enemies. In short, don't I feel convinced that a word, or even a sign, would throw me into the power of men that could send me abroad as a miserable slave for all the rest of my days?"

" And after all we have done," returned Tom Hazle, " you think we would be villains enough to give you up?"

" Place yourself in my situation," exclaimed Kestrel, " and perhaps the same thoughts would cross your mind. However, I don't want to be too hard in my opinions, and, therefore, I'll wait and see what follows; but, remember, if there should appear to be any treachery, I'll have my revenge, if I should be certain to swing for it afterwards!"

" Aye, aye, watch us as closely as you like," replied Hazle, " for we have nothing to fear from it, and, perhaps by and by, you may see reason to acknowledge that you have wronged both of us by the suspicion. For my own part, I would sooner run a risk myself than prove myself a villain against the man that has trusted me."

" Enough said," exclaimed the pedlar, " and now, having so far come to an understanding, I should like to know where I am to hide myself, for it seems I have been traced this way, and I suppose the place will soon be too hot to hold me."

" There'll be a general search, I dare say," answered the landlord, " but what will be the use of that when there's so many places that we can put you into where they'll never think of looking?"

" How do you know what they may do, if once they take it into their heads that the chap they're looking for is close at hand?"

" Why, there's no answering for what may happen," returned the landlord, " but at any rate they've got their match in us, and if they should be too prying, there's plenty of our people close by, and they'll willingly join us if it's to drive away a parcel of fellows that we all look upon as a common enemy. In short, a search hereabouts would not be quite the thing for any of us, for just now we have a large store of goods stowed away in different places, and if they were to be seized in the king's name, we should all be pretty well ruined."

" Are your people to be depended on in case there should be an attack made upon us?" asked Caleb Kestrel.

" They'd fight to the last, like devils," he replied; " and if one may judge from former skirmishes that we've had with the revenue officers, they would have but a queer chance if they come to interfere with our business, or to search for any one that we think proper to shelter."

" Where do you think we can hide him?" asked Tom Hazle.

" I should say, Robin Hood's Cave will be the best place," answered the landlord, " for it's easy to change quarters in case they should take it into their heads to search there, or, if needs be, a boat can be in readiness to take him over to the opposite coast, where he may remain safe enough till he can venture to return here again."

" But I don't want to leave England," answered the pedlar, " for the business I have in hand is just ripe for execution, and I don't wish to be away from the spot when 'Squire Derwent is likely to agree to the proposition I have made him."

"I'll tell you what it is," exclaimed the host, "you seem to fancy that nothing is so easy as to turn and twist him about as you please; but there's a great deal more trouble to be met. with in this affair than you seem to expect."

"Humph!" he ejaculated, "I see how it is, you begin to fancy there may be danger, and would be glad to back out of it, if you could only do so by shuffling and excuses."

"Do you want to quarrel with me, Kestrel?"

"Not I," he replied; "but I should like to know exactly what I've got to look forward to, now that this business seems to be drawing to a close?"

"That'll all depend upon yourself," answered the other, "for if you choose to place your trust in us, we are ready and willing to perform everything we have promised. If, however, on the other hand, you have made up your mind to believe that we don't intend to act as men and comrades, you had better take your own course, and leave us before further danger comes of it."

"Well, then," exclaimed Caleb Kestrel, "come what may of it, I'll trust you, and place myself entirely under your control. So now, make any proposal you like, and I promise not to throw any further obstruction in your way, whatever your plans may be."

Before any reply could be made to this, four or five smugglers came in, and seating themselves at the table, expressed in no very measured terms, their disapproval of the proceedings that were going on. In short, one of them had just before seen Mr. Capsicum and his friend, 'Squire Derwent, as they were proceeding on their return home; and as they knew not the business that had brought them into their immediate neighbourhood, they naturally concluded that mischief was brewing against the smugglers. They even went so far as to tell Kestrel that he must either seek some other hiding place without delay, or take the chance of some among their number betraying him to his enemies, in order to avert the danger from themselves. Tom Haz'e heard them with growing impatience, and then, snatching up one of the pistols that he had laid upon the table, he said

"It seems to me that too many of you are wanting to be masters, and it may now be as well to let you know that, for the present, I shall take that duty upon myself, whether it may be approved of by yourselves or no. You look at me with surprise, gentlemen, but I'm known to be resolute whenever I have made up my mind to anything, and, after this explanation, it will be as much as any man's life is worth, if he attempts to raise a mutiny among us."

This threat was not without its due weight, and the last comers, without venturing to make any further objections, retired to the further part of the room, where they carried on a whispered conversation among themselves. Caleb Kestrel eyed them with a glance of suspicion, and turning towards Hazle, he said in a tone not so loud as to be heard by the others—

"I have not much opinion of those fellows, for where there's dissatisfaction, there is almost sure to be danger, and yonder grumblers may perhaps go and give such information as will bring the enemy upon us when we are least prepared for an attack."

"Never fear it," answered the other, "for though they are not in a very good humour just at this moment, they know their own interest too well to bring people down upon us that can and will rout our whole band the moment they have an opportunity of doing so."

"But they would make a bargain by which they would be excluded from all punishment."

"And of what service would that be to them?" demanded Hazle.

"It's true enough they might sneak out of the consequences of a discovery, but when once men have followed this business of ours, they are never fit for anything else afterwards; and even if they were, who, I should like to know, would give employment to men that had all their lives been setting the laws at open defiance?"

"That may be all very true," answered Kestrel, "but when fellows like these have determined upon mischief, they can always find ways to do it without any one knowing from whom the blow comes. In a word, they can send information of my being here, and before the danger could be avoided we should be surprised by a visit from the people that I am most trying to avoid."

These latter words seemed to have reached the ears of the men to whom they alluded, for the men immediately rose and joined them with as much seeming friendship as if nothing whatever had occurred to mar their harmony.

"You seem to suspect us strangely," said Miles Quested, who had undertaken to be spokesman, "and yet we have no thought whatever of turning traitors against a man that has come here to throw himself under our protection. So here's my hand to your's, Caleb Kestrel, and in future think better of those that are not only glad to find you amongst them, but would fight to the very last if the bloodhounds of the law were to attempt to take you away from 'em."

"I told you so," exclaimed Hazle; "they are trustworthy fellows enough if you place your faith in 'em, but they don't like to be suspected when they know their intentions are good. So now let's have glasses round, my lads, that we may drink to our better understanding, as well as your own escape from the harpies that are upon the look-out to drag you away to the stone-jug."

This was a proposition that the host was perfectly willing to accede to, and and without waiting for a second hint of the wants of his customers, he left the room to execute the orders which he had received. Taking the opportunity that offered, Caleb Kestrel briefly related the cause that had brought him there, and after describing the narrow escapes he had had, he inquired if there was any one among them who would be base enough to give him up to the enemy after he had shown his confidence by coming among them.

"The devil a one is here that would turn informer against you," replied Miles Quested, "so make up your mind as to being safe here so long as you choose to stay with us."

"But just now you seemed to think I was an intruder here."

"Well," replied the fellow, "I believe there was such a notion, but since then we have been talking the matter over among ourselves, and, as it appears that you are willing to pay us handsomely for our risk, out of the money you expect to receive from 'Squire Derwent, we see no reason why we should refuse the shelter you have asked for. But mind—we depend upon your honour, so don't deceive us, or I'll not answer for the consequences."

"Humph!" exclaimed Caleb Kestrel, "I am welcome, then, so long as there is a prospect of being paid for the accommodation?"

"That's about the truth of it," answered the other, "and I believe it's the case all the world over, for money is the golden key that opens all doors, and brings with it its last welcome. But how's this?" he added, suddenly changing his tone, —"here's the host coming back without the grog he went to fetch, and by his frightened looks something has happened that he was not prepared for."

"Gentlemen, we have been betrayed," exclaimed the host, almost breathless with alarm. "Mr. Capsicum and the squire have returned, and brought with them a number of armed revenue officers."

"Then, there's not a moment to lose," cried Kestrel, starting from his seat. "Keep the door secured for a few minutes, and I'll escape from the window, whilst they are parleying for admission."

"It's too late to think of escape now, Kestrel," exclaimed the landlord, "for the men have completely surrounded the house, and if you attempt to make your way out, it will be with the certainty of having about half-a-dozen bullets sent through your body."

"Do you say 'Squire Derwent is with them?"

"He is."

"Then I am lost, unless you are all determined to stand by me to the very last.

I myself am resolute, and not a hand shall be laid upon me whilst I have the mean of "rotecting myself."

Are you mad, that you talk of resisting them, when there's about six to one for us to fight against?"

"I care not how many there may be," exclaimed Caleb Kestrel, "for death is a thousand times preferable to falling into the hands of people that are bent upon my destruction. Listen! they are now clamouring at the door for admission, so go and tell them that we are armed, and that we are determined to defend ourselves, whatever may be the consequences."

"Indeed I shall tell 'em no such thing," answered the host, "for they are determined to perform the errand they have come for, and I have no mind to see deadly strife going on in my house, when I know how heavily the vengeance of the law would fall upon me for it."

"Then you expect I shall give myself up, without attempting to strike a blow in my own defence?"

"I do," answered the landlord, "and you will find it best to follow the recommendation I have given. Resistance would only lead to bloodshed, and that would cost me more than I am likely to sacrifice for the sake of making a useless defence."

"It may be all very well for you to say so," exclaimed Caleb Kestrel, "but if I am taken, there's no saying how far the vengeance of these people may carry them. A prison would be my immediate doom, and that too with the certainty of being convicted, and {sent abroad as a felon for the remainder of my days."

"Leave everything to us, and matters won't turn out half so badly as you expect," answered the other.

"But if no resistance is offered, I must be captured."

"That's very certain," returned the landlord, "but we will watch where they take you to, and you may take my word for it, that within an hour or two afterwards we will collect in such numbers, as to carry you off in triumph, in spite of all their watchfulness. So just surrender yourself quietly as soon as they come in, and depend upon your friends for a speedy deliverance."

Caleb Kestrel had no time to make any reply to this, for at this moment the door was burst open with a sudden crash, and the magistrate, followed by Mr. Derwent and a body of armed men, rushed into the house. Had the pedlar felt inclined to offer the resistance that he first meditated, it would have been utterly impossible to have effected his purpose, for he was instantly seized by three or four of the men, and as speedily deprived of the weapons with which he was armed. He was, in fact, nearly stupified, by the suddenness with which he had been taken, and stood as if deprived of all power of speech or resistance.

"Caleb Kestrel," exclaimed the magistrate, "you are arrested in the King's name, and your companions here will do well not to oppose us in the duty we are bound to perform. They know the consequences of disobeying my injunctions, and their only way to escape the punishment for having harboured and secreted you, is to take no part in this affair that may lead to violence."

"Please your worship," returned the landlord in a most obsequious tone, "we none of us want to interfere in such a case as this. Indeed, we told Kestrel just now, that he must not expect any assistance from us, and it was entirely owing to our counsel that he has suffered himself to be taken prisoner without raising a hand in his own defence. So I hope, sir, you'll take this into consideration, and not get us into trouble afterwards, for harbouring a criminal, when it is well known to every one that a house of this kind is open to all comers."

"What's the use of making a parcel of idle excuses like these, when, as a magistrate, he'll do just as he pleases about it!" exclaimed Kestrel, who by this time had somewhat recovered himself. "For my own part. I'm determined to take my chance whatever may happen, but it don't follow that, because I happen to have got into a little bit of trouble now, I'm never to get out of it."

"You must have extraordinary luck indeed, if you manage to get out of your scrape this time," observed Mr. Capsicum.

"And haven't I generally had good luck when most I've stood in need of it?" exclaimed the pedlar. "So far, I have always been able to laugh at the locks and bolts that have been turned upon me, and I'm greatly mistaken if my career even now has been brought to an end, much as 'Squire Derwent may exult over what I dare say he considers the downfall of his enemy."

"Unfortunately you have always regarded me as a foe," answered the squire, "though I can declare that, much as you have sought to injure me, I never should have commenced this pursuit after you, but for your ever untiring perseverance in persecuting a helpless female, in whose welfare I feel the greatest interest."

"Then I wonder you did not put an end to the persecution, by agreeing to the terms I many times proposed."

"In that I was influenced by many reasons," answered the squire ; "even if your demands were acceded to, the quiet you might have allowed, would not have lasted very long. Money would have been still your cry, so often as you found yourself in want of it, and I should thus have laid myself open to the continual extortion of an unprincipled villain."

"Mind what you're saying there, squire!" exclaimed Caleb Kestrel. "Don't let your language be too severe, for I may not always be as helpless as you see me now ; and if I should happen to get my liberty once more, I shall recollect those that have insulted me, and revenge myself for it in a way they little expect."

"You surely don't expect ever to have your liberty again?" exclaimed the magistrate with surprise.

"And why shouldn't I?" demanded the prisoner, "when a great deal more unlikely things have happened before now."

"But knowing the sort of customer we have to deal with, you will now be watched, so as to prevent all chance of escape."

"Oh, it was not an escape of that kind that I was thinking of," replied Kestrel, " because I've no doubt you'll take care to keep me safe enough till the day of trial comes. But charges don't always happen to be proved to the satifaction of a jury, and unless the witnesses in this case have made up their minds to swear to any lies, I don't see what chance I have of being convicted. Besides, what have I done, that all this fuss should be made about it? In the first instance I was the means of restoring Amy to her property, and, when some sort of reward was expected for my services, I am set down as a villain, and hunted through the country like a wild beast."

"For which you have only yourself to blame," interposed the magistrate; "however, this is neither the time nor place to enter into such an argument, and you will, therefore, now accompany me to my house, where you will be carefully watched and guarded till a full examination into the charge enables me to commit you for trial."

On a sign being given by the old gentleman, Caleb Kestrel, who offered no resistance, was placed in the midst of a body of the revenue officers, and, thus guarded, was marched from the house towards the mansion of Mr. Capsicum, where, as the most convenient place, he was to remain till his removal to the county prison. The landlord and his companions watched them from the door as long as they remained in sight, and then returned once more to the room where the recent occurrences had taken place.

"Well," exclaimed the host, "they've got the devil safe enough now; and now it only remains for us to say whether he is to be sent off to prison or to be set at liberty, as we promised."

"I'll tell you what, my boys," returned Tom Hazle—" we have a pretty chance before us, if we like to use it; and not only can we do a service to Caleb Kestrel, but we may put money into our own pockets at the same time, though not exactly after the fashion that we usually manage such things."

"What the devil have you got into your head now?" demanded Miles Quested, rather puzzled to know what was meant.

"Why something that I rather think will prove to be for the benefit of all of us," replied Hazle; "we don't often break the laws, except by bringing contraband goods ashore; but we have many a time said that if an opportunity offered, it would be worth while getting into old Capsicum's place some of these nights, just by way of easing him of some of the plate that he seems to have so much of."

"Do you want us to join you in a robbery, then?" asked the landlord.

"You've just guessed it," answered Hazle, "and, what's more, I know you are not the man to refuse a good thing when it comes in your way. So confess at once, old fellow, that you see no harm in trying to help Kestrel out of his difficulties, and at the same time making the affair a profitable one, by easing Mr. Capsicum of what he has plenty to spare without being much the poorer for it."

"And even supposing I was to agree to your mad scheme, how are we to get into the house?"

"Leave that to me, and you shall see that it can be managed."

"What!" exclaimed the landlord, "when people will be sitting up to watch the prisoner? and, for aught we know, others will be outside the house to prevent any attempt to escape."

"Ah!" exclaimed Tom Hazle, "you are going to throw difficulties in the way I see; but I happen to have taken a different view of the affair, and it strikes me that nothing can be more easy, if we only set to work the right way. There's plenty of us to take the house by storm, if we like, and as I don't think we have many cowards among our people, I shall collect 'em together presently, and see whether Caleb can't be got out of his difficulties before the time comes that was appointed for his examination."

Upon this, Tom Hazle left the house for the purpose he had spoken of, and the others remained behind to consult among themselves, as to whether they should assist in so hazardous an adventure, or leave it to those who were more reckless than themselves. Losing sight of the smugglers for a brief period, and leaving them to concoct the design with which the reader is now acquainted, we must follow Caleb Kestrel to the place where he was destined to pass some time in all the torments of doubt and uncertainty. Immediately upon entering the house of Mr. Capsicum, fetters were placed upon his legs in order to prevent his escape, which they felt sure would be attempted, and he was then conducted to a chamber, at the door of which a sentinel was placed, whilst another, also armed, was stationed beneath the window, so as to prevent, as far as caution was of any avail, all chance of leaving the house in that direction. Being left alone, the prisoner began to feel more despondent than he had been on any previous occasion, for he had heard the orders given for the utmost vigilance to be observed, and thus every hope that he might otherwise have encouraged, failed him at the moment of his utmost need. Throwing himself upon a seat, he remained for some time with his face buried in his hands, and all his thoughts completely absorbed in the one reflection, that now, indeed, he was past all hope of human succour. Whilst thus lost in thought, he was roused by hearing footsteps in the passage, and presently afterwards, though he raised not his head, he was conscious that three or four persons had entered the chamber.

"So," he heard Mr. Capsicum exclaim, "you see, gentlemen, he is safe thus far, as, indeed, I don't see how it could have been otherwise, after the care that has been taken to prevent his escape, and the well-known vigilance of those that have undertaken the task of keeping a watch over him. So now, my friends, I think there can be no objection to our going to bed for a few hours, for we have all of us had rather a fatiguing day's work, and to-morrow we shall have still more labour to go through."

"If you have no objection, sir," interrupted the clerk, "I'll sit up in case any alarm of an attempted escape should be raised."

"You are very good, Mr. Jones," answered the magistrate, "but I feel perfectly well satisfied with our arrangements, as they at present stand. Everything appears to be progressing in a very satisfactory manner, and I believe the best thing you can do will be to go home and rest yourself against your services are required to-morrow. But how is this?" added the old gentleman, "the prisoner seems to be absorbed in grief for the misfortunes that have befallen him; and perhaps for the first time in his life he discovers that he is in the hands of people who know how to prevent his slipping through their fingers."

"Pray, sir," exclaimed Caleb Kestrel, raising his head as these words were uttered, "does my present helpless condition give you an authority to exult over your victim?"

KESTREL VISITED BY MR. CAPSICUM.

"Don't imagine that I am here for any such purpose," answered Mr. Capsicum, "for, much as I may abhor the conduct you have been guilty of, I am the last man in the world that would add to your punishment by seeming to exult in your downfall."

"Then why are you and Squire Derwent here?"

"Merely to see that you are safe before we retire to bed," answered the magistrate. "In taking that precaution we are only performing our duty, and at the same time we would know whether there is any indulgence you require which we can grant consistently with the duty we owe to those who have a right to inquire into our notions and conduct."

"I want no favour," he replied, "nor will I ask one of those that I know to be my enemies."

"Nonsense, man," exclaimed the magistrate, "we are not your enemies any the more for having caused your capture when the law expected no less from us. Those who do wrong must expect to be punished for it some time or another, and if there is a chance for you to get over this, you may depend upon it, every opportunity for doing so will be afforded you. In short, my friend Mr. Derwent has done nothing more than was necessary for the preservation of himself and the young lady from the plots you had formed, and he will be guilty of a very great act of injustice if he does not take such steps as will secure his own future tranquillity and repose."

"And I," muttered Caleb Kestrel, "should be a fool if I do not endeavour to destroy those schemes of his. However, that is not the question just at present: here I am, completely in his power, and of course he will not feel inclined to let me loose upon the world again."

"You are mistaken there," exclaimed the squire, "for you shall be set at liberty again immediately, on condition that you enter into a solemn promise not to molest Amy any more."

"Well," answered the pedlar, "perhaps I should have no objection to do that on condition that you first of all place in my hands a sum of money that will be sufficient to keep me abroad, without being obliged to have recourse to my old ways again."

"That you will not be allowed to do," exclaimed Mr. Capsicum, "for it would be acting against the law, and, as a magistrate, it is my place to see that everything is conducted in such a manner that no evil consequences arise from it afterwards. So now, Kestrel, you know exactly how matters stand between us;—you are our prisoner, and must remain so till a jury has decided whether this charge of Squire Derwent can be sufficiently substantiated by the evidence he has got to bring forward against you. If he should fail in doing that, you will, of course, be restored to liberty ; but I warn you to be careful, if such should be the case, for a strict watch will be kept upon your actions, and upon the least ground of suspicion you will again find yourself in a position exactly similar to your present one."

Upon this the old gentleman, and all who had accompanied him, left the room, and Caleb Kestrel found himself once more alone to indulge in the thoughts that had been interrupted by the arrival of his visitors. On a sudden he roused himself from his pretended grief, and having removed his fetters, which had been concealed about his person, he placed himself near the window to listen for the expected approach of his companions.

CHAPTER XXXIII.

ACTIVE MEASURES ARE ADOPTED FOR THE RELEASE OF THE PRISONER.—DICK RADCLIFFE AND HIS COMRADES PARTIALLY SUCCEED IN THEIR DESIGNS.—THE CAPTIVE IS RELEASED, AND SQUIRE DERWENT IS SURPRISED BY A VERY UN-LOOKED-FOR TURN IN HIS FORTUNES.—PLUNDER, AND ESCAPE OF THE ROBBER.

HAVING stealthily followed at a distance and watched till they saw Caleb Kestrel taken into the house of Mr. Capsicum, the smugglers, with Dick Ratcliffe at their head, made their way into a thicket, through which they could find their way towards the mansion without any fear of their approach being discovered. In this manner they continued to advance till they perceived the man who had been placed as sentry pacing up and down, and then deeming it prudent to retire to a little distance for the present, they took their station beneath a wide spreading elm tree, where they could consult together as to the safest means for bringing their plan to a successful termination. In this instance, as in most others, Dick Radcliffe took upon himself the chief direction of the business they had in hand. This privilege having been conceded to him, he inquired if the others had made up their minds to liberate their comrade at all hazards.

"As far as I am concerned," replied Miles Quested, "I am determined never to leave a companion in a dilemma as long as I am able to lend him a helping hand. Not but what I think he was foolish to come to this part of the country, where he was sure to be followed by his enemies ; but as finding fault with what is past won't mend matters a bit, I think the best thing we can do is to set about our task with a good heart, and see what can be done for him."

"Done for him !" exclaimed Radcliffe, "why, as a matter of course, the first thing to be done will be to get into the house, and bring him out in spite of any resistance that may be offered."

"Aye, aye," observed the host, "it's all very well to talk about getting into the house, but to me it don't seem to be quite so easy an affair as you imagine it is. Yonder fellow is walking up and down to prevent an attack, and, for aught we know, there may be four or five others inside keeping watch to baulk an attempt that they have every right to suppose will be made."

"And what need we care about that ?" demanded Radcliffe. "We are better armed than they are, I'll be bound to say ; and if matters should come to the worst Kestrel will be able to lend us a helping hand, and with his assistance we should have nothing to fear from much greater odds than we are likely to find there."

"But what right has he to expect us to run all this risk for him ?" demanded Miles Quested.

"He don't look upon it as a right," answered the other ; "but when a poor fellow like him gets into trouble, it's nothing more than right that those who pretend to be his friends should use all their exertions towards getting him out of it."

"It may be all very well for him to expect it," returned the host, "but it's for us to say whether we'll get ourselves into a scrape merely for the sake of assisting him out of one. In a word, he had no business here at all, and if he had remained where he ought to have been, all this disagreeable affair might have been avoided."

"Aye, but he wanted to get a sum of money from the squire, and there was no way of doing that but by keeping him in continual fear of losing the girl he was to marry."

"I suppose the truth of it is, he was over greedy, and demanded a great deal too much," exclaimed Quested.

"Who, I should like to know, has any right to dictate to Caleb Kestrel what sum of money he ought or ought not to ask ?" retorted Dick Radcliffe. "He is one of those sort of chaps that thinks he has a right to have a will of his own, and woe be to those that want to thwart him when a favourite notion is to be carried out !"

"Are we, then, to be frightened and bullied by a fellow that has come among us without either leave or invitation ?" asked the host.

"I don't know what you may feel inclined to do in a case of this kind," answered Radcliffe ; "but remember, we are all of us likely to be in trouble some time in the course of our lives, and we should do by him now as we should expect our comrades would do to us in case their assistance happened to be required."

"Yes, yes," exclaimed Mike Quested, "that argument is a very good one, if there's no danger likely to come from it ; but what have we to do with this Caleb Kestrel, who we never heard of till he got into all sorts of scrapes, and wanted our help to get out of 'em ? In short, I don't believe he'd put out his hand to assist us if it were ever so, in case we should happen to ask him for it, which, by the bye ain't very likely."

" You'd think differently of Kestrel if you knew him as well as I do."

" Very likely," interposed the host ; " but as we don't happen to claim much acquaintance with him, I don't see why he should expect us to run any risk in his behalf."

" Why, you don't suppose he wants a favour to be granted unless he means to pay for it handsomely."

" What does he call paying handsomely ?"

" Ah," replied Dick Radcliffe, " that's a question that I can't very well answer, for Caleb would of course pay in proportion to the sum of money he may happen to receive from Squire Derwent."

" And I have heard," exclaimed Quested, " that he has had the conscience to go up as high as ten thousand pounds."

" I believe he has."

" Then more fool he for his pains," returned the other, " for though a small sum might have been given, a large one is refused without the least chance of any terms being come to. Squire Derwent knows well enough that his enemy will never dare to carry his threats into execution, for the law is always strong enough for his protection, and Caleb Kestrel must in the end fall into the snare that he has laid for others."

" It strikes me he has done that already," returned the landlord.

" Ah," answered Dick Radcliffe, " as for this little affair, it's nothing at all, for nothing will be more easy than to get him out of it, if we only make up our minds not to leave him in his present dilemma. Why half an hour, if we set seriously to work, will be quite sufficient to bring him out of yonder house."

" That is to say," observed Mike Quested, " if all the people in the place are cowards enough to let him escape without making any effort to keep him in safe custody. I, however, can't think it very likely that they will let him get off quite so easily, and if we should venture to enter the house we may expect to meet with a warmer reception than any of us will exactly like."

" If that's the notion you have of it," exclaimed Dick Radcliffe, " what the devil made you come out with us—knowing, as you well did, the purpose that brought us here?"

" Why, the long and the short of it is, a man is allowed to alter his mind if he discovers that he's likely to get himself into an awkward hobble," answered the other. " Now, I happen to see that there's danger in this business, and I should be a precious fool indeed if I was to rush headlong into ruin, merely for the sake of rescuing a chap that I hardly ever saw in my life till this very day."

" Then let's know at once what you mean to do?"

" I'll tell you exactly what he ought to do," interposed the landlord ;—" he ought to take care of Number One before he thinks of anybody else, and the only way to do that will be to keep where he is, and let others that like run themselves into danger."

" So you will leave me to take all the risk upon myself ?"

" Who ought to do it if you don't?" demanded the host ; " this Caleb Kestrel is more your friend than ours, and we are by no means certain that he would pay us for our trouble even if we were to run the chance of getting transported through him. However, to bring matters to an understanding, Mike and I will lend our assistance in this affair as far as the out-of-door business goes, but neither of us will step a foot inside the house, whatever may be said or thought about it."

" And what good can you do outside ?"

" A great deal if you think proper to accept our services."

" Explain yourself."

" That I can do in a minute," answered the landlord, pointing through an opening of the trees ;—"you see yonder man, I suppose, that is pacing up and down by the side of the house ?"

" To be sure I do," replied Dick Radcliffe ;—" he is the fellow that has been entrusted to take care of the prisoner."

" Right ;—and has it struck you what we had better do with him ?"

" That's what has most puzzled me."

" Well, then, I'll tell you what we must do ;—our first care must be to secure him, and, at the same time, prevent his outcries from alarming any other people in the house."

" How is that to be done ?"

" Easily, if it is to be managed at all," answered the host. " We must creep stealthily towards him, and when his back is turned to us, we can rush forward —throw him on the ground—and ensure his silence, by threatening to stab him with our daggers if he ventures to raise even so much as a single cry. That will keep him silent, I warrant you, and then one o the principal obstacles will be removed, and you may make your attempt to get into the house."

" I understand," exclaimed Radcliffe; " whilst I'm engaged in attempting to liberate the prisoner, you will take care that no alarm is raised to disturb me in the midst of my task ?"

" Exactly so."

" And hasn't it struck you," demanded the other, " that by this arrangement of yours you are throwing all the danger and difficulties upon my shoulders ?"

" Perhaps it may be so," answered the landlord ; " and it's nothing more than right, either, for I'll be bound to say you'll take care that more than a propor-tion of whatever Caleb Kestrel may have promised, will find it's way into your pocket."

" And what reason have you for supposing that I would act a dishonourable part towards you ?" he asked.

" We neither of us say you would cheat us out of our rights," answered the other, with a shrug of the shoulders ; " but as we happen to be almost strangers to each other, it's not much to be wondered at if we act in a matter of this kind with a little more than our usual caution. However, you know best whether your intentions are fair and honourable, and if we find they are, why you may depend on it we shall not withhold any assistance you may require."

" But at any rate you will take care that yonder man shall not raise an alarm whilst I am in the house ?"

" If he does, his life shall pay for it."

" Enough !" exclaimed Dick Radcliffe, advancing a step or two forward; " follow me in silence till we approach the sleepy sentinel, and then, with a sudden bound, fall upon and secure him. But, remember, he must not be suffered to utter an exclamation, or the object we have undertaken will be for ever frus-trated."

In a few whispered words they promised to obey this injunction, and then all three of them set forth with such cautious steps, that not the least rustle or sound was to be heard even by themselves. In this manner they advanced to the very edge of the plantation, where they were concealed by the deep shadow that fell from the trees overhead. For a brief period they paused here to watch for a favour-able opportunity, and at length, when the man's back was turned towards them, they all rushed forward with a sudden bound, and ere a second had elapsed the sentry was struck down, and his voice stifled by means of a handkerchief which was forced into his mouth. Thus rendered incapable of raising an alarm, the poor fellow struggled violently to release himself, till the daggers gleamed before his eyes, and a voice whispered in his ear that his life would be instantly sacrificed if he gave utterance to a sound that would bring the assistance he required. This threat was sufficient—the man remained silent under the influence of the most violent alarm ; and Dick Radcliffe, leaving him to the care of his two comrades, advanced towards the house for the purpose of seeing where he would be most likely to obtain an entrance without disturbing those who would endeavour to prevent the object he had in view. Presently he reached the other side of the mansion, where he remained gazing about for a minute or two, unable to decide where to commence his attempt, and still in complete uncertainty as to what part of the building was occupied by Caleb Kestrel. This perplexity was, however, soon put an end to, for his name was pronounced in a low but audible whisper, and turning in the direction from whence the sound came, he perceived the pedlar standing at a window which was situated not far above his head. Not a word of surprise or recognition escaped the lips of Dick Radcliffe as he made this important discovery, but understanding the signs which were made to him by the prisoner, he ran across the garden and soon afterwards returned with a ladder, by means of which he quickly gained access to the room in which Caleb Kestrel had been confined. A few words of friendly greeting sufficed, and the two associates in crime then began to arrange their plans for escaping from a place where they were surrounded by danger. Kestrel was for leaving the house without a moment's delay, but his accomplice had certain visions wandering through his brain of plunder, that was to be gained by a little more hazard, and he expressed a fixed determination not to quit the house if there was even the slightest chance of leaving it richer than he came. The pedlar would have opposed this scheme, but finding that he was immovable upon the subject, he at last yielded unwillingly to the suggestion.

"If it must be so, Dick," he exclaimed, "I'll give in to you; but remember, should any misfortune happen through it you will have no one to blame for it but yourself."

"Psha! what mischief can happen when I have brought with me arms enough for you as well as for myself?"

"We may defend ourselves with these at any rate," exclaimed Kestrel, taking a brace of pistols and a dagger from the hands of his friend, "and if we should happen to be disturbed, I'll take care not to fall into the power of my enemies again whilst I have strength left to defend myself."

"Do you know where the people sleep?" asked Radcliffe.

"Nearly all of them are at the further part of the house," replied the pedlar, "but my mortal enemy, Squire Derwent, sleeps in the next room, for the purpose, as I believe, of preventing any attempt that may be made to set me at liberty."

"Have you heard him move about lately?"

"Within a quarter of an hour before I saw you from this window."

"Then there's no chance of his being asleep?"

"Not the slightest," replied Caleb Kestrel, "for I believe he is sitting up on purpose to keep watch in order that I may not get away from the house. But of what use will that be when I am determined to lose my life in the attempt rather than remain here a prisoner in the hands of those that are resolved on my destruction?"

"Do you happen to know," asked Dick Radcliffe, "whether there is any money or valuables that we can readily lay our hands on?"

"I'm not able to answer that question from any knowledge of my own," replied the other, "but in a house of this kind I should say there can be no doubt of there being plenty of everything. However, why need we run the risk of bringing the whole house upon us when the principal thing we ought to look after is to escape from the place whilst there is a good opportunity for doing so?"

"Why, everything's quiet," whispered his comrade, "and it seems a thousand pities to give away such a golden chance as this, when the whole affair may be managed without much trouble or risk. Besides, I don't want you to assist in looking up the property, for I'm able enough to do that by myself, and whilst I am gone you can sit yourself down here and wait for my return."

"Leave it all to you!" exclaimed Caleb Kestrel. "No, no, you are too rash to be trusted by yourself in such an affair as this; you would be for searching every room in the house, and an alarm being raised, what chance should I have of getting clear off?"

"Psha! do you think I would be fool enough to run the chance of endangering you as well as myself?"

"Not intentionally, I dare say," answered Caleb, "but avarice would tempt you to step beyond the bounds of prudence, and the consequences of such an act are too serious to be lightly thought of."

"Well, for this once I swear to be cautious."

"What makes you so anxious to undertake this alone ?"

"Because two persons are more likely to make a noise than one. That's my only reason, I can assure you; so remain where you are for a few minutes, and I'll return presently with all the swag I can lay my hands upon."

"Without waiting for the permission he had asked for, he snatched up a light and hurried from the room, leaving Caleb Kestrel in the darkness. The latter was restrained from calling upon him to return for fear of alarming the house, and pacing up and down the chamber for a few moments, he gave way to those fears which the rashness of his comrade had given rise to. At length a slight sound in the adjoining room aroused him, and moving towards the door he perceived that the one belonging to the next chamber was partly open, and creeping towards it on tiptoe he saw Mr. Derwent seated by the bed-side, apparently reading from a book which he held in his hand. Previously to leaving his own room, Kestrel had seized a stout cudgel which stood in one corner, and, having concealed his other weapons, he boldly advanced towards the Squire, grasping the stick so as to be ready for immediate use in the event of its services being required. At length the creaking of the boards roused Mr. Derwent, who, starting upon his feet, was about to utter a cry of alarm, when Kestrel seized him by the throat, and by main force drove him back against the bed, where he remained powerless, and nearly choking under the tremendous grasp of his powerful assailant.

"Hear me, Squire Derwent, and utter not a sound to bring assistance, or this hour will be your last," exclaimed the ruffian in a low, suppressed tone, that betrayed the savage feelings by which he was impelled. "My liberty, if not my life itself is now hazarded, and I will not sacrifice either whilst you remain in my power, as at this moment you are."

"What would you ?" asked the other as Kestrel slightly relaxed his hold upon his throat. "Have you come here to murder me, or would you make terms by which to procure your own immediate liberation ?"

"Your life I want not, unless there is reason to believe that you would betray me by raising an alarm," answered the ruffian. "Assure me, upon your honour that you will remain quiet, and your life, as far as I am concerned, is in no danger."

"I do swear it."

"Enough," exclaimed Caleb Kestrel, as he removed his hand from his throat; "I have kept my word with you, 'Squire, and mind that you are as true to the performance of yours. You must not, however, be entirely at liberty," he added, taking up a cord which lay across the table, "for my own life still remains at stake, and if the choice was left to me I would rather die than lose it. So not a word as you value your life, Squire Derwent, and rest content with my assurance that no worse injury awaits you than that of having your arms bound, till the arrival of your friends set you once more free."

"Whilst uttering these words he passed the cord three or four times round the arms and body of Mr. Derwent, and having well secured him, he once more enjoined him to remain silent under a threat of instant death if he disobeyed his injunctions.

"Villain!" muttered Mr. Derwent in a suppressed tone, "do you dare threaten one who has already suffered so severely by the vile schemes you have practised against him ?"

"That I dare do it, you have both seen and heard," answered Caleb Kestrel, "but you know not how much further I may proceed if provoked by any rashness or intemperance of language of your own. But this is no time to talk over our old grievances, though I have much yet to say to you about Amy and the sum of money that was demanded as a bribe to secure that peace for yourself and her which you so anxiously desired."

" Your demand was accompanied by threats," answered Mr. Derwent, " or it is probable it would have been complied with before now."

" In that case," replied Kestrel, " we may now come to an understanding, for I am not going to make use of threats, and by a very few words you may rid yourself of all the annoyance that you and the girl have been made to suffer. Promise me that the money I have named shall be mine, and within four-and-twenty hours afterwards I will be in some foreign country, where you shall never again hear of me."

" I will not consent to anything whilst I am under this restraint," exclaimed Squire Derwent resolutely.

" Can I see you, then, on your return home ?"

" If you choose to do so you can."

" But will there be no danger of being betrayed ?"

" That will depend upon your own conduct," answered Mr. Derwent, " for I would scorn a treacherous act as long as you keep within proper bounds. Call upon me at the Hall whenever you please to enter into this business, and if your terms are less exorbitant than they were, we may perhaps part upon a better understanding."

" In other words, there is a chance that you will at length see the folly of opposing yourself against me ?"

Before Squire Derwent could make any reply to this, Dick Radcliffe entered the room loaded with a large bag, in which he had stowed all the plate and other valuables that happened to have fallen into his way. This, with much seeming unconcern, he laid upon the floor to arrange the articles so as to be more convenient for carrying out of the house. At this sight the squire became enraged in the extreme, and having made a vain effort to liberate his arms, he exclaimed with an emotion he could not control—

" Villains ! I little thought that you had confederates in the house, or never would I have remained silent whilst the house of my friend was being plundered by your infamous comrades. But I will no longer endure this restraint upon the freedom of my own actions ;—you have been followed hither by thieves, and a punishment as speedy as just shall be your reward."

" Stop, stop, squire," cried Caleb Kestrel, holding up his finger in a warning attitude, " let me caution you against raising an alarm, because both my companion and I are well armed, and others are outside, waiting but our signal to enter the house as soon as I think their presence may be necessary. They are bold rough fellows in their way, I can assure you, and would no more mind blowing out your brains than I should myself, if circumstances appeared to render such an act necessary."

" I care not what may be my own fate," exclaimed Mr. Derwent, " murder me in cold blood if you choose, but I will not stand by quietly and see my friend robbed."

" You are determined, then, to raise the house ?"

" I will."

" In spite of the threat I made of taking your life in the event of any disturbance being made ?"

" Aye, in spite of everything ; even though your pistol was levelled at my head I would denounce you."

" In that case," exclaimed Caleb Kestrel, addressing himself to his comrade, " I think we had better give up this plate job till another time, for the squire seems determined to stop everything that he considers dishonest, and as we can't prevent his raising an alarm, the best thing we can do will be to let him have his own way for the present."

" Why haven't you sent your dagger through his heart before now ?" muttered Dick Radcliffe sullenly.

" Because doing that would not have prevented the mischief if he be determined to make a row about it," answered Kestrel ; " one shout from himt and we should have everybody in the house about our ears like a nest of hornets."

"And you may depend upon it, I should raise an alarm," exclaimed Mr. Derwent, "for even if the next moment were sure to be my last, I would raise such a shout that every one in the place should be here before you would have a chance of escaping."

" Then what's to pay me for my trouble in coming here?" asked Radcliffe.

" Your object, I should suppose, is achieved by the release of your friend and comrade," returned the squire.

INTERVIEW BETWEEN AMY AND FRANK MARLDALE.

"As for that," exclaimed Caleb Kestrel, "I wanted no assistance from my friends, for I had already got off my fetters before I knew that anybody was coming to my assistance. In short, I knew how much mercy I had to expect from you ; and no sooner was my room cleared, than I set to and filed off the beautiful ornaments that some of your people had decorated my legs with. So you see I wanted no assistance, nor shall I ever so long as fortune is kind enough not to forsake me."

" You have indeed had most extraordinary good luck," answered Mr. Derwent, " but villany like yours does not thrive for ever, and, depend upon it, the next

No. 37.

time you fall into the hands of the law, you will not be able to boast as you do now."

"That may be all true enough," exclaimed Dick Radcliffe, "but you must not suppose that he's going to be fool enough to run such a risk, when he knows so well what the consequences would be. You'll not catch him again, you may take my word for it; and even if you should lay your hands upon him, there's plenty of friends that are ready to stretch a point rather than see him sacrificed to the revenge of people, that for some reason or other owe him a grudge."

"No one owes him a grudge that I am aware of," answered 'Squire Derwent, "and even if they did, who has he to blame for it but himself?"

"Well," returned Dick Radcliffe, "I neither know nor care what reason there may be for it, but it seems certain that everybody has been pursuing him for some time past, and that being the case, I, for one, am determined to stand his friend whenever he may want one. So, your best course will be to leave him alone, or I can tell you, worse will come of it than you now dream of."

"Everything will depend upon himself," answered Mr. Derwent, "for I have no wish to harm him so long as he abstains from the violence of which he has so often been guilty. Let him remain quiet, and he shall never again have reason to charge me with having feelings of revenge of my own to gratify."

"So then," exclaimed Caleb Kestrel haughtily, "you expect me to yield without making another attempt to force from you what I have a right to expect from your own gratitude. It was I that was the means of restoring Amy to her home, and yet I am to be grudged the sum of money that I have asked for the benefit I have bestowed on her."

"Your demands were too extortionate," answered the squire.

"What can be too extravagant," asked Kestrel, "when rest and security are to be purchased by it? Neither you nor the girl can help yourselves so long as I am determined to have what I consider to be my rights; and even if I should happen to be thrown into gaol, there would still be plenty of my friends left to take up my cause."

"But your friends are known, and unless they take warning in time, they will not fail to meet their deserts. But enough of this;—if your liberty is worth preserving, leave me at once, or, reckless of whatever the consequences may be, I will alarm the household, and consign you both to a well-merited punishment."

"Do that, and you are a dead man!" exclaimed Radcliffe, partly unsheathing a dagger that he had taken from his pocket.

"Aye!" answered Mr. Derwent, "I know I am in your power, and, therefore, I must submit, however repugnant it may be to my feelings to do so. But mark me, sirrahs, this outrage will most assuredly be revenged, for never will I abandon the pursuit till all who have been engaged in the persecution of Amy have received the heaviest doom the law awards to such offenders."

"Oh, never mind his threats," exclaimed Dick Radcliffe, "for it will be our own fault if he has the chance of doing half the mischief that he threatens us with. Besides, we can get far enough out of his reach if we like; and when the next attempt is to be made to carry off the girl, we'll let some of our companions try their hands at it, and perhaps they may succeed better than we have done."

"At all events," said Caleb Kestrel, "we'll not give this gentleman a chance of accusing us of robbery; so let all this plate that you have taken so much trouble to collect together, remain where it is, and then the only charge he can make against me is the old one—that of attempting to take Amy away; which, after all, is not of much consequence, seeing that he has no more right to claim the custody of her than I have myself. So, come along with me, Dick, for some of the people here will be roused presently, and though, with our friends that are waiting for us outside, we are strong enough to defeat all that are likely to oppose us, I wish to avoid all chance of bloodshed, in order that there may be no opportunity given of trying us for our lives."

Having thus expressed himself, and cautioned Mr. Derwent not to raise an alarm till at least ten minutes had elapsed from their departure, he left the room, followed by Dick Radcliffe, and within a very few minutes afterwards, they, with their other comrades, were making their way with all speed towards Robin Hood's Cave, where it seemed to them they would be secure in the event of any pursuit being made after them. Half an hour's sharp walking brought them to the place of which they were in quest, and where the smugglers always kept a good store of brandy and food, to be in readiness on all occasions when they might find it necessary to conceal themselves from the myrmidons of the law. The first thing was to strike a light, and that being done, they seated themselves round a table, with which the place was provided, and over sundry glasses of grog talked over the events of the evening. Miles Quested and the host were, however, not in the best humour, for they had grown impatient at the long time they had been kept waiting, and their temper was by no means improved when they ascertained that the robbery which they looked forward to had not been committed.

"What the devil does all this mean?" exclaimed the host, sullenly. "I thought you went for plunder as much as for anything else—and yet, after all, you return with your hands empty, and we are to get nothing for our pains but disappointment. However, this is the first time I have ever stooped so low as to join in such an affair, and I'll take care it shall be the last, if this is all that is to come of it."

"Well," returned Radcliffe, "all I can say about it is, that it was no fault of of mine, for I had packed away a sack full of things which I should have brought with me, if it had not been for Caleb Kestrel, who was afraid there might be a row about the robbery."

"And so there certainly would," exclaimed the pedlar, "for my enemies would like nothing better than to charge me with assisting to commit a felony, because it would be the most certain means of getting me out of the way for ever. So, as I didn't choose to give them such an opportunity, I persuaded Dick to give up the robbery for the present, and get clear off with me whilst there was a chance of saving ourselves."

"Aye," returned Radcliffe, "but for all that, I wasn't going to give away every chance; and by way of getting my hand into this sort of business, I filled my pockets with some of the most portable of the plate, and between ourselves, I rather think you'll all agree with me, that I have not made such a bad night's work of it."

With that he produced, from several capacious pockets, a number of silver spoons, forks, and other things, which altogether might be expected to realize a tolerable sum, even if sold for the price of old metal. Added to this was a gold drinking cup, two gold watches, and a quantity of jewellery, all of which occupied so little a space as to escape the vigilance of Caleb, who supposed that his companion had left behind him all that he intended to have brought away. He seemed to be thunderstruck when they were now produced before him, and addressing Radcliffe in an angry tone, inquired whether he was aware of the danger this rash act had brought, not only upon himself, but upon all who were connected with him.

"Why, of course, I know they would lag us if any of the property was traced to our possession," he replied, "but we are not such fools as to betray ourselves, when it's so easy to get rid of the swag if any noise should be made about it. There's plenty of places that our friends know of, where we may hide it for the present, and when things get a little quiet again, I know where to find chaps that will be glad to buy all we have got to sell 'em."

"Of course you mean to divide the booty with us?" exclaimed Miles Quested, who had been examining the various articles with an avaricious eye, "for though we didn't get into the house with you, we were of good assistance outside in keeping the fellow that was on the watch from raising an alarm, while you and Kestrel were inside."

"Oh, yes," answered Dick, "you shall both have your proper share of it, so don't trouble yourself about what needn't give you the least alarm. But as I sharnt be in a hurry about disposing of the articles, you had better not make up your mind to a division of the proceeds till I find it quite convenient to look out for a customer for the property."

"Something strikes me," muttered the landlord, "that you are not exactly to be trusted in this affair."

"Does it, indeed!" retorted Dick; "then something strikes me that you'll have guessed right for once, if you don't mind what you are about. Once suspect me, old fellow, and it shall not be without sufficient reason, so you had better be civil about it, or hang me if I don't keep the whole lot of it to myself, and no mistake."

"Come, come," interposed Caleb Kestrel, "this will grow into a serious quarrel presently, and then we shall all be sorry that it was not put an end to in good time."

"Well, then, let's have a cup round to a better understanding between us," exclaimed Mike Quested, "for, after all, I have too good an opinion of Dick Radcliffe to believe that he would act a dishonourable part towards his friends and comrades. 'Here's success to our future endeavours, my lads, and may our next cargo be landed without giving trouble to those that are always interfering with other people's business when they are not wanted.'"

The cups were filled to do honour to the toast, and were as quickly filled again to be in readiness for the next proposition that might be made by any of the company present. It was evident, however, that the host was anything but satisfied with his chance of recovering any part of the booty that had excited his avarice, and it was very easily to be seen that he every now and then regarded Dick Radcliffe with a glance that betokened anything but friendly feelings. This was particularly observed by Kestrel, who, well knowing the evil consequences that might arise out of a quarrel at such a time as this, did all he could to preserve peace, and banish any ill-feeling that might chance to exist.

"This is no time to be gloomy and melancholy," he exclaimed, "for matters are going on tolerably smoothly, and we ought to enjoy ourselves whenever there is an opportunity like the present. Let us drink, then, to our better fortune, and, above all things, let us never give way to quarrels about trifles, for you may take my word for it that the moment we disagree amongst ourselves, there will be no end for ever of our future good prospects."

"That may be all very true," answered the landlord, "but I expect one comrade to behave honourably to another."

"Have you any reasons for supposing that Radcliffe wants to act shabbily towards us?"

"I don't know what you may think about it," replied the other, "but his words just now would make a fellow suspect him; and hang me, if any cheating was practised, but I'd have my revenge, even if I got my own head into a halter through splitting against him."

Seeing that matters were becoming worse instead of better, Miles Quested, by way of lulling the threatening storm, commenced a song, descriptive of the joys and pleasures of a smuggler's life. This soon brought out the others in a roaring chorus that might have proved dangerous had it not been that the roaring of the sea without completely drowned the clamour of the revellers, who kept up their carouse till long after the sun had risen to warn them that they had far exceeded the usual hour for scenes like this.

CHAPTER XXXIV.

ALARMING INTELLIGENCE REACHES DERWENT HALL.—AMY'S DESPAIR IS MITI-
GATED BY THE KINDNESS OF HER FRIENDS.—MR. AND MRS. PEEPS INDULGE IN
A VARIETY OF EXTRAORDINARY NOTIONS.—INTERVIEW BETWEEN FRANK MARL-
DALE AND AMY.—AN OFFER OF ASSISTANCE ; AND THE YOUNG FARMER SETS OFF
ON HIS ERRAND.

OCCUPIED as he and his friends were, in a most active pursuit after Caleb
Kestrel and his lawless companions, three or four days were fairly passed away,
during which Mr. Derwent could find neither time nor opportunity to communicate the result of his labours to those whom he had left behind him at the Hall.
Consequently Amy began to grow uneasy, and her alarm was increased in no trifling
degree by the rumour which occasionally reached her through various channels.
It is true, she could not trace them to any authentic source, yet the uncertainty
was terrible to hear, and it was evident, by her countenance, that she was suffering much more agony of mind than she was willing to confess to those who watched
her with all the attention of the most devoted affection. At length, as the fourth
day of uncertainty was drawing towards a close, Mr. and Mrs. Peeps, who were
sitting with her in the drawing-room, endeavoured to extract from her whether
there was any suggestion that she could make, by which one or both of them
might dissipate the melancholy which they had observed to be hourly increasing.

"Alas !" sighed Amy, "what can the most zealous of my friends do, when,
in my own mind, I begin to feel assured that some terrible catastrophe has
befallen my poor Cecil."

"What can you suppose has happened to him ?" asked Mrs. Peeps.

"That is the chief source of my trouble and anxiety," she replied, "for at
this distance how am I to form any just notion of what may have occurred since
his departure from home ; all we know is, that he went in pursuit of Caleb
Kestrel, and, should they chance to have met, I have but too much reason to
believe that he would fall a victim to the perfidy of his reckless enemy."

"Do you think Kestrel would take his life ?" asked Mr. Peeps.

"Have we not already seen that he would have murdered him, but that his deadly
purpose failed."

"Very true, my dear," answered the ex-proprietor of the Temple of Arts, "he
certainly discharged an air-gun at the squire, and pretty nearly did the job for
him too, if it had not been for the care and skill of our old friend, Mr. Reeve. By
the bye, what can we have been thinking of all this time, to let Caleb Kestrel
remain at large, when he has been all but guilty of a murder ?"

"Ah ! Mr. Peeps," exclaimed his better half. "how easy it is for people to
talk, when they have nothing to do themselves but stay at home and find fault with
other people."

"My dear Mrs. P.," he replied, "don't reproach me for that, because, if I staid
at home, was it not for the sake of being close at hand, in case you and Amy
should be in want of my assistance ? Besides, we don't know that the young
squire is in any danger ; and, as for his being away from home three or four days
longer than was expected, I see nothing at all in that, because there may be a
thousand reasons, any one of which would be sufficient to account for that which
at present may seem strange."

"But he has neither written nor sent a message to us," exclaimed Amy, with
a deep drawn sigh.

"Which only serves to prove that he has been too busy to be able to do either,"
answered the other drily.

"Then you think there is no cause for any alarm ?"

"I don't see any."

"Do you give no credit to the rumours that have reached us ?"

"Oh, as for them," cried Mrs. Peeps, "we can place no reliance in anything but what passes under our own eyes, and as for rumours, I have always found that they are more frequently wrong than right. Mr. Derwent left home for the purpose of going in pursuit of that wretch, Caleb Kestrel, and if he can't find him in one place, of course, he'll go and seek after him in another, till he secures the villain and puts him in a fair way to receive the punishment he deserves."

"Ah, Mrs. P.," exclaimed her husband, "but suppose the other should craftily lead him on from place to place till he gets him to some lonely spot, where he may murder him without fear of discovery?"

"Lor', my dear!' cried the lady, "what in the name of fortune could have put such a notion as that into your head?"

"I don't know what it was," answered her husband, "but the thought came upon me all on a sudden, and——"

"I have myself had thoughts similar to it," exclaimed Amy, "and in spite of my efforts to drive them away, they still haunt my mind with every appearance of a terrible reality. That Cecil is in some danger, I feel but too certain, and yet here I remain without making an effort to discover whether my misgivings are well founded."

"And pray, my dear girl," returned Mrs. Peeps, "what would you do if you were to go in search of him?"

"Not much, perhaps," she replied, "but I might die with him, and thus end this harassing uncertainty, which is almost worse than torture."

"As for dying with him, Amy," observed the ex-showman, "it sounds all very pretty and romantic to talk of such things, but for my own part I can't see any good that would come of it. Besides, I was a foolish fellow to talk in the way I did just now, for I don't suppose the 'squire would run headlong into danger when he knows what an artful scoundrel he has got to deal with."

"Yes, Mr. Peeps," exclaimed his better half, "that's quite true, for Kestrel's schemes are so well known, that I should think Mr. Derwent would be upon his guard when he has so much reason to suspect foul play if an opportunity was given for it. Then, if I mistake not, he intended to act entirely under the advice of Mr. Capsicum, who, as a magistrate, ought to know better than anybody else how to deal with such a character as he has got to do with."

"But Mr. Capsicum cannot control the will of Cecil, if he once resolves upon any steps that he thinks may lead to the apprehension of the man who has occasioned him so much trouble and anxiety."

"That, I suppose, would depend upon circumstances," answered Mr. Peeps, "for no one knows better than Mr. Derwent the sort of person he has got to deal with, and if he suffers himself to be tricked by him it will be strange indeed."

"How was it then," asked Amy, "that you just now thought he might be led into danger?"

"Why," he replied, "the truth is, I was foolish enough to pop out something that there was no foundation whatever for, and now, when too late, I'm heartily sorry for it. However, the only way is to make yourself as easy as you can, and no doubt, before long, we shall have the pleasure of seeing the squire return home safe and sound."

Amy made no reply to this, for she saw it was said only to lull her fears for a time, and, rising from her seat, she left the room to stroll in the gardens, where in solitude she could freely indulge the thoughts that succeeded each other in rapid succession. Mrs. Peeps watched her departure with an anxious look, and would have followed, but she feared to wound where it was her intention to heal, and addressing herself to her liege lord and master, she said—

"I really wonder at you, P., for being so stupid as to say things that you knew would worry and perplex our poor dear girl; I declare if you haven't almost broke her heart with that vindictive notion of your's about Caleb leading the squire into danger."

"Well, my love, you needn't be quite so tart about it," responded her husband, "for the moment I found I had put my foot in it, I did all in my power to remedy the mistake."

"By which you made matters ten times worse, for, of course, she could see well enough what you were doing it for, and now she seems to have made up her mind that some terrible misfortune either has, or is about to happen to her lover."

"Then why don't you follow, and say all you can to convince her that there's danger?"

"Because I know that grief like her's is not to be cured by a parcel of empty words," replied Mrs. Peeps. "Let her have her cry out, and I dare say she will return presently all the better for it."

"Is crying good for grief?"

"Sometimes it is," she replied, "for it relieves the heart, and I have always found that Amy has been the better for giving way to her tears whenever she has had any trouble on her mind."

"Which, by the bye," observed Mr. Peeps, "was very seldom before she had this unexpected turn of good fortune. Why, when she was a poor girl, and supposed herself to be our daughter, she was as happy as the days were long, and I hardly ever remember to have seen her with a tear in her eye."

"Ah, depend on it, those were her happiest days," answered the lady, "for there she had not a care nor a trouble upon her mind, whereas, now, since money h come in the way, she finds herself pursued by an enemy that there's no shaking off unless she and the squire yields to his extravagant demands."

"Which I should have advised them to do before now," exclaimed Mr. Peeps, "but that I saw plainly enough it would only keep him quiet so long as the money lasted. And, judging from what we already know of Caleb Kestrel, it would not serve him long, and then he would be at his old tricks of extortion again."

"Then, I suppose, no relief is to be expected till he has fallen into the hands of those who are in pursuit of him?"

"You may make up your mind about that," answered her husband, "for he is a complete ruffian in his way, and would not stand even at committing a murder if he thought the crime would serve to put money into his pocket. But, hush!—we must bring this subject to an end, for here comes Mr. Brassey Popjoy, and if he should hear us talking of murder, he'd be for packing up and leaving us, just as we want company to relieve our melancholy."

Quitting the worthy couple for the present, we will follow Amy, who, restless and uneasy in mind, wandered up and down the garden, scarcely conscious of the rich flood of moonlight that lit up the scene, almost with the brilliancy of a summer's day. The more she reflected upon the troubles that weighed upon her mind, the more certain she became that something serious had occurred to her lover; and at length, so overpowered did she become by the excess of her alarm, that, leaning for support against a pedestal, she gave way to the tears that she found it impossible to suppress. She had not, however, remained thus for any long time, when footsteps were heard approaching, and Frank Marldale, in another moment, stood before her.

"You are weeping, Amy!" he exclaimed, taking her hand, "and I do not profess myself ignorant of the origin of your grief. You are alarmed at the lengthened absence of your lover, and are anxious to know whether your worst fears are well-founded. Tell me, then—shall I follow him, and ascertain the reason of this extraordinary delay?"

"Alas!" she replied, "we know not where to seek him."

"At any rate, I can make the attempt," he replied; "and doubt not, if I undertake the task, but I will return ere long with news of him."

"Do you know where to go?"

"Yes," he replied, extending his arm in the direction he wished to indicate, "yonder road leads towards the sea coast, and there it is that Caleb Kestrel is supposed to have sought refuge amongst the smugglers who infest that part of the country."

"Then Cecil will follow him there," cried Amy, "and his life will be sacrificed by the lawless ruffians you speak of."

"Nay," answered Frank, "he would not be rash enough to venture there alone, and with the assistance he will be able to obtain in the neighbourhood, there is no doubt but any attempt made upon the smugglers would prove successful; at all events, I will cheerfully afford any assistance towards such an object, and within an hour from this time I shall be on my road towards the sea coast.

"But are you aware Cecil has gone in that direction?"

"At all events, I have every reason to believe so, for I have seen an old Gipsy woman, who has been for some time in this neighbourhood, and she informs me, to a certainty, that he has gone to throw himself upon the protection of the reckless villains who have before afforded him an asylum when he was pursued."

"How did she obtain her information?"

"She saw him and his companions making their way across the moors, and, ing at one time near enough, she heard them speaking of the place to which they were going. They spoke of some cave, the name of which she could not distinctly hear, but that I fancy will matter very little, because we know something of the neighbourhood, and I dare say it will not be very difficult to find people who will be able to give us all the information we require."

"Are there many of these smugglers?" asked Amy.

"Why, I believe they are rather numerous," he replied; "but that signifies very little, for the magistrate will not be slow in affording all the assistance that may be required of him, and with the assistance of the coast guard, there can be no doubt that the smugglers will be so entirely routed that they will never again be able to offer any serious resistance to the authorities, who have hitherto been defeated in every attempt they have made."

"Still," exclaimed our heroine, "Caleb Kestrel may escape, as he has often done before, and in that case, we shall be subjected to the same persecution as ever."

"If he escapes," answered Frank Marldale, "it will be somewhat extraordinary, for the principal object in view is to capture him, and, depend upon it, those who have taken the business in hand will not give up the attempt till they have either succeeded, or he is ascertained to have fled the country."

"And that," returned Amy, "he has sworn never to do whilst Mr. Derwent refuses compliance with his extortionate demands. Rendered still more confident by the repeated successes that have attended his attempts to escape, he will still prosecute his design till he has either brought it to a favourable termination, or discovered that all chances of gaining his object are at an end."

"He need be careful what he is about, though," answered Frank Marldale, "for the reward offered for his apprehension is of a very tempting amount, and there are now hundreds of people who wish for no better opportunity than that of taking him, in order that they may claim the money. So, that being the case, there is no chance of his long eluding justice, and for my own part, I should not be surprised if the next news we hear of him is, that he has fallen into the hands of some of his pursuers."

"That, indeed, would be gratifying information," exclaimed Amy; "but I have so often consoled myself with the reflection that he would not remain much longer at large, that I now begin to fear he will never be taken till he has perpetrated more of those evil designs, which appear to afford him so much gratification. Nay, my fears now carry me so far, that I sometimes feel certain he will murder Cecil, in order to revenge the determination he has expressed, never to yield to his extortionate demands."

"Mr. Derwent himself has no such fears," returned Frank, "and I, therefore hope your fears, in this instance, will prove to be without foundation. At any rate, your lover has the advantage of knowing what sort of an antagonist he has got to deal with, and he will, therefore, be at all times on his guard to prevent so terrible a catastrophe as you anticipate."

"Would that I were certain of it," exclaimed Amy; "but knowing, as we all do, the fiendish malevolence of Kestrel's heart, there is but too much reason for believing that he will watch his opportunity, and, perhaps, execute his design at a moment when he is supposed to be far away from the place."

"In that case," observed Frank Marldale, "there can be no real safety, unless the gibbet at last claims him for its victim. Not that he deserves any pity, however, even if it should come to that, for a more desperate villain I never heard of, nor one who more richly deserves to be made an example of."

CALEB KESTREL IMPLORES PROTECTION FROM THE BEADLE.

"But I am afraid he will act with so much caution that no one will ever be able to take him."

"So I might have thought myself," exclaimed Frank Marldale; "but when so large a reward has been offered for his apprehension, I don't think there can be much chance of his being suffered to remain much longer at large. In short, he must either escape from this country whilst there is an opportunity of doing so, or run a risk that he may afterwards have good reason to repent."

"Repent!" cried Amy. "Would that he had done so before, and we should

No. 38.

have been spared much of the trouble and anxiety that has been heaped upon us, But his heart is too obdurate for repentance, and never can we know repose whilst he has it in his power to work his deadly malice against those whom he hates."

"But his hatred would cease," replied the young man, "if Mr. Derwent would yield to his demands."

"And Mr. Derwent would have done so before now," exclaimed Amy, "but that I interposed to prevent what I considered a most infamous extortion. Had the terms been agreed to, it would have been for my sake, and I would not suffer an imposition to be practised, knowing that it was yielded to, only for the sake of preserving me from the consequences of a refusal."

"That was all very considerate on your part," answered the young farmer, "but peace of mind is worth almost any sacrifice, and for the sake of a few hundred pounds it would have been better to have acceded to the demands of so reckless a ruffian as Kestrel has all along proved himself to be. Not that I have any right to offer an opinion when Mr. Derwent is so much better able to judge of what is to be done in a case of this kind."

"Depend upon it he is in the right," answered our heroine, "for he had every reason to believe that the law was strong enough for his protection, and if he has been deceived, it was because Caleb Kestrel has proved to be even a greater villain than had been anticipated."

"And I am afraid we have not yet seen the worst of what he is capable of doing," exclaimed Frank Marldale, "for he seems to defy all attempts that are made to keep him inside a prison, and, by and by, I expect he will commit some very serious mischief against those that he has vowed to sacrifice to his vengeance."

"Then my earnest hope is that he will be satisfied with letting me be the only sufferer," cried Amy. "It is I alone who have occasioned all the annoyance Mr. Derwent has been subjected to, and since my persecutor is determined not to abandon his base object, I have almost come to the resolution of delivering myself into his hands, on condition that he will no longer continue to harass and annoy those whom I have so many reasons to regard as my best friends."

"Nay," exclaimed the young man, "what do you think Mr. Derwent would say were such a proposition made to him? Besides, Deborah, the Gipsy, has said that even your life would be endangered were you to be again in his power, and even the least violence to be apprehended would be that of carrying you away to some distant place, where you would never again be heard of."

"Which may happen, after all our care to prevent it."

"Very true," answered Frank Marldale. "It's not to be denied that we have a very dangerous fellow to deal with, but I am not without a hope that he may yet fall under that law which he has hitherto succeeded in defying."

"But there is reason for believing that he is again a fugitive; and if that should be the case, what chance is there of his being taken, when people now begin to be afraid of him?"

"There may be some few cowards amongst those who have hitherto taken an an active part in the pursuit," exclaimed Marldale; "but many, I hope, yet remain, who are as resolute as ever they were in following up the villain to any place where he may take shelter. At any rate I can answer for myself; for even if there was a certainty of losing my life, I would not hesitate to grapple with the ruffian, were chance to lead me to his presence."

"And what good would result from such a sacrifice you speak of?" asked our heroine. Have I not already bitter cause to regret the trouble and anxiety that my friends have hitherto gone through on my account, and must I still have to reproach myself for those dangers which I still see too plainly are threatening them in the future."

"Let no such thoughts as these disturb your mind," replied the young man; "for desperate as the villain is that we have to deal with, I believe he has more reason than any of ourselves for taking alarm at the prospect that is before him What can he see but a stern determination on our part to pursue him to death, and if ever he should fall into our hands, his fate will be sealed for ever."

"But, as heretofore, he will take care to avoid all attempts that may be made to discover his place of retreat."

"That he will endeavour to do so, I have no doubt, "answered Frank Marldale "but we now know so many of his lurking places, that he will find no little difficulty in choosing one that will suit his purpose. Even Robin Hood's Cave, with all the smugglers that may be there to assist in his defence, will not be a safe asylum, if there is reason to believe that he has sought a refuge there."

"Will not his associates guard the entrance, to prevent surprise?"

"Probably they may," replied Frank; "but when people are determined to carry out a particular object, it is not so easy as you may imagine to thwart their designs. Besides, knowing the desperate characters of the men we have to deal with, we should not go rashly to work, but take with us a force sufficiently strong to ensure the success of our project, and so be under no apprehension of any misfortune accruing to those who have undertaken to release you from the evil designs of this man; for we will so arrange our plans, that there shall be no chance given to those whom we design to exterminate, or at least to deprive of the power of committing any further mischief. And now, my dear young lady, having given you this assurance, I will take my departure for the sea coast, and in a few days I hope to return with the news that nothing further is to be feared from your vindictive enemy."

"And should you meet with Mr. Derwent, implore him, in my name, not to endanger himself by coming, single-handed, in collision with a man, against whom there is so little chance of succeeding."

"I shall not fail to deliver to him your message," answered Frank Marldale; "but, in the meantime, I hope you will fortify your mind with a firm conviction that the danger we are about to encounter is not so great as your fears have led you to imagine. We shall act with caution as well as determination; and, within a week from this time, I hope you will receive intelligence that will relieve your mind of all fears for the future."

Respectfully pressing her hand to his lips, he bade her good night, and hastening from the grounds where the interview had taken place, took his way homewards, intending from thence to start on the errand which he had so generously undertaken.

CHAPTER XXXV.

CALEB KESTREL SEES REASON TO CHANGE HIS TACTICS.—A RETREAT TO A SEAPORT TOWN.—A DISCOVERY.—THE FLIGHT.—THE SANCTUARY IS CLAIMED.—THE BEADLE PROVES TO BE A FRIEND, BUT IS RATHER TOO INQUISITIVE.—CALEB VENTURES TO LEAVE HIS LURKING PLACE, AND IS AT A LOSS FOR ANOTHER ASYLUM.

IT required no long time to convince the pedlar that the neighbourhood of Robin Hood's Cave no longer offered him any security, and having briefly consulted with Dick Radcliffe upon this momentous question, it was agreed that they should leave that part of the country without delay, and endeavour to obtain a passage by some vessel which would convey them to some foreign land, where they might be concealed till the present pursuit had somewhat relaxed in its activity. Having made up their mind to this step, not a moment's time was lost, and, as no preparations were necessary, they set forth immediately afterwards, without waiting even to inform their smuggling associations of the course they had determined to adopt. We shall not occupy any of our space by describing the few unimportant events that occurred in the course of their journey, but shall content ourselves by observing, that towards the close of the second day they found themselves at the seaport town of Hull. It was on a Sabbath evening, and few persons were walking in the streets, for the churches had just been emptied of their congregations, and most people had returned home to spend the remainder of the day in seclusion and quiet. Nothing could have been more favourable for the two newly arrived travellers, and their present situation would have been most satisfactory, but they were at a loss which public-house to apply at for a night's lodging, as they were not yet certain whether a description of their persons had not arrived there before them. Radcliffe was for going immediately on board one of the ships that were to sail without delay, but his companion saw many reasons for rejecting this suggestion as unwise and hazardous, for he suspected that a watch might be kept upon all the vessels that were preparing for departure, and consequently the risk would be great if they followed the course that had been proposed. Dick, however, still maintained the same opinion.

"What's the use of talking about danger," he said, "when we are just as likely to find it in one place as another, and may perhaps find ourselves in the midst of an enemy, when we are most endeavouring to avoid the danger we want to escape from? At any rate, the town seems a queer sort of a place to think of hiding oneself in, when it's just as likely as not [that the inhabitants are upon the look-out for the sake of the reward that has been offered for our apprehension."

"Fool," exclaimed the pedlar; "what do you talk so loud for, if there's as much danger here as you expect? Don't you see that there are a few passengers left in the street, and if any of 'em should happen to overhear our conversation, it would soon be all over with us."

"Then let's say nothing more just now about our own affairs, but look-out for some public-house where we may get a night's lodging without the fear of being seen by any of the police. Look yonder where a couple of 'em have just come to the end of the street, and are eyeing us in a way that I don't half like."

"Walk a little faster, then, and we shall soon be out of their sight," exclaimed Caleb Kestrel, who had been observing the same two men, and that too with a suspicion hardly less than that which had been expressed by his comrade. They passed down several bye-streets, and having, as they supposed, placed themselves beyond the reach of danger, stopped opposite an ale-house which Dick Radcliffe proposed as a suitable house enough for such plain accommodation as they would require for a few hours. The pedlar, however, was still unwilling to run the risk of entering a place where, as he said, they might both be caught like a couple of rats in a cage."

"For my own part," he said, "I would rather wander about the streets all night than trust myself where I know there is a chance of being grabbed hold of by fellows that are upon the look-out for the reward that has been offered for our apprehension. For my own part, I can't help fancying already that the people here are beginning to look upon us with suspicion, and for that reason I should say the best thing for us to do will be to go down to the quay, and look out for a vessel that is to leave by the next tide."

"And don't you think it's more likely than not that we should be noticed as we went along?"

"Perhaps we might," answered Kestrel, "but at any rate we should have elbow room out of doors, and could fight our way through a crowd if any attempt should be made to seize us. Only give me that chance, and if they take me at all, it shall not be till I have lost my life in my own defence."

"As for that," exclaimed the other. "I am just as determined to defend myself as you can be; but then there's such good reason for securing us alive that we should soon be overpowered by numbers in spite of all we might do in our own defence."

"Humph! you mean to say then, I suppose, that for the sake of the reward our enemies would fight like devils?"

"I'm sure they would."

"Then let 'em try it, that's all," exclaimed Caleb Kestrel, "for I have a notion they would soon take to flight if they saw a few of their comrades laid sprawling by our pistol shots. I know well enough the sort of customers we should have to deal with, and therefore feel very little fear if we only act like men in the affair."

" Why, you talk as if you rather wish to be discovered than otherwise.

" I can't go quite so far as to say that," exclaimed Caleb Kestrel; " but if matters should come to that point, I shall not be one to run off, even if I were sure of being one of the victims of the fray. However, I don't know that there's much chance of any mischief happening if we only mnd what we are about, and keep our own counsel so long as we remain in a place where me may be known."

" But the place over yonder seems to be quiet enough, and, as we must have some sort of shelter for the night, I don't see why we should go farther, where we should most likely fare worse. But who are those two men over there?" he added, slightly inclining his head in the direction to which he had alluded.

" They are the very same fellows that we saw just now," answered Caleb Kestrel in a low tone, and without making the least sign that might betray the discovery which had been made to those it was evident were watching them. " They seem to suspect who we are, and both of us must be upon our guard, or we shall be pounced upon before we can prepare ourselves for a defence."

" A defence !" exclaimed Dick Radcliffe ; " hadn't we better make a bolt of it, and get clear off before worse comes of this ?"

" Let's first of all satisfy ourselves whether our heels will save us," returned the other, " for it would be better for us to run away, if we are to meet with other people in wait for us at the corner of every street we are likely to pass through."

" As for that, we shall be as safe in one place as another," exclaimed Radcliffe, " and, whatever you may think proper to do, I shall not wait here with the chance of being taken up on suspicion of being the man the reward has been offered for."

" Then away with you, and take care of yourself while you can."

" What ! and leave you here alone ?"

" Aye," he replied, " I can take care of myself, no doubt, if you just run down the street on the opposite side of the way. I'll wait and see what effect it has upon the people that seem to be watching us. If they follow in pursuit, I shall know that it's high time for me to be looking after my own safety, and we must afterwards take our chance about finding each other."

Without waiting for a second suggestion of this kind, Dick Radcliffe made a bound in the direction that had been pointed out; but scarcely had he proceeded a dozen paces, when a number of persons, who had evidently been upon the watch, set off after him with loud cries of " stop thief!" At the very same moment another party of constables and townspeople rushed towards Caleb, who was so far taken by surprise, that he had very nearly fallen into their hands, and most certainly would have done so had he not run down a narrow passage, which, fortunately led him into another street. Still, however, the cry was kept up, though the persons who raised it were not within sight ; and Caleb Kestrel would in all probability have fallen into the hands of his pursuers, had not a beadle appeared at the moment at the church doors for the purpose of closing them for the night. The good man stood aghast at the sudden apparition which had then been presented before him, but before he could recover from his surprise, he was forced by the fugitive into the church, and the door closed against any pursuer who might wish to know who it was that had so recently entered the building. The official was at first inclined to give utterance to his indignation at the total want of respect which had been exhibited towards him, but observing that the intruder was more than a match for him, he determined upon being upon his very best behaviour, and with as much civility as he could assume, inquired what had occurred to fill him with so much alarm, and why he had been running so fast, as if there was danger behind. Kestrel scarcely knew what excuse to make, but at length recollecting himself, he stammered out that, whilst talking in the street, a few minutes before, with a friend, they had been suddenly set upon by a mob of ruffians, who would have maltreated them had they not contrived to escape by running off with all speed in different directions.

"And had they no reason for such an act of violence ?" inquired the beadle, rather doubtfully.

"I am not aware of any," replied Caleb Kestrel, "for I and my friend have arrived in this town only within the last hour."

"Humph !—perhaps they mistook you for some other person."

"I don't know how that may have been," answered the pedlar, "but it don't prove much hospitality on the part of your townsfolk, if this is the sort of treatment strangers usually receive from their hands. We were quietly consulting as to where we should look out for a night's resting place, when a sudden rush was made towards us, and we should have received rough treatment had we not taken to our heels as as quickly as we did."

"Well I don't think there was much fear of that," returned the beadle, "for if there was any mistake in the affair, it would soon have been discovered, and there would have been an end of the great danger that you seem to have been so much afraid of."

"But what occasion was there for any violence at all ?"

"Aye," exclaimed the functionary, "that's a question that's a good deal more easily asked than answered ; but perhaps I'm not very wrong in supposing that you and your friend were taken for a couple of precious scoundrels that have been prowling all over the country, and it has been thought they may make their way towards this town for the sake of leaving by one of the vessels that are almost constantly sailing from this port for foreign countries."

"The people must have been fools for supposing we were the persons you speak of," exclaimed Caleb Kestrel ; "and even if we had been the men, why should they have offered violence, if it was imagined that we were about to leave the country."

"I don't know much about the violence that you complain of," replied the beadle, "but I do happen to know that a very large reward has been offered for the two runaway chaps, and I suppose that, as you and your friend were strangers, a notion got abroad that the long-looked-for fellows had arrived at last."

"Do you happen to know the names of these two men that you were speaking of ?" asked the pedlar.

"One of them is called Dick," answered the officer, "and the other is a certain Caleb Kestrel, who is remembered well enough in this town, because he used to come to our fairs and markets as a travelling pedlar. But then he may have disguised himself for aught we know, for, of course, he is aware that bills have been circulated about describing his person and dress, and offering I don't know how much to anybody that will apprehend him."

"And these bills, I suppose, have been about for some time?"

"Oh yes, for the last three or four weeks."

"Well then," answered Kestrel, "depend on it the persons you speak of, have made their escape from England before now, for it's hardly likely they would remain here where it seems from your own words that the whole country is up against them."

"Very right, that I dare say," answered the other, "but suppose there has been such a watch kept all over the country that they have not had an opportunity of getting away?"

"In that case," exclaimed the fugitive, "quick witted people would not have found much trouble in getting away towards some other part of England, where this affair of theirs has never been heard of. By the bye, though, you have not yet told me what great offence these two men have been guilty of."

"Why the truth is, I have not heard much about it," replied the beadle, "but I believe there's some girl that they've been wanting to carry off, and they have even succeeded once or twice, though each time she has been restored to her friends again."

"Is that all ?" demanded Caleb Kestrel with affected surprise.

"All !" echoed the other. "Is it nothing, then for villains and robbers to carry off helpless girls from those that could and would protect them if they were allowed to do so ?"

"Oh, I dare say it may appear very shocking,' answered Kestrel, "but such things don't trouble my head, for the truth is; the world goes on so strangely, that the most unaccountable things are occurring every day that we live. As for those two men that you have been speaking of, they are very bad fellows, I've no doubt, but whether they have already succeeded in escaping, or may yet be taken, is a matter of no consequence to me whatever."

"Then you don't care whether justice is satisfied or not ?"

"To tell you the truth," exclaimed Caleb Kestrel, "I prefer attending to my own business to looking after that of others, and therefore in this instance I, no doubt, differ from a great number of other persons in this world. Some choose to be very inquisitive—some very meddling, but for my own part——"

"I see how it is," interrupted the beadle, "you pity these two worthless fellows, and would rather hear of their escape than that they had fallen into the hands of justice."

"What makes you say that ?" demanded the fugitive.

"I hope I have not given any offence, sir," exclaimed the official, somewhat alarmed by the sharpness with which these words were uttered, and stepping back a pace or two, as if expecting to receive instant punishment for the expression he had made use of.

"Oh, as for that offence," returned Kestrel, carelessly, "it matters very little to me what ignorant people may choose to think of me, and I, therefore, always treat their opinions with perfect indifference."

"Indeed!" retorted the beadle, "that's a very different sort of expression to what you used towards me when first you came rushing into the church! Then you were all civility and submission, but now, when the danger seems to be over, you can forget that a favour was either asked for or granted."

"Favour!" exclaimed Kestrel; "was it any favour to let me come in here, when a parcel of blood-hounds were hunting at my heels ?—However, you and I don't quite understand each other yet, so say no more about this affair, but tell me if anybody seems to be watching near the door ?"

The old man went to a window, looked out, and in a minute or two afterwards returned to the spot he had left.

"I don't see any one near the place," he said.

"But are you quite sure the coast is clear ?"

"There is no one that I can see,' answered the official, "and what's more, I rather think the mob lost sight of you before you came up to this door. At any rate, everything is quite quiet about the place, and I think the sooner you leave it the better, because by and by the people may happen to hear where you came to, and then it would be impossible for me to refuse their admittance."

"Why should you do so ?" demanded Kestrel, abruptly.

"Why should I not do so ?" retorted the other. "Haven't they as much right in here as yourself, and am I to be told to keep 'em out if they want to be satisfied whether you are one of the two chaps that they are hunting after !"

"Surely you don't suspect me to be one of the men for whom a reward has been offered ?"

"How should I know whether you are or not ?" demanded the other, sharply. "We are entirely strangers to each other, and of course it would be impossible for me to say whether you are an honest man or a rogue, though, without much fear of contradiction, I may boldly assert that you are one of the two."

"It seems to me that you are rather inclined to believe that I am a fugitive from justice ?"

"I don't know what you may think about that," answered the beadle, "but if I only thought there was the least chance of your being anything of the kind, I should not have remained talking to you all this time on any consideration whatever."

" Then, perhaps, you will give me a solemn promise not to say to any one'that I have been here to-night ?"

" Holloa !" exclaimed the beadle, " what makes you so much afraid of its being known that you have been here ?"

' As for being afraid of anything of the kind," answered Caleb Kestrel, " I can only say, that, but for'one reason, I should not mind if all the world were acquainted with so trivial a circumstance."

" Then why did you ask me not to say anything about it ?"

" Merely because I have particular business that will require my presence abroad," exclaimed Caleb Kestrel, " and it will prove of the most serious consequence if I were to be delayed by so trivial a circumstance as this. However, I feel sure you will remain silent about it, for you see I am armed, and if any cause or quarrel should arise, you might have sufficient reason to regret the folly of having disobeyed my command."

" Command !"

" Yes; and it is one that must be strictly obeyed, as you have been warned of what the consequences will be."

" Very well sir," e xclaimed the beadle, as Kestrel once more showed him the arms of which he was possessed, " I am quite ready to make any promise you choose to insist on. Only remember, I am acting entirely under compulsion, so that if anything serious should turn out of this, I shall be obliged to excuse myself the best way I can, by explaining exactly how everything took place."

" Perhaps by this time you really suspect that I am one of the persons you have been telling me of ?"

" To tell you the truth, you have guessed my thoughts."

" Then get rid of the notion as soon as you can," exclaimed Caleb Kestrel, " for it is one that will do neither you nor me any good. I am not the person you suspect, but if a word was said to lead to such a conclusion, it might occasion so much inconvenience to me, that I should take an early opportunity of revenging myself."

" Oh, make yourself quite easy upon that point," returned the beadle, " for I can assure you that nothing is further from my thoughts than to say anything that would bring down your anger upon me."

" Remember your promise," exclaimed the fugitive, " for though I am not the man you take me for, I have perhaps as strong passions as he has, and it is, moreover, certain that I shall revenge any injury that may be done me .For the present, then I shall take my leave, and it may be that if this night's adventure is kept secret, I shall reward you for the service that has been performed."

With his half threat and half promise of reward, Caleb Kestrel left the beadle in a state of mingled surprise and terror, that may be very easily imagined. Thick stormy clouds were fast gathering above, but, unmindful of the threatened tempest, the fugitive hastened towards the quay, as the most likely place where he might meet with'his comrade, Dick Radcliffe.

CHAPTER XXXVI.

A STORM ON THE HUMBER.—THE FUGITIVE OVERHEARS A CONVERSATION WHICH DEEPLY INTERESTS HIMSELF.—SQUIRE DERWENT'S RESOLUTION.—THE STRUGGLE IN THE BOAT.—AN UNEXPECTED RESCUE FROM DEATH.—THE BEADLE, DISREGARDING RECENT THREATS, GIVES INFORMATION THAT INFUSES FRESH SPIRIT IN THE PURSUIT.

CAREFULLY leaving the more public thoroughfare, lest he should meet with any of those persons whom he was most anxious to avoid, Caleb Kestrel at length reached the quay, where he thought it probable he might find Radcliffe, who, like himself, had been obliged to start off without the usual ceremony of leave-taking. The quick, anxious glance, however, which he cast round, afforded him little or no satisfaction, for the person he looked for was nowhere to be seen, though several idlers were pacing up and down, all of whom seemed to be looking for friends who were about to leave some of the numerous vessels which were crowded together, either for the purpose of loading or discharging their cargoes. As these persons occasionally directed inquisitive glances towards him, the fugitive arrived at the

DESPERATE ENCOUNTER IN THE BOAT BETWEEN DERWENT AND KESTREL.

speedy conclusion that this was no place for him, and having completely satisfied himself that his myrmidon was nowhere within sight, he directed his way towards a spot which commanded a view of the river Humber, which at that place is several miles in width. Here he paced up and down, so deeply absorbed in his own reflections, that he scarcely knew where he was, till he was startled by a vivid flash of lightning, which was instantly followed by a crash of thunder, so loud that the very earth seemed to tremble at it. Believing that rain would shortly follow, Kestrel sought shelter beneath a penthouse that stood near the river's bank, and had

No. 39.

scarcely taken up his position there, when two persons were seen approaching, one of whom he recognised to be Squire Derwent, and the other Frank Marldale, who, as we have seen, set out in quest of his friend in order to alleviate the fears of our heroine. Gently retreating to the deepest shadow of the building, Kaleb Kestrel could observe all that passed without being himself seen, and as the two persons stopped within a few yards from him, he could easily overhear the conversation in which they were engaged. As may be imagined, he was the theme that occupied their attention, and from what followed, he soon learned that a resolution was formed to pursue him to any part of the world to which he might have fled.

"Then you have discovered at last," said Frank Marldale, "that there will be no security for either yourself or Amy till this monster in human form has been utterly destroyed, or at least sentenced to so long a period of transportation that he will never appear any more in England?"

"I have thought as much almost from the first," answered the squire, "but revenge never formed any part of my disposition, and I was willing to give him an opportunity of retreating, and thus releasing himself from the dungeon to which his own folly and wickedness has exposed him. He has, however, thought proper to scorn the chance I would have given him; and ever since the last attempt he made against Amy, I have resolved to bring his villanous career to a close, even though I may have to pursue him to the farthest extremity of the world."

"Which trouble, I think, will be spared you," returned his friend, "for I have a notion he will be transported, and in that case care will be taken to send him to Botany Bay, which, I believe, is the most distant region of the earth from England."

"Aye," exclaimed Mr. Derwent, "but we have first of all to place him under the strong hands of the law, and that, judging from former experience, may cost us some considerable trouble."

"But you told me just now that there was a reason for believing that he had made his way towards this town for the purpose of trying to obtain a passage to some foreign country."

"And so I still believe."

"Then he will have but a very sorry chance of escaping, unless he has already succeeded in getting on board a vessel, for you have given notice of his expected arrival here, and, of course, the good people of this town will be on the look-out for a man whose apprehension will be handsomely rewarded. However, we must not relax our own endeavours on that account, for the folks here may not be a very bright set, and more may depend upon our own exertions than on theirs."

"Exactly so," exclaimed Mr. Derwent, "and for that reason I am anxious to discover whether any person answering his description has embarked on board any one of the vessels I am told are to sail from this port with the next tide. Nobody, however, is able, so far, to give me any information upon this important point, and I am, therefore, at a loss to decide upon the course it will be best to pursue."

"Suppose," observed Frank Marldale, pointing towards a dark object that was faintly seen in the middle of the river, "suppose he should be in yonder vessel, which seems to be getting under weigh."

"I have had my eye upon it," replied the former, "and my mind is almost made up to go on board her."

"How are you to do so, when none of the watermen are near?"

"I want no assistance from them," replied the squire," for I am not unskilful in the management of a boat, and as one happens to be moored close to the shore, nothing would be more easy than to row myself to the vessel, and inquire if a person answering the description of Caleb Kestrel is on board."

"And supposing he is, would the captain and crew assist you in bringing the prisoner ashore?"

"It would be at their own peril if they refused," answered Mr. Derwent, "for, as a magistrate, I have the power to call upon all persons present to aid in the capture of a fugitive felon. But we are calculating too fast, for we may be deceived in our suspicions, and, on searching the vessel, no such person as we are in quest of may be discovered there."

" Which will give us all our trouble over again."

" Trouble !" exclaimed Mr. Derwent, " what think you I should care for trouble if this, the chief object of my life, was but fully accomplished ? In short, my existence s all be devoted to the capture and punishment of this man, for till this is attained I cannot hope to prove myself worthy the hand of Amy."

" And yet I know there is nothng that affords her more grief than to know that your life is hazarded in the pursuit of this man."

" That I can readily believe," answered the squire, " but how could I reconcile it to myself, if I had not taken up this cause, when the mischief that was intended against her was so palpable ? Has he not already carried her away by violence, and ought not the conduct that he has once pursued to have urged me to adopt every useful measure that I could think of to protect her from further violence ?"

" I have sometimes thought that your marriage with Amy would have put an end for ever to the persecution she has endured."

" So I have argued myself," answered Mr. Derwent, " but she believes all his vengeance would then be directed against me, and for that reason she most positively refuses to consent to the celebration of our nuptials till Caleb Kestrel is deprived of further power to carry out his diabolical designs. Such being the case, I am determined never again to relax in my pursuit till the danger is removed by the just punishment of the heartless villain who has occasioned all this trouble and anxiety."

" And suppose he should escape, so that you may nover more be able to trace out where he is ?"

" In that case, I suppose Amy would alter her present determination as soon as it could be proved that nothing further was to be feared from her vindictive persecutor ?"

" When can she ever venture to hope that her persecutions will be at an end ?" inquired Mr. Derwent. " Whilst that ruffian lives, even supposing he should be banished for the remainder of his existence, there would always be reason to fear his escape, and then, as a matter of course, his first thought would be to revenge himself upon those who were the cause of his punishment."

" But I believe few convicts find means to escape."

" Very few," answered the other ; " but Caleb Kestrel would leave persons behind him who are hardly less vindictive than himself, and through their means the most diabolical schemes might be perpetrated. Indeed, we know that he is surrounded by fellows scarcely inferior in villany to himself, and there is little doubt they would go to any extremity for the sake of revenging the cause of their banished comrade."

" Then why not have them all taken up for being concerned in the same infamous plot ?" asked Frank Marldale.

" Because there is only one of them that we can prove to have been engaged with the pedlar."

" And who is that one ?"

" He is called Richard Radcliffe, and against him a warrant has been issued under which he may be arrested."

" Is it known where he is to be found ?"

" There can be no doubt that he is with Caleb Kestrel," replied the squire, "for I have ascertained that they were both seen together when leaving the neighbourhood of Robin Hood's Cave."

" Have you sufficient ground for believing that they were both making their way towards this place ?"

" I think there cannot be the slightest doubt of it," replied Mr. Derwent, "for England is beginning to get a great deal too hot for them, and it is only fair to imagine that he would get to the nearest sea-port town, in order to embark on board some outward-bound vessel. In fact, I have succeeded in tracing them a considerable part of the way there ; and even some few of the persons that I have met with since my arrival in this town, have seen two strangers prowling through the streets, who bore a great resemblance to the description I gave of the fugitives I am in pursuit of."

" Then I'll be bound they lost no time in seeking refuge on board some of the vessels here," observed Frank Marldale.

"There is at least a great probability that such is the fact," answered the squire ; " but the question is, how we are to discover which ship it is, since the port seems to be more than usually full of them."

" Your inquiries, then, have not led to any information upon that subject ?" replied Squire Derwent. Upon the promise of being handsomely paid, however, several persons have undertaken to make inquiries in every direction, and I am not without hopes that both the scoundrels may be in safe custody by the time we return to our hotel."

"And how soon will that be, squire ?"

"That will depend entirely upon circumstances," he replied, "for I have made up my mind to go on board yonder vessel that we were speaking of just now, and of course I shall not return till I have ascertained whether either or both the fugitives are there."

" I suppose you will not object to my accompanying you ?"

" At any other time I should have been most grateful to you for such an offer," replied Mr. Derwent, " but just now I have a notion that more good may be done by each of us individually, It shall, therefore, be my task to go immediately on board the vessel, while you remain ashore to prosecute your inquiries, and prevent, if you possibly can, the escape of those of whom we are in pursuit."

"And would you venture out in a boat by yourself? '

" Why not ?" asked Mr. Derwent, "when I have told you that I am quite capable of managing such a vessel, even in much rougher water than this is. Besides, with such an object as I have in view, and to prevent the further persecution of a helpless female, I should be a coward indeed to hesitate, merely because there may be a little danger."

" Well," answered the young farmer, " I hope you are not offended with what I said, for I only spoke as I know Miss Amy would have done if she had been present when you spoke of going out on such an errand as this. She is dreadfully alarmed, I know, at the thought of any harm happening to you, and I thought it only my duty to give you a hint before it was too late."

" Your suggestion, my dear friend, was well meant, I have no doubt, and perhaps I spoke with rather too much abruptness, when I declined to act upon it. You, however, know my determination, and all I have now to request of you is that you will inquire for those men through the town, whilst I go to satisfy myself whether they are on board that vessel which is now about to set sail."

" Depend upon it, I shall not fail in my duty," answered Frank Marldale, " but before you go I should like to know what to do with the men if I should happen to hear of one or both of them ?"

" Your first care will be, of course, to secure them," exclaimed the squire, " and that can be easily enough managed if you call for the assistance of as many persons as you see about you."

" Well, and what is to follow if I should happen to succeed so far ?"

"You would then see the prisoners conveyed before a magistrate, if the time would admit of it, but, under any circumstances, the greatest care must be taken not to let the villains escape, if once they should fall into our hands. Again secured, they shall neither of them have another opportunity of carrying on their villanous designs, which were basely plotted for the destruction of a helpless girl."

" Well, sir," exclaimed Frank Marldale, " as far as I am concerned, you may depend upon it no trouble shall be spared to give this precious brace of rascals all the punishment they deserve. I don't mind running the risk of my life, because that's of little consequence, except indeed, to Mary Everett, and she, poor girl, would never forgive me, I know, if I were to fail in my duty after having promised Miss Amy that I would do all I could to lend you my assistance."

"Then you know where to meet me when we each of us return from our pursuit?" exclaimed the squire."

"Oh yes," he replied, "at the hotel where we arranged to stay, whilst we remain in this town. We shall see each other to-night, I suppose, and then lay out our plans for to-morrow."

"To-morrow!" exclaimed the squire; " I hope both the fugitives will be in safe custody before that time."

"For that matter, so do I," exclaimed Frank Marldale; "for otherwise, these chaps may slip through our fingers, and then we should not know which way to look for 'em. However, we had better now see about beginning the tasks we have undertaken, for the ship may sail else before you reach it, and I myself have something to do; if I have to make inquiries all over the town after these two fellows."

"Then it's understood where we are to meet?"

"Perfectly well."

A few other words passed that were not heard by Caleb Kestrel in the place where he had concealed himself, and the friends then separated, Frank Marldale returning towards the town, and the squire making to the boat which was moored close to the shore. The storm, which had abated some of its violence during the last quarter of an hour, now seemed to increase with more than its former force; and it was during this period that Kestrel slowly emerged from the place where he had been concealed. Stealthily advancing in a stooping position, so as not to be seen till his victims were within his grasp, he gained the water's edge, and just as Mr. Derwent was pushing off in his little vessel, sprang forward and threw himself into the boat at the very moment when it was bounding towards the centre of the river. By the force with which this was done, the oars were thrown from the hands of Mr. Derwent, and he fell back into the boat, completely at the mercy of the antagonist with whom he found himself so suddenly engaged. At the same instant a hand forcibly grasped his throat, and by a vivid flash of lightning he recognised the ferocious countenance of Caleb Kestrel, who, with his other hand upraised, was about to dash out his brains with the butt-end of a pistol. To call aloud for assistance was impossible, even if any good would have resulted from it; and the fate of Mr. Derwent seemed to have been sealed, when a terrific flash of lightning burst forth, and, attracted by the steel barrel of the pistol, struck down the arm which had been raised for the destruction of the overpowered victim. Unable to change his position, after the violence he had received, Mr. Derwent saw his assailant leap forward, throw himself into the river, and swim towards the shore, terrified, no doubt, by the awful circumstance which had just prevented him from becoming the murderer of his victim. In a few minutes afterwards another boat came up with Frank Marldale, who had returned to the shore on hearing the outcry that had been raised, and had witnessed nearly the whole of the fearful struggle which we have attempted to describe. On landing he was conveyed to the nearest hotel, and a surgeon being speedily in attendance, he was in a brief period relieved from the pain which had been occasioned by the strong grasp that had been laid upon his throat. A number of persons, attracted together by the extraordinary event which had taken place, were now assembled in the room, and among them our friend the beadle, who was introduced to the reader in our last chapter. With some little pomposity he announced himself as Solomon Grundy, and professed the greatest readiness to assist in discovering the ruffian who had been guilty of so desperate an outrage.

"Did you see the man you speak of?" asked Frank Marldale.

"I did," he replied, "and though it was only by a flash of lightning, I saw quite enough to convince me that it was the same man I had seen at an earlier hour in the evening."

"Then you would be able to recognize the man if you were to see him again?" asked Mr. Derwent.

" Oh yes; I should know him from among a thousand."

" You had an opportunity of observing him well, I suppose ?"

" Oh yes; I was talking to him for a matter of half an hour."

" Pray," exclaimed Frank Marldale, " under what circumstances did you happen to meet with him ?"

" Why, sir, I was just coming out of church, after the congregation had left, when a loud hooting and halloeing was heard, and the person that we are speaking of came running up, and nearly overturning me as I stood upon the steps, bolted past me, and closed the door upon us both before you could say ' Jack Robinson.' "

" Then how was it," asked Mr. Derwent, " that, having such advantage over him, you did not secure your prisoner ?"

" That's easier said than done," answered Solomon Grundy; " for, in the first place he seemed, a dangerous customer to deal with, and in the second, he told me such a story that I really believed I was affording assistance to a very ill-used but deserving gentleman."

" At all events," observed Frank Marldale, " I should suppose you are now convinced to the contrary ?"

" I should rather think I am," answered the beadle, " and all I wish is, that I had known then, as well as I do now, what sort of a fellow I was talking to; for if I had, you may depend on it he would not have got off again quite so easily as he did. But who would have supposed, from what he said, that he was a fellow that would no more object to committing a murder than I should to eating my dinner ?"

" Had you given him up to justice, as you might surely have done," observed Mr. Derwent, " you would have been the means of punishing one of the most consummate villains that this world ever produced."

" I only wish I had known it at the time," exclaimed Solomon, " and hang me, if the door shouldn't have been closed upon him, though he was both younger and stronger than myself. However, there's one thing to be said—I shall know him if we happen to meet again, and he'll not get off quite so easily as he did before."

" Keep your promise in that respect, my friend," returned Mr. Derwent, " and the reward that has been offered for his apprehension will be yours."

" Oho ! so I've lost a good chance then, have I ?"

" An excellent one."

" Confound the fellow, then, for deceiving me with his blarney," exclaimed the beadle, " for if I had only suspected him to have been a rogue, I'll be hanged but I'd have had a tussle with him, rather than lose a prize that was worth having. But never mind, the chance may not be over yet, and if we *should* happen to come to close quarters again, egad ! but I'll have my revenge on him for the lies he told about himself this evening."

" Only fulfil your promise, my friend," returned Mr. Derwent, " and I will cheerfully add another fifty pounds to the reward that has already been offered for his apprehension."

" Fifty pounds !" ejaculated Solomon Grundy, with surprise. " Why, what a terrible villain he must have been for you to promise such a sum as that to have him punished !"

" He is a greater scoundrel than words can describe," observed Frank Marldale, " and if immediate measures are not taken to ensure his apprehension, the life of my friend and another person who is most dear to him, will to a certainty be sacrificed to his deadly hatred."

" Then, of course, there's some old grudge between 'em ?"

" On the contrary," replied the young man, " they were not acquainted with each other till about a month since, when chance caused their meeting at a Harvest Home supper. The villain there recognized a young girl whom he had stolen from her friends when quite a child, and as he was the means of restoring her to a large property, he came to a determination of demanding a considerable share of her fortune as a recompense for what he chooses to consider a favour, but which can only regard as an act of duty that he had long and shamefully delayed."

"Well, I don't understand much of the case, from what you have have been telling me," exclaimed Solomon Grundy, "but it seems to me rather strange that a chap like that should not have been taken up and punished before now."

"He has been taken up, my good fellow, more than once, but each time he has contrived to escape, nobody knows how."

"There must have been carelessness somewhere, I should suppose?"

"Most likely there was," replied the young farmer, "but at the same time it must be acknowledged that he is one of those slippery customers who are not very easily kept hold of. At all events, every care seems to have been taken to prevent his escape, but what with the assistance of his comrades, and his own extraordinary cunning, it is little to be wondered at that he has contrived to elude the vigilance of his keepers."

"Well, he seems to be a strange chap at any rate," exclaimed the beadle, "but for all that, he need have the devil's luck as well as his own if he contrives to escape, after he once finds himself in my gripe. 'Fore George, this large reward has set me all alive, and if I don't take him by hook or by crook, it shall be no fault of mine, that's all I can say about it."

"But, my good fellow," exclaimed Mr. Derwent, "you can have no more idea than we have of where he is to be found."

"That's very likely," he replied, "but the prospect of receiving a thumping reward brightens up a man's wits, and I shall go to work with so much spirit, that I shall be able to nose him out, let him go to what part of England he may."

"You think, then, he will remain in this country?"

"Why," answered Solomon Grundy, "I have no other reason for thinking so, except that he won't find it very easy to get away after the daring attempt to murder that he has made to-night. Besides, if he has any feelings of revenge to serve, I should suppose he'll lie quietly by somewhere, till he has an opportunity of sneaking out from his hiding-place to gratify his malignant feeling."

"It must be admitted there is some truth in that suggestion of your's," exclaimed Mr. Derwent, "and it will be well to keep up a careful watch, in case he should still entertain a notion of carrying out his diabolical purpose. You, my friend, now know the sort of person we have to deal with, and it will be for you to consider whether it will be worth your while to risk yourself in a cause that involves no inconsiderable danger."

"Aye," replied the beadle, "but the profit must not be altogether kept out of sight, and, as a poor man, I can't afford to lose an opportunity that promises so great an advantage."

"Remember," exclaimed Mr. Derwent, "he is revengeful, and will not fail to persecute you as soon as he finds you are ranked amongst the enemies who are bent upon his destruction."

"Very good, sir," answered Solomon Grundy, "but the old proverb says, that to be forewarned is to be fore-armed, and after what I have heard about this fellow I think I shall be able to tackle him with some chance of success. Besides, as I am quite aware of my customer, it will be entirely my own fault if any mischief should happen to me after all I have heard of his evil doings."

"And far be it from me to say aught that would deter anybody from going in pursuit of him," exclaimed the squire; "for I believe the liberty, if not the life, of one whom I regard more than anybody else in the world, is threatened if this monster of iniquity is suffered to be at large after this last defeat that he has sustained. However, all I can say is, that I shall not be niggardly in bestowing my favours upon those who are instrumental in ridding me of a wretch who has caused me so much consternation and alarm."

"But it seems he has comrades, sir, and I suppose you want to get rid of them as well as him?"

"I have sometimes thought it necessary to do so," answered Mr. Derwent "but upon further consideration, I am rather inclined to believe that they will remain quiet enough after the master spirit that has caused all this mischief has been deprived of the power of doing us more harm. If, however, they can be discovered, I shall be glad to have them captured, for I think sufficient evidence may be collected to bring upon them such a punishment as will put an end to all further alarm on their account."

" Will you have the goodness to let me know their names ?'

" Let us be satisfied with hunting after their leader first," replied Mr. Derwent, " and when he has been dealt with according to his just deserts, we shall be able to discover whether any danger is to be apprehended from his associates."

" Perhaps you are right there, sir," exclaimed the beadle, " for I'm inclined to think one iron is quite enough to have in the fire at one time, and when that is done with we can very easily judge as to what ought to be the next step to take. At all events, I have engaged myself to do all I can towards laying the ringleader by the heels, and when that's done you can do as you like about looking after the others."

" But what chance have you of meeting with this Caleb Kestrel ?" inquired Frank Marldale.

" I don't know what to say about my chance," answered the beadle, " but at any rate I can look upon mine being quite as good as any others, for I know every inch of this town, and if the fellow is lurking in any of its holes and corners it will not be long before I get information of it ; and then he had better look out for himself, for as sure as he is alive, I shall be down upon him before he has time to change his quarters."

" Will you allow me to ask you a question ?"

" Yes, sir, as many as you please."

" Then I should like to know if you have any objection to myself and my friend assisting in your search ?"

Solomon Grundy scratched his head, as if rather doubtful.

" I don't mean," continued the squire, who at once saw through the difficulty, "that we should either of us claim any of the merit in the event of your succeeding, for I pledge you my word that all that, as well as the entire reward, shall be yours, if this fugitive should happen to be discovered through your means."

"Oh, if that's all, I don't know that there would be any objection to your bearing me company," answered the beadle ; and then, after a slight pause, he added, —" And yet, on second thoughts, I can't help fancying that it would be better for me to go alone about this job, because it seems we have a cunning fellow to deal with, and if he has any persons on the look-out for him, and it's about a hundred to one but he has—they would be more likely to hear of three persons than one, and then, of course, there would be an end of all chance. But perhaps you fancy that if I go about it alone, I may not do my duty ?"

" No, it was not that," answered Mr. Derwent, " but we are naturally very anxious for the success of this search, and——"

" Well, I dare say you are, gentlemen," he replied, " and for that matter so am I, for there's a good large sum depending on it, and it's hardly likely that I should throw away a good chance by not performing my duty with proper caution and attention."

" In short, you would rather not have our assistance ?"

" To speak my mind fairly, you have just hit it," exclaimed Solomon Grundy. " So now, as we understand each other, perhaps you'll say which way it shall be."

" I will not interfere with you in any way," answered the squire, " for the truth is, we are both well satisfied with your honesty of purpose, and are quite willing to leave the result of this affair entirely in your hands. Here is a note for ten pounds to defray any preliminary expenses that you may find necessary to ensure the success of your undertaking, and if that should be found insufficient to complete all your plans, you have only to send me word, and any other sum that may be required shall be placed at your disposal."

"Well, sir," replied Solomon, "all I can say is, that your confidence in me shall not be misplaced, for I'll do my duty fairly and honestly, whatever may be the result."

"When may we expect to hear from you?"

"Very shortly, sir ; but, of course, I can't say exactly when it will be," answered the other. "I shall, however, begin to make my inquiries before I go

KALEB KESTREL IN DISGUISE.

to bed this night, and if matters turn out at all favourably, I dare say I shall have something pleasant to report before many hours are over. So, good night to you, gentlemen, and my last words at parting are, that I hope, whatever may come of this matter, you will give me the credit of having acted honourably throughout."

Both the squire and Frank Marldale assured him that they placed the utmost reliance in his zeal, and Solomon Grundy left them in order to commence the business he had undertaken.

No. 40.

CHAPTER XXXVII.

THE SEARCH PROCEEDS, BUT WITHOUT ANY VERY SATISFACTORY RESULT ;—SOLOMON GRUNDY REPORTS THEREUPON.—THE HOST OF THE TAVERN RECEIVES A RATHER MYSTERIOUS VISIT.—THE LETTER.—THE THREAT.—A FURTHER DELIBERATION IS HELD.

CONTRARY to the sanguine expectation of the beadle, three or four days passed away without completing the investigation in which he was engaged. Not, be it understood, that he had for a single moment neglected the important charge he had undertaken, for no man could have proved himself to be more indefatigable in the pursuit of his object, but the truth is he had to deal with a very artful personage, and it was therefore hardly to be wondered at that he at last found himself sorely puzzled as to what step he should take next. He was, however, still sanguine in his hopes of ultimate success, and each morning he left home on the same errand determined to succeed if possible in tracing out the place where the fugitive had sought concealment.

"It's very odd," exclaimed Mr. Derwent, as the two friends were sitting together one evening in the hotel in which they were lodging, "that Grundy, who seemed to be very certain of succeeding, is no nearer the attainment of his object than when he commenced it."

"So it has struck me," returned Frank Marldale, "and when people are left in this doubt and uncertainty, it is not much to be wondered at if strange notions now and then come into their heads."

"What do you mean?" asked the other quietly.

"Oh, nothing very unreasonable I assure you," answered Marldale.

"I can guess your meaning though."

"Very likely," replied the young farmer, "for it would be by no means singular if the same thought happened to strike us both. So I'll confess at once that a notion has sometimes occurred to me that this Solomon Grundy may be playing a double game in this affair of ours."

"A double game?"

"Yes—is it at all improbable that he may have seen Caleb Kestrel, and taken a bribe from him not to take any further steps against him?"

"I own the thought never struck me," returned the squire, "nor do I now see any probability of his being a traitor to our cause. In short, he has been tempted by the promised reward, and as Kestrel has no means of out-bidding me in that respect, I believe we may conclude that our ally will prove faithful to us."

"Well," returned Frank Marldale, "let us hope that your opinion of the matter will prove better founded than mine. For my own part, I am willing to believe that the man is honest enough, but the long delay gives rise to suspicions, and I could not help fancying that in the end we may find that we have been deceived. However, when next we see him, I should advise that questions be put, which will set the matter at rest."

"By that time," observed Mr. Derwent, "I hope we shall receive some favourable information from him."

"That will depend on whether he is exerting himself to discover the man we are in quest of."

"And why should we doubt that he is doing his duty, when he expects to be so well paid for it?"

"As I said before, Caleb Kestrel may attempt to dazzle him by a still more tempting offer."

"And as I replied before," exclaimed the squire, "how can he convince him of his ability to outbid us when he has no means? This Solomon Grundy seems to be a worldly-minded man enough, and, depend on it, he will hold the substance instead of grasping at the shadow."

"I am glad you have so much confidence in him," returned Marldale, " and therefore I shall say nothing further to remove your favourable impression till I see more reason than you fancy there is at present. By the bye, my dear sir, I'm afraid our visit to this place will last longer than either of us expected when we left home."

"That I foresee," answered the squire, " but the matter is not of so much consequence, now that Amy and our other friends have heard of our safety, and know the cause that has led to our detention here. At first they were in terrible alarm on my account, believing I had fallen by the hands of Kestrel, but since the receipt of my letter I have had an answer assuring me, that glad as they would be to see me return, they highly commend my determination of waiting here till the fugitive has either been taken or driven to seek shelter in a foreign land."

"Between ourselves, squire," exclaimed Frank, " I see very little use of driving him out of the country, because he would be sure to return the first opportunity, and then we should have all our trouble to go over again, with the disadvantage of not knowing wehn or from what quarter the attack might be made. This fellow is too dangerous to be thought of lightly, and for that reason I am the more anxious that Solomon Grundy should be able to discover his retreat."

"Which I dare say he will do before long."

"Most sincerely do I hope he may," answered the young man ; "for as long as he is able to remain at liberty, you cannot for a moment consider yourself to be free from danger."

"Of what use is liberty to him," asked Mr. Derwent, "when he dare not venture out for fear of being recognized and taken before the magistrate? We know well enough how much reason he has to dread such a turn in his fortune, and may, therefore, with tolerable certainty conclude that he will not venture out from his lurking place merely to accomplish an act of vengeance that must to a certainty terminate in his own distruction."

"Do you think he is still in this neighbourhood ?"

"How can I think otherwise ?" asked the squire, "when all the people in the place are looking out for him, and he could not venture to show himself in the public street without the fear of being immediately apprehended. No, no, Caleb Kestrel is as cunning as he is base, and you may take my word for it that he will not run himself into danger for the mere sake of endeavouring to gratify a revenge that has already involved him in so much peril."

"You may be right enough there, sir," answered Frank Marldale, "but there's no saying what a man of that kind may do when his heart is brimful of hatred and all other evil passions."

"At any rate there can be no reason to believe that he would commit an act that must end in his own destruction, and the consequent overthrow of all his hopes. In a word, I begin to feel tolerably confident that he will within a very short time be taken by some of the numerous persons that are on the look-out for him."

The door was now opened and Solomon Grundy immediately afterwards entered the room. The old gentleman saw that his visit was not an unwelcome one, and seating himself with an air of easy familiarity, he briefly informed the two friends that he had recently ascertained, upon what he conceived to be pretty good authority, that Caleb Kestrel had not yet left the town."

"Are you sure of that, my good friend?" asked Mr. Derwent eagerly.

"As far as a man can be that hasn't seen what he states," answered the beadle, looking gravely.

"But I mean to say, has he been seen by any one ?"

"He has."

"Then, why was he not secured ?"

"Because he took precious good care to prevent it."

"How ?"

"By bolting down a narrow passage that led to the water side, where the devil himself could not have found him."

"Was he pursued ?"

" Aye, that he was," answered Solomon Grundy ; " but you know what sort of chap they had to deal with, and, as you may suppose, he got clear off."

" Then, depend upon it," exclaimed Frank Marldale, " there's more mischief in the wind, for he would not have run the risk of showing himself unless he had some plan to carry out."

" That's just what I have been thinking myself, sir," returned Grundy. " The fellow has got some scheme in his head, and there'll be the deuce to pay soon if I don't contrive some means or another to get him into a snare."

" Have you any project in view ?" asked the squire.

" Why I can't say I have been able to fix upon any plan at present," answered the beadle, " but I thought to myself ' there's wisdom in counsel !' so away I came here directly to tell you what had taken place, and to ask if you had any advice to give me on the subject."

" I know of nothing better to be done," replied Mr. Derwent, " than to go myself and try if chance will throw him in my way."

" Then allow me to advise you not to trust to anything of so fickle a chance," exclaimed Solomon Grundy.

" What reason have you for giving such advise ?"

" Only that I'm afraid he would do you a mischief if you and he happened to come together."

" There can be no doubt of it," exclaimed Frank Marldale, " and therefore I join most heartily in persuading my friend not to trust the risk of an encounter with a ruffian that you well know has a design against your life."

" But if he has the hardihood to venture out after what has occurred, shall I not be in danger from him in one place as well as in another ?" demanded Mr. Derwent.

" I should rather think not," interposed Solomon Grundy, " for he would be a bold fellow indeed if he ventured to follow you to this house, where he would no sooner show himself than he would be taken into custody. So leave the management of this affair to those that have undertaken it, and I'll be bound it will not be very long before you hear of his being locked up."

" I have expected to hear such news before now," replied the squire, " but my hopes in that respect, as almost in all others, have been doomed to disappointment, and I now seem to be no nearer to the attainment of my wishes than I were before."

" My goodness," exclaimed Solomon Grundy, " I hope, sir, you don't think I'm to blame in the matter ?"

" On the contrary, my good sir," answered the squire, " I feel afraid you have done all in your power to accomplish the purpose you have undertaken. I, however, cannot help feeling inpatient at the delay that has occurred, though I do not accuse anybody of being dilatory in the matter."

" All I can say about it is," exclaimed the functionary, " that I have been labouring night and day to discover his retreat, but, of couse, I was obliged to be very cautious in my enquiries, or Keetrel would have been told what was going on, and then a very pretty chance we should have had of finding him."

" Very true," answered Mr. Derwent ; " I cannot but admit that you have acted with sound discretion in the affair, and all I wish is, that you had been more successful in your endeavours. There is, however, still a hope left, for if it is true that my enemy is yet in this town, I believe there is very little chance of his being suffered to escape from it, even should he make the attempt."

" You may make sure of that, sir," returned the beadle, " for bills offering a larger reward have been pasted all over the place, and every one is looking out for him, so that the next time he ventures to show himself will be sufficient to get him into such snug quarters that he will not be able to leave in a hurry."

" For my own part," interposed Frank Marldale, " I can hardly believe it possible that, with all his well known audacity, he would have ventured upon such a rash step as we have been told of. Some other person must have been mistaken for him, and have given to rise the report that has been circulated."

"If he were not the person we are after," asked Solomon, "how was it he ran away upon being detected?"

"Why that certainly is the only fact that gives an air of probability to the story," answered Marldale. "It was strange that he should try to escape, and yet, perhaps, if the matter comes to be inquired into, a very good reason might be given, for it, even though the suspected person were not the one we are looking after."

"Then you still think, sir, there must be some mistake about his having been seen in the streets of this town?"

"I cannot help fancying it," answered the young man, "though, of course, I can have no other ground for it than the very natural doubt that a man should be so fool-hardy as to make a public exhibition of himself, when he knows the consequences of a discovery."

"But perhaps he was looking about the place to see if there was any chance of escaping from it."

"Such might certainly have been the case," answered Frank Marldale, "yet still the rumour that has been spread abroad requires confirmation before I can place much reliance in it. The sum of money offered for his apprehension is a tempting one, and people are ready enough to believe anything that offers them a chance of enriching themselves by assisting to give information of the fugitive."

"Well, sir," exclaimed the beadle, "it's no use argufying the matter any further, if you are determined not to believe it; but, for my own part, I think the report deserves some little credit, and as a proof that I think so, I mean to go directly and try if I can't pick up some more information that may lead to the discovery of the place where this Caleb Kestrel is concealed."

"Do so, my friend," returned Frank, "and believe me, no one can wish you success more sincerely than I do. Go, then, and prosper in your object, for it would afford me the greatest pleasure to hear that the villain had at last been tracked to his lair."

Solomon Grundy rose from his seat to leave the room, when the landlord of the hotel came bustling in with a letter which he placed before Mr. Derwent, with a brief intimation that it was addressed to him. The person to whom he spoke started on casting his eyes over the superscription, and snatching the letter from the table, exclaimed—

"By heavens, this is the handwriting of the very villain we were speaking of!" Then addressing himself to the host, he continued—"From whom did you receive this letter?"

"I never saw the man before in my life; but he was wrapped up in a cloak, and, judging by the fact that a porter was standing by with a load upon his shoulder, I should imagine that the gentleman was about to go on board one of the outward-bound vessels that are lying in our harbour."

"No doubt it is Kestrel," exclaimed Frank Marldale, "so break the seal at once, and let us know without any further delay what the villain has to say to us."

Mr. Derwent was not slow in following this suggestion, and read aloud these few words—

"Squire Derwent,

"You seem determined to hunt me like a wild beast, but know that I am equally determined not to fall into the hands of my mortal enemies. Before you have read this I shall be on board the vessel that is to convey me beyond your reach, so that all further search for me will be in vain. Yet do not comfort yourself with the hope of never seeing or hearing of me again, for I shall follow you as your evil genius, and when least expected will strike the blow that you have hitherto had the good fortune to avoid. Remember my words, for they are uttered by

"YOUR ENEMY TILL DEATH."

"This is just as I expected," exclaimed Mr. Derwent, throwing the letter upon the table as soon as he had read it. "The villain has not feared to venture almost into my presence, and now I suppose all clue to his discovery will be lost!"

"Then all the trouble I have been at is thrown away!" groaned Solomon Grundy, as his vision faded away.

"My good friend," exclaimed Frank Marldale, "don't resign yourself to anything of the kind, for I believe your prospects of gaining the reward are now quite as good as ever they were."

"How can that be," demanded the beadle; "when the man I was looking after has slipped through my fingers?"

"Psha! you must not pay any attention to his letter, for I can see that there is an artful design at the bottom of it."

"What do you mean?" asked Mr. Derwent, who had been roused by these words from a reverie.

"I mean," answered his young friend, "that the letter has been written merely to deceive us."

"In what way?"

"Why, I would not mind wagering my existence that he will not venture on board a vessel."

"Not venture?"

"I think not," exclaimed Frank, "for he knows we should soon follow him there, and that I believe is the reason why he has written that letter to deceive us."

"I understand your meaning," answered Mr. Derwent, "and yet I cannot think your supposition a correct one."

"Still my opinion remains unshaken."

"Then you really imagine that he would give us information of what he might be about to do?"

"Recollect, we have an artful personage to deal with," answered Frank Marldale, "and it would be most unwise of us to place the least reliance upon any communication that he may choose to send us. There is a deep design in all this, and if my advice be taken, you will not suffer yourself to be deceived by it."

"But there was a porter with him with luggage," observed the host, "and that looked as if he were really going away."

"Depend on it," answered Frank, "he would not do things by halves when he had a purpose like this in view. The porter and the baggage were brought to the door merely for the purpose of adding to the deception, and in all probability the man who bore the luggage was one of his comrades."

"Well," exclaimed Mr. Derwent, "your arguments begin almost to convince me that there is some truth in them. It may indeed be that he thinks to escape from the town, and has taken this course to divert our attention into some other direction."

"Then, after all," cried Solomon Grundy, "my chance of taking him is not quite at an end."

"On the contrary, I think it is much better than ever it was," replied Frank Marldale, "for we have now something like a certainty of his being in the neighbourhood, and it only requires a little of your caution and forethought to bring him into your hands. For my own part, I feel more confidence than I did a quarter of an hour ago, and greatly indeed shall I be mistaken if he is able to avoid us much longer."

"So I should think," observed the beadle, "but the worst of it is, we have such a confounded cunning fellow to deal with."

"Then all we have to do is to employ our cunning against his," observed Mr. Derwent, "and if he should be in this town, I believe he will have but a small chance of being able to leave it quite so easily as he may expect."

"But how are you to get over that terrible threat of his?" asked Solomon Grundy.

"As for his threat," returned Mr. Derwent, "I fancy very little uneasiness need be felt at it, for when people tell you beforehand what they are going to do, you may be pretty certain that there is more sound than meaning in what they say. In fact, he thinks to intimidate me from pursuing him any farther, and I dare say the villain imagines that I shall sit myself quietly down whilst he secretly carries on those abominable designs that are intended for the destruction of those against whom he has vowed vengeance."

"Let him think so if he pleases," exclaimed Frank Marldale, "for now that his own letter informs us that he is in this town, we shall have an advantage over him that he never intended to give us. For once, then, Caleb Kestrel has over-reached himself, and before long he will find himself in the very dilemma he was trying to avoid. The host having learnt as much as he cared about, was going to leave the room, when Mr. Derwent said—

"I presume, sir, you are aware how absolutely necessary it is to observe the strictest secrecy in this affair?"

"I do, sir," he replied, "you mean that I am not to say a word about the letter you have just received?"

"Exactly so," answered the squire, "we are now pretty certain that the letter was left here only to deceive us as to the real intention of the person who sent it. He would make it appear that he was about to go on board a vessel that was to convey him to a foreign country, but circumstances have confirmed us in the belief that he has no such intention, but hopes to escape from this place whilst our attention is otherwise occupied. It is, however, of essential importance] that he should not be aware of the discovery we have made, as in that case he would give us more trouble to look for him."

The landlord again promised that he would not mention the affair to any person, and then left the two gentlemen and Solomon Grundy to arrange their future plans.

"It is now pretty certain," exclaimed the squire, "that with little caution we may trace out the person we are in pursuit of, and thus for ever put an end to the doubt and uncertainty in which we have so long lived."

"Then you still think he is concealed somewhere in this town?" observed Solomon Grundy.

"I feel quite certain of it."

"And I am very much inclined to be of the same opinion," interposed Frank Marldale, "for we know money matters must be running very short with him, and it's not likely he will attempt to leave England till he has satisfied himself as to whether he may be able to extort this large sum of money that he has demanded."

"If he expects to bully me into his terms, he will find himself doomed to disappointment," exclaimed Squire Derwent; "had he been more reasonable in his demands, I might probably have made some arrangement with him before now, but he would insist upon depriving me of a full half of my income, and I have, therefore, determined to show him that his threats and intimidation will not serve his purpose so long as he has injustice on his side."

"And, on the contrary," added his friend, "that you will endeavour, by every means in your power, to bring him to justice."

"That he must already know by former experience, and for that reason it is that he would now deceive me by pretending that he is about to flee from this country. I am not, however, to be so easily imposed upon as he may imagine, and in the full belief that he intends to conceal himself till he can make a sudden and unexpected attack, I shall endeavour to be beforehand with him, and so frustrate whatever diabolical scheme he may attempt."

"Leave the matter to me, sir," exclaimed the beadle, "and I promise you there shall be no reason to find fault with me. If he is anywhere in England, I'll find him out, and if not, I shall lose all my trouble as well as the expected reward; you will not only have the satisfaction of saving your money, but there'll be the still further consolation of knowing that your enemy is too far off to reach you."

"I'm not quite so certain about that," murmured Mr. Derwent, "for the man who has become my foe has many comrades in this country, who would be willing to lend him their aid on condition of going shares with him in any sum of money that they might be able to extort. So you or I should not be perfectly safe, even though I should be certain of Kestrel's absence abroad."

"You want to have him arrested, then, in order that he may be sent out of this country for ever?"

"I do."

"Then make yourself quite easy about it," exclaimed Solomon Grundy, "for I am not a man to break my word when I've made a promise, and if this Caleb Kestrel don't fall into my hands before many days are over, it will be something rather remarkable. In short, I must have the reward you have promised, and by hook or by crook it shall be mine, if the fellow has not already left the country."

"But you must have assistance," observed Frank Marldale.

"Ah, it will be time enough to talk of that, sir, when it appears that I am not able to do it by myself," answered the beadle. "Too many cooks, you know, spoil the broth; and I flatter myself, if this is left entirely to my own management, I shall soon have it in my power to convince you that I know what I'm about."

"The truth of it is," observed Squire Derwent, "you are unwilling to divide the money with any person who might assist in capturing the man you are in search of."

"Well," answered Grundy, "it must be confessed I would rather have the honour of doing it all by myself, and as for the reward, of course I should like to make it all my own if possible."

"Perform your task to my satisfaction," exclaimed Mr. Derwent, "and you shall have no reason to complain of any want of liberality on my part. Indeed, to do you justice, I must confess that I place the greatest reliance upon your zeal, and no doubt, when next we meet, you will have a good account to render of the means you have taken to bring this affair to a successful issue."

"I'm very much obliged to you for your confidence in me, sir," replied the beadle, "and I can only say that I'll do all in my power to deserve the good opinion you have formed of me. From this very moment I'll set to with even more determination than ever, and it will be a strange thing to me if I'm not able, in the course of a few hours, to give you a good account of what I've been doing."

Full of self-importance, Solomon Grundy made his very best bow to the two gentlemen, and sallied forth to recommence the search which had hitherto been so unsuccessful. On the other hand, however, it must be confessed that neither Mr. Derwent nor his friend entertained any very sanguine hopes that his exertions would be crowned with the success that was so ardently desired.

———

CHAPTER XXXVIII.

THE CELLAR.—THE TWO WATCHERS.—CALEB KESTREL RETURNS WITH UNFAVOUR-
ABLE INTELLIGENCE.—PREPARATIONS FOR AN ESCAPE.—AN ATTACK, AND THE
CONFEDERATES ARE AGAIN COMPELLED TO RETREAT.

IN a miserable dark cellar, in one of the most obscure streets in Hull, lurked Dick Radcliffe and Jabez Thompson, both of whom were anxiously waiting for the return of Kestrel, who had left them about two hours, for the purpose of delivering the letter, of which we have spoken in the foregoing chapter. Their present hiding-place was as wretched as can be imagined, but they had taken the precaution to provide themselves with a good supply of spirits, with which they frequently regaled themselves, as they talked over their present dangerous situation and their future prospects, which, to confess the truth, were none of the brightest. Both of them were heartily tired of a game that they could see would not end to their advantage, and they now began to debate between themselves whether it was not quite time to give up their present pursuit, and to leave Caleb Kestrel to finish by himself the task which had occasioned himself and his friends so much trouble and danger.

"For my own [part," muttered Jabez Thompson, "I can only look upon myself as a fool for having left my own business to come and look after Kestrel, who seems now to have no better plan to work upon than when he first of all undertook to annoy the poor girl that he wishes to hold under his thumb. If he means anything, why don't he set about it in earnest, and not keep on dangling at his heels, as if he supposed we had nothing to do but to attend to his business."

"Why don't you ask him the question, if you want to know?" demanded Radcliffe, whose temper at the time was none of the best.

"Because there's no getting a decided answer out of him," returned the other, sullenly, "and what he says one day he contradicts the next ; a little while ago, he was red-hot for leaving the country by the first vessel that sailed, and now we find that he is determined to remain in England till he has made another attempt to carry off the girl."

"And a pretty thing it will be if he should happen to fall into the hands of his enemies."

No. 41.

"Very pretty, indeed," exclaimed Jabez; "but he knows the consequence, and it will serve him right whatever may happen, if he is fool-hardy enough to run a risk when there's no occasion for it. For my own part, I have given him the best advice I could, and as he don't think proper to take it, I shall cut the connexion and return home before any mischief happens to me."

"What?" muttered Radcliffe, "you are longing, I suppose, to get back to your old trade of smuggling?"

"Why, to confess the truth, I am," he replied, "for anything is better than constantly running the chance of getting into trouble through a man that is blindly rushing upon his own ruin. If there were any chance of Squire Derwent giving him the money he has demanded, it would be all very well; but as he has refused to put up with anything in the shape of extortion, the wisest plan would be for to give it up for a bad job."

"That's exactly my own notion about it," exclaimed Dick Radcliffe, "but he fancies the squire won't hold out much longer, and for that reason he's determined to give the affair another trial."

"Let him beware in time," answered Jabez, "or he may have to go through another sort of trial that won't prove to be a very pleasant one. There are plenty of people that would be glad to hear of his being transported, and I fancy it won't be long before they are gratified, if he don't mind what he's about."

"And has it never struck you," asked the other, "that you and I should be likely to share the same fate if we should happen to be found in his company? Indeed it's already known that we have been associating with him for some time past, and if we don't get away from this place without loss of time, we shall hardly find an opportunity to get out of this infernal darksome-looking place."

"How did he find this cellar out?" demanded Jabez Thompson.

"I scarcely know," returned the other, "but I believe it belongs to an old acquaintance of his, and we are allowed to remain here till we can find some more agreeable place to retreat to."

"Suppose this acquaintance should take it into his head to betray us to the town authorities?"

"What put such a notion as that into your mind?"

"Why there's nothing very extraordinary in the thought," answered Jabez, "for the reward they have offered is a very tempting one, and I should not at all wonder if the owner of this miserable hole were to turn round and betray us for the sake of what he might make by it."

"Perhaps he might if it could be done safely," returned Dick Radcliffe, "but he knows, I suppose, that we are well armed, and it would not be very lucky for him to show himself whilst I had the means of punishing his treachery; I'd shoot him like a dog, even if I were sure to swing for it afterwards."

"And hanged you would be, without a doubt," exclaimed Jabez, "so take my advice, and have as little to do with bloodshed as possible. Besides, I don't think there's much fear of the fellow betraying us, for if he had been inclined to do anything of the kind, he might have done the mischief before now, instead of letting us remain here, as he has, for the last three or four days."

"How much longer shall we be safe here?" demanded the other, "now that Caleb Kestrel has been fool enough to go and show himself in the public streets, as if there was no chance of being recognized by some of the people that are on the look-out for him."

"As for that," answered Thompson, "I'll be bound he'll take care not to go where he's likely to get into mischief, and his cloak is such a capital disguise, that I don't think any one would know him in it."

"Still," exclaimed the other, "it looks as if it was put on as a disguise, and for that very reason people will be all the more likely to take notice of him. However, he wouldn't take advice, so he must take the consequences, whatever they may be."

"And, for that matter, so must we," replied Jabez, "for if they should recognize him, he would be obliged to retreat to this place, and then, with a mob following at his heels, neither he nor ourselves would have much chance of escaping from the enemy. However, I don't see the use of looking to the worst, so let us hope Kestrel will act with so much caution that he will not get either himself or us into a scrape."

"Whether he does or not," exclaimed Dick Radcliffe, "I'm not going to stay in this miserable place much longer."

"Aye, there you and I agree very well," answered the other; "for I have made up my mind to leave this town as soon as possible, and return to my old way of life, which, after all, suits me better than any other. There's nothing like freedom, to my mind; and who is there that leads such a merry, jolly life as the smuggler?"

At this moment a trap-door from above was hastily raised, and Caleb Kestrel descended quickly a broken flight of steps that led from it. It was evident that something had occurred to alarm him, and throwing himself upon a large stone that served the purpose of a seat, he remained silent for some few moments, as if to recover from the effects of a long and severe chase. The other two men regarded him with a look of alarm, and at length the silence was broken by Dick Radcliffe, who eagerly asked the cause of the haste and agitation with which he had returned.

"There's been cause enough for it, to my thinking," exclaimed Kestrel, "for if I had not made the best use of my legs, I should not have contrived to escape from the devils that came after me."

"You have been pursued, then?"

"And pretty sharply, too."

"Did they trace you to this place?" asked Jabez.

"That's more than I can answer for," he replied. "All I know about it is, that I had to run for it, and at one time I hardly thought my legs would be quick enough to save me."

"Then, of course, they were not far behind when you entered the house?" exclaimed Dick Radcliffe.

"Hang me if I had time to look about me," he replied, "so, of course, I am not able to answer your question. I, however, fancied their voices grew more distant as I ran on, and perhaps it may have been my good fortune to get here without being seen."

"How were you first discovered?" asked Thompson.

"That's more than I can tell you," answered Caleb Kestrel; "but whilst gently walking back, after leaving my letter at the hotel, I was suddenly roused by hearing people running with all speed behind me, and looking back, I saw by the lamp-light that a number of people were in pursuit of me. Of course there was not a moment to be lost, and taking to my heels, I turned down the first narrow street I came to, and made the best of my way towards this place."

"And, I suppose," exclaimed Dick Radcliffe, "they took good care not to lose sight of you for a moment?"

"I can't tell you how that may have been," replied the fugitive, "but at any rate, if they should follow me here they will receive a salutation that they little expect, for let what may happen, I'll rather lose my life than my liberty."

"You must have been a fool to leave this place when there was almost a certainty of your being seen," exclaimed Jabez Thompson; "and as for myself, I deserve anything that may happen for having been such an ass as to follow you to this miserable cellar, that's only a fit place for rats to shelter themselves in. But it's all my own fault, and if I should be fortunate enough to get out of this dilemma, I'll return to my old quarters on the sea coast, and stick to my own business instead of looking after other people."

"What!" muttered Kestrel, "are you beginning to repent of having done me an act of civility?"

"It's enough to make one repent, when it brings a fellow into trouble and difficulty. However, here I am, and as there's no getting out of the scrape, if your pursuers should follow me, I shall make up my mind to fight to the very last, rather than yield myself up quietly to the people that are hunting after us."

"That's well said," exclaimed Caleb Kestrel; "but, between ourselves, I think there'll be no occasion for fighting; however, in close quarters like these, we should not have much chance of getting the best of it, and therefore, though no coward, I fancy the best thing we can do will be to make our escape as quietly as possible."

"But how is that to be done?" asked Radcliffe.

"Through yonder door," answered the pedlar, pointing to a recess that was scarcely to be seen through the murky darkness that obscured the place. "It leads to another vault similar to this one, and from thence is a clear way for us into a court at the back of these premises."

"Suppose watchers should be placed there?"

"Then we must fight our way through them, for we should have no other chance of saving ourselves."

"The game is a very desperate one," exclaimed Jabez Thompson, "and whatever comes of it, we shall have you to thank for it. However, we have got ourselves into the scrape, and now the only way that remains is to get ourselves out of it, in the best way we can."

"Grumbling fool!" muttered Caleb Kestrel, "am I to hear nothing else but your regrets for having given me your assistance on a promise of being well paid for it if I succeeded in getting the money from Squire Derwent?"

"I ought to have known that you had no chance of extorting anything from him," returned Jabez; "and all I can say is, that I deserve all that may happen, for having suffered myself to be so easily led away by your promises."

"Then have nothing more to do with me or my affairs," exclaimed Caleb. "For I would rather give up all my chance of getting money from the squire, than receive the unwilling assistance of a man that would have it in his power to destroy me any time he likes. So, now that we understand each other, you can leave me as soon as you like; only remember one thing, never attempt to play me false; for if you do, I'll have your life as surely as that I now tell you so."

The angry reply that was about to follow was prevented by a loud voice in the upper part of the house, and it soon became certain that the pursuers had found means to obtain an entrance into the place. No time was, therefore, to be lost,—and the quarrel having been lulled for the present, the three companions began to think only of taking care of themselves. This was done by passing through the door, which had been spoken of by Caleb Kestrel, and the passage having been again secured as soon as they were safe on the other side, they made their way across the second vault towards a flight of steps, which formed the only means of access to the place. This, after raising a trap-door, led them to a court, where, luckily for them, no one had been left to look after the fugitives. They, however, heard the sound of many voices, and moving hurriedly away, they reached a lonely spot, near the docks, where they could pause for a few minutes without much fear of being seen by any of those persons they were so anxious to avoid.

"Now, what's to be done next?" exclaimed Dick Radcliffe, after having first looked round to see that no one was near. "We have been regularly scouted from the only place where we could hope to find a shelter, and now, I suppose, we must leave the neighbourhood without having advanced a single step nearer towards getting the money that you was so sure of forcing out of the pocket of Squire Derwent."

"What!" returned the pedlar, "are you going to grumble as well as t'other one?"

"I think it is enough to make people grumble," he replied, "when there's all this trouble and difficulty, and nothing at all to reward us for our pains."

"Psha! The reward will come by and bye, and as it will be a very handsome one, it's surely worth some little trouble before it's earned? I have said that whatever the squire gives shall be equally divided amongst those that are concerned with me, and if you have not patience to wait a short time longer, why you had better give it up at once, and I'll look out for some other fellows to assist me."

"But where are we to look for shelter now?" asked Jabez.

"Why near the old spot, to be sure."

"Where do you mean?"

"In the neighbourhood of Derwent Hall."

'Then it will soon be all over with us," exclaimed Dick Radcliffe, "for they are certain to keep a look-out for us thereabouts, and the moment we show our faces the enemy will pounce upon us."

"Aye, if we are fools enough to show ourselves," answered Caleb, "but as there is no occasion to come out of our hiding-place for some time to come, we can set the foe at defiance till the opportunity comes for carrying the girl away from the hall."

"Are you still determined to run the risk of carrying her off!"

"What great risk is there, Dick," he asked, "if we only contrive the affair with a little caution? However, I forgot that you are going to deprive me of your services, so there is no occasion for me to explain to you exactly the system I am going on."

"I'm not going to leave you," answered Dick Radcliffe, "so don't suppose that I'm a coward just when my services are most required. You'll find me staunch enough so long as I see that everything is going on as it ought to do, but if there should be any chance of the affair failing through a want of caution, I shall then at once give you fair notice of my intention, and cut the business at once."

"Well, that's fair enough; and now what do you say, Jabez, as to your intentions?"

"I shall do as Dick does."

"Then we continue just as we did before, and, of course, there will be no objection to follow me to Derwent Hall?"

"We will," replied Radcliffe, "though I must say that part of your arrangement don't suit me at all, for I see nothing but danger in it, without any good likely to happen."

"The good will be this," exclaimed Caleb Kestrel—"if the girl can be carried away, which I believe may be done easily enough, we shall be sure to make our own terms, though he has obstinately held out so long. So, before long, we may expect to see this affair brought to an end, and then each of us will be rewarded with the share that is to come to him.'

"But how are we to be sure of your keeping faith us?" demanded Jabez Thompson.

"Humph!—you are still suspicious of me then?"

"How can I be otherwise, when we can make no claim upon you, even if this matter should end as you expect?"

"Do you think I have no honour?"

"Honour!"

"Ay; is there not such a thing as honour among thieves as well as amongst a more respectable class of persons? But never mind, doubt me as much as you please, and the surprise will be all the more agreeble when I place the share in your hand.'

"Very likely," returned Jabez, "but unfortunately this affair is so long before it comes to a finish."

"Is that any fault of mine?" demanded Kestrel; "haven't I tried often enough to get the money out of Squire Derwent, and if he chooses to be obstinate, am I to blame for it? In short, we all want the money, so now I am determined not to stand any more nonsense, but to have the money the very first time I see him."

"Which will not be very soon, I'm afraid," exclaimed Dick Radcliffe, "for the squire is in full pursuit, and it would not be very safe for you to put yourself in his power, when I believe he has both the means and the intention to send you abroad for the rest of your life."

"That don't trouble me much," returned Caleb, "for however much I may be indebted to his inclination, you may make up your mind for it that he'll never be rash enough to provoke my anger."

"Psha! what cares he for your anger?"

"Not much, perhaps, as far as he is himself concerned," answered Caleb Kestrel, "but he cares something for the girl though, and he knows very well that she would be taken away from him if he doesn't think proper to come to my terms."

"And what right?" asked Jabez Thompson, "have you to demand this large sum of money from him?"

"I don't know what reason you have to ask my right," he replied, "but at any rate I possess a power over him that he can't help, so the money I have must be very shortly forthcoming, or I shall do something that he will ever afterwards be sorry for."

"You will take her away, I suppose?"

"Aye, and that too without any further delay."

"But suppose he guards her with so much care that you can find no opportunity to carry out your plans?"

"He may be as watchful as he pleases," answered Caleb Kestrel, "but all his care will be thrown away when once I have made up my mind to execute the design that I have been so long thinking of."

"You have been defeated," observed Dick Radcliffe, "and may be so again, if you don't take care."

"Aye, my good fellow, but I will take care, and so the squire will find out to his cost, unless he thinks proper to listen to a little reason. Surely his peace of mind is worth a sacrifice, and he shall never know what it is unless he makes me such an offer as will be worth my acceptance."

"Is it true," asked Thompson, "that you have demanded half his fortune?"

"Yes," he replied, "that's true enough, and I don't see that he has much cause to complain, seeing that he will never know any enjoyment of life as long as he thinks proper to stand out about trifles."

"But he don't seem to think it such a trifle."

"That's because he has not given the affair half the consideration it deserves," answered Caleb Kestrel. "If he loves the girl as he professes to do, he won't think any sacrifice too great to secure her happiness, which it would be well for him to do at once, because I am determined not to lower my demand by even a pound."

"Has the girl ever injured you, that she should have been made to suffer?" demanded Jabez Thompson.

"The girl? Oh, no! she never injured me."

"Then why couldn't you have let her alone?" demanded Jabez.

"Because, through her, I saw a capital chance for myself," answered Caleb Kestrel. "In short, I wanted money, and there was no way that I knew of so certain to bring me in some, as to extort it from the squire by threats and menaces against Amy."

"Well, hang me, if that is not cowardly!" exclaimed Dick Radcliffe.

"Call it what you like," returned the other; "but when a man's hard up for money, he tries many things that he would not otherwise think of. Besides, this girl would never have come to the fortune if it had not been for me, and I've a right to expect something out of it, when I know she has plenty for herself, and enough to spare."

"Did you ever ask her for any?"

"Not I," he replied; "but I have spoken several times to Squire Derwent upon the subject, but he chooses to be obstinate, and refuses to do the slightest thing, though he knows well enough that Amy will never have any rest till I have got all I ask for."

"So you are determined to make her suffer for the obstinacy of her friend?"

"There's no help for it, Jabez," he replied, "as the affair must take it's own course, and those that are afraid to lend me a helping hand must leave it alone, that's all I've got to say about the matter."

"Is it true," asked Thompson, "that the squire is going to marry her?"

"It's quite true that he wants to do so," replied the pedlar, "but it's as certain as that I am now telling you, that he never will marry her unless he thinks proper to come to terms with me."

"Have you ever told him as much?"

"Several times."

"And yet he won't give the money you have asked for?"

"At present he has refused to do anything for me," answered Caleb Kestrel, "but he must, by this time, be tired of the continual annoyance that both he and the girl receive from me, and, before long, I expect he will be glad to come to a fair understanding with me."

"For which purpose you are going to venture once more into the neighbourhood of Derwent Hall?"

"Exactly so."

"With the chance of being taken by some of your pursuers?"

"As for that," answered Caleb Kestrel, "nothing can be done without risk, and those that don't choose to accompany me can leave me to manage the whole affair myself. I don't want your assistance unless it's given with a free will; so now, as we understand each other, perhaps you and Dick Radcliffe will tell me how far I may depend upon your future services."

"Why, of course, we'll stick to you to the very last, my boy," exclaimed the last-named personage, "for having gone through so much trouble on your account, it's not likely we are going to give up just when you fancy the business is about to be settled. So now lead us whereever you please, Caleb, and if we don't do our duty to your entire satisfaction, you will be at liberty to tell us of it afterwards."

Perceiving that the coast was now quite clear, the three confederates moved stealthily away from the place where they had been lurking, and directed their way towards the suburbs, by which they intended to quit the town. Contrary to their anticipations, they found no obstruction whatever in their way, and having at last reached the country, they left the high road and crossed some fields, which led towards the part they were anxious to reach before daybreak.

CHAPTER XXXIX.

SOLOMON GRUNDY LABOURS IN VAIN.—HE TAKES COUNSEL OF A FRIEND, AND LEARNS THAT THE BIRDS HAVE FLOWN.—A VISIT TO THE HOTEL.—THE VIEWS OF SQUIRE DERWENT AND FRANK MARLDALE ARE DEFEATED, AND THEY TAKE THEIR DEPARTURE FOR HOME.

For two entire days did the beadle continue his search from one end of the town to the other, but, as may be imagined, without the slightest success or even any encouragement that his task would be ultimately crowned with success. It is true, if he had spoken to any one upon the subject, he would have heard that in all probability the men were no longer in the town, but Solomon was afraid of doing this, lest he should have to part with any portion of the reward, and he therefore preferred continuing his object in secrecy, little imagining the disappointment that was in store for him. To do him justice, however, he was unremitting in his exertions, commencing his task at an early hour in the morning, and strolling about till late in the evening in search of men who were no longer within his reach. But this was an affair which he had yet to discover, and instead, therefore, of despairing, he kept up his spirits to the very last, believing that the objects he was in pursuit of were not far off, and that in a very short time he would receive as his reward, the large sum of money that had been offered by Squire Derwent for the apprehension of the man he was in quest of. At length, however, the patience of the worthy beadle began to wear out, for it became evident that he had very shy birds to deal with, and he now began to turn it seriously over in his mind whether it would not be better to associate somebody else with him, even though he might have to give up a portion of the expected profits. It was not without considerable regret that Solomon eventually came to that determination, and scarcely was his mind made up when chance threw in his way one Simon Ruddle, the sexton of the same parish to which he was beadle, and between whom there consequently existed some little intimacy. Simon, therefore, was to be his confidant, and to him he cautiously related the prospects he had in view, and the certainty of their both receiving a handsome sum if they only carried on the affair with a little prudence and forethought. Simon Ruddle, who was a bit of a miser in his way, eagerly closed with a proposition that promised him a large share of gold, and having in the first place sworn not to let the secret go any further, he was in the next informed of as much of the affair as Solomon himself knew of it. So far, everything was highly satisfactory to the sexton, and, eager to commence operations without delay, he proposed that they should immediately set about their task in order that it might the sooner be brought to a satisfactory conclusion. Solomon Grundy was quite inclined to accede to this, but unfortunately he was not in a position to say how it would be best for them to commence.

"You must know, Simon," he exclaimed, looking round to see that no one was within ear shot, "that the chaps we have got to deal with are as cunning as the devil, and if we don't go about our work with care they'll discover what's up against them, and neither you nor I will ever touch a farthing of the money."

"Where are they hiding themselves all this time?" demanded the sexton in a whisper.

"That's more than I or anybody else can tell you," replied Solomon, "but I should think we may soon find out where they are if we only go the right way to work. At any rate they are not very far off, so there's some comfort for us, you see."

"How do you know they are not far off?"

"Because one of 'em—and he's the principal of the lot—left a letter at the George Hotel the other night," answered Solomon Grundy. "It's true, he said something in the note about going abroad, but no one believes him, and it is supposed that he only said so for the sake of putting an end to the inquiries that are making about him."

"So then, I see how it is," exclaimed the sexton; "all those fine promises of yours will come to nothing, and before any further trouble is taken in the affair, I shall back out of it."

"Back out of it! Are you afraid of a little trouble, when it's to be paid for on so liberal a scale?"

"Why the long and short of it is, that I don't see my way very clearly," replied Simon Ruddle, "and I must be pretty sure of being well paid before I have anything to do with it."

"Between ourselves, old fellow," exclaimed the sexton, "I don't see but what it would have been as well if we had both of us received a portion of it, because you may depend upon it people will never work well so long as there's any uncertainty about the pay."

"What uncertainty can there be about that," asked the beadle, "when the squire can put his hands upon thousands of pounds at any moment he likes? Besides, we don't want to affront him, and we should be sure to do so if we were to ask for any part of the reward before we have earned it."

"But we are going to earn it, are we not?"

"Aye, aye, that's true enough," replied the beadle, "but just fancy yourself parting with money before anything has been done for it, and then say whether you think any other person would be likely to do it more than yourself. It's out

of all reason I tell you, so if you have a mind to give up this affair at once, say s
and I'll look after somebody else that isn't quite so unreasonable."

"Well," replied Simon Ruddle, "I don't know that I feel at all anxious to hav
any more to do with it, unless I could see my way clearly. Besides, these peop
may not be in the town now, and then a very fine thing it would be for us to ha
thrown away all our time and trouble for nothing."

"But I tell you there's no doubt of their being in the place."

"Have you seen 'em?"

"No; but they were routed out of a hiding place in the town only last night,
and no doubt they have cooped themselves up in some other den, not far off,
where they will be very shortly discovered."

"Even supposing you knew the exact spot, it would be an act of madness for
us to disturb 'em, when we are not sure of being rewarded for our pains. Besides,
neighbour Grundy, I'm not so tired of my life yet as to hazard it, when there's
a chance of our coming off second-best in the business."

No. 42.

" You own yourself a bit of a coward then ?"

" Not I," he replied, " I can boast, perhaps, of as much bravery as here and there one, but as for throwing away my life like a simpleton, is a thing not to be thought of."

" Is it acting like a simpleton, when you know that a good deal of money is to be made with very little difficulty ?"

" Aye," exclaimed Simon, " it's all very fine to tell me how easy it is to be done, but I've a notion that those chaps have made themselves scarce, and if once they're got out of the town, I should like to know where we are to look for 'em."

" Haven't I told you over and over again !" exclaimed a voice—and looking round, they saw a Gipsy woman standing at no great distance off, in the shadow of a building. As no other person was anywhere near, they naturally concluded that it was she who had spoken, and Solomon, advancing towards her, exclaimed—

" How do you know, woman, that they have left the town ?"

" Because I saw them miles away from home at an early hour this morning," she replied.

" Where did you see them ?"

" That is a question that I am not inclined to answer."

" Perhaps you are a friend of theirs ?"

" Perhaps I am," she replied, with the same indifference, " and if so, I am not likely to betray their whereabouts."

" Then why," asked Grundy, " have you told us that they are no longer in this town ?"

" Merely to let you know that it would be useless to take any further trouble in the matter."

" How do you know they are the men we were speaking of ?"

" Because, from the nature of your conversation, I knew that Caleb Kestrel was one of the persons you are in search of."

" I see how it is then," exclaimed the beadle, " he is some relation, whose escape you are anxious to favour, and this assertion of yours has been made merely to put us upon a wrong scent."

" Caleb and I are no friends," she replied, " for I have bitter reasons to curse the hour when he and I became acquainted."

" Then why not tell us where he and his companions are to be found ?"

" Because I am no informer, and would rather suffer the tongue to be cut out of my head than do an injury to the man that I at one time regarded with better feelings than I do now."

" But suppose I take you before a magistrate ?"

" You can do so if you please," answered old Deborah—for she it was who had accosted them—" and when that has been done, what power is there upon earth that can force me to betray a man that is already sufficiently persecuted ?"

" You forget that he is persecuting others ?"

" I have not forgotten it," she replied, " nor has it been through any fault of mine that he has gone on so long in a course that I have warned him against. I would, however, rather favour his escape than say or do anything that would hinder it, and for that reason I have refused to say where I last met him."

" Well," exclaimed Simon Ruddle, who saw an end of his golden dream, " I suppose you will have no objection to tell us whether any people were with him ?"

" There were two men."

" Do you know them ?"

" Yes, both."

" Then, perhaps, you'll tell us where they are to be found ?"

" You'll get nothing from me more than you have already heard," replied the Gipsy, " for it's a rule with our people never to betray a secret when life or liberty depend upon it."

" But we'll pay you liberally for any information that you are inclined to give," exclaimed Solomon Grundy.

" Do you believe then," she exclaimed scornfully, " that I am to be bribed by an offer of blood money ?"

" I don't know what you may call it," answered Simon Ruddle, " but it's my opinion that money in any shape is worth having, and for my own part, I would not refuse it in a case of this kind, because I know how necessary it is to secure these three or four villains who have been setting the law and everything else at defiance."

",What is that to you or I ?" demanded the old woman. " If they have done anything amiss, the law ought to be strong enough to punish 'em for it, and per-haps I should not be one to pity, though I certainly would suffer myself to be tortured to death, rather than be guilty of such an act as you would tempt me to commit."

" But it's not unlikely that murder may be perpetrated before they have done," observed Solomon Grundy.

" You needn't be under any alarm about that," exclaimed the Gipsy, " for I have always my eye upon the one they call Caleb Kestrel, and it shall be my care to prevent any such crime as you have spoken of."

" Perhaps you may be very clever," exclaimed the beadle, " but Squire Der-went expects nothing less, and that's why he is so anxious to secure the fellow under lock and key. So, now, tell us which way to follow these men, and if we take 'em through your information, our employer will not fail to reward you for the service."

" Your employer," she replied, " needs no assistance from anybody, if he sees proper to adopt one course."

" What's that ?"

" Let him give Caleb Kestrel a sum of money, and the chances are that he'll never be troubled by him again."

" Squire Derwent will never do that," answered Solomon, " for if money is to be taken from his pocket, he would rather give it to have the man punished, than to bribe him to drop his villanous proceedings."

" Tell him from me, then, to keep a careful watch upon himself and Amy," she replied, " for I warn him that there is mischief in the wind, and it may soon be too late for him to prevent the evil that is brewing. Forget not my words, for, if heeded, they may save much future trouble and misfortune."

Before Solomon Grundy could make any reply to this, the old woman had dis-appeared, and was not to be seen anywhere near, though she had scarcely been gone an instant. As for the sexton, he had heard quite enough to convince him that nothing was to be gained by affording his assistance to Solomon, and as he turned round to pursue his way homewards, the beadle directed his steps to the hotel in order to inform the squire of all that had taken place since he had seen him last. Mr. Derwent, however, was at first inclined to think some scheme was 'intended by the old woman.

" She appeared like a Gipsy, I think you said ?" he observed to the beadle, after conferring a few moments with Frank Marldale.

" Yes, sir; I'm sure she was one."

" Then I think I have seen the same person in the immediate neighbourhood of my own house," exclaimed the squire. " She is—or, at least has been, an asso-ciate of these men, and, I suppose, comes here to assist in their escape from justice."

" I can't say how that may be, sir," answered Solomon; " but if she came here for any such purpose, she must have been too late, for she says she met them a good many miles away from this town."

" Perhaps that was only a trick to deceive us as to the place where they are really concealing themselves."

" That's just what I thought myself, sir," exclaimed the beadle; " but you, of course, can judge better than myself as to that, and I came away directly to let you know what I have heard."

" It is strange, certainly, that the woman should be here," returned the squire, " when it's not many days since I saw her in the vicinity of my own house. To be sure these Gipsies lead a roving life, and there may not be anything very extraordinary in her having travelled to a large town like this, where she may pursue her vocation with a probability of making a good deal of money."

"I have seen the woman you speak of," interrupted Frank Marldale, " and from two or three conversations I have had with her, it seems that she entertains anything but favourable feelings towards Caleb Kestrel. Indeed, from all I have heard her say, I believe she would not refuse to give us her assistance if she happens to know where they are to be found."

" Don't make too sure of that, sir," exclaimed Solomon Grundy, "for she refused to give me even the slightest hint of where it was that she met the three fellows; and when I gave a hint that she might expect a large reward for any information that it was in her power to give, she was quite huffish, and said she would not turn informer for any bribe that might be offered."

" Perhaps you were too sudden in putting the question ?"

" On the contrary, I was very careful."

" Did she say nothing that might lead one to guess the place where she had seen them ?"

" Not a word," replied Solomon; "and sometimes I feel half inclined to believe she had only invented the story for the purpose of misleading us, and so giving them an opportunity of getting out of this town while our attention is directed elsewhere."

" A very likely suggestion that of yours," exclaimed Frank Marldale, " and I for one am inclined to have a good search all over this place before we go to look for them anywhere else."

" We have already done that sufficiently," returned Mr. Derwent, " and as our labour has been thrown away, I think the wisest course will be to return home, after leaving instructions with this man how to proceed in our absence. A watch may still be kept here, and I needn't say that the reward shall be paid immediately to any parties who apprehend the persons we are after."

" Don't you think it would be better for me to look after the woman I have been speaking about?" asked Solomon.

" I fancy that would be hardly worth while," answered Mr. Derwent, " for I shall most likely see her in the course of a short time, and if nothing has been heard of Caleb Kestrel in the meanwhile, it will then be for us to consider whether we may not prevail upon her to give such information as will lead to his apprehension."

" Wouldn't it be as well to question her upon the subject at once ?" demanded Frank Marldale.

" No, not just yet, certainly," answered his friend, " for she might give him information of what we are doing, and that would so put him upon his guard, that we should have little chance of tracing him out afterwards. We will, therefore, see what course events take in the next four days, and then, I think, we may be able to frame our own projects, so as to obtain the end we are so desirous of reaching."

" I don't know that," exclaimed the young farmer, "for this woman may happen to be a confederate, and in that case all our projects will be exposed to the persons we wish to keep in the dark."

" Perhaps she won't see 'em again for some time to come," observed Solomon Grundy, " for if she is to be believed, they are all in a distant part of the country by this time."

" That may be soon ascertained," exclaimed Mr. Derwent, " because all the town is now alive for their apprehension, who are considered dangerous to the neighbourhood, and if they are anywhere near, we cannot fail to hear something of them before long. At any rate, be where they may, we will not allow them much rest, so that if they should be fortunate enough to elude the search, they will be at length driven to seek shelter and quiet in some foreign country."

"How are they to do that, if they have no money?" asked Frank.

"As for that," answered the squire, "I dare say they have taken care to provide themselves with a tolerable supply of that article, seeing that they are aware how absolutely necessary it will be in the event of their being compelled to go into a strange land. Besides, I'll be bound they would not hesitate to commit a robbery, if there were no other means of raising the wind."

"Have they ever committed a robbery before?" asked Solomon.

"Many, I believe."

"If that's the case, there won't be much difficulty in getting them convicted and sent out of the country."

"My good fellow," exclaimed the squire, "nothing is so easy as to talk of these things, but, on the other hand, nothing is more difficult when you come to try it. Those men can always find lurking places where their pursuers are hardly likely to look for them, and former experience proves that they are too cunning to be taken, unless by officers who are used to deal with such persons."

"Am I to understand," asked Frank Marldale, "that it is likely your old enemy will venture near Derwent Hall?"

"I fancy nothing is more likely," answered his friend, "but, of course, that is a matter that can only be proved after some little delay, and we must, therefore, wait till after we have been at home some few days, when, no doubt, we shall be able to ascertain whether they are skulking about in the neighbourhood."

"Let's hope they'll not go there, at any rate," exclaimed the beadle.

"And why should we hope anything of the kind?" demanded Mr. Derwent; "when, if they should do so, it would be almost certain to lead to their apprehension."

"That's very possible," answered Solomon Grundy, "but it would also lead to my losing the reward that I have been looking forward to; and that's not altogether pleasant after the great trouble I have been at to bring the scoundrels to justice."

"Never mind, my good fellow," exclaimed the squire, "for you have only to continue your search after them, and I will not fail to reward you for the exertions you have, and still may use in my behalf."

"Aye, sir," replied the beadle, "but you forget how impossible it is for me to leave this town."

"Why is it impossible?"

"Why is it impossible! Do you suppose, sir, the townspeople could do without their beadle?"

"I should suppose they might for a short time," answered Mr. Derwent, laughing, "and no doubt a man of your activity and intelligence could be able to trace out these fellows in a very little while. Two or three days ought to be quite enough for an experienced officer like yourself, when once he has got a clue to the persons he is in pursuit of."

"But I have not got a clue, sir, nor anything like one."

"Why," exclaimed Mr. Derwent, "I thought it was agreed among ourselves just now, that there was a very great probability of their having gone back to the neighbourhood of my house."

"So they may, sir," answered the beadle, "but Caleb Kestrel told you in his letter that he was going abroad, and if there's any truth in it, how shall we know where to look for him? In short, I begin to despair of earning the reward, though a few hours ago I thought nothing was more certain than that I should have the pocketing of it."

"Do you often give up so easily, my good fellow?"

"Lor' bless you, sir," exclaimed Solomon, "I always live upon hope as long as there's a chance remaining. But what's the use of hoping when a man has seen one of the prettiest opportunities that he ever had, slipping away from under him?"

" Well, Mr. Grundy," answered the squire, "you have no occasion to lose your chance, for my friend and I are about to return home immediately in a post-chaise, and you are welcome to a seat in it if you fancy that by doing so you will be able to trace out these people that you have been searching after. What say you then—will you accept the hospitalities of Derwent Hall, while you are absent from your own home ?"

" As far as I am concerned," exclaimed the beadle, " I should have been proud to have accepted your invitation ; but the truth is, a man in office has no right to be absent from his duty, for, though I have not anything very particular to call me here at present, there's no saying how suddenly my presence may be required, and then, what would be done if I was nowhere to be found ?''

" Very true," exclaimed the two gentlemen.

" Not but what I consider myself to have been highly honoured," continued the official, " and under any other circumstances I should have jumped at an offer that is as unexpected as it is kind. Another time, however, I may be able to accept your offer, and then——"

" Aye, aye," exclaimed Mr. Derwent, " we shall be happy at all times to see you at the Hall, but I hope whenever you come it will be rather a visit of pleasure than one of business. There's amusement enough to be found in the place and its neighbourhood, and as for a companion, there's one just after your own heart, in the person of Mr. Peeps, who is, and I hope will long continue to be, a resident beneath my roof."

" Peeps !" cried the beadle, " sure I know that name ?"

" I think it not at all unlikely," answered Mr. Derwent, " for he has been used to travel over all parts of the country, and more likely than not he has frequently been in this town."

" Was he a travelling showman ?"

" He was."

" Then I remember him very well," exclaimed Solomon Grundy, " and if I am not much mistaken, his wife and daughter used to travel through the country with him ?"

" His wife did," answered Mr. Derwent, " but the younger female has since proved to be no relation of his."

" No relation ?"

" No more than you are," answered the squire. " It is true he acted towards her with as much kindness as if he was a parent, and she still regards him as if they were related as nearly as was at one time imagined. The fact, however, is that she was stolen from her friends when quite a child by this Caleb Kestrel, and placed under the care of the worthy people we are speaking of. And she would have remained unknown to the present time if it had not been for an unexpected meeting that lately took place at a Harvest Home supper in the neighbourhood of Derwent Hall. This, however, is not a time to enter into an explanation that would take us some time to discuss, and I shall therefore merely observe that from that time to the present Caleb Kestrel has never ceased to persecute her in the expectation of extorting a sum of money as the price of his future forbearance."

" Would he have given up troubling her if you had bribed him ?" asked the beadle.

" So he gave us to understand," replied Mr. Derwent, " but as no promise would be binding on the part of a man like that, I have rufused to submit to the insolent demands he has so often made. Had I acceded to them, I should still have been subjected to his repeated annoyances, and therefore have I resolved to secure future peace by handing him over to the laws that he has so long violated with impunity. You have now heard enough of this singular affair to comprehend its chief points, and as the occasion is a very urgent one, I hope you will exert yourself to the utmost, in order to rid society of a ruffian who is capable of any crime that may further his own purposes."

Solomon Grundy now saw that he had no excuse for staying any longer, and having promised that he would not suffer an opportunity to slip when there was a probability of discovering the retreat of the fugitives, he took his leave with a gentle hint that it was not at all unlikely he might pay a visit to Derwent Hall the first time he could absent himself from the town without particularly inconveniencing the worthy inhabitants. As soon as he was gone Mr. Derwent ordered a postchaise to be immediately got in readiness for him, and within half an hour afterwards he and his friend, Frank Marldale, were, much to their own satisfaction, on their return home. Previously to leaving the hotel, both of them had taken care to look to their pistols in case of a sudden attack by the men they had been in search of. Fortunately, however, nothing occurred to disturb them in the course of their journey, though the road lay through an exceedingly dull part of the country, and they arrived safe on the following morning before the principal entrance of Derwent Hall.

CHAPTER XL.

MR. PEEPS AND HIS LONDON ACQUAINTANCE ENJOY A MORNING'S WALK.—THE ADVENTURE THEY MEET WITH, AND THE ALARM IT OCCASIONS.—THE RETURN HOME.—A SURPRISE.—FRESH MEANS ADOPTED TO ENTRAP THE AUTHOR OF THEIR DISQUIET.

THE absence of their hospitable host was severely felt by both Mr. Peeps and his cockney friend, for though everything was as much at their command as if the house belonged to them, there was a sad want of amusement that made them constantly fidgetty and uneasy. Amy too was never to be seen, for she preferred remaining shut up in her own room so long as her lover was away, and Mrs. Peeps insisted upon being constantly with her, so that the two before mentioned gentlemen were hardly ever enlivened by female society. Sometimes they attempted to play a game at billiards, but as neither of them knew anything about it, they found no amusement beyond that which half an hour would afford. Their chief liversion therefore consisted in walking through the grounds, which, it must be confessed, would have proved agreeable enough, but that they could not help thinking they might on some occasion meet with Caleb Kestrel, who the servants persisted in saying had been seen lurking about the neighbourhood on two or three recent occasions. This, however, was pretty well contradicted by the letters which were received from Mr. Derwent, who expressed a belief that he was concealed somewhere in Hull, and would, before long, be in the power of the law. Somewhat assured by this intimation, they rather extended their walk on the morning in question, and having come within sight of the Ruined Hut, they seated themselves by a style to rest after the fatigue of their walk.

"I say, my boy," exclaimed Brassey Popjoy, returning a brandy flask which they usually carried with them, "this visit of mine must soon come to a close, for hang me if I don't quite long to see London again, after being absent from it all this time."

"Well, for my own part," replied his friend, "I can't think how any one can like such an overgrown place as it is. I know, whenever I have been there,—which is not very often,—I get away as soon as possible, and so, for that matter, does Mrs. P., who prefers the fresh air of this country to such lots of bricks and mortar."

"Then I'm sorry to say,—though I don't wish to be rude,—Mrs. P. must have very bad taste, for, in my opinion, there ain't such another place in all the world! Talk of the country, indeed!—look at your Caleb Kestrels and chaps of that kind. Do you ever see or hear of such ruffians ever showing their faces in London?"

"Where will you find so many scoundrels as you do there?" asked the ex-proprietor of the Temple of Arts.

"Scoundrels there may be," replied Brassey Popjoy, "but they don't come out quite so strong as they do in these sort of places. A man can walk about the streets there without the chance of being knocked down and murdered; and as for women, they are not always in fear of being carried off against their inclination, as has been the case two or three times with Amy."

"But it won't happen again."

"How do you know that?"

"Because I mean to keep a sharp look-out, and if anybody attempts to frighten her any more, I'll have a grapple with him, even if it should cost me my life."

"Psha! Mr. Peeps; I don't suppose you have any more courage than you had before."

"I don't know that," he replied, "for I begin to think this Caleb Kestrel is to be frightened as well as anybody else, and if chance should throw him in my way again, I shall make bold to ask him how long he means to keep up this annoyance."

"And suppose his reply should not be an agreeable one?"

"Why then, I should tell him the sooner he left this part of the country the better, for he can no longer expect to go on as he has been doing, because the people hereabouts are determined to get rid of such a worthless scoundrel as he is."

"You wouldn't venture to call him a scoundrel, would you?"

"Well, I rather think I should, Mr. Popjoy," he replied, "for he and I have been acquainted, on and off, a good many years, and surely one may venture to use the privilege of an old friend."

"You have known him a good while, then?"

"Aye, more years than Amy has numbered."

"And was he always the same desperate ruffian that he is now?"

"To tell you the truth," answered Peeps, in a tone of confidence, "it must be confessed that he has never been any great shakes as long as I can remember anything of him. We lost sight of each other, though, for a long time, and when at last I saw him again, he had just returned home after a seven years' transportation."

"Humph!" exclaimed the cockney, "this seems to be rather a respectable acquaintance of yours."

"Well, I can't say much in his favour, it's true," answered the showman, "but the acquaintance was not of my seeking, and when we did sometimes meet by chance, there was no way of shaking him off, though I would have been very glad to do so. At last he stole the girl, and as you have heard, she was placed under the care of Mrs. Peeps and myself."

"Were you aware at the time that you were receiving stolen goods?" asked the retired pawnbroker.

"Upon my life, I never dreamt of such a thing," exclaimed Peeps; "I always supposed it was his own daughter, till it came out a little while ago that he had stolen her from Mr. Clement Derwent, who was at the time living somewhere in Italy."

"And you brought the girl up as your own daughter, didn't you?"

"I did," he replied, "and for some reasons I almost wish the contrary had never been made to appear when he pounced upon us so suddenly that night at Farmer Brough's. However, I have no right to complain either, for the girl is now well provided for, and nothing ought to give me more pleasure than to see a good, affectionate creature, as she is, on the high road to happiness."

"Do you call it the high road to happiness," asked Brassey Popjoy, "when she has had nothing but misery to go through ever since she came into possession of her property?"

"Well," answered the other, "but it's a long lane that has no turning, and I am in hopes she will have her share of comfort as soon as we can once rid ourselves of Caleb Kestrel."

"Which don't seem likely to happen very soon, if we are to judge by the trouble he has already given us."

"That may be all very well for people to say that have not given the thing much thought," answered Mr. Peeps. "Now I look at these things more philosophically, and my opinion is, that Kestrel will not be able to carry on his games much longer."

"Why do you think so?"

"Because Mr. Derwent is determined to prevent any further annoyance to the girl, and there's plenty of other people that are ready to help him, as has been

already proved. I myself have volunteered my services, and though they were not of much use, they showed a good heart in the cause of an injured female, and when Kestrel sees the determination of all her friends, he'll be glad to give up his schemes, and escape from England whilst there's an opportunity."

"So people have thought before now, and yet, for all that, he may be sneaking about the neighbourhood at this very time."

"Not he!"

"Why not?"

No. 43.

"Because he has made the place too hot to hold him, and it wouldn't be safe to show himself where he's sure to be known and arrested for that affair when he tried to kill the squire with an air gun. That was a black business, Mr. Popjoy; and he ought to have been hung for it, if it were only for the suspicion that fell upon young Frank Marldale, who might have been sent to the gallows but for the lucky circumstance of Mr. Derwent recovering, when everybody fancied that he had been killed outright."

"Isn't it rather strange," asked Brassey Popjoy, "that Kestrel was suffered to make his escape, when everybody knows he ought to have been punished as heavily as the law would allow?"

"Why, there may seem to be a little mystery about that, certainly," replied Mr. Peeps, "but it appears the squire has not a vindictive spirit, and I suppose he had no wish to prosecute his enemy, because he had luckily escaped the fate that was intended for him. And very nicely Caleb Kestrel has returned the favour, hasn't he, by persecuting a poor helpless girl for no better reason than that he is not able to extort the money from Mr. Derwent that he expected?"

"And now the squire has discovered that his kindness was all thrown away upon him."

"He has found that out, I should think," replied Peeps, "and if ever that infernal pedlar should fall into his hands again, I should think there would not be much chance of his meeting with any further mercy from our friend. However, I don't suppose the fellow will venture to show himself any more in this part of the country, for his character is so well known to everybody that he would not have a chance of escaping."

"So one would have fancied before," observed Brassey Popjoy, "and yet he has appeared among us two or three times, when it was thought he had gone away for ever. And it will be the same, depend on it, as long as he is suffered to remain at liberty, and that, to tell you the truth, is one of the principal reasons why I wish to bring my visit here to a close."

"Hadn't you better wait and see how all this will end?" inquired Mr. Peeps.

"It might be all very well to do so," answered the other, "but most unfortuneately I have very particular business to attend to in town—and, in fact, it may be so long before matters are brought to a conclusion, that I'm afraid I shall not be able to wait till Caleb Kestrel is taken."

"Which," returned the ex-showman, "will be before another twelve hours are over, you may depend upon it."

"Are you so sure of that?" exclaimed a voice from one side of them, and turning their heads they saw Caleb Kestrel standing with a brace of pistols in his hands. They scrambled upon their feet, and would have fled in terror, but he advanced, and placing himself before them, exclaimed—"Be not too certain that I am so near the misfortune you speak of, for you see I am still at liberty, and what is better still, I am likely to remain so in spite of the madness that urges men to pursue me to destruction."

"I hope, Mr. Kestrel," exclaimed the terrified cockney, "you don't reckon either myself or this gentleman among your enemies."

"Not so long as you fancy yourselves within my reach," he replied; "but I have reason to know that both by advice, and your own exertions, you have done all you could to bring me into the snare that has been laid for me. Now, however, you are in my grasp, and must be my messengers to Mr. Derwent."

"Mr. Derwent is not at home at present."

"Yes he is," answered Caleb Kestrel, "for I saw him and his friend Marldale in a postchaise just now, going towards the hall. They are tired, I suppose, of their fruitless search after me, and have returned home full of chagrin and disappointment."

"But their disappointment wont last very long when they hear that you are again in this neighbourhood," exclaimed Peeps.

"And who will tell them I am here?" demanded Caleb. "Will you, after my warning to keep my presence here a secret, venture to say a word that will give my pursuers a clue to my place of concealment?"

"N—n—no," stammered the old man; "whatever you command, you may depend on it, I will obey."

"So you may promise now," returned Kestrel, "but will your word be kept when you fancy yourself out of my reach?"

"It shall; indeed—indeed it shall."

"And you," exclaimed the pedlar, turning towards Brassey Popjoy, "can you keep a secret like this?"

"I can do anything," he replied, shaking like an aspen leaf, "if you will but spare my life."

"Do you swear to keep silent about this meeting of ours?"

"I do."

"Well," returned Caleb, "I'll take your word, because I believe it matters little whether you say anything about it or not. In short, I am almost certain that Squire Derwent caught sight of me as he passed, and if so, I may expect that he has by this time commenced fresh operations towards laying me by the heels."

"Then what does it matter whether we say anything about this meeting?" demanded Mr. Peeps.

"Because it would serve to confirm that which at present only rests upon suspicion and doubt," answered Kestrel. "If, however, you should find that they are certain as to having seen me, I have a message for you to deliver for me."

"What is your message, Caleb?"

"A very simple one that will not take much trouble to remember," answered the other. "You have only to tell him that I am as resolute as ever in the pursuit of my object, and he will do well to come to the arrangement that I spoke to him about."

"That is to say, that you are determined not to make any abatement in your demands?"

"Exactly so."

"And suppose he is not inclined to yield to them?"

"In that case you may give him to understand that he must expect a continuance of the annoyance and alarm that he has already suffered through my attempt to force him to my terms."

"But he may be obstinate."

"Very likely," replied Kestrel, "but if he is so, I shall then be compelled to have recourse to more violent means."

"That's quite impossible," exclaimed Mr. Peeps, "for in my opinion you have already done your worst."

"So, in your blindness, you may imagine," replied the pedlar, "but it yet remains to be seen to what excess a disappointed man may be driven. Hitherto I have had some pity for the sufferings of Amy, but when I find that all my hopes are at an end, I will take means of tearing her away from this place, and never again shall she be seen or heard of till the money I demand has been paid.

"Have you no mercy for the girl that you have already injured so deeply?" exclaimed Peeps.

"What have I to do with mercy," he asked, "when I see all my offers treated with scorn and neglect? It is in my power to do mischief, yet I have proposed to give up all further persecution on one condition, that I am to be rewarded for my forbearance."

"Rewarded!" exclaimed Brassey Popjoy, "if you had been properly rewarded, it would have been with a rope long before now."

"Your opinion, at any rate, has not been asked," muttered Caleb Kestrel, "and for your own sake I would advise you not to let your observations be quite so personal. Remember it will not be easy for you to get beyond my reach, so do not excite my wrath, or I may pursue you, even if I should take refuge in the heart of London."

"Begging your pardon," exclaimed the cockney, "but I have seen quite enough of you in the country without feeling any desire to meet with you in the metropolis. However, as far as I am concerned, you have no reason to be afraid of anything I may say, for I would rather do anything than give you one excuse for following me after I have once left this unlucky neighbourhood."

"All that you are required to do," answered Caleb, "is to join with Peeps in persuading Mr. Derwent to take the only step that can preserve him and Amy from the annoyance and trouble that they complain of. Tell him from me that I am determined never to give up this project of mine till I have fully succeeded in it."

"But suppose you happen to be taken by the people that are after you for the sake of the reward?" observed Peeps.

"They have tried to take me for some time past," replied the fugitive, "but so far I have succeeded in defeating my pursuers, and it will be strange to me if I do not still show them that I love my liberty too well to part with it very easily. Nay, rather than fall into the hands of my foes, I would put a pistol to my head, and disappoint their malice for ever."

"It's all very well to say so," answered Peeps, "but if it should ever come to the point, you would think very differently about it, for life is too precious to be thrown away whilst there's a chance of saving it. However, be that as it may, your message shall be delivered, only I would advise you to get out of the way as soon as you can, because I happen to know that Squire Derwent will make no bargain so long as you try to frighten him into it."

"Then tell him he must look out for the consequences of his folly," exclaimed Caleb Kestrel, "and above all things, be careful not to say anything of having seen me, unless he should first of all have admitted that he is aware of my presence here. Remember this my command, and if you disobey it, it will be at your own peril."

This was uttered in a menacing tone, and immediately afterwards the pedlar disappeared with as much suddenness as he had appeared before them. Having satisfied themselves that they were indeed quite at liberty to take their departure, they hurried away with all the speed they could, and made their way to the hall, which they entered nearly out of breath from their exertion. To their surprise they found that Mr. Derwent and Frank Marldale had indeed arrived, as had been announced by Caleb Kestrel. The first greeting being over, they were asked the cause of their apparent alarm, but not a word of explanation could be obtained from them till they had first ascertained that Kestrel had been seen by them whilst he was standing watching them from the roadside. This fact having been ascertained, Peeps and his friend recounted the adventure they had met with, and delivered the message with which they had been charged.

"So, now you see, squire," said Peeps, in continuation, "that the fellow is just as resolute as ever he was to extort the money from you, and it, therefore, only remains for you to say whether you will submit to it or not."

"I will submit to no proposition of the kind," answered Mr. Derwent, "for the fellow has once more thrown himself within my reach, and his good fortune will be most extraordinary if he again succeeds in escaping from me as he has done before."

"But he is such a fellow for concealing himself, that I'm afraid you will look for him in vain."

"At any rate," observed Frank Marldale, "so long as he keeps in concealment we shall not have much to fear from him."

"That is to say," observed Mr. Peeps, "if he has not employed others to do his dirty work for him, which I rather think may be the case, for I'm almost certain I saw two or three of his comrades lurking about as if they were just ready to pounce upon us."

"And I suppose," exclaimed Squire Derwent, "their appearance was quite enough to alarm you?"

"I rather think it was," answered Brassey Popjoy, "and it's little to be wondered at either, for it's no joke to find yourself surrounded by desperate characters when you have no arms to defend yourself with. Besides, this Caleb Kestrel was quite enough to alarm us, for he looked as fierce a desperado as ever I saw, and at one time I verily believed he was going to kill us in order to prevent a rumour being spread abroad that he is in the neighbourhood."

"And the ruffian told you that he had seen us on our return home?" exclaimed Mr. Derwent.

"Oh, yes, he saw you plainly enough," answered Peeps, "and he sent the message by us, warning you that unless his terms are agreed to without delay, he will carry Amy away to some place where you will never see or hear of her again."

"And you may depend upon it he means to keep his word, too," chimed in Brassey Popjoy.

"At all events, I shall not suffer myself to be easily intimidated," answered Mr. Derwent; "for the only reply I shall make to his message, will be a more active search than has hitherto been made for him. So far, it is true, he has contrived to defeat me by his cunning, but now he must look well to himself, for he shall be taken, or all my pains will have been thrown away."

"Hadn't you better see him," asked Frank Marldale, "and try whether some terms may not be come to?"

"I'll make no terms with such a ruffian as he is," exclaimed Mr. Derwent, "for experience has proved to me that he will keep no faith; and, even should money be given to him for the sake of preventing all further annoyance to Amy, it would fail to operate favourably on a man who is destitute of all honourable feelings."

"Then what measures do you mean to adopt next?" asked the young man, eagerly.

"I shall follow him up as I have done before," answered the squire, "for now that I know he is in the neighbourhood, there is some little probability that I may succeed in depriving him of all further power to do us harm. Too long already has he contrived to escape a well merited fate, but at length I begin to see that he will either fall in a vain attempt to defend himself, or, being taken, end his days abroad as a convict."

"I'm afraid he'll give a good deal more trouble before you get rid of him," observed Peeps.

"The trouble will be well bestowed if we only succeed at last," answered Mr. Derwent. "I have not scrupled to follow him from place to place whenever there has appeared a chance of meeting with him, and never will I rest satisfied till he has either fallen into our hands or been driven to flee from England for ever."

"Even if he were to leave this country," observed Frank, "I am afraid we should see him back again before long."

"It would be at his own peril, then," answered his friend, "for there are hundreds who would be glad enough to take him, and his person has been so fully and accurately described that he would be sure to be recognised by anybody who might meet him."

"Well," exclaimed Brassey Popjoy, "I don't want to throw cold water on your hopes, but I can't help thinking you'll have a good deal more trouble with this fellow than you expect. People say he's a very devil when once he is driven into a corner, and in spite of the reward that has been offered for his apprehension, I fancy no one would like to tackle him, unless he were well backed by a good many other desperate fellows."

"But money, my good fellows, works wonders."

"I know that," answered the cockney, "and I know, also, that there's a certain limit that even gold will not drive people beyond. What, I should like to know, would be the use of the reward if the person trying for it was to lose his life in the attempt?"

"Psha!" exclaimed Peeps; "do you think all are cowards because you have not yourself more spirit than a mouse?"

"I flatter myself I have as good a share as you have," retorted the cockney; "and perhaps, if put to it, I might come out a bit as well as here and there one,

But I never boast of my courage, because I always prefer showing it when required."

"At all events we shall be very glad to see a little of it, now that there's so much occasion for every man to do his best," exclaimed Mr. Derwent. "Indeed I have an opinion that coolness and courage are all that is required to bring this affair to a satisfactory conclusion within a very short time."

"That is to say," observed Frank, "if we can by any means discover where this ruffian secretes himself."

"Which, I should imagine, will be no very difficult matter," returned the squire, "for as he is now prowling about the place, we may be very certain that he has more of his devilish mischief in contemplation ; and what will be more easy than to trace him if he leaves the place that he chooses for his temporary concealment ?   At any rate, we shall have plenty of people on the look-out for him, and as there is a large sum attached to his discovery, we may hope that a very brief period will be sufficient to deprive him of the power of doing any further harm."

"Is Amy aware of his being so near her ?" asked Peeps.

" I just now informed her of it," answered Mr. Derwent, "and it has been agreed that she and 'your wife shall not leave this house till all danger is completely at an end.   That, I hope, will be before many days are over, so that her liberty will not be abridged for a period that will prove particularly irksome."

"But, I suppose, the news of his return to this place has filled her with a good deal of alarm."

"She appeared to be rather frightened when first informed of it," replied Mr. Derwent, "but she has a tolerably bold heart of her own, and upon my assuring her that Kestrel should not be suffered to approach the hall, she immediately regained all her composure, and declared her readiness to place herself entirely under my guidance till circumstances permit her to leave the house as usual."

" Then, you think there's nothing to be feared from his accomplices ?"

" I believe his accomplices will be taken at the same time that he is," said the squire ; " and even if they are not, they will remain quiet enough when they find that their leader has no longer the power to direct their movements.   In fact, though the enemy is still at large, I have such a strong hope that he will soon be in custody, that I have almost ceased to believe that we have any further acts of violence to fear from him.   So, now all we have to do is to be careful and vigilant in the discharge of our several duties, and ere long we shall be amply rewarded for all the trouble and anxiety we have been obliged to endure."

Matters having been so far satisfactorily arranged, it was agreed that they should immediately adjourn to the apartment in which the ladies were anxiously waiting their arrival.   There, of course, the all-absorbing subject was renewed, plans were proposed and determined, and the confidence of all parties was in a great degree restored.

CHAPTER XLI.

CALEB KESTREL AND HIS COMRADES ONCE MORE RETURN TO THEIR OLD QUARTERS
    AT THE DESERTED HUT.—A VISIT FROM THE GIPSIES.—THE QUARREL, AND THE
    MURDER.—THE FUNERAL OF DEBORAH, AND THE ARRIVAL OF A PARTY OF
    PURSUERS.—THE RETREAT.—AN ATTEMPT TO DESTROY THE HUT BY FIRE.

HAZARDOUS as it would have been to wander about with the certainty of being seen by those who would report the fact of him being in the neighbourhood, Kestrel and his companions were driven to take up their residence in the Ruined Hut, as the only place where they could obtain the shelter they so much needed.   It is true there was almost a certainty that they would be sought in that place amongst he very first that would be thought of, but as no alternative was afforded them, they resolved to defend themselves to the last in the event of an attack being made upon them. They were aware, too, that there was a ready means offered for their escape even if the worst should happen, for the wood was close by, and if they could once escape to it, as they had done on a former occasion, pursuit would be nearly hopeless in a place that offered so many means for eluding the search of the enemy. Previously to taking up their abode there, they provided themselves with such provisions as they thought would be necessary, and so well were they supplied with arms of various descriptions, that they believed there was little chance of being overcome, even though considerably overmatched by the superior numbers of the enemy.

"Recollect," exclaimed Kestrel to his two companions, who were seated with him, "that we have now a more desperate game than ever to play, and when the time comes we must act with the determination of reckless men, or we must make up our minds to lose all that we have been trying for."

"Oh, you needn't be afraid of us," answered Dick Radcliffe, "for we know what we've got to expect in case of a defeat, and will rather lose our lives, if need be, than yield like cowards to a foe that will show us no mercy if we should fall into their hands."

"That's exactly my own notion upon the subject," rejoined Jabez Thompson, "but I should like to know whether you are going to be rash enough to venture to the hall after the girl, when the people there will be sure to be on the look-out for us?"

"At present I have not made up my mind upon that subject," answered Caleb Kestrel, "but if there should be a favourable opportunity, I think it more likely than not that I should run the risk, rather than lose all chance of completing a plan that has caused us so much trouble. However, those that are afraid of accompanying me had better say so at once, that I may know what sort of assistance I may expect."

"As for that," exclaimed Radcliffe, "I am willing to keep to our contract, but it would be madness to show ourselves at a place when we know the danger that awaits us there."

"Exactly so," chimed in Jabez Thompsom, "and the folly would be all the greater, because we know that by keeping away for a little while we shall meet with the girl in one of her walks, and that then nothing would be easier than to carry her off without running into any unnecessary peril."

— "Do you think it likely, then, that she will venture to leave the house when it's known that we are in the neighbourhood?"

"That will depend upon ourselves," answered Dick Radcliffe; "for if we remain here snug, it will soon be fancied that we knew better than to expose ourselves to the danger of being taken. A few days of quiet will be sufficient to give 'em all the confidence that we can require, and then, the first time she ventures out of the house, we can pounce upon her when nobody is near to protect her."

"And is it likely, think you," asked Kestrel, "that she will venture out of the hall without protection?"

"Perhaps not; but what need we care, if three or four of her friends happen to be with her? Desperate men like us are not to be alarmed at trifles, and if any resistance should be offered, the first pistol that was fired on our side would set her protectors flying."

"Then you think murder may be committed?" exclaimed Jabez Thompsom, with alarm.

"Such a thing may happen if we are driven to it," answered the other coolly; "and if there's no help for it, I don't see why we should be afraid of proceeding to extremities."

"And so get hung for our fool-hardiness?"

"What's the use of looking at the worst, when we don't know that anything of the kind will take place?" demanded Caleb Kestrel, impatiently. "All we have to do is to remain here a few days, and I dare say something will turn up to favour us."

" As for remaining here any time," returned Dick Radcliffe, " I think that's quite out of the question, for by this time it has, no doubt, been rumoured all over the place that we have come back to the neighbourhood, and of course the first spot they search for us will be the one where we have concealed ourselves before."

" Very well," exclaimed the pedlar, " and supposing they do, haven't we plenty of arms to defend ourselves with, and are we going to be such rank cowards as to surrender ourselves quietly when we have the means of beating off the enemy ?"

" Aye," answered Jabez, " but why should we run the risk of being shot, when a little caution would not only preserve our lives, but lead, in the end, to the capture of this girl that you are so anxious to lay hold of. Not that I am afraid of running the risk, if it could only be shown that there's no other way of extorting from the pockets of Squire Derwent the money we all so much need."

" Aye," muttered Kestrel, " you are still, I find, anxious enough to secure your share of the prize, but the devil a bit are you inclined to act in any other way than your own fancy dictates. But remember this, both of you—I must have my way in all that concerns this affair, or not one farthing of the money shall go to the skulking knaves that are afraid to put themselves under my control."

" Is it quite certain that you will keep faith with us, even if we obey your orders ?"

" Humph ! you begin to doubt me, then ?"

" We are not beginning to do so," answered the other, " for the truth is, that both Jabez Thompson and I have for some time had a notion that we should be cheated of our shares."

" Then the best thing we can do will be to part at once," exclaimed Kestrel, sullenly, " for hang me if I want the assistance of men that may deceive me when the time for action comes. It's not too late for you to back out of the affair, and I shall then know exactly what I have got to depend on."

" With all due submission, my boy, we shall not do anything of the kind," answered Dick Radcliffe, " for we have made up our minds to share with you in the spoils that are to be gained by this affair, and we are both determined not to be disappointed, after all the trouble and risk we have been at. So you must be honest with us, or we may do that that you will be sorry for."

" Ha ! so you threaten me ?"

" No ; we only speak out plainly, that's all."

" The long and short of it is this," interposed Jabez Thompson, " we have both gone the whole hog with you, and are still willing to do so, but we see no reason why you should want to carry everything your own way. Let us act cautiously in this affair, and you may rely upon it we will do our duty like men and comrades, but don't run us into danger, for we are not yet so tired of our lives that we would throw them away uselessly."

" Very well," growled Caleb Kestrel, " for this once I'll yield, but you must not expect that I shall always be such an easy fool as to give up my own opinions when I know they are the best. We will, therefore, remain here quietly for three or four days, but if, at the end of that time, we are not likely to meet with Amy out of the house, we must then seek for her there, even if I undertake the task of carrying her away by myself."

" Would you be rash enough to go alone ?" demanded Jabez.

" Why not ?"

" Because you would be sure to be taken."

" They would have a hard matter to do it though," exclaimed Caleb Kestrel, " for I know the fate that would be in store for me, and rather than yield like a coward, I would defend myself as long as a pistol remained undischarged, or my hand was able to grasp a dagger. I have always, perhaps, been a desperate man, but these repeated disappointments have raised my fury to the highest pitch, and I care not if my life is sacrificed, should all hope of succeeding in my object be at an end."

At this juncture they were startled by hearing footsteps stealthily approaching them, and in an instant every man sprang upon his feet and stood, pistol in hand, prepared to defend himself against the anticipated attack. A single glance, however, was sufficient to remove their alarm, for in the intruder they recognised the well-known features of Deborah, the Gipsy.

"How now!" exclaimed Caleb Kestrel, sullenly, "what business has brought you here? Have you come to betray us?"

"That," she replied, "will depend upon whether you listen with favour to the proposition I am about to make."

"Hah! so you have come to insist upon making terms that we are not likely to agree to."

"I have not come to quarrel with you, Caleb," she replied, "but to awaken you to the danger you are running."

"We know all about our danger," answered the pedlar, "and are not to be frightened from the object we have in view by the raving of a mad woman. Leave us, then, before we get into a quarrel, or it may be the worse for you."

"You would murder me, I suppose?"

"No, no," he exclaimed, "I have no wish to shed your blood, Deborah, but

I am not to be thwarted in my schemes now that I see they are so near to completion. Leave me, and never from this time come into my presence again."

"It is but seldom that I appear before you," answered the Gipsy, "nor should I have done so now, but that I know, by the art I profess, you stand on the thresh-hold of danger."

"And does not your art also inform you of the danger you run by coming here?" he asked menacingly.

"I knew there was risk in it," she replied, "but the love I once bore you would not permit me to remain inactive, when by a word of warning I might save you from destruction."

"Don't talk to me of your love, woman!" exclaimed Caleb Kestrel, fiercely "for it is returned on my part only with hatred and contempt. Away, then, from my presence without delay, for I am in no humour to hear you preach of days that I would gladly forget."

"At least let me speak one word in favour of Amy."

"I will hear nothing at all you have to say about her," exclaimed the pedlar. "My mind is resolved upon one thing, and I will carry my object through, let what may happen."

"Then you are lost!"

"If I am, I do not wish to hear it from your lips."

"Are you, then, deaf to reason?"

"To all such reason as you can produce I am," he replied savagely. "My own will is the only guide I have followed through life, and it is not likely that I shall now change my determination through the meddling interference of a woman that I hate, and who I hoped never to have seen again."

"In what have I ever offended you, Caleb?"

"Ask me no questions," he replied, "for I am in no humour to say any more than you have heard. You have now received the only answer I shall give, and I would be alone to confer with those friends of mine upon an affair ot importance."

"I understand," exclaimed the Gipsy; "there is another plot going on for the carrying away of Amy. You have been a bitter source of trouble and misery to her, but the girl has found favour in my sight, and I will preserve her from further misery, even though I commit an act that I would have gladly avoided."

"What do those words mean, woman?" he demanded. "Am I to understand you will betray me to my enemies, unless I give up the prospect of extorting money from Squire Derwent?"

"I have no wish to betray you," she replied, "but I have vowed to save her from further persecution, and I will keep my word whatever may be the conse-quences of the act."

"How will you do it?"

"By a timely warning of your presence here."

"Then, to save her, you would not mind giving me up to destruction?"

"If I had not wished to avoid harming you," she replied, "I should not have ventured here to caution you of what I may be driven to do. At any rate, it shall be my care to prevent the innocent from becoming a prey to the guilty, and you know, Caleb, that I am not to be turned from my object by any threats of vengeance that you can utter. So now, you have heard me, and it only remains for yourself to decide what course I am to take."

"As for that," he replied in a threatening tone, "you know I am not to be intimidated by anything you can say, for I have it in my own power to prevent the mischief you speak of."

"Then prevent it," she replied, turning away to depart, "for since no per-suasions are of any avail, I will now go to the hall and prepare them against the danger that threatens them."

Scarcely were these words uttered when the report of a pistol was heard, and Deborah fell to the ground with a piercing shriek of the most intense agony.

Jabez Thompson sprung forward and raised her up, but her head fell back, and a single glance served to show that the vital spark had flown for ever.'

"Murderer!" exclaimed Radcliffe, who had also advanced to tender his assistance, "you have slain the woman who came here in the hope of saving you the consequences that she foresaw."

"What is it, if I have killed her?" demanded Kestrel sullenly. "The fool provoked her death, for if I had hesitated another moment she would have gone away to raise the alarm against us."

"And couldn't that have been prevented without taking away her life?" demanded the other.

"Ay, if there had been time to think of other means," answered Caleb Kestrel, "but she was just making her way to the hall, and we know what would have followed if once she had gone there to blab the secret that we were about to make another attempt to carry away the girl. At any rate, I knew well enough what we had to expect, and as I am determined not to sacrifice my liberty, I sent a bullet through her body as an act of self-defence."

"What se f-defence will it be," said Jabez Thompson, "if the murder should be discovered?"

"If discovered!" cried his companion; "and what is to hinder the rumour getting abroad that she has been killed?"

"No one can tell who did it though," muttered Caleb Kestrel, "unless either of you think proper to split against me. You think I am in your power, but only let me have reason to suspect that you are going to peach, and d—n me, but I'll serve you both exactly as I have the old woman."

"We are neither of us likely to do that," answered Dick Radcliffe, "for though we are sorry for what has taken place, we are neither of us such sneaks as to inform against a comrade. However, if the thing hadn't taken place so suddenly, I would have wrested the pistol from your grasp, rather than have suffered a murder to take place before my eyes."

"'Tis much better as it is," answered Kestrel, "for if you had interfered it's a hundred to one but I had turned the weapon against your heart! So let's hear no more lamentations for an act that can't be prevented now, and which I should not hesitate to do over again, if there was the same provocation for it."

"But it's my opinion that she never intended to go to the hall."

"Why did she threaten to do so, then?"

"Merely to frighten you into a promise that you would give up persecuting the poor girl."

"Then she deserved her fate for supposing that I was to be intimidated by her threats," answered Caleb Kestrel; "and, much as you may lament her end, I, for my own part, feel no remorse for an act that was forced upon me by her own wilful determination."

"As far as I am concerned," observed Dick Radcliffe, "no one, I believe, can accuse me of being very tender-hearted, but I must own it would have taken a good deal more provocation before I could have committed such an act as you have done. The woman spoke fairly enough till she found that all she had said was thrown away, and even, at last, I believe she only threatened you without having any intention of fulfilling it."

"But you have no proof of it," exclaimed the assassin, "and that being the case, I have a right to believe what I did was done only in self-defence. Was it to be expected that I would suffer her to go away when I had every reason to believe that in an hour or two afterwards the pursuers would be upon me through her treachery."

"Couldn't you have pretended to be moved by her words?"

"I may be a villain," answered Caleb Kestrel," but at any rate, I am no hypocrite, and it was impossible to disguise my feelings any longer when I found there was danger in the way. Besides, who was she, that there should be all this fuss made about her having received the punishment she deserved."

"I have heard," answered Jabez Thompson, " that she was your wife, and tha you deserted her years ago."

"There you were correctly enough informed," he replied, " but I am not to be taunted for having parted from a woman that I couldn't agree with. Our tempers ——— as different as possible, and I left her, rather than live in constant strife. had she been wise she would never have thrown herself in my way again, but as she thought proper to do so, she brought upon herself the fate that you and Dick Radcliffe so deeply deplore."

"——id so will you deplore it when you find the consequences it will be likely to bring upon you."

"Am I to understand that as a threat that you will give information of what has taken place?

"You ought to know me better than to believe that I would do anything to get you into trouble," answered Radcliffe. "The crime is one; that I would have prevented if there had been any means of foreseeing what was going to take place; but as that was quite impossible, I have nothing to blame myself for, though I may be allowed to give my opinion about it."

"Your opinion is not required," exclaimed Caleb Kestrel, " for the old woman has met the fate that she called down upon herself, and all that you can say or do will not bring her to life again."

"What are you going to do with the body?" asked Dick Radcliffe.

"Why, hide it under ground as soon as possible."

"That's more easily said than done," answered Jabez, " for if, when a search is made, the ground should appear to have been lately removed, it would be certain to lead to a discovery of the murder."

"There's no occasion to dig a grave for her," returned Kestrel, "for in the cavern underneath this hut there is an old well that will serve better than anything else for the concealment of the body. She'll rest as well there as anywhere else, and we may make ourselves tolerably safe that no one will find her."

"Well, then, why don't you take her at once?" exclaimed Jabez.

"Because I want somebody to help me."

"Then you won't have our help," muttered the two men.

"Very well," answered Caleb Kestrel, in a tone of anger, "you can do as you like about it, but by-and-by you might want my assistance, and then it will be my turn to refuse it. However, luckily, I have strength enough to manage this job myself, for, having deprived the old woman of life, it will not be much trouble to put her out of sight."

No sooner was this said than he raised the body, and threw it with reckless indifference over his shoulder. Then crossing the room, he snatched up a lighted lamp, which had been placed there so that its rays should not be seen from without, and descending the few broken steps that led to the vault beneath, he bore his lifeless burden to the spot where he intended to conceal it. Without pausing to reflect, he advanced to the brink of the well, and with a jerk released himself of the load with which he was incumbered. From the sound which immediately followed, he ascertained that there was a considerable quantity of water at the bottom, and as that would materially assist in destroying all proof of his crime, he turned away with a feeling of fiendish exultation, and returned to his two comrades, who were debating between themselves whether it would not be advisable to terminate their connexion with a man whose last crime had rendered him too villanous even for such depraved ruffians as they were. Kestrel heard only a few words as he approached them, but the little that met his ears was quite sufficient to inform him of the nature of their conversation.

"So!" he exclaimed, "you are alarmed at what has been done, are you? You would have me be so too, and I suppose, the next thing you do will be to lay an information before a magistrate of what has taken place."

"Why, do you suppose we are going to turn informers?" asked Radcliffe.

"I think there's reason enough for the suspicion," he replied, "for you would not give me any assistance, and that looks pretty much as if you were already afraid of the consequences of what has taken place."

"And so we are," returned Jabez Thompson.

"Then you are a couple of rank cowards for your pains," growled the ruffian, "and I'm only sorry that I was fool enough to take you for anything else. However, I shall be upon my guard against any treachery, so be careful what you do, as desperate men are not very particular, and the moment I see reason to suspect either of you, will be your last."

"Aye, aye, we know all about that," answered Dick Radcliffe, "and being wide awake to your kind intentions we shall spare you the trouble of carrying 'em out. In short, we have neither of us thought of such a thing as informing against you, though we had a notion of parting company, now that we find how dangerous it is to be your associates any longer."

"How could I help killing her, when she threatened to go and give information where I was to be found?"

"Couldn't we have moved away from this place?" asked Jabez.

"Move away!" he exclaimed. "What leave the neighbourhood just when everything is ready for execution!"

"Ah!" retorted Dick Radcliffe, "I see well enough how all this will end. Nothing but the money will satisfy you, and yet I'd stake my existence you never get a farthing of it."

"Then in less than a week the girl will be removed to a place where her friends will never find her."

"That's easier said than done," observed Thompson, "for she has no occasion to leave the house, and it seems there are plenty of people there to prevent our taking her away from it."

"At any rate there can be no harm in trying it."

"Let those do it that like, then," answered Dick Radcliffe, "but for my own part, I see so many chances against our succeeding, that I shall refuse to have any further hand in it."

"Then, why didn't you say so before, and not leave me when everything was ripe for our purpose?"

"For a very sufficient reason; I thought you meant to go more cautiously about the business, and that there was some chance of getting this money from the squire by threatening him. However, you are still determined to follow your own way blindly, and I now begin to see that it's high time to look out for myself."

"I suppose, then, you both mean to leave me?"

"At present it is our intention to do so," answered the other, "but that will depend a good deal upon yourself, for we are still willing to take our share in the matter, if you'll only promise to act cautiously."

"Psha! what's the use of caution, when we find that every preparation is made against us? They know well enough that we have come back to the neighbourhood, and there'll be such a watch kept that we shall not be able to do anything unless we act upon it at once."

"Why not give it up, then, for a time?"

"Because our funds are beginning to get low, and if we delay much longer we we shall be quite without money."

At this juncture Jabez Thompson, who had been watching at the door, came running towards them with an intimation that several lights were to be seen in the distance. No doubt, therefore, could be felt that people were coming to search the place, and the fugitives were once more compelled to deliberate upon the expediency of making another retreat before it was too late.

"We must get into the wood without delay," exclaimed Radcliffe, "for there we shall have plenty of room, and our pursuers will not have much chance of pouncing upon us, if we mind what we are about."

"There's no occasion for us to hurry ourselves," returned Caleb Kestrel, "for I have a little plan of my own to put into execution that may perhaps save us a great deal of trouble afterwards."

"What scheme have you got in your head now?" demanded Dick.

"One that will do us no harm, at any rate," he replied, placing the lamp beneath his cloak so as to conceal the light. I shall watch these people from the other side of the house, and when they have entered, I'll make the place too hot to hold 'em."

"Explain yourself."

"That I can do in a very few words," he replied. "What is more easy than to set fire to the thatch on the roof, and roast yonder fellows when they are looking for us here."

"More blood!" exclaimed Jabez Thompson, shuddering.

"Aye," returned the pedlar, "I thought how it would be. You are afraid of everything I propose, and would rather run the risk of being taken by our enemies than do an act that would relieve us from the dangers that threaten us. Ain't they hunting after us as if we were wild beasts, and is it anything more than natural, that we should try to put an end to the danger we are threatened with?"

"That may be all very well," answered Thompson, "but there has been murder enough for one night already, and I, for one, will take no part in this blood-thirsty scheme of yours."

"What say you to it?" demanded Caleb Kestrel, addressing himself to his other comrade.

"I'm pretty much of the same opinion as Jabez," he replied, "for I can see no reason why we should attempt to destroy all those people, when we have the means of getting out of their reach?"

"Then you don't think people have a right to protect themselves, when a foe is close upon their heels?"

"As far as that goes," he replied, "I'm a rough sort of fellow in my way, and perhaps have been guilty of as desperate acts as most folks. But human blood has never yet been upon my hands, and I'll take care to keep 'em free from it as long as I can."

"In other words then, if this thing is to be done, I must do it without any assistance from you?"

"You must?"

"And I suppose the next I hear will be that we are to part company after this night?"

"It's more than likely we may," he replied, "for you are too desperate in your goings on for us to have anything further to do with you, and the best thing we can do will be to leave you before we break out into an open quarrel. Perhaps, however, you have thought better of it, and if so, we are still ready to lend you a helping hand, on your promising to carry on your plans quietly."

"I shall make no promise," answered Caleb Kestrel, "because my mind is made up to destroy my enemies if I can only do so without the fear of its being suspected whose hand it was that dealt the blow. These people are coming here in the hope of making us their prisoners, and have, therefore, no claim upon our mercy when they throw themselves in our power."

"But what right have we to take away their lives?" demanded Jabez Thompson. "They want to take us, it's true, because they have good reason to believe that we are planning mischief against them, and we may be very well satisfied if we escape, without attempting to destroy their lives."

"Preach to those that are likely to heed you," exclaimed Caleb Kestrel, "but don't attempt to argue me out of what I know will prove to be for the best. Go, both of you, as soon as you like, and in half an hour's time I'll meet you in the wood, where we can come to some sort of an understanding. Away, I say, for the enemy is now close at hand, and in another two or three minutes it will be too late for any of us to make our escape."

There was, indeed, good reason for this exhortation, for the pursuing party was now within a few hundred yards of them, and the glare for their torches rendered it almost impossible to get away without being seen. Dick Radcliffe and

Jabez, therefore, lost not a moment's time, and Kestrel, after observing that they had taken their way towards the wood, strolled round to the back part of the ruin to watch a favourable opportunity of setting fire to the thatch. Leaving him, however, for the present, we will follow in the steps of Mr. Derwent, who, with Frank Marldale and a number of other friends, had come to search the hut in consequence of some information they had received that the pedlar, with his comrades, had sought shelter there. No sooner had the last named person made his escape, than the place was thronged by those who had come to assist in the search, and in a few minutes every corner having been carefully examined, it was announced that their trouble had been all thrown away.

"Not quite thrown away, gentlemen," exclaimed Mr. Derwent, as he stooped and picked up a dagger from the ground, "for this weapon proves that the villains have been here, and the probability is that they only left the place when the light of our torches warned them that their retreat was no longer a safe one."

"Then, of course, they cannot be far off," observed Frank, "and perhaps a search round the place may prove successful."

"I'm afraid that on a dark night like this our chance is but a very poor one," returned the squire, "and as for using our torches, they will serve as a warning to the fugitives of our approach. My advice, therefore, is that we abandon our project for the night, and in the morning we will resume it with, I hope, a fair chance of bringing our labour to a successful termination."

"That's all very well," exclaimed Farmer Brough, who had accompanied the party in their expedition, "but I think, as we have gone so far, it would not be a bad plan to see whether some of the scoundrels may not be lurking somewhere about the place. Indeed, if my eyes didn't deceive me just now, I saw a couple of fellows running with all their might towards the wood, and, I dare say, if we were to go there we should meet with them."

"Very likely they may have fled there," interposed Frank Marldale, "but the wood is a wild sort of a place even in the day time, and at night we should have no chance, because they would slip about from place to place, and, after all, we should have the mortification of discovering that all our labour had been thrown away."

"Well, then," asked the farmer, "what say you to a party of us remaining here to watch, in case they should return?"

"Let those remain who like," exclaimed Frank Marldale, making a movement towards the door, "for the thatched roof is on fire, and the hut will soon be reduced to ashes!"

In an instant all rushed out to avoid the dreadful death they were threatened with, but on reaching the open air it was discovered that the danger was over, for a number of men who had been left to watch the outside of the building, had promptly set themselves to work, and all that part of the thatch which had ignited was quickly torn away and thrown far enough off to prevent any further danger. Some imagined that the fire had been occasioned by the too near approach of the torch bearers, but most were of opinion that the act was a wilful one, and amongst the latter was Mr. Derwent, whose suspicions were immediately directed towards Caleb Kestrel as being the author of the deed.

"I have no doubt whatever of it," he replied, in answer to a question from Frank Marldale, "for we know him to be capable of any crime, and how could he have so well glutted his thirst for vengeance as by setting fire to the place whilst we were in it."

"D—n the scoundrel, then let's after him at once," exclaimed Farmer Brough, "for a cowardly act like that deserves the severest punishment that the law can inflict. Let us scour the whole country till we find him, for we shall never be safe so long as a villain like that is suffered to be at large."

"With daylight to assist us, it would be a proper course to adopt," replied Mr. Derwent, "but, dark as it is, we shall not advance a single step towards the capture of Caleb Kestrel and his comrades. They are, no doubt, safe enough by this time, and we should only run an unnecessary risk by exposing ourselves to their weapons, when we should have no chance of competing against them."

"But by to-morrow they may be far enough off."

"Not so far," replied the squire, "but they may meet with some of the numerous persons who are searching for them. The name and description of Caleb Kestrel are now familiar to most persons, and he cannot hope much longer to escape from the pursuit that is on foot from one end of the country to the other."

"I don't know how that may be," exclaimed the farmer, "but if Kestrel plays his cards well, he may remain at liberty for some time to come. For instance, what chance will there be of his being taken if he chooses to remain snug in some hiding place till the search after him is over ?"

"Believe nothing of the kind, my dear fellow," answered the squire, "for the game he has been carrying on is nearly at an end, and before long we shall have the satisfaction of knowing that a desperate scoundrel has at length been rendered powerless. So, we will now return to the hall, and to-morrow we may learn tidings that will put us on the right scent."

No further opposition was offered to this plan, and it having been first ascertained that no one was lurking near the hut, the party retraced their steps to Derwent Hall. On their way many alarms were raised that the enemy was near, but at length they reached their destination without the occurrence of any important adventure.

CHAPTER XLII.

TRUBBS VENTURES TO REMONSTRATE WITH HIS MASTER, AND RECEIVES ORDERS TO PREPARE FOR THEIR IMMEDIATE DEPARTURE.—SOLOMON GRUNDY RESOLVES NOT TO LOSE HIS CHANCE.—HIS INTERVIEW WITH THE SQUIRE.—JABEZ THOMP-SON ARRIVES AT THE HALL ON AN IMPORTANT MISSION.

If Mr. Brassey Popjoy was alarmed at the threatening look of things, his servant Trubbs was still more so, for he had taken it into his head that there was a conspiracy against his life, and at length his resolution was formed to quit the hall at once, even though by doing so he should be compelled to leave the service of his master. Several times had he resolved to enter his protest against extending the visit to any greater length, but on each occasion his courage had failed him when most it was required, and it was not till two or three days after the occurrences related in the last chapter, that he could muster resolution enough to inform Mr. Popjoy that he thought it was running too great a risk to remain any longer in a place where there had been nothing but danger and violence ever since the day of their arrival. Popjoy was pretty well of the same opinion, or his servant's presumption would have met with a severe rebuke, instead of being listened to quietly.

"Trubbs," he exclaimed, after hearing him to an end, "I have often told you never to presume too far upon my good nature. On the present occasion, however, I shall excuse you, for the truth is, I am heartily tired of this visit, and nothing will afford me greater satisfaction than to find myself once more safe in London."

"When shall I get your luggage ready, sir ?" he asked, delighted at the prospect of a speedy departure.

"Immediately," was the reply.

"Shall I take a place for you in the coach, sir ?"

"Not till you have received my further orders," replied Popjoy. "I must not leave this place like a coward, though it must be confessed I care not how soon we get away."

"Then I shouldn't care for anything they might think of me, sir," exclaimed

Trubbs, "for your life is of more consequence than your honour or reputation, and for my own part, I have come to the determination of turning my back upon Derwent Hall whether you do so or not."

"What's that I hear?" exclaimed Mr. Popjoy indignantly. "Do you dare presume, sir, to give me warning?"

"Indeed, sir, it can't be helped," answered the groom, "for I feel that my life is in danger here, and I would rather run the risk of offending you than take the chance of being killed by that ferocious ruffian that they call Caleb Kestrel."

"Psha!" retorted his master, "do you suppose he would take the life of such a worthless knave as you? No, no, it is I that am in danger, for he knows I have been out searching for him, and the revengeful scoundrel would like to murder me for it."

"And ain't that sufficient to frighten you away?" demanded Trubbs.

"I must own it fills me with uneasy thoughts," answered Popjoy, "but it would not do to show anything like fear, because people would only laugh at me, and coward is, of all things, a name that I could not endure. So I have remained here, suffering like a martyr, merely because I would appear to be as bold as all the others appear to be."

"But what would be the use of all this boldness," asked Trubbs, "if you are to lose your precious life through it? For my part, people may call me what they like, but they won't make me risk my safety whilst I've a chance of changing my quarters."

"At all events you must remain here, sir, till I think proper to take leave of my friends."

"That will depend upon how much longer you are going to stay, sir," answered the groom, "for I've made up my mind upon the matter, and if Caleb Kestrel is not taken in the course of this day, I shall most likely make myself scarce to-morrow."

"If you do anything of the kind, Trubbs, you may make up your mind never to enter my service again."

"I should be sorry to leave my situation," replied the groom, "but a man's safety must be cared for, you know, and be the consequence what it may, I shall bid good bye to this place by the time I just now mentioned."

"Have you heard whether any news has been received of Kestrel?" demanded Brassey Popjoy.

"No, sir," he replied; "people are now as much in the dark about him as ever they were, and it's my opinion that he's lying quietly by, in order that he may pounce upon us when we are least expecting it."

"Then he must be a great fool for his pains," observed his master, "for the whole country is up in arms against him, and if he cares at all about his own safety, he would get away the very first opportunity that offers. In my opinion, he has done so, or I should not remain here after to-morrow."

"Ah, sir," exclaimed Trubbs, "nobody thinks he's gone away but yourself, and, by and by, I'm afraid you'll be sorry that you have stayed here so long."

"I have done so," he replied, "because Mr. Derwent has assured me that I, at any rate, have no reason to be afraid of violence from this Caleb Kestrel."

"And why shouldn't you have as much to fear from him as any body else?" asked Trubbs.

"That's what I should like to know myself," answered his master, "for I believe the fellow has as much spite against one person as another, and that he will have his revenge upon the first person he meets, whether it's myself or any other man."

"And yet you won't go away whilst you are safe and sound."

"But I will go away though, and that, too, as soon as possible," replied his master. "In fact, I'm not staying here through any wish of my own, but that I don't want people to laugh at me, and say I went away through cowardice."

"There's the mischief of it," exclaimed Trubbs; "you are afraid of being laughed at, as if that would matter when you have got your own precious life to take care of."

"Look at my honour, Trubbs."

"Honour!" he replied. "Ah! that's a fine thing for people to talk about, but I could never make out exactly what it is."

"Nor do I pretend to know much about it," answered Mr. Brassey Popjoy, "for it's a bit of a puzzle that no one has ever been able to explain to my satisfaction. However, putting all that out of the question, I shall leave Derwent Hall to-morrow, so you may pack up my luggage, and get everything ready for my journey."

"I'll not be long about that," exclaimed Trubbs, delighted at the prospect of a speedy removal from the scene of danger. "I'll have everything ready, sir, you may depend upon it, and if ever I come back to this place I'll be hanged!"

"Has it never struck you," asked his master, "that the long expected attack upon the hall may be made to night?"

"Upon my life, I never thought of that," exclaimed Trubbs, alarmed at the suggestion which, in truth, was only said to frighten him. "I never gave it a thought till now ; and, since you have mentioned it, wouldn't it be better for you to leave the place without any further delay ?"

"Impossible," replied Brassey Popjoy, enjoying the joke all the more for the success it had met with. It's quite impossible to go away so soon as you wish, for there's no conveyance till the morning, so let the danger be what it may, we must face it out as well as we can."

" Wouldn't the squire lend you his carriage ?"

" Perhaps he might, if I was to ask him," replied his master, " but we happen to know that there's queer company prowling about, and I have no fancy to run the risk of being stopped on the highway."

"There it is again," exclaimed Trubbs despondingly. " Whichever way we turn we are beset with difficulties, and it seems that whether we remain here to-night or go up to town, we shall be in danger of falling into the hands of that Caleb Kestrel and his companions."

" Confound the fellow !" cried Popjoy, " he has been a trouble and an alarm to us ever since we have been in this place, and if once I get safe away from Derwent Hall, nothing shall ever persuade me to pay another visit to it. London, after all, is the only place where a man can live comfortably and without fear, and should I be lucky enough to get there again, I'll stop in it all the rest of my days."

" Then you don't mean to go out shooting any more ?"

" Not I, Trubbs," answered his master. " This last attempt of mine has completely cured me of the folly of attempting what I don't properly understand, and I shall henceforth find my enjoyments in very different pursuits. I have received a great deal of very civil treatment ever since I have been here, it is true, but civility is a poor compensation for all the alarm and inconvenience I have been obliged to put up with."

" And you would have a great deal more to put up with if you were to stay here much longer."

"For which reason I have determined to take my departure without delay," answered Mr. Brassey Popjoy. " You now understand my intentions, Trubbs ? This is to be our last night of staying here, so get everything in readiness as quickly as you can, and at as early an hour as we can in the morning we'll mount the coach and return to town."

This latter declaration was so palatable to the groom that he hurried away to execute his task, and Popjoy, who knew not how to employ himself, strolled out into the garden in the hope that he might there meet with his friend Peeps. In the meantime Mr. Derwent, whilst busy in his study, was informed that a stranger wished to see him immediately. His first thought was that it might be Caleb Kestrel who desired the interview, but the servant who had brought the message was quite positive he was not the person suspected, and orders were therefore given that the visitor should be immediately admitted. In the interval, Mr. Derwent vainly endeavoured to guess who the person could be, and great was his surprise when, at length, the door opened and revealed to him the somewhat portly form of Solomon Grundy. He, however, welcomed him with his usual hospitality, and having desired him to be seated, inquired what business had brought him out on so long a journey.

" Why, the truth is," replied the beadle, with an air of importance, " I have heard something about that fellow, Caleb Kestrel, and I believe he is to be found easily enough if we only go the right away about it."

" Well," exclaimed the squire, " and pray where, according to your information, is he to be found ?"

" In this neighbourhood."

" Indeed," returned Mr. Derwent, with affected surprise, " and so you have come all this distance to look for him ?"

" To be sure I have," answered Grundy, " for I may as well earn the reward that has been offered for his apprehension as anybody else ; so I came here to look after him, and I'm not going to give up my search till I have found him."

"Did you hear as far off as Hull that he was lurking about this neighbourhood?" asked the squire.

"Yes, sir," replied Solomon, "after hunting for him in every hole and corner that I could think of, a rumour began to be spread abroad that he was to be found somewhere about Derwent Hall, and so, resolving to lose no more valuable time in a useless search, I came off at once, determined to make him my prisoner, and then to claim the money you were so liberal as to offer."

"Very well, Mr. Grundy," answered the squire, "I'm glad to find that you have displayed so much energy and good will in this affair, and, believe me, nothing will afford me more pleasure than to pay into your hands the money you have taken so much trouble to earn."

"Have you any reason to believe that he is near this place?" asked Solomon Grundy.

"I have good reason to know he is," answered the squire, "for he has been seen by several persons, and I need hardly say every effort has been tried to discover his lurking place."

"And so far, I suppose, sir, no one has been able to discover him?"

"No," replied Mr. Derwent; "strange to say, we are, to all appearance, no nearer to the attainment of our object than we were when I last saw you at Hull."

"Aye, aye, squire," exclaimed the beadle with a self-satisfied air, "the people hereabouts don't understand the business they have undertaken, I can see. They haven't any gumption when there's any difficulty in the way, but now that I have got the affair in hand you shall soon see this Kestrel deprived of his liberty."

"Do you mean to prosecute your search single-handed?"

"Why, no," replied Solomon Grundy, "it would be hardly wise to do that, because he is a rough fellow to deal with, and it would be doing no good to get myself into his clutches when its most likely he would revenge himself by murdering me. Not that there's any cowardice about me, you must understand, Mr. Derwent, but my life is of some value at home, and Mrs. Grundy charged me before I came away not to expose myself to danger."

"And very prudent advice, too, I should think," answered the squire, laughing. "The good lady, perhaps, knows that your courage sometimes exceeds your prudence, and I dare say she has no very great desire to be left in a state of hopeless widowhood."

"I don't think she'd much like it," answered the beadle, "and, for that matter, I have no wish to put her to the expense of wearing mourning for me. In fact, I'm in hopes of getting the whole of this reward to myself, and if so, I have a notion of giving up my beadleship, and entering into the public line."

"The public line!"

"Yes, sir," replied Solomon, "I flatter myself my form is sufficiently portly to make a tolerably good-looking landlord; and as for Mrs. G., she's exactly cut out for the bar business. She's a perfect picture, sir, and would draw customers from far and near. However, that's neither here nor there, for if we don't come to business at once, we shall never get hold of that fellow Kestrel."

"What do you mean, Mr. Grudy?"

"I would know if you have any sort of clue as to where he is hiding himself all this while?"

"If we had known that," answered Mr. Derwent, "we should have secured him before now; but the truth is, the fellow is playing a very deep game, and I rather think he changes his hiding place pretty nearly every day, so that we may be engaged in this pursuit for some time to come."

"Where was he seen last?" asked Grundy.

"Near a ruined cottage on the moors."

"And has no one been to search the place?" asked the beadle.

"Oh, yes," replied Mr. Derwent, "I myself headed a party for that purpose, but though we had sufficient proof that he had been there very recently, he was not to be found anywhere about the place. Strange to say, however, a fire suddenly burst out in the thatch whilst we were assembled in the cottage, and I have a very strong notion that the fire was occasioned by the hand of Caleb Kestrel, for the base purpose of destroying all of us."

"Mercy on us !" exclaimed Solomon ; "what a wretch he must be !"

"He is no worse now than he has been throughout," answered Mr. Derwent, "for shortly after he came into the neighbourhood he attempted to shoot me with an air gun, and for some time it was imagined that he had succeeded in his diabolical object. Luckily, however, some signs of life were discovered by my steward, and by his skill and attention I was at length restored."

"Wouldn't the commission of a crime like that be sufficient to hang him?" asked Solomon.

"Certainly it would," replied the squire, "but, though we have had him in custody since then, he has contrived to make his escape. In fact, he appears to be more like some infernal demon than a man, and I am apprehensive that he will commit some further heinous offence unless we speedily capture him."

"Very well," exclaimed Solomon Grundy, "you have only to trust to me then, and it shall not be long before we have him safe enough."

"You seem to have great confidence in yourself, Mr. Grundy."

"I have," he replied, "and for that very reason I am the more likely to succeed in laying hold of him. Besides, I have something to look forward to, and if that ain't enough to fill a man with hope, I don't know what is."

"But hope sometimes deceives us."

"True," exclaimed the beadle, "but you may depend upon it that will not be the case in the present instance. All I shall want will be the assistance of three or four of your people, and before many hours are over, I flatter myself I shall be able to convince you, sir, that I have not made any vain or empty boast."

"Every facility shall be afforded you," answered Mr. Derwent, "but I warn you beforehand that the matter you have taken in hand is not quite so easy as you seem to imagine. I have myself already failed in my attempts to capture him, and yet I went out with a firm determination not to be foiled, and was accompanied by persons upon whose courage and fidelity I could rely.'

"Has he made any further attempt to carry off the young lady that you were telling me of?"

"No," replied the squire, "he has not done so yet since his last appearance here, but I know the desperate character of the man, and can therefore hope for no cessation of hostilities so long as he is suffered to remain at large. To be sure, his schemes of success are becoming smaller every day, because the whole neighbourhood has been roused against him, so that at length all his cunning cannot prevent his falling into our hands."

"And what will be the use of that," asked Solomon Grundy, "when it appears he always manages to escape again"

"Aye," answered the squire, "but his having done so on a former occasion is a sufficient reason why he will not be permitted to do so again. We know the consequence, too, of holding him safe, so that the next time we have him, he must make up his mind to suffer whatever punishment the law may inflict."

"And it will not be long first, or I'm much mistaken," returned the beadle, "for it's not often that I fail in my object, when once I set my mind upon anything, and in this instance there's such good reason for exerting myself, that you may be assured I shall neglect nothing that will be likely to ensure success. And it must be done quickly, too, for I must return home before Sunday, because I have not left any substitute to perform my official duties."

"Your resolution pleases me," observed the squire, "and I feel some confidence in the promise you have made, though I still think the difficulties are far greater than you imagine. However, you are determined to make the attempt, and, for my own part, I am ready to afford you every assistanc you may require."

"In the first place," replied Solomon, "I must endeavour to discover where he is to be found."

"Which will not be very easy," exclaimed the squire, "for he is continually changing his quarters, so that if we hear of his being in one place this hour, you may be sure that he will not be there by the time his pursuers reach the spot. And in that has consisted our chief difficulty, for though we have ofen been close upon his heels, he has always received an intimation of our expected arrival, and makes such good use of the information that he is able to defy every effort we have made."

"Aye, aye," returned Solomon Grundy, "he may have been lucky so far, but fortune must forsake him before long, and when that is the case he will fall into our hands in spite of all his cunning. By the by, I believe he has been trying to extort money from you, which you have refused to submit to."

"Exactly so," answered Mr. Derwent, "and many persons have blamed me for standing out so long, because they imagine that, by yielding, I might have spared myself and the young lady all the trouble and inconvenience we have experienced. I, however, am of a very different opinion, for I happen to know that as soon as the money was spent, he would recommence the old game and annoy us as bad, if not worse, than ever."

"Besides," exclaimed the beadle, "you have no right to encourage a villain that has been guilty of so many crimes. All you have to do, therefore, is to lay him up fast in prison, and you may depend on it, the law will prevent you being troubled by him again."

"Such was the thought I used to console myself with," answered Mr. Derwent, "but repeated disappointments have made me at last almost despair of seeing so fortunate a termination of the cruel suspense I have endured. Not, however, that I regard the annoyance so far as concerns myself, but unfortunately his persecutions extend to a young female, whom he previously deprived of the fortune she was entitled to by the will of her cousin, Clement Derwent."

"Was that many years ago, sir?"

"So long, that Amy, who was then a mere child, has no recollection of the fact of his stealing her away from the house which, but for him, would have been a happy one."

"What motive had he for stealing her away?"

"Revenge."

"Had so young a child as she was ever injured him?"

"No," replied Mr. Derwent; "but her adopted father has justly prosecuted him for a felony he had been guilty of, and he afterwards took the steps I have spoken of. The loss of the child had such an effect upon my cousin, that he died shortly afterwards, leaving the whole of his property to his young favourite, on condition that she was found within a certain number of years. The period, however, elapsed without any tidings having been heard of her, and then, according to the tenour of the will, I was entitled to succeed to all the property which had been left."

"Which, I suppose, was rather an awkward affair, when the young lady was afterwards discovered?"

"Not at all," answered Mr. Derwent, "for she was still entitled to half the property, which I, of course, most willingly gave up to her."

"I see," exclaimed Solomon, slyly, "you gave her up the property, but will still keep it in your own possession by marrying the young lady. Not, by-the-bye, that there is anything wrong in that, because she will benefit as well as yourself by the marriage, and the estates will remain whole as they were before. However, that's no business of mine, for all I have to do is too look after that scoundrel Caleb Kestrel, and then you will have every prospect before you of passing the rest of your days happily and comfortable."

They were at this juncture joined by Frank Marldale, who, in passing the hall had looked in to see how matters were going on, and to ask if there was any way in which his services might be rendered useful. The beadle, of course, he immediately recognised as the person he had seen at Hull, and having been informed of the errand which had brought him into that part of the country, he ventured to express an opinion that all his trouble had been taken in vain."

"And pray why do you think so, sir?" asked the beadle, not best pleased at having cold water thrown upon his exertions."

"Because," Frank replied, "there are rumours of Kestrel having escaped abroad immediately after our last search for him had so nearly proved successful."

"Pooh!" exclaimed the beadle, "what have we to do with a parcel of rumours that are raised only to deceive us? I'll not believe a word about his having left the neighbourhood, and shall continue to look after him just the same as if no such report had ever been raised."

"I admire your spirit there, my good friend," answered the young farmer, "for, as you say, the rumour may have no foundation, and it is even very probable that he is lying by to pounce out upon us when we least expect him. In short, I am myself quite willing to combine any exertions, for far better would it be that our trouble should be all thrown away, than that we should afterwards see him triumph in the success of his villany. By-the-bye," he added, "there is rather a painful report abroad, which, if confirmed, will give us stronger reasons than ever to look for Mr. Kestrel.'

"What rumour do you allude to?" asked Mr. Derwent.

"Why, you remember the old Gipsy woman,—Deborah, I think they used to call her."

"Yes, what of her?"

"She is missing, and many people do not hesitate to say that she has been murdered by Caleb Kestrel."

"Well," exclaimed Solomon Grundy, "if there's any truth in that, we ought to find it out at once."

"For my own part," observed the squire, "I don't think the story a very probable one, for we know she followed him to Hull, and it is likely she may be there still."

"So I thought myself, at first," replied Frank Marldale, "but it appears that she has been seen in the neighbourhood since then, and the last tidings we have of her are, that she was met going towards the ruined hut on the night when the fire took place."

"Still," observed Squire Derwent, "no harm may have happened to her, for she belongs to a class of people who seldom remain long in one place, and nothing is more likely than that she may have changed her quarters and gone off to some distant part of the country."

"Your suggestions fall to the ground at once," replied his friend, "for her tent still remains where she pitched it, and from all appearances she has not been there for two or three days. So you see there is ground for suspicion, and I really think immediate steps ought to be taken to discover what has become of her."

"Has anybody been to see if she has taken up her quarters in the hut?" inquired Mr. Derwent.

"Yes," replied the young man, "I and three or four others have been there, but though we searched the place, we believe, thoroughly, we have not been able to discover any trace of the old woman. There were, however, recent marks of blood upon the floor, and I therefore think the affair is one that requires looking into."

"That shall most certainly be done," exclaimed Mr. Derwent; "but even if she should have come to her end by foul means, we have no sort of evidence upon which to charge Kestrel with the act."

"But there's a strong case of suspicion," replied Frank, "because we have pretty good evidence that Caleb was there on the night she was seen going towards the place, and you remember picking up a dagger, which had been dropped by some person on the floor?"

"Which weapon I have by me."

"Did you notice whether there were any marks of blood upon it?"

"I see none whatever," replied the squire, taking the dagger from a drawer and examining it with great care. "It happens to be perfectly clear from all stain, and therefore if the crime you speak of has been committed, it must have been with some other instrument than this."

"At any rate there is much ground for suspicion," observed Frank Marldale, "and I, for one, will devote a considerable portion of my time to search for the man whom I suspect of this unhallowed deed."

"And so will I," exclaimed Solomon Grundy; "for, in spite of what you said just now, I don't believe the fellow has left the country. He is, no doubt, prowling somewhere not very far off, and a little good management may soon bring him within my reach."

"You surely don't intend to undertake this business alone?" cried Frank Marldale.

"Not I, you may depend on it," answered the beadle, "for the more we hear of this Caleb Kestrel, the more desperate scoundrel he appears to be. His hand seems to be in for murder, so I must take Mrs. Grundy's advice, and not run myself headlong into danger."

"Take my advice, and get back to your home as fast as you can," exclaimed Frank Marldale, "for it will require younger and more active men than you to join in an affair like this, that is full of difficulties and danger."

"Young man!" replied the beadle indignantly; "keep your advice, if you please, for those that need it. For my own part, I am not to be turned aside by trifles, and especially when I have put myself so far out of the way as to come here in search of him for the sake of the reward that has been offered for his apprehension."

"And pray, of what use will the money be to you if your life should be sacrificed?"

"Aye," he replied, "it may be all very well for you to try to frighten me out of this, but I fancy myself as well able to take him as anybody else, and I'll do my best towards it, too, rather than be laughed at for a coward when I get home. Besides, isn't it every man's duty to assist when a murderer is to be taken, and shall I, at a time like this, suffer my name to be called in question?"

"We are not quite sure that a murder *has* been committed," observed Squire Derwent.

"At any rate, there's very good grounds for suspicion," retorted Solomon Grundy, "for this old woman has never been seen or heard of since somebody met her going towards the ruined hut, and as Kestrel was believed to have been there about that time, I think we may very fairly suspect that he has been at some more of his foul work. At any rate, I'm ready to do my best towards finding out where he has concealed himself, and if we should lay hold of him we may, perhaps, be able to fix him with a crime that will send him to the gallows; which by the bye, will save Mr. Derwent a great deal of trouble and anxiety afterwards."

"And pray where do you think of looking for him, my good friend?" demanded Frank Marldale.

"Ah!" he replied, "there, I own, you have puzzled me, for I know nothing of this place, and must depend upon chance, I suppose, as a great many other people do when they find themselves in a fix."

"Chance will do very little for you in this instance," answered the young farmer, "for you have an artful scoundrel to deal with, and you may depend on it, he will not remain in the same place very long together. In short, as I told you before, there is a report abroad that he has fled the country."

"That we have heard on former occasions," observed Mr. Derwent, "and it has afterwards appeared that the report originated with himself, and was spread about by his comrades, for the purpose of deceiving those who were bent upon capturing him. However, a very short time, I should imagine, will prove whether he is in England or not, and if he should still be within reach, I will never relax in my efforts till he is taken."

"Nor I," exclaimed Solomon Grundy.

"And most heartily do I wish our efforts may be rewarded with success," rejoined Frank Marldale, "for I know, if he is indeed still in this country, he is plotting further mischief against those whom he has already so cruelly persecuted. Even now I am ready to join any party that may be formed, to search round the country, and, if need be, I will freely devote all my time and exertions till we have either discovered him, or ascertained, beyond a doubt, that he has sought refuge in a foreign land."

"But even if he should have done that," answered Mr. Derwent, "he may return when we are little dreaming of his presence."

"Well," exclaimed Solomon, "all I hope is, that he may not be gone away, for if he should, there's an end of the reward that I thought as safe as if it had been already in my own pocket."

"And yet," observed Frank Marldale, "you know not what might have happened in the event of a rencontre, for Caleb Kestrel is no common enemy to deal with, and, let who may attack him, he will defend himself to the very last, and it

No. 46.

may be that he will shed the blood of some of his pursuers before he submits even to superior force."

"That's rather an awkward consideration certainly," replied Solomon, "but still the prize is worth trying for, and I shall forget the danger in the thought of what is to be gained by risking it."

"Your courage pleases me, my friend," exclaimed Mr. Derwent, "but, at all events, I hope you will not suffer yourself to be carried too far by your anxiety to secure the ruffian. Remember, discretion is sometimes the better part of valour, and that it would be madness on your part to attempt single-handed, that which requires more than an ordinary share of watchfulness and prudence."

"Well," he replied, "I don't want to run myself into danger, of course, but there can be no harm in my inquiring about the neighbourhood if he has been seen by anybody."

"Even that must be done very cautiously," returned Mr. Derwent, "for he may hear of what is going on, and in that case he would obtain an advantage that we should not be able to overcome."

"Then it seems I have thrown away my time and trouble too, in coming this journey."

"Nay, we must not say that, either," answered the squire, "for we shall be glad of the assistance of as many friends as we can get, and you have exhibited a highly praiseworthy zeal in acting so promptly in the matter."

"Oh, if you are satisfied with me, that's enough," exclaimed Solomon Grundy, "for I am ready enough to undertake any part that you may think proper to set me, and you will find I'll act up to my duty, even though there may be some little danger in it."

Before Mr. Derwent had time to make any reply to this, a footman came into the room to announce that some strange man was at the door, who requested to see the squire on business of the utmost importance. Upon a question being asked of the servant if he had ever seen the man before, he replied that he was certain he was not an inhabitant of that neighbourhood, and that, from his manner, it was evident his mind was a good deal disturbed by something that was preying upon it. This immediately conveyed an impression that the man must be one of Kestrel's associates, and the next consideration was whether it would be prudent to admit him to the interview he had requested. After some little hesitation, however, it was decided that his business might be of too much importance to be unheeded, and the servant was dismissed with directions to bring the stranger to the room, and then to remain in the adjoining one in case his assistance should be rendered necessary. Having received this injunction, the footman retired, leaving the others in a state of doubt and perplexity as to the motives that could have led to so unlooked for a visit from a stranger. In a moment or two afterwards, however, footsteps were heard crossing the hall; the door was thrown open, and the person who made his appearance before them was no other than our old acquaintance, Jabez Thompson.

CHAPTER XLIII.

JABEZ REVEALS THE SECRET OF DEBORAH'S MURDER. — A CONFIRMATION OF PREVIOUS RUMOURS.—A PARTY IS FORMED TO SEARCH THE RUINED HUT.— THE DISCOVERY OF THE BODY AND RETURN TO THE HALL, WHERE A FURTHER CONSULTATION TAKES PLACE.

THOMPSON gazed round him sullenly as he entered the chamber, and, perceiving that other persons were present besides Mr. Derwent, his countenance assumed a still darker aspect, and he would have retreated without fulfilling his mission, had not the squire peremptorily commanded him to remain where he was. Contrary to expectation, Jabez obeyed, but it was still evident that he was not

likely to make any communication till he could do so to the only person he wished
to see.   This was perfectly well understood by Mr. Derwent, who, motioning for
him to take a seat, thus addressed him.

"I perceive you are disappointed at finding that I am not alone, but if your
business is of importance, and requires secresy, my friends will retire till our interview is at an end."

"If they do that, sir," he replied, "I have no objection to state the object of
my visit, but before other persons I will not utter a word, lest I should afterwards
be made to feel the consequence of my own folly."

"Have you come to tell us where we may find that scoundrel, Caleb Kestrel?"
asked the beadle.

Thompson looked at him sternly, but deigned not to make any reply to the
question.

"My good sir," exclaimed Mr. Derwent, "you have just heard him say that he
will explain the purpose of his visit in the presence of no other person than
myself.   You and Mr. Marldale will, therefore, have the kindness to leave us
together, and it is very probable that the result of this interview may prove of the
highest importance to all of us."

"I only want to know whether he has any information to give, as to where
the pedlar is to be found."

Vexed at this interruption, Mr. Derwent somewhat impatiently requested that
he would retire with Frank Marldale, during the short interval that was asked for.
Solomon, however, was still inclined to dispute the propriety of leaving him alone
with a stranger, and it was not till he was again desired to leave the room, that
he, unwillingly enough, accompanied the young farmer into an apartment
adjoining that in which the interview was to take place, and where they might
easily overhear all that occurred between them.   As soon as they were thus left
alone, Jabez Thompson, looking earnestly into the countenance of the squire,
demanded whether any advantage would be taken of the communication he was
about to make.

"That will entirely depend upon circumstances," he replied, "for I will not
pledge myself to shield a crime, if you are about to confess yourself guilty of
any."

"But, what if I am not guilty?"

"Then you can have nothing to fear, since what you may have to say cannot
operate against yourself."

"Suppose I happened to be present when a heinous crime was perpetrated?" he
asked.

"In that case you would be guilty of participating in the offence; and I,
therefore, warn you against saying anything more."

"It's all very well to warn me," exclaimed Jabez Thompson, "but when a
man's mind is troubled and harassed as mine is at this moment, the truth will out
in spite of himself.   I have lately been the witness of a horrible murder, and the
thought of that horrible moment haunts me night and day, so that I have no hope
of rest till my bosom has been relieved of the heavy load that oppresses it."

"A murder has been committed, then!" cried Mr. Derwent, startled by the
intelligence he was so little prepared for.

"Aye, sir; a cold and cowardly one."

"How long since?"

"Only three nights."

"In this neighbourhood?"

"Yes, sir; no farther off than the ruined hut."

"Ha!" exclaimed the squire, suddenly recollecting the rumour he had lately
heard from Frank Marldale; "the crime you speak of was committed on that
spot, was it?"

"Aye, sir, as surely so as that there is a heaven above us."

"Then I can, perhaps, guess who the victim is."

"I should hardly think that likely," he replied, "for there were only two other persons present when the murderer slew his victim, and I am sure the secret has not been disclosed till now."

" Then hear me," exclaimed Mr. Derwent, " and be convinced that the secret, if not positively known, was at least guessed at, and means would soon have been in progress to discover whether there was any truth in the rumour. The person murdered was, I believe, a woman ?"

" How, in Heaven's name, did you learn that ?" cried Jabez, startled by this unexpected announcement.

" I have told you," replied the squire, " that rumour is already busy with this affair, and the news—though requiring confirmation—reached me about an hour since. You seem to be surprised at my having so far obtained possession of your secret, but you may perhaps be still more so, when I tell you that the person reported to have been murdered, is no other than Deborah, the old Gipsy woman, who has been lately dwelling in this neighbourhood."

" Right," exclaimed Thompson. almost bewildered by what he heard.- " This matter has somehow got wind, and yet how it should have done so is more than I can understand."

" Then I'll explain to you how it was," answered the squire. " A person saw her on the night in question, going towards the ruined hut, and even watched her till she had entered it."

" Did he see what afterwards took place there ?"

" No," replied Mr. Derwent, " the man was too great a coward to approach any nearer, for it was reported that Caleb Kestrel was lying there in concealment, and the coward would not venture to face a man of whom rumour has told so many extraordinary tales."

" Then, how," asked Jabez, " does the person you speak of know that the female was murdered ?"

" From facts that have since transpired," replied Mr. Derwent. " He watched the place for some time, but Deborah made not her appearance, though it was long after the hour of midnight ere he gave up his task. From that time nothing has been seen or heard of the Gipsy woman—her tent is unoccupied—and the general impression is that the poor creature has been murdered."

" She has indeed been murdered," answered the man, " and I myself stood by a witness of the horrid deed."

" Perhaps you also participated in it ?"

" No, as Heaven is my witness; these hands of mine are as guiltless of the crime as your own."

" How is it, then, that you have not revealed the dreadful secret till three days after the commission of the crime ?"

" Because I couldn't make up my mind till now to inform against a man that was once my comrade."

" Had you no hand in the crime yourself ?"

" If I had," he replied, " it is not likely I should confess as much, knowing as I do what would be the consequence of it. I, however, solemnly declare that I lent no assistance, and was not even aware of what was going to take place till Kestrel fired the pistol that laid her dead at his feet."

" Did you make no attempt to seize him ?"

" No ; he was armed with other weapons, and my life would have been sacrificed if I had taken part against him."

" Who else was present at the time ?"

" One Richard Radcliffe."

" I have both seen and heard of the man," replied Mr. Derwent, " and can hardly doubt that he was willing enough to aid and abet in an act of villany like that."

" You are wrong there for once," replied Jabez Thompson, " for he was no less astonished than myself when he saw the old woman fall under the sudden attack made upon her."

"Surely two of you together would have been enough to overpower the murderer?"

"Very likely we might," answered Thompson, " but we had never any quarrel with him, and it was not likely that we were going to interfere when we knew that he would as likely as not serve us as he had served her. Besides, to tell you the truth, we neither of us thought much of the affair at the time, for the old woman was often troubling him, and I expected beforehand what would happen to her sometime or another."

"You assisted him, I suppose, in concealing the body ?"

"No, we both of us refused to do that, for as we had no share in the murder, we saw no use in mixing ourselves up in the affair by affording our assistance after it was all over."

"What was done with the corpse?"

"That I can only answer from what Caleb Kestrel himself told us," replied the other. "He, however, took the body in his arms, and carried it down into a vault where there is a well, and I believe you will there find all that remains of old Deborah."

" Where is the murderer now lurking ?"

"That's more than I can say," replied Jabez Thompson, " and even if I knew I should not very easily suffer anybody to wring the confession out of me."

" You would prefer, then, to aid a murderer in escaping from the just punishment of his crime ?"

"The truth is, I have had nothing to do with the deed," answered Jabez, " and I consider my confession, as far as it has gone, ought to be quite enough to satisfy you without its being expected that I shall tell where Kestrel is to be found."

" You will be well rewarded for it, if you give the requisite information that will lead to the apprehension of the murderer."

"Neither rewards nor threats, nor anything else, will ever tempt me to give up an old comrade, though conscience brought me here to reveal a crime that I could no longer keep to myself."

" Is Kestrel aware that you intended to betray his secret ?"

"If he had been," replied the other, " it's not very likely that he would have let me live to do it. No, no, I kept all that to myself, and wouldn't even let Dick Radcliffe know I was coming here, for fear he should take it into his head to tell Caleb that I was going to blab about the old woman's murder."

" Well," exclaimed Mr. Derwent, after a pause, " I suppose you are aware that it will be my duty to hold you in custody till a strict inquiry has been made into the truth of your statement ?"

" I know nothing about your duty," replied Thompson, " but it would be a cruel act of treachery to punish me for having come here to make a clear conscience of it."

" But, according to your own showing, you were present whilst a murder was committing, and yet made no effort to prevent it, though you were well enough able to have done so."

" Don't I tell you it took place so suddenly that there was no time to have hindered it ?"

" At all events it was your duty to have given him up to justice immediately, and as you failed to do so, I have no alternative but to secure your person till we have been able to discover whether you had a larger share in the crime than you are willing to acknowledge."

" If I had had anything more to do with it than I have told you, is it likely I should be fool enough to throw myself into your clutches? However, I have not come here to give myself up, and if you deprive me of my liberty it will be a rascally breach of confidence, that's all I know about it."

" As for that," exclaimed Mr. Derwent, "I am a magistrate, and therefore am bound to act in an affair like this to the best of my judgment. Excuse your conduct as you may, you were present when the crime of murder was committed, and yet have taken three days to consider before you make up you mind to relate a secret, that, if it had been earlier discovered, might have led to the punishment of the assassin. Under these circumstances, therefore, I shall detain you in custody till a rigid examination into all the circumstances of the horrible affair has been made."

"In that case," returned Jabez Thompson, "I shall make bold to leave your house without permission. Don't attempt to hinder me, sir, for this is a desperate game that I am obliged to play, and if you dare but to lay a hand upon me it will be all the worse for you."

Roused by this threat, Mr. Derwent started from his seat, and was about to pull the bell for assistance, when Thompson rushed towards him, and would have grasped him by the throat, had not Frank Marldale hastened in from the next room to the assistance of their friend. The latter instantly seized the aggressor, and succeeded in preventing the intended attack till the arrival of several of the domestics, who rendered all further efforts on the part of Jabez Thompson utterly in vain. Immediately afterwards he was conveyed to another room in the upper part of the building, where it would not be easy to escape, and in order to render all chance of a rescue impossible, a strong guard was placed over him, with orders to fire upon any persons who might attempt to liberate him. This having been seen to, and everything appearing to be tolerably safe, Mr. Derwent at length found time to satisfy the curiosity of those who were anxious to know the origin of the struggle which they had fortunately been the means of preventing.

"My friends," exclaimed the squire, to those who were eagerly crowding round him, "the man you have just now rescued me from, has visited me for the purpose of confessing that three nights since he was present when a cruel, cold-blooded murder was committed; and when, as in duty bound, I told him that he must submit to remain for a time my prisoner, he made the attack which might have proved of such serious consequence but for your timely arrival."

"Who is the murderer he told you of?" asked several voices.

"Caleb Kestrel."

"I thought so," exclaimed Frank Marldale, "and no doubt the murdered person was the Gipsy woman, Deborah."

"Aye, that is indeed the person," answered the squire, "and therefore the report you brought here is strictly correct in every particular. The villain, it appears, shot her because he feared she would betray him, and it is now our duty to take immediate steps for the arrest of the assassin."

"There's little doubt about our all being willing enough to assist in doing that," answered Solomon Grundy; "but we should like, first of all, to know where we are to look for him."

"That is what I should have liked to have ascertained myself," returned the squire, "but my informant, though perfectly willing to reveal the fact of the murder, was most positive in his refusal to say where the assassin is to be found."

"Why should he object to one thing more than to another?" asked Frank Marldale, with surprise.

"The fellow would not deign to explain himself upon the subject," answered his friend, "but from what I could gather, it appears that though a sore conscience had urged him to reveal the crime that had been committed, he would not go so far as to betray his former comrade into the hands of his enemies."

"Ah, if that's the case," exclaimed the beadle, "I should not be surprised if the whole story about the murder is a falsehood."

"That can, at any rate, soon be ascertained," answered Mr. Derwent, "for the crime seems to have taken place in the ruined hut, and if this man's word is to be relied on, we shall find the body of the unfortunate woman in a well, into which it was thrown for concealment."

"Whereabouts is the well?" asked Marldale.

"In a vault beneath the hovel."

"Then, of course, you intend to search there?"

'Immediately."

"And if the body should be found there ?"

" In that case we shall have more reason than ever to seek after Caleb Kestrel, and it will be extraordinary indeed if we do not find means to trace him to his lair."

"The long and the short of it is, that we must all make up our minds never to give up the search till we have found him," exclaimed Solomon Grundy. " As far as I am concerned, I'll never give up whilst there's a chance left, and something strikes me very forcibly that it will not be many days, and perhaps only a few hours, before we have the satisfaction of seeing him safe under lock and key. So now, sir, if you are ready for a visit to the hut you speak of, we are all ready to accompany you there, and a short time will serve to prove whether there is any truth in this reported murder."

Finding that all were unanimous in their wish to ascertain the fact of a crime of such deep dye having been perpetrated so near to them, Mr. Derwent ordered a number of torches to be lighted in order that there might be no difficulty in the way of their search. Each vied with the other in forwarding the necessary preparations, and within half an hour afterwards, it was announced that everything was quite ready for their departure from the hall. Upon this they set forth on their errand, and in about half an hour reached the hut, the exterior of which was carefully examined before they again trusted themselves inside with the chance of the place being again set fire to by the inveterate foe they had to deal with. Nothing, however, occurred to show that anybody was watching their movements, and after a few cautions were given by Mr. Derwent, he, accompanied by Frank Marldale, Solomon Grundy, and five or six others, entered the place, leaving about an equal number to guard the house outside, in case an attack on them should be meditated. On gaining the interior, their first care was to examine every corner, so as to satisfy themselves that no enemy was lurking near to rush upon them when their attack was not looked for, and their next course was to descend into the vault or cellar beneath, where it was said the body had been deposited for concealment. Some appeared unwilling to be the first to descend, but Mr. Derwent, who had no idle fears of the kind, instantly volunteered to lead the way, and springing towards the steps, he, torch in hand, made his way towards the spot where such important disclosures were to be expected. His example was quickly followed by the others, and when all were assembled together, they directed their way towards a dark recess, in which they found the well they were in search of. As they stood gazing down into the obscurity a debate took place amongst them as to who should explore the well to its bottom, and it was not till a reward of five guineas was offered by Mr. Derwent that one of his farm-labourers consented to be lowered down by means of a rope, in order to ascertain whether the body of Deborah was at the bottom. Foreseeing that such a thing would be required, a rope of sufficient strength had been brought with them, and one end having been secured to a beam above, the other was fastened round the body of the man who had undertaken to explore the place. At length the word having been given that all was ready, the man was gradually lowered, after having been cautioned to give an alarm the moment anything occurred to render his immediate ascent desirable. During this period the utmost anxiety prevailed amongst those who were awaiting the result of his exploring adventure, but their watching was not of any very long duration, for within two or three minutes after the man had disappeared from their view the rope was observed to be violently agitated, as if by way of signal, and then the voice of the man was heard calling on them to haul him up without delay. This was, of course, promptly obeyed, and all hands being applied to the rope, they soon succeeded in raising their comrade to the brink of the well, and it was then discovered that he bore in his arms the livid corpse of a female. Relieved of his ghastly burden the man was soon assisted on firm ground, and then, as all stood round the dead body, their torches plainly discovered the countenance of the Gipsy woman, Deborah.

" There can be no doubt as to the identity of the body," exclaimed Mr. Derwent, to those who stood about him. "This is, indeed, the poor woman who has been dwelling among us, and we may, therefore, conclude that the story told by Jabez is true in every respect."

"There can be no doubt about the poor creature before us," replied Frank Marldale, "but as far as your information goes, I am not quite certain that his account is entirely correct.

"You don't doubt her having been murdered, I suppose?" observed Solomon Grundy.

"How can I do that when the bullet wound is of itself sufficient to convince me that she has met a violent death?" exclaimed the young man. "There can be no hesitation in saying that a foul murder has been committed by this Jabez Thompson, instead of the person he has accused of it."

"That's possible enough," answered the squire; "but one would hardly believe that Thompson would have let out the secret of the murder if it had been committed by himself."

"I don't know that," observed Solomon, "if he thought to put people off their guard by accusing another. It may have been a deep trick of his to turn away the suspicion from himself, and if my advice is worth being taken, I should say that Jabez Thompson ought not to be set at liberty till we are perfectly satisfied that he had nothing to do with this horrible crime."

"You may depend upon it, my good friend," exclaimed the squire, "that I shall take care to sift this affair to the very bottom, for justice demands a searching examination of every circumstance connected with this diabolical act, and never will I relax my endeavours till the truth has been discovered, and the authors of it brought to condign punishment."

"In the meantime, what is to be done with the body?" enquired Solomon Grundy.

"It will remain here for the present," answered Mr. Derwent, "and in order to prevent the removal of it by any of the persons who have been concerned in the murder, I shall leave half a dozen of our people to watch round the place."

"A good plan that," exclaimed the beadle, 'for Caleb Kestrel may come to take away the corpse, and if so, there will be a capital chance of taking him without much trouble. So if you think proper to allow of it, Mr. Derwent, I should have no objection whatever to make one of the watchers here to-night."

"In order, I suppose," exclaimed the squire, "that you may have the better chance of earning the reward that has been offered for his apprehension?"

"Well, I must confess I think I deserve it as much as anybody," replied the beadle, "for I have spared no trouble in looking after him, and have travelled a good many miles in order that I might have the honour of being his captor. However, be that as it may, I should think Kestrel would have but a poor chance of escaping now that he is accused of this murder."

"That," returned Frank Marldale, "will depend upon whether he is still in England, for if once he gets out of it, there's very little likelihood of his returning when there's such a prospect of being hanged if he should be laid hold of."

"Aye," answered Solomon Grundy, "but the question is, whether we shall be able to get evidence enough against him."

"Why there's Jabez Thompson, at any rate, and he swears that he saw the murder committed on this woman."

"And who will believe him on his oath?"

"Very few, I fancy, would be inclined to take his word," exclaimed Mr. Derwent, "but if his accusation should happen to be confirmed by other testimony there would be reasonable ground for believing that the act was committed by his hand. Indeed, I have no doubt of the fact myself, for though it must be admitted that the evidence of a comrade should always be received with caution, I am not altogether inclined to reject this man's accusation till I have heard or seen something to convince me that he has told a falsehood."

"At all events," observed Frank, "it would be advisable to keep Thompson safe in custody till we are able to decide upon his probable guilt or innocence."

"Which can harldly be done for some time to come," observed the beadle who would still offer an opinion, though within himself he felt very much perplexed, to decide upon which party the greatest weight of proof laid. "There's a considerable difficulty in our way I can see, for the only evidence we yet have is that of Jabez Thompson, and of what use is that when we know that he may have made the accusation only to clear himself from suspicion?"

"You have a notion then, I find, that Caleb Kestrel may not be taken quite so soon as you once thought for."

"I should be very sorry to think that, Mr. Derwent," he replied, "for the longer he is at liberty, the greater will be the danger to those who, like myself, have taken an active part against him. He has marked us all, you may depend on it, and if he only has a chance of serving us out for what we've done, he won't forget to pay off old scores, I'll be bound."

"Well," returned the squire, "if I was in your place, Grundy, I should not let that thought trouble me much, for all the chances are in favour of never being annoyed by him."

No. 47.

"How do you know I shall not be annoyed by him ?"

"Because, if he is luckly enough to be able to preserve his liberty, he will know better than to run any risk of losing it through looking after people that he cares nothing for, and if he happens to fall into the strong hands of the law, he will, of course, have no chance whatever of playing off any of his revengeful tricks. So, in every point of view, you have nothing whatever to fear, though you seem to think yourself in no little danger."

"And who knows," asked the beadle, "but what we are all of us in the greatest danger at this very moment. Aye, you may look at me with surprise," he added, turning round to the people that stood about him, "but we all know what a devil incarnate this Caleb Kestrel is, and it's just as likely as not that he may at this moment be watching us."

"He would be an errant fool for his pains if he was," exclaimed Mr. Derwent, who saw that his people were alarmed by the suggestion that had just been thrown out, "and I only wonder that these people, ignorant as they are, don't laugh at you for giving an opinion that is so absolutely ridiculous."

"Would you have 'em laugh, Squire Derwent," remonstrated the beadle, "with this murdered corpse before their eyes ?"

"Nay, nay," answered Mr. Derwent, "the expression I made use of was, I own a very improper one, but I only wanted to convice you that there is no probability of Caleb Kestrel lurking about this spot at a time like this. What chance, in fact, would he have, if he was to be seen by any of our people, now that he is suspected of being the principal in the barbarous murder of this poor old woman ?"

"Then you think he's gone clear away ?" exclaimed Solomon Grundy, rather chap-fallen at the idea of losing the money he had been so anxiously looking forward to.

"I think, at any rate," he replied, "that the probabilities are very much against his staying in a place where he must continually be in danger of falling into the hands of some of the many persons who are on the look-out for him."

"But suppose he should not be guilty of killing this woman ?"

"Still he would keep away," answered Mr. Derwent, "for he must know that he is suspected, and even that circumstance would subject him to the annoyance, and perhaps the risk of being locked up on a charge that would be so difficult to answer to the satisfaction of those who are prejudiced against him. However, this is a matter that can be considered to-morrow as well as now, and we will therefore return to the hall, leaving the body, as I said before, in the charge of some of these people. By the bye, Mr. Grundy, are you still anxious to remain here as one of the watchers ?"

"I'm by no means anxious for the job," he replied, "unless, indeed, there was a chance that Caleb Kestrel would venture to show himself here in the course of the night. But that's not very likely, it seems, so with your permission, sir, I would rather accompany you back to your house."

Preparations were now made for their departure, and half a dozen of the men having been selected to guard the place till further inquiries had been made into the murder, the others followed Mr. Derwent and his friends back to his home. The news of the shocking discovery that had been made was spread through the neighbourhood by the following morning, and the whole male population of the district were immediately stirring, in the hope of securing the person of the justly execrated Caleb Kestrel.

CHAPTER XLIV.

PURSUIT AFTER THE SUPPOSED MURDERER.—CORONER'S INQUEST ON THE
BODY.—JABEZ THOMPSON REPEATS HIS ACCUSATION, BUT PREVARICATES
IN HIS STORY.—FURTHER EVIDENCE IS HEARD.—THE CASE BECOMES SUS-
PICIOUS, AND THE ACCUSER IS REMANDED FOR A FURTHER EXAMINATION.

NEVER was greater anxiety manifested than by those who had undertaken
the task of dragging before the seat of justice the sanguinary wretch, whose
crime had created so much excitement for many miles round the neighbourhood. The reward promised for his apprehension was, it is true, a great
inducement to many who engaged themselves in the pursuit, but there was a
much better feeling prevailing among the people—that of bringing upon the murderer
the just punishment which his crime demanded. Every place, every corner, where
it was possible he might have concealed himself, was searched with the utmost
strictness, but still nothing was to be seen of Caleb Kestrel, and, what
appeared to be yet more remarkable, no one could be found who had seen or
heard anything of his whereabout, since the day on which it was supposed
the murder had been committed. Still no energy was wanting in an affair of
such absorbing interest to every one, and from morning till night men were
seen hurrying here and there, all intent upon the one object which they had
undertaken with so much resolution and good will. Two days after the discovery of the crime an inquest was appointed to be held upon the body of
the unfortunate woman, and at a stated hour a jury of twelve men assembled
to inquire into the circumstance which had occasioned such a feeling of
horror. The body, which in the meantime had been removed to the public-
house where the inquest was held, was viewed by the jury previous to the
business being entered into, and when all had taken their places at the table,
the coroner addressed them briefly on the case that was now to be brought
before them. He remarked principally on the mystery and uncertainty that at
present involved the affair, the doubt with which the evidence of a man of
notoriously bad character like Jabez Thompson ought to be received, and the duty
which they owed to themselves and the public, to sift every point which might in
any way bear upon the subject. This done, he desired Thompson to be brought
forward, and commenced the proceedings by asking him to describe the circumstances under which the murder had taken place. Jabez, however, seemed to be
in no humour to repeat the accusation now that he was placed under restraint,
and on being a second time desired to make his statement, he replied that he had
done so once, and that before he said anything more upon the subject he must be
set at liberty.

"That," answered the coroner, "is more than I have the power to order, for
you have been placed in confinement by a magistrate, and no doubt he did so
upon what he considered to be very sufficient grounds. You must, therefore,
answer the questions that are put to you, or it is not unlikely that your first story
may be regarded as a fabrication of your own."

"How can it be a fabrication," he demanded, "when the body was found in the
very place I had mentioned."

"The body was found there, no doubt," answered the coroner, "but we must
hear who committed the crime, and whether it was the murderer who placed his
victim in the place where she was discovered."

"I have told you already," said Thompson, "that she was killed by Caleb
Kestrel."

"And you still adhere to that accusation, do you?"

"Why shouldn't I, when it's the truth?"

"You were present at the time, I believe?"

"Of course I was," answered Jabez, "or I shouldn't have been able to swear
who did it."

" Was any other person near when the crime was committed ?"

" Yes."

" What is his name ?"

" Richard Radcliffe."

" Did he take any part in the crime we are inquiring into ?"

" No," answered Thompson, " neither he nor I were aware of what was going to take place till we heard the report of a pistol, and saw the woman fall dead on the ground."

" Had any quarrel occurred between the accused and the deceased woman previous to this event ?"

" They had a few words together, but I little thought of the violence that was going to take place."

" Who was it that afterwards concealed the body in the well ?"

" Caleb Kestrel."

" Was he able to do so without assistance ?"

" Oh, yes, easily enough," answered Jabez. " He has the strength of a giant, and when he found that neither Dick Radcliffe nor I would lend him a hand, he threw the body across his shoulders and went with it down into the vault underneath."

" And after having seen all this done," asked the coroner, " did you make any attempt to secure the prisoner ?"

" No."

" How do you account for that ?"

" Because he was armed with plenty of weapons besides the one he had committed the murder with, and it would have been as much as our lives were worth to have laid our hands upon him, when the devil was raging within him."

" Then it was your duty to have informed some person of it."

" Haven't I done so ?" demanded Jabez, insolently. " If it hadn't been for me, how would it ever have been known that the old woman was murdered ?"

" There is no doubt of your having given information," answered the coroner, " but it was not till two or three days afterwards, and that it is which has thrown some doubt upon your assertions. It was your duty to have denounced the murderer immediately, and then the probability is, that we should have had him in our custody before now."

" I've told Mr. Derwent why I didn't do so," he replied, " and if the same sort of thing was to happen over again, I should still wait long enough to give the accused an opportunity of escaping."

" Be careful what you say," exclaimed the coroner, " for if such an admission is made in the course of your examination, you may probably be committed as an accomplice after the fact."

" Now that I'm in your power, you'll do with me as you like, I suppose," he replied sullenly. " However, be that as it may, I didn't think proper to accuse Caleb Kestrel of the murder till I thought he was far enough out of the reach of the law."

" Then what induced you to say anything about it ? "

" My conscience would not suffer me to have any rest, and I thought to ease it by telling the truth."

" You spoke just now of another person having been present when the murder was committed. Are you aware whether he is ready to support your evidence by his own ?"

" That's more than I can answer for."

" Do you know where we can find him ?"

" No," replied Jabez, " and even if I did, I should not be fool enough to tell anybody."

" Why not ?"

" Because I suppose you would lock him up as you have me, and I don't choose that another shall get into a scrape when I know what sort of people he would have to deal with."

"Let a strict search be made after this Richard Radcliffe," exclaimed the coroner to the three or four constables who were in the room. "This case begins to wear a new aspect, and I am much mistaken if both he and the witness now under examination have not had more to do with the murder than they wish us to know."

"Is this the sort of justice I'm to get from you?" demanded Jabez, invountarily. "You first of all ask questions to draw all you can out of me, and then turn everything I say against me."

"You are not asked questions to criminate yourself," returned the coroner, "but this affair is one of so much importance that we are bound to sift every circumstance connected with it to the very bottom. You have admitted the fact of having been present when the murder was perpetrated, and your evidence, which is admitted only as an approver, must be given without any reservation, or you will certainly be committed as a participator in the crime."

"What! when I had no more to do with it than yourself?"

"You were present, yet, according to your own showing, made no attempt to prevent the crime."

"Shouldn't I have been mad to have interfered when I knew that my life would have been sacrificed?"

"At all events, you might have given information much sooner if you had been inclined. It's no excuse for you to say that you would not get this friend of yours—this Richard Radcliffe—into trouble, for it was your duty to have made known the particulars of this horrible case, in order that immediate steps might have been taken for securing the assassin."

"Am I to understand, then, that you are going to commit me for the crime?" he asked.

"Not upon any statements that you have made, certainly," answered the coroner, "but if other witnesses should be able to prove that you had more to do with the crime than you have admitted, it will then be my duty to commit you, in order that the affair may be tried before a higher tribunal."

"Then, after all," exclaimed Jabez Thompson, "I have done no good for myself by coming forward as I have?"

"The evidence of approvers," answered the coroner, "is admitted only on condition that they withhold nothing which may tend towards the punishment of their accomplices. You have not done all that the law requires from you, and it will, therefore, depend upon the evidence of the next witness whether you will be committed or not for a guilty knowledge of the crime we are inquiring into."

"Who is the next witness?" asked Jabez.

"A man who saw the old woman enter the hut on the night when she was murdered. Let Thomas Thornley be called," he added, turning towards the person who performed the office of crier, and immediately afterwards a young man, having the appearance of a groom, was sworn to give his evidence.

"What do you know respecting the case we are inquiring into?" asked the coroner.

"Nothing of the murder itself, please you, sir," answered the man.

"No, no," exclaimed the other impatiently, "we don't suppose you saw the crime committed, but you can tell us whether the woman who has been slain was seen going towards the hut on the evening when the crime is said to have been committed."

"Yes, sir, I saw her quite plainly."

"Was there sufficient light at the time to enable you to swear that she was the person you saw?"

"I can swear to her, sir, for I was quite near to her."

"Did you speak to the woman?"

"I wished her good night."

"What reply did she make to that?"

"None at all, but I'm positive about the woman, because I had seen her several times before, since she came into this neighbourhood."

"Did you lose sight of her ?"

"Not for a moment, till she entered the hut."

"What did you do then ?"

"I stood a little way off, and watched," he replied, "for I knew the place had had a bad name ever since Caleb Kestrel and his associates have been known to hide there, and I fancied in my own mind that something bad was going to happen."

"You were afraid to go too near the place, I suppose ?"

"Indeed I was, sir," answered Tom Thornley, "because I happened to be pretty close upon the heels of Kestrel three or four times, and I know he owes me a grudge, which he means to pay me the first time he has an opportunity."

"Did you see any other persons go into the house ?"

"Not afterwards, sir."

"Had you seen any one do so previously ?"

"I didn't see 'em go into the house, but I saw 'em when they were going towards it."

"Who do you mean by they ?"

"Caleb Kestrel was one—Dick Radcliffe, the other—and the third was the man that was examined here to-day."

"You are quite positive as to their being the persons ?"

"Quite."

"Now then, tell me if, whilst you were watching, any of these persons came out of the ruined hut ?"

"Not one of 'em, I'm certain."

"Did you hear a report as of a pistol ?"

"I did; but from the distance where I stood I could not be certain whether the sound came from the house or from some other place near it."

"And after that took place, you are sure no one left the house which you had seen them all enter ?"

"I swear no one did."

"This is rather an important fact, gentlemen," said the coroner, addressing himself to the jury, "because it clearly proves that no attempt was made to escape or raise an alarm by either of the two men after they had witnessed the murder of this old woman. If this man's evidence is to be believed, therefore, this Jabez Thompson and Richard Radcliffe were clearly *particeps criminis*, because they took no steps to cause the apprehension of a man who, in their presence, had been guilty of a most heinous crime. Jabez Thompson, as you are aware, has not ventured to swear that he was intimidated by any threats that were held out by the murderer against those who should attempt to arrest him; no warning of this kind was uttered, and therefore it will be for you to ask among yourselves, whilst considering your verdict, whether these two men are not guilty of a wilful omission, when, if they had done their duty, the assassin might have been secured and brought to punishment." Then, again addressing himself to the witness, he asked —"How long did you remain watching the house after you heard the report of the pistol ?"

"Two hours, or more."

"And in those two hours you are positive no person could have left the place ?"

"I am sure no one did."

"How can you be so positive of that ?"

"Because no one can leave the house except from that part which I was watching," answered the witness.

"In short, you mean us to understand that if any person had left the house, you must have seen him ?"

"Exactly so."

"What was the impression upon your mind when you came away from the spot where you had been watching ?"

"I thought there was something very curious about it, and intended to go next day to see if anything was the matter."

"Did you go?"

"I did not, sir."

"How was that?" asked the coroner.

"Because my master was going with some friends to look in another direction after Caleb Kestrel, and I was desired to accompany them."

"Of course, you mentioned to other persons a circumstance that had excited so much of your curiosity?"

"Oh, yes," he replied, "I mentioned it to a good many people, and amongst others to Mr. Frank Marldale, who, I believe, afterwards told my master what he had heard."

"Soon after which, I believe, Mr. Derwent, accompanied by Mr. Marldale and some other persons, went to the deserted cottage to satisfy themselves whether there was any truth in the stories that, through what you had said, were in circulation?"

"Yes sir," replied the witness, "but it was not so much through what I had said, as in consequence of a confession that had been made by Jabez Thompson."

"Did you make one of the party on that occasion?"

"Yes, sir."

"And were present when the body was found in the well?"

"I was."

"I suppose there was no difficulty about identifying the body of the person that was found?"

"Not in the least, sir," answered the witness, "for though the woman had not been long in the neighbourhood, she was well known to almost every one. I knew her directly, and so I should have done, see her wherever I might."

"Was anything else discovered there?"

"Not that I saw," he replied, "but I've heard that Mr. Derwent found a dagger, or something of that sort, in the cottage, when he went to search it a few days before."

"Who was the weapon supposed to belong to?"

"I have been told that one like it was seen in the possession of Caleb Kestrel, but am not able myself to say whether or not such was the case."

This being all the evidence he had to give, Jabez Thompson was again desired to stand forward.

"You have heard," said the coroner, "the depositions of the man who has just been examined, "and I now ask if you have any explanation to give of that part of his evidence in which he says that neither you nor the man you call Richard Radcliffe left the cottage after the report of a pistol was heard?"

"I've told you as much about it as I could already," he replied, "and whatever I have said you seem to turn against me as much as you can."

"On the contrary, I wish to act fairly and impartially," answered the coroner, "and you will do well to reply with openness and candour to all questions that are put towards clearing up the mystery that involves this case."

"And I have done so as far as I know of."

"Of that you are the best judge," exclaimed the coroner, "but in my opinion you seem to withhold everything that will be of real importance to the inquiry we are engaged in. However, you may take my word for it that the truth must come out in spite of whatever may be done to keep it back, and if facts should be disclosed by others than yourself, any hope of pardon that you may have indulged in will prove to be utterly without foundation."

"I see very well how it is," exclaimed Jabez Thompson, sullenly; "you want to get all you can out of me under a promise of pardon, and when that has been done, I shall be given up to the tender mercy of the law."

"Believe nothing of the kind," answered the coroner, "for I again assure you that every promise that has been made will be faithfully fulfilled if you end the cause of justice by bringing the murderer to justice?"

"What more can I do?" asked Jabez.

"At any rate, you can afford a clue by which the retreat of Caleb Kestrel can be discovered."

"I have told you already, Mr. Coroner, that I will never betray a comrade, let what may happen through it."

"We shall see how long that resolution will last, exclaimed the other, "for there is sufficient before me to warrant me in sending you back to prison for a few days, and in the meantime it is likely we may discover the retreat of the men you would shield from punishment. They, perhaps, may not be quite so obstinate in answering my questions, and if so, it is likely you will find yourself in a situation that you will wish yourself out of."

"I should like to know why I am to be locked up when I came forward of my own accord to give the information that has led to the discovery of the body of the old woman?"

"The truth is, you did so through the fear of being discovered by the vigilance of those who are searching for the perpetrators of the crime you acknowledged to have witnessed," answered the coroner. "In fact, the disappearance of the Gipsy woman had been remarked by several persons in the neighbourhood, and as the witness, Thomas Thornley, had seen her enter the ruined cottage, it would have been the first place where a search was made. This you may have suspected, and I, therefore, think it very likely you made a virtue of necessity when you came forward to make your statement.'

"Well," exclaimed the prisoner, "I can only say it's an infernal hard thing to be treated in this way, when I thought I was doing something to deserve reward instead of punishment. But I can see plainly enough how it is, you have got all you can out of me by fair means, and now you want me to betray my friends, and are not ashamed to do so by violence and treachery."

"As far as I am myself concerned," interposed Mr. Derwent—who till now had remained a silent auditor of what was going forward—"I had determined, immediately upon hearing of Deborah's disappearance, to search every part of the neighbourhood where she was likely to be discovered. The hut would, certainly, not have been forgotten, and from the strictness of our investigation, there is no doubt the body would have been discovered."

"Still," answered Jabez, "you would not have known who it was that had killed her."

"But we should have guessed it though," he replied, "for as it was well-known that Caleb Kestrel had been lurking there about the period when Deborah went to the hut, there would have been sufficient ground for us to have attributed the crime to him. At all events, a searching investigation of the affair would have been entered into, and then the truth would, in all probability, have come to light."

"I neither know nor care how that might have been," answered Jabez Thompson, "but no investigation that you might have entered into would have shown that I had anything to do with the murder."

"At any rate," observed the coroner, "you neither attempted to prevent the crime, nor to secure the perpetrator after it had been committed."

"And I should like to know who would be fool enough to lay hands upon an armed and desperate man?" exclaimed the prisoner, "for my own part I am not so tired of life that I would oppose myself against Caleb Kestrel, when once he has been roused to passion."

"But there were two of you present," answered the coroner, "and surely the two together might have interfered when the life of a human creature was at stake. However, that forms no part of our present inquiry, and the jury will, I dare say, agree with me in seeing the propriety of adjourning the inquest for a week."

"And am I to be thrown into prison all that time?"

"Such is the only course we can adopt," answered the coroner, "and I don't see that you have any great hardship to complain of, seeing that the step is only taken to ensure your appearance here when the enquiry is resumed."

"Won't you take bail for me?"

"Bail is never accepted when the person is suspected of having been a party in such a crime as this," replied the other. "You will, however, be treated with as much consideration as the regulations of the prison allow, and if you have any cause for complaint, the magistrates of this district will be at all times ready to hear your wrongs, and, if possible, immediately redress them."

"I shall ask no indulgence," he replied, "for if I am treated with this injustice, I will put up with it till the time comes when I am to be set at liberty."

"Fortunately all men who have not been convicted, have the means in their own power to seek that justice which they may fancy has been denied them," returned the coroner. As far as the present enquiry goes, I am bound to do equal justice between the prisoner and the crown; and as this case has only advanced one step towards completion, I must resort to the only means by which I can ensure your presence before me when a further investigation is to take place. In the meantime, however, a professional adviser, or any friends who may apply to see you, will be admitted into the prison."

No. 48.

"At present I want no lawyers to bother me," he replied, "and as to my friends, I should advise none of 'em to trouble their heads about me, since they may perhaps be suspected as well as myself, and in that case there would be little hesitation about locking them up as you are going to do me."

Perceiving that he was not likely to say anything more, the coroner, with the sanction of the jury, adjourned the inquiry for a week; and the prisoner, who sullenly submitted himself to their custody, was conveyed away to the prison, where he was to remain till the investigation could be completed. Mr. Derwent and Frank Marldale then returned to the hall, there to concert further measures for the discovery of all those who were concerned in the barbarous murder which had been perpetrated. The principal object to which their attention was to be directed was to trace Caleb Kestrel to the place where he had concealed himself; a task which seemed to be full of difficulties, though they would not yet give up all hope of a successful termination of their labours. At all events they were resolved to leave no means untried, and, in order to increase their chance of success, a number of persons were engaged to assist them in their labour.

CHAPTER XLV.

CALEB KESTREL MAKES THE DISCOVERY THAT ONE PLACE, AT LEAST, IS TOO HOT TO HOLD HIM.—HE TAKES HIS FLIGHT WITH DICK RADCLIFFE TO ROBIN HOOD'S CAVE. —HIS RECEPTION BY THE SMUGGLERS IS ANYTHING BUT FRIENDLY.—HE PROPOSES AN ESCAPE OVER THE WATER, BUT FINDING NO ONE WILLING TO TAKE HIM, TAKES UP HIS SOLITARY ABODE IN THE CAVE.

As if under the spell of some powerful infatuation, Caleb Kestrel remained skulking for three or four days in the wood to which he had fled after the murder of Deborah. It seemed to him, indeed, that there was no chance of a discovery of the crime, for the wandering habits of the woman would, he thought, easily account for her absence; and even if any suspicion should arise as to foul play having been practised, he believed it to be most unlikely that her body would be sought for in the place where he had concealed it. Indeed, so little did he dream of danger to himself, that he resolved to remain where he was, till an opportunity presented itself for resuming his hostile attitude against Amy and Squire Derwent. At length, however, news reached him, through Radcliffe, that the only other witness of the crime had given information at the hall of what occurred, and then, cursing the treachery of his comrade, he determined to leave his present retreat without delay.

"It's all very well to talk about cutting away from here," observed Radcliffe, "but the thing ain't quite so easy as you may fancy, for the whole country is up in arms, and you'll be sure to fall into the hands of the enemy the moment you venture to show yourself beyond the boundaries of this wood."

"It can't be helped if I do," answered the other, morosely, "but as good fortune has generally favoured me under similar circumstances, I shall trust to it once more. At any rate, I have more reason than ever to defend myself with determination, and if need be, I will die by my own hand rather than yield to those that I know are bent upon my destruction."

"Well," exclaimed the other, "you know best what ought to be done, but I shall follow wherever you go, and prove that I am not such a sneaking scoundrel as Jabez Thompson, who no sooner sees that there is a little danger, than he turns round and splits all about the murder of an old woman that nobody cares for."

"May I depend upon you?" asked the pedlar, directing a scrutinising glance towards his companion.

"Have I ever been false to you?" he asked.

"Why I cannot say you have," answered Caleb, "and so I might have said a little while ago about Jabez Thompson; but he has turned cur at last, and would have sent me to the gallows if I had not luckily heard of what he had done."

"Hang me if I know what to think of it," exclaimed Dick Radcliffe, "for it seems strange that, as he knew where you meant to conceal yourself, no one has yet been to seek for you."

"Well, and what do you argue from that?"

"Why, I fancy that, through cowardice or some other cause, he has told all about the murder of Deborah, but has not been base enough to say where you might be found."

"That will make little difference," muttered the pedlar, "for now that they know the old woman's fate, it will not be long before they come here, among other places, to look for me. However, come when they may, they shall be disappointed, for I shall take the opportunity of leaving the place at once; so that when my pursuers come they will be disappointed, as has been the case before now."

"And which way do you think of going?"

"To Robin Hood's Cave."

"Psha! the place is known to have been one of your retreats, and they'll be sure to follow there without loss of time."

"Let them come as soon as they please," exclaimed Caleb Kestrel, "for there are plenty of people there to give me information as soon as there's any danger, and when I find it necessary to be off, I can easily engage some of the smugglers to take me over in a boat to the opposite coast."

"And how do you mean to live abroad without money?"

"That is certainly a very natural question," answered the pedlar, "but the difficulty with me is not so great as you imagine, for having travelled a good deal in foreign countries, I know their habits, and should not have much trouble in finding the means to support myself in comfort. The gaming table, for instance, would be one resource, and if that failed, why I could try some of our old schemes that have been so successful in England."

"And don't you think you can remain safely in this country if you take care to go to some distant place, where you are not likely to be recognised?"

"Where can such a place be found," he asked, "when that cursed hue and cry has been raised against me from one end of the country to the other? A description of me has been published in every town and village throughout England, and the reward that has been offered for my apprehension is enough to tempt any man that may have the chance of meeting with me."

"But if you always go well armed, you have not much to fear from the enemies you are likely to encounter."

"That's very true," he replied, "but I don't want to shed more blood if it can possibly be avoided. That old woman's death lies heavily on my conscience, and I feel almost sorry that I suffered myself to be carried away so far by my passion."

"I'm sorry enough, too," answered Dick Radcliffe; "and yet when one thinks of it, the affair can hardly be wondered at either, for she threatened to give you up to your enemies, and if that wasn't enough to enrage a man in your situation, I don't know what would be."

"Very likely," exclaimed the fugitive; "but if they should happen to lay their hands upon me, the provocation would not argue anything in my favour. So, knowing my danger, I am determined to get away from this place as quickly as I can."

"The journey is a long one," observed Dick Radcliffe, "and we shall have many risks to run on the way."

"What of that? Ain't we both well armed?"

"Aye, we are armed, sure enough; but so may be those that we have to encounter."

"You are beginning to show signs of fear."

"I don't deny having my notions that things won't turn out as well as they have," answered Radcliffe, "but for all that you'll find me staunch to the very last, and if matters should come to a struggle, I'll die rather than give in to the enemy."

"Ah!" exclaimed the pedlar, "if that scoundrel, Jabez Thompson, had only proved true, we should not now have been obliged to leave the place where I wished to remain till that affair with Squire Derwent was comfortably arranged. Had that been done, we might have crossed the water with money enough to support us all like gentlemen for the remainder of our lives."

"That's all very true, Kestrel," answered the other, "but for my own part, I can't help thinking that we should have been much better off if we had all been minding our own business instead of trying to get the money that the squire was so unwilling to part wit h. I saw all along that it would get us into trouble, and so it has, but the worst part of the affair is, that no one can possibly say how it's likely to end."

"Leave it all to me," replied Kestrel, "and I'll answer for it we shall have no reason to grumble by and by."

"Do you think, then, Mr. Derwent is likely to submit to your terms by and by?"

"I'm sure he will."

"At all events, I don't feel quite so certain about it," exclaimed Dick Radcliffe, "for he seems to be one of those sort of people that won't give way an inch after they once say nay."

"Perhaps your opinion of him is right in a general way," replied the pedlar, "but he is desperately in love with Amy, and when he finds that she is in danger he will submit to any terms that I insist on, rather than the risk of losing her for ever."

"And pray how are you to insist upon terms," asked Radcliffe, "when you dare not for your life show yourself before him?"

"Others may do it, if I cannot," he replied, "and whilst my chance is as good as it is at present, I shall never despair of gaining the end I have so long had in view. All I want now is to escape from his clutches, and when he finds that I am safe in a foreign, country he will be glad to agree to anything rather than live in a constant state of dread that Amy may be taken away from him."

"You still seem very confident about it," exclaimed Dick Radcliffe, "but men like him are not to be so easily frightened as you think, for the law is strong enough to protect him, and the first man who goes from you with a message to him will be given into custody as an accomplice, or something of that sort."

"So," muttered the pedlar, "you are beginning to look out for your own safety, are you, Dick?"

"I don't know what you may think of it, Kestrel," answered the other, "but I've a notion that it's high time for a man to look after himself when he finds that the officers of justice are dodging at his heels."

"What charge can they bring against you?"

"Not much at present," he replied, "but a good deal will depend upon whether Jabez Thompson has been opening his mind too freely about that affair with the old woman the other night. If he has said that I was present at the time the murder took place, my chance of escaping the fellows will be no better than yours."

"Do you think it's true?" asked Kestrel, without appearing to have heard the last remark, "that they hold him in custody for not having given information of what took place, sooner?"

"Why, the fault is, there's so many difficulties in the way," answered Dick, "that I'm afraid to go and ask my son how the affair stands, because it's very likely they might suspect me if I was to be anxious to learn all that was passing. So, in order to keep myself out of the reach of danger, I pick up my information as well as I can, and, from the little I have been able to learn, it seems pretty certain that Jabez will be committed for trial as one that was concerned in the death of the old woman."

"In that case," exclaimed Kestrel, "the scoundrel will not hesitate to sacrifice you and I."

"That's just what I'm afraid of," answered the other, "and as it would be madness for you and I to get into danger whilst there are means of keeping out of it, I think the best thing we can possibly do will be to disappear from this place without delay."

Caleb Kestrel was about to propose that, as it was sufficiently dark for their purpose, they should commence their journey towards the spot he had proposed ; he was, however, startled by hearing the sound of distant voices, and looking in the direction from whence the danger seemed to come, he saw the reflection of torches gleaming amongst the trees. To retreat at such a moment as this would have been to increase their danger, for the sound of their footsteps might have been heard, and thus lead their pursuers towards the spot where they were. They therefore crouched down among some low bushes, and had scarcely done so when Mr. Derwent, accompanied by a number of armed men, each bearing a torch, passed within a few yards of the place where they were lying concealed. Luckily for the two fugitives the pursuers passed onwards ; the sound of their voices became less and less distinct, and in a few minutes afterwards all was as quiet as the grave. The danger being thus over, Caleb Kestrel once more sprung upon his feet, an example that was quickly followed by Radcliffe, who, feeling somewhat alarmed, suggested that they should remain where they were till they could feel assured that they might pursue their proposed journey in safety.

"What time can we find better for our purpose than the present ?" asked Kestrel; haven't they just searched the wood, and satisfied themselves, as they believe, that we are not here, and can any more favourable opportunity offer itself than now that they have returned home dissatisfied at the disappointment they have met with ?"

"So it may appear to you, Caleb," answered the other, "but every road, turn which way we will, is paraded up and down by a parcel of fellows that have made up their minds not to let us slip through their fingers."

"If they have made up their minds to that," observed Caleb Kestrel, "they'll find themselves confoundedly mistaken, for even if we should happen to meet with any of them, I'll sell my life dearly rather than fall into their clutches."

"But we ought rather to avoid all chances of shedding more blood, since more than enough has been shed already."

"I know that," replied Kestrel, "but you would not be such a fool, I should suppose, as to suffer yourself to be taken whilst you have got arms for your own protection ?"

"If there should be any need for it I shall be as ready as yourself to fight in our defence," he replied.

"Then what have you to be afraid of ?"

"I am not afraid of anything," replied Radcliffe, "except it may be your savage disposition when once put to it. Our only object should be to get away from this place as quietly and as quickly as we can, for should an alarm be given that we are attempting to escape, the enemy would close in upon us, and our game would be brought to an end."

"Well, well," exclaimed Caleb Kestrel, "I see it would be useless for me to argue with you now, so let's say no more about it, but commence our journey towards Robin Hood's Cave without delay. We will go as silently as you like, and, no doubt, if we choose our path with judgment, we shall be able to reach our place of destination in safety."

"You don't mean to keep to the high roads, I suppose ?"

"On the contrary," replied Kestrel, "knowing this part of the country perfectly well, I shall be able to take you a way where we are not likely to meet any one to alarm us. So follow me in silence, and I will wager my life that we arrive safely at the end of our journey."

Dick Radcliffe, though anything but convinced that there was so little danger as his comrade had boasted, followed him in silence, but not without keeping a careful watch around him in case an enemy should appear in sight. At length they succeeded in passing through the wood without meeting a foe, and then the pedlar, who had a thorough knowledge of the country, made his way across the moors, and from thence over a farm, at the further extremity of which he remembered to have seen a barn standing in a lonely place, and which seemed to have been but seldom used. This they reached just as the light of day was beginning to break, and having satisfied themselves that no one was near to observe them, they entered the building, intending to remain there till the darkness of the ensuing night should render it safe for them to re-commence their journey. Here they refreshed themselves with such provisions as they happened to have with them, and then throwing themselves upon some loose litter with which the floor was strewed, they slept off the fatigue which they had encountered during a somewhat long walk. As soon as darkness had again set in, they once more set out on their journey, and, as on the previous evening, pursued the most unfrequented paths, and maintained a strict silence lest the sound of their voices should attract the attention of any persons who might be on the look-out for them. Fortunately for them they met no one on their way, and when the morning again began to break they found themselves within a few miles of the place towards which they were journeying. The ocean lay before them, and a little to the right was the well remembered spot where, on two previous occasions Caleb Kestrel had obtained shelter under circumstances somewhat similar to the present. Within his own mind he had no doubt of meeting with a friendly reception from the smugglers, though Dick Radcliffe was of a contrary opinion, for he knew the men to be selfish when their own interest was concerned, and a suspicion had more than once crossed his mind that no welcome awaited them there, if news had reached the neighbourhood that Caleb Kestrel was now a fugitive for a murder that he had committed. Still, however, he had not ventured to give his opinion, and still proceeding on their way, they at length reached the house which we have previously spoken of as a rendezvous of the smugglers who infested that part of the coast. Entering the room, they found already there assembled, George Laybourne, Tom Hazle, and about half a dozen other smugglers who had all assembled there for the purpose of arranging their plans for the landing of a large cargo of contraband goods which they were in hopes would be effected in safety on the following night. Kestrel, who was the first to show himself among them, was surprised at the want of cordiality with which he was received by his old friends, and his chagrin was still further increased when Hazle refused to take the hand which had been offered him.

"How is this?" exclaimed Kestrel, looking round him as if for an explanation, "am I no longer welcomed by those that I was once proud to call my friends and comrades?"

"Aye," answered Hazle, "that might have been the case at one time, but I have no fancy to take a hand that has human blood on it, and once for all, Caleb Kestrel, I'd rather have your room than your company."

"What do you mean by human blood?" exclaimed the fugitive, startled by the abrupt reception he had met with.

"Of course you would like to make it appear that you are innocent," returned the other contemptuously. "You fancy the news of your evil doings couldn't have reached us here, yet; but we know all about it, and are not inclined to keep company with the murderer of poor old Deborah."

"Who told you I murdered her?"

"Ask George Laybourne who it was that told him," returned the other, "for he it was that heard the news as he was going back in search of you; but who it was that told him of your evil deeds I neither know nor care. He, however, will tell you, I dare say, if you ask him."

"Did you hear this from a stranger?" he asked, turning towards the person who had been named?"

"I did."

"Was it far from here where you met the man who gave you the intelligence of what I had done?"

"About ten or a dozen miles away."

"Was the man a stranger to you?"

"No," replied Laybourne, "I have seen him before, and he remembered me the moment we met."

"Did he ask you about me?"

"Yes, he did," replied the other; "he wanted to know if you were hiding anywhere about this neighbourhood."

"And of course you told him I was not?"

"You may be sure of that," replied Laybourne, "because I could do so with a good conscience. I told him you had not been seen in this neighbourhood, and that it was not very likely you would come to a place where people would be sure to look after you."

"And did he speak of a murder that had been committed somewhere near Derwent Hall?"

"He told me that it was committed in that old hut where you and I and a few more of us have spent so many hours together."

"Aye," exclaimed Tom Hazle, "and as you don't seem to deny it, we have no wish here to keep your company any longer."

"Why it's no use denying that the old woman is dead," answered Caleb Kestrel, "and it's equally certain that she fell by my hand. But then it was all brought about by her own infernal threats of betraying me, and where's the man that would give himself up to his enemies when he knows they would hang him if he fell into their hands?"

"We care nothing at all about that," exclaimed the other, "nor does it matter much that I know of; for, putting aside the worst part of the affair, we are not inclined to receive you among us, when it's certain that they'll trace you out wherever you may be."

"Then you are afraid to shelter a friend when he's in trouble?"

"There's no doubt about that, Kestrel," answered the other;—"we have quite bother enough of our own to take our attention, without bringing more upon ourselves by giving shelter to a man that cares no more about spilling blood than if it was water."

"I tell you I was made mad by her threats and taunts before I thought of committing violence."

"That excuse won't serve you, Kestrel, if it should be your fate to stand before a judge and jury. Murderers receive no pity either from friends or foes, and those that shelter them always receive a heavier punishment than we are inclined to risk."

"What risk can there be, if I stay in the cave till this search for me is at an end?"

"Oh, if you wait till then," replied Hazle, "you must make up your mind never to leave the place any more."

"I should not want to be there more than a week."

"You must not tell me that," answered the other, "for people will never give up the pursuit till they are convinced that you have fled from this country to another. The promised reward will always keep men active, and if ever you should return to show yourself in the world again, it will be with the certainty of being taken."

"It will not be without some trouble, though," exclaimed Caleb Kestrel, "for I am armed, and those that would make me their prisoner will be sure to meet their death. In short, Hazle, I am now a desperate man, and will rather meet my end in an attempt to defend myself, than perish on the scaffold like a dog."

"What! you are not tired, then, of shedding human blood?"

"How can I help it!" he exclaimed. "If people will drive me into extremities, is it to be wondered at that I do things which would not otherwise have been thought of? Besides, if any mischief should happen, you and your comrades must blame yourselves for it, because no life need be sacrificed if you think proper to give me the shelter I have asked for."

"It's no use saying anything more about it," answered Tom Hazle, "for the truth is, you were never any very great favourite here, and now that murder has been added to your other crimes, we are determined to have no more to do with you."

"Humph! it sounds well to hear you and your companions crying out against crime!"

"You may call smuggling a crime, if you like," answered Hazle, "but there's many thousands of people in England who consider that bad laws have brought about the evil, and that it is not much to be wondered at if men are to be found who will risk something for the sake of defeating those that would lay a heavy tax upon every article that we eat, drink, or wear. Indeed, our best customers are to be found amongst those who can best afford to pay a high price, but who see more wrong in paying the price of things, than in our trying to supply our fellow men at a reasonable charge."

"It's all very well to make it appear that there's no harm in smuggling," exclaimed Caleb Kestrel, "but can you tell me that your expeditions never end in bloodshed?"

"Sometimes, no doubt, such a thing occurs," replied the other; "but then the fault is none of ours, for the attack always comes from the side of the Government officers, and it's hardly likely that we should yield like cowards when we have been at trouble and risk enough to bring our cargo over."

"Then you think there's no great harm in killing people who are employed to prevent smuggling?"

"There would be no such a thing as smuggling if it was not for the high duties the people have to pay," answered Tom Hazle; "and therefore every death of violence that takes place in these skirmishes may be said to be caused by those that helped to make bad laws. However, that's nothing at all to do with what we were talking about; this murder you have committed is a different affair altogether, and as we don't choose to get ourselves into trouble about it, you must make up your mind not to stay here."

"Well, if it must be so, it can't be helped," exclaimed Kestrel, "but I suppose some of your people here will not mind taking me across the water in a boat."

"I don't think you'll find anybody very willing to do it.'

"Why not? I have money enough still left to pay them well for their trouble?"

"That may be," replied Hazle, "but we seafaring folks are a good deal given to superstition, and we should fancy the boat must sink if there was a murderer on board."

"I see how it is," exclaimed Caleb Kestrel, "you have been tempted by the reward that has been offered for my apprehension, and I am to be given up, that you may receive the blood money!"

"You know that to be a foul and deliberate lie!" retorted Hazle, fiercely, "for we are not given to treachery, and would always rather shelter than betray a man in his misfortunes. But you have no claim upon our pity, for we like not murderers, nor will we conceal them when the pursuer is at their heels."

"Will you afford me no assistance, then?"

"None, whatever."

"But if I go to the cave, and hide myself there till the hottest part of the pursuit is over, will you inform the enemy where I am to be found?"

"No; you may depend upon us there," answered Hazle, "for we are not likely to betray your secret, though we may abhor you and the crime you have been guilty of. Go then, if you please, but take what provisions you may want for the time you may remain there, for neither I nor any of our people are likely to visit the place while you remain in it."

"What!" exclaimed the guilty wretch, "am I then to be deserted when most I stand in need of a friend?"

"You have no right to expect either pity or friendship," answered Hazle, "for the cold and deliberate shedder of blood will be shunned by all who are not equally fallen as himself. But I want not to add to the misery you must feel, for crime weighs heavily upon your soul, and that is punishment enough for one who is afraid to die, when, by doing so, he would escape from the world's vengeance."

"Only let them drive me into a corner," exclaimed Caleb Kestrel, "and you will see whether I would not rather die than fall into the hands of those who would

hunt me to destruction. At all events, I am determined to cheat the gallows, even though I am driven at last to fall by my own hand."

"What made you come here?"

"Because I expected to have met with a very different reception to the one you have given me," he replied. "When I was last here, you were willing enough to give me shelter and protection as long as I needed it, and I had no reason to believe that you would drive me away now, as if I was a dog."

"You are a murderer, and that is far worse."

No. 49.

"But the murder was not a deliberate one," he replied, "for I swear it was not thought of an instant before the woman fell. I knew not, indeed, that she was going to throw herself in my way, and it was not till she had threatened to give me up to those who were in pursuit of me, that I discharged a pistol at her."

"Well," exclaimed Tom Hazle, "that is a point that I have no wish to inquire into, for the plain truth of it is, we none of us care how soon we are rid of your company. If you want the cave as a place of retreat, there it is at your service, but don't expect any of us to visit you, for if we should be seen to do so, we should be punished as the aiders and abettors of an assassin."

Finding that all he could say or urge in his own behalf would be of no use, Caleb Kestrel purchased from the host such articles as he would require during his sojourn, and having done this, he sullenly left the house, inwardly cursing in his own heart the man who had thus disappointed the hopes he had formed. No one offered to accompany him part of the way; not even Dick Radcliffe, who, not having been charged with having taken any part in the murder, was allowed to remain with the smugglers.

<hr>

CHAPTER XLVI.

INTERVIEW BETWEEN AMY AND HER LOVER.—ARRIVAL OF MR. CAPSICUM WITH NEWS OF THE FUGITIVE.—SUPPOSED DEPARTURE OF CALEB KESTREL FROM ENGLAND.—AMY STILL DOUBTS THE INTELLIGENCE, AS DOES MR. BRASSEY POPJOY, WHO, WITH HIS GROOM, ARE READY PREPARED TO TAKE THEIR DEPARTURE ON THE FOLLOWING MORNING.

AFTER the remand of Jabez Thompson, the search for Kestrel and his companion was prosecuted with increased vigour, for people began to be apprehensive of their own lives, and, to ensure their safety, it was resolved to form themselves into numerous strong parties, each of which was to take a particular district, and to continue the pursuit till they had either secured the assassin, or all trace of him was entirely lost. Mr. Derwent and his friends devoted three days to the same purpose, but without the slightest success, and as it was then suggested that Caleb Kestrel might be lurking somewhere near the Hall, it was determined that they should return thither immediately, in case any further attempt should be made to carry off Amy during their absence. On their arrival there, however, they learnt, to their no small gratification, that nothing had been seen of the ruffian, and that no tidings of him could be heard, though every effort had been made to ascertain the direction he had taken after the murder of old Deborah had been committed. Jabez Thompson, too, had been again questioned upon the subject, in the hope that the imprisonment he had already suffered might have had the effect of changing his mind; but nothing could be drawn from him more than he had already stated at the inquest, and the attempt was therefore given up as hopeless. Yet, in spite of this, the inhabitants of the Hall began to feel more confidence than they had experienced for some time past, and, though the villain was still at large, it was pretty generally believed that he could not again venture near a place where he would be in so much danger. Amy was the only one that still believed he might some day return, and even the persuasion of Mr. Derwent could not alter an opinion that was founded chiefly upon her own fears.

"We have seen enough of him," she replied, in answer to a remonstrance of her lover's, "to know that he will not easily give up a project which he has once vowed to execute. Difficulties and dangers are alike scorned when his own purposes are to be served, and even were we to hear of him for the next ten years, I should still expect every moment to see him present himself before me."

"But no time," answered the squire, "can obliterate the remembrance of the horrible crime he has been guilty of. People will still be upon the look-out after him, and, show himself when he may—which, by-the-bye, I should think he never will—he would be sure to be arrested for the murder he is charged with. And may that time be not very far distant," he added, after a brief pause, "for, though I am not revengeful at heart, I cannot but wish for an exemplary punishment upon the wretch who has committed so much evil."

"Is it quite certain," asked Amy, "that he is not secreted somewhere in this neighbourhood?"

"I think it hardly possible that he can be," answered her lover, "for nothing can exceed the zeal and perseverance of the people hereabouts in their pursuit of this ruffian. Night and day have they willingly devoted their time and exertions to this one object, and it was not till there was every certainty of his having contrived to escape, that they at length gave up the matter as lost."

"And, if I understand you rightly," she exclaimed, "it is supposed that he has left this country."

"Well, so most people are inclined to imagine," replied Mr. Derwent, "but, for my own part, I know not what to say about it. At any rate we have no certain information that we can rely upon, for no one saw him on board any vessel that was about to leave England, and we have, therefore, a right to presume that the report may be without foundation. Nay, for aught we know, it may have been circulated by his own friends and acquaintances, merely for the purpose of misleading us as to the place where he is concealed."

"Then it behoves us to be continually upon our guard," exclaimed Amy; "not so much for my own sake, but for you, upon whom he seems determined to wreak his fiendish revenge."

"As for that," answered the squire, "there are many others besides myself who would have good reason to look after themselves if ever the villain should take it into his head to return to this neighbourhood. In fact, I know not who would have a chance of escaping if they happened to come in his way, for there is scarcely a person near the place who has not taken a more or less active part in trying to lay hands upon him. Mr. and Mrs. Peeps, in particular, have incurred a large share of his vindictive feelings, for he has somehow or another taken it into his head that he might have extorted the money from me but for their interference."

"And why not have allowed me to give up to him all my share of the Derwent property?" she asked. "I never sought or craved for riches, and was far happier as the humble protégé of Mr. and Mrs. Peeps, than I have yet been with wealth and luxuries at my command. It was, indeed, an evil hour for me when Caleb Kestrel arrived here and announced the fact that I was the adopted daughter of your cousin, Clement Derwent."

"Nay," replied her lover, "hitherto it has been unfortunate certainly, but we may expect that the time is not far distant when you will enjoy that which is indisputably your own by right. The persecution you have suffered cannot last much longer, and I am even of opinion that it is over now, since I hope your tormentor will not again venture to show himself near this place."

"That may be," answered Amy, "but I believe he has been heard to say, that, even if he cannot himself pursue me with his vengeance, he will employ others to do so upon whom he can rely. Such, then, is the man at whose mercy I am, and from whom I have not the means of escaping."

"Here, at least, you are safe," exclaimed Mr. Derwent, "for, with all the daring he has manifested, he will not again venture to the house where he knows a strict watch is kept for him."

"So I would have persuaded myself," answered our heroine, "but the more I reflect upon the villanous stratagems he has already practiced, the more certain I feel that there is no act of daring that he would not try, if he could see the least chance of gaining the end he has in view."

"Which end, by the bye, is—money."

"True, but why has he not been appeased, when we know the means by which it can be done?"

"That is a question I have often asked myself," answered Mr. Derwent, "and yet the solution is easy enough when we come to think the matter over carefully.

Had he been moderate in his demands, I should not have hesitated to yield to them, but when I found that they were so extortionate, that not less than half the Derwent property would satisfy his avarice, I at once rejected the terms, and have set him at open defiance ever since."

"And he, having accepted that defiance, has never suffered me to enjoy one moment's repose."

"Thus far he has, indeed, had his own way," exclaimed Mr. Derwent, "but, as was to be expected, the time has now arrived when we may venture to hope that his tyranny is at an end. At any rate we know that he must not venture to show himself for some time, since, if he does so, it will lead almost to the certainty of his falling into the hands of that justice which he has so long defied. And if once he is taken, Amy, you may make up your mind as to what sort of doom he will be sentenced to?"

"I am aware," she replied, "that those who are convicted of murder have no hope of pardon, and the evidence against Kestrel being clear, you think that in the event of his being captured there would be an end of all future fear?"

"Such would, no doubt be the case," exclaimed Mr. Derwent, "and for that reason I am most anxious that he should be taken with as little delay as possible. When that is the case our fears will be at an end, and I may look for that happiness which my anticipated marriage with you has encouraged me to look forward to. Not, however, that I expect to lay hold of him quite so soon as I would wish, but, be that as it may, I will not let any opportunity slip that may bring his villanous career to a speedy termination."

"But if he happens to have left the country, though I don't think he has, we shall still be left in the same state of doubt and anxiety as ever."

"That will depend upon whether we are able to discover the place of his retreat or not," replied Mr. Derwent, I; "however, think there will not be much difficulty in doing that, and, if so, I shall employ some person to watch his movements and give me immediate information of any change that he may be about to make in the place of his abode. Thus you see that we may make ourselves tolerably secure, and by and by, should he venture to return to England, we shall be prepared for any act of treachery that he may have in contemplation."

"Ah!" sighed Amy, "you speak of Caleb Kestrel as if he was no more than a common enemy to deal with. We, however, know him to be ever scheming evil, and though you may keep a watch upon his actions, you cannot dive into those thoughts which will be continually directed against those who have hitherto foiled him, but who will continue to be the objects of his vengeance till he has succeeded in his dark designs."

"He may probably make still more attempts," answered her lover, "but I think a moderate degree of care will be sufficient to prevent any mischief he may be contemplating. However, we are forgetting all this time that even now he may be in the hands of some of the numerous persons that are anxiously looking out for the chance of capturing him."

"Then you don't altogether believe this story of his having succeeded in leaving England?"

"Why, I don't think quite so much of it as I did, it must be confessed," replied Mr. Derwent, "for it would be by no means an easy task for a proscribed ruffian like him to escape when so many persons are on the look-out for him. To be sure, he has probably disguised himself, but even that, I should imagine, would scarcely be of any use, since no disguise that he could assume would deceive those who are determined to prevent his escape. But a few days will serve to set our minds at rest upon that point, and in the meanwhile I shall order renewed exertions to be made towards searching after this most detestable ruffian."

At this moment the door was suddenly thrown open, and Mr. Capsicum, the worthy magistrate who has already been introduced to the reader, entered the room with a countenance wearing a look of the greatest importance.

"My dear friend," he exclaimed, shaking the hand of Mr. Derwent heartily, I have taken the liberty of presenting myself without any announcement ; however, I think the news I bring is of so much importance to you that there is scarcely any need for an apology. In short, we have ascertained to a certainty that Caleb Kestrel has been seen in the neighbourhood of Robin Hood's Cave, and that since then there is no doubt he has been taken over to the opposite coast in one of the smugglers' boats."

"Thank Heaven!" exclaimed the squire, "for if there is any truth in it, we may at last begin to fancy we are safe from any further schemes of his."

"Oh, as to the truth of the report, I don't think there can be much doubt of it," replied Mr. Capiscum, "for it's not very likely he would desire to remain any longer in England when he sees that everything is beginning to look more and more threatening against him. As for remaining in concealment, it was quite out of the question, for where was the place, I should like to know, in which he could remain a week without discovery."

"Do you know anybody that saw him go?"

"Why, I can't exactly say I do," replied the old gentleman, "but at all events the thing is talked of commonly enough by the people in my neighbourhood, and there's not a person in the whole place but would tell you that he is certain Caleb Kestrel is no longer in this country. So now I hope I have made your mind easy, or this long journey of mine will have taken place to very little purpose."

"My dear Mr. Capsicum," answered the squire, "you know how welcome you always are at Derwent Hall, and whether this news of Caleb's flight from England is true or false, I am not the less delighted at the chance that has brought you here. To confess the truth, however, I have no hope that such is the case, and I know Amy, here, will not be inclined to place much confidence in the report, though she would be pleased enough if it could be confirmed."

"Well, all I can say is, that I believe it myself," answered Mr. Capsicum; "for there is not the shadow of a doubt that he has been seen near the smugglers' haunt, and that being the case, I see no reason why he should not have prevailed upon some of them to take him over to the opposite coast."

"The question is, whether he has any money to pay for their services."

"That is certainly a very important affair," answered the magistrate; "but a man like Caleb Kestrel never need be long without money, since we know he don't stand very particular as to the means by which it is to be obtained. There are plenty of houses in our neighbourhood where valuable plate is kept, and he has only to help himself to as much as may be required to assist him in his flight."

"Aye," laughed Mr. Derwent, "but the fellow is too cunning to run such a risk, for he knows the person guilty of such an act would be hotly pursued, and we have had a pretty good proof that he is now anxious to keep out of harm's way."

"No doubt he is anxious enough to do so," answered Mr. Capsicum, "but it don't follow that he will always be able to elude justice. The murder he is supposed to have been concerned in has set people more against him than ever, and the heavy reward that has been offered for his apprehension has put every body upon the *qui vive* to get possession of the prize that is so much coveted."

"As for that," exclaimed the squire, "the whole country has been up in arms against him ever since the time when he made an attempt against my life; people have been pursuing him from place to place with a determination of taking him, and yet we find that they are as far off as ever from their object. And now, it seems, you have heard that he has succeeded in fleeing from the country."

"I only give you the report as I have heard it," he replied. "The opinion is, indeed, very general about our place, and my motive for coming here was to give the earliest information of news that I thought would afford you the greatest satisfaction."

"So it would, my dear sir," answered Mr. Derwent; "but even if he should have got away, as you tell me, I believe there would still be too much fear of a continuation of those persecutions that Amy had so long endured from him. In short, he is determined to extort money from us, and it appears that nothing will ever deter him from the villany he has been carrying on."

" Then how is it, my dear sir, that you have not offered to compromise the affair with him ?"

" Because he is not to be depended on, even if he was to receive the large sum he has demanded."

"Do you believe, then, that if he was to leave England he would ever venture to return ?"

" How can we doubt it," asked Mr. Derwent, " when we know the desperate character of the man we have to deal with ? The money he might extort from me would soon be squandered away in recklessness and dissipation, and when all was gone we should have to undergo a repetition of annoyances that we have already experienced. For that reason I have refused to accede to his terms, and shall continue to do so from a firm conviction that no reliance is to be placed upon any promise he may make."

" Well, my good sir, I don't know but what you are quite right there," answered the old gentleman. " The man is certainly not to be depended on, and therefore I believe the best thing that can happen will be for him to leave the country under such circumstances that he will not be likely to return."

" I am afraid nothing will prevent his coming back if he should be hard driven for money," interposed Amy.

" Then the only way would be to allow him a certain sum of money as long as he continues abroad. This might be paid to him quarterly, and you would then always have a pretty certain knowledge of the part of the world he might be in."

" That might be all very well," exclaimed Mr. Derwent, " but my fear is that he would spend the allowance as soon as it was received, and we should then have him repeating his demands till a further sum of money was extorted from us. In short, there is no knowing how to deal with such a scoundrel as he is, and I now begin to despair of seeing matters satisfactorily arranged as long as he remains at liberty."

" And even if we should succeed in laying hold of him," returned the magistrate, " I am afraid his companions would continue in the same course till all his demands were complied with. The whole affair is, indeed, involved in such difficulties that I can see no end of them, unless there is any truth in the report of his having gone abroad."

" Which, for reasons before mentioned, I am not at all inclined to believe," answered Mr. Derwent. " That he may wish to leave England I have no doubt, but he will not attempt to do so till he has the money I have hitherto refused."

" Have you any notion where he may be hiding himself ?"

" Probably among the smugglers, who, it seems, have befriended him on previous occasions."

" Aye," exclaimed Mr. Capsicum, " they may be all very good friends to him as long as he has money to pay for their services, but only let him go penniless among them, and he would not meet with a very hospitable reception. And just at this this time I should think his pockets must be pretty well empty, so that his only safety will be in getting out of the country."

" But if he has no money, how is he to do that ?"

" I said before that he is not very particular as to the means of supplying himself with cash, and, if driven to it, he would commit a robbery to replenish his exhausted treasury. Be that as it may, however, he will not remain long among the smugglers, who would, as likely as not, betray him if his company proved at all disagreeable. In fact, I have been thinking whether it would not be a good plan for us to visit some of those lawless men, and try whether they are inclined to afford us their assistance on condition of receiving a suitable reward."

" I am afraid we could not place any reliance on them."

" There's no saying what good may be done till we have tried the effect of our promises," answered Mr. Capsicum. " At all events, we may make an attempt, and if the experiment proves to our advantage, there's a probability that Kestrel will soon be deprived of all further power of injuring you ?"

" But how are these smugglers to be met with ?"

"Not very easily, perhaps, but I believe the attempt will not be altogether thrown away."

"Do you ever happen to meet with any of them?"

"Very seldom; but now and then I happen to come across some of them, in spite of their wish to avoid me. The fellows have a natural antipathy against me as a magistrate, but no doubt they may be induced to betray Caleb Kestrel into our hands, if we can only let them understand that their assistance will not fail to meet with a liberal reward."

"Would you run the risk of venturing among them alone?" asked Amy.

"I should not have the least hesitation in doing so," answered the old gentleman, "for though they may not like me as a magistrate, I believe they bear me no particular ill-will as a man and neighbour. When any of them are ill, I have always supplied them with such things as are beyond their limited means, and the consequence is, that I am treated with respect, even by the people who regard me with suspicion."

"Then these fellows never intrude themselves near your house?"

"Never."

"That is rather strange too," observed Mr. Derwent, "for, as you must sometimes act against them in your official capacity, I should have thought they would frequently take the opportunity of retaliating."

"So they might, perhaps, if they dared," answered the old gentleman, "but the truth is, they know I should at once guess who were the offenders, and that they would consequently run the risk of being routed from their quarters, where they have for so long a period carried on their contraband traffic."

"It appears strange," observed Mr. Derwent, "that no efforts have yet succeeded in routing them."

"Why it certainly does appear rather singular," answered the old gentleman, "but for all that, I can assure you no trouble has been spared to rid ourselves of such disagreeable neighbours. However, it may be accounted for, when I tell you that there are a great number of caverns all along that part of the coast, and all our efforts have hitherto failed to discover in which particular one they have stored away their contraband goods. Sometimes they go to one place and sometimes to another, so that we never can tell, with all our watching, in which we are to look for them."

"And yet the coast appears to be strongly guarded by the government officers."

"It is so," answered Mr. Capsicum, "but what is the use of them when they have such cunning knaves to deal with? The smugglers always take care to keep their landing place a secret, and for that purpose they invariably spread abroad a report that they are about to visit a part of the coast, which is far away from the spot they really intend to arrive at."

"But I should have thought the coast-guard would by this time be aware of their tricks."

"So they are, my dear sir," replied Mr. Capsicum, "but the men would be blamed if they were to act contrary to their orders, which are to repair immediately to any place where there is reasonable ground for supposing a landing is to be attempted. The smugglers are all aware of that, and knowing the weakness of their enemies, they profit by it, in spite of all the attempts that have yet been made to suppress the illegal traffic."

"And it is among these men that Caleb Kestrel has sought shelter?"

"It is pretty certain that he has been there," replied Mr. Capsicum, "but, as I before hinted, there is strong ground for supposing that he has left them and gone abroad."

"Probably the report has been circulated only to deceive us as to the real place in which he is concealed. Indeed, I feel quite satisfied in my own mind that he has not yet quitted England, and that, in fact, he has no intention of leaving this country whilst there is a chance of money from me."

"Then what course do you suggest next?"

"Aye, there I own you puzzle me," replied Mr Derwent, "for it seems to me that all our schemes are alike liable to failure."

"Do you think it will be worth our while to make another search among the caverns along the sea coast?"

"I know not what to think about it," answered the squire, "but perhaps it would be as well to do so, because if we gain no other advantage from it, we shall, at all events, satisfy ourselves whether he is still hovering about the place where we know him to have been a very short period since."

"And suppose we should obtain certain information that he has succeeded in escaping abroad?"

"Why, then, all further pursuit of him would be useless, unless he should afterwards venture back to this country."

"Which would be rather unlikely, seeing that the place has grown too hot to hold him. So, if the story I have heard be true, you may fairly venture to hope that all annoyance from this scoundrel is at an end. And a glorious thing it will be for Amy, when she knows she may venture to leave the house, without being in continual dread of meeting with her enemy."

"Alas!" sighed our heroine, "I am almost afraid to believe that I shall ever be rid of this man's persecution."

"Nay," exclaimed Mr. Derwent, "surely you are not going to despair, when your friends are exerting themselves to save you from the machinations of your foe. For the present, it is true, you are compelled to remain within doors, but I firmly believe the time is not far distant when we shall make him our prisoner."

"So I might have believed at one time," replied Amy, "but he has so often escaped from custody, that I am afraid he would do so again, even if he should chance to be taken."

"Aye," exclaimed Mr. Derwent, "he has certainly proved too cunning for us on former occasions, but that is the greater reason why he should not be able to do so again. We now know the sort of customer we have to deal with, and if we have but another chance, it shall not be thrown away, you may depend on it."

Just then, Mr. Brassey Popjoy, who had been fidgetting in and out of the room three or four times during the preceding conversation, once more made his appearance, and inquired if any certain information had yet been heard of the whereabouts of Caleb Kestrel. The alarm he felt was easily to be seen, and Mr. Derwent laughingly replied, that though nothing was yet known of his place of concealment, there was every reason to believe that all further danger from him was entirely at an end.

"How do you know, sir, that he is not lurking about your premises at this very time?" asked the alarmed cockney.

"Because he would not be such a fool as to show himself where he would be sure to get into trouble."

"So I have heard you say before," exclaimed Popjoy, "and yet within a short time afterwards he has made his appearance again, as if nothing had happened. However, I have no fancy for having my throat cut or my brains blown out by the ruffian, so I have been thinking of getting back to London, which, after all, is the only place where I can consider myself safe from him."

"I hope, Mr. Popjoy," returned the squire, "we are not yet to lose the pleasure of your company."

"For the matter of that," he replied, "I should have liked to stay here a week or two longer, if it could have been done with safety. But, unfortunately, I have a notion that this Caleb Kestrel will appear here again, and, as he has taken a dislike to me, I have been thinking that my wisest plan will be to get away as soon as possible."

"I think, on the contrary, that you are perfectly safe from him," replied Mr. Derwent, "for I don't suppose he intends any mischief to you, whatever he may do to anybody else."

"What!" exclaimed Brassey Popjoy, "do you suppose he can ever forget that I was one to go in pursuit of him?"

"I don't know whether he may remember anything of the kind," replied the squire, "but even if he does, he must at the same time acknowledge that he was never in much danger from you. No offence, my dear friend, I hope, but the truth is, you was wise enough at all times to keep yourself beyond the reach of danger."

"Aye," exclaimed the cockney, "I always like to take care of myself when there's danger in the way, for if I didn't do that, there's nobody else would do i

for me. You may laugh at me, squire, as much as you like, but, in my opinion, the man is a fool who runs himself into danger without either rhyme or reason."

"Hasn't it struck you, sir," asked Mr. Capsicum, "that this Caleb Kestrel, may have gone up to London, for the sake of being out of the way, whilst this stir is being made about him?"

"Such a notion has certainly never entered {my head," replied {Popjoy, "nor should I think it very likely he would go to a place where there are so many police officers always prowling about."

No. 50.

"But he can easily avoid them in a large place like that."

"Then you really think it likely that he has gone all the way up to London?" exclaimed the alarmed cockney.

"Mind, I don't state it for a positive fact," answered Mr. Capsicum, "but I think more improbable things have occurred before now."

"Then perhaps, after all, town is not the safest place for me?"

"Between ourselves, my dear sir," answered Mr. Derwent, "I think you cannot do better than remain where you are for the present. At all events, I don't believe Kestrel will venture here, well knowing as he does, that all the people in the neighbourhood are upon the watch for him. So, if my advice is taken, Mr. Popjoy, you will favour me by prolonging your visit at the Hall."

"Well, it's very kind of you to be sure," he replied, "and I have half a mind to accept your invitation, only that I am not quite certain whether Trubbs will remain here any longer."

"Do you usually consult your servant, Mr. Popjoy?" asked the squire.

"Not very often, sir," he replied, "but in this instance his advice seems to be worth taking, because he has proposed that both he and I should keep ourselves on the safe side. Trubbs is a keen fellow when there's danger in the way, and in this instance his motives and mine were pretty much alike."

"But if he thinks any violence is to be apprehended from Caleb Kestrel, surely he can go off to London by himself."

"And what am I to do for a groom?"

"One of mine shall be at your service as long as you remain here," answered Mr. Derwent.

"Well, I'm much obliged to you for your kind invitation," answered Mr. Brassey Popjoy, "and as that suggestion of yours about the likelihood of Kestrel having gone up to London, is a very reasonable one, I'll speak to my servant, and——"

"Ask his advice, of course."

"No, no—I don't go quite so far as that either," exclaimed the cockney, "but I should like very well to hear what he has to say about it, because I would rather have his services whilst I remain here, than lose them. Trubbs has been with me a long time, and though, it must be confessed, he is rather rough in his manner, he is a faithful fellow, and that's more than we can say for most of his class."

"Don't you think he is a little too free in his manners sometimes?" asked Mr. Derwent.

"It's only a way he has got," replied Popjoy, "and I make a point of excusing it on account of his good qualities. Once he and I quarrelled and parted, but we soon made it up again, for neither of us could find ourselves so well suited as when we were together."

"Aye," exclaimed Mr. Derwent, "he fancies you cannot do without him, and for that reason he presumes to take liberties, such as few masters would put up with. Trubbs, perhaps, would not be obliged to me if he knew what I have been saying, but I merely want to persuade you to remain here for some time longer, even if your servant should choose to go away."

"May I, first of all, ask if you are quite certain that Caleb Kestrel is not lurking about this neighbourhood?"

"I believe I can state most positively that he is not," answered Mr. Derwent, "for every place round about has been carefully searched, and as nothing has been either seen or heard of him, we may fairly presume that he has had sense enough to keep himself out of the reach of danger."

"But it seems strange that nothing should have been heard of him ever since he left the place."

"You are wrong there, my good fellow," exclaimed the squire, "for this gentleman has come here on purpose to tell me that he has heard a rumour of Caleb Kestrel having left England to seek safety in a foreign land."

"Where is he gone to?" asked Popjoy anxiously.

"In my opinion," replied Mr. Derwent, "the report is only circulated for the purpose of deceiving us as to his whereabouts."

"Then we are no more safe than we were before?"

"I won't go so far as to say that," replied the squire, "but, at any rate, I feel pretty well satisfied that he will not run the risk of showing himself whilst there are so many people upon the look-out for him. In all probability, he is far enough away from us at this time, and it strikes me, if any further demand for money is made, it will be through some other channel."

"I don't know what your notion may be, sir," answered the other, "but for my own part, I'm afraid he means to murder some of us before very long."

"Do you think yourself in danger, Mr. Popjoy?"

"Indeed, I do, sir," he replied, "or I should not have been so anxious to leave your hospitality all of a sudden. Every one of us are in danger, or Trubbs is very much mistaken."

"Trubbs! what does he know about it?"

"He thinks he knows a good deal," answered his master, "and sometimes I'm inclined to think he is right, for many a thing that he says has come true. When he first saw this Kestrel he told me to beware of him, and we have had proof enough since that he is a very dangerous fellow to have anything to do with."

"We all know that, my good sir," exclaimed Mr. Capsicum, "so your servant might have spared himself the caution, so far as we are concerned. But though Caleb Kestrel is an awkward fellow to have to deal with, he may not always succeed in his evil designs, and I dare say, before long, we shall have the satisfaction of proving to him that he has met more than his match."

"Then you really expect he will be taken?"

"Why, of course, I do, if he is fool enough to remain much longer in this country," answered the magistrate. "Go where he may, he will find the people all up in arms against him, and the more particularly as the reward offered for his apprehension is a very large one."

"Then how is it they have not taken him before now?"

"Aye," replied Mr. Capsicum, "your question, I grant, is a very rational one, but it is not easily to be explained, unless we may suppose that people are afraid of encountering a man whose ferocity is so notorious to everybody. In fact, there is no denying that, let the capture of Caleb Kestrel take place when it may, it will not be effected without a stout resistance on his part."

"Well, then," exclaimed Mr. Brassey Popjoy, "all I know about it is, that I shall not run any risk in the matter."

"A very wise resolution on your part," returned the squire, "for it strikes me you would come off second best if you were to attempt to lay hands upon him."

"But how would it be if I was to happen to meet him?"

"There's very little chance of that, my good fellow," exclaimed Mr. Derwent, "for I expect the pedlar will not venture to show himself out of doors, now that he knows the determination there is to take him the next time he is seen.

"And how about yourself?" asked Popjoy; "do you expect he will give up his schemes against you and Amy?"

"As far as he himself is individually concerned, I think he will," answered the squire; "but he has comrades, who, I fear, are equally worthless as himself, and I am afraid they will not scruple to act as his agents, on condition that they are well paid for their services and the risk they run."

"Do you know any of the fellows?"

"A few of them."

"Then why not have had them taken up before now?"

"Because they have had sense enough to keep out of the way," answered Mr. Derwent. "They know the sort of fate that is in store for them if they happen to fall into the hands of the law, and therefore prefer acting with caution to running themselves headlong into danger."

"Besides," added Mr. Capsicum, "they are more likely to succeed in their designs if they proceed with caution."

"But you don't think they will succeed, I hope."

"Oh! my dear sir, that will entirely depend upon circumstances," answered the magistrate, "We have crafty enemies to deal with, and if we allow ourselves to be taken by surprise, there's no saying where the mischief may end."

"In that case," exclaimed Mr. Brassey Popjoy, "I begin to think my first plan was the best one."

"What plan was that?"

"Why to return to London without delay."

"Do you think, then, you would be more safe there than anywhere else?" asked Mr. Derwent.

"I have a notion I should.'

"But suppose these fellows—which is very probable—should hear where you have gone to?"

"Well, sir, suppose they do?"

"Some of them would follow you there, to a certainty."

"I don't know whether you are laughing at me, Mr. Derwent," cried Brassey Popjoy, "but for my own part, I don't see why they should take the trouble of following me so far."

"Indeed!" laughed the squire; "and yet it was only just now that you said you were known as having assisted in the pursuit of Kestrel."

"True: and now I think of it again, it may perhaps be as well to remain where I am a few days longer."

"Much better, depend upon it, my good sir," exclaimed Mr. Derwent, "for here you are, at all events, among friends, and if there should really be any danger, we have the satisfaction, at least, of knowing that we shall share it in common."

"Ah! my good sir," groaned Popjoy, "I now see the folly of a man trusting himself beyond the sound of Bow-bells! I was happy and comfortable enough so long as I remained in London, but as soon as I ventured, like a fool as I was, into the country, I found myself surrounded with dangers and difficulties."

"Psha!" exclaimed Mr. Capsicum, "what dangers or difficulties either, have you had to encounter?"

"Some people think nothing of getting into a scrape," exclaimed the cockney, "but for my own part, I have always been careful to keep out of harm's way as long as I was able, and now, all through my own folly, I've got into a dilemma that I'm not likely to get out of in a hurry. Ah! after all, London is the only place in the world where a man can live in peace and happiness."

"And yet other people are to be found, who tell you that the country is the only place where true enjoyment is to be found."

"They may believe it that like," answered Mr. Brassey Popjoy, "but for my own part, I'll take care never to venture out of town again, if I have but the good fortune to find my way back to it. Shooting at pheasants and hares, and all that sort of thing, may be all very well in its way, but when I came down here, I never bargained for all the alarm that Caleb Kestrel has constantly kept me in."

"Why," exclaimed Mr. Derwent, "this man appears to be quite a bugbear to you!"

"I don't deny it, squire," answered Popjoy, "and who can wonder at my being alarmed, when it seems pretty certain that he has not shrunk even from a murder?"

"Aye," replied Mr. Derwent, "there's no denying that he is a desperate fellow, but I don't see that you need be at all afraid of him."

"There's not the slightest occasion for it," added Mr. Capsicum, "for his vengeance is directed only against those who have promoted and assisted in the search that has been made for him. Besides, I tell you there is a rumour that he has contrived to get abroad, and if there is truth in that, we may venture to hope that he will never again be heard of."

"Aye," answered the cockney, "but Mr. Derwent has a notion that he is still in England, and if that should be the case, I don't know that my life would be more safe than any other person's."

"In a word," observed the squire, " I suppose you wish to return to London before any mischief befalls you ?"

" That's just what I have been thinking of."

"Well, my dear sir," exclaimed Mr. Derwent, " you will, of course, act as you think proper in the affair, but I hope you will do me the pleasure of repeating your visit at as early an opportunity as possible."

" Thank you, squire, for your kindness," answered Mr. Brassey Popjoy, "but much as I wish to have a few weeks' shooting over these Yorkshire moors, I have a most decided objection to run the risk of coming into contact with Caleb Kestrel. The fellow has frightened me enough already, and I should absolutely die of terror if he and I should ever happen to meet again."

" And you may depend upon it," observed Mr. Capsicum, " that, even if the ruffian is still in England, he will be quite as anxious to avoid meeting with those whose chief anxiety is to render him into the hands of justice. However, I am not saying this to urge your remaining here any longer, for I am a plain spoken, old-fashioned fellow, and between ourselves, Mr. Popjoy, I think you had much better return home, where you will at least be out of harm's reach."

" How do I know that he will not follow me even there ?" demanded the terrified cockney.

"Psha ! do you imagine that he would be fool enough to venture where he would be sure to be caught ? Besides, let Caleb Kestrel be where he may, he has something of far more importance to think about than looking after you or anybody else."

" Well, I hope he may, that's all I know about it," exclaimed Brassey Popjoy ; "but, for my own part, I shall never have an easy mind till I hear that he has fallen into the hands of the law. The fellow has proved himself to be a very fiend of mischief, and nothing will ever put a stop to his pranks as long as he remains at liberty. So, without any further delay, I shall bid good bye to all kind friends here, and hope soon to meet them all in London, where alone a man can find safety and enjoyment."

And Mr. Brassey Popjoy was as good as his word, for leaving the room he went forthwith to take counsel of his man Trubbs, who was no less anxious than his master to get clear away from the neighbourhood. In a very short period afterwards everything was declared to be in a state of readiness, and taking farewell of the squire and other friends, Mr. Brassey Popjoy, accompanied by his servant, was travelling with all speed towards the great metropolis.

***

CHAPTER XLVII.

PEEPS IS THE BEARER OF A MESSAGE FROM CALEB KESTREL.—PREPARATIONS FOR A DEFENCE.—OFFERS OF FRIENDLY ASSISTANCE.—THE PEDLAR IS TRUE TO HIS PROMISE, AND RECEIVES THE REWARD OF HIS VILLANY.—MATTERS ASSUME A SATISFACTORY APPEARANCE.—CERTAIN LONG-TALKED-OF ARRANGEMENTS ARE CONCLUDED, AND ALL PARTIES ARE RENDERED HAPPY.—THE END.

A FEW evenings after the events narrated in the foregoing chapter, Squire Derwent entertained some of his friends and neighbours at the hall in honour of the birthday of Amy, and to celebrate her supposed escape from all further trouble and annoyance. Amongst the guests were Rowland Brough, his pretty niece, Mary Everett, and her lover, Frank Marldale, who had now become an especial favourite of the squire. Mrs. Peeps, too, was one of the party, but her husband, who had left home at an early hour in the afternoon, was most unaccountably absent, though he had promised to return in a short time. This, of course, occasioned no little surprise, which increased as time wore on, till at length it was proposed that some of the servants should be sent to ascertain if any mischief had happened to him. This design was, however, rendered unnecessary by the return of the person who had given rise to all this alarm, when, to their astonishment, his friends learnt that he had been detained by Caleb Kestrel, who he had met at the distance of about a couple of miles from the hall, and who seemed to be, if it were possible, more determined than ever to insist upon the immediate payment of the money he had demanded.

"And I would advise you to agree to his terms, too, squire," continued Peeps, "for he says he's not afraid of anything that may happen to him, and that unless the affair is brought to a close before the next midnight, he will either take your life, or you shall his."

"Did he make any proposition for me to meet him?" asked Mr. Derwent, after a pause.

"He did; and wanted you to go for that purpose to the old cottage that he and his comrades burnt down."

"Can he be mad enough to suppose that I should go there?"

"No," answered Peeps, "for I told him he would have to wait long enough if he staid till you came, and when he found that there was no chance of your being fool enough to obey his insolent demand, he said that it was of little consequence, and that I might give you a message from him, that you may expect to see him here at twelve o'clock to-night, unless things are brought to a settlement."

"If he comes it will be the last moment of liberty that he will ever enjoy," exclaimed Mr. Derwent.

"So I told him," answered Peeps, "but he only gave one of those horrible laughs of his, and told me he was prepared for anything, even if his life should be sacrificed. 'Tell Squire Derwent from me,' he said, 'that he has to do with a a desperate man, who values not his existence, unless he has the means to leave this country at once and for ever. Tell him this from me, and if you possess any influence over him, tell him, also, that any further resistance to my demand will be certain to end in his own immediate destruction.'"

"Was any one with him during this conversation?" asked Mr. Derwent.

"I didn't see anybody," answered Peeps, "but he gave me to understand that his companions were close by, and would come to his assistance in a moment if he only gave the signal."

"Wasn't you frightened, dear?" exclaimed Mrs. Peeps, who had been listening to her husband with breathless attention.

"Terribly so, my love, as you may imagine," returned the other, "but I tried to carry it off with a high hand, and told him that if he had any messages to deliver to Mr. Derwent he had better do it himself. However, he knows better than to do that, so, in order to get out of his company as quickly as I could, I promised to tell the squire everything he had said."

"And do you believe he intends to come?" asked Mr. Derwent.

"As sure as possible he will."

"Then we must be prepared to give him a warm reception," exclaimed Farmer Brough, "for if we let the present opportunity slip, he may obtain an advantage that never ought to be given to him. I know you have plenty of arms in the house, squire, and if my advice is followed, the ruffian will be shot, like a dog as he is, the moment he sets his foot within your house."

"He shall have no quarter here I can assure you," returned Mr. Derwent, "for his determination to do me a mischief is apparent from the fact of his returning to this neighbourhood in spite of the danger with which he is surrounded."

"I hope there's no likelihood of fighting!" exclaimed Mr. Peeps, with alarm.

"The probability is, that we shall have sharp work of it before the night is over," answered Farmer Brough, "and therefore I think it will be advisable for all the females to betake themselves at once to the upper part of the house, where they can remain in safety till this ugly business has been brought to an end."

This suggestion was immediately acted upon, and the females having betaken themselves to that portion of the building which had been alluded to, the men helped themselves to the arms which had in the interim been brought into the room. This done, some of the male domestics were ordered to keep guard over various parts of the hosue, and the arrangements for defence having been completed, Mr. Derwent cautioned his friends against being too rash when the moment for active service should arrive."

"Steadiness and determination are all that I believe will be required," he continued, "for though the enemy may come in considerable force, they have so bad a cause, that they will flee immediately upon seeing that we are prepared for them Besides, they cannot come here without being observed by some of my friends and neighbours, all of whom have volunteered their services whenever I may be in need of them."

"Aye," returned Farmer Brough, "and I can answer for it they will enter heart and soul into your cause; so Caleb Kestrel has nothing but foes to expect here, and they are determined not to let him escape if he should ever come within their reach again. So he had better mind what he's about, or he'll find himself in our hands as soon as he shows himself here."

"For my own part, I propose that no quarter should be shown him," exclaimed Frank Marldale, "for we know he would not hesitate to commit a murder, and therefore, for our own sakes, we ought to shoot him in order that our own lives may be safe."

"Perhaps, under all the circumstances, we might be justified in committing such an act," answered Mr. Derwent, "but for my own part, I would rather that he should be made a prisoner, in order that he may afterwards be made an example of. We must, however, be guided by the events that take place, and of course, if need be, I should not hesitate any more than anybody else to slay him, rather than suffer his escape."

"For my own part," observed Mr. Capsicum, "I think there must be some mistake about this, for desperate as the ruffian has always proved himself to be, it is hardly likely he would venture to come here, when he knows the certainty there is of his falling into our hands."

"At any rate," exclaimed Peeps, rather nettled at a doubt having been implied as to the accuracy of this report, "I have delivered the message exactly as it was given to me, and it's my own opinion that he means to come, let the risk be what it may."

"I have no doubt of it myself," exclaimed Mr. Derwent, "for, after the many proofs he has given of his recklessness of danger, we may now expect that he will fulfil the threat he has sent by our friend. And perhaps it may be better that he should do so, for Amy cannot be safe so long as we know he is skulking in this neighbourhood."

"Don't you think it would have been better if we had all gone out in search of him?" asked Frank Marldale.

"Had it been daylight I should have proposed it myself," answered the squire, "but the darkness of the night would enable him to elude us without difficulty, and he would then attack the house during our absence, when the females were left without any of our protection. Under these circumstances, I think we shall be acting with more prudence by remaining where we are, and giving him such a reception as he will scarcely expect."

"Well," cried Mr. Peeps, "all I can say about it is, that I hope he may fall in with some of our people that are keeping guard round the house, for they would be sure to shoot him down, if it was only for the sake of the reward that has been offered. It would save us a great deal of trouble and danger if they would only do that, and, which is better than all, there would no longer be any obstacle to the marriage of Amy with the man of her choice."

"There is no obstacle even now," answered Mr. Derwent, "and the delay has only taken place because I wished, first of all, to rid her of a foe so vindictive as this Caleb Kestrel. That we shall succeed in doing so before long is, I think, almost certain, and then it is to be hoped she will be rewarded for all the anxiety and alarm to which she has been subjected."

" Ever since the night of Farmer Brough's Harvest Home the poor girl has never known what it is to have a moment's easiness," exclaimed Mr. Peeps, "and some times I have regretted the unlucky chance that brought us into this neighbourhood."

"Why do you call the chance an unlucky one?" asked the squire.

"Because it threw us in the way of Caleb Kestrel, who might never have found us if we had not come here."

" It has certainly led to a great deal of uneasiness," answered Mr. Derwent, "but it has also been productive of very important results, since Amy would never have been restored to her rights, but through the confessions made by the pedlar, villain as he is; we, therefore, owe him some thanks for the discovery he made, though it must be confessed he was induced to make the explanation only by hope that he would be able to extort a large sum of money from her whom he had basely stolen away from her family."

" For which," observed Mr. Capsicum, " if for no other reason, he deserves to be severely punished. And he is going the right way to receive it, too, unless he takes second thoughts, and leaves the place without paying you the visit he has threatened to inflict upon us."

" Depend upon it he will keep his word," answered the squire, " for he must by this time he reduced to the very lowest state of poverty, and it would be impossible for him to leave England without first of all obtaining some money. For that purpose he will doubtless come here, and it will then be for us to take vigorous measures to prevent a repetition of the violence we have so often had to complain of."

" Aye, aye, there must be no child's play now," exclaimed Farmer Brough, " for if we fail either to take or kill him, he will afterwards be guilty of greater crimes than he has hitherto committed."

" I don't know how that can be, when he has shed human blood," observed Peeps. " The fellow stops short of nothing that's bad, and it's now high time that we should put an end to his goings on. If he should be shot, so much the better, for it will be nothing more than he deserves, and will save poor Amy the trouble and alarm that she must be constantly exposed to so long as he remains at liberty."

" That may be all very true," exclaimed Frank Marldale, " but we have a desperate fellow to deal with, and, depend upon it, he will not yield without making a violent effort to slay some of those who oppose themselves against him. I am not saying this to alarm any one, let it be understood, but as a caution that we must act with firmness and determination if he should have the hardihood to come here, as he has threatened to do."

" I believe we have all made up our minds not to show him any quarter if he should venture to approach the house," exclaimed the squire, " and if necessary, I for one shall not hesitate to take his life, for the preservation of my own, and those who have generously come forward to assist me."

" But the poor women will be frightened out of their senses if they should hear a discharge of fire-arms," observed Peeps.

" Unfortunately that cannot be avoided," answered Mr. Derwent, " but their alarm will not last very long, and it is to be hoped they will then have the gratification of learning that we have come off victorious. The capture or fall of Caleb Kestrel will cause immediate alarm among his followers, and even if they should escape, I'll answer for it none of them will ever venture to renew their hostility against me."

" But they had better take care of themselves," observed Mr. Capsicum, " for if any of them should happen to be taken they will be tried as accessories in the murder of the old Gipsy woman. In fact, the men are too dangerous characters to be suffered at large, and it will be my duty, as a magistrate belonging to this county, to pursue them to the justice they so richly deserve."

" I'm glad to hear you say that, sir," exclaimed Peeps, " for I was thinking that while one of them is a liberty, there'll be no safety for any of those that have taken part against them."

"For my own part," observed Frank Marldale, "I can see no danger to be apprehended from any of them, even if they should escape, since it's not very likely they would venture again into a neighbourhood where everybody is to be regarded as an enemy. In fact, I am almost inclined to doubt whether any of them are here at this time."

"Do you think, then, I have told a falsehood about Kestrel having sent a message by me?" asked Peeps.

"I can have no reason for believing that you would practise upon our credulity," answered the young man. "On the contrary, I express my belief that the pedlar has ventured to come back to this neighbourhood, though I cannot imagine it likely that any of his comrades have been fool-hardy enough to follow so dangerous an example."

"He told me they were within sound of his signal."

No, 51.

"That may have been done only because he knew you would bring the information to Mr. Derwent.

"Very likely," replied Peeps, "but for all that, we ought to be prepared to meet a number of his people. It was said, too, just now, that they would run away the moment they saw Caleb Kestrel either killed or taken prisoner, but, for my own part, I believe some of his chaps are quite as desperate as himself, and that they would fight like devils if anything should happen to their leader."

"Well," exclaimed Mr. Derwent, "be that as it may, we are pretty well prepared for them, and being armed, I think we have every reason to believe the victory will be on our side if we only determine to meet them with firmness and courage."

"Perhaps they may not come at all."

"In some respects I hope they may," answered the squire, "for it will put an end to the constant dread with which we have been for some time past anticipating the violence of this implacable enemy. Hitherto all has been doubt and uncertainty, and I would now relieve myself from all further alarm, even at the hazard of losing my own life in a conflict with my foes."

"Don't talk of that, squire," exclaimed Peeps, "for it would break poor Amy's heart at once if anything was to happen to you."

"She has fortitude enough to bear up against misfortune," answered Mr. Derwent, "and would soon conquer her grief, even if the worst was to happen. However, I look forward to a very different result of this nights's affair, and, in my opinion ; we shall have reason to congratulate ourselves upon Kestrel's imprudent determination to pay me this visit. Let him once make his appearance here, and, I'll answer for it, his mischievous career will be brought to an end."

"But I am thinking, squire, that he'll never give up till he has revenged himself upon some of us."

"That he will try to do so, there can be very little doubt," answered Mr. Derwent, "but as we are prepared for his coming, we must take care to seize him the moment he makes his appearance. If that should be found to be impracticable, we must then have recourse to more violent measures, though I wish it to be understood, that I would have his life spared if possible."

"That's doing a great deal more than he would do for you, sir," exclaimed Farmer Brough.

"I know it, my good friend ; but I have a notion that when he finds he has no longer the power of doing me any mischief, he may be induced to confess the motives that have urged him to pursue me with so much bitterness and hostility."

"I thought it was already understood," observed Frank Marldale, "that it was done only to extort from you a large sum of money."

"That was partly his motive, I dare say," answered Mr. Derwent ; "but there must still be something behind, which at present I know nothing about. Besides, I would learn from him whether Amy has anything more to fear from the malice of those who have hitherto obeyed his orders."

A loud report of a gun was at this moment heard, and Mr. Derwent and his friends, starting from their seats at this intimation of danger, stood for a brief period anxiously listening for any sounds that might serve to acquaint them with the cause of alarm. Mr. Peeps showed evident symptoms of uneasiness at the near approach of mischief, and would, no doubt, have run away to find some place of concealment, had it not been for his shame at the idea of being laughed at when all the danger was over. He, however, ventured to suggest that it would be as well to keep watch upon the doors and windows of the room, and to fire upon the first man that ventured to intrude himself.

"My good fellow, there is no occasion for alarm," answered Mr. Derwent, for I have a notion that all the peril you have imagined is at an end. A number of persons seem to have entered the hall, and if the sounds do not deceive me, some of my servants are bringing hither the person at whom the shot was just now fired."

He had scarcely said so, when the door was opened, and Caleb Kestrel, supported between two of the domestics, and bleeding profusely from a wound in the breast, was led slowly into the room, and conducted to a seat, into which he sank, faint and exhausted. It was plain that the injury he had received was mortal, and Mr. Derwent was approaching to satisfy himself with the extent of the injury he had received, when the ruffian waved him back with a gesture of impatience.

" If you think to give me any help, I will have none of it from your hands," he exclaimed. " Leave me where I am, and let me die alone, for it is torture to be gazed upon by those who exult in my fall."

" There are none here that exult," answered Mr. Derwent, " though it must be admitted that your fate has been provoked by your own evil deeds."

" Aye," muttered the other, " 'tis well for you to preach, now that I have no longer the power to help myself. However, if my comrades are true to me after I am dead, they will revenge my fall sooner than you may perhaps expect."

" Did any of them come here with you?" asked Mr. Capsicum.

" Yes."

" Are they still upon these premises ?"

" The cowards ran away as soon as they saw me fall; and not a hand was raised against the man who fired upon me, though he was seen in the very act."

" Then that," observed Mr. Derwent, " is a proof that they are not likely to venture here again."

" Don't make too sure of that," answered the ruffian, " for before coming here, we all swore to be revenged if any one among our number should chance to fall. It has been my destiny to perish, and my companions, though they have run away for the present, will not fail to fulfil the vow they have made. There's some consolation for me in that, and I can die without regret, since, in my last moments, I shall know that both you and the girl Amy will not live many hours afterwards to triumph in my downfall."

" But," observed Mr. Capsicum, " their mischievous intentions may be easily frustrated, since all of them are implicated in your crimes, and it cannot be long before they all fall into the hands of those who are searching for them in every direction."

" They are already taken, sir," exclaimed one of the male domestics who had entered the room whilst these latter words were being spoken.

" How !—taken !" muttered Caleb Kestrel, in a tone of the most bitter disappointment.

" Yes," answered the man ; " we pursued them into a barn, where they had sought concealment, and finding themselves overpowered by numbers, they surrendered themselves without offering any further resistance. Some of our people have since conducted them to the village cage, where they will remain till committed to the county jail for trial."

" Did the cowards make no effort to defend themselves?" asked the pedlar, impatiently.

" How could they do that, when we took good care not to let them out of the place ?" asked the man. " Besides, it would have been of little use if they had, for we were too many for them, and were determined to get rid of such a nest of scoundrels as they are."

" You now see, Kestrel," exclaimed Mr. Derwent, " that all your base schemes have failed, and that those you have persecuted will no longer have to endure the dread of the evil designs you had formed. Repent, therefore, the crimes you have been guilty of, and do not die in the sin that has so long been your guiding-star."

" Repent !" muttered the ruffian. " What's the use of talking to a man like me of repentance ?"

" It is not too late, even now, to ask for pardon from Heaven."

" What good can a man like me do in the few minutes I have to live ?" demanded the other. " What I have done cannot be mended, and the only regret I feel is, that I have not been able to succeed in this last plan that I had formed for your destruction."

"Are your thoughts still upon that ?" asked Mr. Derwent.

" They are."

" And yet I never sought to injure you."

" Perhaps not," he replied; " but I have always borne a deadly hatred against both you and your cousin who died abroad. He it was that caused me to be transported, and during the whole term of my captivity, I thought of little else than how I should best obtain revenge when the period of my punishment expired. At length I once more found myself a free man, and the first use I made of my liberty was to steal away Amy, and so break the heart of Clement Derwent, who loved her as if she had been his own child. The design answered my purpose, for he died of grief shortly afterwards, and you, in your turn, would have been robbed of her this night if an unlucky shot had not brought me to the ground."

" But why seek to injure her who has never been guilty of an offence against you ?"

" There is no time for you now to enter into any further explanation," answered Caleb Kestrel, " and even if there was, I know not that I should gratify your curiosity. Let it suffice that I was guided by my own will, and if I have one thing more than another to regret, it is that I have failed in the design that brought me here to-night. Had I succeeded in taking her away, you must have given me the money I asked for, or the girl's life would have been sacrificed through your own obstinacy."

" Could you have had the heart to kill her ?"

" To be sure I could ; why should her life be cared for more than any other person's ?"

" Because she never did you an injury."

" That weighed very little with me," answered Kestrel, " for I knew that I was looked upon by her with fear and hatred."

" Both of which were caused by your own conduct towards her," answered Mr. Derwent, " and it is little to be wondered at if she was anxious as any of ourselves to hear of your being taken up. Indeed, as long as you remained at liberty, she was in continual dread of being either murdered or carried away, as upon a recent occasion."

" Aye," muttered the other, " if I had not been fool enough to allow her to return home, I should before now have received from you the money I demanded. But I thought she would have urged you to give me the money I asked for, and in that case I should have left England, never to return to it."

" Amy did make the proposition to me," said Mr. Derwent, " but I refused my assent, because I was well aware that we should be subjected to the same threats and intimidations as soon as you had squandered away that which I might give. Being perfectly satisfied of that, I determined to use every effort for your apprehension, knowing that if ever you fell into the hands of the law your life would be made to answer for the crimes you have committed."

" What crimes could you have charged me with ?"

" To mention one act of many others," answered the squire, " I was prepared with pretty conclusive evidence that the old Gipsy woman was murdered by your hands."

" Well," exclaimed Caleb Kestrel, " now that I am so near leaving the world, I don't mind confessing that I did kill the old woman. But she brought it all upon herself, for I had no thought of committing the murder till she threatened to guide the pursuers to the place where I was to be found. I expected to have been hanged for it, and it's most likely I should not have been deceived if one of your people had not this night spared the executioner the trouble."

" Are you sure, then, that your wound is mortal ?"

" Quite."

" And yet you will not offer up a prayer for forgiveness?"

" Don't talk to me about that now," exclaimed the reprobate, " for I am suffering enough pain from my wound, without having the additional agony of looking forward to the future. As I have lived, so will I die, in spite of what you or anybody else may say."

" At last," interposed Mr. Capsicum, " you will not refuse the assistance of a surgeon?"

" What should I do that for?" demanded Caleb Kestrel. " Can I feel any wish to be cured when I know that the gallows would claim its victim directly afterwards? No, no; death, with all its terrors, comes better in this shape than any other."

" Nay," exclaimed Mr. Capsicum, " it is our duty to prevent your evading the penalty you have brought upon yourself."

" No doubt it would be more agreeable to yourself to see me dragged like a dog to the gibbet," returned the pedlar, bitterly, " but even at the moment of my death, I can laugh at the malice of those that I scorn and execrate. No, no, sir, I scorn your proffered aid."

" Have you any confession to make?" asked Mr. Capsicum, taking advantage of a brief pause that followed.

" Confession!" he exclaimed ; " why should I confess any of the deeds I have done, to those that look upon me as a wretch that has met with the fate he deserved? No, no, all the secrets of my life shall perish with me, for I scorn to gratify the idle curiosity of men that I have ever held in the utmost contempt."

" As you will," returned Mr. Derwent, " but I thought it might be a relief to your heart to unburden it at such a moment as this. You, however, refuse to do so, and I, for my own part, will not trouble you any further upon the subject."

" And I," muttered the other in a lower tone of voice, " am growing too faint, through loss of blood, to answer any more of your questions. My last moment is at hand, and the only other words that I shall utter will be to curse, with my dying breath, all those who have taken part against me."

He ceased speaking, and in a few moments a groan, deep and terrible, escaped his lips—his head sunk back, and it was apparent to all that the miserable man was no more. Having witnessed the end of his mortal enemy, Mr. Derwent and his friends left the room, and directions were shortly afterwards given for the removal of the body to a neighbouring cottage, which happened to be vacant. From thence it was shortly conveyed to the churchyard, and deposited in a grave in a part of the ground that was least frequented, so that the remembrance of the man and his evil deeds might be forgotten as soon as possible.—Let us now turn to a subject that we feel assured will prove more agreeable to the reader than any further mention of Caleb Kestrel and his enormities. As will readily be imagined, the aspect of affairs at Derwent Hall assumed a more quiet appearance than had been visible there for some time past. Amy could now ramble about the park and its neighbourhood without fear of being assailed with danger, for Kestrel's companions were securely confined within the walls of the county jail, and there was every certainty of their being convicted and sent out of the country. In these walks, as may be imagined, Cecil Derwent was her frequent companion, and from certain signs of activity that were observable at the hall, rumours were soon spread abroad that the anticipated marriage was very shortly to take place. Others hinted pretty liberally that about the same time Frank Marldale and Mary Everett would exchange their vows at the altar, and soon afterwards the news was confirmed, with the addition, that the nuptial rites were to be solemnised at the same time and place. Honest Farmer Brough now looked, if it were possible, more happy and good-natured than ever, for the marriage was one that afforded him the utmost satisfaction, and he felt assured that, let death come to him when it might, he would leave his niece under the protection of a husband, upon whose never-ceasing love he could rely. All that he possessed, too, in the world would be theirs,—and his wealth was considerable,—so that he could fairly anticipate for the young couple a long life of happiness and prosperity. Mr. Capsicum, too,—warm and impetuous as he sometimes was,—fully entered into the proceedings that were then going on. Business, however, in a day or two afterwards required his presence at home, but he left the hall with a promise to return again on the day preceding that on which the happy event was to take place. In about three weeks after the death of Caleb Kestrel, his companions, who had been taken on the same night, were arraigned for a robbery, and convicted upon the clearest evidence of their guilt. Being dangerous characters, all of them were sentenced to be transported for the remainder of their lives, and the neighbourhood was thus relieved from the further depredations of those who had so long filled it with consternation and alarm. On the morning of the day which preceded that on which they were to be removed, Mr. Derwent sought for and obtained an interview with Dick Radcliffe, who at the trial had manifested a disposition to reveal all the facts connected with the lawless proceedings in which he had been engaged. The squire found him quite willing to answer all questions that were put to him, and was gratified by hearing him declare that there was no fear of any further molestation from those who had been fortunate enough to avoid being taken. He said the smugglers had no further object in view, now that Kestrel was dead, for they had been prevailed upon to join him merely by his promises to reward them with a large sum of money in the event of his being able to extort half the fortune from Mr. Derwent. It was clear, therefore, that they would take no further steps in the affair, but remain quiet, in the hope that they would be suffered to carry on their own lawless occupation without drawing upon themselves the attention which it was their chief object to avoid. This intelligence was most cheering to Mr. Derwent, and with a light heart he returned home to inform Amy of the good news which he had been able to glean. A few more days passed away, and then arrived the important one which was to seal the happiness of the lovers. Mr. Capsicum—true to his promise—had arrived at the hall on the preceding evening ; and, much to the surprise of all parties, Brassey Popjoy and his groom, Trubbs, made their appearance just before the bridal party was about to start for church. There was, indeed, so much good humour blended with the eccentricities of the cockney that he was far from being an unwelcome visitor, and the greeting he received was cordial in the extreme. It appeared that he had read in the newspapers of the death of Caleb Kestrel, and the transportation of his associates, and as there was consequently nothing more to fear from them, he determined to pay another visit to Yorkshire in the perfect assurance that he would be received with the hospitality which had been extended to him on the former occasion. And Mr. Brassey Popjoy was right in his calculations, for there was not a more welcome guest in the hall than the one who had gone there self-invited. When the bridal party returned from the church, who among the assemblage were so happy as our worthy friend Peeps and his equally excellent wife ? It seemed to them both that they had arrived at the very summit of all their earthly wishes, for they had now seen their adopted daughter the wife of the man she loved beyond all others, and she was, besides, the mistress of one of the largest estates in the country. There was nothing, indeed, to alloy their happiness, for it had been agreed that they should pass the remainder of their days with Amy and her husband, so that the toil and privation they had endured so many years would be succeeded by all the comforts which serve to render life a blessing. Farmer Brough, too, was not without his full share of happiness, for he had seen his niece united to one whose many excellent qualities he had had frequent opportunities of witnessing. His latter years were thus left without a single care or anxiety, and when he saw the happiness which had fallen to the lot of Amy, his mind reverted to the events of the last few weeks, and he was gratified beyond measure by seeing that the change of fortune which had befallen our heroine was entirely owing to her being present at his HARVEST HOME.

THE END.